THE JACOBITE TRILOGY

Dorothy K. Broster was born near Liverpool and her family subsequently moved to Cheltenham where she attended Cheltenham Ladies' College. She then went up to St Hilda's, Oxford, and read history. During the First World War she served in France with a Voluntary Franco-American hospital. Later, she returned to Oxford where she remained for several years as secretary to the Regius Professor of History. Her other works include *Chantemerle* and *The Vision Splendid*. She died in 1950.

But the heron's flight is that of a
celestial messenger bearing important, if not happy,
tidings to an expectant people.

'V.', *As You See It*

D.K. BROSTER

THE JACOBITE TRILOGY

THE FLIGHT OF THE HERON

THE GLEAM IN THE NORTH

THE DARK MILE

LOMOND

Lomond

THE JACOBITE TRILOGY
The Flight of the Heron first published in Great Britain
1925 by William Heinemann Ltd
Copyright © the Estate of D. K. Broster 1925
The Gleam in the North first published in Great Britain
1927 by William Heinemann Ltd
Copyright © the Estate of D. K. Broster 1927
The Dark Mile first published in Great Britain
1929 by William Heinemann Ltd
Copyright © the Estate of D. K. Broster 1929
Published in one volume under the title
The Jacobite Trilogy 1984
Copyright © the Estate of D. K. Broster 1984
This edition published 1993
by Mandarin Paperbacks
an imprint of Reed International Books Ltd
Michelin House, 81 Fulham Road, London SW3 6RB
and Auckland, Melbourne, Singapore and Toronto

Reprinted 1996

A CIP catalogue record for this title
is available from the British Library

ISBN 184204 0324

Printed and bound in Great Britain
by Cox & Wyman Ltd, Reading, Berkshire

CONTENTS

THE FLIGHT OF
THE HERON

AUTHOR'S NOTE

For the purposes of this story a certain
amount of licence has been taken with
the character of the Earl of Loudoun in
Part IV, Chapter 5.

CONTENTS

PROLOGUE

A PROMISE OF FAIR WEATHER

THE sun had been up for a couple of hours, and now, by six o'clock, there was scarcely a cloud in the sky; even the peaked summit of Ben Tee, away to the north-east, had no more than the faintest veil floating over it. On all the western slopes the transfiguring light, as it crept lower and lower, was busy picking out the patches of July bell-heather and painting them an even deeper carmine, and the mountains round were smiling (where sometimes they frowned) on Loch na h-Iolaire, today a shining jewel which tomorrow might be a mere blot of grey steel. It was going to be a very fine day, and in the West of Scotland such are none too plentiful.

Loch na h-Iolaire, the Loch of the Eagle, was not large – little more than a mile long, and at its greatest breadth perhaps a quarter of a mile wide. It lay among the encircling hills like a fairy pool come upon in dreams; yet it had not the desolate quality of the high mountain tarns, whose black waters lie shoreless at the foot of precipices. Loch na h-Iolaire was set in a level space as wide as itself. At one end was a multitude of silver-stemmed birches, of whom some loved the loch (or their own reflection) so dearly that they leaned over it until the veil of their hair almost brushed its surface; and with these court ladies stood a guard of very old pines, severe and beautiful, and here and there was the feathered bravery of a rowan tree. Everywhere underfoot lay a carpet of bog-myrtle and cranberry, pressing up to the feet of the pungent-berried junipers and the bushes of the flaming broom, now but dying fires. And where this shore was widest it unexpectedly sent out into the lake a jutting crag of red granite, grown upon in every cranny with heather, and crowned with two immense Scots pines.

The loch's beauty, on this early summer morning of 1745, seemed at first to be a lonely and unappreciated loveliness, yet it was neither. On its northern shore, where the sandy bank, a little

11

hollowed by the water, rose some three feet above it, a dark, wiry young Highlander, in a belted plaid of the Cameron tartan, was standing behind a couple of large juniper bushes with a fowling-piece in his hands. He, however, was plainly not lost in admiration of the scene, for his keen eyes were fixed intently on the tree-grown islet which swam at anchor in the middle of the loch, and he had all the appearance of a hunter waiting for his quarry.

Suddenly he gave an exclamation of dismay. Round the point of the island had just appeared the head, shoulder, and flashing arm of a man swimming, and this man was driving fast through the barely rippled water, and was evidently making for the shore in his direction. The Highlander dropped out of sight behind the junipers, but the swimmer had already seen him.

'Who is there?' he called out, and his voice came ringing imperiously over the water. 'Stand up and show yourself!'

The discovered watcher obeyed, leaving the fowling-piece on the ground, and the swimmer, at some six yards' distance, promptly trod water, the better to see.

'Lachlan!' he exclaimed. 'What are you doing there?'

And as the Highlander did not answer, but suddenly stooped and pushed the fowling-piece deeper into the heather at his feet, the occupant of the loch, with a few vigorous strokes, brought himself in until he was able to stand breast-high in the water.

'Come nearer,' he commanded in Gaelic, 'and tell me what you are doing, skulking there!'

The other advanced to the edge of the bank. 'I was watching yourself, Mac 'ic Ailein,' he replied in the same tongue, and in the sulky tone of one who knows that he will be blamed.

'And why, in the name of the Good Being? Have you never seen me swim before?'

'I had it in my mind that someone might steal your clothes,' answered Lachlan MacMartin, looking aside.

'*Amadain!*' exclaimed the swimmer. 'There is no one between the Garry and the water of Arkaig who would do such a thing, and you know it as well as I! Moreover, my clothes are on the other side, and you cannot even see them! No, the truth, or I will come out and throw you into the loch!' And, balancing his arms, he advanced until he was only waist-deep, young and broad-shouldered and glistening against the bright water and the trees of the island behind him. 'Confess now, and tell me the reason in your heart!'

'If you will not be angry I will be telling you,' replied Lachlan to his chieftain Ewen Cameron, who was also his foster-brother.

'I shall make no promises. Out with it!'

'I cannot shout it to you, Mac 'ic Ailein; it would not be lucky.'

'Do you think that I am coming out to hear it before I have finished my swim?'

'I will walk in to you if you wish,' said Lachlan submissively, and began to unfasten his plaid.

'Do not be a fool!' said the young man in the loch, half laughing, half annoyed; and, wading to the bank, he pulled himself up by the exposed root of a birch-tree, and threw himself unconcernedly down among the heather and bog-myrtle. Now it could be seen that he was some inches over six feet and splendidly made; a swift runner, too, it was likely, for all his height and breadth of shoulder. His thick auburn hair, darkened by the water to brown, was plaited for the nonce into a short pigtail like a soldier's; his deep-set blue eyes looked out of a tanned face, but where the sunburn ended his skin was as fair as a girl's. He had a smiling and determined mouth.

'Now tell me truly why you are lurking here like a grouse on Beinn Tigh,' he repeated.

The half-detected culprit glanced from the naked young man at his feet to the only partially concealed fowling-piece. 'You will not be pleased, I am thinking.'

'All the more reason for knowing, then,' responded his chieftain promptly, hugging his bent knees. 'I shall stay here until you tell me ... *dhé*, how these vegetables prick! No, I do not want your plaid; I want the truth.'

'I am here,' began Lachlan MacMartin with great unwillingness, 'because there is something in the loch which may bring you ill-fortune, and – '

'In the loch! What, an *each uisge*, a water-horse?' He was smiling.

'No, not a water-horse. But my father says – '

'Ah, it is a matter of the two sights? Angus has been "seeing" again! What was the vision?'

But at that moment the speaker himself saw something, though not by the supernatural gift to which he was referring. He stretched out a wet, accusing arm and pointed towards the juniper bush. 'What is that gun doing here?' And at the very plain discomposure on its owner's face a look of amusement came into his own. 'You cannot shoot a water-horse, Lachlan – not with a charge of small shot!'

'It is not a water-horse,' repeated his foster-brother. He suddenly crouched down in the heather close to the swimmer. 'Listen, Mac 'ic Ailein,' he said in a low, tense voice. 'My father is much troubled, for he had a "seeing" last night across the fire, and it concerned you, but whether for good or ill he could not tell; neither would he tell me what it was, save that it had to do with a heron.'

'It is a pity Angus cannot be more particular in his predictions,' observed the young man flippantly, breaking off a sprig of bog-myrtle and smelling it. 'Well?'

'You know that I would put the hair of my head under your feet,' went on Lachlan MacMartin passionately. 'Now on the island yonder there lives a heron – not a pair, but one only – '

The young chieftain laid a damp but forcible hand on his arm. 'I will not have it, Lachlan, do you hear?' he said in English. 'I'll not allow that bird to be shot!'

But Lachlan continued to pour out Gaelic. '*Eoghain*, marrow of my heart, ask me for the blood out of my veins, but do not ask me to let the heron live, now that my father has seen this thing! It is a bird of ill omen – one to be living there alone, and to be spying when you are swimming; and if it is not a *bòchdan*, as I have sometimes thought, it may be a witch. Indeed, if I had one, I would do better to put a silver bullet – '

'Stop!' said the marrow of his heart peremptorily. 'If my father Angus has any warning to give me, he can tell it into my own ear, but I will not have that heron shot, whatever he saw! What do you suppose the poor bird can do to me? Bring your piece here and unload it.'

Out of the juniper bush and the heather, Lachlan, rising, pulled the fowling-piece; and very slowly and reluctantly he removed the priming and the charge.

'Yet it is an evil bird,' he muttered between his teeth. 'You must know that it is unlucky to meet a heron when one sets out on a journey.'

'Yes,' broke in Ewen Cameron impatiently, 'in the same way that it is unlucky to meet a sheep or a pig – or a snake or a rat or a mouse, unless you kill them – or a hare, or a fox, or a woman, or a flat-footed man . . . and I know not what besides! Give me the gun.' He examined it and laid it down. 'Now, Lachlan, as you have not yet promised to respect my wishes in this matter, and a gun is easily reloaded, you shall swear on the iron to obey me – and that quickly, for I am getting cold.'

Startled, the Highlander looked at his young chieftain to see whether he were serious when he suggested the taking of so great and inviolable an oath. But, unable from his expression to be sure, and being blindly, fanatically devoted to him, he obediently drew his dirk from its sheath, and was about to raise it to his lips to kiss it when his foster-brother caught his arm.

'No, I was jesting, Lachlan. And . . . you do not keep your *biodag* very clean!'

'Not clean?' exclaimed its owner, lowering the formidable hiltless blade. Then he bit his lip. '*Dhia gleidh sinn!* you are right – how came that rust there?'

'Rust? It is blood!' Ewen took it from him by its black handle of interlaced design and ran a finger down it. 'No, I am wrong; it was only the early sun on the steel.'

For the weapon lay across his palm, spotless and shining, the whole foot and a half of it.

The dark Lachlan had turned very pale. 'Give it to me, Mac 'ic Ailein, and let me throw it into the loch. It is not well to keep it if we both saw . . . what we saw.'

'No,' said his master with more composure, 'it is a good dirk, and too old a friend for that – and what I imagined can only have been some memory of the times when it has gralloched a deer for us two.' He gave it back. 'We are neither of us *taibhsear* like your father. I forbid you to throw it away. Nor are you to shoot that heron – do you hear?'

15

If his young chief was not, Lachlan MacMartin was plainly shaken by what had happened. He thrust the dirk deep into the heather as though to cleanse it, before he returned it to the sheath. 'I hear,' he muttered.

'Then see that you remember!' Shivering slightly, the young man sprang to his feet. 'Now, as you have forced me to land on this side of the loch, Lachlan, I shall dive off the *creag ruadh!* A score of times have I meant to do it, but I have never been sure if there were enough water below. So, if a water-horse gets me, you will know whose was the fault of it!' And laughing, disregarding entirely his foster-brother's protests, which went so far as the laying of a detaining hand on his bare shoulder, he slid down the bank, ran along the narrow strip of sand below it, and disappeared round a bend of the shore. A moment or two later his white figure was seen clambering up the heather-clad side of the red crag which gave the whole property its name. A pause, then he shot down towards the lake in the perfect dive of the athlete; and the water received him with scarcely a splash.

'The cross of Christ be upon us!' murmured Lachlan, shutting his eyes; and, though he was no papist, he signed himself. When he opened them, the beloved head had reappeared safely, and he watched it till the island once more hid it from his view.

Still tingling with his dive, Ewen Cameron of Ardroy, when he had reached the other side of the little island, suddenly ceased swimming and, turning on his back, gave himself to floating and meditation. He was just six-and-twenty, and very happy, for the sun was shining and he felt full of vigour, and the water was like cold silk about him, and when he went in to breakfast there would be Alison, fresh as the morning, to greet him – a foretaste of the mornings to come when they would greet each other earlier than that. For their marriage contract was even now in his desk at Ardroy awaiting signature, and the Chief of Clan Cameron, Lochiel himself, Mac Dhomhnuill Duibh, Ewen's near kinsman by marriage as well as his overlord, was coming tomorrow from his house of Achnacarry on Loch Arkaig to witness it.

Lochiel indeed, now a man of fifty, had always been to his

young cousin elder brother and father in one, for Ewen's own father had been obliged to flee the country after the abortive little Jacobite attempt of 1719, leaving behind him his wife and the son of whom she had been but three days delivered. Ewen's mother – a Stewart of Appin – did not survive his birth a fortnight, and he was nursed, with her own black-haired Lachlan, by Seonaid Mac-Martin, the wife of his father's piper – no unusual event in a land of fosterage. But after a while arrived Miss Cameron, the laird's sister, to take charge of the deserted house of Ardroy and to look after the motherless boy, who before the year had ended was fatherless too, for John Cameron died of fever in Amsterdam, and the child of six months old became 'Mac 'ic Ailein', the head of the cadet branch of Cameron of Ardroy. Hence Ewen, with Miss Cameron's assistance – and Lochiel's supervision – had ruled his little domain for as long as he could remember, save only for the two years when he was abroad for his education.

It was there, in the Jacobite society of Paris, that he had met Alison Grant, the daughter of a poor, learned, and almost permanently exiled Highland gentleman, a Grant of Glenmoriston, a plotter rather than a fighter. But because Alison, though quite as much in love with her young chieftain as he with her, had refused to leave her father alone in exile – for the brother of sixteen just entering a French regiment could not take her place – Ewen had had to wait for four long years without much prospect of their marriage. But this very spring Mr Grant had received intimation that his return would be winked at by the Government, and accordingly returned; and so there was nothing to stand in the way of his daughter's marriage to the young laird of Ardroy in the autumn. And Alison's presence here now, on a visit with her father, was no doubt the reason that, though her lover was of the same political creed as they, never questioning its fitness, since it was as natural to him as running or breathing, he was not paying very particular attention to the rumours of Prince Charles Edward's plans, which were going about among the initiated.

With deliberate and unnecessary splashings, like a boy, Ewen now turned over again, swam for a while under water, and finally landed, stretched himself in the sun, and got without undue haste

17

into a rather summary costume. There was plenty of time before breakfast to make a more ordered toilet, and his hair would be dry and tied back with a ribbon by then. Perukes and short hair were convenient, but, fashionable or no, he found the former hot. When he was Lochiel's age, perhaps, he would wear one.

Before long he was striding off towards the house, whistling a French air as he went.

*

Between the red crag and the spot where he had rated his foster-brother that morning, Ardroy stood alone now with his betrothed. The loch was almost more beautiful in the sunset light than when its waters had closed over his head all those hours ago, and even with Alison on his arm Ewen was conscious of this, for he adored Loch na h-Iolaire with little less than passion. So they stood, close together, looking at it, while here and there a fish rose and made his little circle, widening until it died out in the glassy infinity, and near shore a shelduck with her tiny bobbing brood swam hastily from one patch of reeds to another.

Presently Ewen took off his plaid and spread it for Alison to sit upon, and threw himself down too on the carpet of cranberries; and now he looked, not at the loch, but at her – his own (or nearly his own) at last. Alison's hand, waited for so patiently . . . no, not always so patiently . . . strayed among the tiny leaves, and Ewen caught the little fingers, with his ring upon the least but one, and kissed them.

'And to think,' he said softly, 'that by this time tomorrow we shall be contracted in writing, and you not able to get away from me!'

Alison looked down at him. In her dark eyes swam all kinds of sweetness, but mischief woke and danced now at the corners of her small, fine, close-shut mouth, which could be so tender too.

'Oh, Ewen, does the contract make you more sure of me? You'd not hold me to a bit of paper, if I were to change my mind one fine morning and say "Ardroy, I'm sweir to tell it, but wed you I cannot"?'

'Would I not hold you to it! Try, and see!'

One of Alison's dimples appeared. 'Indeed, I'm minded to try

18

it, just for that, to see what you would do. What would you do, *Eoghain mhóir*?'

'Carry you off,' replied Ewen promptly.

'And marry me by force?'

'And marry you by force.'

'There speaks the blood of Hieland reivers! I'd think shame to say such a thing!'

'And are you not Hieland yourself, Miss Grant?' inquired her lover. 'And was there never cattle-lifting done in Glenmoriston?'

'Cattle!' exclaimed Alison, the other dimple in evidence. 'That I should be likened, by him that's contracted to be married to me, to a steer or a cow!'

'I likened you to no such thing! You are like a hind, a hind that one sees just a glimpse of before it is gone, drinking at the lake on a misty morning. Oh, my heart's darling,' he went on, dropping into Gaelic,' do not make jests upon our marriage! If I thought that you were in earnest – Alison, say that you are not in earnest!'

Alison Grant looked into the clear blue eyes, which had really grown troubled, and was instantly remorseful. 'Oh, my dear, what a wretch am I to torment you thus! No, no, I was teasing; Loch na h-Iolaire shall run dry before I break my troth to you. I'll never force you to carry me off; 'tis like I'll be at the kirk before you.' She let him draw her head without words upon his shoulder, and they sat there silent, looking at happiness; both the happiness which they knew now, and the greater, the long happiness which was coming to them – as stable and secure in their eyes as the changeless mountains round them.

Yet Alison knew her lover's mind, or at least a part of it, so well that she presently said: 'And yet I am not jesting, Ewen, when I say that I think you would be hard put to it to choose between me and Loch na h-Iolaire – Loch na h-Iolaire and the house of Ardroy.'

His arm tightened round her. 'Alison, how can you – '

'But you'll never have to choose, *m'eudail*. I love this place most dearly already. I have never had a home like it to love, living, as we have for so long, now in France, now in Holland. But your heart is as strongly rooted here as ... the red crag yonder.'

Ewen gave a little sigh. 'You see a long way into my heart, you that are the core of it. Indeed, when I am dying, I think, this is the last place I shall have sight of in my mind. I hope I may be seeing it with my eyes also.'

Alison did not shudder or change the subject, or implore him not to speak of such things, for she was Highland too, with her race's half-mystical preoccupation with the dead. But she thought, 'I hope I'll die the same day, the same hour. . . .'

The shadows on the loch crept a little farther. Behind them Ben Tee changed colour for the hundredth time; his pointed peak seemed to soar. It grew cooler too, and Ewen wrapped the ends of the plaid about his lady.

'On Wednesday we will spend the day at Loch Arkaig,' he announced. 'We will take ponies, and you and Mr Grant shall ride.'

'And Miss Cameron?'

'Aunt Marget detests such jaunts. Meals for the parlour, and the parlour for meals, that is her creed – Alison, are you not cold?'

'In this?' She fingered the plaid where it hung over her shoulders, and added after a moment: 'How strange it will be to wear another tartan than one's own!'

'You shall always wear the Grant if it pleases you better.'

'No, it does not please me better,' answered Alison softly. 'I feel . . . very warm in the Cameron.'

He kissed her for that, smiling, and, raising his head from his kiss, became aware of a dark object beating towards them out of the sunset sky. It was the solitary heron of the island, winging his strong way home, with a deceptive slowness. The sight reminded Ewen of his morning's encounter with Lachlan, and he was about to tell Alison of it when Fate's messenger, who for the last five minutes had been hurrying round the loch, came past the red crag of Ardroy, and Ewen's quick ear caught the snap of a breaking stick under the deerskin brogues. He looked quickly round. A bearded Highlander was trotting towards them under the birches and pines.

'It is Neil – what can he want? Forgive me!' He rose to his feet, and Neil MacMartin, who was Lachlan's elder brother and Ewen's piper, broke into a run.

'Mac Dhomhnuill Duibh has just sent this by a man on horseback,' he said somewhat breathlessly, pulling a letter from his sporran.

Ewen broke the seal. 'Perhaps it is to say that Lochiel cannot come tomorrow,' he observed to his betrothed. But as he read his face showed stupefaction. 'Great God!'

Alison sprang to her feet. 'Ewen! Not bad news?'

'Bad? No, no!' He waved Neil out of hearing and turned to her with sparkling eyes. 'The Prince has landed in Scotland!'

She was at first as amazed as he. 'The Prince! Landed! When ... where?'

Ewen consulted his letter again. 'He landed at Borradale in Arisaig on the twenty-fifth. Lochiel desires me to go to Achnacarry at once.'

'He has come – at last!' said Alison to herself, almost with awe. 'And you will go with Lochiel to kiss his hand, to – Oh, Ewen, how I envy you!'

The light which had come into her lover's eyes died out a little. 'I do not know that Lochiel *is* going to Arisaig, darling.' He glanced at the letter again. 'He is troubled, I can see; there are no troops with the Prince, none of the hoped-for French help.'

'But what of that?' cried the girl. 'It is not to be thought of that Lochiel's sword, of all others, should stay in the scabbard!'

'Lochiel will do what is right and honourable; it is impossible for him ever to act otherwise,' answered Ewen, who was devoted to his Chief. 'And he wants speech with me; I must set out at once. Yes, Clan Cameron will rise, not a doubt of it!'

And, youth and the natural ardour of a fighting race reasserting themselves, he snatched up his bonnet and tossed it into the air. 'Ah, now I know why Lachlan and I thought we saw blood on his dirk this morning!' Then he caught Alison to him. '*My dearest on earth, give me your kiss!*'

It was the title of one of the ancient pibrochs that he was quoting; and the Highland girl put her arms round his neck and gave him what he asked.

Loch na h-Iolaire, bereft of the echoing voices, sank into a silence that was not broken until the heron rose again from the

21

island and began to fly slowly towards the sunset. Then the stillness was rent by a sharp report; the great bird turned over twice, its wings beating wildly, and fell all huddled into the lake. A little boat shot out from the side of the *creag ruadh*, and in a moment or two Lachlan MacMartin, leaving his oars, was bending over the side with the end of a cord in his hand. There was a splash as he threw overboard the large stone to which the cord was fastened; and having thus removed the evidence of his blind effort to outwit destiny, he pulled quickly back to the shelter of the crag of Ardroy.

Soon the same unbroken calm, the same soft lap and ripple, the same gently fading brightness were once more round Loch na h-Iolaire; yet for all those who today had looked on its waters the current of life was changed for ever.

I. THROUGH ENGLISH EYES

> One of them asked ... how he liked the High-
> lands. The question seemed to irritate him, for he
> answered, 'How, sir, can you ask me what obliges
> me to speak unfavourably of a country where I
> have been hospitably entertained? Who *can* like
> the Highlands – I like the inhabitants very well.'
> BOSWELL, *Journal of a Tour to the Hebrides*

Chapter 1

IN all Lochaber – perhaps in all the Western Highlands – there
was no more bored or disgusted man this sixteenth of August
than Captain Keith Windham of the Royal Scots, as he rode
down the Great Glen with a newly-raised company of recruits
from Perth; and no more nervous or unhappy men than the recruits themselves. For the first time in their lives the latter found
themselves far north of 'the Highland line', beyond which, to
Lowland as well as to English minds, there stretched a horrid
region peopled by wild hill tribes, where the King's writ did not
run, and where until General Wade's recent road-making activities, horsed vehicles could not run either. Yesterday only had
they reached Fort Augustus, two companies of them; and this
afternoon, tired and apprehensive, were about half-way through
their thirty-mile march to Fort William. As for the English officer,
he was cursing with all his soul the young Adventurer whose
absurd landing on the coast of Moidart last month had caused
all this pother.

Had it not been for that event, Captain Windham might have
been allowed to return to Flanders, now that his wound of
Fontenoy was healed, to engage in real warfare against civilized
troops, instead of marching through barbarous scenery to be shut
up in a fort. He could not expect any regular fighting, since the
savage hordes of these parts would probably never face a volley.
Nevertheless, had he been in command of a column, he would
have judged it more prudent to have a picket out ahead; but he

23

had already had a slight difference of opinion with Captain Scott, of the other company, who was senior to him, and, being himself of a temper very intolerant of a snub, he did not choose to risk one. Captain Windham had no great love for Scotsmen, though, ironically enough, he bore a Scottish Christian name and served in a Scottish regiment. As it happened, he was no more responsible for the one fact than for the other.

It was hot in the Great Glen, though a languid wind walked occasionally up Loch Lochy, by whose waters they were now marching. From time to time Captain Windham glanced across to its other side, and thought that he had never seen anything more forbidding. The mountain slopes, steep, green, and wrinkled with headlong torrents, followed each other like a procession of elephants, and so much did they also resemble a wall rising from the lake that there did not appear to be space for even a track between them and the water. And, though it was difficult to be sure, he suspected the slopes beneath which they were marching to be very nearly as objectionable. As a route in a potentially hostile country, a defile, astonishingly straight, with a ten-mile lake in the middle of it, did not appeal to him.

However, the mountains on the left did seem to be opening out at last, and General Wade's new military road, upon which they were marching, was in consequence about to leave the lake and proceed over more open moorland country, which pleased Captain Windham better, even though the wide panorama into which they presently emerged was also disfigured by high mountains, in particular by that in front of them, which he had been told was the loftiest in Great Britain. And about twelve miles off, under those bastions, lay Fort William, their destination.

But where was the river which, as he knew, they had first to cross? In this wide, rough landscape Captain Windham could not see a sign of it. Then, farther down the slope and about a mile ahead of them, he discerned a long, thick, winding belt of trees, and remembered to have heard an officer of Guise's regiment at Fort Augustus say last night that the Spean, a very rapid stream, had carved so deep a channel for itself as almost to flow in a ravine, and that Wade must have had some ado to find a spot where he could carry his road over it. He had done so, it appeared, on a narrow stone structure whose elevation above the river-bed had earned it the name of High Bridge. Indeed the Englishman now saw that the road which they were following was making for this deeply sunken river at an angle which suggested that General Wade had had little choice in the position of his bridge.

Ahead of Captain Windham on his mettlesome horse the scarlet ranks tramped down the gently sloping road through the heather; ahead of them again, at the rear of the foremost company, Captain Scott sat his white charger. The English officer looked with an unwilling curiosity at the great mountain mass over Fort William; it actually had traces of snow upon it . . . in August! What a country! Now in Flanders – What the devil was that?

It was, unmistakably, the skirl of a bagpipe, and came from the direction of the still invisible bridge. But if the bridge was not to be seen, something else was – tartan-clad forms moving rapidly in and out of those sheltering trees. Evidently a considerable body of Highlanders was massing by the river.

The senior officer halted his men and came riding back. 'Captain Windham, I believe there is an ambush set for us down yonder.'

'It does not *sound* like an ambush, egad!' replied his colleague rather tartly, as the heathenish skirling grew louder. 'But I certainly think there are Highlanders posted at the bridge to dispute our crossing.'

'I'll just send forward a couple of men to get some notion of their numbers,' said Scott, and rode back again. Keith shrugged his shoulders. 'Somewhat of a tardy precaution!' he thought to himself.

A sergeant and a private were thereupon dispatched by Captain Scott to reconnoitre. Their fate was swift and not encouraging, for they had not gone far ere, before the eyes of all their comrades, they were suddenly pounced upon by two Highlanders who, with a yell, darted out from the trees and hurried them out of sight.

The intimidated recruits began to shuffle and murmur. Captain Windham spoke vigorously to his subaltern, and then rode forward to consult with his senior.

Captain Scott wheeled his horse to meet him. 'This is unco

25

awkward,' he said, dropping his voice. 'The Deil knows how many of those fellows there are down yonder, but do you observe them, Captain Windham, skipping about like coneys among the trees? The bridge, I've heard, is uncommon narrow and high, with naught but rocks and torrent below. I doubt we can get the men over.'

'We *must*!' retorted Keith. 'There's no other means of reaching Fort William. The Royals, to hesitate before a few beggarly cattle-thieves!'

Alas, the Royals did more than hesitate. Even as he spoke there were signs that the half-seen 'cattle-thieves' on the bridge were preparing for a rush, for loud orders could be heard, and the piping swelled hideously. And at that the scarlet-clad ranks on the slope wavered, broke, turned, and began to flee up the rise as fast as their legs could carry them.

It was in vain that their two captains endeavoured to rally them. A man on a horse cannot do much to stem a flood of fugitives, save perhaps on a narrow road, and here the road had unlimited space on either side of it. Helter-skelter the recruits ran, and, despite their fatigue and their accoutrements, never ceased running for two miles, till they stopped, exhausted, by Loch Lochy side once more.

By that time Captain Windham was without suitable words in which to address them; his vocabulary was exhausted. Captain Scott was in like case. There was another hasty consultation beneath the unmoved stare of those steep green mountains. Scott was for sending back to Fort Augustus for a detachment of Guise's regiment to help them force the bridge, and Captain Windham, not seeing what else was to be done, concurred in this opinion. Meanwhile the recruits should be marched at an easy pace in the direction of Fort Augustus to their junction with these reinforcements, which were, of course, to come up with all speed. There had been no sign of pursuit by the successful holders of the bridge, and it might be hoped that in a little the morale of the fugitives would be somewhat restored.

Captain Scott thereupon suggested that Captain Windham should lend one of the lieutenants his horse, which was much faster than his own white charger – no other officers but they being mounted – but Keith objected with truth that a strange rider would never manage his steed, and offered to make over his company to his lieutenant and himself ride back to Fort Augustus if Captain Scott thought good. And Captain Scott hastily agreed to what both officers felt was a somewhat unusual course justified by circumstances.

To a man who, three months ago, had borne his part in the wonderful retreat at Fontenoy, that epic of steadiness under fire, and who had even been complimented by the Duke of Cumberland on his conduct, the last half-hour had been a nightmare of shame, and Keith Windham, glad to be able to extricate himself from it with the confidence that he was not abandoning his men on the eve of a fight, set spurs to his horse with great relief.

He had gone about five miles along the loch – always with those abominable mountains on either side of him – when a report echoed soundingly among them, and a bullet struck the road a little ahead of him. His pulling, nervous horse reared and plunged; and Keith swore. He was not unobserved, then, and might very well be picked off by some unseen marksman up there. Bullets, however, did not discompose him like cowardice, and, cramming his hat farther down upon his head, he merely urged the animal to greater speed.

In the next few miles, as occasional bullets winged their way at varying distances past his person, Keith Windham began to think that the hapless Royals behind him were perhaps being outflanked by some enemy marching parallel to them on the hillside – and marching much faster. The prospect of their being attacked seemed by no means so remote. Still, in any case, it was now his business to go on. But when he came in sight of the village beyond the end of Loch Lochy through which they had passed that morning, he could see armed Highlanders there in such numbers that it was unlikely he would be allowed to ride through it. Gad! he thought, the rout at the bridge had served, then, as a spark to all this tinder! For a moment – since under a mask of indifference and cynicism he was a very hot-tempered young man – the sting of that knowledge prompted him to attempt cutting his way through regardless of consequences. Then common sense triumphed. Better to avoid the enemy altogether by crossing to the farther side of the smaller lake just ahead of him (he did not know its name) on the wide flat isthmus which separated it from Loch Lochy. If there were no ambushes on that side, he would yet reach Fort Augustus, since, as the Highlanders did not appear to have horses, he was safe from mounted pursuit.

It became, however, a question whether he would get to the isthmus in time to evade the enemy ahead, of whom half a dozen or so, suspecting his intention, were running down the road towards him, targe on arm and broadsword in hand, to cut him off. Keith spurred his horse hard, fired at the foremost figure (which he missed), and next moment dropped his own pistol with an exclamation, his arm tingling to the shoulder. A bullet had struck the barrel, ricocheting off Heaven knew where; in any case it was one of the nearest escapes which he had ever experienced. For the moment his right arm was useless; but here, at last, was the end of the waters of this interminable Loch Lochy. He turned his almost frantic horse, and galloped like mad across the green, spongy isthmus, pursued now only by ineffectual yells, which he soon ceased to hear.

The neck of land, though narrow, was longer than he remembered; there were perhaps two miles of it before the next lake came to separate him from his enemies. But, whether or no the fact of his having a fast horse deterred them from pursuit, not one Highlander attempted to cross after him. Possibly they were reserving their forces undiminished, for the attack on the main body of the Royals, a thought which caused the Englishman to maintain his headlong pace. Fortunately this side of the lake seemed deserted; no man was going to stop him now!

And no man did. But he had not gone a mile by the lake side when a large grey-and-white object flapped up suddenly from the water's edge almost under the nose of his excited horse; the beast shied, swerved, crossed its legs, and came heavily down, flinging its rider against a fallen tree with a force which knocked him senseless.

Captain Windham was not stunned for very long, though to him it was an unknown space of time that he lay sprawling in the dust by the side of the pine-trunk. When he dizzily raised himself and looked about him no human being was in sight, but there on the road, within a few feet of him, with snorting nostrils and terrified eyes, lay his unfortunate horse, trying desperately and repeatedly to get to its feet again, despite a broken foreleg. For an instant Keith stared at the poor sweating, plunging brute, then, passing a hand over his bruised and bleeding forehead, he got to his own feet. There was only one thing to be done; though the sound of a shot would very likely draw undesirable attention upon himself, he could not leave the animal there in agony. His remaining pistol was in his holster, and during the process of extracting it he realized that he had twisted an ankle, in his fall. A moment or two later the sound of a shot went ringing over the waters of Loch Oich, and the troubles of Captain Windham's charger were over.

But his were not; indeed he fancied that they had but just begun. Dismounted, his brilliant scarlet-and-blue uniform rendering him in the highest degree conspicuous, his head aching, and in one place excoriated by contact with the tree-trunk, he saw that he could never summon reinforcements in time now; it was doubtful whether he would reach Fort Augustus at all. His ankle, as he soon discovered, was swollen and painful; moreover he had somehow to get back to Wade's road when he reached the end of this lake. With his hand to his head, he glanced in disgust at the prostrate trunk with which it had just made such painful acquaintance. Detestable country, where even the wild-fowl and the vegetation were in league with the inhabitants!

Hearing a sound of water, he looked about, till he found a tiny ice-cold spring between the track and the lake, and, dipping his handkerchief into this, bathed his forehead. Had he known of the seven gory severed heads which had been washed in that innocent-looking little source less than a hundred years before, perhaps he would not have done so. Hardly had he reloaded his pistol, his next care, when a distant noise, like many running feet, sent him hurriedly to the shelter of the steep, tree-clad hillside on his left. Here, among the scanty undergrowth, he crouched as best he could while, some minutes later, a score of armed Highlanders poured past on the track below him. So this side of the lake was gathering, too!

29

Captain Windham waited in his concealment until the way was clear and silent again, and then descended, since it was impossible for him to keep in cover, if he meant to reach Fort Augustus – and where else should he make for? Leaning on the branch of oak which he had broken off to assist his steps, he began to trudge grimly forward.

There soon came in sight, on its rock by the lake-side, the keep of Invergarry Castle. Captain Windham did not know that it belonged to the chief of Glengarry, but he was sure that it was the hold of some robber or other, and that he himself might not improbably see the inside of it. It looked ruinous, but that was no safeguard – on the contrary. And here were some dwellings, little, roughly-thatched buildings, but obviously inhabited. Yet all he saw of their occupants were a few white-haired children who ran screaming away, and one old woman at her door, who crossed herself devoutly at sight of him. So, to add to all their other vices, the people of these parts were papists!

The next obstacle was a river, which he had to cross as best he could on insecure and slippery stones, and the difficulties of doing this with an injured ankle took his mind off remoter possibilities, so that when he was safely over he was surprised to find the ominous tower well behind him, and he went on somewhat cheered. The sun was now getting lower, and though the other side of the glen was in full warm light, this side felt almost cold. Another peculiarity of this repulsively mountainous district. Gently swelling hills one could admire, but masses of rock, scored with useless and inconvenient torrents, had nothing to recommend them. He did not wonder at the melancholy complaints he had heard last night from the officers quartered at Fort Augustus.

And what would the garrison there say, when they heard of this afternoon's disgrace? Captain Windham's thoughts went angrily back to it. What, too, had happened to those chicken-hearted recruits by this time? He pulled out his watch; to his surprise it was after six o'clock. And he still had the watch in his hand when his ear was caught by the sound of horse's hoofs behind him. He stopped to listen. The pace, a smart trot, did not seem hurried; the rider might be some unconcerned traveller. But he might on the other hand be an enemy. Keith Windham looked for cover, but here there was none convenient, as a while ago, and the best he could do was to hobble on ahead to where a solitary oak-tree reared itself by the side of the road, for he was minded to have something to set his back against if necessary.

When he was nearly there he looked round, and saw the rider, a big Highlander on a grey horse. He was not alone, for at his heels came another, keeping up with the horse with long loping strides like a wolf's. To Keith one tartan was as yet like another, so for all he knew these two might be of a friendly clan. He awaited them by the oak-tree.

As the horseman came on, Keith saw that he was young, vigorous-looking, and well-armed. He wore trews, not a kilt like the other. But as he came he rose in his stirrups and shouted something, in which Keith clearly caught the word 'surrender'. So he was not friendly. Very well then! Captain Windham raised the pistol which he had ready, and fired – rather at the horse than the rider. The young Highlander, with a dexterity which he could not but admire, pulled aside the animal in the nick of time, and the shot missed. Keith's sword leapt out as, with a yell, the man on foot flung himself past the horse towards him, dirk in hand. But the rider called out something in Gaelic, which had an immediate effect, for the gillie, or whatever he was, came to an abrupt stop, his eyes glowering and his lips drawn back, as like a wolf about to spring as possible.

Meanwhile, to Keith's surprise, the horseman sprang to earth, flung the reins to his henchman, and came forward empty-handed – a magnificent specimen of young manhood, as the soldier could not help admitting.

'I advise you to surrender, sir,' he said courteously, lifting his bonnet, in which were fastened two eagle's feathers. 'I am sorry to take advantage of an injured man, but I have my Chief's orders. You are completely cut off, and moreover your men are all prisoners – indeed Captain Scott is at this moment in Lochiel's custody. If you will give up your sword, I shall be honoured to take you into mine.'

'The deuce you will!' exclaimed Keith, secretly astonished at the polish of his manner – a man who wore a plaid! 'And who are you, pray?'

31

'Cameron of Ardroy,' answered the young man. 'Lochiel's second cousin,' he added.

'I don't care whose second cousin you are, Mr Cameron of Ardroy,' returned Captain Windham to this, 'but if you think that you are going to have my sword for the asking, you and your cut-throat there, you are vastly mistaken!'

For, provided – but it was a big proviso – that the two did not rush upon him at once, he thought that he could deal with each separately. Splendidly built as this young Highlander was, lean too, and doubtless muscular, he probably knew no more of sword-play than was required to wield that heavy basket-hilted weapon of his, and Captain Windham himself was a good swordsman. Yes, provided Lochiel's second cousin did not use the pistol that he wore (which so far he had made no motion to do), and provided that the wolf-like person remained holding the horse . . .

'Come on and take me,' he said provocatively, flourishing his sword. 'You are not afraid, surely, of a lame man!' And he pointed with it to the rough staff at his feet.

Under his tan, the large young Highlander seemed to flush slightly. 'I know that you are lame; and your forehead is cut. You had a fall: I came upon your dead horse. That is why I do not wish to fight you. Give up your sword, sir; it is no disgrace. We are two to one, and you are disabled. Do not, I pray you, constrain me to disable you further!'

Hang the fellow, why did he behave so out of his cateran's role? 'You are considerate indeed!' retorted Captain Windham mockingly. 'Suppose you try first whether you *can* disable me further! – Now, Mr Cameron, as I don't intend to be stopped on my road by mere words, I must request you to stand out of my way!' And – rashly, no doubt, since in so doing he no longer had one eye on that murderous-looking gillie – he advanced sword in hand upon his reluctant opponent. Frowning, and muttering something under his breath, the young man with the eagle's feathers at last drew his own weapon, and the blades rang together.

Thirty seconds of it, and Keith Windham knew that he had attacked a swordsman quite as good if not better than himself. Breathing hard, he was being forced back to the trunk of the oak again, and neither his aching head nor his damaged ankle was wholly to blame for this. Who said that broadsword play was not capable of finesse? This surprisingly scrupulous young barbarian could have cut him down just then; but he drew back when he had made the opening. The certitude of being spared irritated the soldier; he lost his judgement and began to fight wildly, and so the end came, for his sword was suddenly torn from his hand, sailed up into the oak-tree above him, balanced a moment on a branch, and then fell a couple of yards away. And his adversary had his foot on it in a second.

As for Keith Windham, he leant back against the oak-tree, his head all at once going round like a mill-wheel, with the noise of a sluice, too, in his ears. For a flash everything was blank; then he felt that someone was supporting him by an arm, and a voice said in his ear: 'Drink this, sir, and accept my apologies. But indeed you forced me to it.'

Keith drank, and, though it was only water, sight was restored to him. It was his late opponent who had his arm under his, and who was looking at him with a pair of very blue eyes.

'Yes, I forced you to it,' confessed Captain Windham, drawing a long breath. 'I surrender – I can do nothing else, Mr ... Cameron.'

'Then I will take you home with me, and your hurts can be dressed,' said the Highlander, showing no trace of elation. 'We shall have to go back as far as the pass, but fortunately I have a horse. *Lachuin, thoir dhomh an t'each!*'

The gillie, scowling, brought forward the grey. Keith's captor loosed his arm and held the stirrup. 'Can you mount, sir?'

'But I am not going to ride your horse!' said Keith, astonished. 'It will not carry two of us – and what will you do yourself?'

'I? Oh, I will walk,' answered the victor carelessly. 'I assure you that I am more accustomed to it. But you would never reach Ardroy on foot, lame as you are.' And as Keith hesitated, looking at this disturbing exponent of Highland chivalry, the exponent added, hesitating a little himself: 'There is only one difficulty. If you are mounted, I fear I must ask you for your parole of honour.'

'I give it you – and that willingly,' answered Keith, with a sudden spurt of good feeling. 'Here's my hand on it, if you like, Mr Cameron!'

33

Chapter 2

IF to ride along a road in these mountain solitudes was distasteful, to be following a mere track (and that a very steep one) in amongst their very folds was worse. When he first had seen the path which they were to ascend, and the V-shaped depression, sharp against the sunset sky, up to which it led, Captain Windham had with difficulty repressed an exclamation of alarm. However, he could not really believe that Mr Cameron of Ardroy was taking him up this terrifying route in order to slay him, since he could already have done this with so much less trouble on level ground. Therefore, though he had raised his eyebrows, he had said nothing. After all, it was the horse and not he that had to do the climbing. And now they were half-way up.

The wolf-like attendant, carrying the surrendered sword, kept in the rear, but Captain Windham was almost physically conscious of his frown behind him. This unattractive person was, he felt, no willing party to his capture; he would much have preferred that the redcoat should have been left cold beneath the oak-tree. Meanwhile his master, the young chieftain or whatever he was, walked with a mountaineer's elastic step at the horse's head, occasionally taking hold of the bridle; rather silent, but uncommonly well-made and good-looking, thought his captive again, glancing down at him.

Captain Windham's own dark and rather harsh features were not unpleasing, save when he frowned, which he was somewhat given to doing, nor were they devoid of a certain distinction, and he had really fine hazel eyes. But his mouth had already taken a cynical twist unusual in a young man of thirty. If he had a passion left in life, it was military ambition. Earlier he had known others, and they had brought him nothing but unhappiness. As a boy he had had an extraordinary devotion to his lovely mother – whom he had not been alone in thinking fair. But she too was ambitious, and her second marriage, to the Earl of Stowe, with its attendant advantages, was more to her than the claims of her own son. Then the beautiful boy she bore to Lord Stowe usurped the place

34

which Keith had never had in her heart. So, in respect of affection, sometimes even of ordinary attention, he had passed through a neglected childhood and a starved boyhood, and they had left an indelible mark on him – more indelible, though he did not guess it, than the scars of another woman's betrayal of him four years ago.

The consequence was that at thirty, with a nature at bottom passionate and impulsive, he had become as disillusioned, as little prone to enthusiasms, as a man of twice his age. His creed was that it was a mistake to desire anything very much – a fatal mistake to desire a place in any person's affections, or to admit anyone, man or woman, to a place in your own. By the end of life, no doubt, every human being had discovered this truth; he had done so early, and could count himself the more fortunate.

At the same time it needed a rather different kind of detachment to take his present situation philosophically; and yet, to his own surprise, Keith Windham knew that he was doing so, even though he had by now gleaned from his captor the later history of the day's disaster, and had learnt its mortifying completeness. Matters had fallen out for the unfortunate recruits almost exactly as Captain Windham had afterwards feared; for another body of Highlanders was following them unseen on the hillside, and near the head of Loch Lochy further progress had been barred by those who had attempted to stay Keith himself. Though Captain Scott too had tried to cross the isthmus, it was impossible, since more Highlanders were hastening to the spot from that direction also. Too tired and panic-stricken to use their muskets to good effect, the redcoats had, on the contrary, received a fire which had killed five of them and wounded a dozen, including Captain Scott himself. Some leader called 'Keppoch', Captain Windham heard, had then called on the Royals to surrender, or they would be cut to pieces; and to save his men, Captain Scott had done so. Immediately on this had come up Ewen Cameron's chief, Lochiel (who had been asked for assistance), with a number of his clan including the present narrator, had taken charge of the prisoners, and marched them off to his house of Achnacarry. But as the Highlanders from the far side of Loch Oich reported having seen a dead charger on the road, and one company of the redcoats was plainly captainless, Lochiel had sent his young kinsman, since he happened to be mounted, in pursuit of the missing officer. (And at this point the officer in question had remarked rather stiffly that he trusted Mr Cameron knew that his absence from the scene of conflict was due only to his having gone for reinforcements, and Mr Cameron had replied politely that no other explanation had even occurred to him.)

They were at the top of the pass at last, and had a fine view before them; but the captive did not find it so, the mountains being too high for his taste and the downward path too steep. Stones rolled away from beneath the grey's hoofs; now and then he slipped a trifle, for which his owner, leading him carefully by the bridle, apologized. He would not have come this way, he said, but that it was the shortest from the spot where he and Captain Windham had 'chanced to meet', as he put it. And then all at once the descent was less steep, and they were looking down on a glen among the mountains, with a little lake, some signs of cultivation, grazing sheep and cattle, and in the midst of trees the roof and chimneys of a house, whence a welcome smoke ascended.

'There is Loch na h-Iolaire,' said the young Highlander at Captain Windham's bridle, pointing to the sheet of water; and he paused after he had said it, because, though Captain Windham could not guess it, he never came upon the loch from any point of the compass without a little fountain of joy bubbling up and singing to itself in his heart. 'And there is the house of Ardroy, our destination. I am sure that you will be glad of a meal and a bed, sir.'

Keith admitted it, and the descent continued, in the face of the sunset afterglow. His captor did not live in a cave, then – but the Englishman had abandoned that idea some time ago. Indeed Mr Cameron was apparently a landed proprietor with tenants, for besides sheep, goats, and cows there were a good many roughly constructed cottages scattered about. By and by, skirting the end of the little lake and its birch-trees, they struck into another track, and Keith saw the house in front of him, a simple but not undignified two-storeyed building, of which one end was slightly lower than the other, as if it had been added to. Over the porch was a coat-of-arms, which successive layers of whitewash had made difficult to decipher.

'I expect that my aunt, who keeps house for me, and my guests are already supping,' observed the young owner of this domain, assisting his prisoner to dismount. 'We will join them with as little delay as possible. Excuse me if I precede you.' He walked in and opened a door on his right. 'Aunt Marget, I have brought a visitor with me.'

From behind him, the 'visitor' could see the large raftered room, with a long table spread for a meal, and a generous hearth, by which were standing an elderly man and a girl. But in the foreground was a middle-aged lady, well-dressed and comely, exclaiming: 'My dear Ewen, what possesses you to be so late? And what's this we hear about a brush with the Elector's troops near Loch Lochy? . . . Mercy on us, who's this?'

'A guest whom I have brought home with me from the Glen,' replied the late-comer. 'Yes, there has been a skirmish – Captain Windham, let me present you to my aunt, Miss Cameron, to Miss Grant, and to Mr Grant, sometime of Inverwick.'

Keith bowed, and the two ladies curtsied.

'You are just going to sit down to supper?' queried the master of the house. 'We shall be glad of it; and afterwards, Aunt Marget, pray find some bandages and medicaments for Captain Windham, who has met with a bad fall.'

'I had perhaps better tell you, madam,' interpolated Keith at this point, holding himself rather erect, 'that, though Mr Cameron is kind enough to call me a guest, I am in reality his prisoner – But not one who will put you to any inconvenience of wardership,' he added quickly, seeing the look which passed over the lady's expressive countenance. 'I have given Mr Cameron my parole of honour, and I assure you that even "the Elector's" officers observe that!' (For he believed so then.)

Miss Cameron surveyed him with humour at the corners of her mouth. 'Every country has its own customs, Captain Windham; now I warrant you never speak but of "the Pretender" in London. You are English, sir?'

'I have that disability, madam.'

'Well, well,' said Miss Cameron, breaking into a smile. 'Even

37

at that, no doubt you can eat a Highland supper without choking! But take the Captain, Ewen, and give him some water, for I'm sure he'll be wanting to wash off the traces of battle.'

'I should be grateful indeed,' began Keith uncomfortably, wondering how much blood and dirt still decorated his face; but his captor broke in: 'You must not think that I am responsible for Captain Windham's condition, Aunt Marget. His horse came down as he was riding to fetch reinforcements from Kilcumein, and he was disabled before ever I overtook him.'

'An accident, sir – or was the poor beast shot?' queried Miss Cameron.

'An accident, madam,' responded Keith. 'A heron, I presume it was, rose suddenly from the lake and startled him; I was riding very fast, and he came down, breaking his leg. I twisted my ankle, besides being stunned for a while, so that I must apologize if my appearance – ' And this time he put up his hand to his forehead.

'A heron, did you say?' exclaimed Ewen Cameron's voice beside him, surprised and almost incredulous. 'A *heron* brought your horse down?'

'Yes,' replied Keith, surprised in his turn. 'Why not, Mr Cameron? An unusual mischance, I dare say, and none of my seeking, I assure you; but it is true.'

'I don't doubt your word, sir,' replied the young man; yet there was something puzzled in the gaze which he turned on his prisoner. 'It is . . . yes, unusual, as you say. Herons, as a rule – ' He broke off. 'If you will come with me, Captain Windham, you shall refresh yourself before we eat.'

Captain Windham sat down to a better supper than he had met since he left London, and even in London he would not have tasted such trout and venison, and might well have drunk worse claret. Out of regard for him, perhaps, or out of discretion, the conversation never touched on political matters, though he thought that he could feel a certain excitement simmering below the surface of the talk. (And well it might, he reflected; had not the master of the house this day committed himself to overt hostilities against His Majesty's Government?) The elderly gentleman in the grey wig, who appeared to have been living recently in Paris, discoursed most innocuously of French châteaux and their gardens, with frequent references to Versailles and Marly, and appeals to his daughter – 'You remember the day of our little expedition to the château of Anet, my dear?' Keith would have thought the deserted shrine of St Germains a more likely goal of pilgrimage, for he took Mr Grant, from his mere presence here, to be a Jacobite.

But surely his daughter would have preferred to this mild talk of parterres and façades a recital by Mr Ewen Cameron of his afternoon's prowess! As far as their personal conflict went, Captain Windham was perfectly willing that this encounter should be related by a victor who was evidently disposed to allow the fullest weight to the physical disabilities of the vanquished; yet he was grateful for the tact with which Mr Cameron (in his presence at least) had glossed over the flight of the Royal Scots from the bridge. Only questions, indeed, drew from him the partial information which he furnished. He would tell them more afterwards, no doubt. ... Who was this pretty Miss Grant with the blue fillet in her dark hair – a kinswoman? If she was the future mistress of the house, young Cameron had good taste. So, to be just, had the lady.

But, despite the courtesy shown him, the unwilling guest was not sorry when, very soon after supper, it was suggested that he should retire, for his ankle was painful and one shoulder ached, though he protested that he could look after his own hurts. His conqueror showed him to his bedchamber exactly as a host might have done. The room was of a fair size, and had good old-fashioned furniture; and, presumably because it had been for some time unused, there was even a fire burning. An elderly woman brought up a crock of hot water, a salve, and linen for bandages, and the Englishman was then left to her ministrations. And it was not long before his discreet questions had drawn from this dame, who was not very communicative, and spoke English as though it were a foreign tongue to her, the information that Miss Grant was to marry the laird in the autumn. Keith privately hoped that the prospective bridegroom might not find himself in prison before that time, as a consequence of having laid hands on himself – if of nothing worse – though, after that venison, he resolved that he would not lift a finger to send him there.

When his ankle had been bathed and bound up, and the elderly servant had withdrawn, the soldier removed his sash, coat, and wig, and extended himself in a comfortable chair in front of the fire, with his bandaged foot on another. There were books to his hand, as he discovered by reaching up to a shelf on the wall; but, having pulled some down, he did not, at first, find that the effort had repaid him. He had captured a Terence, a Horace, *Télémaque*, and Montesquieu's *Lettres persanes*. They all had Ewen Cameron's name written in them.

Keith whistled. He was turning over the leaves of the *Lettres*, when there was a knock and his host – or gaoler – re-entered.

'I hope that Marsali has made you comfortable, sir? – Those books are not very entertaining, I am afraid. If you intend reading into the night – which I fear must mean that your foot is paining you – I will see whether I cannot find you something else. I believe that my aunt has Mr Fielding's novel of *Joseph Andrews* somewhere.'

'Pray do not trouble, sir,' replied Keith. 'I intend to go to bed and sleep; it was only idleness which directed my hand to that shelf there. I see that you read French and Latin, Mr Cameron?' And even as he uttered the words he thought how ill-bred was the remark, and the surprise which he had not been able entirely to keep out of his tone.

But the young Highlander answered quite simply, in his gentle, rather slow voice: 'I was partly educated in France – for that, you know, is easier for us Jacobites. As to Latin, yes, I can read it still, though I am afraid that my hexameters would only procure me the ferule nowadays.'

Captain Windham's ideas about the Northern barbarians were undergoing startling changes. He had already noticed that none of the inmates of this house used the vernacular which he was accustomed to hear in the Lowlands; they spoke as good English as himself, if with an unfamiliar and not displeasing lilt. A little to cover his annoyance at his own lack of breeding, he remarked: 'France, yes; I suppose that your connexion is close. And now that the . . . that a certain young gentleman has come thence – '

'Yes?' asked the other in a slightly guarded manner.

'No, perhaps we had best not engage upon that topic,' said Keith, with a slight smile. 'I will imitate your own courteous discretion at supper, Mr Cameron, in saying so little about the episode at the bridge, of which indeed, as a soldier, I am not proud – By the way, having myself introduced that subject, I will ask you if you can make clear a point in connexion with it which has puzzled me ever since. How was it that no attempt at pursuit – or at least no immediate attempt – was made by the body posted there?'

'That is easily explained,' replied Ewen Cameron promptly. 'The Keppoch MacDonalds there dared not let you see how few they were, lest your men should have rallied and crossed the bridge after all.'

'How few?' repeated Captain Windham, thinking he had not heard aright. 'But, Mr Cameron, there were a quantity of Highlanders there, though owing to the trees it was impossible to form an accurate estimate of their numbers.'

'No, that would be so,' said his captor, looking at him rather oddly. 'You may well have thought the bridge strongly held.'

'You mean that it was not?' And, as his informant merely shook his head, Keith said impatiently, but with a sudden very unpleasant misgiving: 'Do you *know* how many men were there, Mr Cameron?'

Mr Cameron had taken up a fresh log, and now placed it carefully in position on the fire before answering. 'I believe,' he said, with what certainly sounded like reluctance, 'that there were not above a dozen there – to be precise, eleven men, and a piper.'

Keith's fingers closed on the arms of his chair. 'Are you jesting, sir?'

'Not in the least,' replied the young man, without any trace either of amusement or of elation. 'I know it to be a fact, because I spoke afterwards with their leader, MacDonald of Tiendrish. They used an old trick, I understand, to pass themselves off as more than they really were.'

He continued to look at the fire. Captain Windham, with a suppressed exclamation, had lowered his injured foot to the ground, and then remained silent, most horribly mortified. Two companies of His Majesty's Foot turning tail before a dozen beggarly Highlanders, with whom they had not even stayed to exchange shots! The solace, such as it had been, of reflecting that the recruits had in the end been surrounded and outnumbered, was swept clean away, for he knew now that they would never have come to this pass but for their initial poltroonery. Keith had lost all desire for further converse, and every instinct of patronage was dead within him. Why the devil had he ever asked that question?

'I think, sir,' observed his captor, turning round at last, 'that it would be better, would it not, if you went to bed? I hope that you have been given everything that is necessary?'

'Everything, thank you,' replied Keith shortly. 'And also, just now, something that I could well have done without.' He tried to speak lightly, yet nothing but vexation, he knew, sounded in his tone.

'I am sorry,' said the Highlander gravely. 'I would not have told you the number had you not pressed me for it. Forget it, sir.' He went to the door. 'I hope that your injured ankle will not keep you awake.'

That ill office was much more likely to be performed by the piece of news which he had presented to the sufferer.

'Eleven men and a piper!' repeated Captain Keith Windham of the Royal Scots when the door was shut; and with his sound leg he drove his heel viciously into the logs of Highland pine.

Chapter 3

CAPTAIN KEITH WINDHAM, unwillingly revisiting the neighbourhood of High Bridge, which was populated with leaping Highlanders about nine feet high, and permeated even in his dream with the dronings and wailings of the bagpipe, woke, hot and angry, to find that the unpleasant strains at least were real, and were coming through the window of the room in which he lay. He remained a moment blinking, wondering if they portended some attack by a hostile clan; and finally got out of bed and hobbled to the window.

In front of the house a bearded piper was marching solemnly up and down, the ribbons on the drones of his instrument fluttering in the morning breeze. There was no sign of any armed gathering. 'Good Gad, it must be the usual reveillé for the household!' thought the Englishman. 'Enough to put a sensitive person out of temper for the rest of the day.' And he returned to bed, and pulled the blankets over his ears.

At breakfast, an excellent meal, and a pleasant one also, where very civil inquiries were made concerning the night he had spent and the state of his injuries, Miss Cameron expressed a hope that he had not been unduly disturbed by Neil MacMartin's *piobaireachd*, adding that he was not as fine a piper as his father Angus had been. Keith was then thankful that he had not heard Angus.

When the meal was over he strayed to the window and looked out, wondering how he should occupy himself all day, but determined upon one thing, that he would not let these Camerons guess how bitterly he was mortified over the matter of the bridge. Outside the porch, his host (save the mark!) was already talking earnestly to a couple of Highlanders, in one of whom Captain Windham had no difficulty in recognizing the 'cut-throat' of the previous day; the other, he fancied, was the musician of the early morning. 'I wish I could persuade myself that Mr Cameron were putting a ban upon that performance,' he thought; but he hardly hoped it.

Presently the young laird came in. He was wearing the kilt today, and for the first time Keith Windham thought that there was something to be said for that article of attire – at least on a man of his proportions.

'Is not that your attendant of yesterday out there?' remarked the soldier idly.

'Lachlan MacMartin? Yes. The other, the piper who, I am afraid, woke you this morning, is his brother Neil. – Captain Windham,' went on the piper's master in a different tone, 'what I am going to tell you may be news to you, or it may not, but in either case the world will soon know it. Today is Saturday, and on Monday the Prince will set up his standard at Glenfinnan.'

There was a second's silence. 'And you, I suppose, Mr Cameron, intend to be present ... and to cross the Rubicon in his company?'

'All Clan Cameron will be there,' was the reply, given with a probably unconscious lift of the head. 'And as, in consequence of this, I shall be pretty much occupied today, and little at home, I would advise you, if I may, not to go out of sight of the house and policies. You might – ' Ewen Cameron hesitated for a moment.

'I might find myself tempted to abscond, you were going to say?' struck in his captive ... and saw at once, from the bleak look which came into those blue eyes, that his pleasantry did not find favour.

'I should not dream of so insulting you,' replied Ardroy coldly. 'I was merely going to say that it might not be oversafe for you, in that uniform, if you did.'

And as he was evidently quite offended at the idea that he could be supposed to harbour such a suspicion of his prisoner, there was nothing for the latter to do but to beg his pardon, and to declare that he had spoken – as indeed he had – in the merest jest.

'But perhaps this young mountaineer cannot take a jest,' he thought to himself when they had parted. 'I'll make no more – at least outwardly.' But he was not to keep this resolution.

And indeed he had little but occasional glimpses of young Ardroy, or of any of the family, that morning. The whole place was in a bustle of preparations and excitement. Tenants were (Keith surmised from various indications) being collected and armed; though only single Highlanders, wild and unintelligible persons, appeared from time to time in the neighbourhood of the house. Miss Cameron and Miss Grant seemed to be equally caught up in the swirl, and Mr Grant was invisible. The only idle person in this turmoil, the captive Englishman sat calmly on the grass plot at a little distance from the house, with *The History of the Adventures of Mr Joseph Andrews* in his hand, half amused to see the inhabitants of this ant-heap – thus he thought of them – so busy over what would certainly come to nothing, like all the other Jacobite attempts.

And yet he reflected that, for all the futility of such preparations, those who made them were like to pay very dearly for them.

Ewen Cameron would get himself outlawed at the least, and somehow he, whom Ewen Cameron had defeated yesterday, would be sorry. The young Highlander had certainly displayed towards his captive foe the most perfect chivalry and courtesy, and to this latter quality Keith Windham, who could himself at will display the most perfect rudeness, was never blind. And yet – a sardonically comforting reflection – a rebel must find the presence of an English soldier not a little embarrassing at this juncture.

It was partly a desire to show that he too possessed tact, and partly pure boredom, which caused Captain Windham, in the latter half of the afternoon, to disregard the warning given him earlier, and to leave the neighbourhood of the house. He helped himself to a stout stick on which to lean in case of necessity, though his ankle was remarkably better and hardly pained him at all, and started to stroll along the bank of the loch. Nobody had witnessed his departure. And in the mild, sometimes obscured sunshine, he followed the path round to the far side, thinking that could the little lake only be transported from these repellent mountains and this ugly purple heather into more civilized and less elevated surroundings, it would not be an ill piece of water.

Arrived on the farther side, he began idly to follow a track which led away from the lake and presently started to wind upwards among the heather. He continued to follow it, without much thinking of what he was doing, until suddenly it brought him round a fold of the mountain side to a space of almost level ground, where beside a group of pine trees stood three low thatched cottages. And there Captain Windham remained staring, not exactly at the cottages, nor at the score or so of Highlanders – men, women, and children – in front of these dwellings, with their backs turned to him, but at the rather puzzling operations which were going forward on top of the largest croft.

At first Captain Windham thought that the man astride the roof and the other on the short ladder must be repairing the thatch, until he saw that, on the contrary, portions of this were being relentlessly torn off. Then the man on the roof plunged in his arm to the shoulder, and drew forth something round and flat, which he handed to the man on the ladder, who passed it down. Next came something long that glittered, then another round object, then an unmistakable musket; and with that Keith realized what he was witnessing – the bringing forth of arms which should have been given up at the Disarming Act of 1725, but which had been concealed and saved for just such an emergency as the present.

Now there came bundling out several broadswords tied together, and another musket. But a man in a bright scarlet coat with blue facings and long white spatter-dashes is altogether too conspicuous a figure in a mountain landscape, and Keith had not in fact been there more than a minute before a boy who had turned to pick up a targe saw him, gave a yell, and, pointing, screamed out something in Gaelic. Every face was instantly turned in the intruder's direction, and moved by the same impulse each man snatched up a weapon and came running towards him, even he on the roof sliding down with haste.

Captain Windham was too proud to turn and flee, nor would it much have advantaged him; but there he was, unarmed save for a staff, not even knowing for certain whether the hornets upon whose nest he had stumbled were Mr Cameron's tenants or no, but pretty sure that they would not understand English, and that he could not therefore convince them of his perfect innocence. Deeply did he curse his folly in that moment.

He had at any rate the courage not to attempt to defend himself; on the contrary, he deliberately threw his stick upon the ground, and held out his hands to show that they were empty. The foremost Highlander, who was brandishing one of those unpleasant basket-hilted swords, hesitated, as Keith had hoped, and shouted something; on which the rest rushed forward, and as many hands as possible laid hold of Captain Windham's person. He staggered under the impact, but made no resistance, for, to his great relief, he had already recognized in the foremost assailant with the broadsword the scowling visage of Lachlan Mac-Martin, and beside him the milder one of his brother Neil, Mr Cameron's piper. Even if they did not understand English, these two would at least know who he was.

'I am your master's prisoner,' he called out, wishing the others would not press so upon him as they clutched his arms. 'You had better do me no harm!'

In Lachlan's face there was a sort of sullen and unwilling recognition. He spoke rapidly to his brother, who nodded and gave what was presumably an order. Reluctantly the clutching hands released their grip of Keith, their owners merely glowering at him; but they did not go away, though the circle now opened out a little. A couple of women had joined the group, and a small child or two; all talked excitedly. Keith had never thought to feel gratitude towards the wolf-like Lachlan, but at this moment he could almost have embraced him, since but for him and Neil his own might well have been the first blood on those resuscitated claymores.

His preserver now advanced, his hand on his dirk, and addressed the soldier, rather to his surprise, in English.

'You may pe the laird's prisoner,' he said between his teeth, 'but why did you come up here? – You came to spy, to spy!' He almost spat the words in the intruder's face. 'And with spiess, who haf seen what they should not haf seen, there iss a ferry short way ... either thiss,' he unsheathed an inch or two of his dirk, 'or the lochan down yonder, with a stone round the neck!'

'I am not a spy,' retorted Captain Windham haughtily. 'I knew nothing of there being cottages here; I was taking a walk, and came upon you entirely by accident.'

'A walk, when yesterday your foot was so hurt that you must ride the laird's horse?' hissed Lachlan, bringing out all the sibilants in this not ineffective retort. 'All thiss way for pleasure, with a foot that iss hurt? And then you will pe going back to the *saighdearan dearg* – to the red soldiers – at Kilcumein and pe telling them. ... Ach, it will certainly pe petter ...' And his fingers closed round the black hilt at his groin; Keith had never seen fingers which more clearly itched to draw and use a weapon.

But at this point Neil the piper intervened, laying his hand on his brother's arm, shaking his head, and speaking earnestly in their native tongue; and Keith, concluding that a professional musician (if that term could possibly be extended to one who produced sounds like this morning's) would be a man of peace, felt more secure, not knowing that in a fray the piper habitually gave his pipes to his boy and fought with the best. But he heartily wished himself back at the house again; it would have been far better had he taken his host's warning to heart, instead of making a foolish jest about it.

During the colloquy, however, there approached the group a handsome, venerable old man whom Keith had not previously noticed. He came towards them tapping the ground with a long staff, as if of uncertain sight, and said something first to Lachlan and then to Neil. The piper appeared to listen with attention, and on that turned to the captive.

'My father iss asking you,' he said, in a manner which suggested that he was seeking for his words in an unfamiliar tongue, 'to permit him to touch you, and to pe speaking with you. He iss almost blind. He hass not the English, but I will pe speaking for him.'

'Certainly, if he wishes it,' replied Captain Windham with resignation, thinking that 'permission' to touch him might well have been asked earlier, and not taken so violently for granted.

Neil took his father's hand, and led him up to the interview. The old man, who was obviously not completely blind, peered into the Englishman's face, while his hands strayed for a moment or two over his shoulders and breast. He then addressed a question to his elder son, who translated it.

'He asks if you wass meeting a *curra* yesterday?'

'If I had any notion what a *curra* was,' returned Keith, 'I might be able to satisfy your father's curiosity. As it is – '

'A *curra*,' explained Neil, struggling, 'iss ... a large bird, having a long ... a long ...'

'It iss called "heron" in the English,' interposed Lachlan. And he added violently: '*Mallachd ort!* wass you meeting a heron yessterday?'

The Erse sounded like an objurgation (which it was) and the speaker's eyes as they glared at Keith had turned to dark coals. It was evidently a crime in these parts to encounter that bird, though to the heron's victim himself it wore rather the aspect of a calamity. Ignoring this almost frenzied query, he replied shortly to the official interpreter: 'Yes, unfortunately I did meet a heron yesterday, which by frightening my horse led to – my being here today.'

48

Lachlan MacMartin smote his hands together with an exclamation which seemed to contain as much dismay as anger, but Neil contented himself with passing on this information to his parent, and after a short colloquy turned once more to the Englishman.

'My father iss *taibhsear*,' he explained. 'That iss, he hass the two sights. He knew that the heron would pe making Mac – the laird to meet with you.'

'Gad, I could wish it had not!' thought Keith; but judged it more politic not to give this aspiration utterance.

'And he asks you whether you wass first meeting Mac 'ic Ailein near watter?'

'If that name denotes Mr Ewen Cameron,' replied Keith. 'I did. Near a good deal of "watter".'

This was passed on to the seer, involving the repetition of a word which sounded to Captain Windham like 'whisky', and roused in his mind a conjecture that the old man was demanding, or about to demand, that beverage. None, however, was produced, and after thanking the Englishman, in a very courtly way, through the medium of his son, the soothsayer departed again, shaking his head and muttering to himself; and Keith saw him, when he reached the cottages, sit down upon a bench outside the largest, and appear to fall into a reverie.

Directly he was safely there, Lachlan MacMartin reverted with startling suddenness to his former character and subject of conversation.

'You haf seen what you should not haf seen, redcoat!' he repeated fiercely. 'Pefore you go away from thiss place, you shall be swearing to keep silence!'

'That I certainly shall not swear to do,' replied Captain Windham promptly. 'I am not accustomed to take an oath at any man's bidding, least of all at a rebel's.'

Again the dark flame shone in the Highlander's eyes.

'And you think that we will pe letting you go, Sassenach?'

'I think that you will be extremely sorry for the consequences if you do not,' returned the soldier. 'You know quite well that if you lay a finger on me, you will have to answer for it to your master or chief, or whatever he is!'

'We are the foster-brothers of Mac 'ic Ailein,' responded

49

Lachlan slowly. ('What, all of you? 'interjected Keith. 'I wish him joy of you!') 'He knows that all we do iss done for him. If we should pe making a misstake, not knowing hiss will . . . or if you should fall by chance into the loch, we should pe sorry, but we could not help it that your foot should pe slipping, for it was hurt yessterday . . . and you would nefer go back to Kilcumein, to tell the *saighdearan dearg* what you haf peen seeing.'

He did not now seem to be threatening, but rather, with a kind of gloomy satisfaction, thinking out a plausible course of action with regard to the intruder, and it was a good deal more disquieting to the latter than his first attitude. So was the expression on the faces of the other men when Lachlan harangued them volubly in his own language. His brother Neil alone appeared to be making some remonstrance, but in the end was evidently convinced, and almost before the unlucky officer realized what was toward, the whole group had launched themselves upon him.

Keith Windham fought desperately, but he had no chance at all, having been surrounded and almost held from the outset, and in a moment he was borne down by sheer weight of numbers. Buttons came off his uniform, his wig was torn bodily from his head by some assailant who probably imagined that he had hold of the Sassenach's own hair, he was buffeted and nearly strangled, and lay at last with his face pressed into the heather, one man kneeling upon his shoulders, while another tied his hands behind his back, and a third, situated upon his legs, secured his ankles. Outraged and breathless, the soldier had time for only two sensations; surprise that no dirk had yet been planted in him, and wonder whether they really meant to take him down and throw him into the lake.

The struggle had been conducted almost in silence; but conversation broke out again now that he was overpowered. Only for a moment, however; then, as suddenly, it ceased, and the heavy, bony knees on Captain Windham's shoulder-blades unexpectedly removed themselves. A sort of awestruck silence succeeded. With faint thoughts of Druids and their sacrifices in his mind, Keith wondered whether the patriarchal soothsayer were now approaching, to drive a knife with due solemnity into his back . . . or, just possibly, to denounce his descendants' violence. But he could not twist himself to look, for the man on his legs, though apparently smitten motionless, was still squatting there.

And then a voice that Keith knew, vibrating with passion, suddenly shouted words in Erse, whose purport he could guess. The man on his legs arose precipitately. And next moment Ewen Cameron was kneeling beside him in the heather, bending over him, a hand on his shoulder.

'Captain Windham, are you hurt? God forgive me, what have they been doing? *Tied!*' And in a moment he had snatched a little knife out of his stocking and was cutting Keith's bonds. 'Oh, why did I let you out of my sight! For God's sake tell me that you are not injured!'

He sounded in the extreme of anxiety – and well he might be, thought the indignant Englishman, who made no haste to reply that, if exhausted, he was as yet unwounded. He made in fact no reply at all, while the young chieftain, white with agitation and anger, helped him to his feet. When at last he stood upright, hot and dishevelled, and very conscious of the fact, Captain Windham said, in no friendly tone:

'You were just in time, I think, Mr Cameron – that is if, now that you are here, your savages will obey you.'

From pale the young man turned red. 'I warned you, if you remember,' he said rather low, and then, leaving Captain Windham to pick up his hat and wig and to restore some order to his attire, strode towards the silent and huddled group of his retainers, who had retreated in a body nearer to the crofts.

Angry and humiliated as Keith felt, it was some consolation to him, as he brushed the pieces of heather off his uniform, and pulled his wig once more over his own short dark hair, to observe that, whatever their master was saying to them in the Erse, it seemed to have a most salutary and withering effect. Even the redoubtable Lachlan, who hoarsely uttered some remark, presumably an excuse, was reduced to complete silence, either by the very terse and vigorous reply which he drew upon himself, or by the threatening attitude of the speaker.

All this time the prophetic elder had sat at his cottage door listening, with his head tilted back in the manner of the blind, but taking no part in the reckoning which was falling upon the offenders, just as (presumably) he had sat throughout the assault. And having made short work of the culprits, the rescuer now seemed in haste to remove the rescued, and came towards him, his eyes still very blue and fierce.

'If you will allow me, Captain Windham, I will take you back to the house, away from these savages, as you rightly call them.'

'Thanks, I can return safely enough, no doubt,' replied Keith indifferently, pulling down his waistcoat. 'There are no more encampments of them, I believe, on the way back.'

'I should prefer to escort you,' returned Ardroy, most acutely vexed, as was evident. And, since his vexation did not at all displease the Englishman, he picked up his staff and preceded him in silence off the plateau.

They had gone some way down the mountain path before Ewen Cameron spoke again.

'I had no right to accept your sword,' he said, in a voice still bitter with mortification, 'if I could not protect you against my own followers. I would not have had this happen for a thousand pounds. I can offer you no apologies that are deep enough for such an outrage.'

'Except for the loss of some buttons, I am not much the worse,' replied Keith dryly without turning his head.

'But I am,' he heard the Highlander say behind him in a low voice.

Nothing more passed between them until they had arrived at the level of the loch, but by that time a rather remarkable change had come upon Keith. Much better and more dignified to make light of the outrage which he had just suffered than to exaggerate it by sulking over it. Besides, he was beginning to be sorry for the palpable distress of that punctilious young man, Mr Cameron of Ardroy, who could not in very justice be blamed for what had happened.

So he stopped and turned round. 'Mr Cameron,' he said frankly, 'I have no one but myself to thank for the rough handling I received up yonder. You warned me not to go far afield; and moreover I acted like a fool in staying there to watch. Will you forgive my ill-temper, and let me assure you that I shall think no more of the episode except to obey your warnings more exactly in future.'

Ardroy's face cleared wonderfully. 'You really mean that, sir?'

'Assuredly. I ran my head into the lion's mouth myself. I shall be obliged if you will not mention my folly to the ladies; a soldier's self-esteem, you know, is easily hurt.' His smile went up a little at the corner.

A sparkle came into Ewen Cameron's eyes. 'You are generous, Captain Windham, and I am not deceived by your plea for silence. I am so ashamed, however, that I welcome it for the sake of my own self-esteem.'

'But I mean what I say,' returned Keith. (He was quick enough in the uptake, this young chief of barbarians!) 'It was the act of an utter fool for me, in this uniform, to stand gaping at . . . at what was going on up there. You know what it was, I presume?' he added, with a lift of the eyebrows.

'Naturally,' said Ewen without embarrassment. 'It was that which brought me up there – most fortunately. But now,' he went on with a frown, 'now I am not sure that I shall allow those arms to be carried by men in my tail who have so disgraced themselves and me. – Let us go on, if you will; for when I have escorted you to the house I shall return to deal with that question.'

'You seemed,' observed Keith, as they went on once more, 'to be dealing with it pretty satisfactorily just now.' (So he proposed, as a punishment, to debar the offenders from the pleasures of armed rebellion!)

'At least, before I consent to their following me on Monday,' said the dispenser of justice, striding on, 'they shall all beg your pardon!'

'Oh, pray excuse them that!' exclaimed Keith, not at all welcoming the prospect. 'I should be horribly embarrassed, I assure you. Moreover, I can almost sympathize with their zeal – now that there is no prospect of my being thrown into the lake here with a stone round my neck.'

His captor stopped. 'Was that what they were going to do?' he asked in a horrified tone.

'They spoke of it, since I would not promise to keep silence on what I had seen. They were quite logical, you know, Mr Cameron, for what I saw was certainly not meant for the eyes of an English officer!'

'You were my prisoner – my guest – they had no excuse whatever!' declared the young man, wrath beginning to seize on him again. 'Neil and Lachlan knew that, if the others did not. And Angus – what was Angus about, not to stop them?'

'Is that the blind veteran who takes such an interest in the natural history of these parts?'

'What do you mean?' asked his companion.

'Why,' answered Keith, who was after all enjoying a kind of secret revenge by quizzing him, 'that he was particular to inquire, through his estimable son, your piper, whether I had encountered a heron before I made your acquaintance yesterday.'

The mention of that fowl appeared for the second time to startle his host (though until that moment Keith had forgotten its effect upon him last night). 'Ah, my foster-father asked you that?' he murmured, and looked upon the Englishman with a rather troubled and speculative gaze. But Keith had found a new subject of interest. 'Is the old gentleman really your foster-father?' he inquired. 'But of course he must be, if his sons are your foster-brothers.'

'I think,' said the foster-son somewhat hastily, 'that you can return safely from here. So, if you will excuse me, Captain Windham, I will now go back to Slochd nan Eun.'

'To execute judgement,' finished Keith with a smile. 'Indeed, I am not so devoid of rancour as to wish to hinder you. But if you do condemn your foster-relations to stay at home,' he added rather meaningly, 'you will be doing them a good turn rather than an ill one.'

It seemed doubtful, however, whether Ewen Cameron had heard this remark, for he was already striding lightly and quickly back in the direction of the mountain path, his kilt swinging about his knees as he went.

It was an odd coincidence that at supper that evening, after Angus MacMartin's name had come up in some talk between Miss Cameron and Mr Grant, the former should turn to Captain Windham and ask if he had seen their *taibhsear* or seer? Seeing

instantly from Ardroy's face that he was regretting the introduction of his foster-father's name into the conversation, Keith
made malicious haste to reply that he had contrived to get as far
as the soothsayer's dwelling, and that his reception there had
been a memorable experience. Immediately the ladies asked if
Angus had 'seen' anything while the visitor was there, to which
Keith, with a glance at his host, replied with great suavity that
such might well have been the case, since he appeared, towards
the end of the visit, to be entirely withdrawn from outward
events.

'He left the honours to his interesting sons,' he explained with
a smile, 'who entertained me so ... so whole-heartedly that if
Mr Cameron had not appeared upon the scene I might be there
still.' But at this point Ewen, with a heightened colour, forcibly
changed the conversation.

Chapter 4

IN spite of a certain amount of turmoil earlier in the day, almost
the usual Sunday calm lay on the house of Ardroy between five
and six that evening, and in it Alison Grant sat at one of the
windows of the long living-room, her arms on the sill, her cheek
on her joined hands. Her father had gone to Achnacarry, Ewen
was she knew not where, her aunt, she believed, in her bedchamber. It would be better, Alison thought, if she were in hers,
upon her knees.

But she could pray here too, looking out on this blue and
purple loveliness of distance, and here she might get a passing
glimpse of Ewen, busy though he was, and would not thus be
missing any of these precious last moments of him. The sands were
slipping so fast now ...

Alison pulled herself up. The sands were indeed running out,
but towards how glorious an hour! Prayed for and wrought for
with so much faith and selfless devotion (as well as with so much
crooked counter-plot and intrigue), it was to strike tomorrow,
when his banner would proclaim to all the winds that the fairy

prince of the hopes of a generation was here at last, on Scottish soil. And tomorrow Ewen would lay his sword at those long-expected feet. Happy Ewen – happy to be among the faithful, when many were forsworn; happy in that he was a man, and could play a man's part. For what could a woman do but hope, and what has she to give but prayers?

Again Alison checked her thoughts, or rather, a new thought came to her. Why, *she* gave what no one else in wide Scotland had to give: Ewen himself!

For a moment she saw herself, as it were, irradiated by the splendour of that priceless gift; then, with a sudden terror, she knew that her will was not to a gift, but to a loan. She was only lending Ewen to the Prince. A gift is gone from one's hands for ever; a loan comes back. She made this loan willingly – more than willingly; but as a free gift, never to be resumed – no, no!

The door in the far corner of the room opened, and Alison swiftly withdrew the hands that she was pressing over her eyes. Miss Cameron came in, looking exactly as usual in her Sunday paduasoy, not a hair out of place beneath her cap, and no sign of agitation or excitement on her firm-featured, pleasant visage. By only one thing was this Sunday of last preparations marked off from any other, that she wore at her waist the capacious black silk pocket in which she kept the household keys.

'Ah, there you are, child! Your father is not returned, I suppose? Where is Ewen?'

'I do not know, Aunt Margaret.' Alison's voice seemed to herself a little unsteady, so, with some idea of covering this deviation from the usual she added: 'Nor do I know where Captain Windham is got to, either.'

'Captain Windham is down by the loch, my dear; I saw him set out in that direction. And I have my reasons for thinking he'll not have gone farther.' There was an odd tone in Miss Cameron's voice, and a twinkle in her eye, as she sat down on the window seat by the girl, plunging her hand into that capacious pocket of hers. ''Twas our redcoat that I came to speak to you about. Alison, do you know what these are?'

She laid on the window-sill between them two buttons covered with gold thread.

'They look', said Alison, studying them, 'like the buttons on the lapels of Captain Windham's uniform. I noticed this morning that some were missing. How did you come by them, Aunt Margaret?'

'Neil MacMartin brought them to me about half an hour ago. Before that they were reposing in the heather up at Slochd nan Eun, where their owner also reposed, very uncomfortably, I fear, yesterday afternoon. I can't keep from laughing when I think of it!' declared Miss Cameron. 'And, Alison, are not men the sly creatures? To think that Ewen knew of this yesterday evening, and said never a word!'

'Knew of what, Aunt Margaret?'

'I will tell you,' said Aunt Margaret, with visible enjoyment of the prospect. 'It seems that yesterday afternoon my fine Captain very incautiously walked up to Slochd nan Eun by his lane, and arrived there just as the arms were being taken out of Angus's thatch. Not unnaturally the MacMartins and the others thought that he was a Government spy, so they fell upon him, tied him up, and might have proceeded to I know not what extremities if Ardroy had not appeared in the very nick of time.'

'Oh, what a dreadful thing!' said Alison, aghast.

'Exactly Ewen's view, as you may imagine. He has not yet forgiven the two MacMartins, whom he holds most to blame. Neil, in the greatest despair, has just been to beg me to intercede for him and Lachlan, and seemed to think that the restoration of these buttons, torn off, so I gathered, in the struggle, would go to prove their penitence.'

'Was Captain Windham at all hurt, do you think?'

'No, I do not think so, though I can quite believe that it was not his mother's bosom he was in – you know the Erse saying. Neil admits that they had him on his face in the heather when they trussed him up, and that two of them sat upon him. Well, they are paying for it now. As you know, Ardroy is not in general easily angered, but when he is, he is not easily pacified neither. Neil looks like a whipped dog; 'tis really comical, and I dare say Lachlan is ready to cut his own throat. I think you had best do the interceding, my dear; and you can give Ewen the buttons to return, for we women cannot restore them to Captain Windham without his knowing that his misadventure is no longer the secret that he and Ewen hoped it was.'

But Alison left the buttons on the sill as if she dreaded to touch them. 'I wish, oh, I wish that mishap had not befallen Captain Windham!'

'Never fash yourself about Captain Windham, my lass; I warrant he can fend for himself. Ewen should not have brought him here, at a moment so inopportune – just what a man would do, without thought of consequences! At the least he might have locked him up somewhere out of harm's way, and not made all this parade of his being a guest and the like.'

'*I* think it fine of Ewen to have behaved so,' retorted Alison, rather mutinously.

'Bless you, child,' said Miss Cameron, smiling, 'so it is! I'd not have him a churl. But they must have made a compact, the two deceitful bodies, not to let us know. And to think that I asked the Captain at supper last night had he seen our *taibhsear* – do you mind of it? And he smiling and saying he was well entertained up at Slochd nan Eun!'

'But Ewen did not smile,' amended Alison. 'He was displeased; I saw it, and wondered why.'

'Now that you mention it, I remember I saw him glower a wee. He's not so deep as yon Englishman, I'm thinking. All the same, he can keep a secret. . . . Alison, my bonny lass, do you think he'll have secrets from you, when you are wed?'

'No,' said Alison, shaking her dark curls with a half-secret smile. 'Or if he has, I'll know 'tis something I had best be ignorant of.'

'Then you'll make a dutiful wife, my dear,' pronounced Miss Cameron, smiling too.

'If ever I am a wife at all!' suddenly came from Alison with a catch of the breath, and she turned her head away.

Margaret Cameron, who was never known to show much emotion, who even now, at this last hour before what might prove so tremendous a dawn, seemed mainly occupied with amusement at Captain Windham's misfortune, gazed at that little dark head, so beautifully and proudly set on its long neck, and a profound change came over her cheerful and practical face.

Thirty years ago, in the Fifteen, she too had stood where Alison stood now, and had seen her lover go from her down the dark defile. She had never seen him return. . . . Alison did not know this, and even Ewen, though he had heard the story, thought that Aunt Margaret had long ago forgotten her tragedy.

'Oh, my dear, do not say that!'

Struck by the unfamiliar note in the elder woman's voice, Alison turned her head quickly, and met the look in those eyes, nearly as blue as Ewen's. It was a surprise to her, and yet – how could she have imagined that Aunt Margaret did not realize what she, Alison, risked . . . what they both risked!

'I did not mean that,' she exclaimed rather tremulously. 'To be sure Ewen will come back, and we shall be wed some day; but I cannot help knowing, as he does, how even Lochiel himself has been torn in two by the Prince's coming without the aid that was promised. But when Ewen goes tomorrow, he shall never guess how cowardly my heart is.'

Miss Cameron bent forward and kissed her.

'That's my brave lass! We shall both be as gay as the laverock, I dare say, till he's fairly away; and then we can be as hare-hearted as we please, with no one to see. Hark, there's the boy's step! I'll leave you, my dear; don't forget to put in a word for poor Neil!'

'Till he is fairly away.' It echoed in the girl's ears as Miss Cameron slipped from the room. Why, one could not even imagine what the house of Ardroy would be like without Ewen!

'Heart's darling, are you there?' He had come in by the door from the hall, and now threw himself down beside her on the window-seat. 'Hardly a word have I had with you this live-long day! And now I must ride over to Achnacarry for Mac Dhomhnuill Duibh's final orders, and shall not be back till late, I fear me. But all's ready here, I think.'

'I wish I were more ready,' thought Alison, devouring him with her eyes. His bright hair grew down in such an enchanting square on his wide forehead; and a desire came upon her to pass her hand over some of its thick waves. 'Ah, to see the Prince at last, at last, Ewen, with one's own eyes!'

'You'll see him yourself before long, Alison, I hope, in Edinburgh, or maybe Perth – or even, before that, at Achnacarry, if he honours it. Who knows? Meanwhile you can be practising your curtsy, *m'eudail*!'

'You do not know what His Royal Highness will do after the standard is set up?'

'I've not a notion. But I shall contrive to send you word of our movements, never fear. I suppose that somewhere or other we shall be obliged to try conclusions with Sir John Cope and the Government troops.'

The words reminded Alison of the commission just laid upon her. She took up the buttons from the window-sill and held them out towards him.

'Ewen, these have just been brought down from Slochd nan Eun.'

Her lover looked at them with a surprise not quite free from embarrassment. 'They must have come off Captain Windham's uniform,' he observed non-committally. 'I will give them back to him.' And he took them from her.

'I must tell you that I have just heard how it was that he lost them,' confessed the girl.

Ewen's mouth tightened. He laid the buttons on the sill again. 'How came that? I had hoped – '

'Yes, dearest, I know; but the matter came out by reason of Neil's bringing the buttons to Aunt Marget this afternoon, as a kind of peace-offering, it would seem. But, Ewen, what a shocking thing to have happened! I do not wonder that you were angry.'

By the laird of Ardroy's looks, he was angry still. Alison trusted that he would never look at her, on her own account, in that stern way; and perhaps indeed Ewen realized that he was frowning on the innocent, for his brow relaxed, and he took her hand into his as if in apology.

'Indeed, Alison, my heart was in my mouth when I came upon the MacMartins and the rest up there yesterday; for all I knew they had dirked Captain Windham. It seems they had thought of throwing him into the loch. He should not have gone so far from the house; I had warned him against it. But he behaved very well over the affair, and we agreed not to tell you or Aunt Marget, so you must neither of you say a word to him about the matter this evening.'

'But he must have been greatly offended and incensed. It is true that he was very agreeable at supper, even though Aunt Marget asked him had he seen Angus.' She paused, wrinkling her brows. 'Ewen, do you think that he was only feigning?'

'No, I do not think so, although he was very angry at first -- and naturally. Afterwards he made to treat the affair almost as a joke. But I do not think that in his heart he can have considered it as a joke. And considering that his person should have been held sacred, it was a very black disgrace for me, and I did well to be angry. I am still angry,' he added somewhat unnecessarily, 'and I have not yet resolved whether I shall allow the two MacMartins to accompany me tomorrow.'

'Not take Neil and Lachlan to Glenfinnan – not take your piper and your right-hand man!' exclaimed Alison, almost incredulous. 'But, Ewen, dearest, you will break their hearts for ever if you leave them behind! That punishment is too great! It was surely in ignorance that they sinned; you yourself said that Captain Windham should not have gone there, and in that uniform, they must naturally have thought – '

'Neil and Lachlan did *not* sin in ignorance,' interrupted Ewen sternly. 'I had particularly told them that morning what was Captain Windham's position here. The others, if you like, had more excuse, though why Angus did not prevent their setting upon him, as he could have done, I cannot think. The reason he gave was so – ' He broke off, and pushed about the buttons on the sill for a moment or two, then, raising his head, said: 'I have not yet told you, Alison, how Angus "saw" last month that this fellow Windham and I would meet.'

'Angus "saw" that you would meet!' repeated Alison, wide-eyed. 'Oh, Ewen, why did you not tell me?'

'Because I forgot all about it, till last Friday night. Yes, and what is more, it appears that we are to keep on meeting, confound him!'

'Do you then dislike Captain Windham so much?' asked Alison quickly.

'I do not dislike him at all,' Ewen assured her, 'though I

confess that I cannot quite make him out. But I have no desire for the continual rencontres with him which Angus promises me. And I am sure that Captain Windham cannot possibly view me with anything but dislike for capturing him – and now comes yesterday's affair. – Don't look so troubled, my heart!'

'Tell me what Angus said.'

Ewen looked at her a moment as if considering. 'But you must not believe it too implicitly, darling; I do not. Though I admit,' he added, as though wishing to be quite just, 'that the old man's predictions have sometimes fulfilled themselves in an extra-ordinary way. . . . This one began by something about a heron.'

'That, then, was why you were so much surprised on Friday evening,' interpolated Alison in a flash. 'I mean, when Captain Windham said that a heron had brought down his horse. I saw it, Ewen. But how – '

'I will tell you from the beginning,' said her betrothed. He got up and put a knee on the window seat. 'It was that day at the end of last month when Lochiel's message came about the Prince's landing – you remember? Early that morning Lachlan had been very troublesome, wanting to shoot the heron that lives on the island in the loch, because his father had been having a vision about one. I forbade him to do it. – That reminds me, I have not seen the bird of late, but I do not think that Lachlan dare have disobeyed me. – After I had taken leave of you that evening, darling, and was just about to set off to Achnacarry, I met Angus by the Allt Buidhe brun. He had come down from Slochd nan Eun on purpose to see me, and he told me very solemnly that I should soon meet with a man whose destiny would in some unknown way be bound up with mine, and that I should meet him through the agency of a heron. Angus went on to say: "And as the threads are twisted at your first meeting, foster-son, so will they always shape themselves at all the rest – a thread of one colour, a thread of another." I said on that: "At all the rest, Angus? How many more, then?" and he thought a while and answered: "I saw you meeting five times. The first time and the last were by water . . . but always the place changed. Oh, my son, if only I could know what it means!" I asked then whether I ought to avoid this man, and Angus said: "You will not be able to avoid him; the heron by the waterside will bring you to him." "Ah," said I, "that then is why Lachlan wanted to shoot the *curra* this morning!" But Angus shook his head and muttered: "A man cannot change the future in that way. What is to be will be."

'I thought at the time, Alison,' went on Ewen explanatorily, looking down at her intent face, 'that I should come on this man some day, if ever I did, when I was out with a fowling-piece, or something of the sort, and then, to tell truth, I forgot all about the matter in the stir of the news from Moidart; and thus it never crossed my mind when I encountered Captain Windham that he could be the man ... till he mentioned the heron which startled his horse, and so indirectly – or directly, if you will – led to my overtaking him by Loch Oich, and our fight.'

'And is that all that Angus said?' asked Alison breathlessly.

'There was one thing more, I remember, for when, after he had assured me that I should not be able to avoid this man, I said: "He is an enemy, then?" Angus replied: "That I cannot see. He will do you a great service, yet he will cause you bitter grief. It is dark." You know how vexatious it is when one with the two sights cannot see any more. It is like beginning to read a book of which the last pages are lost.'

'I do not think that I should wish to read any more,' said the girl, shivering a little, and she too got up from the window seat. 'I have never before met anyone who had the gift so strongly as Angus, and indeed it is not canny. You are used to it, Ewen, since you have known him all your life, and I think you do not believe in it very much, either.'

'No, I do not,' admitted her lover. 'But it would not be kind to tell my foster-father so.'

Alison looked out of the window for a moment, biting her lip hard. 'Ewen, when a *taibhsear* "sees" any person it is nearly always a warning of that person's imminent death.'

Ewen put his arm round her. 'No, you are wrong, my dear. A *taibhsear* has been known to see a man's future wife – sometimes his own. I wonder Angus never "saw" you, sitting by the hearth here in the days when you were in Paris ... long days those were for me, *mo chridhe*! Moreover, in this matter of the heron, he "saw" two people; and neither Captain Windham nor I can be going to die very soon, can we, if we must meet each other four times more?'

She looked up and met his expression, tender but half quizzical. 'No, that is true.'

'Angus said nothing about death,' went on Ewen reassuringly. 'And he seemed completely puzzled by his vision – or visions. If it were not for that heron by Loch Oich, I vow I should think that he had dreamed the whole business.'

'Have you told Captain Windham any of this?' asked Alison.

'Not I. He would only laugh at it, and I am sure, too, that he has no desire to meet me again, so that I should not be telling him anything to pleasure him.'

'Do you think,' suggested Alison slowly, 'that Angus did not hinder his sons and the others from attacking Captain Windham because he thought that he would be better out of the way – on your account?'

Her lover looked at her with a rather startled expression. 'I never thought of that. . . . But no, I do not believe that was the reason – it would not have been, unless he was lying over the reason he gave me.'

'And what was that?'

'It was outrageous enough. He said that there was no cause for interference, because he knew that the *saighdear dearg* and I had yet several times to meet, so he would take no harm. What do you think of that? Had he not been an old man, and nearly blind, and my foster-father to boot, I declare that I could have shaken him, when I went back to Slochd nan Eun and upbraided him, and was given that for justification. It might very well have been Captain Windham's wraith that I was to tryst with!' He glanced at the clock. 'I must go, darling.'

'What will become of Captain Windham tomorrow?' asked Alison with a tiny frown.

'I do not know; it is a question I have to ask Lochiel.'

'One thing more, Ewen; did not Angus, after he had seen Captain Windham in the flesh yesterday, as I suppose he did – did he not tell you any more about him and . . . and the future?'

'Not a word. No, as I say, the last pages of the book are torn out ... but then it is so with every book in which our lives are written.'

He had both his arms round her now, and Alison hid her eyes against his breast, for he was so tall that even the top of her head was scarcely level with his chin. 'Why do you say that, Ewen? Oh, Ewen, why do you say that?'

'What ails you, heart's darling?' he asked, looking down at the dark head tenderly. 'It is true. You're not thinking, surely, that at the end of the book I can care for you any less, little white love? That's impossible ... and I think it's impossible that I should care for you more, either,' he added, and put a kiss on the soft hair.

Alison clung to him, saying nothing, mindful of her proud promise to Aunt Margaret, but shaken with the knowledge of the red close of many a life across whose pages the name of Stuart had been written. Devotion to that name and cause was the religion in which she had been reared; but the claims of religion can some-times make the heart quail ... and Ewen was so splendid, so real and so dear! She forced a smile, and raised her head; her eyes were quite dry. 'I must not keep you from Lochiel; but when you return, Ewen, will you not tell your foster-brothers that you have remitted their punishment?'

'For your sake, Alison?'

'No, for his who is waiting for them! Is he not needing every sword that we can bring him?'

Ewen smiled down at her appreciatively. 'You find clever argument, miss! I never said that they should not join me later.'

'As ghosts? You may find yourselves trysting with wraiths, as you spoke of doing a while ago! Are they not capable of drowning themselves in the loch, particularly Lachlan, if you put that shame upon them, Ewen?'

'Yes,' said Ewen after a moment's silence, 'I'll not deny that Lachlan, at least, might throw himself into Loch na h-Iolaire. I suppose that I must allow them to come with me, and if you see them before my return, you can tell them so, rose of my heart.'

The room was empty once more, almost as empty as it would

be tomorrow. And, since there was no one to see, Alison put her head down upon her arms on the window-sill.

When she raised it again after some moments a small object rolled off the sill and fell tinkling to the floor – one of Captain Windham's unfortunate buttons, which Ewen had forgotten after all to take with him. As Alison stooped to recover it the thought of its owner came sharply and forbiddingly into her mind, accompanied by all that she had just heard about him. Ewen's destiny bound up with his . . . and he, yesterday, disgracefully handled by Ewen's followers! Surely, however he had passed it off, he must retain a grudge about that; and it might be that in the future he would seize an opportunity of repaying the outrage. Alison wished for a moment that she were not Highland, and that belief in second sight did not run so in her blood. She could not shake from her mind the conviction that for old Angus to have seen the doubles of Ewen and the English officer meant the death of one or both of them within the year. It was true that the prediction had not seemed to trouble Ewen much, but he was a man, and had his head full of Glenfinnan at present. Yet there was Captain Windham, with nothing to do but to brood over the injury. Already, as Ewen had felt, he might well have a dislike to his captor. And did it not seem as though he had a horrid gift for dissimulation if, so soon afterwards, he could pretend to find amusement in the mortifying thing which had happened to him? What sort of a man was he really, this stranger who was to cause her Ewen bitter grief?

Alison jumped to her feet and stood with clasped hands. 'I'll go along the loch side, as though I were taking a walk; and if he is still there I'll engage him in talk, and perhaps I can find out a little about him.' For in the house she could not so easily get speech with him alone, and tomorrow he would surely be gone altogether. Yes, she would do that; Captain Windham would never guess that she had come on purpose. She slipped the buttons into her pocket and left the room.

Chapter 5

It was not difficult to find Captain Windham by the loch, for the delicate veils of birch foliage made no effective screen for his strong scarlet. Alison saw him, therefore, before he was aware of her presence. He was sitting a yard or two from the edge of Loch na h-Iolaire, on the stump of a felled pine, with his arms folded on his breast, staring at the water. Was he thinking of yesterday – meditating some revenge? She would never know, because she dared not refer, even indirectly, to that unlucky contretemps. The buttons were in her pocket only for safe keeping.

Alison came very slowly along the ribbon of track through the heather, her eyes fixed on the soldier's unconscious figure. Ewen's destiny in *his* hands? No. Angus had not said that exactly. Nor had Angus said that he was an enemy; on the contrary, he was to render Ewen a great service. . . . Technical enemy, of course, he was. She had his profile now, clear against a reddish pine-trunk; he looked rather sad. He was an enigma, neither friend nor enemy; and she would find out nothing, do no good ... and wished she had not come.

Then the best was to turn and go back again. No, it was too late for that now. At that very moment Captain Windham must have heard her step, for he turned his head, sprang up, and, uncovering, came towards her between the pines.

'Pray do not let me drive Miss Grant away,' he said civilly.

'I ... I fear I disturb you, sir,' said Miss Grant, really discomposed.

'Disturb me! But I was not asleep, I assure you, and in breaking into my meditations you may have been doing me a service.'

He smiled a little as he said it, but Alison looked at him warily, wondering what he meant by that remark. Here they were, alone together, and neither could see what was uppermost in the other's mind. *He* did not know that strange thing prophesied of him, linking him to an enemy; nor could *she* in the least read what were his feelings with regard to Ewen, although it was a matter which concerned her so vitally. But, notwithstanding that she had a moment ago turned away like a coward from this interview,

67

now she resolved to pursue it. Surely her wits could point out some road by which she might arrive at Captain Windham's real sentiments?

Quite close to her was another convenient pine-stump, so she sank down upon it, murmuring about resting for a moment. Captain Windham stood beside her, his hands behind his back and his head bent, and before she had settled upon her own line of attack startled her by saying slowly, and even a trifle hesitatingly, that he had for the last hour been greatly wishing for the privilege of a few minutes' conversation with her.

Considerably surprised at this reversal of parts, Alison glanced up at him. Was this remark a prelude to compliments or gallantry of some kind? No; Captain Windham's manner quite disposed of that idea. Yet he said again, gravely: 'I desire to ask a favour of you, Miss Grant.'

'Pray ask it, sir,' replied Alison, just a trifle stiffly.

There was a moment's pause. 'I believe that Mr Cameron – Ardroy, I suppose, I should say – has ridden off to see his Chief, has he not?' said the soldier.

'Yes,' said Alison, still less encouragingly.

'And by this time tomorrow – ' Captain Windham left the sentence unfinished, and, to her surprise, walked away from her with bent head, and stood at a little distance carefully pushing two or three fallen fir-cones together with his foot. Finally he stooped, picked up one, and came back, twirling it in his fingers.

'Miss Grant,' he said, studying it with apparent absorption, 'I wish that I could make Ardroy some return for his generous treatment of me. This is not a mere figure of speech; I am in complete earnest. But the only return that I can make, he would never take at my hands.' He raised his eyes and looked at her musingly. 'What I wonder is, whether he would take it at yours.'

'What do you mean, sir?' asked Alison, lifting her head a trifle haughtily. Surely he was not going to offer Ewen money! She must prevent that at all costs, or Heaven knew what might happen!

Captain Windham threw away the fir-cone. 'Will you believe, Miss Grant, that in what I am going to say I speak as a friend might (though I dare not presume to call myself one) and that I have but one aim in speaking – Mr Cameron's good and yours?'

Alison met his eyes, and they convinced her of his sincerity. She had scarcely time to be amazed. 'Yes, I do believe it,' she said in a softened tone. 'Please say what you wish, Captain Windham.'

'Then let me ask you,' said the Englishman earnestly, 'whether you and Ardroy realize on what a hopeless adventure he is embarking? Is it possible that, on the strength of having captured two wretched companies of raw recruits – for indeed they were no more than that – the clans of these parts think that they will be able to defy the whole military force of the Crown? Yes, Miss Grant, it is advice that I should like to give Mr Cameron; if he would only take it. Cannot you use your interest with him? Forgive me if I trespass on delicate ground, but . . . this is to be your home together, is it not? Think again before you let him stake it on so hazardous a throw! You know what happens to the property of a declared rebel. And he stakes more than his property, Miss Grant!'

His voice was very grave. Alison, who had heard him through, answered firmly: 'Yes, I know that.' But the lovely colour was gone from her cheeks, and her hands were holding each other tightly.

'It is not too late, even now,' urged her companion. 'If I choose to suppress the fact that I was brought here as Mr Cameron's prisoner, who is to gainsay my assertion that I came as a guest? Only keep him back from this crazy rendezvous tomorrow, which can but herald disaster, and he may be able – '

'Keep him back!' exclaimed Alison. She had got up from her tree-stump. 'Do you suppose that I *could*? Do you suppose that if I could, I *would*?' Her voice trembled a little.

'But, Miss Grant, consider! If this young man, this Prince of yours, had come with an army – '

'Then it would have been safe to declare for him!' broke in Alison, and her dark eyes flashed. 'Oh, if that is the English way of thinking, it is not the Highland! Because he comes alone, and trusts himself to us, is not that the best of reasons why we should follow him who has the right, Captain Windham, and who may yet prove to have the might also?'

There was a short silence between them. On the other side of the loch a curlew uttered its plaintive, liquid cry. Captain Windham drew himself up a little.

'If you feel thus about the matter, Miss Grant,' he said rather dryly, 'there is no more to be said. I see that you will not take my offering. The best I can wish you, then, is that the affair may burn itself out as quickly as possible, for the longer it lasts the more victims there are likely to be ... afterwards. And I would give much, believe me, to know that Mr Cameron of Ardroy will not be among them.'

Alison held out her hand impulsively. And she had been thinking that he was brooding on revenge! 'I thank you for those words, sir,' she said with great sweetness, 'because I believe that you mean them. But, though I shall not easily forget your kindness, it is – forgive me – useless to discuss the matter further.'

Captain Windham kissed her hand in silence, and offered her his arm back to the house, if she were returning thither. Alison took it readily enough, and as they left the loch, conversing on indifferent topics, she had time to taste the surprise and relief which had come to her there. If Fate's chosen instrument – supposing he were really that – were so well disposed towards Ewen, how could he in the future be used against him?

And yet, later in the evening, waiting for Ewen's return, she found that, unreasonably perhaps, she disliked Captain Windham's presumption that she could, if she tried, influence her lover to betray his convictions, even more than the supposition that she could be induced to try. She felt that the soldier understood neither Highlanders nor Jacobites. But for his kindly and even generous intentions, she had nothing but gratitude.

As for Keith Windham, whose meditations by Loch na h-Iolaire had moved him to an effort which surprised him, he told himself that he had never expected any other result. They were all blinded and besotted, these Jacobites. He wondered whether Miss Grant would tell her betrothed of his attempt. With Ardroy himself he naturally should not think of expostulating; to do so would be mere waste of breath.

There was no Ardroy at supper, though it appeared that he was expected back at any moment, and Keith shortly afterwards excused himself and withdrew to his own bedchamber, having no wish to be an intruder on the lovers' last hours together, rebels though they were. But it was too early to go to bed, so once more he pulled a couple of books at random from the shelf on the wall, and settled down by the window to read. One of them he opened before he realized what it was, and found himself staring at 'Most heartily do we beseech Thee with Thy favour to behold our most gracious Sovereign Lord, King – ' but 'James' had been neatly pasted over the 'George'.

Captain Windham smiled. He held in his hand the Book of Common Prayer as used and amended by the nonjuring Episco-palian Jacobites, and saw with his own eyes the treason to which his ears might have listened earlier in the day. For though, on rising, he had forgotten that it was Sunday, this was a fact of which he had not long been suffered to remain ignorant, since after breakfast Miss Cameron had said to him in matter-of-fact tones – they were alone for the moment: 'I doubt you will wish to attend Morning Prayer with us, Captain Windham, even if you be an Episcopalian, like most of the English; for I must not dis-guise from you that we pray, not for King George, but for King James.'

'"Morning Prayer",' Keith had stammered. 'Is – do you – I had thought that you were all Presbyterians hereabouts . . . or Papists,' he added, suddenly remembering the old woman on Friday.

'Ah, not at all,' replied Miss Cameron composedly. 'The Mac-Donalds of the mainland and the most of the Frasers indeed are Papists, but we Camerons are Episcopalians, and so are our neighbours, the Stewarts of Appin. But we can get to kirk but rarely, and today in especial being, as you will understand, some-what throng, we shall be obliged to worship at home.'

'And who – '

'Why, my nephew the laird, naturally,' replied Miss Cameron. 'Though as Mr Grant is with us, 'tis possible he may read the service today.'

'Leaving your nephew free to preach, no doubt?' suggested Keith, trying to control a twitch of the lip.

'Now you are laughing at us, sir,' observed Miss Cameron shrewdly, but with perfect good humour. 'No, Ardroy does not preach. But I have the habit of reading a sermon to myself of a Sunday afternoon, and if you scoff any more 'tis likely the same exercise would benefit you, and I'll be happy to lend you a volume of some English divine – Bishop Jeremy Taylor, for instance.'

Keith bowed, and gravely assured her that if she saw fit to do this he would duly read a homily. But he had gone out into the garden smiling to himself. That model young man – he could not be more than five- or six-and-twenty – reading the Church service every Sunday to his household! He thought of the young men of his acquaintance in the army, or in the fashionable world of London, the careless, loose-living subalterns, the young beaux of White's. Ye gods, what ribald laughter would have gone up at the tale! . . . Yes, but not one of those potential mockers could have beaten Ardroy in stature or looks, or at swordplay. Keith would not forget Loch Oich side in a hurry.

But he had not attended Morning Prayer.

Now he was rather wishing that he had done so, for he supposed that he would never again have the chance of seeing a young man who could fight in that style acting as chaplain. But perhaps Mr Grant had superseded him; Keith had not inquired. At any rate Ewen Cameron was not engaged on particularly prayerful business at this moment, over at his Chief's house, nor would he be on his knees tomorrow. Afterwards . . . well, it was likely that his relatives would have need to pray for *him*!

He turned over the Prayer Book idly, and it opened next at the feast of the Conversion of St Paul, and the words of the Gospel leapt at him: 'Every one that hath forsaken houses, or brethren, or sisters, or father, or mother, or wife, or children, or lands, for my Name's sake . . .'

Though not much of a church-goer himself, Captain Windham was shocked at the analogy which occurred to him, and closing the Prayer Book hastily, fell to wondering what was going to be done with him tomorrow; also, whose hand had retrieved and laid upon his dressing-table the two missing buttons from his uniform, which he had found there a short while ago.

It was nearly ten o'clock when he heard the beat of hoofs. They stopped in front of the porch, but he did not look out. Someone dismounted, then Keith heard Miss Grant's voice, with her heart in it: 'Ewen, you are come at last; it has been a long evening!'

'And will be a short night, Alison,' came the half-exultant reply. 'We march at daybreak for Glenfinnan!'

And from the sudden silence, Keith guessed that the girl was in her lover's arms. He moved away from the window and began to pace up and down. So there was to be no holding back. Ah, what a pity, what a pity!

Half an hour later he was back in his old place reading, but with a lighted candle at his elbow now, when there was a knock, and Ardroy himself came in, a big branched candlestick in his hand.

'You are not abed, Captain Windham! I must apologize, none the less, for so late a visit.'

There was a kind of suppressed elation about him, and his eyes were as blue as the sea.

'Your Highland nights are so light,' returned Keith, as he rose to his feet, 'that it is hard to believe it late.' Why should he, who cared for no human being, feel regret that this young man was going to destruction?

'My excuse', went on Ewen, setting down the light he carried, 'is that I leave this house again in a few hours, and must speak with you first on a matter that concerns you.'

'You will be setting out for – the rendezvous of which you told me?'

'Yes. And before I go – '

'Mr Cameron,' broke in the Englishman, 'you gave me a warning yesterday, to which I should have done well to listen. I suppose it is too much to hope that, at this eleventh hour, you will listen to one from me?'

As he said it he knew that he was a fool for his pains; that his words, uttered on that astonishing impulse, so contrary to his intention, were as useless as the little puff of air which at that moment entered by the open window and set the candles a-quiver.

73

And over the bending flames the Highlander, looking very tall, gazed at him straight and unyieldingly.

'You are too kind, Captain Windham. But if the matter of your warning be what I suppose, you must forgive me for saying that you would only be wasting your time.' His tone was courteous but very cold.

Keith shrugged his shoulders. After all, if a man *would* rush on his doom it was his own affair. 'My time is far from valuable at present,' he replied flippantly, 'but yours no doubt is precious, Mr Cameron. On what matter did you wish to speak to me?'

'I have come to tell you from my Chief, Lochiel, that you are free from tomorrow – on one condition.'

'And that is?'

'That you engage not to bear arms against the Prince, for the remainder of the campaign. Lochiel will accept an assurance given to me.'

' "For the remainder of the campaign"!' exclaimed Keith rather indignantly. 'An impossible condition, on my soul!' He gave a short laugh. 'It is true that your "campaign" is not like to be of long duration!'

Ewen ignored the sneer. 'You cannot tell, sir,' he replied gravely. 'But those are the terms which I am to offer you. Captain Scott has accepted them, and has today gone to Fort William to have his wound cared for.'

'Precisely,' retorted Keith. 'Captain Scott is wounded; I am not.' There was still indignation in his voice; nevertheless he was thinking that if he accepted the offer he would be able to leave the Highlands and return to Flanders and real warfare. It was a temptation. But some deep-rooted soldierly instinct revolted.

He shook his head. 'My sword is the King's, and I cannot enter into an indefinite engagement not to use it against his enemies. Indeed it is fully time that I should ask you, Mr Cameron, to restore me the parole of honour which I gave you. I should prefer henceforward to be your prisoner upon ordinary terms.'

But at this his gaoler seemed taken aback. 'I fear that is impossible at present, sir,' he replied with some hesitation. 'If I left you behind here, there would be no one to guard you. As you will not accept your freedom on the condition which is offered you, I have no choice but to take you with me tomorrow – still on parole, if you please,' he added, looking his captive straight in the face.

'I have requested you to give me back my parole, Mr Cameron!'

'And I have already said that I cannot do so, Captain Windham!'

Once more they were facing each other across the candle flames. Keith began to feel annoyance.

'Am I then to go ranging the mountains with you for ever? You will find me a great nuisance, Mr Cameron.' (Mr Cameron looked at that moment as if he shared this opinion.) 'But perhaps this is your way of forcing Lochiel's offer on me, for, by Gad, that is what it comes to!'

'No, no,' said Ewen hastily, and with a frown. 'I had no such intention. I will consult Lochiel again about the matter tomorrow and – '

'Can't you do anything on your own responsibility, Mr Cameron of Ardroy? Must you always consult your Chief?'

He had goaded him at last. Ardroy's head went up. 'Had you not a commanding officer in your regiment, Captain Windham?' he inquired haughtily.

'*Touché!*' said Keith, with good humour. (It was a mutual hit, though.) He liked to see his civilized young barbarian on the high horse. 'But suppose, Mr Cameron, that I do not choose to wait so long, and tell you frankly that, if you will not restore my parole to me, I shall myself withdraw it from midnight tonight?'

'In that case,' said the barbarian with great promptitude, 'I shall put two of my gillies in here with you, lock the door, and sleep across it myself. . . . Do you tell me that you withdraw it?'

There was a second or two's silence, while Keith envisaged himself thus spending the remainder of the night. It was on the tip of his tongue to inquire whether the amiable Lachlan would be one of his guards, but he suppressed the query. 'No,' he said with a little grimace, 'you may keep my parole, and I will keep my privacy. Let us hope that your "commanding officer's" wisdom will be able to cut the knot tomorrow. I am to be ready, then, to accompany you at daybreak?'

'If you please,' said Ardroy stiffly. 'I am sorry that I can do nothing else. Good night.' He took up the candlestick, and stalked out.

Captain Keith Windham remained staring for a moment at the closed door and then began to smile rather ruefully. 'A droll captivity, 'pon my honour! Had I known that I was to be trailed about in this fashion my attempt at warning might have been less disinterested than it was. But I shall not make another.'

Chapter 6

FOUR days later, Captain Windham was sitting at evening in a dark little hut on the shores of Loch Eil, studying a pocket-book by the light of a small lantern hung on the wattled wall behind him. A pile of heather was all his seat; outside it was pouring with rain, but he, unlike almost everyone else, was at least under cover and secure, as he had not been lately, from the attentions of the rapacious Highland midges.

It was Thursday, the twenty-second of August, and since Monday he had gone with Clan Cameron wherever it went. First of all Ardroy and his contingent had rendezvoused with the main body of the clan at the very place where Keith Windham now found himself again, Kinlochiel, at the upper end of Loch Eil. Here, on that eventful Monday, Keith had had his first meeting with the courteous and polished gentleman whom Clan Cameron followed, Donald Cameron of Lochiel, nineteenth of the name. And Lochiel had appeared so much distressed at the idea of the English officer's continued conveyance with them under guard, even possibly in bonds, for they had no place in which they could conveniently leave him behind, that Keith had been prevailed upon to extend the parole which he had tried to take back from Ardroy, and to regard it as given for the space of one week, dating from the day and hour of his capture in the Great Glen. When that week was up, his gaolers seemed to think that they would be able to make other arrangements about his custody.

After the rendezvous, the clan had proceeded westwards in the direction of the coast, along a difficult road between close-pressed craggy mountains, where the grey rock pushed in a myriad places through its sparse covering, and came at last in the afternoon to the trysting place at Glenfinnan. Though he was treated with every civility, and rode in comfort on a horse of Ardroy's, it had been a mortifying journey for Captain Windham. Between the ranks of Camerons marched sulkily the captured recruits of the Royals, without their arms – like himself – and even Captain Scott's white charger formed part of the procession, to be offered to the 'Prince'. As well, thought the Englishman, be the prisoner of wandering Arabs.

So, scornful, but half interested too, Keith Windham had been present at a scene which, a week ago, he could little have imagined himself witnessing, when, on the stretch of level ground at the head of Loch Shiel, among that wild and lonely scenery, a thousand Highland throats acclaimed the fair-haired young man standing below the folds of his banner, and the very air seemed to flash with the glitter of their drawn blades. It was very romantical and absurd, of course, besides being rank rebellion; but there was no denying that these deluded and shaggy mountaineers were in earnest, and Lochiel too, who was neither shaggy nor – so it seemed to the observer – deluded in quite the same sense . . . and certainly not absurd.

None observing or hindering him during the following days, Captain Windham had taken the opportunity of keeping a fragmentary journal in his pocket-book, and it was these notes which, for want of anything better to do, he was now reading over in the wet twilight.

'What an Army! 'tis purely laughable!' he had written on 20th August. 'The Men are fine, tall Fellows enough, particularly the Camerons – but their Weapons! I have seen Muskets with broken Locks, Muskets with broken Stocks, Muskets without Ramrods, and Men without Muskets at all. There can't be more than a Score of Saddlehorses all told, and the Draught Horses are quite insufficient for Transport over such a Road. Moreover the so-call'd "Army" is as yet compos'd of two Clans only, the Camerons and some Part of the Macdonalds, its Number being, I suppose, about thirteen hundred Men.

'The Pretender's Son I must admit to be a very personable

77

young Man indeed, with the *Bel Air*; they all appear craz'd about him. My own young Achilles, still very well-bred and agreeable, like his Chief. I never lookt to see so much native Polish as Lochiel exhibits. Achilles, if I mistake not, pretty well adores him. There is also a younger brother of the Chief's, whom they call Doctor Archibald; with him also my Warrior seems on very friendly Terms.'

Captain Windham turned over to the next two days' records, which were briefer, and brought him up to the present date.

'August the 21st. Set out at last from that curst Spot, Glenfinnan. But, after an Advance of one Mile, the Road was found to be so bad, and the Horses so few, that the Rebels were oblig'd to leave twelve out of their Score of Swivel Guns behind, and spent some Hours burying 'em in a Bog. As their total March today, to a Place call'd Kinlochiel, was no more than four miles, it looks as though 'twould be some Weeks before the Breechless reach Civilization.'

'August the 22nd. At Kinlochiel all day. Prodigious Rain. Much-needed Attempts seen to be going forward to organize the Transport. Wagons and Carts of all Sorts being collected. Have scarce seen E.C. all day.'

But he had hardly come to these last words, when a tall wet figure appeared without warning in the low doorway, and the diarist restored his notebook somewhat hastily to his pocket. Ardroy stooped his head to enter, taking off his bonnet and swinging it to remove the raindrops. The dampness of the rest of his attire appeared to give him no concern.

'Good evening, Mr Cameron! Have you been burying any more cannon?' inquired the soldier pleasantly.

Ardroy, reddening slightly, made no reply beyond returning the 'Good evening', but hung up his bonnet on a nail and began to unfasten the shoulder-brooch of his plaid. There was not a very great deal of satisfaction for Captain Windham to be got out of baiting this 'young Achilles' of his, because Achilles kept so tight a hold upon his temper and his tongue. Or was it that he was naturally impassive? Hardly, for Keith was sure that he felt the points of the darts which he contrived from time to time to plant in him. Perhaps Ardroy thought that the best way to meet his captive's malice was to appear unaware of it; and indeed the archer himself had to confess that this course rather baffled him. He followed up his first shaft by another.

'You must admit that you should not have brought me here, if you did not wish me to learn your military dispositions – if such I am to call that measure!'

And if the Highlander went on pretending that the unpinning of his plaid was engaging his whole attention, Keith would feel that he had drawn blood. He knew that his own conduct verged on the puerile, but the pleasure of pursuing it was too strong.

The big brooch, however, was undone at last, and Ewen said rather dryly: 'I am glad that your spirits are not suffering from the weather, Captain Windham.'

'On the contrary,' said his prisoner cheerfully, leaning back against the wall of the hut, his hands behind his head. 'I am entertaining myself by trying to recall any other great commander who began his campaign by burying most of his artillery in a swamp; but I have failed. Yet, by Gad, the plan might work a revolution in warfare – in fact 'twould end it altogether, if it were carried out to its logical conclusion. Armies would take the field only to bury their muskets – and perhaps', he added, maliciously, 'that *will* be your next step. I protest that some of them would not take much harm by the interment!'

Ewen swung off his plaid. 'Your mirth at our lack of equipment is very natural,' he replied with complete equanimity. 'But perhaps our ill provision may not be widely known to our enemies. And is it not a fact within your own military experience, Captain Windham,' he went on, looking him in the face, 'that it is what one supposes an enemy's forces to be, rather than what they actually are, which sometimes turns the scale?'

It was the Englishman who coloured this time. In its absence of specific reference to the mishap at High Bridge the retort was just sufficiently veiled to enable him, had he chosen, to affect unconsciousness of its sting. But he was too proud to do this.

'I deserved that,' he admitted, scrambling to his feet with the words. 'I am not such a dolt as to be unaware to what you allude. That you feel obliged to remind me of last Friday's disgrace, proves that my own remarks were not in the best of taste – and I apologize for them.'

But his tormentor's apology appeared to embarrass Ewen Cameron much more than his thrusts. 'I am sorry I said that, Captain Windham!' he exclaimed, with a vivacity which rather astonished the other. 'I ought not to have taunted you with a calamity for which you were not to blame. That was in worse taste still.'

'Egad, Mr Cameron, you are too punctilious,' said Keith carelessly. 'But if you are of that mind – I don't say that I am – we may fairly cry quits.'

'For after all,' pursued Ewen, throwing down his plaid, 'since you are not witnessing our preparations of your own free will, I suppose you are at liberty to make what observations you please upon them.'

'You seem bent upon making allowances for me!' returned Keith with a smile. 'However, I do not complain of that; and if Fate should ever reverse our positions, and give you, for instance, into my hands, I hope I may be able to show the same generosity.'

Ardroy, who was now unbuckling his broadsword, stopped and gazed at him rather intently in the feeble lantern-light, feeble because it still had to contend with a measure of wet daylight. 'Why, do you then expect our meeting again, Captain Windham?' he asked after a moment.

'I expect nothing, Mr Cameron. I am no wizard to foretell the future. Yet, but for the fact that we could not meet save as enemies, I vow 'twould give me pleasure to think that we might one day encounter each other again.' But, feeling somehow that the young man standing there looking at him took this for a mere *façon de parler*, he added, with a return to his bantering tone: 'You can have no notion how much this tour – albeit a trifle too reminiscent of a Roman triumph – has been alleviated by having so agreeable a cicerone. Though indeed in the last twenty-four hours my glimpses of you have been few – too few.'

So expressed, his sentiments had of course small chance of being taken for sincere. The Highlander, indeed, for all reply gave a little shrug that was almost like a Frenchman's, spread his plaid upon the bare earth floor, and laid his broadsword beside it.

'Surely you are not going to sleep in that plaid!' exclaimed Keith, stirred out of his levity. 'Why, 'tis drenched! Take my cloak, I have no mind to sleep yet, and shall not need it.'

But Ewen, without stiffness, declined, saying that a wet plaid was of no consequence, and indeed but kept one the warmer. Some, he added, and the Englishman gasped at the information, wrung them out at night in water for that reason. All he would accept was some handfuls of heather for a pillow, and then, lying down, his sword convenient to his hand, he wrapped himself in the folds of damp tartan and in five minutes was fast asleep.

But Keith, as he said, was not sleepy; and after a while, feeling restless, he strolled to the doorway – door, the hut had none. When he got there he was aware of a rigid figure, muffled in a plaid, standing in the rain, just out of the direct line of vision – the inevitable Lachlan watching over his master's slumbers. He turned his head, and Keith could see a contraction pass over his dark features. But the English officer was not to be intimidated by a scowl from studying, if he wished, the sodden, cloud-enfolded landscape, and the sheets of rain driving in the twilight over the waters of Loch Eil, though it was not a cheerful prospect.

What was going to happen to him when his parole expired tomorrow? At the far end of Loch Eil, Loch Linnhe joined it at right angles, and on Loch Linnhe was Fort William with its loyal garrison. Tomorrow the Highland force would proceed along Loch Eil, and every step would bring him nearer to his friends. . . .

He left the doorway after a few moments, and looked down at the sleeper on the floor, his head sunk in the bundle of heather and his arm lying across his broadsword. 'The embraces of the goddess of ague seem to be agreeable,' he thought. 'I shall be sorry to say farewell tomorrow, my friend – deuce take me if I quite know why – but I hardly think *you* will!'

Then at last he went and lay down on his heap of heather, and listened to the sound of the rain, always since he was a boy, connected with the worst memories of his life. There was the dismal day of his father's funeral; he had been but five then, yet he remembered it perfectly; rain, rain on the nodding plumes of the great black carriage which had taken his father away; the day some years later on which his childish mind first realized that his adored mother cared nothing for him – rain, a soft mist of it. And the night in London, four years past now, the night that he had discovered what Lydia Shelmerdine really was. Against the closely-curtained windows of her boudoir it could be heard to dash in fury (for there was a great wind that evening) every time that there came a pause in her high, frightened, lying speech, which ran on the more, that he stood there saying so little. The rose had slipped loose from her close-gathered powdered hair, her gauze and ivory fan lay snapped at her feet . . . and the rain sluiced pitilessly against the windows.

Into that tempest Keith Windham had presently gone out, and, once away from the scented room, had known nothing of its fury, though it drenched him to the skin; and he had forced his way all dripping into the presence of the man who had seduced her . . . no, the man whom she had seduced . . . and had told him to his face that he was welcome to his conquest, that he did not propose to dispute it with him, nor even to demand satisfaction. The lady was not worth fighting about; 'not worth the risking of a man's life – *even of yours!*' There had been witnesses, vastly surprised witnesses, of conduct so unusual. But he thought his way of dealing with the situation more effective than the ordinary; and perhaps it was. He never again saw either of the two who had betrayed him.

Riding behind his young Achilles next afternoon, Keith Windham kept looking at Loch Eil, now shining and placid, the seaweed of its level shore orange in the sun, and the great mountain miles away over Fort William mirrored upside down, as clear as the original. If only he could reach Fort William! But Ardroy, to whom his word of honour still bound him, would certainly see to it that at the expiry of his parole this evening he was secured in some other way.

'I dare say he will make it as little irksome for me as he can,' thought Keith, looking at the tall easy figure sitting the horse just ahead of him, on whose gay tartan and ribbon-tied autumn hair the westering sun was shining full. He's an uncommon good fellow . . . and we shall never see each other again, I suppose.'

And again he thought: 'Not that he will care – and why the devil should I?'

Then the stream of men and conveyances began to leave the loch side, making towards Mr John Cameron's house of Fasse-fern, standing where Glen Suilag made a breach into the mountains; though Lochiel's burgess brother, who would not join the Prince, had carried his prudence to the length of absenting himself from his property, lest he should be open to the charge of having entertained that compromising guest. It was not until they came to the gate in their turn that Ardroy slewed round in his saddle to speak to the captive, and said that he would do what he could for him in the way of accommodation, if he did not object to waiting a little. So Keith gave up his horse to one of Ewen's gillies, and, working his way through the press, waited under a tree and revolved plans. But in truth he could make none until he knew how he was to be secured.

Sooner than he had expected his warden reappeared and, taking him in at a side entry, conducted him to the very top of the humming house.

'I thought this little room might serve for us,' he said, opening the door of a small, half-furnished garret, and Keith saw that their mails were already there. 'I do not know how many others may be thrust in here, but there is at least one bed.' And so there was, a sort of pallet. 'You had best establish your claim to it at once, Captain Windham, or, better still, I will do it for you.' And, mindful as ever of his prisoner's comfort, he unfastened his plaid and tossed it on to the mattress. 'I will come and fetch you to supper; I suppose there will be some.'

Keith could not help looking after his departing figure with a smile which held both amusement and liking. He could not, however, afford to let sensibility interfere with what was in his mind now. Whatever were the reason, Ardroy seemed to have completely forgotten that in – Keith consulted his watch – in another twenty minutes his captive's parole would expire, and he would be free to take himself off . . . if he could. Or was it that he had not mentioned the coming change of conditions from some feeling of delicacy, because it would involve setting a guard?

The Englishman sat down upon the pallet and considered his

chances. They depended almost entirely upon whether in twenty minutes' time there was a Highlander posted at the door of this room. But Ardroy had spoken of fetching him to supper. Heaven send, then, that supper was delayed! Perhaps he could creep out of the garret and conceal himself elsewhere, until he found an opportunity of getting clear away later in the evening. Yet there was no special advantage in waiting for nightfall (even if Ardroy's forgetfulness extended so far), because the nights were apt to be so disconcertingly light. No, the great difficulty at any hour was his uniform. . . .

And here he found himself looking at the roll from Ewen Cameron's saddle, lying on the solitary half-broken chair.

But Keith Windham was much too proud a man not to have a strict regard for his pledged word. He could hardly prevent the entrance of a plan of escape into a brain which was as yet on parole, but he would not take the smallest step to put it into execution before the appointed hour should strike. To pass the time he would scribble a note to explain his conduct; and, wondering the while whether he should not have to destroy it even before he had finished it, he tore out a leaf from his pocket-book and began:

Dear Mr Cameron,

To justify my unadvertis'd Departure I am fain to put you in Mind that I gave my Parole of Honour for the Space of a Se'nnight from the Day and Hour of my Capture by you in the Evening of last Friday. In ten Minutes more that Period will have expir'd, and I trust you will not think it any Infraction of Military Honour that, without having previously recall'd that Fact to your Memory, I intend at half after six to attempt my Freedom.

I shall always retain the most cordial Remembrance of your Hospitality, and though the Pilgrimage of the last few Days has been somewhat prolonged, it has enabled me to be present upon a more interesting Occasion.

Adieu, and forgive me for supposing that when you are more accustom'd to a military Life, you will not repeat the Oversight by which I am hoping to profit.

Your most obedient, humble Servant,
Keith Windham, *Captain*

When he had finished this effusion, of which the last paragraph it cannot be denied, afforded him a special pleasure, he still waited, watch in hand. At half past six exactly, he rose from the pallet and, feeling remarkably like a footpad, opened Ardroy's modest baggage with hasty fingers. It proved to contain a clean shirt, a pair of stockings, a few odds and ends, and – a kilt. The plunderer held this up in some dismay, for he would very greatly have preferred trews, such as Ardroy was wearing at present, but it was this nether garment or his own; and in a remarkably short space of time he was surveying his bare knees with equal disgust and misgiving. No knees that he had seen this week under tartan were as white as that! Happily the garret was dusty, and therefore his legs, if not respectably tanned, could at least look dirty. He thought at first of retaining his uniform coat, which he fancied could be fairly well hidden by Ardroy's plaid – how he blessed him for leaving it behind – but the skirts were a little too long, and the blue cuffs with their galons too conspicuous; and so he decided to go coatless. Thereupon he began experiments with the plaid – what a devil of a lot of it there was! He wished he had a bonnet to pull forward on his brows . . . but one could not expect everything to be provided. The want, however, reminded him of his incongruous wig, and he took this off and placed it, with his discarded uniform, under the mattress. And so there he was, clad in a costume he would as soon have assumed as the trappings of a Red Indian – and clad very insecurely too, he feared, for Ardroy's kilt was too big for him, and he could not fasten it any tighter.

Still no sign of any person coming. Keith looked doubtfully at his host's rifled baggage. It was his duty to regain his liberty by any lawful means, but he had certainly acted the part of a pickpocket. The only compensation in his power was to pay for the clothes he had taken, since those he had left behind were no adequate exchange. He pulled out his purse, having small idea of the worth of the purloined garments, and still less of how Ardroy would view the payment; he suspected that the Highlander might not relish it, but for his own peace of mind he felt constrained to make it. And so he wrapped three guineas in his farewell letter and laid the letter on the chair. Then he softly opened the garret door, went to the head of the stairs, and listened.

The immediate neighbourhood of the little room was deserted, and the sounds from below suggested that the bustle which existed in Fassefern House that evening was more likely to help than to hinder a pretended Cameron who desired to slip out unnoticed. Captain Windham settled the plaid more to his satisfaction, and began with an unconcerned air to descend the stairs. But he was clutching nervously at the top of the philabeg, and his legs felt abominably cold.

Some three-quarters of an hour later Donald Cameron of Lochiel and Alexander MacDonald of Keppoch, he whose clansman had held High Bridge, were talking together outside the front of Fassefern House. About an hour previously it had been arranged that the heavy baggage was to go forward that night along Loch Eil side with a strong convoy of Camerons; a large escort was required, because at Corpach they would have to run the gauntlet of the neighbourhood of Fort William on the other side of the water – a danger which the Prince and the rest of the little force would avoid next day, by taking a route through Glen Suilag impossible to the baggage train.

'And I am sending my young cousin Ardroy in command of it,' concluded Lochiel, 'though the news was something of the suddenest to him. But he will be ready; he is a very punctual person, is Ewen.'

And they went on to speak of other matters: of Macleod of Macleod's refusal to observe his solemn engagement to join the prince (even if he came alone), which was still more resented than the withdrawal of Sir Alexander MacDonald of the Isles; and of what Sir John Cope would do, and where he would elect to give them battle. For that the English general would take his alarmed way up to Inverness without daring to face them had not occurred to the most sanguine.

Lochiel, indeed, was looking very grave. Keith Windham's flash of insight had been correct; he was not deluded. His was the case of a man who was risking everything – life, fortune, lands, the future of his young family – against his better judgement because, more scrupulous of his plighted word than the Chief of Macleod or MacDonald of Sleat, he felt himself too deeply engaged to draw back without loss of honour. Yet, unlike Macleod's, his engagement only pledged his support in the case that the Prince came with French assistance – and he had come without it. The fate of his whole clan lay on Lochiel's shoulders – more, the fate of every man in the rising, for if he had held back the spark would have been quenched at the outset for lack of fuel. That knowledge was a heavy burden to be laid on a man who, far from being a freebooting chief, had striven all his life for the betterment of his people.

'Yes,' he was saying for the second time, 'if we can reach and hold the pass over the Corryarrick before Cope – '

At that moment there was a rapid step behind the two men, Lochiel heard his name uttered in sharp accents, and turning quickly, beheld the young commander of the baggage convoy in a state of high discomposure.

'My dear Ewen, what is wrong?'

'He's gone!' And so agitated was Ardroy's tone, so black his brow, that Lochiel's own colour changed. 'Who – not the Prince!'

'The English officer – my prisoner . . . he's escaped! His parole expired at half past six this evening, and I, fool that I was, had forgot it, over this business of the escort. He'll go straight to Fort William, with information of our numbers and our arms. . . . Oh, I deserve you should dismiss me, Lochiel! He's been away near an hour, I suppose. Shall I ride after him! . . . No, I cannot, unless you give the convoy to someone else – and truly I think I am not fit – '

Lochiel broke in, laying a hand on his arm. ''Tis not worth while pursuing him, my dear Ewen, nor any very great loss to be rid of him. I doubt not, too, that they have already at Fort William all the information that Captain Windham can give. But how, with that uniform, did he get away?'

The enraged young man ground his teeth. 'He was not wearing his uniform. He stole some clothes from me – a philabeg and my plaid. And he left me a damned impertinent letter . . . and these.' He unclosed a hand and held out three gold coins. 'Isn't that the final insult, that he must leave so much more than the things were worth, as though to – ' He appeared unable to finish the sentence. 'If I ever meet him again – ' Back went his arm, and Captain Windham's guineas hurtled violently into the shrubbery of Fassefern House.

II. FLOOD-TIDE

To wanton me, to wanton me,
Ken ye what maist would wanton me?
To see King James at Edinburgh Cross,
Wi' fifty thousand foot and horse,
And the usurper forced to flee –
Oh this is what maist would wanton me.
                              – *Jacobite Song*

Chapter 1

THE dusk of early October had fallen on the city of Edinburgh, that stately city, which for some three weeks now had been experiencing a situation as odd as any in its varied and turbulent history. For Prince Charles and his Highlanders held the town, but not the Castle, secure on its lofty and impregnable rock; this they could neither storm, owing to its position, nor, from lack of artillery, batter down; while King George's military representatives in the Castle were, for their part, unable to regain control of the city below them. The stalemate thus established was perfectly in harmony with the spirit of unconscious comedy which had reigned throughout these weeks, beginning with the ludicrous indecisions and terrors of the city fathers on the news of the Highland advance, and the casual method by which the city had suffered itself to be captured, or rather walked into, by Lochiel and his men. For the opening of the Netherbow Port very early on the morning of the 17th of September, just as the Highlanders outside were preparing to withdraw disappointed, was due to nothing more momentous than the exit of a hackney carriage on its way to its stable in the Canongate – though it is true that it was the carriage which had just brought back the discomfited envoys sent to interview the Prince at Gray's Mill.

Yesterday only had come to an end the latest (and not entirely humorous) episode, of some days' duration, when, the Prince having 'blockaded' the Castle, in other words, having cut off daily supplies, the garrison had retaliated by firing on the town, killing some innocent inhabitants, striking terror into them all, and making it very undesirable to be seen in the neighbourhood of the Castle in the company of a Highlander. Violent representations on the part of the city to the Prince, embodying 'the most hideous complaints against the garrison', had brought this uncomfortable state of affairs to an end by the raising of the 'blockade' – itself originated, so the story went, by the discovery of smuggled information in a pat of butter destined for the valetudinarian General Guest, for whom milk and eggs were permitted to pass daily into the Castle. Yet the old gentleman's treacherous butter was only one of the many whimsical touches of the goddess Thalia, who had devised, during these weeks of occupation, such ingenious surprises as the descent of a soldier from the Castle, by means of a rope, into Livingston's Yard, where he set a house on fire and returned in triumph, by the same method, with a couple of captured Jacobite muskets; the discomfiture, by a sudden illumination from above, of three Camerons sent experimentally to scale the Castle rock under the cover of darkness; and – perhaps the most genuinely comic of all – the solemn paying out to the cashier and directors of the Royal Bank of Scotland, within the very walls of the Castle, and in exchange for Prince Charles's notes, of the ready money which had been taken there for safety, but the lack of which inconvenienced the Edinburgh shopkeepers as much as anybody. This transaction had taken place, under the white flag, during the blockade itself.

But tonight, the guns being silent, and General Joshua Guest once more in possession of his invalid diet, the lately terrified citizens, in the high crammed houses with their unsavoury approaches, were preparing to sleep without fear of bombardment next day by their own defenders. Those outposts of the invading foe, which always kept a wary eye upon the Castle and its approaches – and which had not passed through a very enviable time the last few days – the Highland guard at the Weigh-house, the West Bow, and elsewhere, had received their night relief, and Mr Patrick Crichton, saddler and ironmonger, was writing in his diary further caustic and originally spelt remarks anent these 'scownderalls', 'scurlewheelers' and 'hillskipers'. Inside the walls all was quiet.

But at the other end of the town Holyrood House was lit up, for there was dancing tonight in the long gallery under the eyes of that unprepossessing series of early Scottish kings due to the brush of an ill-inspired Dutchman ... and under a pair of much more sparkling ones. For the Prince was gay tonight, as he was not always; and though, following his usual custom, he himself did not dance, it was plain that the growing accessions to his cause during the last few days had raised his spirits. For besides all those who had joined him soon after Glenfinnan – Stewarts of Appin, MacDonalds of Glengarry, Grants of Glenmoriston – two days ago had come in fierce old Gordon of Glenbucket with four hundred men, and the day before that young Lord Ogilvy, the Earl of Airlie's son, with six hundred, and Farquharson of Balmoral with two hundred, and his kinsman of Monaltrie with more. And others were coming. Whatever the future might hold, he was here as by a miracle in the palace of his ancestors, having defeated in a quarter of an hour the general who had slipped out of his path in August and returned by sea to the drubbing which awaited him among the morasses and the cornstubble of Prestonpans.

So there, at the end of the gallery nearest to his own apartments, in a costume half satin, half tartan, stood the living embodiment of Scotland's ancient dynasty, and drew to himself from time to time the gaze of every lady in the room. But it was to those of his own sex that he chiefly talked.

At the other end of the gallery, which looked out on to the garden and the chapel, Alison Grant, very fine in her hoop and powder, her flowered brocade of blue and silver, with a scarf of silken tartan and a white autumn rose on her breast, was talking with animation to three young men, one of whom, in a French uniform, bore a strong resemblance to her, and was in fact her young brother Hector, just come over from France. The others were distant kinsmen, Grants of Glenmoriston and Shewglie respectively. Right in the corner, on a gilded chair, sat Mr Grant in a not very new coat (for it was more fitting that Alison should go braw than he). His hands rested on his cane, and his lined face, half shrewd and half childlike, wrinkled into a smile as he saw the likelihood that neither young Glenmoriston nor young Shewglie, who seemed to be disputing in a friendly way for the honour of the next dance, would obtain it, since someone else was making his way between the knots of talkers to this corner. To judge by the glances cast at him as he passed, it appeared that Alison was not the only lady there to think that a certain tall cadet of Clan Cameron, a captain in Lochiel's regiment and one of the Prince's aides-de-camp, who wore powder for the nonce and amber satin instead of tartan, was the match of any other gentleman in the room – except, of course, of him with the star on his breast.

Yet Alison, for some reason, gave the newcomer the briefest glance now, though it was a sweet one enough; then her eyes wandered away again. The two Grants, evidently thinking their cause hopeless, took themselves off.

'Alison, here is your cavalier come to claim you,' said her father from his corner.

'Alison has not a look or a thought to give to me nowadays,' observed Ewen, looking at his love from behind, at the back of her white neck, where the sacque fell in imposing folds from the square of the bodice, and where two little unruly tendrils of hair, having shaken off their powder, were beginning to show their true colour. 'Like the rest of the ladies, she has eyes only for the Prince. 'Tis pity I am not a Whig, for then she might pay me some attention, if only in order to convert me.'

At that Alison turned round, laughing.

'Well, sir,' she said, looking him up and down, 'your costume, I vow, is almost Whiggish. In those clothes, and without a scrap of tartan upon you, you might be an Englishman?'

'Or a Frenchman,' suggested her father from his corner.

But this accusation Alison repudiated somewhat indignantly. 'No; Frenchmen are all little men!' Yet, having lived so much in France, she must have known better.

'No one could call Ardroy little, I admit,' agreed Mr Grant. 'And he has not the French physiognomy. But in that dress he has quite the French air.'

'Thank you, sir,' said Ewen, bowing, 'since I suppose I am to take that as a compliment.'

'There are some tall fellows in my regiment,' declared Hector Grant, drawing up his slim and active figure. 'For my part, I've no ambition to attain the height of a pine tree. Alison, is it customary in Scotland, think you, for a brother to lead out his sister?'

'Not unless they are so unlike that the company cannot guess the kinship,' responded Ewen for his betrothed. 'Not, therefore in this case, Eachain!'

'Proprietary airs already, I see,' retorted the young soldier, a smile in the dark eyes which were Alison's too. '*Eh bien*, if I may not have Alison, I vow I'll dance with the oldest dame present. I like not your young misses.' And away he went, while Ewen, offering his hand, carried off his lady for the minuet which was just about to begin.

And, intoxicated by the violins, the lights, the shimmer of satin and silk – with just enough tartan to show the gathering's heart – thinking of Cope soundly beaten, Edinburgh in their hands, Ewen distinguished by the Prince for Lochiel's sake, Alison felt that she was stepping on rosy clouds instead of on a mortal floor. Her feet ached to dance a reel rather than this stately measure. And Ewen – the darling, how handsome, though how different, he looked in powder! – did he too know this pulsing exhilaration? He always kept his feelings under control. Yet when his eyes met hers she could see in them, far down, an exultation profounder, perhaps, than her own.

The music ceased; her betrothed bowed low, and Alison sank smiling in a deep curtsy that spread her azure petticoat about her like a great blue blossom. Then she took his hand, and they went aside.

'Now you must fan yourself, must you not, whether you be hot or no? What are these little figures on your fan – Cupids or humans?' asked Ewen.

'Mercy on us!' exclaimed Miss Grant suddenly, looking towards the end of the apartment, 'the Prince is no longer here!'

'Is he not?' responded Ewen calmly. 'I had not observed.'

'And you one of his aides-de-camp! Fie on you!' cried Alison, and took her fan out of his hand.

'I was looking at you, *mo chridhe*,' said her lover in his deep, gentle voice, and offered no other excuse.

'But where can His Royal Highness have got to?'

'My dear, His Royal Highness is under no vow that I know of to watch us dance any longer than he pleases. However, there's another of his aides-de-camp, Dr Cameron; perhaps he can assuage your anxiety. Archie!'

Dr Archibald Cameron, Lochiel's brother, turned round at his kinsman's summons. He was a man only a dozen years or so older than Ewen himself, with much of Lochiel's own wisdom and serenity, and Ewen had for him a respect and affection second only to that which he bore his Chief.

'Archie, come and protect me from Miss Grant! She declares that I am a Whig because I am wearing neither trews nor phila-beg, and unworthy of the position I occupy towards the Prince because I had not observed his withdrawal, nor can tell her the reason for it.'

But already the fiddles had struck up for another dance, and one of the young Grants had returned and was proffering his request anew. So Ewen relinquished his lady and watched her carried off, sailing away like a fair ship.

'Taken to task so soon!' said Dr Cameron with a twinkle. He was a married man himself, with several children. 'No doubt if my Jean were here I should be in like case, for though I knew the Prince had withdrawn I have not fashed myself about it.'

Neither did Ewen now. 'Is it true,' he asked, 'that Donald will not be here tonight at all?'

'Yes; I left him by his own fireside in the Canongate.'

'He's not ill, Archie?'

'No, no; he's older and wiser than we, that's all.' And giving his young cousin a nod and a little smile Dr Cameron went off.

Ewen abode where he was, for it was too late to secure a partner. Suddenly, hearing his name uttered in a low tone behind him, he turned to see Mr Francis Strickland, one of the 'seven men of Moidart', the gentlemen who had landed with the Prince in the west.

'Captain Cameron,' said he, coming closer and speaking still lower, though at the moment there was no one within a couple

93

of yards or so, 'Captain Cameron, the Prince desires that in a quarter of an hour you will station yourself at the door of the ante-room leading to his bedchamber, and see to it that no one approaches his room. His Royal Highness finds himself indisposed, and obliged to withdraw from the ball; but he particularly wishes that no attention shall be called to his absence. Do you understand?'

Ewen stared at him, a good deal astonished at this commission. There was something furtive, too, about Mr Strickland's manner which he did not relish; and in common with many of the Highland chiefs, he was coming to dislike and mistrust the Irish followers of the Prince – though Strickland, to be accurate, was an Englishman.

'This indisposition is very sudden, Mr Strickland,' he observed. 'A short while ago the Prince was in the best of health and spirits.'

'I suppose, sir,' retorted Strickland tartly, 'that you scarcely consider yourself to be a better judge of the Prince's state of health than he is himself?'

'No,' returned Ewen, his Highland pride all at once up in arms, 'but I do conceive that, as his personal aide-de-camp, I take my orders from His Royal Highness himself, and not from any . . . intermediary.'

Mr Strickland's eye kindled. 'You are not very polite, Captain Cameron,' he observed with truth. Indeed he seemed to be repressing a warmer retort. 'I am to tell the Prince, then, that you refuse the honour of his commands, and that he must find another aide-de-camp to execute them?'

'No, since I have not refused,' said Ewen with brevity, and he turned upon his heel. But Strickland clutched at his arm. 'Not yet – you are not to go yet! In a quarter of an hour's time.'

And Ewen stopped. 'The Prince intends to be indisposed in a quarter of an hour's time!' he exclaimed. 'Then indeed 'tis a very strange seizure; I doubt Dr Cameron would be better for the post.'

'For God's sake, Captain Cameron!' said Strickland in an agitated whisper, pulling Ewen by the sleeve. 'For God's sake show some discretion – moderate your voice!' And he murmured something about a delicate task and a wrong choice, which only inflamed Ewen's suspicions the more. What intrigue was afoot that the Prince's door should be guarded, under plea of illness, in a quarter of an hour's time? He was expecting a visit, perhaps – from whom? Ewen liked the sound of it very little, the less so that Strickland was plainly now in a fever of nervousness.

'Pray let go my arm, sir,' he said, and, the Englishman not at once complying, added meaningly, 'if you do not wish me to be still more indiscreet!' On which Mr Strickland hastily removed his grasp, and Ewen turned and began to make his way down the room, careless whether Strickland were following or no, since if that gentleman's desire for secrecy were sincere he dared not make an open protest among the dancers.

As he went, Ewen very much regretted Lochiel's absence tonight, and also the indisposition of Mr Murray of Broughton, the Prince's secretary, who had delicate health. Mr Strickland must be aware of both those facts. . . . And if Strickland were in this business, whatever it might be, it was fairly certain that Colonel O'Sullivan, the Irish Quartermaster-General, was in it also. For a second or so the young man hesitated, and glanced about for Dr Cameron, but he was nowhere to be seen now. Then he himself would try to get to the bottom of what was going on; and as, when his mind was made up, an earthquake would scarcely have turned him from his path, Mr Cameron of Ardroy made straight for the Prince's bedchamber with that intention.

The drawing-room leading directly from the picture gallery had about a dozen couples in it; the ante-room which gave at right angles from this was fortunately empty, although the door between was open. The investigator went quietly through, closing this, marched across the ante-room, and knocked at the Prince's door.

'*Avanti!*' cried a voice, and Ewen went into the bedchamber which had once been the ill-fated Darnley's. The Prince was sitting on the other side of the gilded and embroidery-hung bed, with his back to the door, engaged, it seemed, in the absence of Morrison his valet, in pulling on his own boots. A black cloak and plain three-cornered hat lay upon the gold and silver coverlet.

'Is that you, O'Sullivan?' he asked without turning his head. 'I shall be ready in a moment.'

Ewen thought: 'I was right; O'Sullivan is in it!... Your Royal Highness...' he said aloud.

At that, the Prince looked quickly behind him, then, still seated on the bed, turned half round, leaning on one hand. 'My orders, Captain Cameron, were for you to post yourself at the outer door. There has evidently been some mistake, either on your part or on Mr Strickland's.'

'On mine, then, may it please Your Highness,' admitted Ewen coolly. 'As the order puzzled me somewhat, I have ventured to ask that I may receive it from Your Royal Highness's own mouth.'

The mouth in question betrayed annoyance, and the Prince arose from his position on the bed and faced his aide-de-camp across it. '*Mon Dieu*, I thought it was plain enough! You will have the goodness to station yourself outside the farther door and to let no one attempt to see me. I am indisposed.'

'And the quarter of an hour's interval of which Mr Strickland spoke, sir?'

'That is of no moment now. You can take up your place at once, Captain Cameron.' And with a gesture of dismissal the Prince turned his back, and walked across the room towards the curtained window. It was thus plainly to be seen that he had his boots on.

He was not then expecting a visit; he was going to pay one! Hence the sentinel before the outer door, that his absence might not be known. Ewen looked at the cloak on the bed, thought of the dark Edinburgh streets, the hundred and one narrow little entries, the chance of a scuffle, of an encounter with some unexpected patrol from the Castle, and took the plunge.

'Your Royal Highness is going out – at this hour?'

The Prince spun round. 'Who told you that I was going out? And if I were, what possible affair is it of yours, sir?'

'Only that, as your aide-de-camp, it is my great privilege to watch over your Royal Highness's person,' answered Ewen respectfully but firmly. 'And if you are going out into the streets of Edinburgh at night without a guard – '

Charles Edward came nearer. His brown eyes, striking in so fair-complexioned a young man, sparkled with anger. 'Captain Cameron, when I appointed you my aide-de-camp, I did not think that I was hampering myself with a s—' He bit off the short, pregnant word, that aide-de-camp's suddenly paling face evidently recalling to him whither he was going. But he instantly started off again on the same road. '*Dieu me damne!*' he said irritably, 'am I to have your clan always at my elbow? Lochiel may have walked first into Edinburgh, but he was not the first to declare for me. He sent his brother to beg me to go back again! I think you Camerons would do well to remem—' Again he broke off, for there had come a knock at the door.

But Ewen, white to the very lips, had put his hand behind him and turned the key. 'Will your Royal Highness kindly give your orders to some other man?' he asked, in a voice which he did not succeed in keeping steady. 'I'll not endure to hear either my Chief or myself insulted, no, not though it be by my future King!'

The Prince was brought up short. His aide-de-camp might have taken upon himself a good deal more than his position warranted, but to offend a chieftain of Clan Cameron at this juncture was madness. Charles was not yet a slave to the petulant temper which from his boyhood had given anxiety to those about him, and which in later unhappy years was to work so much disaster, and his great personal charm was still undimmed.

'Wait a little!' he called through the door, and then looked with appeal in his beautiful eyes at the tall figure in front of it, rigid with the stillness of a consuming anger. 'Ardroy, forgive me for a moment of irritation! I scarce knew what I was saying. You cannot think that there is any thought in my breast for my good Lochiel but gratitude – all the greater gratitude, that he knew and weighed the risk he ran, and yet drew that true sword of his! And as for you, how did I insult you?'

'I think,' said Ewen, still very pale and haughty, and using to the full the physical advantage which he had – not very many had it – of being able to look down on his Prince, 'I think that your Royal Highness was near calling me ... something that no gentleman can possibly call another.'

'Why, then, I could not have been near it – since I hope I am a gentleman!' The Prince smiled his vanquishing smile. 'And to prove that you are imagining vain things, my dear Ardroy, I will tell you on what errand I am bound tonight, and you shall accompany me, if you still insist upon your right to watch over my royal person.'

Ewen was not vanquished. 'Your Royal Highness is too good,' he answered, bowing, 'but I should not dream of claiming that right any longer, and I will withdraw.'

'I always heard that you Highlanders were unforgiving,' lamented the Prince, between jest and earnest. (Devoted though they were, they were certainly not easy to manage.) 'Come, Ardroy, you are much of an age with myself, I imagine – do you never say in heat what you designed not – and regret the moment after?'

Their eyes met, the warm Southern brown, and the blue.

'Yes, my Prince,' said Ewen suddenly. 'Give me what orders you will, and they shall be obeyed.'

'I am forgiven then?' asked the Prince quickly, and he held out his hand as though to clasp his aide-de-camp's. But Ewen bent his knee and put his lips to it.

During this touching scene of reconciliation, it was evident from various discreet but not too patient taps upon the door that the excluded person on the other side still desired admittance.

'Open the door, *mon ami*,' said Charles Edward, and Ewen, unlocking it, did so; and in walked Colonel John William O'Sullivan, not too pleased, as was obvious, at his exclusion. He carried a cloak over his arm.

'I thought your Royal Highness was admitting no one except –' He stopped and looked in dumb annoyance at the intruder. Ewen showed a stony front. There was no love lost between the Quartermaster-General and the Camerons, whom he had posted so badly at Tranent before the recent battle.

'Strickland has not come yet,' observed the Prince, and added, with a spice of malice, 'I think it well to take an aide-de-camp with me, O'Sullivan. We shall therefore be a *partie carrée*.'

'As Your Highness pleases, of course,' said O'Sullivan stiffly.

'And in that case,' went on his Royal Highness, 'he had best know whither we are bound. We are going, my dear Ardroy, to pay a visit to a lady.'

Ewen was astonished, for he had seen enough since their coming to Edinburgh to make him conclude that the Prince was

– perhaps fortunately – very cold where women were concerned, no matter how much incense they burnt before him. Then disgust succeeded to astonishment: was this the time for intrigues of that nature? But the latter emotion, at least, was very transitory, for the Prince went on almost at once: "Tis the Jacobite widow of a Whig Lord of Session – an old lady, but no doubt charming, and certainly loyal – who dwells at the corner of the West Bow and the Grassmarket.'

'So near the Castle!' broke from Ewen in spite of himself.

'*Donc*, the last place in which I shall be looked for! Moreover,' said the young Prince gaily, 'I am borrowing Murray's name, since Lady Easterhall is his kinswoman, and is expecting a visit from him – though not, I'm bound to say, tonight. You look blank, Captain Cameron' (and Ewen had no doubt he did). 'See then, read the old lady's letter to Murray.'

Ewen took the paper which the Prince drew from his pocket, and read the following, written in a slightly tremulous hand:

My dear John,

It will no doubt be your Labours in His Royal Highness's Service that have hitherto hindered you frae waiting upon an old Woman who has not set Eyes upon you since you were a Lad. I see I'll e'en have to bid you to my House, and maybe set a Bait to bring you there. Well then – do you mind of William Craig of Craigmains, him that's sib to your Uncle Dickson on the Mother's Side, with a pretty Fortune, and Kin that went out, severals of them, in the Fifteen? He comes to Edinburgh today on Affairs, and will likely stay two-three Days with me; and I'm thinking that could he be gained for the Good Cause others of the Fife Lairds might follow his Example. Forbye there's his Siller. Try then could you not dine with me the morn at three of the Clock, and have a bit Crack with Craigmains, and tell him how well Things go for our bonny Prince, and you'll maybe do as good an Afternoon's Work as writing Proclamations.

Your loving Great-aunt,
Anna Easterhall

This letter was superscribed 'To Mr John Murray of Broughton at Holyrood House', and was of the same day's date. Ewen gave it back to his royal hand in silence.

'Mr Murray is indisposed and keeps his room, and I am going to pay his great-aunt a visit in his stead,' said the Prince, going to the bed and taking up his cloak. 'And "our bonny Prince" himself will have the necessary bit crack with this Fife laird of the moneybags. You can see from the letter that Lady Easterhall thinks a little persuasion might induce him to open them, and I flatter myself that he'll yield to me sooner than to Murray.'

'But your Royal Highness could cause this kinsman of Mr Murray's to come here, instead of venturing yourself in the Grassmarket,' objected Ewen, to whom this Haroun-al-Raschid scheme – unknown, he felt sure, to the secretary himself – did not at all appeal.

'Not before he had made up his mind, man! He would not; your Lowland Scot is too canny.'

'But would not a visit to this lady tomorrow – '

'Would you have me approach the Castle in daylight, my friend?'

'But consider the other dwellers in the house,' urged Ewen. 'Your Royal Highness knows that nearly all Edinburgh lives pell-mell, one above the other. Lady Easterhall's neighbour on the next land may well be a Whig gentleman, or – '

'My dear Ulysses,' said the Prince, laying a hand familiarly on his aide-de-camp's arm, 'you may have an old head on young shoulders, but so have I too! Lady Easterhall is very singular; she has a whole house to herself. I found this out from Murray. And if report says true, the house itself is singular also.'

At that moment there was another discreet tap at the door, and O'Sullivan, who had been listening to this conversation in a sardonic silence, opened it to admit Mr Francis Strickland, in a cloak. In response to the displeased query on the last-comer's face the Quartermaster-General observed that Captain Cameron was going with them, 'though one gathers that he disapproves.'

'He has my leave to disapprove,' said the Prince lightly, 'provided he comes too.' He was evidently in great spirits at the prospect of this escapade, as pleased as a boy at stealing a march on his bedridden secretary – relieved too, perhaps, at having laid the storm which he had himself raised; and when Ewen asked him whether he should not procure him a chair, scouted the idea. He would go on his own feet, as less likely to attract attention. 'And when I have my cloak so' – he threw it round his face up to the very eyes – 'who will know me? I learnt the trick in Rome,' he added.

But his gaze then fell upon his aide-de-camp's attire. 'Faith, Ardroy, you must have a cloak, too, to cover up that finery – nay, you cannot go to fetch one now. I know where Morrison keeps another of mine.'

'And the sentinel at your Royal Highness's ante-chamber door?' inquired Strickland in an injured voice.

'The door must go wanting one after all – unless you yourself covet the post, Strickland? In that case you can lend *your* cloak to Captain Cameron.' And at the look on Strickland's face he laughed. 'I was but jesting. Like the man in the Gospel, I have two cloaks – here, Ardroy, if 'twill serve for that excessive height of yours. . . . Now for my great-great-great-grandsire's private stair!'

Chapter 2

THE three men followed him in silence down the narrow, twisting stair, Ewen bringing up the rear, and wondering why disapproval made one feel so old. And, after O'Sullivan had given the word of the day and passed them out of Holyrood House, they were soon walking briskly, not up the Canongate itself, but up the slope parallel to it, the 'back of the Canongate', the Prince in front with the Irishman, Ewen behind with Strickland, both the latter very silent. Flurries of the October wind plucked at their cloaks as they went in the semi-darkness, sometimes swooping at them from the open grassy spaces of the King's Park on their left, at others appearing to originate mysteriously in the tall line of houses of the Canongate, with their intervening gardens, on the right. They met nobody until they came to the Cowgate Port, and, O'Sullivan again giving the word to the guard, were admitted within the town walls and the nightly stenches of Edinburgh proper.

In the Cowgate there were still a few folk abroad, and a couple of drunkards, emerging unexpectedly from a close, all but knocked into the Prince. As he moved quickly aside to avoid collision, a man passing in the opposite direction was obliged to step into the gutter. It was quite natural that this man should turn his head to see the reason for being thus incommoded, but unfortunate that the Prince's cloak should at that instant slip from its position. Ewen could only hope that the passer-by had not recognized him; there was at least nothing to indicate that he had. He went on his way without a pause, and the four adventurers resumed theirs.

As they emerged into the Grassmarket, the great mass of the Castle Rock, half distinguishable against the sky, and crowned with a few lights, lifted itself as if in menace; but a few steps farther and it was blocked from view by the houses on the other side of that wide open space. Lights still burned in some of these, but everything was quiet.

'That is the house,' said the Prince in a low voice, but it was not easy to know at which he was pointing across the Grassmarket, since they all adjoined each other. 'The entrance, however, is neither here nor in the West Bow, but up a close leading out of the Grassmarket, so Murray says.'

Holding their fluttering cloaks about them they crossed the Grassmarket. Away to their right, when they were over, wound the curve of the West Bow. At the mouth of the close which the Prince indicated, Ewen, seeing that O'Sullivan seemed to be going to allow his master to walk first up the dark passage, strode forward, and without apology placed himself in front, and so preceded them all up the alley, his hand on his sword. He liked this place not at all.

In a moment he felt a twitch on his cloak from behind. 'This will be the door of the house,' said the Prince's voice. 'See if you can summon someone. They keep uncommonly early hours hereabouts; I trust the household is not already abed.'

But Ewen, tirling the risp on the door in the gloom, welcomed this suggestion with delight, since if it were so the Prince would be obliged to go home again. And for some little time it did appear as if his hope were to be fulfilled, for no one came in answer to his summons. He peered up the close; it seemed to him possible that its upper end debouched on the Castle Hill itself. It was madness to have come here.

The Prince himself then seized the ring and rasped it impatiently up and down, and very soon Ewen's heart sank again, as he heard bolts being withdrawn inside. An old serving-man opened the door a little way and put his head out.

'Will Lady Easterhall receive her kinsman, Mr Murray of Broughton, and his friends?' asked Mr Murray's impersonator.

The ancient servitor opened the door a little wider. 'Ou, ay, Mr Murray o' Broughton,' he said, stifling a yawn. 'Mr Murray o' Broughton,' he repeated, in an owl-like manner which hinted at recent refreshment. 'An' Mr Murray's frien's,' he added, with another yawn, but no motion to admit the visitors. 'Hoo mony o' ye wull there be then – is yon anither?' For footsteps had been coming up the close, and at the words a man passed the group, walking quickly. He did not glance at them, and it was too dark in the alley to see faces; but Ewen felt an uncomfortable suspicion that it was the same man who had passed them in the Cowgate and had looked at the Prince. But no, surely this man was shorter; moreover he had betrayed no interest in them.

'Come, man, conduct us to Lady Easterhall,' said O'Sullivan sharply. 'Or is she abed?'

'Nay, her leddyship's taking a hand at the cartes or playing at the dambrod wi' Miss Isobel. Come ben then, sirs. Which o' ye wull be Mr Murray?'

But nobody answered him. They followed him towards the staircase, up which he began laboriously to toil. 'Forbye her leddyship's no' expectin' Mr Murray till the morn,' they heard him mutter to himself, but soon he did little save cough as he panted and stumbled upwards, pausing once to announce that whiles he had a sair hoast.

'Take heart, my Nestor,' said the Prince in Ewen's ear, as they arrived at the first floor. 'It may be difficult to get into this house, but I have heard that it is easy to get out of it.'

Before he could explain himself the old man had opened the door of a large room, economically and most insufficiently lit by the flickering firelight and a couple of candles on a small table near the hearth, at which sat an old lady and a young playing draughts. There was no one else in the room.

'My leddy, here's yer leddyship's kinsman, Mr Murray o'

Broughton, and a wheen frin's tae veesit ye. Wull I bring some refreshment?'

From the island of light the old lady looked up, surprised. 'Ye veesit ower late, nephew,' she said in a little, cracked, but authoritative voice, in the Scots common even to persons of breeding. 'Nane the less ye are welcome. But did ye no get my letter the day? Saunders, light the sconces and bring wine.' And, as one or two candles on the walls sprang to life and the Prince took a few steps forward, she leant from her easy chair. 'Eh, John, ye've made a finer figure of a man than aince I thocht ye like to do! But hae ye the toothache, that ye are sae happed up? Come and present your friends, and I'll make ye acquainted with Miss Isobel Cochran, your aunt Margaret's niece. Bestir yersel' now wi' the candles, Saunders – dinna don'er, man!'

The Prince removed his cloak from the lower part of his face. 'Madam,' he said, bowing, 'I must crave your pardon for having used your great-nephew's name as a passport. I am not Mr Murray, and – though I hope indeed that you will not be so cruel – I await only your word to have your good Saunders show us the door again.'

The old lady peered still farther into the only half-dispelled dimness. 'Presairve us – wha's gotten intil the hoose?' she exclaimed. 'Wha is't ... I canna see ...'

But the girl was on her feet, the colour rushing into her face. 'Great-aunt, great-aunt, 'tis the Prince himself!'

Even Ewen's disapproval was hardly proof against the scene that followed. Old Lady Easterhall rose tremulously on her ebony stick, her face working almost painfully, and attempted to kneel, which the Prince of course would not allow; while Miss Cochran, from pale that she was become, had the colour restored to her cheeks by the salute which he set on her hand, as she rose from the deepest curtsy of her life. In a short time Saunders, babbling joyfully, had lit every sconce in the room, till the candlelight swam and glittered on the well-polished furniture and the half-seen satins of the visitors' coats, seeming to concentrate itself upon the winking star of St Andrew which – most ill-advisedly, thought the aide-de-camp – still adorned the royal breast. And when chairs had been set, and wine brought, then at last, in a warm atmosphere of loyalty and emotion, the Prince tactfully explained his errand.

Lady Easterhall shook her becapped head. 'Ah, I jaloused 'twas not to see an auld woman that your Royal Highness came here! But Craigmains is no' come yet; he wasna to reach the toun till noon the morn. I thocht I had writ that in my letter to my nephew. Sae your Royal Highness has come here for nae-thing.'

The Prince's face had indeed fallen, but he recovered himself quickly. 'Do not say that, madam. Have I not gained the pleasure of your acquaintance, and of Miss Cochran's, not to speak of drinking tne best claret I have tasted since I came to Edinburgh? So let us pledge the missing guest, gentlemen, and the real Murray shall deal with him tomorrow.'

On which, lifting his glass, he drank again, and Colonel O'Sullivan and Mr Strickland followed his example. But Ewen did not; he had risen, and now remained standing behind the Prince's chair, as one awaiting the signal to depart. Now that he had learnt the uselessness of his escapade, His Highness would no doubt speedily withdraw. But that young gentleman showed no sign of such an intention. On the contrary, he began in an animated manner to question Lady Easterhall on her recollec-tions of the Fifteen, while Miss Cochran's hand played nervously with the neglected draughtsmen on the little table, though her eyes, wide and glamour-stricken, never left the unbidden guest. She at least, even if she knew it not, was uneasy.

And after a few minutes the Prince became aware of his aide-de-camp's attitude. He turned his head.

'What a plague ails you, Captain Cameron, standing there like a grenadier! Sit down, man, and do not so insult our hostess's excellent vintage.'

'I had rather, with Your Highness's and Lady Easterhall's leave,' replied Captain Cameron, 'post myself in some part of the house whence I can get a view of the approach to it. Does not the close run up towards the Castle Hill, madam?'

'You are very nervous, sir,' commented O'Sullivan, half-sneeringly. 'Why should the nearness of the Castle trouble Lady

Easterhall, since his Royal Highness's presence cannot possibly be known there? And of what use is the guard at the Weigh-house – your own clansmen, too – if they cannot prevent the garrison from coming out?'

But Lady Easterhall herself seemed of Ewen's opinion. 'The young gentleman is verra richt,' she declared. 'He shall keep watch if he's minded tae, though, as ye say, sir, the Castle's little likely to trouble my hoose. Isobel, gang ye with Captain Cameron and show him the best windy for the purpose. Though even if they should send a picket here,' she added, smiling, 'His Royal Highness and all could be oot of the hoose before they could win entrance. There's a secret stair, gentlemen, leads frae this verra room doun under the hoose to a bit door in the West Bow, and the entry to't lies ahint yon screwtore at the side of the chimley, sae ye may be easy.'

All eyes turned towards the spot indicated, where, not far from the hearth, an ebony writing-table with inlay of metal and tor-toiseshell – evidently a French importation – stood against the panelling. 'A secret stair!' exclaimed the Prince, and, in a lower tone, '*Ma foi*, rumour was right! – You hear, Ardroy? So now you need not deprive us of your society . . . nor of Miss Coch-ran's.'

'Miss Cochran's I need not in any case take from your Royal Highness,' responded Ewen, preparing to leave the room, 'for I doubt not I can find a suitable lookout without troubling her. But, even with the secret stair, I think it would be better to post a sentry.' A laugh from O'Sullivan followed him as he closed the door, and stirred his simmering wrath against the Quartermaster-General and Strickland to a still higher temperature. That they should without remonstrance allow the Prince to remain here, under the very shadow of the Castle, for no more valid object than to drink Lady Easterhall's claret – and, of course, to give her pleasure by the honour done to her – was monstrous! It was true that it needed a certain amount of skill and courage to make a dash from the Castle, on account of the Highland guards in its neighbourhood, but it was dark, and he was still uneasy about the man who had passed them in the close.

The landing and stairway were ill lit, and he hesitated; he had better summon Saunders, perhaps. Then the door behind him opened and shut, a rather timid voice said 'Captain Cameron –' and turning, he beheld Miss Isobel Cochran with a lighted candle in her hand.

'I came, sir, because I thought you would need this.' She held it out, none too steadily. 'Oh, sir, you are the only one right of all of us! The Prince should not abide longer; it is too dangerous.'

'So I think,' said Ewen, looking down at her gravely. 'I thank you, Miss Cochran.' He took the light from her. 'Could you not persuade Lady Easterhall to hasten his departure?'

'Hardly,' answered the girl regretfully. 'You can see what it means to her to have the Prince under her roof. . . . If you will go along that passage, sir, you will find a window out of which you can see some way up the close. . . . Stay, I will show you, since I am here.'

She slipped along the passage in front of him, and he followed with the candlestick.

'There,' said Miss Cochran, 'this window.' She unlatched it, Ewen setting down the light at some distance. He saw the girl put her head out . . . and then draw back, her hand over her mouth as though to stifle a scream. 'Too late, too late already! Look, look!'

Ewen leaned out. Down the dark alley, already echoing to the quick tramp of feet, a file of soldiers were advancing two by two, an officer leading. He drew in his head.

'Go back at once and warn the Prince, madam. I will stay a moment to watch. Blow out the light, if you please; I do not want them to see me.'

Obeying him, the girl fled, while Ewen, crouching by the open window, held his breath as the heavy, hasty footsteps drew nearer and nearer, and he was looking down at last on three-cornered hats and tilted bayonets. There were fully a score of soldiers, and they were stopping at Lady Easterhall's entrance; he saw the officer raise a lantern to make sure of the door. Waiting no longer, he ran back along the passage and pelted down the stairs. 'Saunders, Saunders!'

Fortunately the old man heard him at once, and emerged from some lair of his own on the ground-floor. 'What's to do, sir?'

'There are soldiers from the Castle at the door. Don't admit them, on your life! Théy are after . . . "Mr Murray". Is the door stout?'

'No' by-ordinar' stout. Dod, they'll be for coming in; nae doot o' that!' For a sword-hilt, it might have been, was clamouring on the door. 'If I'm no' tae open, they'll ding the door doun!'

'Let them,' commanded Ewen. ''Twill take some time to do it. And remember, you know nothing at all about her ladyship's visitors!'

He ran up again, thanking Heaven with all his heart for the secret passage, and its exit in a spot where the redcoats would never dare to show their faces – since there was a Highland post in the West Bow also.

Three minutes, perhaps, had elapsed since the first discovery and Miss Cochran's return to the drawing-room; Ewen hoped, therefore, as he burst into that apartment, to find no one but the ladies remaining. To his dismay, however, they were all there, in a group against the wall on the right of the hearth. The writing-table had been pushed aside, Strickland was holding a candle close to a panel, and O'Sullivan seemed to be struggling with something in the carving of this. Lady Easterhall, looking incredibly old, was clinging to her great-niece, and the eyes of both were fixed agonizedly on the Irishman and his efforts. The Prince, though he too was watching O'Sullivan narrowly, appeared the most unconcerned of the five.

'Ah, Ardroy, it seems you were justified of your nervousness, then,' he observed coolly. 'And the spring of the panel is unfortunately stiff. It is long, evidently,' he added in a lower tone, 'since a lover left this house by that road!'

'The soldiers are at the door,' said Ewen in a stifled voice. His heart felt like hot lead within him; was all to end thus, so foolishly, and so soon? The dull sound of battering came up from below.

'Let Miss Cochran try,' suggested the Prince. 'I think it is rather skill than strength which is needed.' And O'Sullivan relinquished his place to the girl. He was very pale, and Strickland had obvious difficulty in keeping the candle upright.

'Isobel, Isobel, can ye no' stir it?' exclaimed Lady Easterhall, wringing her old hands.

The girl's slender fingers were striving with the boss of carved woodwork which concealed the spring. 'O God!' she whispered, and shut her eyes. 'Is there no other possible hiding-place – ' Ewen was beginning in desperation when, with a loud grinding noise, the panel ran back, revealing a dark wall and the first few steps of a winding stair, which plunged steeply downwards.

'Quick!' said O'Sullivan, seizing Strickland by the arm. 'You first, to light the stair. Now, your Highness!' The Prince stepped through the aperture, and O'Sullivan himself followed. But Ewen lingered a moment on the threshold of safety.

'Madam,' he said earnestly to the shaken old lady, 'if I may advise, do not you or Miss Cochran stay a moment longer in this room! To be in your bedchambers retiring for the night, when the soldiers succeed in forcing an entrance, as I fear they will, is the best answer you can make to the charge of entertaining the Prince. Do not, I beg of you, be found here – for he has still to get clear of the house!'

'Ye're richt,' said Lady Easterhall. The frozen terror had left her face now. ''Tis you hae had the wits all along, young sir! In wi' ye! Noo, Isobel, pit tae the door – and then let's rin for it!'

Behind Ewen came grinding and a snap, and he was left in almost complete darkness to find his way as best he could down the stair. Somewhere below he heard echoing steps and cautious voices, so the Prince and his companions were still in the house. There must, indeed, be a passage as well as a stair, if one was to emerge into the West Bow right on the other side of it. For him there was no hurry; it was just as well to play rearguard. He started leisurely to descend, feeling his way by the newel, and hoping that he would never again go through another five minutes like the last.

He had certainly not accomplished more than a dozen steps of the descent when he stopped and stiffened, his heart jumping into his throat. There had suddenly floated down from above an ominous dragging, rasping sound which he had heard too recently not to recognize. It was the panel sliding open again! Had the soldiers found it already? It seemed almost impossible.

Tugging at his sword, Ewen half leapt, half stumbled, up the dark twisting stair again, and was met by an oblong of light, barred across its lower half by the replaced writing-table. But, as he was instantly aware, the room, though still brilliantly lit – for there had been no time to extinguish the sconces – was empty, and silent save for the sounds of furious battering which came up from below through its closed door. It was clear what had happened. The spring of the secret entrance, damaged perhaps, had failed to catch, and after the hurried departure of the two ladies it had released the panel again . . . and so the first thing to attract the notice of anyone entering the room would be that yawning gap in the wall.

Ewen sprang at the sliding door and tried to push it to again, but on its smooth inner surface there was nothing by which to get sufficient purchase. Closed it must be, at whatever cost, and on whichever side of it he was left. He thrust aside the escritoire, stepped out into the room, and pressed the boss which concealed the spring. The panel obediently returned . . . to within half an inch of its place. By getting hold of a projecting line of carving with his nails, Ewen feverishly contrived to push it completely home, but was instantly aware that it would no longer engage itself securely in whatever mechanism usually kept it fast there – in short that, having first refused to open, it now refused to shut. And if the Prince were not yet clear of the passage down below, if the fastenings of the door into the West Bow, for instance, were rusty from disuse, as well they might be, he would yet be taken.

There was a final crash from below; the door was undoubtedly down and the invaders in the house. If only the existence of the sliding panel could be concealed for a few moments longer! To stand before it sword in hand (as was Ewen's impulse) were only to advertise its presence. He looked round in desperation. Perhaps the corner of the escritoire, pressed well against the line of carving, would eliminate that betraying crack in the woodwork? Yes, the escritoire was sufficiently heavy to keep the panel in place, and, provided that it was not itself moved away from its position, all might yet be well . . . though not for him, who must now throw himself to the wolves to keep the secret inviolate.

To ensure that the writing-table stayed as he had put it he must be near it, and have a reasonable excuse, too, for his position.

110

The most natural was the best; so, throwing off his hat and cloak, he pulled up a chair, sat down – unfortunately this necessitated his having his back to the door – and, seizing a sheet of paper and a quill, began hastily to write a letter. His heart might be beating faster than usual, but his hand, as he saw with pleasure, was quite steady.

'My dear Aunt Margaret – I told you in my last Letter of the Victory gain'd – ' They were coming up the stairs now, and at the noise of their approach he realized how unnatural it would look to be found writing a letter in the midst of such a disturbance as had been going on below. He let his head sink forward on his arm as if he were overcome by sleep; and so was sitting when a second or two later the door was flung violently open, heavy feet came tumbling in, and there was a triumphant shout of: 'Here's one o' them, sir.'

Ewen judged it time to wake. He lifted his head and turned in his chair with a start; and then sprang to his feet in simulated astonishment. '*Soldiers!* What are you doing here?'

There were a sergeant and three men of Lascelles' regiment in Lady Easterhall's drawing-room, and the sergeant advanced resolutely towards the tall gentleman in amber satin. ''Tis for us to ask that of you, sir.' Then he stopped, his face lighting up with a sort of incredulous joy. 'Lord, it's him himself!' he exclaimed. 'Call the officer quick, one of ye! Bide where ye are, sir,' he said with a mixture of triumph and respect. 'If ye don't stir, ye'll not be harmed.'

Ewen saw that the man took him for the Prince – a mistake well worth encouraging if possible, though it was not very likely that an officer from the Castle would make the same mistake. In any case he had no intention of stirring from his place; as it was he imagined that the crack of the panel was widening behind his back, and dared not turn his head to look. What would be the end of this? Edinburgh Castle and captivity, at the best; perhaps a fate even less agreeable.

Ah, here was the officer pushing eagerly through the soldiers round the doorway. One glance at the figure in front of the escritoire and that eagerness was wiped away.

'That is not the Prince, you fool!' he said to the sergeant.

111

'What was he doing when you came in – did he offer any resistance?'

Through the sergeant's reply that the gentleman was sitting at the table and seemed to be asleep, Ewen was striving not to manifest a surprise which, this time, was perfectly genuine. For, however he had become part of the marooned garrison of Edinburgh Castle, his captor was no officer of Lascelles' regiment from that fortress; he was Captain Keith Windham of the Royal Scots.

Chapter 3

BUT Ewen's own powder, satin, and lace were, apparently, as good as a disguise to him, for it was quite clear that Captain Windham had not recognized in this fine gentleman the tartan-clad victor of Loch Oich side, nor even his seven days' host – no, even though he was now looking at his capture more directly, and saying, with military abruptness: 'You are my prisoner, sir!'

Ewen drew himself up. 'By what right, if you please?' he demanded. 'By what right, indeed, do you break at all into a private house? The Lord Provost shall know of this tomorrow,' he went on, with a sudden idea of passing himself off as an ordinary peaceful burgess. 'The Lord Provost shall know of it, and will require an explanation from General Guest.'

Alas, his voice, at any rate, was not unfamiliar, like his hair and costume. Captain Windham suddenly strode forward, gave an exclamation, and recoiled a little. 'What! It is *you*, Ardroy! Then I know that the Pretender's son is in this house, for you are one of his aides-de-camp! Sergeant, leave a couple of men here, and search the next floor with the others; I will follow in a moment.'

'Is that your pretext for breaking into an old lady's house at this hour of night?' asked Ewen with a fine show of indignation, as the sergeant withdrew. 'Surely you know the way to Holyrood House, Captain Windham – though in truth it may not be so easy to force an entrance there!'

In spite of his anxiety, he was able to view with pleasure Captain

Windham's visible annoyance at this speech. 'Mr Cameron,' said the soldier, with a steely light in his eyes, 'I am not to be played with like this! The Pretender's son, with three companions, was seen to enter this house a short while – '

'I am sorry to disappoint you, sir,' broke in Ewen, 'but it was *I* who entered with three companions. As you see, I have just been mistaken anew for the Prince. My three friends have left – yes, those are their wine-glasses on the table – Lady Easterhall has retired, and I was beginning to write a letter, when I fell into the doze which your noisy and illegal entry has cut short.'

'I don't believe you,' said Keith starkly, though at the mention of the letter his eyes had strayed for a second to the escritoire – and Ewen immediately wished he had not called attention to it. 'Nor do I believe that our informant mistook you for the Pretender's son; tall though he is, you are much taller. He is somewhere hidden in this house.'

'Tall . . . taller . . .' observed Ewen meditatively. 'Ah, yes, I was forgetting your opportunities of observation at Glenfinnan. I suppose you were able to tell them his exact height at Fort William, after you had so craftily given me the slip.'

This effort at provoking an argument about the ethics of that action was unsuccessful, though he could see that his late prisoner did not relish the expression which he had applied to it. But Captain Windham merely repeated, with more emphasis: 'He is somewhere hidden in this house!'

'If so, then perhaps you will have the good fortune to find and recognize him,' said Ewen with an air of levity. 'Or if not His Royal Highness, one of the other two, perhaps.'

'I have no doubt I shall,' replied Keith shortly. 'Meanwhile – your sword, if you please, Mr Cameron!'

This object Ewen had not the slightest intention of surrendering. But any kind of parley with the enemy gained time, which was the important matter. So, after a long look at the floor, as though seeking counsel there, he put his hand to the hilt, and very slowly drew the small-sword from its velvet sheath. But, once the blade was out, his fingers retained their grip.

'After all, I find that I dislike making you an unconditional gift of it,' he announced coolly, while the candlelight played menacingly up and down the steel. 'But I cannot prevent your *taking* it, Captain Windham – if you think it worth the trouble.' And with his free hand he tucked his lace ruffle out of the way.

But, as he had expected – half hoped, yet half feared, for at bottom he was pining for a fight – the Prince's pursuer did not wish to engage either himself or his men in personal conflict, while part of the house still remained unexplored. 'I'll deal with you later, Mr Cameron,' he replied curtly, and turned to the soldiers. 'See that the prisoner does not move from that spot, men! I am going to fasten the door.' He went out and, sure enough, could be heard to bolt the door on the outside.

Ewen smiled to himself to think how little he desired to quit his self-chosen position. 'You'll not object to my sitting down, I hope?' he observed politely to his two guardians, and turning round the chair from which he had risen – casting, too, a quick glance at the panel behind him, still in place – he sat down, facing his gaolers, his sword across his knees. Though they had no orders to that effect, he thought it just possible that they might attempt to disarm him, but they showed no sign of such a desire, standing stiffly by the door with their muskets and screwed bayonets, and glancing nervously at him out of the corners of their eyes, mere young north-country English lads, overawed by his dress and his air. Had they not been there, however, he could have decamped through the secret door, and what a charming surprise that would have been for Captain Windham when he returned – Fassefern House the other way round! But on second thoughts Ewen was obliged to admit to himself that this withdrawal would not have been feasible in any case, because he could not close the panel from the inside.

Meanwhile Captain Windham, in pursuit of a prey already (please God!) out of the snare, was presumably searching Lady Easterhall's bedchamber, and, a still more delicate matter, Miss Cochran's. Ewen could not suppose that the task would be to his liking, and the thought of his opponent's embarrassment afforded him much pleasure, as he sat there with one silk-stockinged leg crossed over the other. His ill-temper had gone. Too young a man to have at all enjoyed the role of disapproving critic forced upon him this evening, with his two elders covertly sneering at his prudence, and even the Prince amused at him, he was more than relieved to be free of his ungrateful part. Events had most amply justified his attitude, and now, with rising spirits, he was free to try what his wits – and perhaps, in the end, his arm – could accomplish against Captain Windham and his myrmidons. It was true that, short of getting himself killed outright, he did not see much prospect of escaping imprisonment in the Castle, but at any rate he might first have the satisfaction of a good fight – though it was to be regretted that he had not his broadsword, instead of this slender court weapon. Still, to get the chance of using it, against what he knew to be overwhelming odds, was better than having to submit to being told that he had an old head on young shoulders!

Sooner than he had expected, he heard returning feet, and now Captain Windham and he would really come to grips! It was by this time, he guessed, some twenty minutes since the Prince had slipped down the stair, and, provided that there had been no difficulty about exit, he must be almost back at Holyrood House by this time. But one could not be sure of that. And in any case Ewen had no mind to have the way he took discovered. Here, at last, was an opportunity of repaying to Captain Windham the discomfiture which he had caused him last August over his expired parole, perhaps even of wiping out, somehow, the insult of the money which he had left behind. The young man waited with rather pleasurable anticipations.

And Captain Windham came in this time, as Ewen knew he would, with an overcast brow and a set mouth. He was followed in silence by the sergeant and five men, so that the room now contained nine soldiers in all.

'Ah, I was afraid that you would have no luck,' observed Ewen sympathetically. He was still sitting very much at his ease, despite his drawn sword. 'A pity that you would not believe me. However, you have wasted time.'

Keith Windham shot a quick, annoyed, questioning glance at him, but made no reply. His gaze ran rapidly round Lady Easterhall's drawing-room, but there was in it no article of furniture large enough to afford a hiding-place to a man, and no other

115

visible door. He turned to the two soldiers whom he had left there. 'Has the prisoner made any suspicious movement?'

'He has not moved from yonder chair,' he was assured in a strong Lancashire accent.

'And yet this is the room they were in,' muttered the Englishman to himself, looking at the disordered chairs and the used wine-glasses. After frowning for a moment he started to tap the panelling on his side of the room, a proceeding which made Ewen uneasy. Had they heard up at the Castle of the existence of a secret passage somewhere in this house? It was unpleasantly possible. But when Captain Windham came to the three windows giving on to the Grassmarket he naturally desisted. And the farther side of the room – that where Ewen and his writing-table were situated – faced, obviously, down the close by which the soldiers had entered, so (if the Highlander followed his reasoning correctly) Captain Windham concluded that there was no room there for a hiding-place, and did not trouble to sound the wall.

Ewen, however, judged it time to rise from his chair. 'I told you, Captain Windham, that my friends had gone,' he remarked, brushing some fallen powder off his coat. 'Will you not now take your own departure, and allow an old lady to resume the rest which I suppose you have just further disturbed?'

He saw with satisfaction that the invader (who was, after all, a gentleman) did not like that thrust. However, the latter returned it by responding dryly: 'You can render that departure both speedier and quieter, Mr Cameron, by surrendering yourself without resistance.'

'And why, pray, should I be more accommodating than you were last August?' inquired Ewen with some pertinence.

Keith Windham coloured. 'To bring back the memory of that day, sir, is to remind me that you then put me under a deep obligation, and to make my present task the more odious. But I must carry it out. Your sword, if you please!'

Ewen shrugged his shoulders in the way Miss Cameron condemned as outlandish. 'I had no intention, sir, of reminding you of an obligation which I assure you I had never regarded as one. But why *should* I render your task, as you call it, more pleasant? And why make a task of it at all? The Prince, as you see, is not here, and Generals Guest and Preston will find me a very disappointing substitute.'

Keith Windham came nearer and dropped his voice. His face looked genuinely troubled. 'I wish, Ardroy, for your own sake, that you would let me take you unharmed! Take you I must; you are a chieftain and the Prince's aide-de-camp, as I happen to know. It is the fortune of war, as it was last August, when our positions were reversed. So, for the sake of the courtesy and hospitality which I then received from you – '

'My sorrow!' burst out Ewen. 'Must my past good conduct, as you are pleased to consider it, lead to my undoing now! ... And I very much doubt whether our positions *are* reversed, and whether any further disturbance – and you have made not a little already – do not bring the guard from the West Bow about your ears. If I might give advice in my turn, it would be to get back to the Castle while yet you can!'

'Thank you,' said Keith with extreme dryness; 'we will. Sergeant, have your men secure the prisoner.'

He stood back a little. Ewen had already decided in the event of a fight to abandon his post by the writing-table, where, on one side at least, he could be taken in flank, and where any shifting of the table itself, highly probable in a struggle, would cause the panel to reveal its secret. (Not that that would greatly matter now.) Immediately the Englishman stepped back, therefore, he darted across the room and ensconced himself in the corner by the nearest window, hastily wrapping his cloak, which he had snatched up for the purpose, round his left arm. His eyes sparkled; he was going to have his fight!

'I am ready,' he remarked cheerfully, seeing the much slower preparations of his assailants. 'Is it to be a charge with the bayonet, or are you going to use the butt, my friends?'

'You'll not use either!' said Keith sharply to his men. 'I do not wish this gentleman injured.'

'Then make him put up his sword, sir,' retorted the sergeant in justifiable indignation. 'Else it's ourselves will be injured, I'm thinking!'

Ewen was about to endorse this opinion when a familiar and most welcome sound came to him through the closed window behind him. No mistaking that strain; and that the soldiers should hear it too, he turned a little and dashed his elbow, protected by the curtain, through the nearest pane of glass. In it flowed, wailing and menacing; the Cameron rant: 'Sons of the dogs, come hither, come hither and you shall have flesh . . .'

'I think you had best call off your men altogether, Captain Windham, if they are to save their own skins!' And in the uneasy silence which he had procured Ewen added, with some exultation: 'It is my own clan, the Camerons; they are coming down the West Bow into the Grassmarket. There will not be much left of you, my good fellows, if you so much as scratch me!' And, seeing the effect of his words, he tugged aside the curtain, flung open the partly shattered casement, and called out in Gaelic to the line of kilted figures just emerging from the West Bow.

The long yell of the slogan answered him, as he swung quickly back on guard. But there was no need of his sword. Prestonpans had taught the Castle garrison exaggerated terror of those who uttered such cries. The soldiers, the sergeant included, were already huddling towards the door, and Keith Windham was not in time to get between them and the exit. He stamped his foot in fury.

'Do your duty, you dirty cowards!' he shouted, pointing at the figure by the window. But a second heart-shaking yell came up from the Grassmarket.

'*Chlanna nan con, thigibh an so! Thigibh an so . . .*'

Perfectly deaf to their officer's objurgations, the English soldiers were occupied only with the question of which should be first from the room. Keith seized the last fugitive by the collar, but the only result of this appeal to force was that the man, who was very powerful, shook him off, thrust him back with small regard for his rank, and banged the door behind himself. Captain Windham, livid, threw himself upon the handle to pluck it open again – but the knob merely turned in his hand. The violent slam had evidently shot to the bolt on the outside. Hunter and quarry – only now it was hard to know which was which – were equally prisoners.

Ewen, over at the window, laughed aloud; he could not help it. 'You seem always to be unfortunate in your men, Captain Windham,' he remarked, and, shaking the cloak off his left arm, slid his blade back into the scabbard. 'I fear it is I who shall have to ask you for *your* sword. Would you prefer to give it up to me before the guard arrives?'

He got it ... but not in the fashion which he had expected. Keith, quite beside himself with mortification and rage, had already whipped out his weapon, while Ewen, with bent head, was sheathing his own; and now, really blind to the fact that the Highlander was for the moment defenceless and off his guard, Captain Windham sprang furiously at him without warning of any sort. Ewen had no chance to draw again, no space to spring aside, no time for anything but to catch wildly at the blade in the hope of diverting it. At the cost of a badly cut right hand he succeeded in saving himself from being spitted, and the deflected point, sliding through his clutching fingers, went by his hip into the panelling where, both men loosing their hold at the same moment, the weapon stuck for the fraction of a second, and then fell ringing to the floor.

Horrified and sobered, Keith had sprung back; Ewen, after a first instinctive movement to catch him by the throat, had checked himself, and, clasping his bleeding hand tightly with the other, leant back against the wall and looked at him with a mixture of sternness and inquiry. His breath was coming rather quickly, but, compared with his assailant, he was the image of calm.

'My God!' stammered the Englishman, as white as a sheet. 'I never saw ...' He indicated Ardroy's sheathed sword. 'I might have killed you....' He took a long breath and drew a hand across his eyes. Still looking at him curiously, his victim fished out his lace-bordered handkerchief and began to wrap it round his palm, a very inadequate precaution, for in a moment the cambric was crimson.

In another Keith was at his side. 'How deeply is it cut? Let me ...' And he pulled out his own more solid handkerchief.

'I don't know,' answered Ewen composedly, putting back his Mechlin ruffle, which had slipped down again. 'Pretty deeply, it seems.' He surrendered his hand. 'Thanks; over mine, then – tie it tighter still.'

'Good God, I might have killed you!' said Keith again under

his breath as he bandaged and knotted. 'I . . . I lost my temper, but, as Heaven's my witness, I thought you had your sword out.'

'Why, so I had, a moment earlier,' replied Ewen. 'You did not intend murder, then?'

'I deserve that you should think so,' murmured the soldier, still very much shaken. 'Perhaps, as it is, I have disabled you for life.'

Ewen had nearly retorted: 'Why should that trouble you?' but he was so much astonished at the depth of feeling in his enemy's tone that he merely stared at his bent head as he tied the last knot.

'These handkerchiefs are not enough,' said Keith suddenly, relinquishing the wounded hand. He pushed aside the little brass gorget at his neck, untied and unwound his own lace cravat, and bound that over all. Then he stood back.

'You will soon get attention now, Ardroy. Keep your hand up, so. . . . There is my sword.' He made a jerky movement towards the floor, and walking abruptly away to the hearth, stood there with his back turned.

For a moment or two Ewen also stood quite still where he was, looking at that back. That Captain Windham was ashamed of his attack on a practically unarmed man he could understand; he would have had precisely the same scruples in his place, and he would certainly have felt the same rage and humiliation had he been deserted by his followers in so disgraceful a manner (though he could not imagine Highlanders ever acting so). And, observing the dejection revealed in Captain Windham's attitude, where he stood with bowed head and folded arms by the dying fire, and the complete absence in him of any of that mocking irony with which he himself had more than once made acquaintance at Ardroy, Ewen began to feel less vindictive about the incident of the guineas. Captain Windham, being an Englishman, did not understand Highland pride, and had probably never intended any insult at all. And now, with this sudden turning of the tables, he was again a prisoner, made in rather an absurd and ignominious fashion. Ewen could find it in his heart to be sorry for him. And what would be the advantage of yet another prisoner? The officers taken at Gladsmuir had had to be paroled and sent away. . . .

He picked up the fallen sword, faintly smeared with red along its edges, and went over to the hearth.

'Captain Windham!'

The scarlet-clad figure turned. 'Your Camerons are very tardy!' he said with a bitter intonation. 'Or are those yells all we are to know of them?' It was indeed sufficiently surprising that the rescuers had not entered the house some minutes ago, particularly as the door was broken open.

Ewen listened. 'I think that they are possibly chasing ... a retreating enemy. But in any case' – he held out Keith's sword – 'I cannot stomach taking advantage of your being left in the lurch by those rascals. Put on your sword again, and I'll convey you safely out of the house.'

A dull flush swept over the English soldier's face. 'You mean that I am to run the gauntlet of those caterans, when they return, under your protection? No; I have been humiliated enough this evening. It would be less galling to go as a prisoner. Keep my sword; 'tis the second of mine you have had, Mr Cameron.'

Yes, he was sore, and no wonder! Ewen decided that he would not even mention the objectionable guineas.

'I cannot hold this sword much longer,' he said lightly, 'having but the one hand at present. – No, the caterans shall not see you at all, Captain Windham, and you shall go alone. Only, for Heaven's sake, be quick, for some of them must soon be here!'

Bewildered, half reluctant, Keith closed his fingers on the hilt held out to him, and Ewen drew him to the escritoire on the right of the hearth. When he pushed it aside the panel behind slid slowly back.

Keith Windham stood before the gap momentarily speechless. 'That, then – ' he began at last, thickly.

'Yes, that is the way my friends went. But you can use the same road. It comes out, I understand, in the West Bow; there you will have to trust to chance, but it seems a dark night. Here, take my cloak,' – he went and picked it up – ''twill cover your uniform. And you must have a candle to light you down.'

To these directions, and the proffered candlestick and cloak, the baffled hunter paid no heed. 'Your friends!' he said between his teeth. 'The Pretender's son, you mean! He *was* here this evening, then, in this very room!'

'Yes, but he was gone a little time before you entered,' answered Ewen soothingly. 'I was only troubled lest the door should slide open and betray the path he took. But 'tis of no moment now.'

'No, it's of no moment now!' repeated Windham bitterly. Wrath, reluctant admiration, disappointment, and concern for what he had so nearly done – and not in fair fight – to the man before him strove openly in his tone, as he went on: 'Is this your revenge for –' he pointed to the swathed right hand – 'and for my outwitting you last August? It's a sharp one, for all that it's generous. . . . Yes, you have fairly outmanoeuvred me, Ardroy, with your secret stair and your clansmen so pat to the moment, like a stage play! But I warn you that this mumming will turn to grim earnest some day; there'll be a bloody curtain to the comedy, and you will regret that ever you played a part in it!'

'That depends, does it not, on how many more battles of Gladsmuir we have?' retorted Ewen, with a smile on his lips and a sparkle in his eyes. 'But go – go!' for at last there had come a rush of feet up the stairs, and the rescue party (oblivious of the bolt) were hammering upon the door with cries. He thrust the candlestick and the cloak – the Prince's cloak – into the Englishman's hands, calling out something in Gaelic over his shoulder the while. 'Go – they'll have the door down in another minute!'

He almost pushed Captain Windham into the aperture, pressed the spring, and wedged the returning panel with the table, only a second or two before the unfortunate door of Lady Easterhall's drawing-room fell inwards with a crash, and Cameron kilts plunged over it.

Chapter 4

WALKING home with her father next day up the crowded Canongate after rain, Miss Alison Grant suddenly became aware of a tall Highland officer striding up the street some way ahead. From the occasional glimpses of him, which were all that she was able to obtain in the moving throng, it seemed to be her betrothed; but, if so, he was carrying his right arm in a sling. This was disturbing. Moreover, Ewen, if it were he – and at any rate the officer was a Cameron – was walking at such a pace that Alison and her parent would never overtake him, unless indeed he were on his way to visit them where they lodged in Hyndford's Close, a little beyond the Netherbow.

'Papa,' whispered Alison, 'let us walk quicker; yonder's Ewen, unless I am much mistaken, on his way to wait upon us, and he must not find us from home.'

They quickened their pace, without much visible effect, when lo! their quarry was brought to a standstill by two gentlemen coming downwards, who encountered and stopped him.

'Now let us go more slowly, sir,' suggested Alison, dragging at her father's arm. To which Mr Grant, complying, said: 'My dear, to be alternately a greyhound and a snail is hard upon a man of my years, nor do I understand why you should be stalking Ardroy in this fashion.'

'Ewen *is* rather like a stag,' thought Alison; 'he carries his head like one – Papa,' she explained, 'I want to know – I *must* know – why he wears his arm in a sling! Look, now that he has turned a little you can see it plainly. And, you remember, he disappeared so strangely last night.'

And now, crawl as they would, they must pass the three gentlemen, who made way for them instantly, not to turn the lady with her hooped petticoats into the swirling gutter. As Ewen – for it was he – raised his bonnet with his left hand, Alison cast a swift and comprehensive glance over him, though she did not pause for the fraction of a second, but, acknowledging his salutation and those of his companions, went on her way with dignity.

But she walked ever slower and slower, and when she came to the narrow entrance of their close she stopped. Yet even then she did not look back down the Canongate.

'Papa, did you hear, those gentlemen were asking Ewen what had befallen him. I heard something about "disturbance" and "Grassmarket". You saw his hand was all bandaged about. He looked pale, I thought. What can he have been at last night – not fighting a duel, surely!'

'Well, my dear, here he is, so he can tell us – that is, if he is disposed to do so,' observed Mr Grant. 'Good day, Ardroy; were you coming in-bye?'

'I intended it, later on,' replied Ewen, with more truth than tact, 'but – '

'But now you see that you behove to at this moment,' finished Alison, with determination, looking very significantly at his arm; and Ewen, without another word, went obediently up the close with them, secretly admired from above by a well-known Whig lady who happened to be at her window, and who remarked to her maid that the Jacobite Miss lodging overhead had a braw lover, for all he was a wild Hielandman.

And presently the wild Hielandman was standing in the middle of Mr Grant's parlour, and the Jacobite Miss was declaring that she could shake him, so little could she get out of him. 'They say you can ask anything of a Cameron save butter,' she said indignantly, 'but it's clear that there are other things too you'll never get from them!'

Ewen smiled down at her, screwing up his eyes in the way she loved. He was a little pale, for the pain of his cut hand had kept him wakeful, but he was not ill-pleased with life this afternoon.

'Yes, other people's secrets, to wit,' he said teasingly; and then, feigning to catch himself up: 'My sorrow, have I not the unlucky tongue to mention that word in a woman's hearing! What I have told you, *m'eudail*, is the truth; I had an encounter last night with some of the Castle garrison, and my hand, as I say, was hurt – scratched, that is, as I warrant you have sometimes scratched yourself with a needle or a bodkin.'

'The needle's never been threaded whose scratch required as much bandaging as *that*!' retorted Alison, with her eyes on the muffled member in the sling. 'And what was yon I heard as I passed about a disturbance in the Grassmarket?'

'Has she not the ears of a hare?' observed Ewen to Mr Grant. ''Tis true, there was a disturbance in the Grassmarket.'

'If that is so, then I'll learn more of it before the day's out,' deduced Alison, with satisfaction. 'And you, sir, that ought to know better, brawling in the town at such an hour! I thought the Prince had summoned you last night. Not that I remarked your absence from the ball,' she added. 'I was quite unaware of it, I assure you, in the society of my cousins of Glenmoriston.'

Ewen looked across at Mr Grant and smiled. 'My dear,' protested the old gentleman, 'an encounter with the Castle garrison can scarce be called brawling. We are, it may be said, at war with them.'

'But are they not all as mild as milk up there now that the Prince has lifted the blockade?' inquired Alison. 'And how could Ewen have met any of them in the Grassmarket? The poor men dare not show their faces there; the place is hotching with Camerons and MacDonalds!'

'Who said I met them in the Grassmarket?' retorted Ewen. 'But never fret, Miss Curiosity; some day I'll be free to tell you where it was.'

'Wherever it was,' said Miss Grant, with decision, 'I'll be bound 'twas you provoked the disturbance!'

Her lover continued to smile at her with real amusement. In a sense there was truth in this last accusation. 'It's a fine character you give me, indeed! I think I'd best be taking my leave until you appreciate me better!' And he put out his left hand to take his bonnet from the table where he had laid it. Something sparkled on the hand as he moved it.

'Who gave you that ring?' exclaimed Alison. 'Nay, *that* I have a right to know!'

Ewen put his hand behind him. 'No woman, Alison.'

'Then you can tell me who it was. . . . Come, *Eoghain mhóir*, if there be a mystery over the ring also, why, you should not be wearing it for all the world to see!'

'That's true,' said Ardroy, and he relinquished his hand. 'Yes, you can take it off. 'Tis not so plain as it looks, neither. There is a spring beneath.'

'Oh!' breathed Alison, her eyes very wide. The chased gold centre of the ring had moved aside in the midst of the rose diamonds, and it was a tiny miniature of the Prince which she held. 'Ewen, *he* gave you this?'

'I did not steal it, my dear. Yes, he gave it me this morning.'

'For . . . on account of what happened last night?'

Ewen nodded. 'For my prudence. You see, the Prince does not write me down so turbulent as you do.'

There was something like tears in Alison's eyes. 'Prudence? No! It was because you gained that "needle-scratch" for him!' She kissed the ring, and, taking the strong, passive hand, slipped it on again. 'I will not plague you any more. Does the wound pain you, dearest heart?'

But next day Hector Grant came into possession of the story, more or less correct, which was flying about Edinburgh, and presented his sister with a fine picture of her lover, alone against a score of the Castle redcoats, standing with his back to the secret stair hewing down the foe until his sword broke in his hand, and the Cameron guard rushed in only just in time to save him. And Alison unveiling this composition to the hero himself at their next meeting, Ewen was constrained in the interests of truth to paint out this flamboyant battle-piece and to substitute a more correct but sufficiently startling scene. Alison certainly found his sober account quite lurid enough.

'And you let the English officer go, after that!' she exclaimed breathlessly. 'But, Ewen dearest, why?'

'For one reason, because 'twas such curst ill luck that his men should run away for the second time!' replied Ewen, settling his silken sling more comfortably.

'For the second time?'

'I have not yet told you who the officer was. Cannot you guess?'

'Surely 'twas not . . . *Captain Windham* . . . here in Edinburgh?'

'It was Captain Windham himself. I have no notion how he got here; it must have been before we took the town. But I was sorry for him, poor man, and it was quite plain that he had no real intention of killing me; indeed he was greatly discomposed over the affair. So you must not lay that to his charge, Alison.'

'And so you *have* met again!' said Alison slowly, her eyes fastened on her lover. ('A great service' . . . 'a bitter grief' . . . This was neither.) 'It was not then because of your foster-father's prophecy, that you let him go?'

And now Ewen stared at her. 'Faith, no, darling, for I had clean forgot about it. *Dhé!* It begins to fulfil itself then!'

Bright and cold, or wet and windy, the October days went by in Edinburgh. Ewen's hand healed, and that secret fear which he had mentioned to no one save Dr Cameron, who dressed it, that he would never be able to grip a broadsword again, passed also. And having waited upon Lady Easterhall and Miss Cochran a day or two after the fracas, to ask how they did (not that he had omitted to reassure himself of this on the night itself, before he left) he then, by the old lady's desire, carried Alison to visit them also. And it is possible that Miss Cochran envied Miss Grant.

But up at the Castle the days went a great deal more slowly, particularly for Captain Keith Windham, who had little to do but to pace the battlements and look down, as he was doing this morning, when October was almost sped, on that unrivalled vista of which he was now heartily sick, and remember all the mortifications, professional as well as personal, which he had suffered there since the end of August, when he had made his way thither from Fort William with the news of the Highland advance. For after the startling tidings of Cope's avoidance of the rebels, leaving the road open before them to Edinburgh, Keith, secure but chafing, had endured the spectacle of vain attempts by the frightened citizens to repair and man the walls, and to raise a body of volunteers (almost immediately disbanded, lest their lives should be endangered), and the sight of two regiments of His Majesty's dragoons in full flight along the Lang Dykes with no man pursuing. Finally, to complete and symbolize the great scandal and shock of Cope's lightning defeat, he had with his own eyes seen, struck defiantly into the outer gate of the Castle, the dirk of the single Jacobite officer who on that occasion had chased a party of terrified troopers thither like rabbits to their burrow.

On top of all this had come his own personal humiliation and disappointment, and of this Ewen Cameron and no other had been the cause. The soldiers of Lascelles' regiment who had so shamefully deserted the officer in charge of them had been severely punished, but this did little to heal the very sore place in Captain Windham's memory. Sometimes it was only anger which coloured his recollections of that scene in Lady Easterhall's house, sometimes it was shame. Sometimes he wondered if he had not permanently injured Ardroy, and though, as a loyal subject of King George, he ought no doubt to have been glad of the possibility, in view of how the hurt had been inflicted and of the Highlander's subsequent behaviour, the idea filled him with a feeling far removed from satisfaction. And even worse might easily have come of his onslaught. Keith was inclined to shudder still when he thought of that contingency, and not merely because with Ewen dead or dying on the floor, he himself would have received short shrift from the Camerons when they broke in.

How nearly he had succeeded in capturing the Prince, he supposed he would never know, but there was no doubt that it was Ardroy who had destroyed whatever chance he might have had. Chosen as Keith had been to lead the flying raid that evening because he was the only officer in the Castle who had seen Charles Edward Stuart face to face, he could then have blessed Fate for having sent him to Glenfinnan. Thus, he had reflected as they marched stealthily down the close, does profit come out of the unpleasant. Already he saw his name in every news sheet as the captor of the Pretender's son. . . . Alas, he had merely come anew into collision with the same stubborn and generous character, and once again, though their positions this time had seemed to be reversed, he had had the worst of it. And on this occasion the Highlander had shown him a new and unsuspected side of himself, for it was Ardroy who had played with *him*, sitting so coolly in front of that table on which hung the secret. God! if he had only guessed.

And so Keith had come back empty-handed, with the knowledge that but for Ardroy's quixotry he would not have come back at all. Huddled in his enemy's own cloak (for its real ownership, luckily for his peace of mind, he never discovered), pushed ignominiously to safety down the very passage by which his quarry had eluded him, he had been ever since weighed down by a debt which was well-nigh a grievance. There were times when he almost regretted that he had not remained and been made prisoner . . . and always times when he asked himself why Ewen Cameron had acted as he did. He was sure that he himself would not have been so foolish. The days of chivalry were over; one did not go about in this century behaving like the knights in the old romances. An enemy was an enemy – at least to a professional soldier – and it was one's business to treat him as such.

The cursed part of it was that people who were insane enough to behave as Ardroy had behaved, somehow attained a position of superiority which was distinctly galling. And galling also was it to realize, as Keith Windham suddenly did at this moment, how much time he spent in speculating what that curious young man might be doing down there in the city spread out like a map. ... Strange that he had not at first recognized him that night – extraordinarily handsome Ardroy had looked, and devilish cool he had kept, too, in a tight place! ... Fool that he was, he was at it again. Keith turned from the battlements, glad of a diversion, for he had become aware of the approach of a wheeled chair, which he knew to contain the aged but spirited form of General Preston.

General George Preston, deputy-governor of Edinburgh Castle since 1715, to whom, old and infirm though he was, it was likely that his Hanoverian Majesty owed it that that fortress had not been surrendered to the invaders, was a veteran of Marlborough's wars bearing in fact souvenirs of Ramillies which had ever since affected his health and his prospects of promotion. He was eighty-six years of age, even older than General Guest (now, since Cope's flight, commander-in-chief); but whereas that warrior had scarcely left his quarters since he had removed for safety into the Castle, Preston, during the more strenuous days of the 'blockade', had caused himself to be wheeled round in a chair every two hours to supervise and encourage. Since Colonel Philip Windham, Keith's father, had also fought under Marlborough, Keith had on one occasion asked the old soldier some questions about the great Duke's battles, and found Preston very ready to hold forth on them, and in particular on that bloody fight of Malplaquet, where he had commanded the Cameronian regiment. And Keith remembered suddenly that the Scottish friend of his father's after whom he himself was named had met his death at Malplaquet; and he spoke to the old soldier about that misty John Keith of whom he knew so little.

'Aye,' said the General, a Perthshire man himself. 'I wondered that ye should bear a Scots name in front of an English, Captain Windham. I suppose yon Keith will have been in a Scottish regiment, but I don't mind of him. 'Tis thirty-six years syne, ye ken – a lang time, more than your hale lifetime, young man.'

So John Keith, who had fallen on a Flanders battlefield nearly forty years before, became more misty than ever. But Captain Windham's pre-natal connexion with a Scot of Malplaquet had interested old Preston in him, and he announced an intention of reporting on the zeal and vigilance which the officer of the Royals had displayed in the defence of the Castle.

From his chair the old General beckoned to that officer now, and sent his servant out of hearing.

'Captain Windham, a word in your ear!' And, as Keith stooped, he said gleefully. ''Tis a good work, if ever there was one. I've reason to believe that Edinburgh will be free of these Highland pests the morn!'

Keith gave an exclamation. 'They are evacuating the city, sir?'

The veteran chuckled. 'They intend marching for England, whence I pray not a man of 'em will return alive. The news has just come in by a sure hand, but I had jaloused it already. In a day or two ye'll not see a plaid between Greyfriars and the Nor' Loch!'

General Preston's sure hand had carried perfectly correct tidings. Against the wishes and the instincts of the Chiefs, Prince Charles was about to march into England, believing that he would thus rally to his standard those cautious English Jacobites on whose promised support he built such large hopes, and many others too, who had made no promises but who would surely declare for him when he appeared in person to lead them against their alien ruler.

And early on the morning of the first of November, Ewen took his farewell of Alison in Hyndford's Close. Lochiel's regiment, like the bulk of the army, was already assembled at Dalkeith; for since Prestonpans the Prince had never quartered troops in the city to any great extent, and he himself was already gone. But Ewen, in order to be with his own men in this strange country to

130

which they were bound, had resigned his position as aide-de-camp, had remained behind in order to bring away the Cameron guard, who would presently march out of Edinburgh with colours flying and the pipes playing.

But here there was no martial display, only a knowledge that this, and not the farewell at Ardroy in August, was the real parting. Ewen was setting off today for something much more portentous than a mere rendezvous – armed invasion. Yet some unspoken instinct made them both try to be very matter-of-fact, especially Alison.

'Here is a sprig of oak for your bonnet, Ewen – you'll be wearing your clan badge now, I'm thinking. I picked it yesterday.' And she fastened beside the eagle's feathers a little bunch of sere leaves. 'And see, I have made you a new cockade ... I doubt you'll get your clothes mended properly. England's a dour place, I'm sure. Oh, I wish you were not crossing the Border!'

'Nothing venture, nothing win,' replied Ewen tritely, looking down at his bonnet, about which her fingers were busy. 'I doubt, for my part, that those oak-leaves will bide long on their stalks, Alison, but you may be sure I'll wear them as long as they do. And the cockade – 'tis a very fine one, my dear – I'll bring back to you somehow. Or maybe you'll get your first sight of it again in London!'

'I wonder will you meet Captain Windham anywhere in England?' said Alison.

'How that fellow runs in your head, my darling! I vow I shall soon be jealous of him. And I marching away and leaving him here in the Castle – for I suppose he is there still. Make him my compliments, if you should meet him before setting out for Ardroy,' said Ewen, smiling. For to Ardroy were his betrothed and her father retiring in a day or two.

'Ewen,' said the girl seriously, taking him by the swordbelt that crossed his breast, 'will you not tell me something? Was there ever a danger that, from the injury Captain Windham did you, you might never have had the full use of your hand again?'

'Why, what put that notion into your head?'

'A word you let fall once, and an expression on Dr Cameron's face one day when I mentioned the hurt to him.'

131

'For a day or two Archie did think it might be so,' conceded her lover rather unwillingly. 'And I feared it myself for longer than that, and was in a fine fright about it, as you may imagine. – But Alison,' he added quickly, as, exclaiming, 'Oh, my poor darling!' she laid her head against him, 'you are not to cast that up against Captain Windham. It was I that took hold of his blade, as I told you, and I am sure that he never meant – '

'No, no,' cried Alison, lifting her head, 'you mistake me. No, I am glad of what you tell me, because that hurt he did you is perhaps the fulfilment of the "bitter grief" which Angus said that he should cause you . . . only happily it is averted,' she added, taking his right hand and looking earnestly at the two red puckered seams across palm and fingers. 'For that *would* have caused you bitter grief, Ewen, my darling.' She covered the scars with her own soft little hands, held the captive hand to her breast, and went on, eagerly pursuing her exegesis. 'Indeed, if for a time you believed that you would be disabled always – how dare you have kept that from me? – he has already caused you great grief . . . and so, that part is over, and now he will only do you a service!'

But Ewen, laughing and touched, caught her to him with his other arm.

'The best service Captain Windham can do is never to let me see his face again, or I may remember how angry I was with him when I found his letter and his guineas that night at Fassefern. Nor do I think he'll want to see mine, for in his soul he was not best pleased, I'll undertake, at being so lightly let off the other evening and shown down the very secret stair he could not find. – But now, *mo chridhe*, do not let us talk of the tiresome fellow any more. . . .'

And five minutes later, when Hector Grant in his French uniform appeared at the door, they had forgotten everything except that they were parting.

'Come, Ardroy, you'll be left behind,' he called gaily. 'Dry your tears, Alison, and let him go; we've eight good miles to cover.'

'I was not greeting, never think it,' said Alison as she was released. 'But oh, I'm wishing sore I could come with you two!'

'Indeed, I wish you could,' said Hector. 'For I doubt the English ladies cannot dance the reel.'

Alison looked from her brother to her lover and back again. She might not have been crying, but there was little gaiety in her. 'There'll be more than dancing over the Border, Hector!'

'There'll be *better* than dancing, you mean, my lass,' said Hector Grant, and his left hand fell meaningly on his sword-hilt. 'I suppose I may take a kiss of her, Ardroy?'

III. THE EBB

Then all went to wreck.
— The Lyon in Morning

Chapter 1

THERE was a bitter wind sweeping across the Beauly Firth, and Inverness on the farther shore lay shivering under a leaden sky. The Kessock ferryman had to tug at his oars, although he carried but one passenger, a gaunt, broad-shouldered young man, fully armed, who sat looking across at the little town with rather harassed blue eyes.

Four months – four months and a week over – for today was the seventh of March – since, full of hope and determination, the Prince's army had set out on the road to England. Of what avail those hopes? England had not risen for the Stuarts, had not stirred. And yet, just when it seemed that, if the invaders had put their fortunes to the touch and pushed on, they might have gained a kingdom, they found themselves turning their backs on their goal and trailing home again over the Border. Little more than forty days had been spent on the other side, and, save for the rearguard action near Penrith, the sword had not left its sheath there. The invasion had been a failure.

Yet, in spite of weariness and heartburnings, the little army had at least recrossed Esk in safety – except those of it so mistakenly left to garrison Carlisle – and many were not sorry to be back on Scottish soil. But to have retreated once more after beating Hawley at Falkirk in January, even though the bad weather had hindered pursuit and prevented a more decisive victory, to have left Stirling, after failing to take it, in such haste and disorder that the withdrawal had been more like a rout, what name best befitted that strategy? For gradually all the Lowlands had been occupied in their rear, and there was a slow tide setting northwards after them, which one day might be slow no longer.

The Prince, maddened at the decision to withdraw north, which was against his every instinct, had been told that the daily desertions were so great as to leave no choice, that the only course was to master the forts in the north, keep together a force until the spring, and then increase it to fighting strength. But had the desertions been so extensive? It was hard to judge, yet, from his own experience, Ardroy would not have said so. Still, there were other difficulties, other divisions; there was the preponderating influence of the Irish favourites, who always had the Prince's ear, because they always fell in with his opinions; there was the growing ill-feeling between him and his able but hot-tempered general-in-chief, so acute that Ewen had with his own ears heard Charles Edward charge Lord George Murray behind his back with treachery. Yet Lochiel had been for withdrawal, and whatever Lochiel did was right in Ewen's eyes. He was wondering today whether the Chief were still of the same opinion; he had not seen him for over a fortnight.

The ferryman's voice broke in on his passenger's reflections. ''Tis all much changed in Inverness now, sir, and for the better.' Evidently, like most of the inhabitants, he was Jacobite at heart. 'To think that only two weeks ago I ferried Lord Loudoun and the Lord President and the Chief of Macleod over in this very boat, and all their troops crossing helter-skelter too, to get away from the Prince. ... You'll be yourself, perhaps, from chasing after Lord Loudoun yonder?' he added tentatively.

'Yes,' answered Ewen, his eyes still fixed on Inverness, 'I am from Lord Cromarty's force.'

The reason why the Earl of Loudoun, commanding the district for the Government, had evacuated Inverness without a battle, was really due to the somewhat ludicrous failure of his attempt to seize the person of the Prince when, in mid-February, the latter was the guest of Lady Mackintosh at Moy Hall. Conceiving the idea of surprising him there, the Earl had set out secretly at night with a force of fifteen hundred men for that purpose. But timely warning having been sent from Inverness, the Prince slipped out of Moy Hall, and the whole of Lord Loudoun's force was thrown into confusion, and a part of it into headlong flight, by the ruse of Donald Fraser, the Moy blacksmith, and four of Lady Mackintosh's Highland servants, who, by firing off their pieces in the dark and calling to imaginary regiments to come up, re-enacted the comedy of High Bridge on an even more piquant scale. Not only was the Earl obliged to return ignominiously to Inverness, but the desertions from his Highland companies consequent upon this affair were so great that he thought it better to await Cumberland's advance among the Whig clans of Ross and Cromarty, to which he and his force accordingly retired; and Prince Charles's army had entered Inverness without a blow.

The water lapped the sides of the ferryboat impatiently. The sky looked full of snow, and nearly as dark as on the day of Falkirk, while the wind was even colder than Ewen remembered it as they had plodded over Shap Fell in the December retreat from England. In Caesar's time, as he used to read in his boyhood, armies went into winter quarters. But all *their* marching and fighting had been done in the severest season of the year, in autumn and winter; and who knew what awaited them in the not less cruel rigours of a Highland spring? For Cumberland, he knew, had been at Aberdeen since the end of February.

Ewen frowned, and his thoughts went back to the somewhat comic warfare from which he had just been recalled. For when Lord Cromarty had been sent with a Jacobite force over the Moray Firth after Lord Loudoun, the latter, retreating farther north into Sutherland, established himself at Dornoch on the other side of the deep-winding firth of that name, which Cromarty, having no boats, could not cross. But directly Cromarty attempted to go round by the head of the firth Lord Loudoun sent his men across by ferry to Tain, on the Ross-shire side, once more; and when Lord Cromarty returned to Ross, Lord Loudoun recalled his followers to Dornoch. And thus a vexatious and absurd game of catch-as-catch-can had been going on, and might go on for ever, unless the Prince could send another detachment to hold Tain. No, Ewen was not sorry that Lochiel had recalled him.

He pulled his bonnet with the draggled eagle's feathers and the soiled cockade farther down on his brows, and wrapped his plaid round him, for they were now in the icy middle of the firth. The ferryman babbled on, telling him for the most part things he knew already; how, for instance, when the Prince had had the castle here blown up after its surrender, an unfortunate French engineer had been blown up with it. It was useless to ask the man what he really wanted to know, how Miss Alison Grant did over there in Inverness, Alison on whom he had not set eyes since Hector and he had said farewell to her last All Hallows in Edinburgh. It was a question whether they three would ever meet again, for Hector had been one of the officers left behind as part of the ill-fated garrison of Carlisle, and since the thirtieth of December he had been a prisoner in English hands. How Alison was bearing this ill news Ewen could only guess; it was all the heavier for her, too, because her father was in France, having been dispatched thither on a mission by the Prince directly after Falkirk.

Ewen knew that Alison and his aunt had come to Inverness in the hopes of seeing him, immediately on the news of the town's surrender to the Highland army on 18 February, but as it was before their arrival that Ewen himself had been sent off with Lord Cromarty's composite force, the meeting had not taken place. Miss Cameron, as a letter had since told him, had thought it best on that to return to Ardroy, but, feeling sure that sooner or later Ewen's duties would bring him to Inverness, she had left Alison there, in the care of Lady Ogilvy, whose husband, with his regiment, was on the other side of the Spey. And now Lochiel had recalled Ewen – but only to accompany him on another enterprise. Of his approaching return Ewen had told Alison in a letter which he had dispatched yesterday by Lachlan, but he had not told her how brief his stay would be, nor had he broached the project which was in his own mind – the determination which had been growing there since the retreat northward.

But, as he thought of what that was, the harassed look went out of his eyes, and he became deafer than ever to the ferryman's chatter.

At the guardhouse by the bridge over the Ness, Ewen stopped to inquire where Lady Ogilvy was to be found, for he was not sure of her lodging, and as he was talking to the officer there, he heard a youthful voice behind him asking exactly the same question in Gaelic.

Ewen turned quickly, for he knew that voice. There in the entry stood a half-shy, half-excited boy of fifteen, who had never been in a town before – young Angus, Neil MacMartin's eldest son. His face lit up, and he darted forward. 'Letters, Mac 'ic Ailein!' And out of an old sporran too big for him he produced two, none the better for their sojourn in that receptacle.

With a smile and a kind word, his master took them. One was from Miss Cameron to himself, the other, addressed to Miss Alison Grant at Ardroy, in an unknown and foreign-seeming hand, had been redirected by his aunt to Inverness. He put them both in his pocket, gave the lad money to procure himself food and lodging and a new pair of brogues to go home in, told him where to find his father and not to return to Ardroy without seeing him again, and himself set off in haste for Lady Ogilvy's lodging.

But Angus *Og*, footsore and hungry though he was, seeing his young chieftain quite unaccompanied, pattered at a little distance behind him with all the air of a bodyguard, his head full of wild plans for joining his father and uncle in this place of many houses, instead of returning to Slochd nan Eun. If they were in Mac 'ic Ailein's tail, why not he?

Young Lady Ogilvy lodged in one of the larger houses at the lower end of Kirk Street, and as Ewen passed the many-paned projecting window on the ground floor he caught sight of a blue ribbon confining dark curls. After that he was not much conscious of being admitted, or of anything, until he found its wearer in his arms.

'Oh, my darling! ... You were expecting me – Lachlan brought you my letter?'

Alison nodded, holding very fast to him, her eyes closed like one surrendered to ecstasy. Much as they had to say to one another, for a time neither said it; it was enough merely to be together again, after the months of strain and waiting and endurance and disillusioned hopes. But when they had their fill of looking at each other, they began to talk.

'I knew that you would come back to Inverness,' said Alison happily. They were both sitting on the window seat now. And she added, with all her old gaiety. 'If Lochiel would permit so forward an act, I would kiss him for having recalled you from Lord Cromarty's force!'

'But he has not recalled me in order to stay in Inverness, darling – at least not for more than a couple of days. He and Keppoch are shortly going with reinforcements to the siege of Fort William, and I go too.'

All the peace and content was dashed out of Alison's face. 'Oh, Ewen . . . and I thought you would be staying here!' She bit her lip and the tears came into her eyes.

Her hand was in Ewen's, and he sat a moment silent, looking down with some intentness at his ring upon it. 'But we shall have two days together, *meudail*. And . . . do you not think those two days are long enough . . . that the time has come . . . to change this ring of my mother's for another?'

The colour ran over Alison's face, and her hand made a movement as if to withdraw itself. 'Oh, my dear,' she said rather breathlessly, 'not when my father is absent – not till he comes back! And not when . . . when one does not know what will befall next!'

'But, my heart,' said Ewen quietly, 'that is just why I want to make you my wife. Do you not see that? Why, you should have been mine these six months. I have waited even longer than I had thought to wait, and God knows that was long enough.' And as Alison said nothing, but looked down, twisting her ring, he went on, suppressing a little sigh: 'There are many reasons why we should be wed without further loss of time, and these two days that we have now seem designed for that. Our marriage could easily be arranged in the time; Mr Hay, the Episcopal minister of Inverness is, I believe, in the town; Lochiel would take your father's place. And I could carry you back to Ardroy, as its mistress, when we start for Fort William . . . Alison dear love, say yes!'

He was very gentle as he pleaded, for she seemed oddly reluctant, considering that they had been formally contracted since last July, and should indeed have been married in the autumn. She even mentioned Hector and his perilous situation, rather tentatively, as a reason for delay; but Ewen told her that her brother's prospects were ten times better than those of most who wore the white cockade, for he held a French commission, and could not be treated otherwise than as a prisoner-of-war. And finally Alison said that she would ask Lady Ogilvy's opinion.

Ewen tried not to be hurt. Since he had not the mistaken conviction of some young men that he knew all about women, even Alison's feelings were sometimes a mystery to him. He longed to say '*I* have not a French commission, Alison' and leave her to draw a conclusion which might get the better of her hesitancy, but it would have been cruel. And as he looked at her in perplexity, he remembered a commission of another kind, and put his hand into his pocket.

'When I saw you, Alison, everything else went out of my head. But here is a letter I should have given you ere this; forgive me. It was sent to you at Ardroy, and Aunt Marget dispatched one of the MacMartin lads hither with it; and meeting me by the bridge just now, he gave it to me for you. It is from France, I think.'

'I do not know the hand,' said Alison, studying the superscription, and finally breaking the seal. Ewen looked out of the window; but he did not see any of the passers-by.

Suddenly there was an exclamation from the girl beside him on the window seat. He turned; her face was drained of colour.

'My father ... Ewen, Ewen, I must go at once – he is very ill ... dying, they think. Oh, read!'

Horrified, Ewen read a hasty French letter, already more than two weeks old, which said that Monsieur Grant, on the point of leaving France again, had been taken seriously ill at Havre-de-Grâce; the writer, apparently a recent French acquaintance of his, appealed to Mlle Grant to sail for France at once, if she wanted to see her father alive – not that the state of Monsieur Grant at the moment was desperate, but because the doctor held out small hope of ultimate recovery.

Alison had sprung to her feet, and clasping and unclasping her hands, was walking up and down the room.

'Ewen, Ewen, what if I am not in time! My dearest, dearest father, ill and quite alone over there – no Hector anywhere near him now! I must go at once. I heard Lady Ogilvy say that there was a French vessel in port here, due to sail for France in a day or two; I could go in that. Perhaps the captain could be persuaded to sail earlier . . .'

In contrast to her restlessness Ewen was standing quite still by the window.

'Ewen,' she began again, 'help me! Will you make inquiries of the captain of the ship? I think she is for St Maloes, but that would serve; I could post on into Normandy. Will you find out the captain now – this afternoon? . . . Ewen, what ails you?'

For her lover was gazing at her with an expression which was quite new to her.

'I am deeply sorry to hear this ill news of Mr Grant,' he said in a low voice, and seemed to find a difficulty in speaking, ' – more sorry than I have words for. But, Alison, what of *me*?'

'You would not wish to keep me back, surely?'

'What do you think?' asked the young man rather grimly. 'But I will not – no, it would not be right. I will let you go, but only as my wife. You'll marry me tomorrow, Alison!'

There was no pleading about him now. He moved a step or two nearer, having to keep a tight hold on himself, neither to frighten her nor to let slip a word against this other claim, which much as he respected it, was coming in once more to sweep her away from him, when he had waited so long. Whatever might be read on his face, his actions were perfectly gentle.

And Alison came to him, the tears running down her cheeks, and put her two hands in his. 'Yes, Ewen, I am ready. Heart's darling, I wish it, too; you must not think I am unwilling. . . . And you said that you would carry me off by force, if I were,' she added, laughing a little hysterically, as he folded her once again in his arms.

So next day they were married in the little Episcopal meeting-house of Inverness. Only a very few people were present, but the Prince was among them: not the light-hearted adventurer of the escapade in Edinburgh, in which the bridegroom had played so belauded a part, but a young man who looked what the last three months had made him, soured and distrustful. Yet he gave them a glimpse of his old charming smile after the ceremony, when he kissed the bride and wished them both happiness.

'I would I were venerable enough to give you my blessing, my friends,' he said, 'since 'tis all I have to give; but I think I am somewhat the junior of your husband, Lady Ardroy; and in any case how could I bestow my benediction upon a bridegroom who has the bad taste to be so much taller than his future King!'

'But you know that I am at your feet, my Prince,' said Ewen, smiling, and he kissed once more the hand which he had kissed that night at Holyrood.

Last of all Lochiel, grave and gentle, who had given Alison away, kissed her too, and said: 'Ewen is a very fortunate man, my dear; but I think you are to be congratulated also.'

For their brief wedded life a little house which Mr Grant had hired the previous summer had been hastily prepared; it was bare almost to penury, a tent for a night or two, meet shelter for those who must part so soon. And Ewen had no gift ready for his bride – save one. When they came home, he put on her middle finger the ring which the Prince had given him in Edinburgh.

Next day was theirs, to play at housekeeping, and they were a great deal more gay over it than Jeanie Wishart, Alison's woman, who went about her work perpetually murmuring: 'Puir young things!' In the afternoon, since the March sun had come out to look at them, they wandered among the Islands and gazed down at Ness, hurrying past, broad and clear and shallow, to the firth. That evening they had thought to spend alone by their own fireside; yet nothing would serve Lady Ogilvy save to give a supper for the new-married pair, and Lady Ardroy, in a rose-coloured gown, was toasted by not a few who would never drink a pledge again; and all the Jacobite songs were sung ... but not, somehow, that only too appropriate, 'Oh, this is my departing time, for here nae longer maun I stay', with which gatherings were wont to conclude.

Yet Ewen and Alison sat by their fire after all, sat there until the last peat crumbled, and it began to grow cold; but Alison, as once before, was warm in the Cameron tartan, for Ewen had wrapped it round her knees over her pretty gown. He sat at her feet, looking very long and large, the firelight, while it lasted, playing on the shining golden brown of his hair, accentuating too the faint hollow in his cheek, the slight suggestion of a line between the brows, which the last two months had set there.

'Ewen, I want to tell you something.' Alison hesitated and a tinge of colour stole over her face. 'Do you know, *m'eudail*, that you talk in your sleep?'

He looked up at her surprised. 'Do I? No, dearest, I did not know. Did I talk much – to disturb you?'

She shook her head. Ewen seemed to turn over this information for a moment. 'I believe,' he said thoughtfully, 'that as a boy I used to do it sometimes, so Aunt Marget said, but I thought that I had outgrown it. What did I talk of – you, sweetheart, I'll warrant?'

'No,' said Alison, smiling down upon him. 'Not a word of your wife. You seemed to think that you were speaking to someone of whom she may well be jealous; and what is more, when I spoke to you, thinking for a moment that you were awake, you answered quite sensibly.'

'Jealous!' exclaimed Ewen, turning his clear, candid gaze full upon her. 'My little white love, there's no one in this world of whom you have occasion to be jealous, nor ever has been. Do not pretend to be ignorant of where my heart is kept!' He took her clasped hands, opened them gently, and kissed the palms. 'The space is small,' he said, looking critically at it, 'but, such as the heart is, all of it lies *there*.'

Alison enveloped him in a warm, sweet smile, and slid the hands round his neck. 'All? No; there's a corner you have kept for someone else, and in it you have set up a little shrine, as the papists do, for your saint – for Lochiel. But I am not jealous,' she added very softly. 'I understand.'

Ewen gave her a look, put his own hands over those clasped round his neck, and dropped his head on to her knee in silence. After a while she put her cheek against the thick, warm waves of his hair. Joy and apprehension had so clasped hands about Alison Cameron this day that it was hard to know which was the stronger.

But in the night she knew. The icy fingers of foreboding seemed gripped about her heart. Not even Ewen's quiet, unhurried breathing beside her, not even the touch of his hand, over which

her fingers stole in search of comfort, could reassure her; his
nearness but made the pain the sharper. Oh, to have him hers,
only to lose him so soon! But her father – alone, dying, over the
seas! She reached out and lit a candle, that she might look once
more at the husband she was leaving for her father's sake, for
God knew whether she should ever see him asleep beside her
again. It was not the seas alone which were about to sunder
them. . . .

Ewen was sleeping so soundly, too, so quietly; and he looked
as young and untroubled as the boy she had known five years ago
in Paris. There was no sign on his face, in its rather austere
repose, of the trouble which had forced its way through his unconscious lips last night. Alison had not told him by the fire, that
on their bridal night he had uttered protests, bewildered question-
ings, against that double retreat in which he had shared. 'Must
we go back, Lochiel – must we go back?'

She gazed at him a long time, until for tears she could see him
no longer, and, blowing out the light, lay and sobbed under her
breath. She thought she should die of her unhappiness; she almost
wished that she might; yet she sobbed quietly, lest she should
wake Ewen to unhappiness also. But quite suddenly, though he
had not stirred, she heard his voice in the darkness; and then she
was in his arms, and he was comforting her in their own Highland
tongue, with all its soft endearments and little words of love. And
there at last she fell asleep.

But Ewen stayed awake, until the grudging March daylight
crept into the little room where he lay wide-eyed, with Alison's
dark curls on his heart, and within it a chilly sword that turned
and turned. He would never hold her thus again; he was sure of
it.

The morning was very cold, and when he took Alison to the
French brig a little snow was falling; the gang-plank was slippery
too with rime. He carried her bodily over it, and down to the
cabin which she would share with Jean Wishart.

There under the low beams Alison's courage broke at last.
Clinging to him convulsively, she said, in a voice that was not
hers, that he must come with her; that she could not go without

him – she could not! He must come too, and then he would be safe . . .

Ewen turned even paler than she. 'My darling, my heart's darling, you don't mean that!'

Alison swayed; her eyes closed. Alarmed, he put her on a seat against the bulkhead, and, kneeling by her, began to chafe her hands. Soon they clenched in his, and she opened her eyes, dark pools of sorrow, and said firmly through colourless lips: 'No, no, I did not mean it! I know that you cannot come. Will you . . . can you forget what I said, Ewen?'

'It is forgotten. It was not you who spoke,' he answered, trying to keep his own voice steady as he knelt there, holding her hands very tightly. There was a trampling sound on deck; how long had they for all the thousand thousand things that remained to say? There was no time to say even one. He bent his head and pressed his lips passionately upon the hands he held. Anguish though it was to lose her, it was better that she should go. For since he had urged her to marry him, that he might take her back to Ardroy, he saw with different eyes. The future looked blacker than he had realized; away in Ross he had not known of the desperate want of money, even of food, the gradually thinning ranks. He knew of these now, and saw even Cumberland's delay at Aberdeen in a sinister light, as if the Hanoverian commander knew that the fates were working on his side and that there was no need for haste. . . .

Above him Alison's voice said suddenly: 'Ewen . . . Ewen, why do you not say: "Stay then in Scotland with me – do not go to France yourself!"?'

He was startled; had she read his thoughts? 'Why, my darling,' he answered as readily as he could, 'because your father needs you so sorely.'

Her voice sank still lower. 'There is another reason, too – do not deny it! You think that I am safer away!'

And Ewen did not answer.

'And you gave me this ring – the Prince's ring – not only as a wedding gift, but because you feared that one day . . . soon . . . it might be taken from you!'

After a pause he said: 'Partly, perhaps.'

'Then . . . I cannot leave you, even for my father!' said Alison, and sprang up. 'I must stay in Scotland, beside you. I am your wife. Take me back to the quay – Ewen – tell Mrs Wishart . . .'

But Ewen, on his feet too, caught her in his arms. 'No, darling, no! Think of your father, whom you may never see again. And, love of my heart' – he tried to make his voice light – 'you cannot come besieging Fort William with me! When we have beaten Cumberland, as we beat Cope and Hawley, I will come to France, and fetch you home to Ardroy.'

'When we have beaten Cumberland.' Alison looked up into her husband's eyes with a moist insistent question in her own. But he did not answer the question, though he knew very well what it was, for he said gently: 'How can one see into the future, darling? One can only . . . do one's duty.'

Even as he uttered that rigorous word, there came a knock at the cabin door, and a gruff French voice announced that they would be casting off in another minute or two, and that if Monsieur wished to land he must be quick.

So the sword slid down between them. Ewen's grasp tightened.

'Alison, white love, rose of my heart, we are one for ever now! You will know, I think, what befalls me.'

Her face was hidden on his breast, so close that he could not even kiss it. 'Darling, darling, let me go . . .' he whispered. But it was rather a question, he felt, whether he could ever unloose his own clasp and cast his heart from him. And men were running about shouting overhead; the hawser was coming inboard . . .

Suddenly Alison lifted her face, and it was almost transfigured. 'Yes, I shall know . . . for I think you will come back to me, God keeping you.' She took her arms from his shoulders; he bent to her lips for the kiss that first turned his heart to water and then ran through it like wine, loosed his hold of her, and walked straight out of the cabin without another word or look. With the same unchecked movement he crossed the gang-plank from the deck, as if he could not trust himself to remain the moment or so longer that it would take the sailors to cast off the second hawser.

But on the quay he turned, wishing they would be quick, and make it impossible for him to leap on board again, though the plank was now withdrawn, and be carried off with Alison. And

146

at last, after an eternity which was all too short, the end of the rope splashed into the water. More sails went up; the distance began to widen. Alison was going from him.

He stood there motionless, long after the brig had left the shore, watching her move to the waters of the firth. The sparse snow-flakes whirled relentlessly against him, but they melted as soon as they came to rest, as brief in their stay as his two days' happiness.

From the quay Ewen went straight to Lochiel's headquarters and reported himself for duty. Two hours later his body was marching out of Inverness in the van of the Cameron reinforcements. Where his soul was he hardly knew.

Chapter 2

To rid the Great Glen of both its obnoxious English forts was an enterprise which highly commended itself to those clans whom they chiefly incommoded, the Camerons and the Glangarry and Keppoch MacDonalds. There had been jubilation among these when, on 5 March, Fort Augustus had surrendered after two days' siege, and what artillery the besiegers possessed was free to be turned against Fort William.

But Fort William, between Inverlochy Castle and the little town of Maryburgh, was not so accommodating as its fellow. For one thing, it was in a better position to defend itself, since sloops of war could come up Loch Linnhe to revictual it, even though the Highlanders held the narrows at Corran. It had a garrison of five hundred men, both regulars and Argyll militia, plenty of guns, and after the middle of March, that zealous officer Captain Carolina Scott to assist Major-General Campbell in the defence. Already, by the time that Ewen arrived with Lochiel and the reinforcements, there had been some severe skirmishes, and the Highlanders had fought an engagement with the soldiers from the fort and the sailors from the *Baltimore* and *Serpent* sloops, in which the latter succeeded in landing and destroying the ferry-house and several small villages on the Ardgour side. On this, the Camerons ensconced themselves at Corpach, where Loch Linnhe bends to its junction with Loch Eil, and there beat off an armed flotilla of boats with such success that the *Baltimore* was ordered thither to open fire and cover a landing. But the Highlanders' position was so good that the bombardment made no impression, and Captain How had to withdraw baffled.

Ewen was with these adventurers at Corpach, enjoying himself and finding in conflict an anodyne for his thoughts; it made the blood run pleasantly, and enabled him to forget Alison for an hour or so. But the ordinary business of the siege was less stimulating, since he had nothing to do with the artillery under Stapleton and Grant and their Franco-Irish gunners, and the only chance of hand-to-hand fighting lay in repelling the constant raids of the garrison and trying to protect the unfortunate dwellers in the countryside who suffered by them. He seemed to himself to live in a series of disconnected scenes, sometimes here in Lochaber, where Ben Nevis, thickly capped with snow, looked down impartially on assailants and defenders alike, sometimes back in Inverness, going through every moment of those two short days with Alison. But no one who did not observe him constantly and closely could have guessed this. Lochiel, who knew him well and did observe him closely, gave him as much to do as possible.

But it was certainly not Lochiel who enjoined on him the feat which brought his share in the siege to an abrupt end.

It was a fine morning in the latter half of March, blown through with a gusty wind. Brigadier Stapleton, having got some mortars into position on one of the little eminences about half a mile from the fort, had started to shell it from that point, and the fort was replying. Since its fire was directed towards destroying the hostile batteries, there was no great danger from it to those not serving the guns, and the Highlanders had no doubt grown a little careless, which might account for the fact that near the crest of another hillock, about a quarter of a mile away from Stapleton's mortars, and the same distance as they from Fort William, Lochiel and Keppoch were standing unconcernedly in the midst of a little group of Camerons and MacDonalds. Below them, on the slope looking towards the fort, a half-ruined stone wall hinted at a bygone attempt at cultivation or enclosure. The two chiefs were interested in some rather suspicious activities on board the *Baltimore* sloop, visible at anchor in the loch, beyond the counterscarp and bastions of the fort.

'I vow it seems like another raid preparing,' said Alexander MacDonald. 'Do you look, Lochiel.'

He passed the Cameron his spyglass. Ewen, who was sitting comfortably in the heather at a few yards' distance, nearer the battery, rested his elbows on his knees and shaded his eyes the better to see also, his brain at these words busy with a vision of a possibly gratified desire for what he considered real fighting.

Suddenly, as it were with half an eye, he became aware of something unusual in the fort, where, a mere eight hundred yards away, movements were perfectly visible. Surely the defenders had altered the position of one of their six-pounders . . . could they be intending . . . Lochiel standing there with the glass to his eye, looking at the sloop, was fully exposed to their view . . .

In a second Ewen was on his feet, shouting a warning, but as he sprang came the flash and the roar. 'God!' he cried in agony, and with another bound was up on the crest of the hillock, his arms wide. Could one man's body suffice?

There was a crash as the shot pitched into the ruined wall on the slope below, breaking and scattering the big rough stones in all directions. Ewen never saw what struck him, but at the moment of impact, which seemed to drive his soul from his body, he had just time to think: 'It is for *him*! Alison, forgive me . . .' Then he went into darkness.

When he came out of it again, he found himself lying on the farther slope in the midst of a group of people, with his head on someone's arm and hands unfastening his coat. A voice said: 'No, the head wound is only slight; 'tis here on the breast that the large stone must have struck him.'

Ewen tried to get his own voice. It was difficult, and the world heaved. 'Is . . . Lochiel safe?'

Archibald Cameron, kneeling beside him, looked up for a second. 'He is holding you at this moment, dear lad. No – lie still!' He went on with his examination.

But Ewen disobediently turned his swimming head a little, and saw that he was indeed in Lochiel's hold, so Lochiel must be unharmed. Why then had he his other hand over his eyes? Puzzled but content, he shut his own again.

When next he thought much about his surroundings, he was lying in the same place, wrapped in a plaid, with Lachlan squatting near, gazing at him with anguished eyes. Over the level top of Ben Nevis clouds as white as the snow which crowned it were hurrying against the blue. It came back to Ewen that he had heard Archie say that he was greatly bruised, but that no bones seemed broken and no internal injury, he hoped, inflicted; so after speaking a word or two of reassurance to his foster-brother, he relapsed into his state of happy content, with pain every time he drew a breath, and a violent headache. But Lochiel was safe.

Presently he felt his hand taken, and there was Lochiel himself kneeling by him, and Lachlan on the other side removing himself respectfully to a distance.

'Ewen, Ewen,' said the well-beloved voice, with trouble in it, 'you should not have done it!'

Ewen gave him a radiant smile. He felt neither penitence nor any need for it.

'I saw . . . what was going to happen,' he observed.

'I do not think that anything would have reached me. No one was struck but you, who deliberately threw yourself in the way of the fragments, and one of Keppoch's gillies, slightly. If you had been killed on my behalf – ' Lochiel left the sentence unfinished, and glanced down at the cuff of his coat; there was a stain on it.

Ewen's eyes had followed his. 'Do not say that you are hurt after all!' he exclaimed, in a tone of horror.

'It is your own blood, Ewen. Your head was not much cut, Archie says. But oh, my child, if I had had your death too at my door, when there is so much that I must answer for!'

And the young man saw that his Chief was moved – more deeply moved than he had ever seen him; but, being still stupid from the blow on the head, he thought: 'Why does he say that . . . whose death is at his door?' And he lay looking with a mixture of affection and perplexity at the kinsman who was still as much his pattern of all that was noble, wise, and generous as when he himself had been a boy under his tutelage. Then the fort fired one of its twelve-pounders at the battery, and through the din Lochiel told him that a litter had been sent for, to take him to Glen Nevis House, where he should see him again later.

Soon after, therefore, four of his men carried Ewen to that house of Alexander Cameron's, at the opening of the glen which Lochiel and Keppoch had made their headquarters; and he heard the voice of the Nevis, telling of the heights from which it had descended; and a little later, when that had faded from his hearing, a less agreeable one, Lowland and educated, saying how disgraceful it was that a peaceful writer could not go a mile from Maryburgh to visit a client without being seized by cattle-thieves; that indeed the said thieves could do no less than send him back under escort and safe-conduct. And here the indignant speaker's gaze must have fallen upon the litter with its burden, for his next remark was: 'What have we here – another of ye killed? I'm rejoiced to see it!'

Ewen felt constrained to deny this imputation. 'I am not in the least killed,' he rejoined with annoyance, opening his eyes to find himself almost at the door of Glen Nevis House, and to see, in the midst of a group of rather shamefaced Highlanders, Mr Chalmers, the Whig notary of Maryburgh, whom he knew and who knew him. The lawyer gave an exclamation.

'Gude sakes, 'tis Mr Ewen Cameron of Ardroy! I'm unco sorry to see you in this condition – and in such company, Ardroy!'

'Why, what other company do you suppose I should be in?' asked Ewen, and shut his eyes again and heard no more of Mr Chalmers and his grievances. But that chance meeting was to mean a great deal to him afterwards.

What meant more to him at the moment, however, was that Dr Cameron kept him in bed longer than he had expected, and he had not been on his legs again for more than a day or two, when the siege of Fort William was suddenly abandoned. The defenders were too resolute, the besiegers unfortunate, and their artillery not sufficiently powerful; and in the night of 3 April, after spiking their remaining cannon, the attacking force withdrew. And, since they were in their own land of Lochaber, and it was seed-time or past it, Lochiel and Keppoch gave permission to their men to go home for a few days. So Ewen and his little force returned to Ardroy, and he saw Loch na h-Iolaire again, and caused Neil to row him upon it, for it was too cold for a swim; in the middle of which voyage he was struck by a sudden suspicion, and, landing on the islet, examined it for traces of the heron. There were none; and the nest, up at the top of the tallest pine-tree, must long have been uninhabited, for the winds had blown it nearly all away.

Shortly afterwards Lachlan had a singularly unpleasant interview with his chieftain, in which, upbraided with the most direct disobedience, he replied that his concern for the being he loved best on earth was even stronger than his wish to obey him; after which, in a dramatic but perfectly sincere manner, he drew his dirk and said that rather than Mac 'ic Ailein should look at him with such anger he would plunge it into his own heart. In the end Ewen was constrained to forgive him, after pointing out how little his disobedience had availed. There were more herons than one in Lochaber.

And other officers than Captain Windham in King George's army, he might have added. His twice-held prisoner had indeed passed from his thoughts these many weeks; the question of the slaughtered heron necessarily brought him back there for a moment, but without any permanence. Ewen did not expect another meeting with him, for were Angus's prophecy going to be fulfilled to the letter, they would surely have encountered each other in the confusion of Falkirk fight, where the second battalion of the Royals had – until it fled – faced the Camerons across the ravine. No; that two meetings should come to pass out of the five predicted was quite a reasonable achievement for the old *taibhsear*.

And then one afternoon, when he was absorbed in thoughts of Alison, with all the final suddenness of the expected came a panting messenger from Achnacarry, with a scrawl in Lochiel's writing: 'Gather your men and march at once. Cumberland is moving. God send we reach Inverness in time!'

A bad dream is sometimes only a dream to the sleeper; he may know it to be such, and tell himself so. But this, though it held some of the elements of nightmare, was no dream; it was reality, this tramping of a tired and half-starved army through the night in a hopeless attempt to surprise the Duke of Cumberland's camp – hopeless, because it was plain that they would never get to Nairn before daylight now. Aide-de-camp after aide-de-camp, officer after officer, had come riding past to the head of the column of Highlanders and Atholl men, to urge Lord George Murray to halt, for the rear could not keep up. And yet, thought Ewen rather scornfully, they had not just marched more than fifty miles over mountainous country in two days, as most of Clan Cameron had.

It was by this feat of endurance and speed that Lochiel and his men had reached Inverness the previous evening, to learn to their dismay that Cumberland had been allowed to cross the Spey unopposed. Despite fatigue, they had made but a brief halt in the town and had proceeded to Culloden House, whither the Prince had gone earlier in the day. A warm welcome had been theirs, for he was becoming alarmed at their non-appearance, the more so that by no means all his scattered forces were yet returned from the various enterprises on which they had been dispatched. Cromarty, the Macgregors, and the Mackinnons were still north of the Moray Firth, no one knew where, and Keppoch had not yet appeared, nor the Frasers, nor Cluny Macpherson and his men. Today, since early morning, the whole army had been drawn up on the chosen ground on Drumossie Moor, in the belief that Cumberland would advance that day and attempt to reach Inverness. But the hours went by and the enemy did not appear, and then the cravings of hunger began to be felt, for all the food which had passed any man's lips that day was a single biscuit served out at noon. And at last it was clear that, the fifteenth of April being his birthday, Cumberland was remaining at Nairn to allow his troops fitly to celebrate it. The Prince's hungry forces therefore withdrew from the moor again, to the vicinity of Duncan Forbes's mansion.

It was known that Lord George Murray had not liked the ground chosen for their stand, and Brigadier Stapleton and Colonel Ker of Graden, the ablest staff officer the Prince possessed, had crossed the water of Nairn that morning to seek for a better. They reported that the boggy, hilly ground there was much more suitable than the open moor for receiving the Hanoverian attack, since it was almost impossible for cavalry and artillery, and the foot might perhaps be tempted into some pass where they could be fallen upon and annihilated. On the other hand, it was urged that, if the Highlanders withdrew over the stream into the hills, Cumberland would almost certainly slip by them to Inverness, seize the baggage and stores, and starve them out. The matter was still unsettled when, at an informal council of officers in the afternoon, someone (Ewen was not clear who) had proposed to surprise the Hanoverian camp by a night attack. Most of the soldiers there, it was thought, would be more or less drunk after the festivities of the birthday. Lord George Murray and the Prince were both found to be in favour of the idea; moreover, owing to the scandalous neglect of the commissariat shown by Hay of Restalrig, who had succeeded Murray of Broughton as secretary, there was not a crumb of food for the men next day. Objections to the plan there were indeed: the distance – a good ten miles – the danger of a spy's carrying the news to the English camp, the absence of so many contingents. But the arrival of Keppoch, with two hundred MacDonalds, when the meeting was in progress clinched the matter, and the night attack was resolved upon.

The decision had purposely been kept from the men themselves, and it was with remorseful knowledge of the futility of their preparations that Ewen had watched his own little company choosing the driest spots on the heathery hillside for a night's repose, making a fire and rolling themselves supperless in their plaids to seek in sleep a palliative for the gnawing hunger which possessed them. Perhaps it would have been better if the rank and file had been told what was afoot, for by the time planned for the start, seven o'clock, it was found that hundreds of them had stolen off in search of food. And to the mounted officers sent out in the utmost haste to beat them up and bring them back – no easy task – many had replied that the officers might shoot them if they pleased, but go back they would not until they had had meat. The Prince was urged to give up the plan, but he refused; and as those who had remained were assembled, the word had been given to march off.

It was an excellent night for a surprise, dark and misty; but it was also very favourable for tired and hungry men to drop un-observed out of the ranks, and many of them did so. Ewen was as tired and hungry as anyone else, but he shut his mouth and plodded on like an automaton at the head of his company. Lochiel was in front, and where Lochiel went he followed, as a matter of course. And close on his heels came Neil and Lachlan, of the same mind regarding him.

Although Lord George had never consented actually to stop, he had been obliged to march slower and slower in consequence of the messages from the rear; but now at last there came a halt, and a prolonged one. The Duke of Perth rode past, and presently Hay of Restalrig. Discussion was evidently going forward in the van. And meanwhile the unwished-for light was growing in the east; not yet daybreak, but its harbinger. Faces began to be distinct, and haggard faces they were.

And here came back one of the Mackintosh guides, the same who, not long before, had brought the order to attack with the sword only. Before he spoke to him, Ewen guessed what orders he brought now. They were to retrace their steps; the surprise was being abandoned. Too much time had been lost on the way, and to attack in daylight would be madness. All the nightmare effort had been for nothing – for worse than nothing . . .

Between five and six of that cold, grey morning, Ewen found himself once more before the gates of Culloden House. Men were dropping where they stood; some, he knew, were lying worn out along the roadside. He was in no better case himself; in some ways, indeed, in a worse, for it was not three weeks since he had left his bed after his experience at Fort William. But in anger and desperation he dispatched Neil and Lachlan, who still seemed capable of movement, to Inverness with orders to get food for their comrades if they had to steal it. It was all he could do, and when he got inside the house he sat down exhausted in the hall and fell asleep with his head on a table. He was hardly conscious of the stir a little later, when the Prince arrived, tired, dispirited, and sore from the complaints which he could not avoid hearing. But from scraps of talk about him (for the place was full of officers in the same plight as himself) Ewen's weary brain did receive the welcome impression that they would at least have some hours to rest and recuperate – and later, please Heaven, to get some food – for Cumberland was evidently not going to attack today.

He was dreaming that he was at home and sitting down to a good meal, when he felt someone shaking him, and, raising his head, saw one of his own cousins from Appin, Ian Stewart.

'What is it?' he asked stupidly.

'A straggler has just come in with news that some troops are advancing from Nairn. He did not know whether it was the main body or only skirmishers . . .'

Ewen dragged himself to his feet. All round the hall others were doing the same, but some would require more to rouse them than a mere rumour. It was broad daylight; a clock near marked nine o'clock. 'It cannot be the main body – the attack!' he said incredulously. 'There was no sign of general movement at Nairn; the camp fires were burning – we could see them four miles away. However, the truth can soon be discovered.'

The weary-faced Appin lad shrugged his shoulders. 'It will not be very easy to make sure,' he said. 'FitzJames's Horse is all dispersed after fugitives and food. I tell you, Ardroy, I do not much care which it is, if only I can get an hour's sleep.'

'I must find Lochiel,' said Ewen. He had no idea where he was – a sufficient comment on his own state – but was told that he was upstairs with the Prince, who on coming in had thrown himself just as he was upon his bed. Half dizzy with sleep and hunger, Ewen went up the wide staircase, hearing everywhere voices discussing the report and arguing and wondering what was to be done, and declaring that the speakers disbelieved the news – because they desired to disbelieve it.

When he reached the landing, the door of the Prince's bedchamber opened and Lord George Murray and Ker of Graden came out together, the latter looking very grim, Lord George plainly in a rage. They went down the stairs to the encumbered hall, Lord George calling for his aides-de-camp. The door meanwhile had been left ajar; loud voices came through it, and Ewen had a glimpse of the Prince, sitting on the edge of his bed, still booted, with Sir Thomas Sheridan, his old tutor, beside him. He was speaking, not to him, but to someone invisible.

'I tell you,' his voice came sharply, edged with fatigue and obstinacy, 'I tell you the English will be seized with panic when they come to close quarters. They cannot face my Highlanders in the charge; 'twill be again as it was at Gladsmuir, and –'

Then the door shut behind Lochiel, coming slowly out. He did not see the young man waiting for him, and on his tired unguarded face Ewen could read the most profound discouragement.

As he crossed the landing, Ewen took a couple of strides after him, laying hold of his plaid, and the Chief stopped.

'Is it true, Donald?'

'I suppose so,' answered Lochiel quietly. 'At any rate we must take up our positions at once.'

'Over the water of Nairn, then, I hope?'

'No. The Prince is immovable on that point. We are to take our stand on our old positions of yesterday, on the moor.'

'When you and Lord George disapprove? – It's the doing, no doubt, of the same men who were for it yesterday, those who have nothing to lose, the French and Irish officers!'

Lochiel glanced over his shoulder. 'Don't speak so loud, Ewen. But you are right – may God forgive them!'

'May God – reward them!' said Ewen savagely. 'We are to march our companies back to the moor then?'

'Yes. And we and Atholl are to be on the right wing today.'

Ewen was surprised, the MacDonalds always claiming and being conceded this privilege. But he did not seek the reason for the change, and followed his Chief in silence down the stairs. The confusion in the hall had increased, and yet some officers were still lying on the floor without stirring, so spent were they.

'Find me Dungallon and Torcastle,' said Lochiel. 'By the way, have you had anything to eat, Ewen, since noon yesterday?'

'Have *you*, which is more to the point?' asked Ewen.

Lochiel smiled and shook his head. 'But fortunately a little bread and whisky was discovered for the Prince.'

Ewen found Ludovic Cameron of Torcastle, the Chief's uncle, and Cameron of Dungallon, major of the regiment, and himself went out in a shower of sleet to rouse his men, having in several cases to pull them up from the ground. He had got them into some kind of stupefied order when he saw Lochiel and Dungallon come by. A body of MacDonalds was collecting near, and as the two Camerons passed – Ewen scarcely realized it then, but he remembered it afterwards – there were muttered words and a black look or two.

But he himself was thinking bitterly: 'I wonder are we all fey? We had the advantage of a good natural barrier, the Spey, and we let Cumberland cross it like walking over a burn. Now we might put the Nairn water between him and us – and we will not!' An insistent question suddenly leapt up in his heart; he looked round, and by good fortune Lochiel came by again, alone. Ewen intercepted and stopped him.

'For God's sake, one moment!' He drew his Chief a little apart towards the high wall which separated the house from the parks. 'If the day should go against us, Lochiel, if we have all to take to the heather –'

'Yes?' said his cousin gravely, not repudiating the possibility.

'Where will you make for? Give us a rendezvous – give *me* one, at all events!'

'Why, my dear boy, I shall make for Achnacarry.'

'But that is just where you would be sought for by the Elector's troops!'

'Yet I must be where the clan can find me,' said the Chief. 'Loch Arkaig is the best rallying point. 'Tis not easy, either, to come at it suddenly in force, because there is always the Lochy to ford. And if I were strictly sought for in person, there are plenty of skulking places round Achnacarry, as you know.'

'But none beyond the wit of man to discover, Donald – and most of them known to too many.'

'Of the clan, perhaps, yes. But you do not imagine, surely, that any of them would be betrayed by a Cameron! Moreover, Archie came on a new one the other day when we were there; he showed it to me. Truly I do not think the wit of man could find that unaided, and no one knows of it but he and I. So set your mind at rest, dear lad.' He took a step or two away. 'I'll tell you too, Ewen.'

The young man's face, which had become a little wistful, lit up. 'Oh, Donald . . .'

'Listen,' said Lochiel, dropping his voice, and coming closer

158

to the wall. 'Half-way up the southern slope of Beinn Bhreac, about a hundred paces to the right of the little waterfall. . . .'

And Ewen, listening eagerly, heard of an overhanging birch tree whose old roots grasped like hinges an apparently immovable block of stone, which could be moved if one knew just where to push it, and of a cave, long disused, which Dr Cameron had found behind it – a place whose existence could never be suspected. And there, if hard pressed . . .

'Yes, surely there you would be safe!' said Ewen with satisfaction. 'That is a thousand times better than any of the old places. I thank you for telling me; I shall not forget.'

'Whom should I tell if not you, my dear Ewen?' said his Chief, laying his hand for a moment on his shoulder. 'You have always been to me – ' More he did not say, for Dungallon was at his elbow, urgently summoning him. But perhaps, also, he could not.

Ewen pulled his bonnet lower on his brows, and, bending his head against the sleety blast, set his face with the rest towards the fatal stretch of moorland, the last earthly landscape that many a man there would ever see. But over that possibility he was not troubling himself; he was wondering whether it were possible to be much hungrier, and what his foster-brothers would do when they returned and found him gone into battle without them. And like a litany he repeated to himself, to be sure that he remembered them aright, the directions Mac Dhomhnuill Duibh had given him: 'Half-way up the southern slope of Beinn Bhreac, about a hundred paces to the right of the waterfall . . .'

Just as they were all taking up their positions, a gleam of sun shot through the heavy, hurrying clouds and fell bright upon the moving tartans, Stewart and Cameron, Fraser, Mackintosh, Maclean, and MacDonald, lighting too the distant hills of Ross across the firth, whence Cromarty came not, and the high ground over the Nairn water on the other hand, where Cluny Macpherson was hurrying towards them with his clan, to arrive too late. Then the gleam went out, and the wind howled anew in the faces of those who should spend themselves to death unavailingly, and those who should hold back for a grudge; it fluttered plaid and tugged at eagle's feather and whipped about him the cloak of the young man for whom the flower of the North stood here to be slain; and faint upon it, too, came now and then the kettledrums of Cumberland's advance.

Chapter 3

ONCE more Keith Windham – but he was Major Windham now, and on General Hawley's staff – was riding towards Lochaber. This time, however, he was thankful to find himself so occupied, for it was a boon to get away from what Inverness had become since the Duke of Cumberland's victory a couple of weeks ago – a little town crammed with suffering and despair, and with men who not only gloated over the suffering but who did their best to intensify it by neglect. One could not pass the horrible over-crowded little prison under the bridge without hearing pitiful voices always crying out for water. And as for last Sunday's cause-less procession of those poor wretches, in their shirts or less, the wounded too, carried by their comrades, simply to be jeered at – well, Major Windham, feigning twinges from his wound of Fontenoy, had withdrawn, sick with disgust, from the neighbour-hood of the uproariously laughing Hawley.

And not only was he enjoying a respite, if only of a few days, from what was so repugnant to him, but he had been chosen by the Duke himself to carry a dispatch to the Earl of Albemarle at Perth. It seemed that the Duke remembered a certain little inci-dent at Fontenoy. General Hawley, relinquishing his aide-de-camp for the mission, had slapped him on the shoulder and wished him good luck. The errand seemed to promise transference to the Duke's own staff; and, if that should occur, it meant real advancement at last, and when Cumberland returned to Flanders, a return with him.

So Keith was in better spirits than he had been for the last week. Surely the end of this horrid Scottish business was approaching for him! Falkirk – a bitter memory – was more than avenged, for the late victory on the moor of Culloden could not have been completer – he only wished he could get out of his mind some of the details of its completion. But there was this to be said for ruthless methods of suppression, that they were the sooner finished with.

To tell truth, Major Windham's immediate situation was also exercising his mind a good deal. Wade's road from Fort Augustus to Dalwhinnie and Perth ran over the steep Corryarrick Pass into Badenoch, and he had been told that somewhere in the neighbourhood of the Pass he would find a military post under a certain Major Guthrie of Campbell's regiment, in which bivouac he proposed to spend the night. (There had been a time last August when Sir John Cope with all his force dared not risk crossing the Corryarrick; it was different now.) Keith had first, of course, to get to Fort Augustus, and had set out from Inverness with that intention; but about half-way there, just before the road reared itself from the levels of Whitebridge to climb to its highest elevation, he had been inexplicably tempted by a track which followed a stream up a valley to the left, and, on an impulse which now seemed to him insane, had decided to pursue this rather than the main road. His Highland orderly, a Mackay from Lord Reay's country, only too pleased, like all his race, to get off a high road, even though he was riding a shod horse, jumped at the suggestion, averring in his not always ready English that he knew the track to be a shorter way to the Corryarrick road. So they had ridden up that tempting corridor.

It was a most unwise proceeding. At first all had gone well, but by this time it was clear to Keith that he and his orderly, if not lost, were within measurable distance of becoming so. The original track had ceased, the stream had divided, and they knew not which branch to follow; and either only seemed to take them higher and higher towards its source. Bare and menacing, the mountainsides closed in more and more straitly upon the foolhardy travellers. The Highlander was of use as a pioneer, but Keith had expected him to be a guide, whereas it soon appeared that he had no qualifications for the post, never having been in these parts before, despite his confident assertion of an hour ago. Every now and then they were obliged to lead their horses, and they were continually making detours to avoid boggy ground. Keith trudged on, silent with annoyance at his own folly, his orderly voluble in assurances that 'herself' need not be alarmed; there were worse places than this in Sutherland, yet Dougal the son of Dougal had never lost himself.

It was hard to believe that it was the first of May, so cold was it; not only were the surrounding mountains capped with snow, but it lay in all the creases of the northern slopes to quite a low level. There were even patches not far above the route which the travellers were painfully making out for themselves. And it was actually a pocket of snow in a sort of overhanging hollow·some way off to their left, a little above them, which drew Keith's eyes in that direction. Then he saw, to his surprise, that there was a figure with a plaid drawn over its head sitting in the hollow – a woman, apparently.

He called Mackay's attention to it at once 'Ask her if she can tell us the best way to the Corryarrick road.'

The Highlander shouted out something in his own tongue, but there was no answer, and the woman huddled in her plaid, which completely hid her face, did not move. 'She will pe asleep, whateffer,' observed Mackay. '*A bhean!* – Woman, woman!'

But another thought had struck the Englishman. Tossing the reins of his horse to Mackay, he strode up to the hollow where the woman sat, and stooping, laid a hand on her shoulder. For any warmth that struck through the tartan he might as well have touched the rock against which she leant. He gave an exclamation, and, after a moment, drew the folds of the plaid a little apart.

If the young woman who sat crouched within it, stiff now, like the year-old child in her arms, knew the way anywhere, it was not to the Pass of Corryarrick. There was a little wreath of half-melted snow in a cranny near her head; it was no whiter than her face. The upper half of her body was almost naked, for she had stripped herself to wrap all she could round the little bundle which she was still clasping tightly to her breast. But it was only a bundle now, with one tiny, rigid waxen hand emerging to show what it had been.

Keith removed his three-cornered hat, and signed to Mackay to leave the horses and come.

'The poor woman is dead,' he said in a hushed voice, ' – has been dead for some time. Can she have met with an accident?'

'I think she will haf peen starfed,' said his orderly, looking at the pinched face. 'I haf heard that there are many women wandering in the hills of Lochaber and Badenoch, and there iss no food and it hass been fery cold.'

'But why should she have gone wandering like this, with her child, too?'

The Mackay turned surprised eyes upon him. 'Because you English from Fort William will haf burnt her house and perhaps killed her man,' he replied bluntly. 'Then she wass going trying to find shelter for herself and the wean. . . . And now there iss no one to streak her and to lay the platter of salt on her prest. It iss a pity.'

He, too, with the innate reverence of his race for the dead, was standing bareheaded.

'I wish we could bury them,' said Keith. But it was out of the question; they had neither the implements nor the time; indeed, but for the food that they carried, and their horses, the same end might almost be awaiting them in these solitudes. So Mackay replaced the plaid, and they went silently back to the horses and continued their journey.

'You English' – we English – have done this; we whose boast it has always been that we do not war with women and children; we English whose vengeance (Keith had realized it ere this) is edged by the remembrance of past panic, of the disgrace of Prestonpans and Falkirk and invasion. He went on his way with a sensation of being branded.

Yes, he had been too true a prophet. The comedy *had* turned to grim and bloody earnest. And, despite relief and natural exhilaration at victory – of which there was not much left in him now – despite the liberation of his native country from a menace which she affected to despise, but which in the end had terrified her, despite the vindication, at last, of the worth of trained troops, Keith Windham could say with all his heart: 'Would God we were back in the days of farce!' Yes, even in the days when last he was in Lochaber; for the very mortification of the rout at High Bridge last summer and of his subsequent captivity had been easier to bear than the feeling that he belonged now to a band of executioners – was indeed closely connected with the most brutal of them all. He had been gratified when Hawley, on his arrival at

Edinburgh, had, on Preston's recommendation, chosen him to fill a vacancy on his staff; but during the last two weeks he had come to loathe the position. Yet his ambitious regard for his own career forbade him to damage it by asking permission to resign his post; indeed, had he taken such a remarkable step, he would not now be on his way to Perth, having turned his back for a while on what had so sickened him.

Another half-hour passed, and the memories which had been sweeping like dark clouds over Keith's mind began to give way to a real sensation of alarm, not so much for his personal safety as for the carrying out of his mission. Suppose they did not find their way before nightfall out of this accursed maze into which he had so blindly ventured! He consulted anew with Mackay, and they resolved to abandon the line which they had been taking, and try instead to find a way over a spur on their right, for the mountain which sent it forth was neither craggy nor strewn with scree, and the slope of the spur was such that it was even possible to make use of their horses. At the worst, its summit would give them a view, and they might then be able to strike out a better route for themselves.

As Keith was putting his foot in the stirrup, Dougal Mackay caught his arm and said excitedly: 'I wass hearing a shout, sir!'

'I heard nothing,' responded Major Windham, listening. 'Where did it come from?'

The orderly pointed ahead. 'The men that shouted will pe round the other side of this *beinn*. Let uss make haste, sir!'

Praying that the Highlander was not mistaken Keith scrambled into the saddle, and his horse began to strain up the slope. He himself could hear nothing but the melancholy notes of a disturbed plover, which was wheeling not far above their heads, and he cursed the bird for drowning more distant sounds. Then, sharp through the mournful cry, there did come a sound, the crack of a shot – of two shots – and the mountains re-echoed with it.

For a moment both Keith and his orderly instinctively checked their horses; then Keith struck spurs into his, and in a few minutes the panting beast had carried him to the top of the shoulder . . . and he had his view.

Directly before him rose another mountainside, much greener

than the rest, and this greenness extended downwards into the almost level depression between it and the slope whose summit he had now reached. Below him, in this narrow upland valley, stood a small group of rough huts for use when the cattle were driven up to the summer pasture, and in front of these was drawn up a body of redcoats, to whom a mounted officer was shouting orders. On the ground near the entrance of the largest shieling lay a motionless Highlander. The shots thus explained themselves; the soldiers were at their usual work, and Keith had ridden into the midst of it. He felt weariness and disgust, but he needed direction too badly not to be glad to meet with those who could give it. Presumably the detachment was from the post on Wade's road, and the officer might even be Major Guthrie himself. Hoping that the worst was now over, he rode slowly down the hillside through the bloomless heather, unnoticed by the group below.

The fern-thatched roof of one of the shielings had already been fired, and at its first cracklings Keith realized with distaste that the butchery was not yet finished. Three or four scarlet-clad figures came out of the hut before which the dead man lay, half carrying, half dragging another Highlander, alive, but evidently wounded. The officer pointed, and they followed the usual summary method in such cases, and, after planting him against the dry-stone wall of the building itself, withdrew, leaving him face to face with the firing-party. But apparently their victim could not stand unsupported, for a moment or so after they had retired he slid to one knee, and then to the ground.

'Detestable!' said Major Windham to himself. He had recognized the tartan now – the one of all others that he would never mistake, for he had worn it himself – the Cameron. But that did not surprise him. The doomed Highlander was now struggling to his feet again; he gained them unaided, and, steadying himself with one hand against the wall behind him, stood once more upright, so tall that his head was well above the edge of the low thatch. Now Keith was near enough to see the lower end of a dirty bandage round his left thigh, and the whole of another on his sword arm, for all that he had upon him was a kilt and a ragged shirt. And –

'Good God!' exclaimed the Englishman aloud; and calling out

at the top of his voice 'Stop! stop!' he drove the spurs into his horse, came slithering down the last part of the slope, raced towards the shieling, leapt off, and holding up his hand – but all faces were now turned towards him – ran in between the already levelled muskets and Ewen Cameron.

Ewen alone had not seen him. His face was the colour of the wall behind him; his eyes were half closed, his teeth set in his lower lip, and it was plain that only his force of will was keeping him upright there. A tiny trickle of blood was beginning to course down his bare leg. And even the blind instinct to face death standing could keep him there no longer; for the second time he swayed, and the wounded leg gave way under him again. But this time Keith's arms caught him as he sank.

Oblivious of the stupefaction which had descended upon the soldiers, and of the more than stupefaction manifested by the officer behind them, Keith lowered that dead weight to the ground and knelt beside it. In Ardroy's gaunt face a line of white showed under the closed lids, and Keith's hand, pressed on the torn shirt, found a heart-beat so faint that he thought: 'He was dying when they dragged him out, the brutes!' Perhaps he had not been in time after all. He remembered that there was brandy in his holster, and looked up with an idea of summoning Mackay.

But by this time the officer had ridden up, and was there a pace or two away, towering over the pair by the wall.

'Am I tae tak ye for a surgeon, sir?' he inquired in a strong Lowland accent, and in a tone compounded of hot rage and cold. 'If sae, an' ye'll hae the kindness tae shift yersel' oot o' the way for a meenut, there'll be nae further need o' yer sairvices!'

Keith laid Ewen's head down on the grass, and, standing up, regarded the rider, a neat, fair-complexioned Scot of about five-and-forty with little light eyes under sandy brows.

'Major Guthrie, I think?' he suggested, and saluted him. 'I am Major Keith Windham of the Royals, on General Hawley's staff, and now on my way with dispatches from His Royal Highness to Perth.'

'I care little if ye hae dispatches frae God Himsel'!' retorted Major Guthrie with increasing fury. 'And this isna Perth . . . Haud awa frae yon wa' – unless ye've a fancy tae be shot tae!'

But Keith did not move. 'This is not a common Highlander, sir,' he said, as calmly as he could. 'He is an officer, despite his dress.' For officers, as Major Guthrie must know, were not shot in cold blood – now.

'What's that tae me?' inquired Guthrie. He turned. 'Here, ye sumphs, pit him up afore the wa' again!'

Two of the men made an undecided move forwards, but the sight of this other officer of equal rank standing so resolutely in front of the prostrate Highlander daunted them.

'But listen, Major Guthrie,' pleaded Keith, keeping a tight hold upon his own rapidly rising temper and disgust, 'this gentleman is really of more than ordinary importance, for he was at one time aide-de-camp to the Pretender's son, and he is Lochiel's near kinsman – some kind of cousin, I think. You surely would not – '

'Lochiel's near kinsman, did ye say?' interrupted Guthrie, bending down a little. 'Hoo is he called?'

'Cameron of Ardroy, a captain in Lochiel's regiment. I am sure,' went on Keith, eager to follow up the impression which Lochiel's name appeared to have made, 'I am sure you will recognize, Major, that the Duke would not wish him to be shot out of hand like this!'

'Indeed I'm obliged tae ye, Major Somebody or ither, for sae kindly instructing His Royal Highness's wishes tae me,' retorted the Lowlander, but he bent still farther from the saddle, and gazed down for a moment at what was lying so still by the wall – at the dirty, bloodstained, half-clothed figure which Keith had last seen so gallant in powder and satin, cool, smiling and triumphant. The plea he had offered – the only plea that he could think of – was it going to save Ewen Cameron from lying there stiller yet? He tried to read Guthrie's intentions on his face, but all that he could see there was its innate meanness and cruelty.

The saddle creaked as the rider came upright again. He looked down at Keith himself now, with eyes that seemed to hold a flickering light.

'This is God's truth ye're tellin' me, that yon' – he pointed contemptuously – 'is Lochiel's cousin?'

'Yes, on my honour as an officer.'

'And may I speri hoo ye ken it?'

167

'Because I have met him before. I assure you, sir, that if they knew at Inverness – '

'This is nae mair Inverness than it is Perth, Major – Keith! I'm actin' here on my ain authority, and if yon lousy rebel lying there had the Duke's ain protection on him, I wudna regard it, if I thocht fit. Still and on, I'm weel aware that as Lochiel's near kinsman he may be of mair value alive than deid – we shall see of hoo much in a day or two. . . . Aye, I doot they'll be wishing they had him at Inverness!'

'But you cannot send him all the way to Inverness,' protested Keith, rather alarmed. 'He is evidently badly wounded – ill. . . .' He dropped on one knee beside Ewen again.

Guthrie gave a short laugh. 'Did I say I was gaun to? Ye maun tak me for a fule, Major. Findin's keepin', as they say. – But deil kens,' he added, suddenly dismounting, 'hoo I'm tae transport the man even to my ain camp the nicht; I've naething tae carry him on, and I dinna jalouse – ' Here he too came and stooped over the unconscious figure. 'Aye, *he*'s no' for sittin' a horse, that's plain. I'm thinkin' I'll e'en hae to leave him here till the morn, and send doun a party wi' a litter. There's ane thing,' he added coolly, raising himself with a shrug of his shoulders, 'he'll no' rin awa', and there's naebody left aboot the place. Aye, that's what I'll dae.'

'You are going to leave him here alone all night, in this state?' exclaimed Keith, loosing the almost pulseless wrist.

Guthrie stared angrily at him. 'Upon my saul, Major! Are ye expectin' a spital on Ben Loy? For a man on Hawley's staff, ye're unco tender tae a rebel! If I canna tak the prisoner wi' me, I've nae choice but leave him here . . . unless ye'd prefer me tae blaw his harns oot after a'. It's nane too late for it yet, ye ken.' And he laid a hand on one of his own pistols.

'No, you are quite right, sir,' said Keith hastily, almost humbly. 'I see that you can do nothing else but leave him till the morning.'

'Sergeant,' called out Major Guthrie, 'pit the prisoner ben the hoose again, and dinna fire yon shieling. Noo, Major Keith, in payment for the guid turn ye've done me, I'll hae the pleasure of offerin' ye hospeetality for the nicht, and settin' ye on the richt road for Perth, which ye're no' on the noo, ye ken!'

'I am much beholden to you, sir,' replied Keith stiffly. 'But I am not aware of having laid you under any obligation.'

Guthrie raised his sandy eyebrows. 'Are ye no'? Aweel, ye may be richt; we'll see, we'll see. – Aye, sergeant, fire the lave o' them; we mauna leave ony bield for the rebels.'

The thatch of the next shieling, going up with a roar, lit sharply the uniforms of the men who, roughly enough, lifted Ardroy from the ground, and, staggering a little, for he was no light weight, disappeared with him round the corner of the miserable little dwelling. Biting his lip, Keith watched them go; and then Mackay brought up his horse, restive at the flames. The men came out again.

'Well, Major, are ye no' satisfied!' asked Guthrie, already back in the saddle.

Satisfied? No. But he was on such dangerous ground; this man's mercy, if so it could be called, was like a bog; at any moment there might be no more foothold. A little more pressing for better treatment, and he would have Ardroy shot out of mere spite; Keith was sure of it. But – left alone, scarcely breathing . . . and in what condition *had* Ewen been left in there?

'I'll ride after you in a moment, sir,' he said. 'You see, I am under a sort of obligation to this young Cameron. I'll just go in and leave him my brandy-flask.'

Really Major Guthrie of Campbell's regiment had the most unpleasant eyes he had ever encountered! 'As ye will, sir,' he returned. 'I doot he'll no' be able tae thank ye. But I advise ye no' tae be ower lang wi' him, for I canna wait, and 'tis for me tae warn ye this time that the Duke'll no' be verra pleased if ye lose the way tae Perth again.' He turned his horse; Keith took the flask out of his holster, said a word to Mackay, and went round to the door of the shieling.

It was Neil MacMartin who lay shot not far from the entrance; Keith recognized him instantly. No doubt it was only over his dead body that they had been able to get at his wounded foster-brother. Inside the tiny place, it was so dark that for a moment Keith could hardly see anything; then, by a sudden red glow from without, he distinguished Ewen's body in the far corner, on a heap of something which proved to be dried fern and heather. The soldiers had flung him back there with little regard for his wounds or for the coming of night. But there was a plaid lying in a heap on the floor; Keith picked this up and spread it over him. Ardroy was still senseless, but when Keith tried to arrange him more comfortably he moaned; yet it was only the faintest trickle of brandy which the Englishman could get down his throat. He desisted finally, for fear of choking him, and closed his cold, nerveless hand round the flask instead. Looking about he saw not a trace of food nor even of water, though there was an overturned bowl on the floor; he hurried out with this to the burn which he had noticed, filled it and placed it within reach. But it seemed rather a mockery, now that the only hand which might have held it to Ewen Cameron's lips was lifeless outside. Had he done Ardroy a kindness after all in saving him from the volley?

Mackay was in the doorway. 'The redcoats iss all gone, Major. I am not seeing them now.'

Keith jumped up. His duty came before an enemy's plight, whatever were his feelings towards that enemy. He could do no more.

The leaping flames outside had died down to mere incandescence, and the dead man and the senseless were left in possession of the darkening hollow where the burn's voice, babbling on in protest or unconcern, was now the only sound to break the silence.

Chapter 4

'WEEL, sir, and was yer *frien'* able tae thank ye?' inquired Major Guthrie when the Englishman overtook him at the end of the little column as it wound along the mountainside. Keith said No, that he had not yet recovered his senses.

''Tis tae be hoped he'll hae gotten them again when I send for him,' commented the Lowlander. 'He'll no' be o' muckle use else. But are ye sure, Major, that he kens whaur Lochiel is the noo?'

'How do I know what he knows? And use – of what use do you expect him to be?' asked Keith shortly.

'What use?' Guthrie reined up. 'Losh, man, dinna ye ken there's a thousand punds on Lochiel's heid, that he's likely skulking somewhere round Achnacarry or Loch Arkaig, and that tae ken his hiding-place wad be half-way tae the apprehension o' the man himsel'! Gin ye come frae Inverness ye canna be ignorant o' that! – And why for else did ye lay sic a stress upon yon rebel bein' sib tae Lochiel, if ye didna mean that he wad be o' use tae us in that capacity?'

Keith sat his horse like a statue, and stared at the speaker with feelings which slowly whitened his own cheek. 'Is it possible you imagined that I thought Ewen Cameron, a Highlander and a gentleman, would turn informer against his own Chief?'

'Then for what ither reason,' retorted Guthrie, 'when ye came wi' yer damned interference, did ye insist on his kinship wi' Lochiel, and imply that he kenned o' his whereaboots?'

'I never implied such a thing!' burst out Keith indignantly. 'Not for a moment! You must most strangely have mistaken me, Major Guthrie. And if Cameron of Ardroy did know, he would never dream of betraying his knowledge!'

'Ah,' commented Guthrie, surveying him slowly. 'Then it's no' worth the fash o' sendin' for him the morn.' And smiling crookedly he touched his horse with his heel, and moved on again after his men.

But Keith Windham remained behind on the mountain path, almost stunned with disgust. That he should be thought capable of suggesting such a reason for sparing Ewen Cameron's life! This then was the cause of Major Guthrie's change of intention at the mention of Lochiel's name, the meaning of his reference to the 'good turn' which Major Windham had done him! Keith's impulse was to leave the very path which Guthrie's horse had trodden. But he could not gratify this desire; he was dependent on Guthrie's guidance. Besides, Ardroy lay helpless and utterly alone in the hut; he had not saved him yet. Great heavens, what line was he to take to that end now?

He moved on slowly after the Lowlander, who took no notice of him. On the narrow path they were obliged to ride in single file, but soon the track, descending to a lower level, joined a wider one, and here the Major waited for him to come abreast.

'Since your object in hinderin' the execution a while syne wasna zeal for His Majesty's sairvice, as I thocht,' he observed, 'ye maun gie me leave to say, Major . . . I didna richtly get yer name – that I find yer conduct unco strange.'

'I am fully prepared to answer to my superiors for my conduct, sir,' replied Keith very stiffly. 'As I told you just now, I am under an obligation to that young Cameron, such as any soldier may owe to an enemy without dishonour. He spared my life when it was his for the taking, and as his prisoner last year I received very different treatment from that which we are now giving to ours!'

'Ah, sae ye were his prisoner?' repeated Guthrie, fixing his little ferret eyes upon him. 'When micht that hae been?'

'It was after the affair at High Bridge last summer,' answered Keith shortly.

'High Bridge!' A light seemed to dawn on Guthrie's face – not a pleasant light. 'What, it's *you* that lost the twa companies of Sinclair's there, along wi' Scott last August – ye'll be Major Windrum then?'

'Windham,' corrected Keith, still more shortly.

'Ou aye, Windham. Tae think I didna ken the man I was gangin' wi', me that's aye been ettlin' tae meet ye, for I mind hearin' ye were pit on Hawley's staff after yon tuilzie – ha, ha! Aye, I mind hearin' that verra weel. – Nae offence meant, Major Windham' – for Keith's expression was distinctly stormy – 'we all hae oor meelitary misfortunes . . . but we dinna a' get promoted for them! – And ye were sayin' yon rebel made ye prisoner. What did he dae wi' ye?'

'He accepted my parole,' said the Englishman between his teeth.

'And let ye gang?'

'No. I was at his house for some days, and afterwards accompanied him to Glenfinnan.'

'Ye seem tae hae been chief wi' him! And whaur was this hoose of his, if ye please?'

'Can that be of any moment to you, sir?' retorted Keith, goaded by this interrogatory.

'Dod! I should think sae! It's o' moment tae me tae ken hoo far it lay frae Lochiel's ain hoose of Achnacarry.'

172

'Well, that I am afraid I cannot tell you,' replied Keith sourly. 'I was never at Achnacarry, and I have no knowledge of the neighbourhood. I am not a Scotsman.'

'Fine I ken that! But e'en a Southron has lugs tae his heid, and he maun hae heard tell the name o' the district whaur yon rebel's hoose was situate? If we canna tell me that, I'll be forced tae think – ' He broke off with a grin.

'And what, pray, will you be forced to think?' demanded Keith, surveying him from under his lids.

'Aweel, I suld think ye could jalouse that,' was Guthrie's reply. 'Come noo, Major, ye can surely mind some landmark or ither?'

It was no use fencing any more. 'Mr Cameron's house was near a little lake called the Eagle's Lake, in the mountains some way to the north of Loch Arkaig.'

'Ah, thank ye, Major Windham, for the effort,' said Guthrie with another grin. 'I hae a map in the camp. ... And syne ye couldna be pairted frae yer rebel frien', but gaed wi' him to Glenfinnan tae see the ploy there?'

'Do you suppose I went willingly? I have told you that I was his prisoner.'

'But ye were at Glenfinnan wi' him, and that's o' moment too, for nae doot ye'd see him an' Lochiel thegither. Did ye no'?'

'Once or twice.'

'And hoo did they seem – on intimate terrms wi' ane anither?'

'I was not concerned to spy upon them,' retorted Keith, who had an instant picture of the Chief as he had once seen him, with an affectionate hand on Ewen's shoulder, a picture he was not going to pass on. 'I have told you that they were cousins.'

'Aye, ye tellt me that. But ilka Highlander is cousin tae twenty mair.' They rode on for perhaps a moment in silence, and then Guthrie began again. 'See here, Major Windham, what the de'il's the gude o' tellin' me the Cameron's this and that, and syne, when ye've hindered me frae shootin' him as he desairves, tae begin makin' oot he's naething o' the sort? I suppose ye'll say noo he wasna aide-de-camp tae the Pretender's son neither?'

'I am not in the habit of telling lies,' replied Keith. 'He *was* aide-de-camp to the Pretender's son, at least when the Highland army occupied Edinburgh, and that, as I said, and say still, is an excellent reason for not shooting him out of hand.'

'Ye met him in Enbra, then?'

'I did.'

'As an enemy or a frien'?'

'As an enemy, of course.' Keith was having to keep a tight hold of himself. 'Yet there again he put me under an obligation.' And at Guthrie's expression he was unable to resist adding: 'But I dare warrant the recognition of an obligation is no part of your creed, sir.'

Guthrie met this thrust instantly. 'And me that gleg the noo tae allow mine tae ye! Fie, Major! But as a plain soldier I'm thinkin' there's ower muckle obleegation atween you and yer Cameron; ye're gey frien'ly wi' him for an enemy, rinnin' in like that when ye micht hae gotten a ball in yer ain wame. But since ye assure me he'll no' tell what he kens aboot Lochiel, he maun e'en bide in yon shieling and rot there, for it's no' worth a brass bodle tae bring him in.'

Keith's heart sank at these words. Yet he could not bring himself to assert that Ardroy would impart his knowledge (if he had any), for he was certain that he would rather die than do such a thing. Yet somehow he *must* be got out of that desolate place.

He summoned up all his own powers of dissimulation.

'You are quite mistaken, Major Guthrie,' he said carelessly. 'I am not a friend of Mr Cameron's in the sense that you imply, and I should be as glad as anyone to hear of Lochiel's capture – if it would advance His Majesty's affairs in this kingdom.' He added this qualifying clause to salve his own conscience, since Lochiel's capture was about the last he would rejoice at. But he had to say something worse than this, and he did it with loathing, and a hesitation which perhaps served him better than he knew, fidgeting meanwhile with his horse's reins. 'You know, sir, that although I am sure Mr Cameron would never answer a direct question, he might perhaps drop . . . inadvertently drop . . . some hint or other – and I presume you have a certain measure of knowledge, and might find a hint valuable – I mean that it might, by good luck, complete your information. At least I should think that it would be worth your while to bring him into camp on the chance of it.'

It sounded to him so desperately feeble a bait that it was surely to no purpose that he had soiled his lips with its utterance. Yet Guthrie appeared to respond to the suggestion with surprising alacrity.

'Drap a hint,' he said meditatively, rubbing his chin. 'Aye, maybe. Thank ye for the notion, Major; I'll e'en think it ower. I could aiblins drap a hint mysel'.' And they rode on in silence for a few minutes after that, Keith not knowing whether he more detested himself or the man beside him.

But by the time that they came in sight of the little river Tarff, which they must ford before they could get up to the Corryarrick road, Major Guthrie was busy weaving what he evidently considered a highly diverting explanation of his companion's interest in 'yon rebel', which he now refused to attribute to the alleged 'obligation' under which Major Windham professed to labour. 'I see it a',' he chuckled. 'He had a bonny sister, and she was kind tae ye, Major – kind as yon ither lass of a Cameron was kind to the Pretender's son. Or a wife maybe? Oot wi' it, ye sly dog – ' And for a moment or two he gave rein to a fancy so coarse that Keith, no Puritan himself, yet innately fastidious, longed to shut his mouth.

'And that's how ye repaid his hospitality, Major,' finished the humorist as they splashed through the Tarff. ''Tis a guilty conscience, not gratitude, garred ye save him!'

After that he reverted to the subject of his companion's staff appointment, which seemed to possess a sort of fascination for him, and tapped a very galling and indeed insulting vein of pleasantry in regard to it. And Keith, who would not have endured a quarter of this insolence from anyone else in the world, no, not from the Duke of Cumberland himself, swallowed it because he knew that Ewen Cameron's life hung on this man's pleasure. First of all his companion supposed that General Hawley did not know what a viper he was cherishing in his bosom, in the shape of an officer who possessed a weakness for rebels which could certainly not be attributed to that commander himself; of this Keith took no notice, so Major Guthrie passed on to affect to find something mightily amusing in the distinction of staff rank having been bestowed on a man who had run away at the first shot of the campaign. He actually used the expression, but at once safeguarded himself by adding, with a laugh: 'Nae offence, my dear Major! I ken weel the twa companies o' Sinclair's just spat and gied ower, and you and Scott could dae nae less but gang wi' them – 'twas yer duty.' But after a moment he added with a chuckle: 'Forbye ye rinned farther than the rest, I've heard!'

Ardroy or no Ardroy, this was too much. Keith reined up. Yet, since it seemed deliberate provocation, he kept surprisingly cool. 'Major Guthrie, I'd have you know I do not take such insinuations from any man alive! If you know so much about me, you must know also that Captain Scott sent me back to fetch reinforcements from Fort Augustus.'

Guthrie, pulling up too, smote himself upon the thigh. 'Aye, I micht ha' kent it! Forgie me, Major Windham – yon was a pleasantry. I aye likit ma joke!'

'Allow me to say, then, that I do not share your taste,' riposted Keith, with a brow like thunder. 'If we were not both on active service at the moment – '

'Ye'd gar me draw, eh? Dinna be that hot, man! 'Twas an ill joke, I confess, and I ask yer pardon for it,' said Guthrie, with complete good humour. 'See, yonder's the camp, and ye're gaun tae sup wi' me.'

Keith wished with all his heart that he were not. But he felt, rightly or wrongly, that he must preserve a certain measure of amenity in his relations with the arbiter of Ardroy's fate, and, though it seemed to him that he had never done anything more repugnant (except make his recent speech about the possibility of Ewen's dropping a hint) he affected a demeanour modelled in some remote degree upon his companion's, and insincerely declared that he was foolish not to see that Major Guthrie was joking, and that he bore him no ill-will for his jest.

What baffled him was the reason for the ill-will which he could hardly doubt that Guthrie bore *him*. Was it because he had hindered the shooting of a rebel? But, according to his own showing, Major Guthrie hoped to find the rebel more useful alive than dead.

It was certainly no deprivation to the Englishman when he discovered, on arriving at Guthrie's camp athwart the road, some miles from the top of the pass, that he was not to share the commanding officer's tent. Finding, as he now did, that the distance from the mountainside where he had come upon the soldiers was not so great as he had feared, he would much have preferred to push on over the pass to Meallgarva, but his horse and his orderly's were too obviously in need of rest for this to be prudent, and when he was offered a vacant bed in another tent (for it appeared that the captain of the company had gone to Fort Augustus for the night), his worst apprehensions were relieved. The lieutenant, indeed, who made a third at the meal which he was nevertheless obliged to share with Guthrie, was of a different stamp entirely, an open-faced lad from the Tweed, named Paton, whom Keith at once suspected of disliking his major very heartily.

On the plea that he must make an early start, the guest afterwards excused himself from playing cards with Guthrie and his subaltern, and withdrew to Lieutenant Paton's tent. Once there, however, he made no attempt to undress, but flung himself on the camp bed and lay staring at the lantern on the tent-pole. A few miles away, on the other side of the Tarff, the man whom he had tried so hard to save lay dying, perhaps, for want of food and care. What Guthrie's real intentions were about fetching him in tomorrow he, probably of set purpose, had not allowed his visitor to know. And the question rather was, would Ewen Cameron be alive at all in the morning – he seemed at so low an ebb, and the nights were still so cold. Do what Keith would, he could not get him out of his head. It was useless to tell himself that he had, alas, witnessed worse episodes; that it was the fortune of war; that he was womanish to be so much distracted by the thought of an enemy's situation. He had been that enemy's guest; he had seen his domestic circumstances, met his future wife, knew what his very furniture looked like. Was not all that even more of a tie than that double debt which he felt he owed him? His instincts were stronger than his judgement, and when, an hour or so later, Lieutenant Paton slipped quietly through the flap of the tent, he rose up and abruptly addressed him.

'Mr Paton, you look as if you had the natural sentiments of

humanity still left in you. Can you tell me where I could procure some food, and if possible some dressings, for that unfortunate rebel left alone upon the mountainside, about whom you heard at supper?'

The young man looked considerably taken aback, as well he might. 'But how would you propose, sir, to get them to him? And the Major, I thought, spoke of fetching him into camp tomorrow.'

'I am not at all sure that he will, however,' replied Keith. 'And even if he does I fear he may fetch in a corpse. If I can get some food and wine I propose to take them to him myself; I think I can find the way back without difficulty, and my orderly is a Highlander.' And as Lieutenant Paton looked still more astonished, he added: 'You must not think me a mere philanthropist, Mr Paton. I owe the man in that hut a good deal, and I cannot endure the thought of having turned my back upon him in such a plight. In any case I should be making an early start for Dalwhinnie. Is there any cottage in this neighbourhood where I could buy bread?'

'No, but I could procure you some in the camp, sir,' said the boy quite eagerly. 'And, as for dressings, you are welcome to tear up a shirt of mine. I . . . I confess I don't like these extreme measures, even with rebels, and I should be very glad to help you.'

'You'll not get into trouble, eh?'

'Not tonight, at any rate, sir; the Major is in bed by now. And tomorrow, if it is discovered, I can say that you ordered me to do it, and that I dared not dispute the orders of a staff officer.'

Chapter 5

AND thus it was that a few hours later Major Windham started back to Beinn Laoigh again, with bread and meat and wine, and an orderly who plainly thought him mad. Lieutenant Paton had seen them clear of the camp, whose commander was fortunately wrapped in slumber. Keith would not need to pass its sentries on his return, for the track up from the Tarff joined the road to the pass on the farther side of it.

He found that he had noted the position of the shieling hut better than he could have hoped, considering the disagreeable preoccupation of his mind during the ride thence with Major Guthrie, and by good chance there was a moon not much past the full. In her cold light the mountains looked inexpressibly lonely and remote as Keith rode up the sheep track to the pasture where the harmless little shelters had stood. A faint exhausted smoke yet lifted itself from one or two of the blackened ruins. The stream was chanting its changeless little song, and in the moonlight Neil MacMartin still lay on guard outside the broken door of the one unburnt shieling. Keith bent over him as he passed; he was stiffening already in the plaid which was his only garment. And Ardroy?

Taking from Mackay the lantern which he had brought for the purpose, and food and wine, Keith went rather apprehensively into the dark, low-roofed place. Except that he had flung his left arm clear, its occupant was lying as he had left him, long and quiet under the tartan covering; his eyes were closed, and he did not look very different from his dead foster-brother outside. But as the light fell on his face he moved a little and faintly said some words in Gaelic, among which Keith thought he heard Lachlan's name. He stooped over him.

'Ardroy,' he said gently, and laid a hand on the arm emerging from the tattered shirt-sleeve.

At the touch, Ewen opened his eyes. But all that he saw, evidently, in the lantern-light, was the bright scarlet uniform above him. 'What, again!' he said, with an accent of profound weariness. 'Shoot me in here, then; I cannot stand. Have you not . . . a pistol?'

Keith set the lantern on the floor and knelt down by him. 'Ardroy, don't you know me – Windham of the Royals? I am not come for that, but to help you, if I can.'

The dried fern rustled as the wounded man turned his head a little. Very hollow in their orbits, but blue as Keith remembered them, his eyes stared up full of unbelief. '*Windham!*' he said at last, feebly; 'no, it's not possible. You are . . . someone else.'

'No,' said Keith, wondering how clear his mind might be. 'It is really Windham, come to help you.' He was searching meanwhile for the flask of brandy which he had left, and finding it slipped down, untouched, among the sprigs of heather, he wetted Ewen's lips with a little of the spirit.

'Yes, it *is* Windham,' said Ewen to himself. His eyes had never left his visitor's face. 'But . . . there were other soldiers here before . . . they took me out to shoot . . . I think I must have . . . swooned. Then I was . . . back in this place. . . . I do not know why. . . . Are you sure you . . . have not orders to . . . take me out again?'

'Good God, no!' said Keith. 'I have nothing to do with shootings; I am alone, carrying dispatches. Tell me, you are wounded – how severely?'

'My right arm . . . that is nothing much. . . . This thigh . . . badly. I cannot . . . move myself.'

'And what of food?' queried Keith. 'I do not see any here – but I have brought some with me.' He began to get it out. 'Are you not hungry?'

'Not now,' answered Ewen. 'I was once . . . Captain Windham,' he went on, apparently gathering together what forces he had, 'your coming . . . this charity . . . I cannot . . .'

'Do not try!' put in Keith quickly. 'Not hungry? How long, then, is it since you have eaten?'

'Eaten!' said the Highlander, and what might be interpreted as a smile dawned on his bony face. 'There is no food . . . in these hills. I have had nothing but water . . . for three days . . . I think. . . . That is why Lachlan has gone . . . to try . . .' The words tailed off as the spark of astonishment and animation in him went out quite suddenly, leaving his face the mask it had been when Keith entered.

Three days! No wonder that he was weak. Keith threw the water out of the bowl, poured some wine into it, and lifting Ewen's head from the bracken held it to his lips. 'Drink this!' he commanded, and had to say it two or three times before Ewen obeyed.

'But this is wine, Lachlan,' he murmured confusedly. 'How did you come by wine?' Then his eyes turned on Keith as if he recognized him again, and the recognition was only a source of bewilderment.

Keith meanwhile was breaking bread into the wine. He knew that one must not give a starving man too much food at first. But the fugitive, far from being ravenous, seemed to find it difficult to swallow the sops which were put to his lips. Keith, however, persevered, and even added some meat to the bread, and patiently fed him with that, till Ewen intimated that he could eat no more. Keith's next intention was then announced.

'Now I am going to dress your wounds, if they need it,' he said. 'You'll permit me?'

'*Permit* you!' repeated Ewen, gazing at him with a renewal of his former wonder.

Keith took the bowl, and went out for water. The moon was hidden behind a bank of cloud, but a planet hung like a great flower over one of the black mountain-tops. The grazing horses lifted their heads inquiringly, and Mackay, sitting propped against the shieling wall, scrambled sleepily to his feet.

'No, I am not going on yet. Get me that torn linen from my saddle-bag.'

To his surprise, when he went back into the hut after even so momentary an absence, Ewen had fallen asleep, perhaps as the result of eating after so long a fast. Keith decided not to rouse him, and waited. But five minutes saw the end of the snatch of feverish slumber, for Ardroy woke with a little cry and some remark about the English artillery which showed that he had been back at Culloden Moor. However, he knew Keith instantly, and when the Englishman began to unbandage his wounded sword-arm, murmured: 'That was a bayonet-thrust.'

The arm had indeed been transfixed, and looked very swollen and painful, but, as far as Keith could judge, gave no particular cause for anxiety. He washed the wound, and as he bound it up again saw clearly in the rays of the lantern, which for greater convenience he had set upon an old stool that he had found, a curious white seam on the palm of the hand; another ran across the fingers. He wondered for a moment what they were; then he guessed.

But when he came round and unbandaged Ewen's thigh – and

miserably enough was it bandaged – and found there a deep gash, in no satisfactory state, he was somewhat horrified. This injury called for a surgeon, and he nearly said so; but, reddening, checked himself, recalling the deliberate denial of care to the Jacobite wounded at Inverness, and the actual removal of their instruments from the few of their own surgeons imprisoned with them. Would Ewen Cameron get real attention in Major Guthrie's hands?

He glanced at him, lying with his eyes shut and his hands gripped together on his breast, but making neither sound nor movement, and wondered whether he were hurting him intolerably, and what he should do if he went off into another of those long swoons, and thereupon finished his task as quickly as he could and had recourse to the brandy flask once more. And then he sat down at the bottom of the rough bed – for the heather and fern was spread on a rude wooden framework standing about a foot from the floor – and gazed at him with a furrowed brow. The lantern on the stool beside him revealed the Highlander's pallor and exhaustion to the full, but though his eyes were closed and he lay quiet for a considerable time, he was not asleep, for he suddenly opened them and said:

'I cannot understand; did you know that I was here, Captain Windham . . . or is it chance that has brought you . . . so opportunely?'

'It was chance the first time – for this is the second time that I have been here,' replied Keith. 'I will tell you about it. I was on my way this afternoon from Inverness to Perth when some impulse made me attempt a very foolish short cut among the mountains. I think now that it must have been the finger of Fate pushing me, for thus I came upon this place just a moment or two before they dragged you out and set you against the wall . . . only just in time, in fact. I protested and argued with the officer in charge – a Major Guthrie, who has a camp on the Corryarrick road up there – and was fortunately able to prevent his shooting you in cold blood.' And as Ewen gave a little exclamation, he hurried on in order not to give him time to ask (should he think of it) how he had accomplished this feat. 'But he intends – at least I think he intends – to send a party in the morning and

take you prisoner; and indeed, brute though he is, I hope that
he will do so, for otherwise what will become of you, alone
here?'

But Ewen left that question unanswered, and was equally far
from asking on what ground he had been spared. The fact itself
seemed enough for him, for he was trying agitatedly to raise himself a little. 'It was you ... though I saw no one ... you saved
my life, then!' he exclaimed rather incoherently. 'And now ... is
it possible that you have come back *again* ... out of your way?
Captain Windham, this debt ... this more than kindness ...'
He struggled to go on, but between emotion, weakness, and recent
pain it was more than he could do; and seeing him almost on the
point of breaking down Keith stopped him quickly.

'For God's sake don't talk of debts, Ardroy – or, if you must,
remember what I owe you! See, you are horribly weak; could you
not eat a little more now?'

Ewen nodded, not trusting himself to speak, and put out a
shaky left hand, apparently to show that he could feed himself.
And while he nibbled in a rather half-hearted way at the slice of
bread and meat which Keith put into it, Major Windham himself wandered slowly about the hovel. The ashes of last summer's
fires lay white in the middle of the floor, and through the hole in
the room which was the only outlet for the smoke a star looked
in as it passed.

It seemed to Keith that before he went on his way, he must tell
Ardroy the means he had used to save him. Surely there was
nothing blameworthy or unnatural in his having revealed who
Ewen was, when he stood between him and imminent death?
But from telling him the reason which Guthrie supposed, or
feigned to suppose, lay at the back of his action, he mentally shied
away like a nervous horse, the Lowlander had rendered the whole
subject so horribly distasteful to him. Moreover it was not
Guthrie who had suggested that Cameron of Ardroy might 'inadvertently drop a hint'. How *could* he tell Ewen that he had said
that about him?

He turned round, miserably undecided. Ewen had finished his
pretence at a meal, and his eyes were fixed on his visitor. Keith
had a sudden access of panic; he was sure that the Jacobite was

going to ask him on what plea he had stopped his execution. He would put a question to him instead.

'How did you get so far with a wound like that?' he asked, coming back to his former place, and sitting down again. 'You had Neil MacMartin to help you, I suppose? You mentioned Lachlan, too, just now.'

He had not anticipated more than a brief reply, but Ewen, once started, told him the whole story – not, indeed, with any superfluity of words, and slowly, with pauses here and there. But the narrative was quite connected, though the speaker gave a certain dreamy impression of having half forgotten his listener, and of going on as if he were living his experiences over again rather than narrating them.

It appeared that he had received both his wounds in that desperate charge into which the clans of the right wing had broken, maddened by the cruel artillery pounding which they had endured, a charge so furious that it had pierced and scattered the English front line of regiments, only to dash itself to pieces – on the bayonets of Sempill's behind them. At the second and severer injury he fell, and was unable to get to his feet again, for it seemed as if a muscle had been severed in his thigh, and he was besides losing blood very fast. Only the devotion of one of his followers got him away from the heap of dead and wounded strewn about like seaweed along the front of the second line; this man, powerful and unhurt, tied up the gash as best he could, and succeeded in carrying his chieftain a little out of the carnage, but in doing so he was shot dead, and once more Ewen was on the ground among the fallen. This time he was lying among the dead and wounded of the Atholl men, with none of his own clan to succour him, and here a strange – and yet ultimately a lucky – mischance befell him. For a wounded Stewart, half crazed no doubt by a terrible cut on the head, crawled to him where he lay across his dead clansman and, cursing him for one of the Campbells who had taken them in flank, dealt him a furious blow on the forehead with the butt of a pistol. The result for Ewen was hours of unconsciousness, during which he was stripped by some redcoats who would certainly have finished him off had they not thought him dead already. He came to his senses in the very early morning, naked and stiff with cold, but so thirsty that he contrived to drag himself as far as the little burn which crossed the end of the English line in the direction of their own. There, almost in the stream, and unconscious again, Lachlan and his brother, who had been searching for him since evening, almost miraculously found him.

His foster-brothers carried him to a farmhouse on the moor, where, indeed, he was not the only wounded fugitive, but by noon that day, fearing (and with good reason) a search and a massacre, they somehow procured an old worn-out horse, and taking turns to ride it and to hold him on its back, succeeded in crossing the Water of Nairn and gaining the slopes of the Monadhliath Mountains. What happened then Ewen was not quite clear about; between pain, loss of blood, and exposure he was always more or less fevered, but he remembered an eternity of effort and of going on. At last the old horse fell dead; for a whole day Neil and Lachlan carried him between them till, weakened by want of food, they could get him no farther, and had taken shelter on Beinn Laoigh because the shieling hut at least gave him a roof from the cold and the rain. They did not know of Guthrie's camp on the Corryarrick road, which indeed was pitched after they got to Beinn Laoigh; in any case they could not entirely avoid the road, for it would have to be crossed somewhere if they were ever to get back to Ardroy. But in these lonely mountains they were really faced with starvation, and Lachlan had at last been forced to go out scouting for food, and must either have gone far afield or have met with disaster, for he had been gone since the day before.

'But if he still breathes,' finished Ewen, 'I know that he will return; and if he is in time perhaps he can contrive to get me away to some other hiding-place before the soldiers come for me tomorrow. But in any case, Captain Windham – no, I see that it is Major – I am not likely to forget this extraordinary charity of yours . . . nor your intervention yesterday. . . . Was it yesterday?' he added rather vaguely.

'Yes, since it must now be after midnight. The tartans attracted my notice first,' said Keith, 'and then, by great good fortune, I looked again, and recognized you.'

'This is Neil's kilt that I have on,' said Ewen with a faint smile. 'There was not a stitch of my own left upon me. ... You wore the philabeg too, once ... it seems a long time ago. ... But I do not think,' he went on, rather feverishly talkative now, 'that you would have recognized me the day before, with a two weeks' beard on me. It happened, however, that I had made poor Neil shave me as best he could with his *sgian*.'

'That was good fortune, too,' agreed Keith. 'Certainly I should not have known you bearded.'

'And it is because I had been shaved that I am alive now?' Ewen gave a little laugh. 'Do you know, Windham, that before ever I met you old Angus, my foster-father – you remember him? – predicted that our lives would cross ... I think he said five times. And this is ... I can't count. ... How many times have we met already?'

'The old man predicted five meetings!' exclaimed Keith, struck. 'How strange! This is the third ... yes, the third time we have met. If he is right, then we shall meet again, and more than once. I hope it may be in happier circumstances.'

'And that I can thank you more fitly,' murmured Ewen. 'Last time ... do you remember the house in the Grassmarket? ... You told me the comedy would end some day, and the players be sorry they ever took part in it.'

Keith nodded. It was not the first time in the last twelve hours that he had remembered the house in the Grassmarket.

'But I, for one, do not regret it,' went on Ewen, with a touch of defiance. 'Not for myself, that is. I would do it again. Yet there is poor Neil outside, killed defending me ... and so many others on that horrible moor. ... You were there, I suppose?'

'I was there,' said Keith. 'But *my* hands are clean of the blood of massacre!' he added almost fiercely. 'If I could have stopped – We'd best not speak of it. But your cause is lost, Ardroy, and I suppose you know it. It only remains for you to escape the consequences, if you can.'

'I do not seem to be in very good trim for doing that,' said Ewen, and again he gave the shadow of a smile. 'But, since we speak so frankly, I cannot think that our cause is lost while the Prince and Lochiel remain at large. We may be scattered, but –

The Prince has not been captured, has he?' he asked sharply, having evidently seen the change which the mention not of the Prince but of Lochiel, had brought to Keith's face.

'No, no, nor is it known where he is.'

'Thank God! And Lochiel?'

Keith shrank inwardly. Now it was coming. His momentary hesitation had a cruel effect on Ewen, who dragged himself to his elbow. 'Windham,' he said hoarsely and imploringly, 'surely he's not ... what have you heard? ... My God, don't keep me in suspense like this! If he's captured tell me!'

'You mistake me,' said Keith, nearly as hoarsely. 'He has not been captured. ... I am sorry if I misled you.'

Ewen had relapsed again, and put a hand over his eyes. It was fairly clear that his Chief's fate was even more to him than that of his Prince. And now that odious information must be imparted.

Keith tried to gain a little time first. 'But Lochiel was wounded in the battle. Did you know that?'

Ewen removed his hand. 'Yes, and have thanked God for it, since it caused him to be early carried off the field.'

'You saw him fall?'

'No, but afterwards we met with some of the clan, and got news of him.'

'That must have been a great relief to you,' murmured the Englishman. Suddenly he was possessed with a desire to find out how much Ewen knew about Lochiel. Half of him hoped that he knew very little – why, he could not have said – but the other half thought: If he knows a certain amount, Guthrie will take better care of him. 'But you can have had no news of your Chief since then?' he hazarded.

'No,' answered the Highlander. 'There has been no opportunity.'

Keith looked at him nervously. Ardroy was lying gazing upwards; perhaps he could see that peering star. Would it be possible to advise him, if he found himself in Major Guthrie's custody, to pretend to have definite knowledge of Lochiel's whereabouts, even though that were not the case? Dare he suggest such a thing? It was not one-half as offensive as what he had already suggested to Guthrie!

Ewen himself broke the silence. 'Since we speak as friends,' he said, his eyes travelling to the open doorway ' – and how could I regard you as an enemy after this? – I may tell you that I have, none the less, the consolation of knowing where Lochiel is at this moment – God bless him and keep him safe!'

Keith's mouth felt suddenly dry. His unspoken question was answered, and the frankness of the acknowledgement rather took his breath away. Yet certainly, if Ardroy was as frank with Guthrie, it might serve him well.

'You know where Lochiel is?' he half stammered.

Ewen shut his eyes and smiled, an almost happy smile. 'I think he is where (please God) he will never be found by any redcoat.'

'You mean that he has gone overseas?' asked Keith, almost without thinking.

Ardroy's eyes opened quickly, and for a second, as he looked up at the speaker, there was a startled expression in them. 'You are not expecting me to tell you – '

'No, no,' broke in Keith, very hastily indeed. 'Of course not! But I should be glad if he were so gone, for on my soul there is none of your leaders whom I should be so sorry to see captured.'

Yet with the words he got up and went to the doorway. Yes, Ardroy *had* the secret; and he wished, somehow, that he had not. The moment could no longer be postponed when he must tell him of his conversation with Guthrie, were it only to put him on his guard. Bitterly as he was ashamed, it must be done.

He stood in the doorway a moment, choosing the words in which he should do it, and they were hatefully hard to choose. Hateful, too, was it to leave Ardroy here helpless, but there was no alternative, since he could not possibly take him with him. Yet if Lachlan returned, and in time, and especially if he returned with assistance, he might be able to get his foster-brother away somewhere. Then Ewen Cameron would never fall into Guthrie's hands. In that case what use to torment him with prospects of an interrogatory which might never take place, and which could only be very short?

No; it was mere cowardice to invent excuses for silence; he must do it. He came back very slowly to the pallet.

'I must tell you – ' he began in a low voice, and then stopped.

Ewen's lashes were lying on his sunken cheeks, and did not lift at the address. It was plain that he had fallen anew into one of those sudden exhausted little slumbers, and had not heard even the sentence which was to herald Keith's confession. It would be unnecessarily cruel to rouse him in order to make it. One must wait until he woke naturally, as he had done from the last of these dozes.

Keith took the lantern off the stool and sat down there. And soon the wounded man's sleep became full of disjointed scraps of talk, mostly incoherent; at one time he seemed to think that he was out after the deer on the hills with Lachlan; then he half woke up and muttered: 'But it's we that are the deer now,' and immediately fell into another doze in which he murmured the name of Alison. Gradually, however, his slumber grew more sound; he ceased to mutter and to make little restless movements, and in about five minutes he was in the deep sleep of real repose, which he had not known, perhaps, for many nights – a sleep to make a watcher thankful.

But Keith Windham, frowning, sat watching it with his chin on his hand, conscious that his time was growing very short, that it was light outside, and almost light in this dusky hovel, and that the pool of lantern-shine on the uneven earth floor looked strange and sickly there. He glanced at his watch. No, indeed, he ought not to delay any longer. He took up and blew out the lantern, went outside and roused Mackay, washed the bowl and, filling it with water, placed it and the rest of the food and wine within reach.

His movements had not roused the sleeper in the least. For the last time Keith stooped over him and slipped a hand round his wrist. He knew nothing of medicine, but undoubtedly the beat there was stronger. It would be criminal to wake Ardroy merely in order to tell him something unpleasant. There came to the soldier a momentary idea of scribbling a warning on a page of his pocket-book and leaving this on the sleeper's breast; but it was quite possible that the first person to read such a document would be Guthrie himself.

He rearranged the plaid carefully, and stood for a moment longer looking at the fugitive where he lay at his feet, his head sunk in the dried fern. And he remembered the hut at Kinlochiel last summer, where he had done much the same thing. He had talked somewhat earlier on that occasion, had he not, of obligation and repayment; well, he had more than repaid. Ewen Cameron owed him his life – owed it him, very likely, twice over. Yet Keith was conscious again that no thought of obligation had drawn him to dash in front of those muskets yesterday, nor had the idea of a debt really brought him back now. What then? . . . Absurd! He was a man who prided himself on being unencumbered with friends. Moreover, Ewen Cameron was an enemy.

It was strange, then, with what reluctance, with what half-hopes, half-apprehensions, he got into the saddle and rode away under the paling stars, leaving his enemy to rescue or capture; very strange, since that enemy was likewise a rebel, that he should so greatly have desired the former.

IV. 'YOUR DEBTOR, EWEN CAMERON'

So, in this snare which holds me and appals me,
Where honour hardly lives nor loves remain . . .
    - H. BELLOC, *On Battersea Bridge*

Chapter 1

THE mist shrouded every mountain-top, sagging downwards in some places like the roof of a tent, and in others, where a perpetual draught blew down a corrie, streaming out like smoke. How different from last week, when, cold as it was up there, the top of the Corryarrick Pass had presented to Major Windham's eyes a view from Badenoch to the hills of Skye. Today, recrossing it, and looking back, he could hardly distinguish through the greyish-white blanket more than three or four of its many traverses winding away below him.

But here, on the lower levels of the mountain road, where it prepared to debouch into that which ran along the Great Glen, this clogging mist had become a fine and most penetrating rain, bedewing every inch of the rider's cloak and uniform, the edges of his wig, his very eyebrows and lashes, and insinuating itself down his collar. Major Windham did not know which was the more objectionable form of moisture, and wished it were late enough in the day to cease exposing himself to either, and to put up for the night at Fort Augustus, which he should reach in another twenty minutes or so. But it was still too early for that, and, bearer as he was of a dispatch from Lord Albemarle to the Duke of Cumberland, he must push on beyond Fort Augustus before nightfall; must, indeed, reach the only halting-place between that spot and Inverness, the tiny inn known, from Wade's occupation of it when he was making the road, as the General's Hut. However, he intended to stop at Fort Augustus to bait the horses – and to make an inquiry.

It was six days since he had left Guthrie's camp, and he was not altogether surprised today to find it gone, but, to judge from

191

the litter lying about, only recently gone. There was, therefore, no one to give him news of Ardroy, but he was sure that, if the Jacobite had been made prisoner, he would have been sent or taken to Fort Augustus, and he could get news of him there.

That night in the shieling, just a week ago, seemed to Keith much farther off than that, and the emotions he had known then to have lost their edge. 'Gad, what a fit of philanthropy I had on me that day!' he reflected. If 'Hangman' Hawley came to know of it, how he would sneer at him, and the rest of the staff too. Luckily they would not know. So consoling himself, and cursing the rain anew, he came to Fort Augustus, or rather to what remained of it. Its Highland captors, who during their attack upon it had partially demolished the new fort, had on the summons to face Cumberland blown up and fired most of the residue. A small temporary garrison had been sent there after the victory, to secure the abandoned stronghold for the Government; but it had now been taken possession of by a larger force, in the shape of the Earl of Loudoun's regiment, under the Earl himself, and eighteen 'independent companies'. These had only marched in a few hours before, in consequence of which influx the whole place was in a state of great turmoil.

There was so little accommodation in the ruined fort that a small village of tents was being erected in the meadows by the mouth of the Tarff, and between the confusion of camp-pitching and the fact that nearly everyone whom he encountered was a newcomer, Keith found it difficult to discover who was or had been responsible for prisoners sent in before Lord Loudoun's arrival. He did, however, elicit the information that Major Guthrie's detachment was now somewhere on the road between Fort Augustus and Inverness. And at last, though he did not succeed in seeing anybody directly responsible, he was told that a wounded Cameron, said to be the head of one of the cadet branches of the clan, had been captured the previous week and sent in by that very detachment, and that he had been given proper care and was progressing favourably.

That was all Keith wanted to know for the moment, and he delayed no longer. A certain vague disquiet which had teased him during the past week about Guthrie's possible treatment of his prisoner was allayed. For the rest, he had already made his plans about Ardroy. It was at Inverness, with Cumberland, that he could really do Ewen service, especially if the Duke did take him on to his personal staff. To His Royal Highness he could then represent what he owed to the captured rebel, and, before he himself returned with the Commander-in-Chief to Flanders, he might very well have the satisfaction of knowing that the object of his 'philanthropy' had been set at liberty.

As he turned away from Fort Augustus, where the vista of Loch Ness was completely blotted out in rain, and addressed himself to the long steep climb up the Inverness road, Keith's thoughts went back to the Earl of Albemarle in Perth, craving like himself to get overseas once more – whence, though colonel of the Cold-stream Guards, he had come to serve as a volunteer under Cumberland. His lordship, who had, moreover, greatly preferred commanding the front line in the recent battle to his present post with the Hessian troops in Perth, had lamented his situation quite openly to Cumberland's messenger; he detested Scotland, he announced, and had fears, from a sentence in the dispatch which that messenger had delivered to him, that he might be appointed to succeed Hawley in this uncongenial country. Having thus somewhat unwisely betrayed his sentiments to Major Windham, he was more or less obliged to beg his discretion, in promising which Keith had revealed his own fellow-feeling about the North. When they parted, therefore, Lord Albemarle had observed with much graciousness that if this horrid fate of succeeding General Hawley should overtake him, he would not forget Major Windham, though he supposed that the latter might not then be in Scotland for him to remember. No; Keith, though grateful for his lordship's goodwill, distinctly hoped that he would not. He trusted to be by then in a dryer climate and a country less afflicted with steep roads ... less afflicted also with punitive measures, though, since Perth was not Inverness, he was not so much dominated by those painful impressions of brutality as he had been a week ago.

The greater part of the lengthy and tiresome ascent from the level of Loch Ness was now over, and Keith and Dougal Mackay

193

found themselves again more or less in the region of mist, but on a flat stretch of road with a strip of moorland on one hand. Water glimmered ahead on the left: it was little Loch Tarff, its charms dimmed by the weather. Keith just noticed its presence, tightened his reins, and, trotting forward on the welcome level, continued his dreams about the future.

Twenty-five yards farther, and these were brought abruptly to a close. Without the slightest warning there was a sharp report on his right, and a bullet sped in front of him, so close that it frightened his horse. Himself considerably startled too, he tried simultaneously to soothe the beast and to tug out a pistol from his holster. Meanwhile, Dougal Mackay, with great promptitude and loud Gaelic cries, was urging his more docile steed over the heather towards a boulder which he evidently suspected of harbouring the marksman.

As soon as he could get his horse under control, Keith also made over the strip of moorland, and arrived in time to see a wild, tattered, tartan-clad figure, with a musket in its hands, slide down from the top of the boulder, drop on to hands and knees among the heather and bog-myrtle, and begin to wriggle away like a snake. Major Windham levelled his pistol and fired, somewhat at random, for his horse was still plunging; and the Highlander collapsed and lay still. Keith trotted towards him; the man had already abandoned his musket and lay in a heap on his side. The Englishman was just going to dismount when shouts from Dougal Mackay, who had ridden round the boulder, stayed him. 'Do not pe going near him, sir; the man will not pe hit whateffer!' And as this statement coincided with Keith's own impression that his bullet had gone wide, he stayed in the saddle and covered the would-be assassin with his other pistol, while Mackay, who certainly did not lack courage, slid off his own horse and came running.

And it was even as Mackay had said. At the sound of the feet swishing through the heather the heap of dirty tartan lying there was suddenly, with one bound, a living figure which, leaping up dirk in hand, rushed straight, not at the dismounted orderly, but at the officer on the horse. Had Keith not had his pistol ready he could hardly have saved himself, mounted though he was, from

a deadly thrust. The man was at his horse's head when he fired.
. . . This time he did not miss; he could not. . . .

'I suppose I have blown his head to pieces,' he said next moment, with a slightly shaken laugh.

'Inteet, I will pe thinking so,' replied Mackay, on his knees in the heather. 'But it will be pest to make sure.' And he put his hand to his own dirk.

'No, no!' commanded Keith, as he bent from the saddle, for somehow the idea of stabbing a dead man, even a potential murderer, was repugnant to him. 'It is not necessary; he was killed instantly.'

There could be small doubt of that. One side of the Highlander's bearded face was all blackened by the explosion, and as he lay there, his eyes wide and fixed, the blood ran backwards through his scorched and tangled hair like a brook among waterweeds. The ball had struck high up on the brow. It came to Keith with a sense of shock that the very torn and faded philabeg which he wore was of the Cameron tartan. He was sorry. . . .

Deterred, unwillingly, from the use of his dirk, the zealous Mackay next inquired whether he should not put the cateran's body over his horse and bring him to Inverness, so that, dead or alive, he could be hanged at the Cross there as a warning.

'No. Leave him, poor devil,' said Keith, turning his horse. 'No need for that; he has paid the price already. Let him lie.' He felt curiously little resentment, and wondered at the fact.

Dougal Mackay, however, was not going to leave the musket lying too.

'*Ta gunna* – she is Sassenach,' he announced, examining it.

'Take it, then,' said Keith. 'Come, we must get on to the General's Hut before this mist grows thicker.'

So they rode away, leaving the baffled assailant staring into vacancy, his dirk still gripped in his hand, and under his head the heather in flower before its time.

Once more the road mounted; then fell by a long steep gradient. The General's Hut, a small and very unpretentious hostelry, of the kind known as a 'creel house', was at Boleskine, down on its lower levels, and before Keith reached it he could see that its outbuildings were occupied by soldiers. They were probably

Major Guthrie's detachment. Indeed, as he dismounted, a uniformed figure which he knew came round the corner of the inn, but it stopped dead on seeing him, then, with no further sign of recognition, turned abruptly and disappeared again. It was Lieutenant Paton.

So these *were* Guthrie's men, and he could hear more of Ardroy. But he would have preferred to hear it from Paton rather than from Guthrie, and wished that he had been quick enough to stop that young man.

The first person whom Keith saw when he entered the dirty little parlour was Guthrie himself – or rather, the back of him – just sitting down to table.

'Come awa', Foster, is that you?' he called out. 'Quick noo; the brose is getting cauld.' Receiving no response he turned round. 'Dod! 'tis Major Windham!'

Keith came forward perforce. 'Good evening, Major Guthrie. Yes, I am on my way back to Inverness.'

'Back frae Perth, eh?' commented Guthrie. 'By the high road this time, then, I'm thinkin'. Sit ye doun, Major, and Luckie whate'er she ca's hersel' shall bring anither cover. Ah, here comes Foster – let me present Captain Foster of ma regiment tae ye, Major Windham. Whaur's yon lang-leggit birkie of a Paton?'

'Not coming to supper, sir,' replied Captain Foster, saluting the new arrival. 'He begs you to excuse him; he has a letter to write, or he is feeling indisposed – I forget which.'

'Indeed!' said Guthrie, raising his sandy eyebrows. 'He was well eneugh and free o' correspondence a while syne. However, it's an ill wind – Ye ken the rest. Major Windham can hae his place and his meat.'

Keith sat down, with as good a grace as he could command, at the rough, clothless table. This Foster was presumably the officer whose bed he had occupied in the camp, a man more of Guthrie's stamp than of Paton's, but better mannered. Lieutenant Paton's absence, coupled with his abrupt disappearance, was significant, but why should the young man not wish to meet Major Keith Windham? Perhaps because the latter had got him into trouble after all over his 'philanthropy'.

Between the three the talk ran on general topics, and it

was not until the meal was half over that Guthrie suddenly
said:

'Weel, Major, I brocht in yer Cameron frien' after ye left.'

Keith murmured that he was glad to hear it.

'But I got little for ma pains,' continued Guthrie, pouring
himself out a glass of wine – only his second, for, to Keith's surprise, he appeared to be an abstemious man. He set down the
bottle and looked hard at the Englishman. 'But ye yersel' were
nae luckier, it seems.'

Keith returned his look. 'I am afraid that I do not understand.'

'Ye see, I ken ye went back tae the shieling yon nicht.'

'Yes, I imagined that you would discover it,' said Keith coolly.
'I trust that you received my message of apology for departing
without taking leave of you?'

'Yer message of apology!' repeated Major Guthrie. 'Ha, ha!
Unfortunately ye didn't apologize for the richt offence! Ye suld
hae apologized for stealing a march on me ahint ma back. 'Twas
a pawky notion, yon, was it no', Captain Foster?'

'I must repeat that I am completely in the dark as to your
meaning, Major Guthrie!' said Keith in growing irritation.

'Isna he the innocent man! But I forgive ye, Major – since ye
gained naething by gangin' back.'

'*Gained!*' ejaculated Keith. 'What do you mean, sir? I did not
go back to the shieling to gain anything. I went – '

'Aye, I ken what ye said ye gaed for,' interrupted Guthrie with
a wink. ''Twas devilish canny, as I said, and deceived the rebel
himsel' for a while. All yon ride in the nicht juist tae tak' him
food and dress his wounds! And when ye were there tendin' him
sae kindly ye never speired aboot Lochiel and what he kennt o'
him, and whaur the chief micht be hidin', did ye? – Never deny
it, Major, for the rebel didna when I pit it tae him!'

'You devil!' exclaimed Keith, springing up. 'What did you
say to him about me?'

Guthrie kept his seat, and pulled down Captain Foster, who,
murmuring 'Gentlemen, gentlemen!' had risen too. 'Nae need
tae be sae distrubel'd Captain Foster; I'm na. That's for them
that hae uneasy consciences. What did I say tae him? Why, I

tellt him the truth, Major Windham: why ye set such store on saving his life, and how ye thocht he might be persuaded tae "drap a hint" aboot Lochiel. Forbye he didna believe that at first.'

Keith caught his breath. 'You told him those lies ... to his face ... and he believed ...' He could get no farther.

'Lies, were they?' asked Guthrie, leaning over the table. 'Ye ne'er advised me tae bring him into camp tae "complete ma knowledge"? Eh, I hae ye there fine! Aweel, I did ma best, Major Windham; nane can dae mair. But I doot he has the laugh of us, the callant, for he tellt me naething, either by hints or ony ither gait, a' the time I had him in ma care. So I e'en sent him wi' a bit report tae Fort Augustus, and there he is the noo, as ye may have heard, if ye speired news o' him when ye came by.'

Keith had turned very white. 'I might have known that you would play some dirty trick or other!' he said, and flung straight out of the room.

Fool, unspeakable fool that he was not to have foreseen something of this kind, with a man of Guthrie's stamp! He *had* had moments of uneasiness at the thought of Ardroy's probable interview with him, but he had never anticipated anything quite so base as this. 'Take me to Lieutenant Paton at once!' he said peremptorily to the first soldier he came across.

The man led him towards a barn looming through the mist at a little distance. The door was ajar, and Keith went in, to see a dimly lit space with trusses of straw laid down in rows for the men, and at one end three horses, his own among them, with a soldier watering them. The young lieutenant, his hands behind his back, was watching the process. Keith went straight up to him.

'Can I have a word with you alone, Mr Paton?'

The young man stiffened and flushed; then, with obvious reluctance, ordered the soldier out. And when the man with his clanging buckets had left the building, Paton stood rather nervously smoothing the flank of one of the horses – not at all anxious to talk.

'Mr Paton,' said Keith without preamble, 'what devil's work went on in your camp over the prisoner from Ben Loy?' And then, at sight of the look on Paton's face, he cried out, 'Good

God, man, do you think that I had a hand in it, and is that why you would not break bread with me?'

Lieutenant Paton looked at the ground. 'I . . . indeed I found it hard to believe that you could act so, when you seemed so concerned for the prisoner, but – '

'In Heaven's name, let us have this out!' cried Keith. 'What did Major Guthrie say to Mr Cameron? He appears to have tried to make him believe an infamous thing of me – that I went back to the shieling that night merely in order to get information out of him! Surely he did not succeed in making him think so – even if he succeeded with you? . . . Answer me, if you please!'

The younger man seemed very ill at ease. 'I cannot say, sir, what Mr Cameron believed about you in the end. He certainly refused, and indignantly, to believe it at first.'

'He *cannot* have believed it!' said Keith passionately. ' "In the end"? How long, then, did Major Guthrie have him in his custody?'

'He kept him for twenty-four hours, sir – in order to see if he would make any disclosures about Lochiel.' And Lieutenant Paton added, in a very dry tone, turning away and busying himself with a horse's headstall: 'A course which it seems that you advised.'

Keith gave a sound like a groan. 'Did the Major tell Mr Cameron that also?'

Paton nodded. 'Yes, he did – and more, too: whether true or not I have no means of judging.'

Keith had the sensation that the barn, or something less material, was closing in round him. This honest boy, too – 'Look here, Mr Paton, I will be frank with you. I was so desperately afraid that Ardroy would be left to die in the shieling that I did suggest to Major Guthrie that it might be of advantage to bring him into camp, though I knew that he would have his trouble for nothing. Though I unfortunately recommended that course, I was perfectly certain that Mr Cameron would not give the slightest inkling of any knowledge that he might have.'

'No, it was plain from the beginning that he would not,' said the young man, 'and that was why . . .' He broke off. 'If Mr Cameron is a friend of yours, it is a good thing that you were not in our camp that morning ... or no, perhaps a misfortune, because you might have succeeded in stopping it sooner. I could not.'

'Succeeded in stopping what?' asked Keith. Then the inner flavour of some of Guthrie's recent words began to be apparent to him. He caught Paton by the arm. 'You surely do not mean that Major Guthrie resorted to – violent measures? It's impossible!'

Thus captured, the young soldier turned and faced him. 'Reassure yourself, sir,' he said quickly, seeing the horror and disgust on his companion's face. 'He could not carry them out; the prisoner was in no state for it. He could only threaten, and ... question.'

'He threatened to shoot him after all?'

'No, not to shoot him, to flog him.' And as Keith gave an exclamation and loosed his hold, Paton added: 'And he went very near doing it, too.'

'Threatened to *flog* him! Mr Paton, you are jesting!' said Keith incredulously. 'Flog a badly wounded prisoner, and a gentleman – a chieftain – to boot!'

'I am not jesting, sir; I wish I were. But I am thankful to say that it was not carried out. – Now, if you will excuse me, Major Windham, I must be about my duties.' His tone indicated that he would be glad to leave a distasteful subject.

But Keith made a movement to bar his passage. 'Mr Paton, forgive my insistence, but your duties must wait a little. You cannot leave the matter there! For my own sake I must know what was said to Mr Cameron. You see how nearly it concerns my honour. I implore you to try to recall everything that passed!'

Reluctantly the young man yielded. 'Very well, sir; but I had best speak to the sergeant, to ensure that we are not disturbed, for this barn is the men's quarters.'

He went out to give an order. Hardly knowing what he did, Keith turned to his horse, busy pulling hay from the rack, and looked him over to see that Mackay had rubbed him down properly. Threatened with flogging – Ewen Cameron!

Paton came back, closed the door and brought up a couple of pails, which he inverted and suggested as seats. 'You must be

tired, Major, after your long ride, and I am afraid that this will
be a bit of a sederunt.' So Keith sat down in the stall to hear
what his ill-omened suggestion had brought on the man whom
he had saved.

Chapter 2

IT appeared that Major Guthrie, on learning next morning of
Major Windham's departure on his errand of mercy, had been
not only exceedingly angry, but suspicious as well – 'or at least,'
said Paton, 'he declared that he was suspicious' – and sent off a
party almost immediately to fetch in the wounded rebel from the
shieling. About a couple of hours later they returned, carrying
him on a litter, which they deposited outside their commander's
tent, where Paton happened to be at the moment. Guthrie
immediately went out to him, and said – the narrator remembered his first words exactly – 'Well, my fine fellow, and so you
know where Lochiel is like to be skulking!' The prisoner replied
by asking whether Major Guthrie thought he should tell him, if
he did. Major Guthrie retorted, with a grin, that he knew it was
the thing to begin with a little bluster of the sort, but that they
had better get to business without wasting time. 'And he added,
sir,' said the young soldier, looking away, ' "I know that you
know; Major Windham says so." '

Keith had put his hand over his eyes. 'Yes; go on,' he said
after a moment.

'This was plainly rather a blow to Mr Cameron,' continued
Paton. 'I saw the blood rush to his face. "*What* did you say?"
he asked. The Major replied that you, sir, being a loyal subject
of King George, were just as eager to secure Lochiel as himself,
which was the reason why you had very properly stopped him
from having the prisoner shot. To that Mr Cameron replied,
short and sharp, "I don't believe it!" The Major affected to mis-
understand this, and ... well, sir, he said a good many things
incriminating you in the affair, twisting what you had perhaps
said ...'

'Try, for God's sake, to remember what those things were,' begged Keith miserably, without looking up.

The young man paused a moment, evidently trying to remember accurately.

'First, I think, he told Mr Cameron that you had said he was Cameron of Ardroy, Lochiel's cousin, and had had you as his prisoner after the affair at High Bridge, and he added, "I doubt he wanted to get even with you for that!" And to make his assertion more credible he asked Mr Cameron how otherwise he should have known who he was, since he took him for a gillie when he had him up against the shieling wall. And the Major went on to say that for the news of Mr Cameron's identity he was grateful to you, but not so grateful when he found that you had stolen a march on him by sneaking back to the shieling by night in order to get information out of the prisoner before he could. But at that Mr Cameron tried to raise himself on the litter, and burst out, "That's a lie!" And then the Major silenced him by what I can only suppose was an arrow drawn at a venture, since you . . . I don't suppose that you . . .' Paton began to stumble.

'Let me have it!' said Keith, looking up this time.

'He said, "And so he never speired about Lochiel . . . where he was . . . if yu kenned where he was?" '

Keith stared at the narrator half dazed. 'How did he know that . . . he *could* not have known it!'

'As I say, it seemed to silence Mr Cameron altogether,' continued Paton, glancing at him with a sort of pity. 'He looked quite dizzy as he dropped back on the litter. But the Major laughed. And he went on, in that bantering way he has: "I hope you did not tell him, for I want you to tell *me*. Did you tell him?" The rebel took no notice of this question; he had shut his eyes. It was as I looked at him then, sir, and saw the effect which that question had had on him, that I first began, I confess, to have doubts of your good faith.'

'You had cause,' answered Keith with a groan. 'I did ask him about Lochiel – in all innocence. My God, what he must think of me!' He took his head between his hands. 'Go on!'

'Finding that Mr Cameron was silent,' resumed Paton, 'Major Guthrie went nearer and said something, I do not exactly re-

member what, about dropping a hint inadvertently with regard
to Lochiel's hiding-place, which it was easy to do, he said, and
which he should give the prisoner every opportunity of doing,
keeping him there, indeed, until he did. He kept harping for
awhile on this question of dropping a hint, and he brought you
even into that, for he said that it was your suggestion, that you
had advised him to bring the rebel into camp and watch him
well for that purpose. . . . And from what you have just told me,
sir, it seems that that was true.'

Paton paused; but Keith, his head between his hands, said
nothing; he was beyond it. This was what came of doing evil in
order to accomplish good!

'Still Mr Cameron took no notice,' pursued Paton, 'even
when the Major went on to say in so many words that you had
betrayed him – Mr Cameron – and had then ridden off, leaving
him the dirty work to do. Then he changed his tone, and said:
"But I shall not flinch from it; 'tis my duty. Do you know, Mr
Cameron of Ardroy, how we deal with folk that have valuable
information and will not part with it?" At that the prisoner did
open his eyes, and said with a good deal of contempt that, from
what he had seen of the Major, he could very well guess.

'The Major at that bent over him and gripped him by the
nearer arm. He may not have observed that it was bandaged – I
cannot say – and repeated: "Ah, you can quite imagine, can you?
D'you think you'll like it?" Mr Cameron did not answer; perhaps he could not, for he was biting his lip, and I saw the sweat
come out on his brow. Major Guthrie let go and stood up again,
and said that a flogging with belts would soon loosen his tongue;
and that did rouse Mr Cameron, for he coloured hotly and said
he thought the Major forgot that he was a gentleman. But the
Major replied with a chuckle that he looked so little like one at
present that it was easy to assume that he was not. Then he asked
him whether he intended to save himself from this unpleasant experience, as he easily could do; Mr Cameron's look was sufficient
answer to that. So, to my horror, the Major sent for the drummers
and ordered a tent to be struck, in order to have the pole available
to tie him up to.'

'This is intolerable!' exclaimed Keith, starting up. 'Stop! I had rather not – ' He pulled himself together. 'No, I have got to hear it. Go on!'

'I assure you that I did not enjoy it,' said the young officer, 'for *I* thought that the matter was going through. They lifted Mr Cameron off the litter; he could not stand, it appeared, owing to the wound in his thigh, and the men were obliged to support him. But the Major said to him that he would not be able to fall this time, as he had done yesterday, because we had ropes here. . . . I myself, who would willingly have interfered before, sir, had there been any chance of being listened to, now took the Major by the arm and told him plainly that he would kill the prisoner if he was so barbarous as to have him flogged in his present condition. But he shook me off, and said, when everything was ready (except Mr Cameron himself, who was still held up there, facing him, as white as you please, but perfectly unyielding and defiant): "Now, before you make acquaintance with His Majesty's leather, will you tell me what you know about Lochiel?" And the rebel, with his eyes blazing, said, in a sudden access of fury: "Not if you cut me to pieces!"

'Well, sir, though I am convinced that the Major was *not* acting a part and merely threatening, but that he really meant to go through with the horrid business, I think it must have come to him then that, if he did, he would have Mr Cameron dead on his hands, as I had warned him, and there would be an end to that source of information. (It is possible, too, that he thought he might be called to account for it afterwards.) And even the men were looking uneasy and murmuring a little. So he said that he would postpone the flogging until the afternoon. He had the prisoner carried into his own tent, not much, I fear, the better for this scene; and in his tent Mr Cameron was all the rest of the day and the night. I do not know what passed in there, for whenever I made an effort to go in, I was stopped; but I am sure the Major questioned him pretty continuously. He still spoke of the flogging taking place, but it never did. Next morning I was not surprised to hear that the prisoner seemed worse, and in a fever, so that the Major resolved to be rid of him, and sent him to Fort Augustus. I was heartily glad, for his own sake, to see Mr Cameron taken away. And at Fort Augustus he must have had care, or he would not be alive now, which he is, for I asked news of him yesterday, as we came by. But that I should be ashamed to meet him, I would fain have seen him to ask his pardon.'

Paton's voice ceased; in the silence one of the horses near them stamped and blew out its nostrils. Keith, standing there very still, released his own tightly gripped elbows.

'Mr Paton, I thank you most heartily for your frankness. I, too, am ashamed – with much more cause than you, I think – yet I am going back to Fort Augustus to see Mr Cameron.'

'Back to Fort Augustus – tonight!' said Paton, rather startled.

'Yes, tonight. My horse,' he glanced at that animal, 'can still carry me so far – a matter of ten or twelve miles, is it not? I intended to lie here tonight, and to start about six o'clock tomorrow morning for Inverness. I shall lie at Fort Augustus instead, and start proportionately earlier, that is all. I must find my orderly at once, but I shall not take him back with me.'

Paton said no more, and they went out of the barn together, by which evacuation the waiting soldiers outside, huddled against its wall for shelter, were enabled to enter their sleeping-place. While the surprised Mackay resaddled his officer's horse, Keith strode back to the inn parlour. But just outside, where he could hear Guthrie's voice in conversation, he paused. If he meant to get back to Fort Augustus, he must not enter Guthrie's presence first; the fury and resentment which possessed him could have but one result – a quarrel with the Lowlander. Moreover, Lieutenant Paton might suffer for his communicativeness. Clenching his hands, Keith turned away from temptation.

But there was one last question to ask.

'Mr Paton,' he said in a low voice as his horse was brought towards him, 'have you any notion why Major Guthrie hates me so, for it is plain that he does?'

And to his surprise the young man answered, in a voice equally low:

'I have a very good notion why, sir. He had had great hopes of securing that post on General Hawley's staff which was eventually given to you. Your obtaining it was a very sore point with him, because he thought his claims superior to those of an officer who – who ...' Paton hesitated.

'Yes, I understand,' said Keith, his mouth tightening. 'Who had lost one of the companies at High Bridge.' Guthrie's sneers on that fatal ride were explained now. 'So that was my offence!' he said under his breath, as he swung into the saddle. 'And this is how he has avenged himself!'

The wind had risen greatly in the last hour, and the rain was no longer a fine, almost caressing, drizzle, it beat upon the rider as he urged his horse back along the lower levels with a vehemence which predicted real difficulty in proceeding when he should reach the higher. But he did not notice it.

There could not be the slightest doubt that Ewen Cameron must believe him to have acted in a manner unspeakably treacherous and vile. From the deadly success of Guthrie's 'arrow at a venture', as Paton had rightly called it, he must even think that his visitor had gone straight back from tending him in the shieling to Guthrie's camp with the news that he had succeeded in gaining the fugitive's confidence, and had ascertained that he did know of Lochiel's hiding-place. It was an absolutely intolerable thought, and nothing, nothing should stop him until he had seen Ardroy and assured him of his innocence – neither the rising storm nor fatigue, nor the possible danger in riding thus alone at night (though to that, despite the afternoon's attempt on his life, he gave scarcely a thought), nor Lord Albemarle's dispatch. It was a mercy that this contained, as he knew, nothing of urgency, nothing but a mere expression of compliments, and that he could therefore retrace his steps consistently with his military obligations. In any case, the letter would reach Inverness no later than if he had spent the night at the General's Hut, so on that score at least his mind was at rest.

It was certainly the only score on which it was. The more Keith thought of the situation, the more it horrified him. Why, good God, Ardroy might even imagine that the infamous proposal of flogging, which turned him hot to think of, came from *him*! Guthrie was evidently quite capable of stating that it had, and though Paton had not reported him as having done so in his hearing, who knew what had been said, what had been done, during the rest of the twenty-four hours in Guthrie's tent? He was utterly without scruple, and Ardroy completely helpless.

Yet even now Keith could hardly blame himself for his total absence of suspicion that Guthrie might be tempted to do more than question his prisoner ... rather closely perhaps. No, he told himself again and again, he could not have guessed to what he was delivering up Ardroy. A prisoner-of-war – above all, an officer – in a Christian country and a civilized century, stood in no danger of such proceedings. It was true that there had been barbarity after the battle, barbarity which had sickened him, but there had never been any suggestion of deliberately torturing prisoners in order to extract information. (For Major Lockhart of Cholmondeley's regiment, Captain Carolina Scott of Guise's, and Captain Ferguson of H.M.S. *Furness* – all Scots, too – had still to win their spurs in this field.)

Keith was up on the higher levels now, where the wind was really savage, and the rain stung like missiles. It seemed as though the elements desired to oppose his return. But his thoughts ran ahead of him to Fort Augustus. Would there be difficulty in getting access to the prisoner? There might be some, but an officer on Hawley's staff, riding on the Duke's business, would be hard to gainsay. If necessary he should approach the Earl of Loudoun himself. And in what state should he find Ardroy? What sort of a captivity had been his now that he was out of that scoundrel Guthrie's clutches? Remembrances of Inverness, very sinister remembrances, kept floating into his mind. No, it would be different here; and, as Paton had pointed out, they must have taken good care of the Highlander, or he would hardly be alive now, judging from his state a week ago – a state which must have been, which evidently had been, rendered even more precarious by Guthrie's damnable proceedings. On Guthrie himself he hardly dared allow his mind to dwell; but there could not be another like him at Fort Augustus!

And when he had got access to Ardroy? Surely it would not be difficult to convince him that it was Major Guthrie's almost incredible spite and jealousy which had wrought this mischief, that nothing in the world had been farther from his own thoughts than the belief that Ewen would betray his Chief? Yes, but unfortunately, though he could deny everything else (save the mere fact of having been forced to establish Ardroy's identity) he could not deny that most unlucky suggestion to which, in desperation, he had been reduced on the hillside. Oh, if only he had not shirked telling Ewen Cameron of it that night in the shieling! Better, far better, to have faced a measure of shame on that occasion, than to have left in Major Guthrie's hands a weapon capable of working this havoc!

For Guthrie, it was clear, had, in his calculated spite, struck at him through Ewen, and at Ewen through him. He had evidently *wished* the Highlander to believe himself betrayed. Did he then think the ties between them so close, when they were only . . . What were they then? Was it really only philanthropy, as Keith had assured himself a few hours ago, which had sent him back to the shieling that night? It was certainly not philanthropy which was driving him to Fort Augustus now.

At nine o'clock, wet and buffeted, he was back in the lines of Loudoun's camp, still humming with life. Mentioning that he was on the staff, he asked, as he had asked that afternoon, to see the officer in charge of prisoners there. Once again there was an obstacle; this time it appeared that the officer, a certain Captain Greening, was closeted with Lord Loudoun, who was very busy, and not to be disturbed save for a matter of great importance.

Keith still retained enough sense of proportion to realize that private inquiry after the well-being of a rebel prisoner was not likely to wear that aspect in the eyes of Cope's late adjutant-general. However, perhaps he could arrive at seeing Ardroy without the consent of Captain Greening, so he said to his informant, the officer of the guard:

'I wish to see a certain Mr Ewen Cameron of Ardroy, who lies here a prisoner. He was taken last week not far from the Corryarrick Pass. Do you think this would be possible without deranging Captain Greening?'

'Cameron of Ardroy?' said the lieutenant with an accent of enlightenment. 'Oh, have you come from Inverness about the question of Lochiel's capture, sir? Then you will be glad to hear that we have got the necessary information at last.'

Keith's heart gave a great twist – foolishly, surely! 'Ah, from whom?'

'Why, from him – from Cameron of Ardroy, naturally. We knew that he had it.'

This time Keith's heart did not twist – it seemed to die in his breast. 'Got it from him – from *him*!' he faltered with cold lips. 'When?'

'Last night, I believe,' answered the lieutenant carelessly, pulling his cloak closer to him. 'But I fear that I cannot give you permission to visit him, sir, and as Captain Greening is – '

But to his surprise the staff officer was gripping him hard by the arm. 'Tell me, in God's name, what means you used? Ardroy would never – ' He seemed unable to finish.

'Means? I really don't know,' replied the lieutenant, still more surprised. 'I should be obliged if you would let go my arm, sir! I have nothing to do with the prisoners. Perhaps this Cameron was promised his liberty or something of the sort – but on my soul I don't know ... or care,' he muttered under his breath, rubbing his arm as Keith released it.

'Promised!' cried Keith in a tempest of fury and horror. 'No, he has been tortured into it! – that is the only possible explanation of his giving that information – if it be true that he has done so. My God, what has this campaign reduced men to! Take me to Lord Loudoun at once!'

'I cannot, sir,' protested the lieutenant. 'He has given the strictest orders – '

'Take me to him at once,' repeated Keith in a dangerous voice; and the young officer, probably thinking that the safest way to deal with a superior who seemed off his balance was to humour him, shrugged his shoulders, and began to lead him in the rain between the tents.

Last night! That meant, then, that for nearly a week they had been trying ... and had succeeded at last in wresting the secret from a man badly wounded, ill from starvation, and now, perhaps, dying – dying as much of a broken heart as from their usage of him. It was with that unbearable picture of Ewen Cameron in his mind that after parleys with sentries, of which he heard nothing, Keith stepped into the Earl of Loudoun's presence without any clear idea of what he was going to do there.

He found himself in a large, well-furnished tent, with a brazier

209

burning in one corner, and, round a table, several officers of various ranks (most of them, like the Earl himself, wearing tartan), was announced as an officer of the staff from Inverness, and, duly saluting, gave his name and regiment.

The Earl of Loudoun – more Lowland Scot than Highlander in his appearance – looked less annoyed at the interruption than might have been expected; indeed his air showed that he supposed the intruder to be the bearer of some tidings of importance from headquarters.

'You are on His Royal Highness's staff, Major Windham?' he asked.

'On General Hawley's, my Lord,' replied Keith. 'I am on my way back to Inverness from Perth, and I have ventured to ask for this interview because – '

'You have not a dispatch for me from the Duke, then – or from General Hawley?'

'No, my Lord. I have but seized this opportunity of appealing to your Lordship on behalf of a prisoner here' – the Earl's homely, blunt-featured face changed – 'who, if he has really made any disclosures, can only have done so under violent measures, taken unknown to your Lordship, and I – '

'What is all this about a prisoner?' interrupted Loudoun, frowning. 'You mean to say, Major Windham, that you are here on a purely private matter, when I especially gave orders – Who admitted you to me under false pretences?'

But the officer of the guard had discreetly vanished.

'Is it a purely private matter, my Lord,' retorted Keith hotly, 'that a badly wounded Highland gentleman should be tortured into giving information against his own Chief? It seems to me a matter affecting the good name of the whole army. I only hope that I have been misinformed, and that no such disclosures have been dragged from him.'

'Have you come here, sir,' asked Lord Loudoun with increasing displeasure, 'and on no one's authority but your own, to dictate to me on the treatment of prisoners?'

'No, indeed, my Lord,' replied Keith, making an effort to be properly deferential. 'I have come, on the contrary, because I feel sure that your Lordship – '

'If you want news of any prisoner,' interrupted his Lordship with a wave of the hand, 'you must wait until Captain Greening here is at liberty. Meanwhile you will perhaps have the goodness to remember that I only marched in to Fort Augustus this morning, and am still so pressed with business that I see small chance of sleep tonight, if I am to be interrupted in this manner.'

It was a dismissal: less harsh than at one moment had seemed likely, but proving to Keith that he had gained nothing. He tried another tack.

'My Lord, give me permission then, I implore you, to visit the prisoner in question, Mr Ewen Cameron of Ardroy.'

Loudoun's eyebrows went up. 'Is there anyone of that name confined here, Captain Greening?' he asked in an annoyed voice, turning to a fair, rather womanish-looking young man on his left.

Captain Greening smiled a peculiar little smile. 'Oh, yes, my Lord; he has been here nearly a week. Major Windham has already made inquiries for him once today, so I hear – when he passed on his way to Inverness this afternoon. I was out of camp at the time.'

'What!' exclaimed the Earl, looking from the officer to Keith in astonishment. 'Major Windham has been through Fort Augustus once already today? This is very singular! Instead of *your* questioning *me*, Major Windham, I will ask you to explain your own conduct. Kindly tell me on what errand you originally left headquarters?'

Keith saw a possible gulf opening for himself now. But he was too passionately indignant to care much. 'I have been to Perth, my Lord, with a dispatch from His Royal Highness to Lord Albemarle. I was on my way back to Inverness today when I heard that Cameron of Ardroy –'

'Leave Cameron of Ardroy out of it, if you please!' said Lord Loudoun in growing anger. 'What I want, Major Windham, is some explanation of your own extraordinary behaviour. I gather that you are now on your way back from Perth. Are you carrying dispatches from Lord Albemarle to His Royal Highness, or are you empty-handed?'

'I have a letter, of no particular moment, from Lord Albemarle to the Duke,' replied Keith more warily.

'You have, at any rate, a dispatch, sir. You have passed this place already on your way to Inverness, carrying it. Some hours later you are back again, making fresh inquiries about a rebel. Had you confided your dispatch to another hand in the interval?'

'No, my Lord,' confessed Keith. 'Knowing that the matter was not urgent, and that it was impossible for me to reach Inverness tonight, I resolved to lie at the General's Hut. There I heard something which determined me to have more reliable news of Mr Cameron of Ardroy, to whom I owe it that I am alive at all today. Instead of going to bed at the General's Hut I rode back here, and whether I start from Boleskine at six or from Fort Augustus at half past four, Lord Albemarle's letter will reach His Royal Highness's hands at exactly the same hour.'

'You seem to have a strangely easy idea of your military duties, Major Windham,' commented Lord Loudoun, drumming on the table. 'May I ask how long you have borne His Majesty's commission?'

'Twelve years,' answered Keith curtly.

'And in all those years you have not learnt the sacredness of a dispatch! You are entrusted with one to the Commander-in-Chief, and you take upon yourself to turn back in order to assure yourself of the welfare of a rebel prisoner! – Is it true that this man has made a disclosure?' he asked suddenly of Captain Greening.

'Quite true, my Lord,' responded the fair young officer. 'I have notes of it here; it was one of the matters which I desired to bring to your Lordship's notice. It relates to Lochiel's hiding-place near Loch Arkaig, and will prove of the greatest service in your Lordship's future operations.'

At that reply all thoughts of his own situation abandoned Keith; he was caught up again in a wave of fury and shame. 'My God!' he cried, striding forward, his eyes fixed on Captain Greening, 'are there devils here too? You have tortured him into it ... never deny it, I'll not believe you! As well be in a camp of Red Indians or African savages! Inverness was bad enough, with its prisons stuffed with purposely neglected wounded; then that man Guthrie, and now –'

Lord Loudoun sprang up, very threatening of aspect. 'Major

Windham, may I ask you to remember where you are! I'll not be spoken to in such a manner!'

'I was not addressing you, my Lord,' said Keith fiercely. 'I know that you only reached Fort Augustus this morning. You are not responsible for what has been going on – God knows what it was – before you came. But this officer here –'

'Be silent, sir!' shouted the Earl of Loudoun. 'Neither will I have aspersions cast on officers now under my command . . . and by a member of General Hawley's staff, too! Are your own hands so clean, pray? You do not deserve that I should reply to your insinuations, but – Captain Greening, *was* this information got from the Cameron prisoner by unlawful means?'

'No, my Lord, I assure you that it was not. He gave it . . . voluntarily.' But again there was that little smile.

'There, you hear, sir!' said the Earl. 'Your charges –'

'I don't believe it,' said Keith in the same moment. 'I will not believe it until I hear it from Ardroy himself!'

And at that Lord Loudoun completely lost his temper. 'God's name, am I to suffer you to browbeat me in my own tent? – you, who have just behaved in a manner unpardonable in a soldier! Major Windham, I place you under arrest for insubordination. You will kindly give up your sword!'

It was as if a douche of cold water had descended on Keith's head. His left hand went to his sword-hilt. 'Insubordination, my Lord? No, I protest!'

'Very well, it shall be for neglect of duty, then,' said the Earl, still very angry. 'Lord Albemarle's dispatch is in truth not safe with a man who can go twenty miles out of his way while carrying it. I shall send it on by one of my own aides-de-camp tonight. Give it up at once, if you do not wish to be searched. Captain Munro, call a guard!'

Like rain upon a bonfire, the cold douche had, after a temporary extinction, only inflamed Keith Windham's rage. He unhooked his sword, scabbard and all, and flung it at Loudoun's feet, saying that he was glad to be rid of it. By this time – seeing too that the falling weapon had nearly caught his Lordship on the toes – every officer in the tent was rushing towards him. 'Reassure yourselves, gentlemen,' said Keith, laughing angrily, and, opening his uniform, took out Lord Albemarle's dispatch and tendered it to the nearest. Then, without more ado, he followed the guard out into the rain, his last memory, as he left the lighted tent, not of Lord Loudoun's affronted, angry face, but of Captain Greening's, with that sly, secretly amused smile round his girlish mouth.

Chapter 3

THE early morning bugle, close at hand, woke Keith Windham with a start. He had had little sleep during the night, and was all the deeper buried now. Where was he? He stared round the tent – an unfamiliar one. Then he remembered.

And all that endless day he sat in his canvas prison and did little else save remember. For the first time in his life he was in the midst of camp routine without a share in it – with no right to a share in it. No sword hung upon the tent-pole, and a sentry paced outside whose business was not to keep intruders out, but *him* in.

Had he not still been sustained by rage, he might have felt more dejection than he did. The rage was not against Lord Loudoun, to whose severity he could not deny some justification, nor was it on his own account; it was against the effeminate Captain Greening and other persons unknown. Not for a moment did he believe that officer's half-sniggering asseveration of voluntary betrayal on the part of Ewen Cameron . . . though at times the other alternative haunted him so horribly that he almost wished he could believe it. Far better to have let Ardroy go down riddled by bullets on the mountainside than to have saved him for agony and dishonour; far better had he *not* come upon him in time!

And where *was* Ardroy? Unable to make personal investigations, Keith could not well ask the soldier who brought him his meals. And, even if he discovered, even if he were allowed an interview with the prisoner – very improbable now – was he so sure that he himself wanted it? Could he bear to see the Highlander again, in the state which must be his by now?

His own plight seemed negligible in comparison. He thought

of it, indeed, but only with a sort of dull wonder. Up till now his own advancement had been for him the one star in a grey heaven. Now the heaven was black and there was no star at all.

A rainy yellow sunset was smearing the sky when the flap of the tent was pulled aside and an officer came in – a very stiff young aide-de-camp.

'I am to inform you, sir,' he said, 'that as this tent is required tonight a room has been prepared for you in the fort. And Major-General Lord Loudoun supposes that rather than be marched through the camp under escort, you will agree to make no attempt to escape *en route*, in which case I am to conduct you there now myself.'

'His Lordship is extremely considerate,' replied Keith. 'I am only surprised that he is willing to rely on my word. But no doubt he is aware that I should hardly better my situation by deserting.'

'Then if you will kindly follow me,' said the aide-de-camp still more stiffly, 'I will lead you to the fort.'

But, for all his own sarcastic words, for all the absence of an escort, Keith did not enjoy that short journey very much. Everyone whom they met, either among the tents or on the brief stretch of muddy road, must know why he went thus without a sword, and whither he was going; and it was with some instinct of avoiding their scrutiny that he tried to lag behind two lieutenants of independent companies who were strolling ahead of him deep in talk. It was impossible, however, not to overtake them in the end; and, as he and his escort drew nearer, scraps of their conversation floated backwards to the Englishman's ears, bearing, so he thought, the word 'Cameron'. Instantly he strained his ears to catch more; perhaps they were discussing Ardroy. As he drew still nearer he found that he was mistaken, but that one officer must be concluding an account of his experiences in a scouting party from which he had recently returned.

'. . . The same everywhere by Loch Lochy; and there's not a doubt the rebels are much more numerous in that neighbourhood than we had any notion of – Camerons and MacDonalds, too. 'Tis thought they even contemplate making a stand in a few days' time. His Lordship will be sending out a fresh reconnaissance . . .'

Here they passed the speaker, and the rest was lost; but what he had heard did not particularly interest Major Windham. Only one Cameron was in his mind at present.

And now they were at the shell of the fort, where the remains of the burnt-out buildings within the enceinte hardly looked as if they could afford any accommodation at all.

'I suppose,' said Keith carelessly to his guide, 'that the rebel prisoners, if you have any, are confined here?'

'Yes. But you must not think, sir,' explained the ever-correct aide-de-camp, 'that Lord Loudoun has any wish to put your case on a level with theirs. We are indeed short of tents, and you will not, I believe, find the room assigned to you in the fort any less comfortable.'

Keith thanked him for the assurance, but he was not really listening. Ewen Cameron was somewhere in this half-ruined enclosure.

His new quarters turned out to be bare, but not more so, certainly, than the tent. In the night, tossing on the camp bed, he made up his mind that if it proved impossible to obtain access to Ardroy in person, he would at least contrive to get a letter smuggled in to him somehow. Surely he could find a venal sentry or gaoler. He wondered what his own custodian was like, for on arrival, being much absorbed in his own thoughts, he had only received an impression of someone stout and middle-aged.

Morning and breakfast revealed him; a sergeant who might have been a well-to-do sufferer from gout, so painfully did he hobble in with the meal. Talkative upon encouragement, and apologetic for his bodily shortcomings, he explained that his lameness was due to a wound in the foot received when Fort Augustus was besieged by the Highlanders, he being a sergeant of Guise's regiment, three companies of which then held it. When they surrendered and marched out, he was left behind. 'And though I looked to have my throat cut, sir, by the wild MacDonalds and what not, I was very well treated, and my wound cared for. Is this what you wish for breakfast, sir?'

'I am not in a position to exercise much choice,' said Keith. 'You know that Lord Loudoun has put me under arrest?'

The stout sergeant seemed shocked at this blunt reference to an

216

unfortunate fact. 'If I may presume on your being English, sir, same as I am myself – '

'You may,' replied Keith.

'I would say, sir, that it don't seem right that a Scotchman should be able – ' But there he stopped, aware no doubt that he was about to make a remark even blunter.

Keith could not help smiling. 'I think, my friend, that we had better not pursue that subject. May I ask whether it is by a delicate attention of the authorities that you have been detailed to wait upon me?'

'No, sir; I only come to the fort yesterday, the corporal that was here before having gone off duty sick; and me not being capable of much at present with this foot, I was told off in his place.'

'Are the ordinary prisoners – the rebels, I mean – in your charge?'

'Yes, sir, so I find; though there's only a few, picked up in the last week. Them's in the rooms below, the dungeons as we call 'em – all but a young man as has been kept by himself at the top of this very building; he's been ill, I understand.'

Small doubt who that was. 'You have seen this young man already, I suppose, sergeant,' asked Keith, making no attempt to begin his breakfast. 'How did he seem? I am interested in him.'

'Indeed, sir! Well, he looks in but a poor way, and seems very melancholy like.'

'You do not know . . . you have not heard – anything particular about his previous treatment?' asked Keith, his heart suddenly beating hard. 'You have not heard, for instance, that . . . that forcible measures have been used to wring certain information out of him?'

'Lord, no, sir! Have they so? Yes, 'tis true he looks as though something of the sort might have happened to him, but I put it down to his having been ill with his wound.'

Keith had turned away his face. 'Do you mean,' he said after a moment, 'that he is actually in this very corner of the fort?'

'Yes, sir; up a-top of you, as it were. 'Tis the least damaged portion, and even at that there's some holes in it. You know them

Highlanders used near twenty barrels of powder a-blowing of this place up? – Have you all you want, sir?'

'By the way,' said Keith, as his attendant was hobbling out, 'do not tell the young man – Mr Cameron of Ardroy – that I was asking about him.'

'No, sir, I won't mention it. Mr Cameron, is that his name now? Why, 'twas a Dr Cameron dressed my foot; a very kind gentleman he was, too.'

Keith's breakfast was totally cold before he began it, and when the sergeant appeared again he opened his campaign at once. His guardian proved much less obdurate than he had feared. Obdurate indeed he was not; it was quite natural caution on his own behalf which withheld him from acceding sooner to Major Windham's request to be taken up to see the rebel prisoner 'up a-top of him'. It was fortunate for Keith's case that Sergeant Mullins was unaware of the close connexion between that prisoner and the English Major's arrest; he believed the latter to be suffering merely for hot words to General Lord Loudoun, cause unknown. The fact of Keith's being a fellow-countryman went for something, as did also the remembrance of the Highlanders' good treatment of himself. Finally he yielded, on condition that he chose his own time for letting the sequestered officer out of his room, and that Major Windham gave him his word of honour not to take any steps to help the rebel to escape. Keith promised without difficulty that he would not even speak of such a thing; it was the past, and not the future, which was more likely to engage his tongue.

So about six o'clock in the evening he followed his limping guide up the stair and found himself standing, with real dread in his heart, outside a door which the sergeant unlocked, saying to an unseen occupant.

'I have brought someone to see you, Mr Cameron.'

The room was light and airy – rather too airy, for one wall had in it a good-sized breach, across which a piece of canvas had been stretched in an attempt to keep out rain and wind. Facing the door was a semicircular embrasure pierced with three narrow windows, and having a stone seat running round it. And on the floor of this embrasure, on some sort of a pallet, with his back propped against the seat, his legs stretched out in front of him, and his eyes fixed on the slit of window opposite him (though from his position on the floor he could not have seen anything but a strip of sky) Ewen Cameron was sitting motionless. He did not turn his head or even move his eyes when the door opened and closed again; and Keith stood equally motionless, staring at a haggard and unshaven profile which he found difficulty in recognizing.

At last he took a few steps forward. Ewen turned his head indifferently ... and then was as suddenly frozen as one who looks on Medusa. There was a long shivering pause.

'Why are you here ... *Judas*?'

Half prepared though he was, Keith felt slashed across the face. He caught his breath.

'If I were that, I should not be here,' he answered unsteadily. 'I have come ... I came directly I had news of you, to explain ... to put right if I could ...' But the words died on his lips; it seemed a mockery to talk of putting anything right now.

'To *explain*!' repeated Ewen with an indescribable intonation. 'To explain why you told your confederate Major Guthrie everything you knew about me, to explain why you came back that night and fooled me, why you urged him to tear from me what I knew, having first made sure that I knew it – it needs no explanation! You wanted to pay off old scores – Edinburgh, Loch Oich side. Be content, you have done it – you have more than done it!'

'Ardroy, no, no, as God's my witness,' struck in Keith desperately, 'I had no such thought!' But he was not heeded, for Ewen tore on hoarsely:

'Since you desired so greatly to be even with me for a moment of triumph, could you not have let me be shot, and watched it? Or was that not sufficient for you, because I did not know that you were there? ... Oh, if God would but give me back that moment against the shieling wall, and allow it to finish as it was meant to! Then I should not be today what you have made me – a worse traitor than you are yourself!'

After that there was silence. What use in talking of his good faith and his charitable intentions when they had resulted in this!

219

For it was true then – Ardroy *had* given the information. Indeed, the fact was written on his haunted face.

But at last Keith said, in a scarcely audible voice and with his eyes on the floor: 'What did they . . . do to you?'

There was no answer, and, looking up, he saw that the wounded man's outburst had exhausted him; breathing fast, he had put his head back against the edge of the seat behind him, and his eyes were half shut. His appearance was so ghastly that Keith went forward and seized a bowl of water from the floor beside him.

But a shaking hand came up to keep him off, and he hesitated. 'What, are you trying to act *that night* over again?' asked Ewen bitterly. And Keith stood there helpless, his fingers tightening on the bowl. Was this anguished hostility utterly to defeat him?

The Highlander looked as if he had not slept for nights and nights; his eyes, naturally rather deep-set, were fearfully sunk, and glittered with a feverish brilliance. All his courtesy, all his self-command, his usual rather gentle address, every quality which Keith had observed and carelessly admired in him, seemed obliterated by the event which had brought him almost to breaking-point. 'Will you not go?' he gasped out, clenching his hands: 'Will you not go, now that you are satisfied?'

Keith put down the bowl; the action seemed symbolic. 'Ardroy, if you would only listen for a moment!' he pleaded. 'Indeed it is not as you think! I never betrayed you – I would as soon betray my own brother! There has been a horrible – '

'Why must I endure this, too, after all the rest?' broke out Ewen violently. 'You cannot make a fool of me again, Major Windham! Have a little pity at the last, and leave me!'

'No! For your own sake you *must* hear me!' urged Keith. 'It is Major Guthrie who is respon—'

But Ewen Cameron, with a face like stone (save that no stone image ever had eyes like that), had put his hands over his ears.

It was hopeless then! Baffled, Keith slowly turned and went to the door. He had wrecked his own career to no purpose. . . . But it was not of that catastrophe which he thought as, having rapped to be let out, he stood there with bent head. He was not even conscious of resentment at the more than taunts which had been flung at him, for it was he who had brought the man who uttered them to this pass.

He knocked again, louder; but the sergeant must have gone away, possibly to keep watch below. It came to Keith dimly, like a shape seen through fog, that Ardroy and he had once before been locked in together. ... Then he was aware that the half-prostrate man on the floor had moved a little, that he was leaning on his left hand, and that those glittering blue eyes were on him again.

'Cannot you get out?' There was impatience in the icy voice.

'No, for I also am locked in,' answered Keith very low.

'You – the informer!'

Keith swallowed hard. 'I am a prisoner ... like you.' But the words would hardly come.

'Why?'

'For neglect of duty,' replied Keith wearily. 'For turning back while carrying a dispatch.'

'So you cannot even serve your own side faithfully!' observed Ewen with contempt.

Keith turned a little whiter and gripped the handle of the locked door. For an instant the flame of his hot temper flickered, only to subside among the ashes. 'No,' he answered after a moment; 'no, so it seems. I have disgraced myself, as well as ruining you. ... The gaoler must have gone away, I am afraid, and I cannot relieve you of my presence until he returns.'

'It is of no moment,' replied Ewen coldly, and he shifted himself a trifle so as to look at his visitor no longer, and propped his head on his clenched fist. The plaid in which he was partly wrapped had slipped from his shoulders when he put his hands up to his ears, and there was now nothing to hide his torn and dirty shirt – which, after all, was only of a piece with the general neglect of his person. The only evidence of care or cleanliness was the fresh bandage round his sword-arm. ... 'So that has been recently dressed,' thought Keith, 'and he can use it. ... That must be the plaid which I spread over him in the shieling. He was a very different man then. ...'

He was surprised, after another appreciable silence, to find himself being addressed again, though not looked at.

'Why did you turn back?'

'What is the use of telling you – you will not believe me! Indeed I wonder whether you believe me when I say that I am under arrest; that might be a lie also.'

He had at least succeeded in gaining Ardroy's attention, for the latter dropped his arm and once again looked across the room at him. 'I should like to know why you turned back?' he repeated, without comment on the reply which he had drawn forth.

Yes, that at all events he should hear! Keith left the door, where there was no sound of Sergeant Mullins's approach.

'Cannot you guess? I came because of you – because, a dozen miles beyond here, on my way back to Inverness, I learnt both of the abominable way in which you had been treated in Guthrie's camp, and of the manner in which that scoundrel had twisted my words, and my actions, in order to misrepresent me to you. It was the night before last; it was late, but I resaddled and came back at once – neglecting my duty, Lord Loudoun said. I rode back in the greatest haste to see you, I was in such apprehension about you. When I got here I heard that you – ' Ewen drew his breath sharply, and the sentence was not finished. 'I insisted on seeing Lord Loudoun at once, and when I was told that you had . . . had made disclosures of your own free will, I demanded to see you. I said that I would never believe that, unless you told me so yourself. Then there was a scene of some violence, and I had to give up my sword and my dispatch – and I suppose that in a few days my commission will go the same road. Should I have acted so – so madly against my own interest, if I had been what you think me? . . . But I am forgetting; you will say that this is false also, though every officer in Fort Augustus should tell you that it is true!'

Ewen had put his head down on his updrawn right knee. A shaft of sunlight, striking through one of the narrow windows, fell across its auburn disorder. And, looking with something more painful than pity at the utter desolation of his aspect, Keith thought that life could scarcely hold anything more terrible for a gallant man than to feel himself at once a traitor and betrayed. But betrayed he had not been! If only he could be brought to see that!

222

And perhaps Ewen was being brought to it, for from his huddled figure there came a long sigh, and, after another silence, words which sounded as though they were wrung from his very heart:

'I wish to God that I *could* trust you again!'

Chapter 4

KEITH ventured nearer. 'Why is it so difficult? You trusted me that night.' His own voice was not much less moved than the Highlander's. 'I am not changed: it is circumstances which have brought about this horrible situation.'

The head stirred, but did not raise itself. 'Yes ... that night I thought you ... generous, kind, charitable beyond anything that could be imagined. ... It was not what I should have expected from you. Afterwards I saw what a simpleton I was, to think you could have done all that for me without some very good reason ... for by that time next day I had learnt what that reason was.'

'Is it fair, is it just,' pleaded Keith, 'to believe what a brute, and my enemy, said of me behind my back, rather than to judge me by my own actions, Ardroy?'

'You were ... too humane,' said the voice dully. 'And you *did* ask me about Lochiel ...'

'And must I have had an ill motive behind my humanity, as you call it? You cannot say I pressed you for information about your Chief!'

'But you found out that I had it!'

It was so difficult to answer this that Keith did not attempt it. 'What motive, then,' he urged, 'brought me hastening back here, into disgrace, into complete ruin, perhaps? Is there nothing in your own heart to tell you? When you hear that I have been broke for neglecting my duty and offending my superior officer on your behalf, Ardroy, will you still think that I betrayed you to Major Guthrie?'

Ewen raised his ravaged face. 'Will you swear to me on your

word of honour that you never told him that I knew Lochiel's hiding-place?'

'I do most solemnly swear it, on my honour as a gentleman. I never saw Guthrie again till the day before yesterday.'

'And will you swear, too, that you had not *already* suggested to him that I knew it, and would tell?' asked Ewen, narrowing his eyes.

'No, I never suggested that,' answered Keith, with a steady mien but a sinking heart. Nothing but the naked truth would avail now . . . and yet its nakedness might prove too ugly. 'I am going to tell you exactly what I did suggest.'

'You will not swear it – I thought as much!'

'No, I will not swear until I have made clear to you what I am swearing to. – Yes, you must listen, Ardroy; 'tis as much for your own sake as for mine!' He dragged forward a stool for himself. 'Go back to that scene on the mountain – if you can remember it. Do you think it was easy for me to find weapons to save you with? When I rushed in and caught you, as you sank down by the wall, when I stood between you and the firing-party, with that scoundrel cursing me and ordering me out of the way and telling the men to set you up there again, I had to snatch at anything, *anything*, to stop your execution. I told Guthrie who you were – too important to shoot out of hand like that. Afterwards, *he* asserted that I had implied that you, as Lochiel's kinsman, would give information about him. As God sees us, such an impossible notion never entered my head, and I said that you would never do it. It was as we were riding away; so he replied, that devil: "Then it is not worth my while to fetch him into camp tomorrow; he can rot there in the hut for all I care!" And I saw that you *would* rot there, unless I could persuade him to send for you. Being at my wits' end, I made a most disastrous suggestion, and said, loathing myself the while for saying it, that it might perhaps be worth his while to fetch you into camp on the chance of your . . . of your dropping some hint by inadvertence. And he –'

Ewen had given a sharp exclamation. 'You said that – you *did* say that! It was true, then, what he told me! God! And how much more?'

'No more,' said Keith, wincing. 'No more, on my soul. And I

only said that to hoodwink him into sending for you. You cannot think that I –'

'You advised him to take me for that reason!' interrupted Ewen, dropping out every word, while his eyes, which had softened, began to turn to ice again. 'And, when you came back that night, you never told me what you had done. Is not that . . . somewhat difficult to explain?'

'No,' said Keith with a sigh, 'it is easy. I was ashamed to tell you – that is the explanation . . . and yet I only made the suggestion because your life, so it seemed to me, was in the balance. When at last I had brought myself to the point of confession, you had fallen into the sleep in which I left you. If I had guessed – But of what use is regret now! And, Ardroy, you cannot imagine that I really thought that you would . . . or that anyone would try by force to . . .' He suddenly covered his eyes with his hand.

And presently he heard the Highlander say, in a strange, dry, reflective tone: 'Yes, it ill becomes me to accuse another man of treachery.' And then, even more quietly: 'You say you did not believe it, when they told you that I had made a disclosure . . . voluntarily. I ought to thank you for that.'

The tired voice seemed for the moment empty of emotion; and yet it wrung Keith's heart, as its frenzied reproaches had not. He uncovered his eyes. 'Nor do I believe it now,' he said vehemently. 'If it is true that they have got your secret from you, then I know that they must have . . . half killed you first.'

'No,' said Ardroy in the same dull tone, 'they have not laid a finger on me here. . . . Yet I have told them what Major Guthrie nearly flogged me to get from me.'

If Keith had seen a visitant from the dead, he could not have stared more wildly. 'That's impossible!' he stammered. 'I don't believe it – you don't know what you are saying!'

Ewen's lip twisted a little. 'Why, by your own admission you said that I might drop a hint inadvertently!' The shaft went visibly deep. 'Forgive me!' he exclaimed hastily. 'It is true – I think I do not know what I am saying!'

'Oh, let it pass,' said Keith, recovering himself. 'Only, in God's name, tell me what happened!'

Ewen shut his eyes. 'It is quite simple, after all. It seems that I still at times talk in my sleep, as I used when a boy. I was warned of it, not so very . . . not so very long ago.' He paused; Keith gave a stifled ejaculation, and had time to taste the immensity of his own relief. This, then, was the explanation of what had been to him so inexplicable – or else so abhorrent. Under his breath he murmured: 'Thank God!'

But Ewen, his eyes open now, and fixed on the other side of the room, was going on.

'When I was first brought here, I was too ill and feverish to realize what they wanted of me. Afterwards, when I knew well enough (since they openly asked me for it so óften, and it was what Major Guthrie had wanted too) and when I felt that the secret might slip from me in sleep, because it was so perpetually in my mind, I resolved never to allow myself to go to sleep, except when I was alone. But I so seldom was alone. At first I thought, very foolishly, that this was from care for me; then I discovered the real reason, for I think they must have been hoping for this result from the first. Perhaps I talked when I was in Guthrie's hands; I do not know. But, for all my endeavours,' he gave a dreary smile, 'it seems that one *must* sleep some time or other. And the fifth night – two nights ago – I could hold out no longer, and being left by myself I went to sleep . . . and slept a long time, soundly. I had thought that I was safe, that I should wake if anyone came in.' Ewen stopped. 'I ought to have cut my tongue out before I did it. . . . And I would have died for him – died for him!' His head went down on his knee again.

'Good God!' murmured Keith to himself. The methods that he feared might not have been used, but those which *had* been were pretty vile. And though their victim had neither given the information voluntarily – not, at least, in the true meaning of the word – nor had had it dragged out of him by violence, his distress was not less terrible. Yet surely –

'Ardroy,' he said quickly, and touched him on the shoulder, 'are you not leaping too hastily to conclusions? No doubt you may have said *something* about your secret, since it was so much on your mind; but that in your sleep you can have given any precise information about it, I cannot believe. Granted that you were told that you had – perhaps in hopes that you would really betray yourself – why did you believe it, and give yourself all this torment?'

Ewen raised his head, and out of his sunken, dark-rimmed eyes gave Keith a look which wavered away from him as if undecided, and then came back to his face and stayed there. Despair sat in those blue windows, but behind despair could be caught now a glimpse of a more natural craving for sympathy, which had not been there before.

'Because,' he answered, his hand gripping hard the plaid over his legs, 'they had written down every word I said – every word. In the morning they read it over to me. Of course I denied that it was correct . . . but there it all was – the secret that only I and one other besides Lochiel himself knew. Never having seen the actual spot myself, I had learnt the directions off by heart; 'twas the last thing I did before the battle.' He shuddered violently, and once more dropped his head on to his knee. 'O God, that ever I was brought away from Drumossie Moor!'

'Devils!' said Keith under his breath, 'cold-blooded devils!' But who had first suggested that Ardroy should be watched? He sprang up, and began to pace distractedly about the room; but that thought could not so be shaken off. Yet a rather stinging consolation dawned on him: since the prisoner had acknowledged to him, what he had denied to his inquisitors, that the information was correct, he must trust him again – he must indeed, for he had thus put it in his power to go and betray him afresh.

'You'll tell me, I suppose,' began Ewen's dragging voice again, 'that a man cannot be expected to control his tongue in sleep, and it is true; he cannot. But they will keep that part out, and Lochiel, all the clan, will hear that I gave the information of my own free will. Is not that what you have been told already?' And as Keith, unable to deny this, did not answer, Ewen went on with passion: 'However it was done, it has been done; I have betrayed my Chief; and he will know it. . . . If I were only sure that it would kill me outright, I would crawl to the breach there and throw myself down. I wish I had done it two nights ago!'

From the camp, where a drum was idly thudding, there came the sound of cheering, and the broken room where this agony beat its wings in vain was flooded with warm light, as the sun began to slip down to the sea behind the hills of Morven, miles away. And Keith remembered, with wonder at his obtuseness, that he had once decided that Ewen Cameron was probably a very impassive person. . . .

What was he to say? For indeed the result of Ardroy's disclosure might very well be just the same for Lochiel as if he had made it when in full possession of his senses. One argument, however, leapt unbidden to Keith's lips: his Chief would never believe that Ardroy had willingly betrayed him. Would Ardroy believe such a thing of him, he asked.

But Ewen shook his head, uncomforted. 'Lochiel would not have allowed himself to go to sleep – I did.'

'But you must have gone to sleep sooner or later!' expostulated Keith. 'Lochiel himself would have done the same, for no human being can go very long without sleep.'

'How do you know?' asked Ewen listlessly. 'I cannot sleep now, when I wish to . . . when it is of no moment if I do.'

Keith looked at him in concern. That admission explained a good deal in his appearance. If this continued, he might go out of his mind; and yet one was so powerless to help him; for indeed, as Ardroy had said, what was done, was done. He began to pace the room again.

Suddenly he stopped and swung round. Perhaps he was not so impotent to help after all. Somehow that idle drum, still beating out there, with its suggestion of march and movement, had revived a memory only twenty-four hours old.

'Listen to me, Ardroy,' he said quickly, coming back and sitting down again. 'But tell me first: you would only expect Lochiel to take to this refuge, would you not, if he were skulking, as the phrase goes here, not if he had a considerable body of followers with him?'

'No,' admitted Ewen, looking faintly surprised. 'Only if he were alone, or nearly so. But he is alone; or at the best, he can have but a handful with him.'

'It is there that I think you are wrong,' retorted Keith. 'Though that may have been the case at first, it is evidently so no longer. That is what I overheard yesterday.'

And he told him, word for word, what had fallen from the

officer who had been scouting down the Glen. Ardroy listened with the look of a drowning man sighting a distant spar.

'My God, if only that is true! No, if the clan has rallied some-what, he would not be in hiding. Yet, after a skirmish, or if he were surprised – '

'But consider', urged Keith, 'that, if they are so numerous, only an attack in force would be possible; and Lochiel could hardly be surprised by that: he would have scouts posted, surely. And after a skirmish, supposing the results unfavourable to him, he would probably withdraw altogether with his men, not go to earth in the neighbourhood. If the place is searched, believe me, it will be found empty!'

The eagerness with which Ewen hung upon his words was pathetic to witness.

'You are not,' he asked painfully, 'inventing this story . . . out of compassion?'

'No, no; I heard it exactly as I have told it to you, and I can see no reason why the speaker's statement should not have been true.'

(And whether true or no, he thought, it will have served a very good purpose if it prevents this too tightly stretched string from snapping altogether.)

Ewen drew a long breath and passed his hand over his eyes as if to wipe out a sight which was too much there. Then his head sank back against the edge of the seat behind him, his hand fell away, and Keith saw that he had fainted, or as near it as made little difference. He supposed that his attentions would be per-mitted now, and, grabbing up the bowl, dashed some of the water in the Highlander's face; then, putting his arms round him, succeeded in shifting him so that he could lay him flat upon the pallet.

But Ardroy was not gone far. In a moment or two he raised a hand to his head as he lay there, and murmured something about a ray of hope. Then his eyes opened, and looking straight up into Keith's face as he bent over him he said clearly, but with a catch of the breath: 'Forgive me – if you can!'

'I have so much to be forgiven myself,' answered Keith, look-ing down unhappily at the dirty, haggard wreck of his young

Achilles, 'that I can scarce resent what you, of all people, have thought of me. Oh, Ardroy, what a curst tangle it has been! – Are you well like that – your wounded leg . . .?'

The blue eyes held on to him. 'You have not answered my question. If you could forgive me for so wronging you . . . I know I have said unpardonable things to you . . . you who saved my life!'

Keith took into his own the hand he had scarred. 'Forgotten – if you will forget what I said of you.'

'But what have I to forget?' asked Ewen, and he suddenly bit his lip to keep it steady. 'I think I have to remember! And indeed, indeed, Windham, I did not doubt you lightly! I fought against it; but it all fitted together so devilishly . . . and I was not sound in mind or body. And now – selfish wretch that I am – if you are broke through what you have done for me – '

But it seemed as if it were a third person who fancied himself in more imminent danger of that fate, for Ardroy had got no farther when there were hasty, hobbling steps outside the door, a fumbling with the lock, and there stood Sergeant Mullins, much flustered.

'If you please, Major,' he said, sadly out of breath, 'will you come away at once? I misdoubt you'll be found up here if you stay a minute longer, for I saw Lord Loudoun's aide-de-camp coming along the road – and I shall be sent packing without the pension that's been promised me!'

'Go – go quickly, Windham,' said Ewen earnestly. 'It will do *you* no good, either, to be found up here.'

There was nothing for it. 'Yes, I'm coming, Sergeant. – We cannot undo the past, Ardroy, but for God's sake try to torment yourself less about a calamity which may never befall – a certain person.'

Ewen looked up at him with a faint, forlorn smile. 'And *your* calamity?' he asked.

'I must endeavour to take my own advice,' said his visitor rather grimly. 'I shall try to see you again if possible . . . that is, if you . . .' he hesitated.

Ewen's left hand reached up and gripped his wrist. 'You say the past cannot be undone. There are some hours in it which I

230

am glad I can never lose again – that night in the shieling, now I
know that you were . . . what at the time I thought you!'

Three minutes after Keith had got back to his quarters, the
correct aide-de-camp appeared to announce to him that he would
be taken to Inverness under escort early next morning, as he had
been sent for from headquarters. Keith shrugged his shoulders.
That meant a court-martial, in all probability, and the loss of his
commission. But at any rate the sacrifice was not all in vain, for
he had cleared himself, in Ewen Cameron's eyes, of charges far
worse than any court-martial could bring against him.

All evening he thought of Ardroy up there, destitute in body
and tormented in mind – though less tormented, fortunately, by
the time he had left him. . . . Yet why, he asked himself, should he
care what Ardroy was suffering, now that he had cleared his
account with him? Was it because he had somehow become
responsible for him by snatching him from death? God knew.

But that, he supposed, was why, when Mullins hobbled in with
his supper, he handed the sergeant a sheet of paper.

'I want you to take this to Mr Cameron tonight, Sergeant.
Read it, and you can satisfy yourself that it contains nothing
which it should not.'

The note briefly said that the writer would not be able to see the
recipient again, since he was obliged to go to Inverness next
morning, but that he would go thither with a mind vastly more
at peace than he had come; and would go even more cheerfully
if he were permitted to leave with the sergeant a sum of money
sufficient to provide for the captive's immediate needs in the way
of food and clothes. 'You can repay it at your convenience,'
Keith had added, 'but, if you will not accept this loan, I shall
depart feeling that you have not truly forgiven me.'

As he expected, Sergeant Mullins made no bones about delivering a missive, when he had connived at a much more serious
breach of discipline. But when, on his return, he handed his letter
back to Keith, the Englishman's heart fell, until he saw that
Ardroy, having no writing materials of his own, had used the
back of it for his reply. And thereon was scrawled with a blunt
pencil of the sergeant's these words:

If there is any Justice on Earth, you should not only be re-instated but advanc'd at Inverness. I pray you to inform me, if you can, of what happens. I accept your Loan with Gratitude; it is for me to ask your Forgiveness still. Perhaps I shall sleep tonight.

Your Debtor,

Ewen Cameron

Keith at any rate slept, though he was rather bitterly amused at the idea of being given advancement by the Duke of Cumberland because he had got himself into a scrape for the sake of a rebel. The cause of his dereliction of duty would be the chief count in his probable disgrace.

Chapter 5

IT was raining hard, and blowing too, and rain and wind kept up a constant siege of the inadequate canvas stretched over the breach in Ewen's place of confinement, the drops pattering against it like small shot. Ewen himself, shaved and wearing a clean shirt, but the same disreputable kilt, was sitting on the seat which ran round the embrasure, to which, with some difficulty, he could now hoist himself. His object in so doing was to see out, but this morning there was little to see when he had got there.

Ten days had passed since his momentous interview with Major Windham, ten days of wearing, grinding suspense. Every hour, almost, he had expected to learn of Lochiel's capture. But, as day followed day, and nothing of the sort occurred, nor, from what Sergeant Mullins told him, was any attempt being made against Achnacarry, the spar of hope which his visitor had flung to him began to have more sustaining qualities. It did look as if Windham's information were correct, and that the clan was known to be in such force that it was not a mere question of hunting down the wounded Chief, of plucking him out of the refuge whose secret was a secret no longer. For the comfort of that thought he had to thank the generosity of an enemy whom he had accused to his face of an infamous action.

Major Windham had always been something of an enigma to

Ewen, and the depth of the concern which he had shown the other day still surprised him. That he had personally attracted the English soldier would never have occurred to him. Apart from wishing to clear himself of the charge of treachery, Major Windham, he supposed, felt a somewhat exaggerated sense of obligation for having been allowed to go free in Edinburgh – though indeed some men might have resented that clemency, and there had been a time when Guthrie's insinuations had driven Ewen to the belief that this was so. Yet now the remembrance of the night in the shieling hut was no longer a draught of poison, but what it had been at the time, that cup of cold water which holds a double blessing.

But it was strange how accurate had been his foster-father's prophecy, that the man to whom the heron would bring him should alike do him a great service and cause him bitter grief. Both predictions had been fulfilled; and by the same act on Major Windham's part.

Ewen himself seemed to have been forgotten by the authorities. The same military surgeon came from time to time, and grumblingly dressed his wounds, but, though rough and quite devoid of consideration, he was tolerably skilful, and the patient's own splendid physique was doing the rest, now that he had proper care and that his mind was a little more at ease. Old Mullins mindful alike of a substantial *douceur* from Major Windham and of his own good treatment by the Highlanders, looked after him to the best of his ability, particularly when he discovered him to be Dr Cameron's cousin. He still boggled, however, at procuring the captive entirely new clothes (for how, he said, should he account to Captain Greening for having the money to pay for them?), but he brought him better food than was provided, a couple of clean shirts, and a second blanket, and shaved him every other day. But Captain Greening, whom Ewen loathed, he thought, even more than he had loathed the brute Guthrie, never came near him now. He had got what he wanted, presumably, and troubled no more about the prisoner whom at one time he had had so assiduously watched.

The outcome of those horrible days and nights remained deeply branded on Ewen's soul: he was a traitor, if an unconscious and most unwilling one; but the actual memory of them, and of the twenty-four hours in Guthrie's hands, he was now beginning, with the natural instinct of a healthy mind, to put behind him. And with the slight relaxation of tension due to Major Windham's suggestion and the inactivity of the authorities – due also to the wild hope which sometimes visited him, that Lochiel was no longer near Achnacarry at all, and that they knew it – he was beginning to feel the pressure of captivity, and would spend hours peering hungrily through the narrow slits of windows. Even if, as today, he could see little for the rain and mist, he could always smell the blessed air, and he now screwed himself into a still more uncomfortable position in an endeavour to get as much of this as possible. Yes, the rain, as he thought, was stopping; the wind was blowing it away. Often, on such a morning, on the braes above Loch na h-Iolaire –

Several people seemed to be coming quickly up the stairs. The surgeon and others? Ewen turned his head. No; when the door was unlocked and flung open there came in three officers all unknown to him. The foremost was of high rank, and Ewen, after a second's astonishment, realized that he could be none other than the Earl of Loudoun himself.

Sitting there, he instinctively stiffened. With the opening of the door the wind had swooped through the breach in the wall, and even the Earl's dark, heavy tartans fluttered for a moment. There was a sheet of paper in his hand, and he wore a look of great annoyance.

'Mr Cameron,' he said, like a man too much pressed for time to indulge in any preamble, 'when you gave us this information about Lochiel's hiding-place a couple of weeks since,' he tapped the paper, 'why did you name as the spot a mountainside which does not exist anywhere near Loch Arkaig?'

Ewen's heart gave a bound so sudden and violent that he thought it must suffocate him. What did Lord Loudoun mean? He stared at him breathlessly.

'Come, sir,' said the Earl impatiently, 'do not play the innocent! On 7 May you gave Captain Greening a detailed account of a cave on a mountainside which Lochiel would be apt to use in an emergency, how its whereabouts could be recognized, its concealed opening found, and the rest. The mountain, according to you, was called Ben Loy. But you made a slip – or something more intentional – for guides who know the district well declare that there is no mountain of that name in the neighbourhood, though it is true that there is a Glen Loy farther down the Lochy, but much too far to serve as a convenient refuge from Achnacarry. This makes nonsense of your information.' His voice was warm with a sense of injury. 'The mistake has only been discovered in the nick of time. . . . Why, what's wrong with you, man?'

For Ewen, with an exclamation, had leant forward and buried his face in his hands. Was it possible that his rebel tongue had, all unknown to himself and to his inquisitor, undone so much of the harm it had wrought? And how had he not realized it himself?

Lord Loudoun much mistook the cause of his emotion. 'The slip can easily be repaired, Mr Cameron,' he said impatiently. 'You cannot possibly have meant any of the heights of Glen Loy – none of which, moreover, appears to be called Ben Loy. It must be one of the other names I have on this paper – Come, my time is precious! I am about to set out for Achnacarry today.' And as Ewen, really too much overcome by his 'slip' to pay much attention to these adjurations, still remained with his face hidden, a new note crept into the Earl's voice. 'You are not, I hope, indulging in scruples *now*, Mr Cameron? 'Tis too late for that; nor is it any manner of use to withhold a part when you have told us so much. We shall know the place when we come upon it.'

Ewen raised his head at last and looked at him, but still dizzily. '*Withhold!*' he said. 'Is it possible, Lord Loudoun, that you do not know how such information as you have was extracted from me?'

'Extracted from you!' repeated the Earl. 'Why, you gave it of your own free will when you were asked for it; I have Captain Greening's word for that.'

'My own free will! Did Captain Greening tell your Lordship that he had me watched and questioned day and night for nearly a week, hoping that I should tell it in my sleep, as at last I did, unknowingly? While I had life in my body, he should never have

235

got it otherwise!' And, seeing clearly from Loudoun's face that this was indeed news to him, Ewen went on with more heat, 'Whatever lies you were told by your English underlings, how dare you, my Lord, believe that a Cameron would ever willingly betray Mac Dhomhnuill Duibh?'

'Go and see if you cannot find Captain Greening this time, and bring him here,' said the Earl to one of the officers. He took a turn up and down, his hands behind his back, looking very much disturbed.

'I had no idea of this; 'tis a method which should never have been used,' he muttered after a moment. It was evident that he entirely believed the prisoner's assertion. 'But you must admit, Mr Cameron,' he went on mildly, 'that I am not to blame for it, seeing that I was not here at the time. And, as to believing that you made the disclosure willingly, I confess that I ought to have remembered – since I have the honour to be one myself – that a Highland gentleman does not willingly betray his Chief.'

Yet, having elicited this *amende*, Ewen said nothing, his racial distrust of a Campbell inclining him to wait for what was to come next.

'I cannot pretend, however,' began the Earl again, 'that I am sorry to possess this information, since I am a soldier, and must obey orders. In accordance with these, I set out today with two thousand men for Loch Arkaig and Achnacarry.' He gave time for this news to sink in. 'But, Mr Cameron, though our clans have unfortunately been at enmity in the past, that shall not prevent me from treating Lochiel, when he is in my hands, with all the regard due to his position and merit.'

'As his kinsman,' replied Ewen to this, 'I thank your Lordship for the intention, even though I trust that you may never have the chance of carrying it out.' Why had the Campbell become thus smooth-spoken, and was it true that he was going with so overwhelmingly large a force against Lochiel?

Before Lord Loudoun could offer any further remarks, Captain Greening came in, apologizing that he should have been sought for twice, and evidently ignorant of what was in store for him. The Earl cut short his excuses.

'Why did you assure me, Captain Greening, that the information about Lochiel obtained from Mr Cameron of Ardroy here was given of his own free will? Mr Cameron tells me that, as the result of unceasing persecution on your part, it was dragged out of him in sleep; which is a very different matter!'

Somehow Captain Greening, while appearing to have his eyes fixed respectfully on his superior, contrived to shoot a glance of a very different nature at Ewen.

'If your Lordship believes that story,' he said with a scarcely believed sneer, 'it does credit to your Lordship's nobility of disposition – as well as to Mr Cameron's powers of invention! Sleep! As if he could have given all that detail in his sleep! But the tale may serve to patch the hole in his reputation, though I'll wager he was no more asleep than you or I!'

'You are a pretty consummate scoundrel, are you not!' observed Ewen softly.

'Yet, whether he was asleep or awake, my Lord,' went on Greening quickly, 'I submit that what I said was perfectly correct – no force of any kind was used. I certainly had no intention of misleading your Lordship on that point, when you asked me that question in order to satisfy ... a somewhat indiscreet inquirer after Mr Cameron.'

But Lord Loudoun, frowning heavily, declined to be drawn into a side issue. 'It was playing with words, sir, to call information thus given "voluntary". I am very much displeased at the means employed. And even so, as might have been foreseen, the matter was bungled, for the information itself, on which you led me to rely, is not complete!'

'Not complete!' stammered Greening, flushing. 'My Lord – '

'No, sir, it is not complete – and only now, within an hour or so of setting out for the neighbourhood, has its insufficiency been discovered! The guide, who knows that district well, swears that there is no mountain of the name of Ben Loy anywhere near. And Ben Loy is the name you have written here.'

Captain Greening almost snatched the paper from the Earl's hand, and ran his eyes feverishly over it.

'My Lord, the guide is perhaps mis—'

'I tell you that he knows that part of the country like the palm of his hand,' interrupted Lord Loudoun angrily. 'It might, he says, be any of the three mountains whose names are written below. But how can I hope to surprise Lochiel if I have to go searching every brae-side near Loch Arkaig for this cave? And I tell you further, Captain Greening, that this ridiculous wrong name, occurring thus, gives me very much to doubt whether the whole description be not the product of ... of a dream, or of imagination – whether this cave near a waterfall is to be found on any mountainside whatever, be the mountain called what it may!'

In the extremely mortified silence which ensued on Captain Greening's part at this, Ewen saw his opportunity.

'I was wondering,' he observed mockingly, 'how long your Lordship would be before you discovered the real value of Captain Greening's dirty work!'

'Do not believe him, my Lord,' urged Greening, his light, womanish voice roughened by rage and disappointment. 'If I cannot answer for the name of the mountain, I can, by God, for the rest! Had you seen the prisoner's face when I read over to him next morning what he had told me, you would know that his description was accurate enough. It is only a question of finding out which mountain he had in mind; and if your Lordship will give me half an hour or so with him – '

Lord Loudoun turned on him. 'You have mismanaged this business quite enough,' he snapped. 'I do not desire you, Captain Greening, to meddle with it any further. Nor is Mr Cameron asleep *now*.'

There was that in Captain Greening's expression as he turned away, biting his lip, which suggested that he would not consider that state necessary for his purpose.

Ewen shut his eyes and leant his head against the wall. The Earl and his two officers were talking together in low voices, and he longed for them to go away and leave him to turn over, as if it were a grain of gold out of a muddy river, the thought of this wonderful and saving slip of the tongue. He could not understand how he came to have stumbled so mercifully; was it because in his illness he fancied himself at times back in the shieling on that mountain, which was, he believed, called Beinn Laoigh, the calf's mountain? That he had not himself noticed the mistake in

the name when Captain Greening read over to him next morning
what he was pleased to call his deposition, he could after all
understand; the horror of the accuracy of the rest had too much
swamped his soul. He tried to now calculate how much security
was given back to the secret place by his happy blunder; but it
was not easy.

Then he heard a movement to the door. Thank God, they had
done with him! No; feet were approaching him again. He opened
his eyes and saw Lord Loudoun standing looking out through
one of the narrow windows only a few feet away. Save for him,
the room was empty, though the door remained ajar. Evidently
the Earl desired a measure of privacy.

'I am very sorry about your treatment, Mr Cameron,' he
began, his eyes still fixed on the narrow slit. 'It has been an unfortunate business.'

'Which, my Lord,' asked Ewen coolly, 'my treatment or the
information which proves to be worthless?'

'I referred, naturally, to your treatment,' said Lord Loudoun
with dignity (but Ewen did not feel so sure). 'However, you must
admit that I may fairly consider the other affair a . . . disappointment. As a soldier, with my duty to carry out, I must avail myself
of any weapon to my hand.'

'Evidently,' commented his prisoner. 'Even of one which is
not very clean!'

Lord Loudoun sighed. 'Alas, one cannot always choose. You
yourself, Mr Cameron, had no choice in the matter of your disclosure, and are therefore in no sense to blame. . . . I should wish
everyone to know that,' he added graciously, turning round and
looking down at him.

'Then our wishes coincide, my Lord, which is gratifying,'
observed Ardroy. 'And is it to discuss with me some means of
compassing this end that your Lordship is good enough to spare
time for this interview now?'

Although Lord Loudoun could not possibly have been insensi-
tive to the irony of this query, it apparently suited him to ignore
it. In fact he sat down upon the stone bench, on the opposite side
of the embrasure.

'Chance made your revelation incomplete, Mr Cameron,' he

239

said, giving him a rather curious look. 'Yet, if the missing link in the chain *had* been there, the same . . . blamelessness would have covered it.'

Ewen, his eyes fixed upon him, said something under his breath and gripped the edge of the seat. But the Earl went on meaningly: 'There is still time for the true name of that mountain to have been . . . *spoken by you in your sleep!*'

. And still his captive merely looked at him; yet Lord Loudoun evidently enjoyed his gaze so little that his own seemed to be caught by the breach in the wall, and stayed there.

'This room appears a very insecure place of confinement,' he murmured. 'Has that thought never occurred to you?'

Ewen was still looking at him. 'I cannot walk, much less climb, my Lord.'

'But with a little help from outside, a little connivance,' suggested the Earl, gazing at the breach. 'Sentries, I am afraid, are sometimes both venal and careless . . . especially when the commander is away. But I dare say the negligence would be overlooked at headquarters, in view of the – the exceptional circumstances.' There was a little silence as he turned his head and at last looked the Highlander in the face again. 'Is it useless to hope that you will see reason, Mr Cameron?'

'*Reason!*' exclaimed Ewen. Contempt had warmed to rage by this time. '*Treason* is what you mean, you false Campbell!' With difficulty he shuffled himself along the seat to a greater distance. 'I wish I had the use of both my legs! I like ill at any time to sit upon the same seat with a son of Diarmaid; and to sit near one who after all that fine talk tries to bribe me to betray my Chief, who offers me my liberty as the price of his – ' And he somehow dragged himself to his feet, and stood clutching at the corner of the wall, breathless with anger and effort.

Lord Loudoun, his smile completely vanished, was on his feet, too, as flushed as his prisoner was pale. 'You *have* betrayed him, Cameron – what use to take that tone? You might as well complete the disclosure . . . and if your pride will not stomach the gift, I'll not offer you your liberty in exchange. I had already made you an offer which would mend your self-esteem, not hurt it. Here's another: tell me what is the real name of that mountain and I'll engage that Lochiel shall never know who told us of the cave upon it!'

'And I'm to rely on nothing but a Campbell's word for that!' cried Ewen, still at white heat, but sinking down again on the seat despite himself. 'No, thank you, my Lord; the security's not good enough! Nor am I going to tell you the name on any security, so you were best not waste your time.'

'Then,' said the Earl, and there was a new and dangerous note in his voice, 'I warn you that Cameron of Lochiel will have the mortification of knowing that it was a Cameron who betrayed him. But I repeat that if you give it to me – '

'There is one place the name of which I feel at liberty to give you,' interrupted Ewen, half closing his eyes, in which the light of battle was gleaming. 'I think I should be doing my Chief no harm if I told you the way – ' He paused as if uncertain, after all, whether to go on, and Greening and the two other officers, who, hearing voices raised, had reappeared in the doorway, pressed quickly forward.

Lord Loudoun fell into the trap. 'The way to where?' he asked eagerly.

'The way to Moy,' answered Ewen, and the glint in his eyes was plain to see now. 'To Moy in Lochaber – there *is* a place of that name there. Though whether you will encounter a second Donald Fraser too I don't know.'

Lord Loudoun gave a stifled exclamation and grew very red. Consternation overcame his officers. The too-famous 'rout of Moy', as Ewen had well guessed, was not mentioned in the Earl's hearing. But the Earl was the first to recover himself.

'You are not only insolent but foolish, Mr Cameron. When Lochiel falls into my hands, I shall not now be inclined to keep silence on the subject of his refuge, whether he is found in it or no, and it will depend upon me whether he is told that you made your disclosure about it involuntarily, as you declare that you did, or of your own free will.'

And thus did the Earl of Loudoun, a not ill-natured nor inhumane man, who in calmer moments would have been ashamed of such an impulse, threaten to use a calumny which he knew to be such, in order to bring a captive foe to heel. The merest sign

241

of pleading on the Cameron's part, and he would have relented. But nothing was farther from Ardroy's mind than pleading. All he craved, in his wrath, was a fresh weapon with which to draw blood. He found it.

'But you may not capture Lochiel at all,' he said with an appearance of carelessness. 'He may have followed your Lordship's example when, after your amusing performances on the Dornoch Firth, you ran away from your captured troops and sought safety in Skye! Only,' he added venomously, 'in my Chief's case, it will be *after* the battle, not, as in yours, John Campbell, *before* it!'

The effect on Lord Loudoun, who was no coward, of this really undeserved interpretation of his misfortunes was all that Ewen could have wished. His hand clenched on his swordhilt. 'By God, sir, if we were ... elsewhere ... I'd make you pay for that!'

And alike from him, fourth earl of his line, representative peer of Scotland and royal aide-de-camp, and from the defiant, ragged young man on the seat before him, with his French training and his natural courtesy (which an Englishman had not long ago thought almost excessive), there slipped for a moment the whole cloak of eighteenth-century civilization, and they were merely two Highlanders, heirs of an age-long feud, waiting to spring at each other, dirk in hand, amongst the heather. The metamorphosis lasted but a second or two, and they were themselves again, but John Campbell had had his answer; he knew better now the temper with which he had to deal than to expect an appeal for mercy, much less the revelation he coveted.

'I am only sorry that your future is not likely to allow of your giving me satisfaction for that insult, Mr Cameron,' he said grimly, and turned his back upon him. 'Captain Greening, you will have the prisoner removed from this room to some securer place of confinement. But bear in mind, if you please, that he is not to be ill-treated.' And, without another look behind him, he left the room. Nor was his going devoid of dignity.

As the hated Diarmaid tartan vanished, Ewen's whole body relaxed against the wall. But he soon became aware that Captain Greening had stayed behind, and was standing there in Loudoun's place addressing him, his delicate features contorted with rage.

'If I had only guessed, you dirty cattle-thief, that you had fooled me after all! It would not have taken a fortnight to get the real name out of you somehow!' His teeth ground together. 'Perhaps in the dungeons you'll learn at least to keep a civil tongue in your head, as long as it is on your shoulders.' He flung away towards the door, then turned again. 'Yes, smile while you can! "Not to be ill-treated", eh? We'll see about that when the Earl is gone, my fine Highlander!'

As the door slammed behind his guardian, the contemptuous smile died off Ewen's face, and, lowering himself with some difficulty from the stone bench, he lay down on the pallet below and pulled his plaid over his head. Now that the clash of the interview was over, he felt shaken and sick. A great consolation had indeed emerged from it, but even that consolation could do little for him against the immediate anguish of knowing that the hounds were on the trail at last, and the quarry perhaps unsuspecting. How could Lochiel escape so large a force? He and his few hundreds would be surrounded as in a net; he would be killed or captured, even if he did not take to the cave on Beinn Bhreac. And, if he did, chance might always lead the pursuers straight to it. Could Ewen in that hour have sent a message to Lochiel he would willingly have bought the privilege not merely by his own death – that went without saying – but by a death in any manner protracted and horrible. Yet no suffering could buy that chance; there was nothing to do but lie there helpless, at the lowest ebb of dejection, and hear from the camp the drums and bugles of departure.

At last came evening, and Mullins with food and water.

'Is there any news, Sergeant?' asked Ewen, raising himself.

'Yes, sir, His Royal Highness the Duke's expected here to-morrow with nine regiments of foot and some horse. And Captain Greening ain't in charge of prisoners no longer; his Lordship saw to that before he left – seems he was annoyed with the Captain about something or other. I can't say as I'm sorry. But I'm afraid, Mr Cameron, you're going to be moved from here tomorrow, and put in one of them nasty places they call the dungeons, though they ain't scarcely that, so to speak, and – '

Ewen cut short the bulletin. 'You can put me in my grave, for

243

all I care at present. It's the expedition to Loch Arkaig I want news of. Is there *none*?'

'No, sir. How could there be, so soon? – Bless me, how wild you look. Have you kin in those parts?'

'More than kin,' said Ewen brokenly. 'My heart and my honour . . . O God, send a mist, a storm – send someone to warn him!'

Next day Cumberland and his ten regiments marched in from Inverness. But of this great stir Ewen heard nothing. He was down in a damp little cell under the fort, with fever once more in his blood, fighting a desire to knock his head against the wall. The old sergeant, who still had charge of him, could tell him nothing of what he wanted to know, save that there was report of great burnings going on down the Glen, and of quantities of cattle driven off.

So Ewen had to endure the suspense as best he might, until the following morning, when a light suddenly streamed through the open door, and a kilted figure was roughly pushed down the steps by a couple of redcoats. But in the short-lived radiance Ewen had recognized the tartan of his own clan.

'Who is it – are you from Loch Arkaig?' he asked hoarsely, raising himself on his heap of straw.

'Aye; Alexander Cameron from Murlaggan,' answered the newcomer. 'My sorrow, but it is dark in here! Who are you – a Cameron also?'

Ewen dragged himself to one knee. 'Lochiel . . . Lochiel – is he safe? Tell me quickly, for God's sake!'

The Cameron groped his way to the corner. 'Yes, God be praised! There were but a handful of us captured; the rest scattered while the redcoats were fording the river of Lochy. – There honest man, sure that's good news, not bad!'

For – the first time in his grown life – Ewen was shaken by uncontrollable sobs, by a thankfulness which tore at his heart like a grief. Alexander Cameron sat down by him in the straw, seeming very well to understand his emotion, and told him more fully the story of what had happened: how the Argyll militia with Lord Loudoun had at first been mistaken for a body of MacDonald reinforcements which were expected, but distinguished in time by the red crosses on their bonnets; how the Camerons had thought of disputing the passage over Lochy, but, realizing the overwhelming force of the enemy, had withdrawn swiftly along the northern shore of Loch Arkaig, so that by the time the latter got to the neighbourhood of Achnacarry the Chief must have been well on his way to the wild country at the head of the loch, where they would never pursue him. But the burnings and pillagings had begun already, and one could guess only too well the heavy measure of vengeance which was going to be meted out in Lochaber.

The two men lay close together that night under one plaid for warmth, and Ewen at last knew a dreamless sleep. Not only had Lochiel escaped, but he was not likely ever to hear now that the secret of the cave by the waterfall had been partly betrayed; nor, if he had left the district altogether, would he be tempted to make use of it in the future. The horror was lifted.

Chapter 6

IT was the seventeenth of July, and Keith Windham in his quarters at Inverness was turning over an official letter which had just come to him from Fort Augustus. It was, he saw, in the handwriting of Sir Everard Faulkner, Cumberland's secretary, and as he looked at it hope whispered to him that it might, perhaps, portend the lifting of the cloud under which he had lived for the last two months. And, not to silence that voice too soon, he left the letter unopened for a minute or two, and sat staring at it.

His case had never come before a court-martial; it had been privately dealt with by Hawley and the Duke. Three things had combined to save him from being cashiered; the fact that Cumberland was graciously pleased to set his conduct at Fontenoy against his present lapse, that Lord Albemarle had written some words of appreciation of him in that dispatch which Keith had never delivered, and that Hawley had regarded, and succeeded in making Cumberland regard Lord Loudoun's action in putting his staff-officer under arrest as high-handed and to be resented. 'I can't understand your conduct, Windham,' he had said angrily to his erring subordinate, 'but I'm damned if I'll stand Lord Loudoun's!' Hawley chafed all the more, because he knew his own star to be on the decline; and thus military jealousy played no small part in saving Keith from complete disaster.

But all was over, naturally, with his chance of being appointed to Cumberland's staff, nor could Hawley keep him on his, even for the short time that should elapse before he resigned his own none-too-fortunate command. Although Major Windham's might be regarded as a mere technical offence – and even Cumberland, severe as he was showing himself in matters of discipline, did not seem to regard it as more – Lord Loudoun's treatment of it had given it so much publicity that for appearances' sake the defaulter had to be punished. Keith had hoped that he might escape from Scotland by being sent back to his own battalion of the Royals, now in Kent, or that perhaps he would be attached to the second, just proceeding to Perth; but he was offered instead a vacancy in Battereau's regiment, which was to remain behind with Blakeney's when the bulk of the army should move with Cumberland to Fort Augustus. He was, in short, put on the shelf; but he was very plainly shown that it was a choice between accepting this position or sending in his papers altogether. He might indeed count himself extremely lucky that he had escaped being broke, and so the Duke himself had told him.

The last week in May, therefore, had found him left behind in Inverness, no longer the centre of military activity now that Cumberland was gone, but rather a depot for prisoners, entailing on the two regiments remaining in the town duties which were both dull and – to Keith Windham at least – hateful. But the shelf has an uncommonly sobering effect upon a hot-tempered and ambitious man, and it did not require two months of it to bring reflection to Major Windham. Before they were half over, he was viewing his own irregular conduct in a much more critical light, and from cursing his impetuosity he had come to marvelling at his folly. Saving Ewen Cameron's life he did not for an instant regret; he would have done the same again without a moment's hesitation, nor did he regret his return to the shieling in the guise of

246

the Good Samaritan; but to have dashed in that manner back to Fort Augustus while carrying a dispatch, still more to have thrust himself into Lord Loudoun's presence and almost to have brawled there – was it any wonder that he had found himself under arrest? Prudence could not undo the past, but it might modify the future, and he therefore set himself to practise this virtue in Inverness, much as it went against the grain. Warned by the fate of an officer who was court-martialled for having shown the wretched captives there some kindness, he did not go out of his way to emulate him, nor did his old wound again furnish a pretext for his withdrawal from scenes which he disliked. If the officers of Battereau's had known him previously they would have thought him remarkably changed. General Blakeney, a hard man, had no fault to find with Hawley's disgraced staff-officer.

The first-fruit of this new prudence had been Keith's abstention not only from writing to Ewen Cameron, but even from sending him a direct message. He had sent instead by an acquaintance in Bligh's regiment, when it proceeded to Fort Augustus, a verbal recommendation to Sergeant Mullins to be faithful to the 'commission' which he had given him, in the hope that the sergeant would, besides obeying this injunction, pass on unsolicited to Ardroy the scanty news of himself which his messenger was instructed to add. A man under a cloud could not, he felt, afford to compromise himself still further in the matter of open friendship with a rebel – though to Cumberland and Hawley he had vigorously denied any such relations with Ewen Cameron. Made wary by his experiences with Guthrie, and afraid of giving a handle against Ewen, he had merely urged in defence of his own conduct a not unnatural anxiety about a Scottish acquaintance – the name, of course, he had been unable to withhold – who had shown him hospitality and kindness *before* the raising of the standard of rebellion. It was disingenuous, but in the absence of close questioning the version had served its purpose.

And as the weeks went by, he had not only made no attempt to communicate in any way with the captive Jacobite, but was careful never to inquire for him by name whenever an officer came from Fort Augustus, whence indisposition (induced, so they asserted, by their melancholy surroundings) was always bringing a few. Yet, as the clearing out of Lochaber and Babenoch proceeded, he did his best always to ascertain what prisoners were arriving at Inverness for transhipment to England, but he never found Ewen Cameron's name among them. And at last, since he felt sure that the latter would never have been kept until July at Fort Augustus, he came to the conclusion that he must have overlooked his name in the lists, and that he had been shipped off from Inverness without his knowledge – unless he had been dispatched by land from Fort Augustus to Edinburgh. Keith hoped indeed that the latter course had been taken, for he knew something of the horrible condition in which the prisoners were kept in the ships, packed together like cattle, with nothing to lie upon but the stones and earth of the ballast. He was sorry, very sorry, that he had not been able to see Ardroy once more, but it was the fortune of war; and there was no denying the fact, once recognized, that this young man, to whom he had been so unusually attracted, had brought him nothing but ill-luck.

The letter, its seal broken at last, merely said that His Royal Highness the Duke of Cumberland commanded Major Windham's attendance without delay at Fort Augustus. Now Cumberland, as Keith knew, was on the very eve of departure for England; the summons must evidently have some connexion with that fact, and it was full of the most hopeful speculations that he went at once to procure leave of absence from his colonel.

And when, some five hours later, he came down the descent to Loch Ness, he could not but remember the last time that he had ridden into Fort Augustus, on that wet night in May, on fire with indignation and disgust. Well, he had learnt his lesson now!

Since Cumberland's advent, Fort Augustus had naturally become an armed camp of a much greater size; there were hundreds more tents pitched by the Tarff, and besides these, the women's quarters, the horse lines of the dragoon regiment of Kingston's horse, and quantities of cattle and ponies driven in from the ravaged countryside. As had been foreshadowed, the Earl of Albemarle, who had already been there for some time, was to succeed the Duke as commander-in-chief on the latter's departure tomorrow. Remembering his lamentations at Perth in

May, Keith wondered whether his Lordship were more reconciled to the prospect now.

But the Duke sending for *him* at this juncture – it *must* mean something to his own advantage.

He asked, as he had been instructed to do, for Sir Everard Faulkner, and found the ex-banker, ex-ambassador to Constantinople, and patron of Voltaire at a table in a tent, very busy writing.

'Good afternoon, Major Windham,' said he, looking up. 'You have made good speed hither, which is commendable.'

'So your letter bade me, sir.'

'Yes,' said Sir Everard, laying down his pen. 'I sent for you by His Royal Highness's recommendation, to request your assistance on a certain matter of importance to His Majesty's Government. If you can give it, you will lay not only me, but the Duke also, under a considerable obligation.'

'If you will tell me what the matter is ...' murmured Keith, amazed. To be able to lay Cumberland under an obligation was a chance not to be made light of, but he could not for the life of him imagine how he had it in his power to do so unlikely a thing.

'I have for some time,' proceeded Sir Everard, fingering the sheets before him, 'been collecting evidence against such prisoners in Inverness and elsewhere as are to be sent to England in order to take their trials. Yesterday I received a letter from the Lord Justice Clerk in Edinburgh transmitting a copy of the Duke of Newcastle's order that prisoners are to set out as soon as may be, and that particular care is to be taken that the witnesses sent to give evidence against them should be able to prove' – he took up a paper and read from it – ' "that they had seen the prisoners do some hostile act on the part of the rebels, or marching with the rebel army". You appreciate that point, of course?'

'Certainly,' agreed Keith. 'But surely there is no lack of such evidence?'

'No, in most cases there is not,' replied the secretary. 'But – to come to the point – we have here in Fort Augustus a prisoner of some importance, who is most undoubtedly guilty of overt acts of hostility in this late unnatural rebellion, but to my chagrin (and His Royal Highness's) I cannot put my hand on any person who

249

actually saw him commit such acts, though there must be numbers who witnessed them – not even on anyone who observed him in the company of the rebels. There is indeed a probability – but only a probability – that if he is sent to Fort William he may be identified by someone or other as having taken part in the attack upon it in the spring, for it is pretty certain that he was there with Cameron of Lochiel. The prisoner's name, by the way,' he added, with a carelessness too complete to be quite natural, 'is also Cameron – Ewen Cameron of Ardroy.'

There was a silence in the tent. 'So he *is* still here!' said Keith under his breath. 'And that is why you have sent for me, Sir Everard; – because you think that I can supply the evidence which will bring Cameron of Ardroy to the scaffold?' He checked himself, and added, in a studiously expressionless tone, 'Why, to what do you suppose that I can witness against him?'

Deceived perhaps by the manner of his last words, Sir Everard referred complacently to his notes.

'I understand that you can testify to his taking you prisoner by force on the outbreak of hostilities at High Bridge in Lochaber. That in itself would be more than sufficient, but it seems that you also encountered him in Edinburgh, and can therefore bear witness to his being in the Pretender's son's so-called army.'

Keith stared at Sir Everard Faulkner's wig, which was awry, with dismay in his soul. Surely Ardroy could not have been so mad as to have admitted these facts – which *he* had so carefully suppressed – to anyone at Fort Augustus! 'Who told you these details, sir – not that I admit their truth?'

'Major Guthrie of Campbell's regiment was so obliging as to mention to me the service which you could render to the Government in this matter. And he had the facts, it seems, from you yourself, shortly after the victory on Culloden Moor. Release from your duties at Inverness,' pursued Sir Everard amiably, 'can easily be obtained, Major Windham, and no expense would be incurred by you for your journey to Carlisle; it would be defrayed ...'

But Keith was not listening; he was wishing that he had Guthrie in some private spot with a couple of swords between them –

no, better, one horsewhip! This was his crowning piece of malevolence!

Sir Everard stopped short in his beguiling recital, which had reached the assurance that the Duke would not forget the service which the hearer was about to render. 'What is the matter, Major Windham?' he inquired. 'You seem discomposed. Has Major Guthrie misinformed me?'

Keith did not answer that question. 'Why does not Major Guthrie go as witness himself?' he asked in a half-choked voice.

'Because he cannot testify to overt acts, as you can,' explained Sir Everard. 'It is true that he captured Cameron of Ardroy, badly wounded – and there is no room for doubt when he took those wounds – but a jury might not convict on that evidence alone, whereas you, Major Windham – '

'Whereas mine – supposing it to be what you say – would successfully hang him?' finished Keith, looking straight at the secretary.

Sir Everard nodded with a gratified expression. 'You would have the satisfaction of rendering that service to His Majesty, and at the same time – if you'll permit me to be frank, Major Windham – of purging yourself of any suspicion of undue tenderness towards the rebels. I fancy,' he added with an air of finesse, 'that the accusation arose in connexion with this very man, Ewen Cameron, did it not? You see how triumphantly you could clear your honour of any such aspersions.' And Sir Everard smiled good-humouredly.

.'My honour must be in a sad case, sir,' said Keith, 'if to act hangman to a man who spared my own life will cleanse it! I am obliged to you for your solicitude, but I must beg to decline. Had it been some other rebel I might perhaps have been able to gratify you, but against Cameron of Ardroy I cannot and will not give evidence. I will therefore wish you good day.' He bowed and turned to go, inwardly seething.

'Stop, stop!' cried Sir Everard, jumping up; but it was not his summons which stayed Keith (in whose head at that moment was some wild idea of going to search for Major Guthrie), but the fact that he almost collided with a stout young officer of exalted rank just coming through the aperture of the tent. Keith hastily drew back, came to attention, and saluted respectfully, for it was Cumberland himself.

The Duke took no notice of him, but went straight over to his secretary. There had come in with him another stout officer of high rank, twenty years or so his senior, in whom Keith recognized the Earl of Albemarle. The couple of aides-de-camp who followed posted themselves just inside the tent door.

'I hope you have completed those damned tiresome notes about evidence, Faulkner,' said the Prince rather fretfully, 'for there are a thousand and one matters to be attended to before tomorrow, and Lord Albemarle also desires some talk with you.'

'All are in order, your Royal Highness,' responded Sir Everard deferentially, 'save the case of Cameron of Ardroy, for which we shall have to rely on evidence at Fort William. With your permission, my Lord,' he turned to the Earl of Albemarle, 'I will speak to your secretary about it.'

'But have you not summoned Major Windham from Inverness, as I bade you?' exclaimed the Duke. 'You told me yourself that his testimony would be invaluable. Why the devil didn't you send for him?'

'Your Royal Highness's commands were obeyed to the letter,' responded Sir Everard with some stiffness. 'But it seems that Major Windham has scruples about giving his testimony – as he can explain in person to your Royal Highness, since he is present.'

Cumberland swung round his bulk with an alertness which showed his five-and-twenty years. He glanced at Keith, standing motionless at the side of the tent. 'Won't give it – scruples? Nonsense! You must have misunderstood him, Faulkner. Write a line to Major-General Blakeney at once, informing him that Major Windham is seconded, as he sets out with me for England tomorrow. Now, Major, you see how easy it is to leave your new regiment, so no difficulty remains, eh?'

Keith's head went round. Advancement at last – and good-bye to Scotland! But his heart was cold. There was a condition to this favour, impossible of fulfilment.

He came forward a little. 'If the honour your Royal Highness designs to do me,' he said in a very low voice, 'depends upon my giving evidence against Cameron of Ardroy, I must beg leave, with the greatest respect, to decline it. But if it is without such a condition, your Royal Highness has no more grateful servant.'

'Condition, sir – what do you mean?' demanded the Prince sharply. 'Are you trying to bargain with me?'

'Indeed, no, your Royal Highness. I thought,' ventured Keith, still very respectfully, 'that it was rather the other way about . . . But I was no doubt mistaken.'

The pale, prominent eyes stared at him a moment, and their owner gave vent to what in any other but a scion of royalty would have been termed a snort. 'Indeed you are mistaken, sir! I do not bargain with officers under my command; I give them orders. Be ready to start for Edinburgh tomorrow with the rest of my staff at the time I design to leave Fort Augustus. In England leave will be given you for the purpose of attending the trial of this rebel at Carlisle, whenever it shall take place. After that you will rejoin my staff and accompany me – or follow me, as the case may be – to the Continent. It is part of the duty of a commander-in-chief, gentlemen,' went on the Duke, addressing the remainder of the company, 'to remember and reward individual merit, and Major Windham's gallantry at Fontenoy has not passed from my mind, although I have not until now been able to recompense it as it deserves.'

The aides-de-camp, Sir Everard and even Lord Albemarle, expressed in murmurs or in dumb show their appreciation of His Royal Highness's gracious good memory. As for Keith, he was conscious of an almost physical nausea, so sickened was he by the unblushing hypocrisy of the bribe – it was nothing less. He looked at the ground as he answered.

'Your Royal Highness overwhelms me, and I hope to show my gratitude by always doing my duty – which is no more than I did at Fontenoy. But there are private reasons why I cannot give evidence against Cameron of Ardroy; I am too much in his debt for services rendered in the past. I appeal therefore to your Highness's generosity to spare me so odious a task.'

The Duke frowned. 'You forget, I think, Major Windham, with what kind of men we are dealing – bloody and unnatural rebels, who have to be exterminated like vermin – like vermin, sir! Here is a chance to getting rid of one rat the more, and you ask that your private sentiments shall be allowed to excuse you from that duty! No, Major Windham, I tell you that they shall not!'

Keith drew himself up, and this time he met Cumberland's gaze full.

'I would beg leave to say to your Royal Highness, speaking as a soldier to the most distinguished soldier in Britain, that it is no part of military duty, even in the crushing of a rebellion, to play the informer.'

The faces of the aides-de-camp, one of them a most elegant young man, expressed the kind of shock produced on a refined mind by an exhibition of bad taste; Lord Albemarle shook his head and put his hand over his mouth, but Sir Everard Faulkner's demonstration of horror could not be seen, since he was behind his royal master, and the latter had almost visibly swollen in size.

'What, you damned impertinent dog, are you to tell *me* what is a soldier's duty!' he got out. 'Why, this is mutiny!'

'Nothing is farther from my thoughts,' replied Keith quietly and firmly. 'Give me any order that a soldier may fitly execute, and your Royal Highness will soon see that. But I have been accustomed to meet the enemies of my country in the field, and not in the dock.' And as the Duke was still incoherent from fury and incredulity he repeated: 'With the utmost respect, I must decline to give evidence in this case.'

'Damn your respect, sir!' shouted the Commander-in-Chief, finding his tongue again. 'You're little better than a rebel yourself! A soldier – any soldier – under my command does what he is ordered, or I'll know the reason why!' He stamped his royal foot. 'By Heaven, you *shall* go to Carlisle, if I have to send you there under guard! But you need not flatter yourself that there will be any vacancy for you on my staff after this. Now, will you go willingly, or must the provost-marshal take you?'

Keith measured his princely and well-fed opponent, the adulated victor, the bloodstained executioner. He was tolerably certain that the Duke, for all his powers, could not force him to give evidence, and that this talk of sending him to Carlisle by force was only a threat. But he knew that civilians, at all events, could be subpoenaed as witnesses, and was not too sure of his own ultimate position. He brought out therefore a new and unexpected weapon.

'If my presence should be constrained at the trial, I must take leave to observe to your Royal Highness that I shall then be obliged to give the whole of my testimony – how Mr Cameron spared my life when he had me at his mercy after the disaster at High Bridge last summer, and how, in Edinburgh, he saved me from the hands of the Cameron guard and gave me my liberty when I was abandoned by the soldiers with me and trapped. Since those facts would undoubtedly have some influence on an English jury, I cannot think that I should prove an altogether satisfactory witness for the Crown.'

The victor of Culloden stood a moment stupefied with rage. When he could command his voice he turned to his secretary. 'Is this true, Faulkner, what this – mutineer says?' (For indeed, owing to Keith's calculated reticence at Inverness, it was news to him.) To Sir Everard's reply that he did not know, the Duke returned furiously: 'It's your business to know, you blockhead!' and after that the storm was loosed on Keith, and a flood of most unprincely invective it was. The names he was called, however, passed him by without really wounding him much. They were nothing compared to those he would have called himself had he sold Ardroy's life as the price of his own advancement.

But it was pretty clear that he had finally consummated his own ruin, and when he heard the angry voice declaring its owner's regret that he had overlooked his previous ill-conduct with regard to this misbegotten rebel, Keith fully expected the Duke to add that he intended to break him for his present behaviour. Perhaps that would come later; for the moment the Duke contented himself with requesting him, in language more suggestive of the guardroom than the palace, to take his — face where he would never see it again. 'And you need not think,' he finished, out of breath, 'that you will save the rascally rebel who has suborned you from your duty; there are plenty other witnesses who will see to it that he hangs!'

But that Keith did not believe, or the Duke and Sir Everard would not have been so eager to secure his evidence. And as, at last, he saluted and rather dizzily left the tent where he had completed the wreck of his ambitions, it was resentment which burnt in him more fiercely than any other emotion. That it should be supposed that anyone – even a Prince of the blood – could bribe him into an action which revolted him!

Late as it was, he would much have preferred to start back to Inverness that evening, but his horse had to be considered. And, while he was seeing that the beast was being properly looked after, he was surprised to find himself accosted by an elegant young officer, whom he recognized as one of the two aides-de-camp present at the recent scene.

'Major Windham, is it not? General Lord Albemarle requests that you will not leave the camp without further orders, and that you will wait upon him at some time after His Royal Highness's departure tomorrow.'

'Do you mean, sir,' asked Keith bluntly, 'that I am to consider myself under arrest?'

'Oh, my dear Major, by no means!' answered the young man, greatly shocked. 'On the contrary! His Lordship – but I am being prodigious indiscreet – recognized in you, it seems, an acquaintance, so do not fail to wait upon him tomorrow.'

'I will do so,' said Keith. 'Meanwhile, can you tell me if a certain Major Guthrie of Campbell's regiment is in camp?'

'Major Guthrie – la, sir, I've not the pleasure of his acquaintance. But stay, part of Campbell's regiment marched the day before yesterday for Badenoch, so it is like the Major is gone with them.'

'If it be a question of further burnings and floggings, I am sure he will be gone with them,' commented Keith. 'Perhaps it is as well. ... Tell his Lordship that I will certainly obey his commands tomorrow.'

Once again he spent a night at Fort Augustus after a clash with authority. But this time it was a collision with a much more devastating force than Lord Loudoun. Cumberland was not likely to forget or forgive. And Keith felt quite reckless, and glad to be rid of the prudence which had shackled him since May. He had no more to lose now. If he could have shaken the life out of Guthrie it would have been some consolation. From Lord Albemarle's message it did not seem as if he were going to be relieved of his commission after all; but, if he were, then, by God, he would get at Guthrie somehow, and challenge him!

When Cumberland first came to Fort Augustus he had been housed in a 'neat bower' which was specially constructed for him, and Lieutenant-General Lord Albemarle evidently preferred this abode of his predecessor's to a tent. It was there, at any rate, that he received Major Windham next afternoon when the racket of the Duke's departure was over.

William Anne Keppel, second Earl of Albemarle, the son of King William's Dutch favourite, was at this time forty-two years of age, but his portly habit of body made him look older. Plain as well as stout, he gave the impression of a kind but easily flustered nature.

'We met at Perth, did we not, Major Windham?' he asked, and as Keith bowed and assented the Earl said pleasantly: 'I should like a few minutes' conversation with you. You can leave us, Captain Ferrers.'

And when the elegant aide-de-camp had withdrawn, Albemarle, pacing up and down with short steps, his hands behind his broad back, began: 'I must say that I am very sorry, Major Windham, that you felt constrained to take up such an attitude towards His Royal Highness yesterday.'

'So am I, my Lord,' returned the culprit, with truth. 'But I had no choice. I hope your Lordship is not going to renew the same request, for there are some things which a man cannot do, and one of those is to help hang a man who has spared his own life.'

'Is that so – the prisoner in question spared your life?' asked Albemarle with an appearance of surprise, though, thought Keith, unless he had not been listening he must have learnt that fact yesterday. 'Surely you did not make that clear to His Royal Highness, who is as remarkable for clemency as for just severity!'

Keith looked at him askance; was my Lord Albemarle joking or sincere?

'No, Major Windham,' went on the new Commander-in-Chief, 'I do not intend to renew the request, for I should not presume to flatter myself that I could succeed where one with so

257

much stronger a claim on your obedience has failed. Your reveal-ing this fact alters matters; I sympathize with your scrupulosity, and so must the excellent Prince have done, had you but presented the case fairly to him. A pity, Major Windham!'

Keith inclined his head, but said nothing. A grim amusement possessed him, and he could not imagine why Lord Albemarle should be at pains to make this elaborate pretence.

'His Royal Highness's zeal has been wonderful,' pursued the Earl. He sighed, sat down, and began to drum his fingers on the table beside him. 'How I am expected to replace him I do not know. He has indeed accomplished most of his great task, but I am left with part of it still upon my hands – the capturing of the Pretender's son, if indeed he has escaped the last search party of fifteen hundred men sent out from here and from Fort William three days ago. . . . And again, I fear that relations with the Scottish authorities may be sadly difficult. *L'Écosse est ma bête,* Major Windham, as I think I said to you before, on a certain occasion when I was very indiscreet. Had I then had an indiscreet listener I might have harmed myself by my imprudence.' He stopped drumming and looked up. 'I shall see what I can do for you, Major Windham,' he concluded, with a suddenness which took Keith's breath away.

'Your Lordship . . .' he stammered, and found no more words. Albemarle smiled.

'The opportunity may shortly present itself of employing you. I must see. Meanwhile I wish you to remain here; I will arrange that with Major-General Blakeney and your colonel.'

And Keith murmured he knew not what. It seemed impossible that at Perth he should have made an impression so deep as to lead to this; and in a moment it appeared that there was another factor in the case, for Lord Albemarle, fidgeting with the sandbox on the table, revealed it.

'Years ago,' he said reflectively, 'when I was a younger man, I used to know a lady – the most beautiful, I think, whom I have ever met in my life. Perhaps you can guess whom I mean? . . . I did not know when you brought me the dispatch at Perth, Major Windham, that Lady Stowe was your mother; I have learnt it since. It would give me pleasure to extend to her son a trifle of help at a crisis in his fortunes. – No, say no more about it, Windham; 'tis but the payment of a debt to Beauty, who allowed unreproved worship at her shrine!'

And he raised his eyes to the roof of the neat bower, apparently absorbed in sentimental retrospect, while Keith, startled, grateful, yet sardonically amused, tried to picture this plain and unwieldy Anglo-Dutch peer paying his devoirs to a lady who had almost certainly made game of him behind his back. Or had she found him useful, like Lord Orkney, who when Keith was a mere boy had promised the pair of colours in the Royal Scots which had saved his mother so much trouble and expense – and had deprived him of any choice in the matter of a regiment.

But the adorer in question at this moment had now brought his eyes to the ordinary level again.

'You are not like the Countess, Major Windham,' he observed.

'My Lord, I am only too well aware of that. My half-brother Aveling resembles her much more closely. He is a very handsome youth.'

'I must make Lord Aveling's acquaintance some day,' said the Earl rising. 'Commend me meanwhile to Lady Stowe.'

'I shall not fail to do so, my Lord,' replied Keith, preparing to withdraw, but hesitating. Yes, this unlooked-for and melting mood was certainly that in which to proffer his request. 'Your Lordship's extreme generosity towards a disgraced man,' he went on, 'emboldens me to ask a small favour, which is, that I may see Cameron of Ardroy once before he goes south to his trial – giving my most sacred word of honour that nothing shall pass between us relative to escape. I desire only to say farewell to him, and your Lordship, who has shown yourself so sensible of my obligation towards him – '

'Yes, yes,' interrupted his Lordship, putting up a plump hand. 'Yes, before he goes you shall see him, I promise you, Major Windham. But not at present – not at present,' he added, as if he felt that the line of his complaisance must be drawn somewhere. 'Send me in Captain Ferrers, if you please, as you go out.'

So Keith left, meditating on the hopeful change in his outlook. It was strange that Lord Albemarle did not fear Cumberland's wrath, if the Duke ever learnt of the favour shown to a man under his extremest displeasure. If it was solely for the sake of the beautiful Countess of Stowe that his Lordship was braving this possibility, the situation was still more ironical, for Keith knew well that his mother would not feel any particular gratitude for this clemency towards her elder son. She would rather that some special token of favour had fallen on the head of his young halfbrother, who had no need of it.

The next few days went slowly by, and Keith began to wonder whether Lord Albemarle's lenity were not going to end in nothing but the assurance to him of an idle existence at Fort Augustus. He was glad, however, to be there, for he could fairly well assure himself that Ardroy was not taken away without his knowledge. Inquiries revealed the fact that old Sergeant Mullins was no longer his gaoler, but Keith got speech with his successor, a Scot, and learnt that Ewen was to be taken on the twenty-fifth of the month to Fort William to be identified. On the morning of the twenty-fourth, fearing to wait any longer, he sought out the exquisite Captain Ferrers and begged him to recall to Lord Albemarle's mind his promise that he should see the prisoner before departure; and in the afternoon was duly handed a signed order permitting an interview.

Chapter 7

IN thinking of Ewen, Keith had always pictured him where last he had seen him, in the upper room, light and wind-blown, and when he was conducted to the regions under the remains of the fort, he realized with something approaching dismay that Ardroy's quarters had not been changed for the better. And as the door was opened, and he saw before him, down a few steps, a sort of cellar which seemed darker than it really was, and which smelt of damp, he was horrified, though in reality, the fort being of quite recent construction, its 'dungeons' were not nearly as noisome as their name suggested.

There was one small grated window, high up, and under this Ewen was sitting on a stool with his back to the door, reading, though there hardly appeared sufficient light for it. He did not turn his head. 'Is that supper already, Corporal?' he asked. 'What time is it then?'

'No, Mr Cameron, nae supper, but an officer tae veesit ye. – Hae a care o' yon steps, sir!'

But Ewen had turned on his stool, had seen who his visitor was, and was getting to his feet. He clashed as he moved, for he was in irons.

'Windham!' he exclaimed with an accent of surprise and pleasure. 'This is very good of you! Where have you come from?'

And as Keith, distressed by everything, the darkness, the want of accommodation and the chains, stood rooted, Ewen, with more jangling, limped towards him, holding out a fettered hand. He was blanched by two months of semi-darkness, worn down by illness and insufficient food to the framework of himself, but he was shaven and respectably clothed, and he had all his old erectness of poise.

Keith took the proffered hand. 'How long have you had *those* on?' was his first question.

'These irons? Only for a few days. They have just come off a man, imprisoned for a short time with me, who had the distinction of helping the Prince to escape when he was in Skye, MacDonald of Kingsburgh, and when he was carried to Edinburgh they put them on me. I was flattered, not having the same qualification for them. Sit down, Major, on the stool he had, which still remains to me – or take mine, if you consider that less treasonable. Faith, no, I suppose Kingsburgh, who was never "out", is less of a rebel than I.' He laughed, shuffled to a corner, and came back with another stool. 'Now tell me how you came here, and what your situation is now? Mullins gave me some news of you – very scanty – in May. Are you quit of the cloud you drew upon yourself for my sake?'

'It is of yourself that we must speak,' said Keith, hoarsely, thrown off his balance by this unaffected cheerfulness, and deeply ashamed, all at once, of the cowardly 'prudence' which had left Ardroy without a letter. 'Sit down; you should not stand, I am sure. How does your wound?'

Rather stiffly, Ewen sat down. 'Quite healed, though the leg is weak. However, I am to ride thirty miles tomorrow, for I go to Fort William to be identified, thence to Carlisle for trial – by what means of transport I do not know.'

'You think that you will be identified by this man at Fort William?'

'Man? There is more than one; indeed there'll be a measure of jealousy, I'm thinking, who shall travel to Carlisle on my affair at the expense of the Government. – Why, I vow it never occurred to me before that *you* might go, Windham, and save me the journey to Fort William; for you can identify me, none better!'

Keith winced. 'Don't jest,' he said in a sombre voice; 'don't jest on such a theme, I beg of you. And, Ardroy,' he added earnestly, 'I doubt whether the authorities here really place very much reliance on this testimony from Fort William, or they would not have – ' He pulled up, biting his lip, for he had no intention of speaking of his encounter with Cumberland. Though he had no cause for shame, he was ashamed; moreover he did not wish to parade his own self-abnegation.

In the dim light, momentarily becoming to Keith, however, a little less dim, the prisoner looked at him with those clear eyes of his. Then, with a jangle, he laid his bony hand on the Englishman's wrist. 'My sorrow, I believe my jest went near the truth! They did want you to go as a witness against me – was not that what you were about to say? Why, then, did you not comply?'

Keith turned on him almost savagely. 'How dare you ask me that, Ewen Cameron! Do you think I baulked Guthrie, only to go in cold blood and bring you to the scaffold myself? Are you like the Duke, that you can fancy I would do such a thing for any consideration on earth ... and witness moreover to acts by which I had been the gainer?'

'I beg your pardon,' said Ewen mildly. 'In truth I was not thinking of the implications of what I said. But, Windham,' he went on anxiously, 'has not your refusal involved you once more in Cumberland's displeasure? I'm sure it has!'

'No, no,' said Keith mendaciously. 'He was angry, but he has not punished me further. He could not force me to be a witness; and Lord Albemarle has subsequently shown me some favour, and holds out hopes of employing me, which is why I am here at

Fort Augustus. As far as I am concerned, therefore, good may yet come out of evil. – But, tell me, to what does this evidence at Fort William amount?'

But Ewen replied by another question. 'What was the bribe which Cumberland offered you to give evidence against me?'

'Bribe!' exclaimed Keith, rather over-hastily. 'I said nothing about a bribe. I want to hear about these witnesses at Fort William.'

'But *I* want to know what you have sacrificed for my sake? Or perhaps it would be truer to say, for the sake of your own self-respect – Cumberland did offer you something, did he not?'

'Nothing of consequence,' answered Keith carelessly.

'You will not tell me what it was? Then I know that it was something which you coveted. I seem fated to bring you misfortune, Windham,' said the Highlander rather sadly. 'And yet I never really wished you other than well.'

'But I have brought you even more,' said Keith; 'and indeed I wished you well, too.' His eyes were on the heap of straw in the corner which constituted Ewen's bed. 'If I had not ridden by the shieling hut that day, you would be lying quietly among the mountains of your own land and not – not about to set out for the chance, at least, of a death far away, and ... and much less merciful. I should like to hear you say that you forgive me for that.'

'Forgive you for saving my life!' exclaimed Ewen. 'My dear Windham, you are really absurd! Don't, for God's sake, go recalling the crazy things I said to you at our last meeting! You must remember that I was nearly out of my senses then.'

'I know that, and I have never given them another thought, I assure you. But there is a count,' said Keith rather hesitatingly, 'on which you must find it hard to forgive me – suffering of the mind, for which I must always hold myself in a measure responsible. You know to what I refer.'

Ewen looked down at the floor. 'I had some dark days, it is true. ... Yes, they were very dark ... but not so dark after your return. You gave me hope; and above all you gave me back that night in the hut.' He smiled. 'I often think of it. I think of it when I hear very different stories of the English. And I suppose you

263

know that nothing came of my betrayal – they never even searched the place for Lochiel, I believe. And, moreover' – he suddenly looked almost boyishly elated and mischievous – 'by some wonderful mischance I never gave the name of the mountain where the secret place was. In my sleep I presented them with the name of Ben Loy, where you came upon me, and they did not discover the error until too late.'

Keith put his hand on the speaker's knee. 'I heard at Inverness, to my satisfaction, that Lochiel had escaped capture. Then that is all over, and your mind at rest; I am thankful.'

Ewen looked grave again. 'No, it cannot be at rest until I am sure that Lochiel knows the truth.'

'But why should he ever hear anything at all about the matter?'

'And I have thought that at my trial,' went on Ewen without taking notice of the interruption, 'I may get the chance of publicly denying that I gave the information knowingly. And then I believe that I could die in peace.'

Keith withdrew his hand. 'Why do you make so sure of your condemnation?' he asked almost irritably. 'Of what real worth is the testimony of persons who imagine that they saw you during a siege? No one could swear to you, out of so many Camerons!'

'You think we are all as alike as sheep?' queried Ewen, looking amused. 'But I had at least one hand-to-hand conflict with the Argyll militia, and another day I encountered a writer of Maryburgh with whom I had had dealings; he knew me at once, and will be only too glad to give evidence against me; I cannot think how they have not got hold of it already. – No, Windham, 'tis better to face the truth; once I reach Fort William I am certainly for Carlisle, and with such good evidence against me, I have small chance of acquittal. I have known that for the last ten days; though naturally I have not acquainted the authorities with the excellent case they are like to have.'

And to this Keith found nothing to say. It was strange, it was alarming, to feel, as by this time he did, how strongly their intimacy had progressed in two months of absence and, on his side, of deliberate abstention from communication – like the roots of two trees growing secretly towards each other in darkness. But it was so; and now the roots must be severed.

'I hear that some of the prisoners at Inverness intend to swear that they were forced out,' he remarked after a silence.

'I dare say that may be true of some of them,' replied Ewen with composure. 'But you are not suggesting that I should employ that plea, are you?'

'I know too well that you would not,' returned his visitor, and then murmured something about transportation, as a possible alternative to a worse fate.

'Transportation!' exclaimed the Highlander. 'To be sent to work in the plantations overseas as an indentured servant! I'd far liefer be hanged and quartered!'

Keith sighed heavily. 'Yes, I have brought you nothing but harm. I would give my right hand to save you – and I can do nothing!'

Ewen twisted round on his stool. 'How can you say that? Who knows what the want of your evidence at Carlisle may mean to me? For there is always a chance that the witnesses at Fort William may have left or died.'

'You have just said that once you reached Fort William there was no chance of escaping Carlisle. I am not a child, Ardroy!' retorted Keith, glowering at him in his own pain.

'Neither am I,' replied Ewen with a sudden smile. 'Do not, therefore, talk about wishing in vain to give your right hand for my sake, for I strongly suspect that you have already given what means as much or more to you.'

Keith got up, that the speaker might not see in his face how near this guess went to the truth. 'Even in my refusal to witness against you,' he said gloomily, 'I begin to think that I acted like a fool. For, as I told His Royal Highness, if he sent me to Carlisle by force, as he threatened to do, nothing should have prevented my testifying also to your granting me my life in Lochaber and my liberty in Edinburgh. I have thought since that, on that score, it might have been better to agree to go. . . . But no, I could not have done it!' he added.

Ewen smiled up at him with a look that was almost affection, and laid his manacled hand on his cuff. 'I almost wish that you had consented, so that we might meet again. For, if old Angus is right, this is our last meeting – I have counted them many times.

And, indeed, I do not see how it could be otherwise. So' – his voice was very gentle – 'we cannot bring each other misfortune any more.'

The words knocked sharply at Keith's heart. And how young the speaker looked, for all his half-starved air; a boy going to extinction, while he, only four years his senior, felt as if he were middle-aged. (But no, at their last meeting, when he had trembled before him, Ewen had not been a boy.)

'Is there nothing I can do for you?' he asked painfully. 'Do your kindred know of your situation; I suppose so?'

'I am not sure if my aunt knows. If she does, she has no doubt tried to communicate with my wife in France, but –'

'Your wife! Then you –'

'Yes. Miss Grant and I were married at Inverness in March. She is in France with her sick father, and since the battle I have been unable to write to her, so that, unless my aunt has contrived to do so, she may not know whether I am alive or dead. If *you* would write to her, Windham – you remember her, no doubt – that would indeed be a kindness. Will you?'

'Certainly, if you wish it,' answered Keith, though he did not like the prospect. 'But,' he went on with a little hesitation, 'why do you not write yourself, and I would use my best endeavours that the letter should reach her.'

'I cannot write,' said Ewen. 'They will not allow me the materials; I have often tried to come by them. You must tell her of me, if you will; and I particularly charge you not to omit how you saved my life and visited me, and ... and all the rest that you have done,' he concluded a trifle unsteadily. 'That is a last command, Windham.'

But Keith had drawn a pencil from his pocket. 'You had a book in your hand when I came in; can you not tear out a blank page and write upon that? I promise you that, if I can compass it, no eye shall see the letter but your wife's.'

'A book?' queried Ewen. 'Ah, yes, but 'tis only a little Gaelic psalter which I contrived to get hold of. However –' He took it out of his pocket, remarking that the pages were but small, and, carefully tearing out the fly-leaf, accepted the proffered pencil. Keith, unable to withdraw as he would have wished, walked slowly up and down the narrow place with bent head. 'I have saved him for this!' was still the burden of his thoughts. Had Ardroy been shot that day, he would have known little about it; he was barely conscious. It would have been over in a moment, and it would have been a man's death, too. Now . . . he shuddered to think of the alternative, purposely prolonged and horrible, the death of an animal in the shambles. He hoped with all his heart that Alison Cameron, away in France, did not know, and would never hear, the details of the English sentence for treason.

Ewen did not write much, for there was not a great deal of space on his paper. He read it over very composedly and signed his name. Then he folded the letter, stooped his head and put his lips to it. Keith turned his back, but the distance between them was so small that he knew that the writer, after that, had buried his face in his hands.

Ah, if only he had listened to him on that evening last summer, which now seemed such centuries ago, he would not now be giving up his love, as well as his life and lands!

But there was a clashing behind him; Ewen was getting to his feet. 'I beg your pardon for keeping you waiting so long. Since you are so good, I think that I should like to send my wife also the only remembrance that I can send. Have you a knife, and can you trust me with it? – or better still, will you cut off a piece of this for her?'

He indicated his hair, and, coming closer, bent his head. So Keith, with a rather blunt penknife, and not particularly good eyesight at the moment, sawed off a little lock on his temple.

'Women like such things,' said the young man half apologetically as Keith, his mouth tight shut, wrapped the trophy in his handkerchief. 'And the more of which one can cheat Carlisle gate, the better.' He spoke quite lightly and calmly, but his little letter, which he gave Keith the moment after, had been so tightly held in his hand that it was marked with his nail-prints. 'I have written the direction upon it,' he went on, watching the Englishman put it carefully away. 'Perhaps I may be able to write to her once more from Carlisle, but who knows? And the messenger might not be trustworthy, whereas I know that you are. – Now,

Windham, there is another matter. The money you so generously left for my use – '

'For God's sake don't think of that now!' cried Keith, quite distracted.

'But I must! Miss Cameron, if I can communicate with her, which may be allowed at Carlisle – '

'Will you waste time over a few guineas? In Heaven's name, take them as a gift – cannot you see that it would be kinder to me?'

Ewen evidently saw; he could hardly fail to see it. 'Very well, then I will; and thank you for the gift. After all, I took a greater at your hands on Beinn Laoigh. And do you remember the money you left as payment for my clothes at Fassefern House? My sorrow, but I was angry with you! I threw it away into the bushes, and Clanranald's and Keppoch's men hunted for it all night, so I heard afterwards.' His tone suddenly changed. 'Do you mean to leave this penknife here – is that a gift, too?'

He pointed to that object, lying where Keith had laid it down on one of the stools in order to have both hands free to wrap up the lock of hair. The Englishman hesitated, looking from it to the prisoner, and read, plain to see in his eyes, the value which he would set on even so small and blunt a weapon tomorrow. For a moment he was tempted, against honour and duty.

'Why did you put me in mind of it?' he asked reproachfully 'I had indeed honestly forgotten it, and had I so left it, you could have taken it with you tomorrow! . . . But I gave Lord Albemarle my word not to help you in any way to escape . . .'

Ewen instantly picked up the penknife, shut it, and held it out to him. 'Take it. They are sure, too, to search me before I go tomorrow. Come,' he still held it out, 'you have sacrificed enough for me; your honour you shall not sacrifice!'

As Keith reluctantly took the knife from the shackled hand, he had a shock as if a lightning flash had stabbed asunder the sky above him and shown him something he had never seen – never wished to see – before. The barren and solitary path which he had marked out for himself through life was *not* the best. Here was a man who would never willingly fail friend or lover, much less play them false. Now, at this their last meeting, when friendship with him was a thing impossible of realization, he knew that he would have asked nothing better – he who never wished for a friend.

Like a lightning flash too in its speed, the revelation was over. Mechanically he put the penknife away, and Ewen limped the few paces back to his stool. 'Come and sit down again, Windham,' he said, 'for once more you cannot get out if you wish to. And there is a matter about which I have long been curious. Why do you bear a Scots name – if I may ask without indiscretion? Have you perhaps Scottish kin?'

Keith, sitting down beside him again, shook his head. 'There's not a soul of my blood north of Tweed. But my father, who was a soldier also, had once a Scottish friend, killed at Malplaquet before I was born, for whom he must have had a great affection, since he gave me his name.'

They looked at each other, and the shadowy dead Scot of Marlborough's wars seemed, to his namesake at least, to assume the shape of a symbol or a prophecy. Keith shivered suddenly.

'I can hardly hope,' said the Jacobite, 'that you will care to name your son after me when I have ended . . . not on a battle-field . . . but I should like to feel that you will remember some-times, not me, but what you did for me. For whereas you think but poorly of your fellow-men and yourself – or am I wrong? – you act, Keith Windham, very much otherwise!'

Moved and startled, Keith dropped his gaze and stared be-tween his knees at the floor. Yes, they might have been friends; they were meant to be friends – Ardroy felt that too, did he? 'I . . . in truth I do not well know what I think,' he murmured; 'and, as for my actions, why, I seem to have failed on every side. – But one thing I do know,' he went on with a touch of defiance, 'and that is, that I do not believe in your Highland second sight. Who can say that we shall not meet again – and you a free man?'

Ewen looked hard at him a moment. Outside the jangling of keys could be heard coming nearer. 'I wish very much that I could think so too,' he answered simply, as he rose to his feet with a corresponding clashing. And again the strange constriction in his throat betrayed Keith into irritation.

'Are you so superstitious, Ardroy, that you'll read into an old man's maunderings a menace that was never there? Did your foster-father say a word about death in his precious prophecy? I warrant he did not!'

Ewen smiled. 'My dear Windham, at bottom I believe as little in the two sights as you. But surely 'tis not superstition to realize that I am at least threatened with that fate. Yet who knows? If it pass me by, and we ever meet again in this world, then maybe I'll have more time to thank you fitly for all you have done and given up for me. Yet I do thank you now, from my heart – from my inmost heart!'

He held out his fettered hands, and Keith as he took them was hardly capable of speech.

'I have failed in everything,' he muttered. 'But your letter – I promise you it shall go by a safe hand. I . . . I . . .' The door, opening, recalled him to an Englishman's last obligation, the suppression of emotion before witnesses. 'Tomorrow,' he said, loosing his grasp, and in a tolerably composed voice, 'tomorrow you will at least be out of this dismal place and free of those irons.'

'Aye, will he,' commented the gaoler in the doorway. 'And riding a braw horse forbye!'

'I doubt I'll make much show as a horseman,' replied Ewen. 'I fear I shall fall off.'

'Ye're no like tae hae the chance, Mr Cameron,' replied the man dryly. 'Ye'll be tied on. – Noo, sir, if ye please.'

'What time is he to start?' asked Keith.

'Sax o' the clock.' The keys jingled impatiently.

Keith took a resolve. But he did not put it into words. All he said was 'Good-bye', and, for fear of being totally unmanned, stole only the most cursory glance at the pale, gravely-smiling face under the rather untidy auburn hair.

But Ewen held out his hand again. '*Beannachd leat*, as we say in the Erse. "Blessings go with you; may a straight path be before you, and a happy end to your journey"!'

Without answering Keith wrung the hand and went quickly up the steps past the gaoler and into the passage. He was hardly there before the heavy door clanged to between him and his last meeting with Ewen Cameron.

'A peety,' said the gaoler reflectively, taking the key from the lock, 'a peety yon muckle young man behoves to hae a rope aboot his thrapple. But there, wha will tae Cupar maun tae Cupar ... Yon's the way up, sir.'

At twenty minutes to seven next morning Keith Windham, having propped himself upon one elbow in his camp bed, was staring with incredulous and remorseful eyes at the watch which he had just drawn from beneath his pillow. That he should not wake in time to catch a final glimpse of Ardroy as he rode away had never occurred to him; the question last night had rather been whether he should ever get to sleep ...

Well, evidently old Angus MacMartin's fates were determined that he should not see Ewen Cameron again. And after all, he thought, trying to stifle regret, did I really desire to see him carried away, bound upon a horse, by Kingston's dragoons?

When he was dressed he went to the door of the tent, which opened towards Loch Ness, and looked out. It was a beautiful, fresh morning, and the loch was smiling up at the flanking hills. Even the ruins of the fort, rearing themselves against that brightness, looked less blackened in the sunshine. But for Keith those gutted buildings held nothing now; and the busy camp around him was empty, too. How far on the road were they got by this time, and were the troopers riding too fast ...?

He dropped the flap of the tent and, going over to the table, took out from the breast of his uniform the handkerchief with the curl of hair and the scrap of a letter, and sealed them up carefully in a little packet, first copying down the address and scrupulously averting his eyes from the rest of the torn fly-leaf in doing so. Then, wondering how soon and in what manner he should find an opportunity of fulfilling his trust, he sat on, staring at the packet, now directed in his own hand to Mrs Ewen Cameron at an address in Havre-de-Grâce.

What was it that Ardroy had wished him yesterday – a straight path and a happy end to his journey? Ewen's own path seemed straighter than his, now, but the end to which it led? Keith had a sudden horrible vision, corollary of those which had haunted him in the night. He pressed his hands over his eyes and bade it begone, bade himself be as little perturbed at the prospect as Ewen himself had been yesterday – Ewen who would certainly go cheerfully and courageously to that ghastly business, but who, had it not been for his interference, might be lying now unmutilated under the turf of Ben Loy, with only the plovers and the curlews to disturb his rest.

Keith suddenly got up and began to pace restlessly to and fro, his head on his breast. He was finding his self-defensive philosophy of a very meagre assistance now. If he were again the child he had been, the child who every night at his nurse's knee asked so simply and naturally for what he desired, it would have been easy to utter the prayer in his heart. But of what use such supplication to the Power whose only concern with the world was that He had set it a-rolling? Yet it was some time before he came to a standstill, and, with a heavy sigh, replaced in his breast the little packet for Ewen Cameron's wife; with this for consolation in his mind, that he who was riding southward was not yet condemned, and that till the sentence was spoken his case was not hopeless.

All that afternoon there came marching wearily back to Fort Augustus, in a woeful state of fatigue and rags, the various units of the fifteen hundred men whom Cumberland had sent out in his last battue for Prince Charles nearly a fortnight before. They had met with no success whatever.

At nine o'clock that evening Keith, to his surprise, received a summons from Lord Albemarle, and found him heated and discomposed.

''Tis a most extraordinary and vexatious thing,' declared the Earl, pacing up and down his quarters with his heavy tread. 'It seems as though the Pretender's son must have broken through the chain of sentry posts round Clanranald's country, and yet I can scarce believe it, they were so close together. I shall make a fresh effort, with fresh men; these poor fellows are quite worn out with their exertions. For my part, Major Windham, I declare that to capture that young man, source of all our woes, I should with infinite pleasure walk barefoot from Pole to Pole!'

Had Lord Albemarle but known, no such heroic pilgrimage

was required of him; a ten-mile expedition that night to a certain cave in Glenmoriston would have been sufficient.

'Your Lordship's zeal is common knowledge,' murmured Keith, wondering what the Commander-in-Chief wanted him for. 'If it could only be crowned with success. . . .'

'Aye, if only it could! One report says,' continued the Earl, going to a table and turning over some papers, 'that the Pretender's son is in Badenoch on his way to the east coast; another that he has gone north to Caithness. Some say he is still in Morar and Knoidart; and the very latest of all declares that he has gone back to the Long Island – as you know they call that chain of islands from South Uist to Lewis. It is distracting!'

It was; but Keith could not think why he should have been summoned to hear this truth.

'Why, bless my soul,' said Albemarle, as if he had read his thoughts, 'I am so prodigiously put about that I have forgotten, I believe, to tell you, Major Windham, that you are one of the officers whom I design to employ in my new effort.'

'My Lord!' ejaculated Keith, flushing.

'Yes, I intend to send you without delay to the neighbourhood of Arisaig, not because I think that the young man is there at the moment, though one report says so, but because I think it not unlikely he may try in the end to escape from the very spot where he landed last July.'

'Your Lordship is really too good,' stammered Keith, rather overcome. 'If the most active vigilance – '

'Yes,' cut in Albemarle, 'I depend upon you to show that, Major Windham. Your future is in your own hands, and my reputation, too. For reasons upon which I touched the other day, it is you whom I am sending to what I cannot but consider the most likely spot for securing the person of the arch-rebel. The day that you bring him back a prisoner, your difference with His Royal Highness will be no more remembered against you. And perhaps I, too,' added the Earl with a sigh, 'shall be able to leave this most distasteful country.'

'I assure your Lordship,' said Keith with a beating heart, 'that failure shall not be due to any want of exertion on my part. Your generous selection of me for this expedition overwhelms me with gratitude, and whether I secure the prize or no, I shall be your Lordship's lifelong debtor for the opportunity.'

Lord Albemarle nodded, pleased as one who knows that he confers a benefit. 'You will march at daybreak with a hundred men. I do not say that you are to station yourself exclusively at this Loch nan – on my soul, I cannot pronounce its outlandish name. Dispose your men as you think best. My secretary is preparing a few notes for your guidance. The devil of it is, however,' confessed the harassed commander in a further burst of confidence, 'that these informations, when one receives them, are always a se'nnight or two out of date.' And, after adding a few more recommendations as to Keith's conduct, he said kindly: 'Now go and get some sleep, Windham – and good luck to your endeavours!'

Keith went out as one who walks on air. A chance at last – the greatest, if only he could seize it! So the day which had taken from him something which he felt that he had never really possessed had brought him ... no, not compensation for the loss, for that, perhaps, he could never have, but opportunity to do more than purge his disgrace – to make himself the most envied man in the three kingdoms.

V. THE HERON'S FLIGHT IS ENDED

> Hereafter, in a better world than this,
> I shall desire more love and knowledge of you.
> — SHAKESPEARE

Chapter 1

IT was fortunate for Ewen that the sorrel horse on which he was tied had easy paces, and that the troopers did not ride fast; fortunate too that his arms had been bound to his sides and not behind his back, as had at first been proposed when, limping badly and shielding his eyes against the unaccustomed daylight, he was brought out into the courtyard of the fort to be mounted. For by midday so many hours in the saddle under a July sun were making heavy demands on a man come straight from close confinement and not long recovered of a severe wound.

But from Ewen's spirit a much heavier toll was being exacted; not by the prospect of the death which was in all likelihood awaiting him, not even by the remembrance of his lost Alison, but by the pain which was actually tearing at him now, this taking leave of what he loved better than life, the lakes and mountains of his home. This was the real death, and he kept his lips locked lest he should cry out at its sharpness.

The picture which had been tormenting Keith Windham he could look at without undue shrinking; or rather, he did not trouble to look at it any more now. Like the man who had saved him, he could not avoid the thought that Guthrie's musket balls would have been more merciful, but the choice had not lain in his hands; and for the last two months it had been more important to try to keep his equanimity day after day in the cold and darkness of his prison than to think what he should do or feel when he came to stand in the hangman's cart. And the parting with Alison was over; and because he had known that the kiss in the cabin of the brig might be their last, it had held the solemnity which had enwrapped their hurried marriage and the bridal night whose memory was so holy to him. Alison had been his, though for so brief a space; and one day, as he firmly believed, they would meet again. But Beinn Tigh . . . would he ever see again, in *that* world, his beloved sentinel of the stars?

Ever since its peak had appeared, all flushed by the morning sun, as they began to ride by Loch Oich, he had kept his eyes hungrily upon it, praying that the horses might go slower, or that one might cast a shoe; watching it like a lover as it revealed more of its shapeliness and dominated the shoulder, between it and the loch, behind which, as they went farther, it would inevitably sink. And Loch na h-Iolaire, *his* loch, away behind there, invisible, secluded by its own mountains! If only he could get free of these cords, swim the water between, climb those intervening miles of scree and heather, and see the Eagle's Lake once more! No, never again; neither in this world nor the next. For Loch na h-Iolaire was not like Alison and him; it had not a soul free of time and space. Loch na h-Iolaire existed over there, only there, on that one spot of earth, and in all the fields of heaven there would be no lake so lovely, and in heaven the grey mists would never swoop down on one who ambushed the deer.

At Laggan-ach-drum they had halted and rested and eaten. It was Glengarry's country, yet on the border of the Cameron, and Ardroy was known there; but in the burnt and ravaged clachan there seemed to be no man left, and no risk of a rescue. The troopers of Kingston's Horse had shown themselves rough but not unkindly, and the sergeant, probably thinking that unless they gave the prisoner some attention they would hardly get him to Fort William at the end of the day, had had him unfastened and taken off the sorrel and set down amongst them by the roadside with food and drink. But they were very careful of him, tying his ankles together, and putting a cord from one wrist to the belt of the next man. And Ewen had eaten and drunk in silence, looking at the sunlit desolation. *This* was what had been done in the Glen . . . done in all the countryside . . .

A young girl had passed once or twice to a half-burnt croft, carrying a bucket of water, and presently the sergeant, wanting some for the horses, called to ask where the water came from, since here they were no longer by a lakeside. Setting down the heavy bucket, she came and stood before him, looking on the troopers with eyes like coals, and only once at their prisoner. (But the softness of evening was in them then.) The sergeant, without harshness, put his question, but the girl shook her head, and Ewen knew that she had not the English. Already he had seen a sight that set his heart beating, for as she stooped to put down the bucket he had caught a glimpse of the black handle of a *sgian dubh* in her bosom.

'Shall I ask her for you?' he suggested to the sergeant, and, hardly waiting for the answer, he spoke rapidly to her in Gaelic, putting the question about water indeed, but adding at the end of it: 'Try to give me your knife when I am on the horse again – if you have another for yourself!'

The girl gave him a glance of comprehension, and turned away to show where to fetch the water; and the sergeant had no inkling that another question besides his had been put and answered. He even threw a word of thanks to the interpreter.

But while they were tying Ewen on again the girl came among them, as if curiosity had brought her to see the sight, and, heedless of the jests which she did not understand, slipped nearer and nearer among the horses until she seemed to be jostled against the sorrel's shoulder. And Ewen felt the little knife, warm from its hiding-place, slide into his right stocking; it was only with an effort that he kept his eyes averted and seemed unaware of her presence. But he turned his head as they rode away, and saw her standing at gaze with her hands joined, as though she were praying.

That was an hour agone and more. How he should ever get at, much less use, the blade against his leg he had no idea, seeing that his arms were immovably pinioned, but to know it there made a world of difference. His thoughts reverted to Major Windham, to that interview yesterday. They might have been friends had Fate willed it otherwise; indeed he could not but think of him already as a friend, and with wonder at what he had done for him. But why had Angus's heron brought them together to so little purpose, to meet, and meet, and then to part for ever, as they had met at first, 'by the side of water' – Loch Oich and Loch Ness? Yet he owed his life to one of those encounters; there was no possible doubt of that. But it was still a mystery to him why the Englishman should have cared so much for his fate as to wreck his own career over it. He had really behaved to Loudoun and (as far as he could make out) to Cumberland – all honour to him for it – as if he were fey. And he had seemed at the outset of their acquaintance of so mocking a temper, so lightly contemptuous as scarcely even to be hostile. One saw him with different eyes now.

But Keith Windham was swept from his thoughts again, as he realized afresh that he was going for the last time along Loch Lochy side. It was bright pain to look at it, but Ewen looked greedily, trying to burn those high green slopes for ever on his memory, to be imaged there as long as that memory itself was undissolved. There was the steep corrie and the wall shutting out his home. What though the house of Ardroy were ashes now, like Achnacarry and a score of others, there were things the marauders could not touch, things dearer even than the old house – the sweeps of fern and heather, the hundred little burns sliding and tinkling among stones and mosses, the dark pine-trees, the birches stepping delicately down the torrent side, the mist and the wind, the very mountain air itself. But these, though they would remain, were not for him any more.

And then Ewen bit his lip hard, for, to his horror, his eyes had begun to fill, and, since he could not move a hand, all that was left was to bow his head and pray desperately that the troopers on either side might not observe his weakness. But they were just then absorbed in heartfelt complaints at the detour which they were obliged to make on his account, instead of setting out with the rest of Kingston's Horse, in two days' time, for Edinburgh; and Ewen quickly swallowed the salt upon his lips, thinking: 'Since I am so little of a man, I must fix my mind on something else.' Yet here, in this dear and familiar neighbourhood, he could think of nothing else but what was before his eyes; and his eyes told him now that the radiance of the morning was gone, and that clouds were coming up the Glen from the south-west, from Loch Linnhe, with that rapidity which he knew so well of old. In an hour it would very likely be raining hard; in less, for beyond the Loch Arkaig break he could see that it *was* raining . . .

Here he was, looking just as intently at the hills as before! So he shut his eyes, afraid lest moisture should spring into them again; and also a little because the waters of Loch Lochy, still bright, despite the advancing clouds, were beginning queerly to dazzle him. And when his eyes were shut he realized with increasing clearness that physically too he was nearing the boundary-line of endurance. He had wondered himself how he should ever accomplish the thirty-mile ride, but the problem had not troubled him much, and the untying and rest at Laggan had been a relief. Now – and they still had a long way to go – it was astonishing how the sea of faintness seemed to be gaining upon him. He reopened his eyes as he felt himself give a great lurch in the saddle.

'Hold up!' said the trooper who had the reins. 'Were ye asleep?'

Ewen shook his head. But what curious specks were floating over the darkening landscape! He fixed his eyes on his horse's ears; but once or twice the whole head of the animal disappeared from his sight altogether; and the second time that this phenomenon occurred he felt a grip on his arm, and found the soldier on the other side looking at him curiously. However, the man released him, saying nothing, and Ewen, mute also, tried to straighten himself in the saddle, and looked ahead in the direction of Ben Nevis, since perhaps it was a mistake to look at anything close at hand. The mountain's top was veiled. The last time that he had seen it ... with Lochiel ...

But that memory had poison in it now. Oh, to have speech with Lochiel once before he went hence! Ewen set his teeth, as waves of faintness and of mental pain broke on him together. If he could only say to Donald ...

And there followed on that, surprisingly, a period in which he thought he was speaking to Lochiel; but it must have been by some waterfall – the waterfall near the hiding-place, perhaps – and through the noise of the rushing water he could not make Lochiel hear what he was saying to him. He tried and tried ... Then all at once someone was holding him round the body, and a voice called out, miles away, yet close: 'He was near off that time, Sergeant!'

Ewen left the waterfall and became conscious, to his astonishment, that they were away from Lochy and within full sight of Ben Nevis and all his brethren. Also that the whole escort had stopped. Landscape and horses then whirled violently round. His head fell on a trooper's shoulder.

'The prisoner's swounding, Sergeant! What are we to do?'

Swearing under his breath, the sergeant brought his horse alongside. 'Shamming? No, he ain't shamming. Here,' he brought out something from his holster, 'give him a drink of his own Highland whisky – nasty stuff it is!'

They held up Ewen's head and put the spirit to his lips. It revived him a little, and he tried to say something, but he himself did not know what it was. The sergeant eyed him doubtfully.

'I'll tell you what,' he remarked to his men, 'we'll untie his arms – not his feet, mind you – and maybe then he can help himself by taking a holt of the mane – Can ye do that?'

Ewen nodded, too sick and dizzy to realize what possibilities would thus be put within his reach.

The dragoons unfastened the cords round his arms and body, gave him some more spirit, rubbed his cramped arms, and in a little while he was able to do what the sergeant suggested; and presently, he leaning hard upon the sorrel's crest, his fingers twined in the mane, they were going slowly down the moorland slope toward the Spean. Ewen felt less faint now, after the whisky and the release of his arms; the fine misty rain which had now set in was refreshing, too, so, although the landscape showed a disposition to swim at times, he could certainly keep in the saddle – indeed, how could he fall off, he thought, with this rope passing from ankle to ankle beneath the horse's belly? And he began to think about High Bridge, still unseen, which they were approaching, and of the part which it had played in this great and ill-fated adventure – and in his own private fortunes, too. For down there the first spark of revolt had flashed out; down there Keith Windham had been turned back by MacDonald of Tiendrish and his men; and because he had been turned back, Ewen himself was alive today, and not mouldering by Neil MacMartin's side on Beinn Laoigh.

But he was none the less on his way to death, and there was no one to stay the redcoats from passing High Bridge now. Tiendrish, marked for the scaffold, lay already in Edinburgh Castle; Keppoch, his chief, slept with his broken heart among the heather on Culloden Moor; Lochiel was a wounded outlaw with a price on his head. The gods had taken rigorous dues from all who had been concerned in the doings of that August day here by the Spean. Yes, strangely enough, even from Keith Windham, who was on the other side. They had made him pay for having dared to show compassion to those whom they pursued. It was singular.

Unconsciously Ewen was back in the dungeon again, seeing the Englishman's troubled face, hearing his voice as it asked him why he had put him in mind of the forgotten penknife . . .

And then Keith Windham's face and voice were blotted out in an instant by a thought which made him draw a long breath and clutch the sorrel's mane almost convulsively. He had something better than a blunt penknife on his person at this very moment, and now, now that his arms were untied, he could perhaps get it into his hand. For the last hour he had completely forgotten the girl's *sgian* in his stocking; and indeed, until recently it might as well not have been there. But now, if he could draw it out unobserved . . .

And then? Rags of a wild, a desperate plan began to flutter before his eyes. And only here, by the Spean, could the plan be put into execution, because, High Bridge once crossed, it was all open moorland to Fort William. Only by the Spean, racing along between its steep, thickly wooded banks, was there a chance of shelter, if one could gain it. It was a mad scheme, and would very likely result in his being shot dead, but, if they stopped at the little change-house on the other side of Spean, as they surely would, he would risk that. Better to die by a bullet than by the rope and the knife. How his body would carry out the orders of his brain he did not know; very ill, probably, to judge from his late experiences. Yet, as he hastily plotted out what he would do, and every moment was carried nearer to High Bridge, Ewen had an illusory feeling of vigour; but he knew that he must not show it. On the contrary, his present partially unbound condition being due to his recent only too real faintness, he must continue to simulate what for the moment he no longer felt. If only the faintness did not come on again in earnest!

Here was the Spean in its ravine, and here the narrow bridge reared on its two arches, its central pier rising from a large rock in the river-bed. They clattered over it, three abreast. The bridge was invisible, as Ewen knew, when one was fairly up the other side, because the approach was at so sharp an angle, and the trees so thick. And as they went up that steep approach the trees seemed even thicker than he remembered them. If Spean did not save him, nothing could.

The change-house came into view above them, a little low building by the side of the road, and for a moment the prisoner knew an agonizing doubt whether the escort were going to halt there after all. Yes, thank God, they were! Indeed, it would have been remarkable had they passed it.

The moment the troopers stopped it was evident how little they considered that their prisoner needed guarding now; it was very different from the care which they had bestowed in this particular at Laggan. Drink was brought out; nearly all swung off their horses, and broke into jests and laughter among themselves. Ewen's all but collapse of a few miles back, his real and evident exhaustion now, served him as nothing else could have done. Realizing this, he let himself slide slowly farther over his horse's neck as though he could scarcely sit in the saddle at all; and in fact this manoeuvre called for but little dissimulation.

And at that point the trooper who had charge of his reins, a young man, not so boisterous as the others, was apparently smitten with compassion. His own half-finished chopin in his hand, he looked up at the drooping figure. 'You'd be the better of another drink, eh? Shall I fetch you one?'

Not quite sure whether this solicitude was to his advantage, Ewen intimated that he would be glad of a cup of water. The dragoon finished his draught, tossed the reins to one of his fellows, and sauntered off. But the other man was too careless or too much occupied to catch the reins, and they swung forward below the sorrel's head, free. This was a piece of quite unforeseen good luck. Ewen's head sank right on to his horse's crest; already his right hand, apparently dangling helpless, had slipped the little black knife out of his stocking; now he was able unsuspected to reach the rope round his right ankle. ... Five seconds, and it was cut through, and the next instant his horse was snorting and rearing from a violent prick with the steel. The dismounted men near scattered involuntarily; Ewen reached forward, caught a rein, turned the horse, and, before the startled troopers in the least realized what was happening, was racing down the slope and had disappeared in the thick fringe of trees about the bridge.

The sorrel was so maddened that to slip off before he reached the bridge, as he intended, was going to be a matter of difficulty, if not of danger. But it had to be done; he threw himself across the saddle and did it. As he reached ground he staggered and fell, wrenching his damaged thigh, but the horse continued its wild career across the bridge and up the farther slope, as he had designed. Ewen had but a second or two in which to pick himself up and lurch into the thick undergrowth of the gorge ere the first of a stream of cursing horsemen came tearing down the slope. But, as he hoped, having heard hoof-beats on the bridge, they all went straight over it, in pursuit of the now vanished horse, never dreaming that it was riderless.

Once they were over, Ewen cut away the trailing rope from his other ankle, pocketed it, and started to plunge on as fast as he could among the birch and rowan trees, the moss-covered stones, and the undergrowth of Spean side. He was fairly sure that he was invisible from above, though not, perhaps, from the other side, if and when the troopers returned. But the farther from the bridge, the better. His breath came in gasps, the jar of throwing himself off the horse had caused him great pain and made him lamer than ever, and at last he was forced to go forward on his hands and knees, dragging his injured leg after him. But as he went he thought how hopeless it was; how the dragoons would soon overtake the horse, or see from a distance that he was no longer on its back, and, returning, would search along the river-bank and find him. And he could not possibly go much farther, weak and out of condition as he was, with the sweat pouring off him, and Spean below seeming to make a noise much louder than its diminished summer clamour.

Thus crawling, he finally came up against a huge green boulder, and the obstacle daunted him. He would stop here . . . just round the farther side. He dragged himself round somehow, and saw that what he had thought to be one stone was two, leaning together. He tried to creep into the dark hollow between them, a place like the tomb, but it was too narrow for his breadth of shoulder. So he sank down by it, and lay there with his cheek to the damp mould, and wondered whether he were dying. Louder and louder roared the Spean below, and he somehow was tossing in its stream. Then at least he could die in Scotland after all. Best not to struggle . . . best to think that he was in Alison's arms. She would know how spent he was . . . and how cold . . . The brawling of the river died away into darkness.

Chapter 2

WHEN Ewen came fully to himself again, it was night, the pale Highland summer night; he could not guess the hour. He had not been discovered, then! He lay listening; there was no sound anywhere save the rushing of the river below him, nothing to tell him whether the troopers had returned or no. But now was undoubtedly the time to quit his lair and get back over the bridge and along the short but dangerous stretch of high road, until he could leave it and make for the river Lochy. When he had forded Lochy and was on the other side of the Great Glen, he would be safer.

Alas, the next few minutes implanted in him a horrible doubt whether he would ever ford Lochy, seeing that between the swimming head of exhaustion, and the twist which he had given his damaged leg in throwing himself off the horse, he could scarcely even stand, much less walk. And although the people up at the change-house, almost within call, were, unless they had been removed, of a Cameron sept, he dared not risk attracting their attention, for a double reason: soldiers, his own escort or others from Fort William, might very well halt there. And to shelter him would probably in any case be disastrous to the poor folk themselves.

His prospects did not seem too bright. All his hope was that he might feel more vigorous after a little more of this not very comfortable rest. Huddled together on his side under the lee of the boulder, to get what shelter he could from the soft, misty rain which he felt rather than saw, he said a prayer and fell into the sleep of the worn-out.

He was wakened by a strange, sharp noise above him, and the sensation of something warm and damp passing over his face. Stiff and bewildered, he opened his eyes and saw in the now undoubted though misty daylight the author of these two phenomena, an agitated sheep-dog, of a breed unknown to him. As he raised himself on an elbow the dog gave another excited bark, and immediately darted away up the tree-grown bank.

So numbed and exhausted was the fugitive that it took him a few seconds to realize that he was discovered. But by whom? Not by soldiers, certainly; nor could that be the dog from the change-house. He dragged himself into a sitting posture, got his back against the boulder, pulled the little black knife, his only resource, from his stocking, and waited.

Feet were coming down the steep bank, and soon two men could be seen plunging through the birch and alder, shouting to each other in an unfamiliar accent; in front of them plunged and capered the sheep-dog, with its tail held high, and Ewen heard a loud hearty voice saying: 'Clivver lass – aye, good bitch th'art indeed! See-ye, yon's rebel, Jan!' He reflected: 'I can kill the dog, but what good would that do me? Moreover, I have no wish to.' And as the intelligent creature came bounding right up to him, wagging a friendly tail, and apparently proud of his accomplishment in having found him, he held out his left hand in invitation. The dog sniffed once, and then licked it.

'See thon!' cried the former voice. 'Dang it, see Lassie so freendly and all!'

'Yet you had best not come too near!' called Ewen threateningly. 'I am armed!' He raised his right hand.

The larger of the men, pushing through an alder bush, instantly lifted a stout cudgel. 'If thou harmst t' bitch – Coom here, Lassie!'

'No, I will not harm her,' said Ewen, fending off the dog's demonstrations with his other arm. 'But call her off; I owe her no gratitude.'

'For foindin' thee, thou meanst,' supplied Lassie's owner. 'Aye, thou'st the fellow that gie t' sogers the slip yesterday; we heerd all aboot thee oop at t' little hoose yonder. Eh, but thou'rt a reet smart lad!' There was genuine admiration in his tone. ''Twere smart ti hide thee here, so near an' all, 'stead o' gooin' ower t' brig – eh, Jan?'

'Main smart,' agreed the smaller man. 'Too smart fur th' redcoats, Ah lay!'

The smart lad, very grim in the face, and rather grey to boot, sat there against his boulder with the *sgian* clutched to his breast, point outwards, and eyed the two men with a desperate attention, as they stood a little way higher up amid the tangle of bushes, stones, and protruding tree-roots, and looked at him. They had the appearance of well-to-do farmers, particularly the larger, who was a tremendously burly and powerful man with a good-tempered but masterful expression. The smaller was of a more weazened type, and older.

'See-thee, young man,' said the burly stranger suddenly, ''tis no manner o' use ti deny that thou'rt one of these danged Highland rebels, seein' we's heerd all the tale oop yonder.'

Ewen's breath came quickly. 'But I'll not be retaken without resistance!'

'Who says we be gooin' ti taake thee? Happen we've summit else ti moind. Coom here, Lassie, wilt thou! Dunnot be so freendly tiv a chap wi' a knife in 'is hand!'

'I tell you the dog has nothing to fear from me,' repeated Ewen. 'See then!' And on a sudden impulse he planted the *sgian* in the damp soil beside him and left it sticking there.

'Ah, that's reet, yoong man – that's jannock!' exclaimed the large stranger in evident approval and relief. 'Happen we can 'ev some clack together noo. Hoo dost thou rackon ti get away fra this tod's den o' thine?'

Here, quite suddenly, the little man began to giggle. 'He, he! maakes me laugh to think of it – t' sogers chasing reet away ower t' brig and Lord knaws wheer beyond! They nivver coom back, so t' folk oop yonder tells.'

'Aye, a good tale to tell when we gan back ower Tyne,' agreed the large man, shaking gently with a more subdued mirth. And as Ewen, for his part, realized that the reference to Tyne must mean that the strangers were English, though he could not imagine what they were doing in Lochaber, this large one burst into a great rumbling upheaval of laughter, causing the sheep-dog to bark in sympathy.

'Quiet, lass!' commanded her master, making a grab at her. 'Thy new freend here has no wish for thy noise, Ah'll lay.' He looked straight at the fugitive sitting there. 'Hadn't thee best get thee gone, lad, before 'tis onny loighter?' he asked.

Was the man playing with him, or was he genuinely friendly? Ewen's heart gave a great bound. A momentary mist passed before his eyes. When it cleared the large man was stooping over him, a bottle in his hand.

'Thoo'rt nigh clemmed, lad, or ma name's not Robert Fosdyke. Here's 't stuff for thee – reet Nantes. Tak' a good soop of it!'

The fiery spirit ran like lightning through Ewen's cramped limbs. 'Why . . . why do you treat me so kindly?' he gasped, half stupid between the brandy and astonishment, as he returned the bottle. 'You are English, are you not? Why do you not give me up?'

Mr Fosdyke, who had now seated himself on a large stone near, struck his knee with some vehemence. 'Ah'll tell thee whoy! First, because t' bitch here foond thee and took ti thee, and thou didna stick yon knife o' thine intiv her – but Ah'd 'ev driven in thy skool if thou hadst . . . second, because thou'rt a sharp lad and a bold one, too; and last because Ah've seen and heerd tell o' things yonder at Fort Augustus, wheer we went ti buy cattle, that Ah 'evn't loiked at all. No, Ah didn't loike what Ah heerd of goings on – Aye, and foorthly, t' cattle was woorth danged little when we'd gotten 'em: all t' best were sold awready.'

Ewen knew what cattle they would be; the one possession of many a poor Highland home, as well as the herds of the gentry. He remembered now having heard that some of the many thousands collected from Lochaber and Badenoch were sold to English and Lowland dealers. Apparently, then, these men were on their way south through Glencoe and Breadalbane with such as they

287

had bought, and now he knew why once or twice during this conversation he had fancied that he heard sounds of lowing at no great distance.

'I wonder if mine are all gone!' he said half to himself.

'Thou hadst cattle of thy own, lad?' inquired Mr Fosdyke. 'If thou canst see onny o' thine among oors oop there thou shalt have them back again – and that's none so generous as thou medst think, for there's some Ah'd as soon give away as drive all t' waay ower t' Border.'

Ewen gave a weak laugh. 'What should I do with cattle now? I cannot get home myself, much less drive cattle there.'

'And whoy canst thou not get home, when thou'st put summut in thy belly?' asked the Yorkshireman.

Ewen told him why he should find it difficult, if not impossible, and why he dared not go to the change-house either. The farmer pronounced that he was right in the latter course, and then made the astonishing suggestion that 'Jan Prescott here' should run up to the house and bring the fugitive something to eat and drink. 'Dunnot say who 'tis for, Jan; say Ah've a moind ti eat by river, if thou loikes.' And while Jan, with amazing docility, removed the birch twig which he had been twisting between his lips and betook himself up the bank, his companion questioned Ewen further as to the direction of his home.

'T' other soide of t' other river? T' other river's nobbit a couple of moiles away. . . . Tell thee what, lad,' he exclaimed, slapping himself once more, 'Ah'll tak thee as far as t' river on one of t' nags. Happen thou canst sit a horse still?'

'Take me there!' Ewen could only stare in amazement.

'Aye. And when thou'st gotten to this river o' thine, hoo medst thou cross it; happen there's brig, or ferry?'

'No, there is a ford. The ford by which we all . . .' His voice died away. How long ago it seemed, that elated crossing last August after Glenfinnan!

'And when thou'rt on t' other soide?' pursued Mr Fosdyke.

'I'll reach my home somehow, if I have to crawl there.'

'And who'lt thou foind theer – thy parents?'

'My aunt, who brought me up. My parents are dead.'

'No wife nor childer?'

'My wife is in France.' And why he added: 'We were only married two days before parting,' Ewen did not know.

'Poor lad,' said Mr Fosdyke. 'Whoy didstna stop at home loike a wise man?'

Ewen, his head resting against the boulder, said: 'That I could not do,' his eyes meanwhile fixed on the form of Mr Jan Prescott, already descending the slope with a tankard in his hand and two large bannocks clasped to his person. Mr Fosdyke turned and hailed him, and in another moment Ewen had started upon the bannocks, finding that he was famished, having tasted nothing solid since the halt at Laggan yesterday morning. And while he ate, Mr Robert Fosdyke unfolded his intention to his companion, who raised no objection, except to remark: 'Happen thou'lt meet redcoats on t' road.'

'Ah shall say t' lad's a drover o' mine, then.'

'In yon petticoat thing?' queried Mr Prescott, pointing at Ewen's kilt.

'He shall have thy great-coat ti cover him oop.'

'Ah dunno hoo he'll get intiv it, then,' returned Mr Prescott. 'See ye, Robert, Ah'd sooner he had a horse blanket than split ma coat.'

'He can have t' loan of ma coat then,' said Mr Fosdyke. 'He'll not split that. – Beasts all reet oop there?' he inquired.

'As reet as ivver they'll be,' returned his partner, with gloom.

'Ah knawed as we peed too mooch for them,' growled Mr Fosdyke in a voice like subterranean thunder. 'Goviment notice saays – well, nivver moind what, but 'twere main different fra what t' cattle were loike. Hooivver, Ah weren't comin' all the way fra t' other soide o' York for nowt.'

'York?' asked Ewen, with his mouth full, since this information seemed addressed to him. 'You come from York, sir?'

'Fra near-by. Dost thou knaw the toon?'

'No,' said Ewen.

'T' sogers werena takin' thee there yistiday?'

'It was Carlisle that I was going to in the end.'

'Ah!' said Mr Fosdyke comprehendingly. 'But some poor devils are setting oot for York, too, we hear. Thou's best coom

289

along wi' us.' And giving his great laugh he began to embroider his pleasantry.

'Thou doesna loike the notion? Whoy not? York's a foine toon, Ah can tell thee, and more gates tiv it for setting rebels' heads on than Carlisle. Ah lay we have a row o' them ower Micklegate Bar come Christmas. And thou'st not wishful ti add thine?'

Ewen shook the imperilled head in question with a smile.

'No,' agreed Mr Fosdyke, 'best keep it, ti lay on t' pillow besoide thy wife's. If she's in France, then thou'rt not a poor man, eh?'

'I am what you call a gentleman,' replied Ewen, 'though I expect that I am poor enough now.'

'If thou'rt a gentleman,' pronounced Mr Fosdyke, 'then thou dost reet ti keep away fra York and Carlisle, aye, and fra Lunnon, too – Noo, Jan, we'll gan and see aboot t' nags. Thou medst bide here, lad. Come on, Lassie.'

With tramplings and cracklings they were gone, dog and all, and, but for the yet unfinished food and drink, which were putting new life into Ewen, the whole encounter might have been a dream. As he waited there for their return he wondered whether Alison's prayers had sent these good angels, which, to his simple and straightforward faith, seemed quite likely.

Presently the larger of the angels came back and helped him along the slope to the scene of his exploits at the bridge. Here was the satellite Jan with two stout nags, a flea-bitten grey and a black. A long and ample coat (certainly not Mr Prescott's) was provided for the Jacobite. 'If thou wert clothed like a Christian there'd ha' been no need for this,' said Mr Fosdyke with frankness as he helped him into it; and then, the difficulty of getting into the saddle surmounted, Ewen found himself half incredulously riding behind the broad back of his benefactor over the brawling Spean, in his hand a stout cattle goad to assist his steps when he should be on his feet again.

In the two miles before they came to the river Lochy, they had the luck to meet no one. There the clouds hung so low that the other side of the Great Glen was scarcely visible. When they came to the ford, Ewen pulled up and made to dismount. But Mr

Fosdyke caught him by the arm. 'Nay, if thou canst scarce walk on land, Ah doot thou'll walk thruff water! Daisy will tak thee ower. Coom on, mare.'

The two horses splashed placidly through in the mist. On the other side Ewen struggled off, and got out of the coat.

'I cannot possibly recompense you, Mr Fosdyke,' he began, handing it up to him.

'If thou offer me money,' said Mr Fosdyke threateningly, 'danged if Ah don't tak thee back ti wheer Ah foond thee!'

'You can be reassured,' said Ewen smiling, 'for I have none. But in any case, money does not pass between gentlemen for a service like this. I only pray God that you will not suffer for it.'

'Ah'd loike ti see the mon that's going ti mak me,' was the Yorkshireman's reply. 'And Ah feel noo as Ah've got even wi' Goviment in t' matter of t' cattle,' he added with immense satisfaction. 'And thou think'st me a gentleman? Well, Ah'm nobbut a farmer, but Ah'm mooch obliged ti thee for the compliment.' He shook Ewen's hand. 'Good luck ti thee, ma lad. . . . If thou lived a few hoondred moiles nearer, danged if Ah wouldna gie thee a pup o' Lassie's – but thou'rt ower far away, ower far!' He chuckled, caught the bridle of the grey, and the eight hoofs could be heard splashing back through the ford. Then silence settled down again, silence, and the soft folds of mist; and after a moment Ewen, leaning heavily on his goad, began his difficult pilgrimage.

Twenty-four hours later, very nearly at the end of his tether, he was hobbling slowly along the last mile of that distance which ordinarily he would have covered between one meal and the next. So slow and painful had been his progress, and with such frequent halts, that it had been late afternoon before he reached Loch Arkaig. And there he had seen the pitiful charred remains, left by vengeance, of Lochiel's house of Achnacarry, almost as dear to him as his own. In that neighbourhood above all others he had feared to come on soldiers, but the Campbells in Government pay who had burnt and ravaged here had long ago done their work, and the place was deserted; there was nothing to guard now, and none against whom to hold it. A poor Cameron woman, whose husband had been shot in cold blood as he was working in his little field, had given Ewen shelter for the night. She told him, what he expected to hear, that the house of Ardroy had been burnt down by a detachment of redcoats; this she knew because the soldiers had returned that way, and she had heard them boasting how they had left the place in flames. Of Miss Cameron's fate she knew nothing; but then she never saw anyone, now that her man was gone; the burnt countryside was nearly depopulated. That Ewen had seen for himself already. And she said with tears, as, thanking her from his soul for her hospitality, he turned away from her door in the morning grey: 'Oh Mac 'ic Ailein, for the Chief and the Chief's kin I'd give the last rag, the last mouthful that's left to me – but I'm asking God why He ever let Prince Tearlach come to Scotland.' And Ewen had no heart to find an answer.

Against his will, the question had haunted him as he hobbled on. Just a year ago he had the news of that coming; yes, just a year ago he had sat with Alison by the loch and been happy – too happy perhaps. So his father's house was gone! But all the more was his mind set to reach Ardroy, to find out what had befallen those who had remained behind there: Aunt Marget first and foremost, the servants, old Angus and his grandchildren, the womenfolk, the fugitives from Drumossie Moor. . . . And here at last he was, going incredibly slowly, and accompanied by a dull pain in the thigh which by this time seemed an inseparable part of himself, but come to the spot where, after crossing the Allt Buidhe burn, one used to discern the chimneys of the house of Ardroy between the pines of the avenue. Since he knew that he would never see them thus again, Ewen did not look up, but he thought, as he crossed the burn on the stepping-stones, nearly over-balancing from fatigue, that one thing, at least, would be the same, for not even Cumberland could set fire to Loch na h-Iolaire.

Then, unable for the moment to get farther, he sank down among the welcoming heather for a rest. That, just coming into bloom, was unchanged; 'thou art the same and thy years shall not fail' – the words floated into his head and out again, as he felt its springy resistance give beneath his body. Then, half lying there, twisting a tuft round and round the fingers of one hand for the pleasure of feeling it again, Ewen let his eyes stray to the spot where his father's house and his had stood. And so strange were habit and memory that he could see its roof and chimneys still. He put a hand over his eyes to rub away the false sight ... but when he removed it the chimneys were still there, and from one there floated a wisp of smoke. ... Trembling, he dragged himself clumsily to his feet.

Like a man who dreams the impossible, he stood a little later outside the entrance door of Ardroy. The whole affair was like a dream; for fire had certainly passed upon the house, and yet it was unharmed. The lintel, the sides of the stone porch were blackened with smoke; the ivy was brown and shrivelled, but not even the woodwork was injured. The house seemed occupied; the door stood open as on fine days it was wont to do; but there was not a creature about. Where was Aunt Marget?

Slowly Ewen went over the threshold, feeling the stone and wood like a blind man to make sure that it was real. He could have kissed it – his house that was not burnt after all. The sun was pouring into the long room; there was a meal laid on the table – for Aunt Marget? Then where was she? The place was very silent. Perhaps – a horrible notion – strangers held Ardroy now, enemies. He would rather it were burnt. ... But had harm befallen Aunt Marget? He must find her; shame on him to be thinking first of the house!

He was giddy with hunger and fatigue, but he had no thought of approaching the table; he left the room and, holding very tightly by the rail, went up the stairs. The door of Miss Cameron's room was a little ajar, so he pushed it gently open, too confused to knock. Where, where was she?

And he stood in the doorway rooted, because, so unexpectedly, everything in that neat, sunny room which he had known from a child was just as he had always known it ... even to Aunt Marget herself, sitting there by the window reading a chapter in her big Bible, as she always did before breakfast. The surprise of its usualness after his experiences and his fears almost stunned him, and he remained there motionless, propping himself by the doorpost.

It was odd, however, that Aunt Marget had not heard him, for she had not used to be deaf. The thought came to Ewen that he was perhaps become a ghost without knowing it, and he seriously considered the idea for a second or two. Then he took a cautious step forward.

'Aunt Marget!'

He was not a ghost! She heard and looked up ... it was true that her face was almost frightened ...

'I have come back!' said Ewen baldly. 'May I ... may I sit on your bed!'

He crashed on to it rather than sat upon it, hitting his head against the post at the bottom, since all at once he could not see very well.

But Aunt Marget did not scold him; in fact he perceived, after a little, that she was crying as she sat beside him, and attempting, as if he were a child again, to kiss his head where he had struck it. 'Oh, Ewen, my boy – my darling, darling boy!'

'Then did that poor woman dream that the house was burnt down?' asked Ewen some quarter of an hour later, gazing at Miss Cameron in perplexity, as she planted before him, ensconced as he was in the easy-chair in her bedroom, the last components of a large repast. For allow him to descend and eat downstairs she would not; indeed, after the first questions and emotions were over, she was for hustling him up to the attics and hiding him there. But, Ewen having announced with great firmness that he was too lame to climb a stair that was little better than a ladder, she compromised on her bedchamber for the moment, and with Marsali's assistance brought up thither the first really satisfying meal which Ewen had seen for more than three months.

In answer to his question, she now began to laugh, though her eyes were still moist. 'The house was set fire to – in a way. Eat, *Eoghain*, for you look starving; and you shall hear the tale of its escape.'

Ewen obeyed her and was told the story. But not yet having, so it seemed to him, the full use of his faculties, he was not quite clear how much of the house's immunity was due to chance, to connivance on the part of the officer commanding the detachment sent to burn it, and to the blandishments of Miss Cameron herself.

At any rate, after searching, though not plundering, the house of Ardroy from top to bottom (for whom or what was not quite clear to Ewen, since at that date he was safely a prisoner at Fort Augustus), firing about half the crofts near, collecting what cattle they could lay their hands on, the most having already been sent up into the folds of the mountains, and slaying a dozen or so of Miss Cameron's hens, they had piled wood against the front of the house, with what intention was obvious. It was a moment of great anguish for Miss Cameron. But the soldiers were almost ready to march ere the fuel was lighted. And as they were setting fire to the pine-branches and the green ash-boughs the officer approached her and said in a low voice: 'Madam, I have carried out my instructions – and it is not my fault if this wood is damp. That's enough, Sergeant; 'twill burn finely. Column, march!'

Directly they were out of sight Miss Cameron and Marsali, the younger maidservants and the old gardener, seizing rakes and brooms and fire-irons, had pulled away the thickly smoking but as yet harmless branches. 'And then I bethought me, Ewen, that 'twould be proper there should be as much smoke as possible, to convince the world, and especially the redcoats, should they take a look back. A house cannot burn, even in a spot so remote as this, without there being some evidence of it in the air. So we made a great pile of all that stuff at a safe distance from the house – and, my grief, the trouble it was to get it to burn! Most of the day we tended it; and a nasty thick reek it made, and a blaze in the end. That's how the house was burnt. ... What ails you, my bairn?'

But this time Ewen was able hastily to dash the back of his hand over his eyes. He could face her, therefore, unashamed, and reaching out for her hand, put his lips to it in silence.

Chapter 3

NOT infrequently in the past had Miss Marget Cameron animadverted on the obstinacy which lay hidden (as his temper was hidden) under her nephew's usually gentle speech and ways. And now, at the greatest crisis in his life, when that life itself might hang upon his prudence, poor Miss Cameron was faced in her young relative with a display of this quality which really distracted her.

On that joyful and wonderful morning of his return, she had allowed him (she put it so) to retire to his own bed in his own room 'just for the once'; the garrets, the cellar or a bothy on the braeside being designated as his future residences. Ewen did not argue – indeed he was not capable of it; he fell into his bed, and slept for fourteen hours without waking.

Once he was there, and so obviously in need of rest and attention, Miss Cameron had not, of course, the heart to turn him out; but she kept a guard of young MacMartins and others round the house, ready to give tongue in case of a surprise, and promised herself to banish the returned fugitive to more secluded regions directly he was able to leave his room. But when after three days Ewen did so, it was not to retire into this destined seclusion; on the contrary, he began at once to limp about, acquainting himself with what had happened to his tenants in his absence, trying to discover the fate of those who had never returned – among whom was Lachlan MacMartin – visiting the nearer crofts in person, and interviewing the inhabitants of the farther at the house. Presently, he said, he would 'take to the heather', perhaps; but, as his aunt could see, he was yet too lame for it; and, as for the garrets or the cellar, he was just as safe in his own bedchamber as in those uncomfortable retreats.

Yielding on this point with what she hoped was the wisdom of the serpent, Miss Cameron then returned to a subject much nearer her heart: Ardroy's departure for France or Holland, which he would attempt, she assumed, as soon as he could hear of a likely vessel and was fit to undertake the journey to the coast.

'France?' queried Ewen, as if he had heard this suggestion for the first time. It was the fifth evening after his return; Miss Cameron was sitting knitting in the long parlour, and he stretched in a chair opposite to her. The windows were closely curtained, and young Angus MacMartin and a still younger brother prowled delightedly in the avenue keeping watch. 'France, Aunt Marget? What put that into your head?'

Miss Cameron laid down her knitting. 'Because you cannot stay here, Ewen. And France is in my head rather than Holland or Denmark because – well, surely you can guess – because your wife is there.'

Ewen got out of his chair and limped to one of the windows. 'I am not leaving Scotland at present,' he said quietly, and drew aside the curtains. 'We need not therefore discuss the claims of one country over another.'

'You cannot mean to stay here at Ardroy! Ewen, are you daft? And, in the name of the Good Being, don't show yourself at a lighted window like that!'

' 'Tis so light outside that the candles do not carry,' returned her nephew. Indeed, but for Miss Cameron's prudence they would not have been sitting thus curtained, but in daylight. 'Moreover no one will come to look for me here; the house has been "burnt",' he went on, using the argument he had already used half a dozen times. And he continued to look out; at least Marget Cameron thought that he was looking out. In reality he had his eyes shut, that he might not see Alison's face – a vain device, for he saw it all the clearer.

His aunt was silent for a moment, for he had implanted in her mind a most disturbing doubt.

'Well,' she said at last dryly, 'I should think that if Major Windham, to whom you owe so much, knew of this freak of yours, he would regret the sacrifices which he had made in order to save you, when this is the use to which you put your liberty.'

'I think Major Windham would understand,' said Ewen rather shortly.

'Understand what?'

There was no answer. 'Then I doubt if the ghost of poor Neil, who died for you, or of Lachlan, would understand!'

Ewen turned at that, but stayed where he was. 'Poor Neil indeed; may his share of Paradise be his!' he said in a softened tone. 'And Lachlan, too, if he be dead. Since you speak of my foster-brothers, Aunt Marget, and reproachfully, then you must know that this is one reason why I do not wish to leave Ardroy, because it shames me to take ship for France myself and desert those others who cannot flee, for whose fate I am responsible.

Moreover, I have started the rebuilding of the burnt crofts, and – '

'Trust a man to think that he is the only being who can oversee anything practical! I wonder,' observed Miss Cameron, 'how much of rebuilding and repairs I have not ordered and supervised, when you were nothing but a small wild boy, Ewen, falling into the loch and losing yourself on the braes above it!'

He hobbled over to her. 'I know, I know. No laird ever had a better factor than you, Aunt Marget!'

Miss Cameron's knitting slid to the floor. 'Had! Aye, I'm getting an old wife now, 'tis plain, that you dare not leave the reins to me for a year or so, while you take your head out of the lion's mouth for a while.'

'No, no, you know that's not my thought,' said Ewen, distressed. 'I'd leave Ardroy to you as blithely as I did a year ago – I will so leave it . . . presently.'

'Aye, that you will do presently – but not by your own will. You'll go off from this door as you left Fort Augustus a week ago, tied on a horse again, and your father's house really in flames behind you – and all because you will not listen to advice!'

'You make me out more obstinate than I am,' said Ewen gently. 'Your advice is excellent, Aunt Marget, but you do not know . . . all the circumstances.'

'That can easily be remedied,' said Miss Cameron with meaning. But to that suggestion Ewen made no reply.

Miss Cameron turned round in her chair, and then got up and faced him. 'Ewen, my dear, what is wrong? What is it that is keeping you from getting out of the country? Surely it is not . . . that there is something amiss between you and Alison?'

Ewen did not meet her eyes. But he shook his head. 'Alison and I – ' he began, but never finished. How put into words what Alison was to him? Moreover, that which was keeping him back did stand between him and her – at least in his own soul. 'Some day, perhaps, I will tell you, Aunt Marget,' he said quietly. 'But I'd be glad if you would not discuss my departure just now. – You have dropped your knitting.'

He picked it up for her, and Marget Cameron stood quite still, looking up uneasily at the height of him, at his brow all wrinkled with some pain of whose nature she was quite ignorant, at the

298

sudden lines round his young mouth. She ended her survey with a sigh.

'And to think that – since we cannot get a letter to her – the lassie may be breaking her heart over there, believing that you are dead!'

Ewen took a step away, with a movement as though to ward off a blow. Then he translated the movement into a design to snuff the candles on the table behind him. After a moment his voice came unsteady and hurt: 'Aunt Marget, you are very cruel.' And his hand must have been unsteady, too, for he snuffed the flame right out.

' 'Tis for your own good,' replied Miss Cameron, winking hard at the engraving of King James the Third as a young man over the mantleshelf in front of her. Ewen relighted from another the candle he had slain, saying nothing, and with the air of one who does not quite know what he is doing. 'At least, I'm sure 'tis not for mine,' went on Miss Cameron, and now, little given to tears as she was, she surreptitiously applied a corner of a handkerchief to one eye. 'You cannot think that I *want* you to go away again . . . and leave the house the . . . the mere shell of emptiness it is when you are not here!'

Ewen looked round and saw the scrap of cambric. In an instant, despite the pain it cost him, he had knelt down by her side and was taking her hands into his, and saying how sorry he was to grieve her, and assuring her that there was nothing, nothing whatever wrong between him and Alison.

Yet even then he made no promises about departure.

Nor had he made any a week later, when, one hot afternoon, he lay, reflecting deeply, on the bed in his own room, with his hands behind his head. Although his wounded leg was already much stronger, it rebelled with effect against unremitting use all day, and to Ewen's intense disgust he found it imperative to spend a portion of the afternoon thus. He regarded this necessity as not only burdensome but disgraceful.

The wind soughed faintly through the pines of the little avenue, and then passed on to ruffle the ivy outside his open window. A little brown, some of them, after their fiery ordeal, the topmost of those tough leaves were still there, and made just the same rustling noise as of old. And there Ewen lay, apparently at peace; back in his own room, among his modest possessions, his life and liberty snatched from the enemy, his home unharmed after all, and over the seas his young wife waiting for him in safety, the call of the sword no longer keeping him back from her, since the sword was shattered.

But he was by no means at peace; there was unceasing war in his breast. The way to Alison was barred by a spectre which he could not lay. It was in vain to tell himself that, by God's mercy, his most unwilling lapse at Fort Augustus had done no harm, that no one of his own party knew of it, that it was not even a complete revelation. To his acutely sensitive Highland pride, the mere fact of the betrayal of his Chief's trust was agony. Alison could not heal that wound, which, now that Ewen was back again in his old surroundings, almost in his old life, seemed to have broken out bleeding afresh. There was only one man who could draw the poison from it, and Ewen knew neither where he was nor how he could come at him.

And meanwhile his dreams were full of Alison; and a night or two ago he had even seemed to hear her voice in one, asking in so pitiful and faint an accent why he delayed to come to her, now that honour no longer forbade it. She was so lonely . . .

Ewen sighed deeply, and withdrew his hands from beneath his head. The double scar on his right palm caught his eye for an instant. He wondered, not by any means for the first time, whether Windham had heard of his escape; if he had, he would know that he had indeed given him his life – yes, even by his refusal to witness against him, since that was the direct cause of the prisoner's being taken over the Spean, where he had met and seized his great opportunity. To judge by the Englishman's palpable distress at their farewell interview, Windham would be exceedingly glad of the news of his escape. Some day, perhaps, he might contrive to get a letter conveyed to his hands. He would like to tell him in person. But he was never to see him again, so it seemed, for the five meetings were over. Again he counted them: here, at Edinburgh, on Beinn Laoigh, at Fort Augustus. And suddenly his pulse quickened with pleasure – that made four, only four! . . . No, of course, there had been two at Fort Augustus. . . . Yet what (save his own recapture) stood now in the way of their meeting again some day?

But the ivy leaves went on rubbing their hands together, and through the window at the other side of the room came the clucking of Miss Cameron's remaining hens, drowsy sounds both, and Ewen, pondering this question, began to fall asleep. Yet, just before he lost consciousness, there shot through his mind, apparently from nowhere, a last flicker of Angus's prediction of a year ago . . . something about twisted threads . . . a thread of one colour and a thread of another. It had meant nothing at the time and he had totally forgotten it since. Now, between the two worlds of sleep and waking, it not only came back to him, but, with the curious pictorial clarity sometimes vouchsafed in that state, he seemed to see what it meant. Then picture and meaning faded, and he slept.

He slept quietly for a while, and then dreamt that a man had come into the room and was standing looking down at him. Yet somehow he knew that it was not a dream, that there was really someone there. He tried to rouse himself, but could not; and then the man laid a hand on his wrist. And at that, still half in a dream, he began to struggle and to speak.

'Let go my arm, you damned torturer? . . . No, not if you cut me in pieces! . . . Ah, my God, but there's another way . . . another way!'

The hand had left his wrist quickly, and now it was laid on his shoulder, and a voice – Lochiel's voice – said: 'Ewen, wake up. No one is hurting you.'

He woke instantly, crying: 'Donald! Donald!' half sure, all the time, that it was but a dream. Then he caught his breath and lay staring upwards. It was not indeed Lochiel, but it was his brother who stood there, looking down at him with a good deal of attention.

'*Archie!*' he gasped in the most complete astonishment. 'You here? Why?'

'Don't you think you would be the better of a doctor, my dear Ewen?' inquired his cousin cheerfully. 'That is why I am here.'

'But there's a price on your head,' protested Ewen. 'You should not, should not have come here!'

Archibald Cameron smiled his gentle, quizzical smile and sat down on the bed. 'I understand from Miss Marget that you daily affirm the house of Ardroy to be perfectly safe. Moreover, one does not dictate to a physician, my dear boy, how and when he shall visit his patients. I heard how you escaped as you were being carried to Fort William, and I did not believe that it was your body which was found some days after in one of the pools of Spean. (You do not know, perhaps, that that is what has been given out at Fort Augustus.) But I guessed that that same body needed attention, so, being yesterday in Glendessary, I made my way hither. Now, let me look at those wounds of yours.'

And, though Ewen protested that these were quite healed and that he was only a trifle lame, Dr Cameron insisted. The extent of the lameness, very patent when he made the young man walk about the room, evidently displeased him.

'When you get to France, Ewen, you must have the care of a good surgeon. I greatly fear that an important muscle in the thigh has been severed; but with proper treatment it may reunite again.'

'I suppose you have been talking to Aunt Marget,' remarked his patient, sitting down upon the bed. 'But, as I have told her, I am not going to France – yet. The muscle must reunite at home.'

Archie looked at him keenly. He *had* been talking to Aunt Marget. 'I am not advising France solely in the interests of your lameness, Ewen.'

'Well I know that! But I shall stay in Scotland for the present.'

'Until you are captured again, I suppose?' said Dr Cameron, crossing one leg over the other and leaning back against the post at the bottom of the bed. 'But I do not know on what grounds you assume that you will have so lucky an escape a second time.'

'Oh, I shall not be captured here,' said Ewen carelessly. 'And when I can walk a little better, I shall very likely take to the heather for a while – like you!' And as Archibald Cameron raised his eyebrows he said with more warmth: 'My God, Archie, I'd rather skulk in sight of Loch na h-Iolaire with nothing but my plaid and a handful of meal, even were there a redcoat behind every whin-bush, than lie in the French King's bed at Versailles!'

'No doubt,' responded his cousin, unmoved. 'And so would I. Yet I shall certainly make for France - if God will - when my tasks here are done. I hope indeed that it may not be for long; who knows but next year may see another and a more successful effort, with support from the French. The Prince - '

'Yes, indeed,' said Ewen eagerly, 'what of the Prince? My last news of him was from a fellow-prisoner at Fort Augustus, Mac-Donald of Kingsburgh, who, though he is Sleat's factor, brought him to his own house in Skye disguised as the maidservant of one Miss Flora MacDonald, and was arrested in consequence. I heard much from him, and laughable some of it was, too, for Kingsburgh's wife and daughter seem to have been frightened at the queer figure that His Royal Highness made in his petticoats. But you will have later news of him, Archie?'

'The Prince was at the end of July in Glenmoriston,' said Dr Cameron, 'but he is now, I think, in Chisholm's country, farther north. There is so plainly a Providence watching over him that I have no doubt he will be preserved from his enemies to the end; and it is therefore the duty of his friends to preserve themselves, too. Yes, I am going to read you a lecture, *Eoghain mhóir*, so you had better lie down again; I shall not begin until you do.' He waited until Ewen had grumblingly complied, and then began, ticking off the points on his fingers.

'*Imprimis*, you stubborn young man, there is this house, almost miraculously preserved from destruction, and, if you keep clear of it, likely to continue immune. There is your good aunt, who can well continue to look after it, but who, if you are found under its roof, will certainly be driven out of it and very possibly imprisoned. You are not on the list of attainted persons, and you have the advantage at this moment of an official report declaring you drowned. Most of all, have you not someone already in France who is breaking her heart for a sight of you?'

Lying there, Ewen changed colour perceptibly, and it was only after a moment that he answered: 'There are broken hearts in plenty, Archie, in Lochaber.'

'But I do not see, my dear lad, how they are to be mended by your offering up the fragments of Alison's - and your own.'

Ewen uttered a sound like a groan, and, twisting over, buried his face in the pillow; and presently there emerged some muffled words to the effect that he longed to go to Alison, but that ... and then something wholly unintelligible in which the word 'honour' was alone distinguishable.

Dr Cameron looked down at the back of the uneasy auburn head with the affectionate tolerance which one might display to the caprices of a younger brother. 'No, Ewen, to my mind honour points to your going – aye, and duty and common sense as well. You cannot help your tenants by remaining here; Miss Cameron can now do that much more effectively – so long as you do not compromise her by your presence. You cannot help the Cause or the Prince; you cannot help Lochiel;' – the head gave a sudden movement – 'he is for France with me when the opportunity comes. Another day – that is a different tale; but 'tis likely there will never be another day for you if you persist in remaining here now. ... And there is another point, which I hope you will pardon me for mentioning: is your wife going to bear you a child, Ewen?'

'How do I know?' answered Ewen in a stifled voice from the pillow. 'Our happiness was so short ... and I have had no letter.'

'Then, before you throw your life uselessly away,' said Archibald Cameron gravely, 'it is your duty to make sure that there will be a son to follow you here, Mac 'ic Ailein. Do you wish your ghost to see strangers at Ardroy?'

No Highlander could ever affect to disregard that argument, and Ewen remained silent.

'And Alison – do you suppose that she found her wedded happiness any longer or more satisfying than you did? God knows, my dear Ewen, I hold that neither wife, children, nor home should stand in a man's way when duty and loyalty call him – for, as you know, I have turned my back on all mine – but when duty and loyalty are silent, then he does very wrong if he neglects those ties of nature.'

And on that Archibald Cameron, conceiving that he had preached long enough, got up from the bed. Ewen was still lying with his face hidden: was there something on his mind, as Miss Cameron affirmed? The doctor went and looked out of the far window, and saw the lady in question scattering meal to her hens.

'Archie,' came from the bed after a moment or two, 'if I go, it is only on one condition, which you can grant.'

'I?' said Dr Cameron, turning round, rather surprised. Ewen had raised himself on to an elbow. He looked oddly pale and strained. 'What is the condition, *ille*?'

'That I see Lochiel first.' And over his fair skin there swept a wave of red.

It occurred to Dr Archibald then how strange it was that Ewen, for all his intense devotion, had not yet asked news of his kinsman and Chief. But he looked doubtful. 'I am afraid that would be difficult, because you are both disabled; you cannot travel to him, nor he to you.'

'Yes, I had thought of that,' said Ewen, now quite pale again. 'But I must contrive it somehow.' And as Archie was silent, reflecting, he added, with a sharp note in his voice, 'Is there any other reason why I should not ?'

'Of course not – save that you will meet in France, please God.'

'That will not serve. I must see him before I leave Scotland. I know that he is no longer in Lochaber.' The short phrases were jerked out; even more so the last one: 'Archie, where *is* he?'

'He – ' Archie was beginning, when unfortunately he heard Miss Cameron calling to him from below, possibly uttering a warning of some kind. He turned sharply to the window and never finished. But on Ewen the effect was of a man who has second thoughts about answering a question, and is not only mute, but turns his back upon the questioner.

In his present state of mind, it was quite enough, and next moment, to his visitor's amazement, he had thrown himself off the bed with such violence that he staggered. 'I knew it!' he exclaimed hoarsely. 'You will not tell me where he is, because you have heard what I did at Fort Augustus – because Lochiel has heard it. I am not to be trusted! That is why you came, I believe – why you want me gone at any price from Scotland!' And as Archibald Cameron, already swung round again from the window, stared at him in consternation, Ewen added, clenching his hands, 'I'll not go! I'll not be got rid of like that! I'll get myself killed here in Lochaber ... the only thing I can do in expiation.' And with that he sank down on the side of the bed and hid his face in his hands.

Dr Cameron hastily left the window, but before his amazement allowed him words, Ewen was adding, in a strangled voice: 'You are quite right, from your point of view, neither to let me see him nor to tell me where he is. But, Archie, I swear to you by my father's memory that I did not do it willingly! How can he believe that of me?'

His cousin stooped and put a hand on his shoulder. 'Ewen,' he said with great gentleness, 'I have not the least notion what you are talking about. What did you do at Fort Augustus? Nothing, I'd stake my soul, that your father's son need ever be ashamed of. You would have let yourself be "cut in pieces" first, eh? I was just on the point of telling you where Lochiel was; he is in Badenoch, hiding in a hut on Ben Alder with Macpherson of Cluny. Now,' he sat down and slipped his arm completely along the bowed shoulders, 'will you tell me what is on your mind, and why you must see him?'

Chapter 4

THINKING it over afterwards, Ewen knew why it had been such a comfort to tell Archie; it was that Dr Cameron seemed to understand so well what he had suffered that he never tried to belittle the cause of it. Instead of attempting to minimize this he said that he would have felt exactly the same had such a terrible mischance befallen him. Only how could Ewen at any stage have imagined that Donald, if he heard of his lapse, would ever believe that he had made a disclosure willingly?

'I blame you for *that*, my poor Ewen,' he said, shaking his head. 'You must surely have known that he would as soon suspect me as you, who have been like an elder son to him, who so nearly threw away your life for him at Fort William. . . . I think that's the worst part of your confession, but as you say that I am not to suppress anything I must tell him that too, though it will hurt him.'

Ewen raised his colourless face, to which, however, a measure of tranquillity had already returned. 'I am sorry for that; but you must not keep back a word. Tell him how I allowed myself to fall asleep when I suspicioned it might be dangerous; tell him that I insulted Lord Loudoun somewhat unworthily – *he* would not have done that – tell him everything. You are only a proxy, you know, Archie – though a very satisfactory one,' he added gratefully. 'There's no other man save Lochiel that I could have told. *Dhé*, but I feel as if Ben Nevis had been lifted off me!'

Archibald Cameron gave his arm a little pressure. 'Now 'tis my turn to make a confession to you. When I first came into this room I found myself emulating that Captain Greening of yours – whom, by the way, I should rejoice to meet on some good lonely brae, with a precipice near by. But, like your talking, my dear lad, my overhearing was accidental.'

'Do you mean that I was saying things in my sleep again? Archie, this is intolerable!'

'You bade me loose your arm when I touched you, and spoke of preferring to be "cut in pieces" and of "another way". You have just told me what that "other way" was. Ewen, what was the first way, and who took it with you? You have not told me everything, after all.'

The young man was looking on the floor, and there was colour enough in his face now. 'I do not very much wish to revive that memory. . . . But if you must know, I was near being flogged by order of the Lowland officer who captured me. He had been going to shoot me first – I'll tell you of that anon. It was because he wanted . . . what they wanted and got at Fort Augustus. – No, do not look so horrified, Archie; he did not carry it out, though I'll admit I believed he was going to. It was only a threat.'

'Then, if it was only a threat,' remarked Dr Cameron, looking at him closely, 'why did you call me a "damned torturer" when I touched you?'

'I . . . Really, Archie, I cannot be responsible for everything I say in my sleep. I apologize, but if you were worth your salt, you would give me some drug to cure me of the cursed habit!'

'I'm afraid the drug does not exist, my dear boy. When your mind is at peace, you will not do it any more. And don't you think that it would conduce to that state if you told me why you called me so unpleasant a name?'

Ewen gave him a little shake. '*Mo thruaigh*, Archie Cameron,' he said with vivacity, 'I begin to think it was because you merit it, with this persistence of yours! If I said that, I suppose I must have been remembering that when one has had a bayonet through one's arm not long before, it is conveniently sensitive, that is all. But after a few experiments, Major Guthrie found that it was not sensitive enough. They knew better how to do things at Fort Augustus.'

Archibald Cameron still gazed at him, compressing his lips. 'So the Lowlander tried "experiments", did he? And do you still consider yourself a traitor, Ewen? I'd give you a rather different name, and so, I fancy, will Lochiel.'

'But I don't mean you to tell Lochiel *that*! No, Archie, that was not confession – you got it out of me unfairly!'

'Unfortunately you made me promise to tell him everything,' retorted his cousin, smiling. 'To turn to another aspect of this matter, then,' for Ewen was really looking unhappy, 'it was, I suppose, to this Major Guthrie with a fancy for experiments that you were betrayed by the English officer who was your prisoner here – I might also say your guest – last August. I hope that he did not go so far as to take part in these proceedings, too? – Bless us, what is wrong now?'

For this partial change of topic had proved far from soothing. With a sharp exclamation Ewen had got up from the bed.

'Good God, Archie, how did you hear that story? It's not true – Major Windham did not betray me – he saved me!'

'Did he? Well, I'd far liefer hear that than the other thing. But that was what Lachlan MacMartin told us, when he came hotfoot to us at Achnacarry at the beginning of May.'

'Lachlan – *Lachlan* went to Achnacarry!' exclaimed Ewen in amazement.

'Yes, he appeared there one day, nearly crazy with rage and remorse, because you had been captured while he had left you in order to get food. He wanted Donald to march against Fort Augustus and deliver you.'

. Ewen had begun to limp distractedly about the room. 'I did not know that. But, great heavens, what a story to get abroad about Major Windham! Archie, he saved my life at the last minute; I was actually up against the wall before the firing-party, when he dashed in between at the risk of his own life. I should not be here now for you to bully, but for him. It is true that I, too, God forgive me, was deluded enough for a short time to think his goodness calculated treachery, but at least I did not spread it abroad. And that is only part of what he has done and given up for me.' He gave his cousin a sketch of the rest. 'I cannot think how Lachlan got such a mistaken notion into his head, for he was not there when I was found and taken, and he can hardly have met with that scoundrel Guthrie, who is capable of any lie.'

'What has become of Lachlan – is he here at Ardroy?'

'No, he has never returned, and no one knows anything of him; he has undoubtedly been either captured or killed, and much more probably killed, I fear. But I wish he had not spread this slander; 'tis at least to be hoped that no word of it reaches poor Windham!'

'I like to see in you, Ewen,' said his cousin, 'the same concern for another man's honour as for your own. But you know the Erse proverb, "A lie goes but on one leg".'

'Like me,' commented Ewen with a smile. 'Yet you think that in France I may go on two again?'

'You will certainly have a better chance of it. Then I may tell Lochiel, when I get back to Badenoch, that you consent to be reasonable?'

'Yes, thanks to you, I will go – since he is going. But I must wait a chance of getting off.'

'There's a chance now,' said his cousin quickly; 'but you must start for the coast tomorrow.'

'Tomorrow!' Ewen's face fell. 'So soon!' His glance swept round the room and lingered for a moment on the heathery distances visible through the window. 'Very well,' he said with a little sigh. 'Tell me what I must do – No,' he caught himself up, 'first tell me a little about Donald. Those wounds of his, are they healed? Archie, I hope due care is being taken of him on Ben Alder?'

'You look as if you think I ought not to have left him,' said

Dr Cameron, smiling. 'But he has had Sir Stuart Threipland of Edinburgh with him, and the wounds are healing, though slowly. And I assure you that I have been too busy following Mercury of late to pay much attention to Aesculapius; I have been to and fro in Lochaber and Moidart a great deal more regularly than the post. More by token, I am become a sort of banker. For I suppose you did not hear in your captivity, Ewen, that at the beginning of May two French ships landed six barrels of gold – forty thousand *louis d'or* – in Moidart for the Prince; and with some ado, owing to the reluctance of Clanranald's people to lose sight of it, I got it conveyed to Loch Arkaig, and it has been buried there against future requirements. – I know what you are going to say. "If only we had had that money earlier, when we needed it so!"'

Those were indeed the words which leapt to the young man's lips. Yet since over the ruined fortunes of today there still danced like will-of-the-wisps the hopes of tomorrow, he fell to discussing the possible uses of this money with the man to whose endeavours (as he soon discovered) it was due that the French had not carried it off again, when they heard the news of the disaster at Culloden. Archibald Cameron had indeed played post and banker to some purpose! Ewen looked at him with admiration not free from concern.

'Archie, are you duly careful of your own safety in these constant journeyings of yours, seeing that you are proscribed by name?'

His cousin smiled. 'You may be sure that I am careful. Am I not pre-eminently a man of peace?'

Nevertheless, not even Balmerino, the dauntless old soldier, was to make a more memorable end on the scaffold than Archibald Cameron. But his time was not yet – not by seven years; though, all unknowing, he had just been talking of what was to bring him there – the belated French treasure, fatal as the fabled gold of the river maidens to nearly every man who touched it.

'Now for your getting off to France,' he resumed. 'There has lately been a French privateer off Loch Broom, and she may very well be hanging off the coast farther south, therefore you should start for Moidart without a day's delay. Since the twenty-fifth of

July the coast is not so closely watched for the Prince as it was; the cordon of sentries has been removed. Make for Arisaig or Morar; at either you will be able to find a fisherman to take you off at night to the French vessel if she is still there. You speak French, so the rest should be easy.'

'And will Lochiel and the Prince try to leave by her?'

'I doubt it, for I fear she will be gone by the time Donald could reach the coast, or His Royal Highness either. But do not delay your departure on that account, Ewen, for the larger the party getting off from shore, the more hazardous is the attempt – at least, if there are any soldiers left in those parts now. There cannot, at any rate, be many. Now I must be getting on my way.'

'You will not pass the night with us?' suggested Ewen. 'Aunt Marget seems to have a high opinion of the garrets as a refuge.'

Dr Cameron shook his head. 'I must push on; 'tis only five o'clock. God bless you, my dear Ewen, and bring us to meet again – even though it be not in Scotland!'

'I wish I were coming with you to Ben Alder,' said Ewen rather wistfully, halting after his visitor down the stairs.

'Trust me to do your business with Donald as well as you could do it yourself – nay, better, for I suspect that you would leave out certain episodes. – You'll be rid of this fellow at last, Miss Marget,' he said to the figure waiting at the foot of the stairs. 'I've sorted him!'

''Tis you have the skill, Archibald Cameron,' replied the lady, beaming on him. 'None of *my* prayers would move him. You'll drink a health with us before you go?'

And under the picture of King James the Third and Eighth the three of them drained their glasses to the Cause which had already taken its last, its mortal wound.

Next day Ewen kept his word, and set about his departure. A garron was found for him to ride, and two of his men who had followed him through the campaign were to accompany him to the coast. Yielding to pressure, he had agreed to take young Angus MacMartin with him to France as his personal servant. He could not refuse it to Neil's memory and to old Angus's prayers that a MacMartin should be about him still.

He was to leave at dusk, since travelling by night would be less hazardous, and a little before sundown he went up to Slochd nan Eun to take leave of his foster-father, with whom he had had little converse since his return, for Angus had been ill and clouded in mind. But he had borne the loss of his two sons with an almost fierce resignation; it seemed as if he had asked no better fate for them, especially for Neil. He had recovered from his illness now, but he was rather frail and still at times a little confused. A daughter looked after him in the old cottage which had once rung with the laughter of many children, and with Ewen's own; but the old man was alone, crouched over the fire with a plaid across his knees, when Ewen, helping himself on the ascent with a staff, arrived at the door.

Half blind though he was, Angus's hearing was as keen as ever, and even with the unfamiliar halt in it, he knew his foster-son's step.

'Mac 'ic Ailein, is it you? Blessings on your head! You have come to say farewell to me, who shall never see you again.'

Tremblingly and slowly, he arose and embraced the young man. 'Neil and Lachlan shall go with you, son of my heart, that you take no harm before you embark on the great water.'

'Neil is dead, foster-father, do you not remember?' asked Ewen gently. 'He gave his life for me. And Lachlan – I fear Lachlan is dead also.'

'It is true that I do not see them any more,' replied the old man, with a singular detachment, 'for I grow blinder every day; yet I hear Neil's pipes very well still, and when the fire burns up I know that Lachlan has put on a fresh peat for me. Good sons both, but I have between my hands a son who is dearer, though I did not beget him – O my tall and beautiful one, glad was the day when you came back after the slaughter, but gladder this day, for you carry your head out of reach of your foes!' He passed his hand lingeringly over the bright locks. 'And yet ... all is not well. I do not know why, but all is not well. There is grief on the white sand ... grief and mourning, and a sound of tears in the wind that blows there.'

'Indeed there is grief,' said Ewen sighing, 'grief enough in my heart at going, at leaving Alba and my father's house. I was almost for staying, Angus, did I take to the heather; but the brother of Mac Dhomhnuill Duibh has been here, and he bids me go. The Chief himself is going. But we shall return – '

'Some will return,' broke in Angus, sinking his head upon his breast. 'Aye, some will return.' Sitting there, he stared with his almost sightless eyes into the fire.

Ewen stood looking down at him. 'Shall *I* return?' he asked after a moment.

'I shall not see you, treasure of my heart ... But these eyes will see my own son come back to me, and he too grieving.'

'But I fear that Lachlan is dead, foster-father,' repeated Ewen, kneeling on one knee beside him. 'Is it not his wraith that puts the peats on the fire for you?'

'It may be,' answered the old man. 'It may well be, for when I speak to him he never answers. Yet one night he stood here in the flesh, and swore the holy oath on his dirk to be avenged on the man who betrayed you to the *saighdearan dearg*. My own two eyes beheld him, my two ears heard him, and I prayed the Blessed One to give strength to his arm – for it was then that you were gone from us, darling of my heart, and fast in prison.'

'But you surely do not mean, Angus,' said his foster-son, puzzled, 'that Lachlan came back here after I was captured? You mean that you saw his *taibhs*. For in the flesh he has never returned to Slochd nan Eun.'

'Yes, for one night he returned,' persisted the old man, 'for one night in the darkness. None saw him but I, who opened to him; and he would not go near the house of Ardroy, nor let any see him but his father, because he was sick with grief and shame that he had left you on Beinn Laoigh to the will of your enemy. Ah, Mac 'ic Ailein, did I not feel that many things would come upon you because of the man to whom the heron led you! But that I never saw – that he would betray you to the *saighdearan dearg*! May Lachlan soon keep his oath, and the raven pick out the traitor's eyes! May his bones never rest! May his ghost – '

Ewen had sprung up, horrified. 'Angus, stop! What are you saying! That man, the English officer, did not betray me: he saved me, at great risk to himself. But for him, the redcoats would have shot me like a dog – but for him, I should not have escaped

from their hands on the way to Inverlochy. Take back the curse
. . . and for Heaven's sake tell me that you are mistaken, that
Lachlan did not swear vengeance on *him*, but on the man who
took me prisoner, a Lowland Scot named Guthrie. That is what
you mean, Angus, is it not?'

But Angus shook his grey head. 'My son swore vengeance on
the man who was your guest, the English officer who found you
in the bothy on Beinn Laoigh, and delivered you up, and told the
soldiers who you were. Lachlan found this out from the talk, as
he skulked round the Lowlander's camp in the dark. Vengeance
he meant to have if he could, but he swore it for certain against
the other, the English officer, because he had broken your bread.
So he took oath on the iron to rest neither day nor night till that
evil deed was repaid to him – he swore it here on the *biodag* on
which you both saw blood that day by the lochan, and which you
bade him not throw away. I think he meant to hasten back and
lie in wait for the English officer as he returned over the pass of
Corryarrick, and to shoot him with the musket which he had
stolen from one of the redcoats. But whether he ever did it I do
not know.'

Bewildered, and with a creeping sense of chill, Ewen had
listened mutely in order that he might, perhaps, contrive to dis-
entangle the true from the false in this fruit of the old man's
clouded brain. But with these last words came a gleam of comfort.
No, Lachlan had not succeeded in any such attempt, thank God.
And since then – for it was in May that Windham had returned
over the Corryarrick – his complete disappearance pointed to
one conclusion, that he was gone where he could never keep his
dreadful and deluded vow. Ewen drew a long breath of relief;
yet it was rather terrible to hope that his foster-brother was dead.

Still, he would take what precaution he could.

'If, when I am gone, Angus,' he said, 'Lachlan should return
here, charge him most straightly from me that he abandon this
idea of vengeance; tell him that but for the English officer I
should be lying today where poor Neil is lying – I wonder if
anyone gave Neil burial,' he added under his breath.

But Angus heard. He raised himself. 'Lachlan buried him when
he came there after yourself, *Eoghain*, and found you gone, and

was near driving the dirk into his own heart, as he told me. Yes, he stayed to bury his brother, and so when he came to the camp of the redcoats, they had taken you to Kilcumein. But all night long he prowled round the tents, and heard the redcoats talk – he having the English very well, as you know – and tried to get into the tent of their commander to kill him while he slept, and could not. So he hastened to Achnacarry, and found Mac Dhomhnuill Duibh, and besought him to go with the clan and besiege the fort of Kilcumein and take you out of it; but the Chief had not enough men. So Lachlan came here secretly, to tell me that he had not been able to stay the redcoats from taking you, and that Neil had been happier than he, for he had died outside the door before they entered to you; and all that was left for him was to slay the Englishman – and so he vowed. But now, it seems, the Englishman is not to be slain?'

'A thousand times, no!' cried Ewen, who had listened very attentively to this recital, which certainly sounded as if it had come originally from Lachlan's own lips, and some of which, as he knew from Archie, was true. 'Remember that, if Lachlan should come here. – But I cannot understand,' he went on, frowning, 'how, if Lachlan overheard so much of the soldier's talk, he did not overhear the truth, and learn how Major Windham ran in and saved me from being shot. Surely that is the matter which must have engaged their tongues, and in that there was no question of delivering me up.'

'I do not know what more my son heard,' said Angus slowly, 'but, when a man hates another, does not his ear seek to hear the evil he may have done rather than the good?'

'Yes, I suppose he did hate Major Windham,' said Ewen thoughtfully. 'That was the reason then – he wanted a pretext. ... Indeed I must thank God that he never got a chance of carrying out his vow. And, from his long absence, I fear – nay, I am sure – that he has joined poor Neil. Alas, both my brothers slain through me, and Neil's children fatherless!'

'But Angus *Og* goes with you, is it not, son of my heart, that he too may put his breast between you and your foes?'

'That he shall never do,' thought Ewen. 'Yes, he goes with me. Give me your blessing, foster-father; and when I come again, even if your eyes do not see me, shall your hands not touch me, as they do now?' And he guided the old hands to his shoulders as he knelt there.

'No, I shall not touch you, treasure of my heart,' said Angus, while his fingers roved over him. 'And I cannot see whether you will ever come back again, nor even whether you will sail over the great water away from your foes. All is dark ... and the wind that comes off the sea is full of sorrow.' He put his hands on Ewen's head. 'But I bless you, my son, with all the blessings of Bridget and Michael; the charm Mary put round her Son, and Bridget put in her banners, and Michael put in his shield ... edge will not cleave thee, sea will not drown thee. . . .' He had slid into reciting scraps of a *sian* or protective charm, but he did not go through to the end; his hands fell on to his knees again, and he leant back and closed his eyes.

Ewen bent forward and threw some peats on to the fire. 'Tell me one thing, foster-father,' he said, looking at him again. 'Even if I never leave the shores of Moidart, but am slain there, or am drowned in the sea, which is perhaps the meaning of the wind that you hear moaning, tell me, in the days to come shall a stranger, or a son of mine, rule here at Ardroy?'

Angus opened his eyes; but he was so long silent that Ewen's hands began to clench themselves harder and harder. Yet at last the old man spoke.

'I have seen a child running by the brink of Loch na h-Iolaire, and his name is your name.'

Ewen drew a long breath and rose, and, his foster-father rising too with his assistance, he kissed him on both cheeks.

'Whatever you have need of, Angus, ask of Miss Cameron as you would of me.'

'You are taking away from me the only thing of which I have need,' said the old man sadly. 'Nevertheless, it must be. Blessings, blessings go with you, and carry you safely away from the white sands to her who waits for you ... and may my blessings draw you back again, even though I do not greet you at your returning.'

When Ewen came slowly down the path again he found himself thinking of how he had descended it last August behind Keith

Windham, nearly a year ago. The story of Lachlan's vow had perturbed him, but now he saw it in a far less menacing light. Either his foster-brother's unquiet spirit was by this time at rest, or the whole thing was a dream of that troubled imagination of the old seer's, where the distinction between the living and the dead was so tenuous.

Soon he forgot Keith Windham, Angus and everyone. Loch na h-Iolaire lay before him under the sunset, a sunset so tranquil and so smiling that in its sleepy brightness, which mirrored all the mountains round, the loch seemed to hold the very heart of content. Ewen had the sensation that his heart, too, was drowned there. And by his own will he was saying farewell to loch and mountain, island and red crag. He remembered how Alison had said that he would be hard put to it to choose between her and them. Was she right?

There was a place where for a little there was no bank, but marshy ground, and where the water came brimming into the reeds and grasses, setting them faintly swaying. He went to it, and, stooping with difficulty, dipped a cupped hand into the water and raised it to his lips. Perhaps that sacramental draught would give him to see this scene as bright and sharp in dreams, over there in the land of exile whither, like his father, like all who had not counted the cost, he was going.

As he drank there was a loud croak over his head, and, looking up, he saw a heron winging its slow, strong way over the loch towards the sunset. It might almost have been the same heron which he and Alison had watched that evening last summer, when it had seemed to arrive from the western coast like a herald from him who had landed there. Now it was going towards the coast once more, as he, the outlaw, was going, and as his Chief and his fugitive Prince would soon be going. In a little year, between two flights of a heron seen over Loch na h-Iolaire, the whole adventure of ruin had been begun and consummated.

Well, if one's life remained to one, it was in order to come back some day and renew the struggle. Ewen took off his bonnet. 'God save King James!' he said firmly, and turned away from the mirrored mountains to take the same path as the heron.

Chapter 5

THIS sea-fog Keith Windham decided, was worse than the inland mist; thicker, more woolly, more capricious. Yesterday, for instance, one had wakened to it, and all day it had cloaked sea and shore and the wild, tumbled mountains of the 'Rough Bounds'. Yet towards evening it had suddenly lifted, and the night had been clear and moonlit. But this morning the white veil was down again, and only now, some hours after sunset, was it clearing away.

And this was all the more vexatious because in the silver clearness of last night he had distinctly made out a strange vessel – a Frenchman, he was sure – anchored somewhere off the isle of Rum. But in the day, thanks to that muffling fog, who knew whether she was still off the coast or no? Yet in a few minutes more, when the moon came up from behind the mountains, he hoped to be able to see as far as her anchorage; meanwhile, followed by his orderly, he rode slowly along the flat shore in the direction of Morar.*

No one could accuse Major Keith Windham of neglecting Lord Albemarle's instructions; if anything, he went beyond them in his ceaseless vigilance. Quartered himself at Arisaig, he thence patrolled the coast in both directions, from Loch nan Uamh, the Adventurer's original landing-place, to Morar of the white sands on the other, and had his grumbling men out in all weathers, at all hours of the day and night, and for any kind of false alarm. But he spared himself still less than them, taking little sleep and covering miles every day, often on foot. If fatigue, like virtue, were its own reward, then he had that recompense. And so far it was his only one.

But at least Keith felt tolerably certain that no fugitives had yet made their escape from his strip of coast, no fugitives of any kind. For, apart from using every endeavour to secure the person of the Pretender's son, he had been instructed to prevent all communication with French vessels, of whom one or two might al-

* Pronounced Móar.

318

ways be hovering off the coast. These nights, therefore, that this ghostly ship was visible, it naturally behoved him to be extraordinarily vigilant, since it was unlikely that she was there by chance; she was probably hanging about in hope of taking off the prize that he was after, and he was duly grateful to the moon last night for showing her to him. And surely it was time for the moon to appear now! Keith put his hand impatiently into the breast of his uniform for a little almanac which he carried there, and encountering a packet which he also carried, was swept at the touch of it away for a moment from shore and ship and moonrise.

Having left Fort Augustus for the coast so soon after Ewen Cameron had confided to his care the letter to his wife, Keith had had no opportunity of dispatching it; moreover, why send that farewell letter, now that its writer had escaped? So, not knowing where else to dispose it, he still carried the packet with the lock of hair upon him, a material token of the tie between him and the foe who had captured him a year ago, and had held him in a species of bondage ever since. The thought had never formulated itself so definitely until tonight, but, by gad, it was true!

He had been hard put to it to conceal his exultation when just before setting out from Fort Augustus for Moidart, he had heard of Ewen's escape and disappearance; and this news had ever since been a source of the most unfeigned pleasure to him. His sacrifices had not been in vain; they had been well worth the making. He thought of Ewen back at Ardroy – *his* doing, that! Ewen would recognize it, too. He had not failed in everything!

And now he pictured Ewen lying hid in the mountains round Loch na h-Iolaire until the worst of the storm had blown over. He could not imagine him leaving Ardroy unless he were obliged, and surely, not being on the list of proscribed, he could contrive to elude capture in those wilds. His wife would doubtless get news of him somehow, return to Scotland and visit him secretly; and in the end, when the price had been paid by those who had not had his good fortune, and there was for the others an amnesty or some act of indemnity, he might be able to occupy his home again in peace. It had so happened, Keith believed, after the Fifteen.

Was then his hope, that they should meet again some day, so impossible of fulfilment now? It was true that if he himself succeeded in capturing the 'Prince', Ewen would not readily take his hand. However, no need to face that dilemma yet. But, in a sense, every day that 'the young gentleman' was still in Scotland brought nearer the hour when he must try to leave it, and if Lord Albemarle were right in supposing that he would make for this stretch of coast, already familiar to him, he must soon approach the snare laid for him there.

And the presence of that unknown ship last night seemed to indicate that the actual moment of that approach was very near. Ah! now at last he would be able to look for her, for the moon had pushed up over the craggy eastern summits at his back into a cloudless sky.

Keith gave his horse to his orderly, and going along a low spur of rock, gazed out to sea. The fantastic peaks of Rum were even more unreal in the moonlight than in the day, and the Isle of Eigg of an even odder shape. At first he thought that the stranger was gone, and then all at once he saw her, a ghostly bark on the rippling silver. She seemed to be off Morar, and, since some of her square-sails appeared to be set, he doubted if she was at anchor; but she was certainly not sailing away.

Keith had to make a rapid decision. At Morar he had an officer and thirty men stationed. That, surely, was enough. He could, if he wished, send back to Arisaig and bring up some more from there; yet should Arisaig and not Morar prove after all the destined spot, and he had denuded Arisaig of watchers, he would be undone. Loch nan Uamh, the original landing-place, was also provided with a quota, but the distance did not admit of bringing any soldiers thence tonight.

He returned to his orderly and mounted his horse. 'I shall ride on to Morar. Go back to Arisaig and tell the Captain so; desire him to keep a close watch on the shore, for the Frenchman is lying off the coast again and nearer in than last night.'

The man saluted and rode off along the rough sandy road, and Keith was left alone with the ship, the moonlight and his own excited thoughts. Not that he stayed to contemplate any of these; he pushed on at a smart trot for Morar, turning over the question of a boat, without which no fugitive could, naturally, reach the ship. He had temporarily confiscated every boat on this stretch of coast, except such as were genuinely needed for fishing, to which he had granted a permit. Even of the owners of these he was not sure, for they were all MacDonald of Clanranald's dependents. It would no doubt have been better to have burnt every one of their craft. Yet even then a vessel could easily dispatch one of her own, at the risk of being fired on.

Keith took a last look at the burnished and gently moving expanse of which he must now lose sight, for here the track turned sharply to the right, to run round the deep little inlet of Morar. But there was no visible speck upon the sea which might be a boat.

And before long he was approaching the shoreward end of the inlet, on the rough sandy track of a road bordered by dense undergrowth which ran round, a little higher than the level shore, under trees of no great stature. The tide was coming in fast over the dazzling white sands of Morar, snow under the moon, and drowning the little river which tumbled from the wild, deep freshwater loch behind, where Lord Lovat had sought his last refuge. It was so intensely quiet, and the tide was slipping in so noiselessly, that the roar of the double falls was carried very clearly over the water. Reining up, Major Windham listened for some sign of the patrol which should be going its rounds from the quarters on the other side of the bay, across the river; and, to his displeasure, he could detect none. This, on a night when a French ship was off the coast! The men must be got out at once.

He touched his horse with the spur and then pulled up again. What was that dark shape down there on the sand? A small boat, and so near the incoming tide that in another quarter of an hour or so it would be afloat. No fisherman could have been so careless as to leave it there, unless it were secured in some way. Brimful of suspicion as Keith was tonight, he had jumped off his horse in an instant, and thrown the bridle over a convenient branch. He knew better than to take the animal plunging into the soft, dry sand of the slope, he was almost up to his ankles himself before he was down.

Yes, he was right; the boat was there for no purpose authorized by him. It had only recently been brought there, for it was not made fast to anything. There were oars in it, but no nets or fishing-lines. It needed no more evidence to convince him that the little craft had been placed there in readiness to take off some person or persons tonight to the strange vessel.

The most lively anger seized Major Windham. What was that damned patrol about, not to have discovered this? He must certainly gallop round to their quarters without a moment's delay and turn out the lazy brutes. His pulses leaping, he plunged up the yielding sand to the tree-shadowed road, turned to throw himself into the saddle – and stood staring like a man bewitched. His horse was gone . . . gone as if swallowed up!

'It is not possible!' said Keith to himself. 'I have not been down there two minutes!'

But, evidently, it *was* possible. Black though the shadows were under the trees, he could tell that they held nothing so solid as a horse. He looked up and down the empty white track, streaked and dappled with those hard shadows; he examined the branch. It was not broken, and the beast could certainly not have twitched his bridle off it. Someone had been watching him, then, and human hands had conveyed the animal away – whither?

Furious, he began to run back along the road; its sandy surface was already too much churned up to show any hoof-marks. He did not remember passing any crofts as he came. Though a man could hide in the thick bushes on the seaward side, a horse could not be concealed in them. He turned abruptly and went back again, remembering that there was a dwelling or two farther along, between him and the river. If some of these MacDonalds had stolen his horse and hidden it there, by Heaven it should be the worse for them!

What, however, was of paramount importance now was not the finding of his horse, but the beating-up of the patrol, with the least possible delay. Yet by the time that he, on foot, could get round to their quarters, or at least by the time that the soldiers arrived on the spot, the boat would probably have put out with her freight. That was why his horse had been spirited away, by the ambushed spy in league with tonight's fugitives.

Keith set his jaw, and cursed himself most fervently for having come alone. The extraordinarily skilful way in which his horse had been made to vanish, joined to the inexplicable lateness of the patrol, only confirmed his conviction that it was the Pretender's son for whom that boat was waiting. Then, at all costs, he must delay its putting out. . . . Could he disable it in some way? Not easily, without tools, but he would do his best.

Once more he plunged down the sandy slope. But the boat, though old, was solid. A knife, a sword, could make no impression on those timbers. Keith had a moment of angry despair; then he remembered having seen in one of these craft the other day a plugged hole, designed to allow water to drain out if necessary. Suppose this boat had one!

Getting in, he peered and felt over the bottom, and at last, to his joy, his fingers encountered, towards the after end, a rough peg of wood sticking up like a cork. After some tugging, he succeeded in wrenching it out, and slipped it into his pocket. He could get his thumb through the hole he had thus unplugged. He leapt out and ran towards the slope again in triumph. One of two things would happen now; either the Pretender's son and his companions would discover what had been done, and a new plug would have to be fashioned to fit the hole, which would delay them not a little, or – what seemed to Keith more probable – they would launch the boat and pull off without examining it, on which it would almost immediately fill and sink, and its occupants be forced to struggle back at a disadvantage to a shore by that time, it was hoped, straitly guarded.

Keith was half-way up the slope again, when he stopped abruptly, for in the stillness he had distinctly heard voices – low voices at no very great distance. The patrol at last, perhaps? He did not think so. The speakers seemed to be coming along the tree-shadowed road between him and the end of the inlet, the very road along which he was preparing to hasten. A party of Jacobite fugitives would most certainly not allow a soldier in uniform to run past them if they could help it. Was the prize going to slip through his fingers after all?

No, hardly, in that unseaworthy boat! But he must perforce let the owners of these cautious voices pass him and get on to the beach, before he started for the quarters of the patrol. Had the tide not already been so high, he could have cut across the sands and swum or waded the river, but that was out of the question now; he could only go by the road. He looked round for shelter and slipped cautiously into a high bush of hazel which itself stood in a patch of shadow so deep that he felt sure of being invisible.

Not only voices, but muffled footsteps were audible by this time, and presently a man – a fisherman, he thought – ran down the slope towards the boat. He had scarcely passed before it came to Keith with a gust of despair that he had set himself an almost impossible task. Now that the fugitives were already here, before he had even started, he could never get round and fetch the patrol in time, for if the Jacobites were left to embark undisturbed they would discover and repair the loss of the plug – that man down there was probably discovering it now. But there was another way of rousing his dilatory men, for, unbelievably negligent as they were this evening, they could not fail to hear a pistol-shot. That would bring them to the place in double-quick time; and although to fire would naturally alarm the fugitives, and make them embark with all the greater dispatch, there was gain in that, since – if it were not already done – they would pretty certainly not discover the loss of the plug. Keith drew the loaded pistol from his belt, but he put it at half-cock only, because he must wait until the party was well past him before firing, seeing that he was only one against he knew not how many.

Centuries seemed to pass while he waited, and considered, only to dismiss it, the idea of deliberately shooting at the Pretender's son with a view to disabling him; for he could not in this light be sure of stopping short at that. His heart beat faster than ever it had done at Fontenoy or Culloden Moor, for this business was fraught for him with issues more momentous than any battle. What happened in the next quarter of an hour would decide his whole future – and no fighting had done that for him.

A sudden fall of sand behind him startled him for a moment, but he dared not turn his head to look what had caused it, for three . . . four dim shapes were coming at last out of the shadows above and beyond him, and beginning to descend the slope. The tallest was limping badly; and he was also the principal figure, for the others, he could see now, were only gillies, and one was a boy.

Had the Pretender's son gone lame in his wanderings? It was quite possible.

Or ... or ... God of Heaven! The sand seemed to swim under Keith's feet. It was not Charles Edward Stuart, it was Ewen Cameron who had walked into his trap, Ewen Cameron who had just limped down past him on the arm of one of the gillies ... Ewen, his friend, whom he had thought safely hidden in Lochaber!

The bitter disappointment and the disastrous surprise of it overwhelmed Keith, and he stood there stupefied. Once more he had come on a fool's errand – not the first since he had watched the coast. This was Edinburgh over again ... but a much more sinister repetition of it. For the net which he had spread for the arch-rebel was not empty; it held a lesser but indubitable prize – a chieftain, Lochiel's kinsman. With a wild sense of being in a net himself, he realized the cogency of the arguments which he had used against Guthrie; if Ewen Cameron was too important to shoot out of hand, he was also too important to let go. .... And he saw Ewen sent back to the scaffold after all, and by him: tied on a horse again, by his hands. ... Or since the boat was holed, and Ewen was lame, he would drown, perhaps, when it sank ... the men were already pushing it nearer to the water....

Stabbed to alarm by that thought, he stepped almost unconsciously out of his sheltering hazel bush, and stood at the edge of the shadow with some vague notion of shouting to warn Ardroy. No, what he had to do was to fire, and bring the patrol here quickly, and arrest him. He was to stop all communication, to allow no one to leave ... much less a chieftain and a kinsman of Lochiel's ...

'God help me!' he said aloud, and put a hand over his eyes.

There was a sudden crackling of broken stems, a fierce exclamation behind him; something glittered out of the shadow, and Keith swung quickly round, just as the man who had been tracking him for over a week sprang down upon him. And so he did not receive Lachlan MacMartin's dirk between the shoulders, as Lachlan had intended, but in his breast.

Leaning on young Angus's shoulder by the boat, Ewen watched the Morar fisherman hastily fitting in the spare plug which he had brought with him (because, as he had explained, the redcoats had

325

played the trick of removing one from Ranald Mor's boat the other night). The fates had indeed been kind – no patrol this evening – if they were quick they would get out of the bay without a single shot being fired at them.

The boat was being pushed down to the water, when all at once the lad Angus gave a little cry, clutched at his master's arm and pointed up the beach. Ewen, turning his head, saw two men locked together on the sandy slope, saw one drop and roll over, had a dim impression that he wore uniform, and a much clearer one of a wild figure running over the sand towards him with a naked dirk in his hand. Young Angus tried to throw himself in front of his chieftain, but the grip on his shoulder, suddenly tightening, stayed him. Moreover, in another moment the spectre with the dirk was on his knees at Ewen's feet, holding up the weapon, and, half sobbing with excitement, was pouring out a flood of words as hot as lava:

'Mac 'ic Ailein, I have kept my vow, I have avenged you – and saved you, too, though I knew not till the *biogad* was bare in my hand that it was you who had passed. The Englishman would have betrayed you a second time . . . but he lies there, and will not rise again. Oh, make haste, make haste to embark, for there are redcoats at Morar!'

Despite his disfigured face, Ewen had recognized him at once, and the meaning of his words, for all their tumbling haste, was clearer still – horribly clear. Frozen, he tried to beat that meaning from him.

'God's curse on you, what have you done!' he exclaimed, seizing his foster-brother by the shoulder. 'If you have really harmed Major Windham –' But the moon showed him the bloody dirk. With a shudder, he thrust the murderer violently from him, and, deaf to young Angus's shrill remonstrance, started to run haltingly back towards the slope. Surely, surely Lachlan had mistaken his victim, for what could Windham be doing here at Morar?

But it *was* Keith Windham. He was lying on his side, full in the moonlight, almost at the bottom of the slope, as if he had been thrown there . . . stunned, perhaps, thought Ewen wildly, with a recollection of how he himself had lain on Culloden Moor

– though how a dirk could stun him, God alone knew. Half-way down the slope lay a pistol. Calling his name, he knelt and took him into his arms. Oh, no hope; it was a matter of minutes! Lachlan had used that long blade too well.

As he was lifted, Keith came back from a moment's dream of a shore with long green rollers roaring loudly under a blood-red sunset, to pain and difficult breath, and Ewen's arms. He knew him.

'I . . . I did not have to . . . fire,' he gasped: but Ewen could not realize what lay behind the words. 'Go . . . go before . . . they come from Morar . . .'

'My God, my God!' exclaimed Ewen, trying to staunch the blood which that spotless sand was already drinking. 'Oh, Windham, if I could only have warned you – if I had known that *he* was here . . .'

'There is a hole . . . in the boat,' said Keith with increasing difficulty. 'I . . . took out . . . the plug.'

'They have put in another – one they had in readiness. Windham, for God's sake try to – '

Try to do what? 'Your letter . . . is still . . . I had no . . .'

'Duncan – Angus!' called Ewen desperately, 'have none of you any brandy?'

But his men, who had run up, were intent on another matter. 'Come, the boat is ready – and I think the redcoats are stirring over the river,' said Duncan Cameron, laying a hand on his shoulder. 'Come, Mac 'ic Ailein, come!'

Ewen answered him in Gaelic. 'I shall not stir while he breathes.'

But the dying man seemed to understand. 'Go . . . Ardroy! . . . I implore you!' He began to fumble at one hand with the other, and managed to pull off the signet-ring which he always wore, and to hold it out a little way. Ewen took it, not knowing what he did.

'I was watching for . . . the Pretender's son,' went on Keith, lower and lower; 'then I saw . . . it was you . . . and I had to try . . . to decide . . . duty . . . no, it is just as well . . . I could not . . . have borne . . .' He sighed and shut his eyes.

Ewen held him closer, still trying to stay the flood, and trying, as he knew, in vain. Yet Keith only seemed to be going to sleep.

He was murmuring something now which Ewen had to stoop his head close to hear. And then all that he could catch were the words: '. . . desire . . . friends . . . always . . .'

'Yes, yes, always,' he answered in anguish. 'Always!' But there would be no 'always'. 'Oh, if only you had not been in that madman's path!'

But that, at least, was not fortuitous. Yet to Keith the assassin had only been some man of Morar in league with the embarkation.

He reopened his eyes. 'Your hand . . .' Ewen gave it to him, and saw a little smile in the moonlight. 'Have you been . . . burying any more cannon? . . . I always liked you,' said his enemy clearly; and a moment after, with his hand in Ewen's, was gone to that place 'where an enemy never entered and from whence a friend never went away'.

Ewen laid him back on the patched sand, and, getting to his feet, stood looking down at the man to whom the heron had brought him – foe, enigma, saviour, victim of a terrible mistake. And friend – yes; but it was too late for friendship now. It had already been too late at their last meeting – which had not been the last after all – when he himself, as he thought, was standing on the threshold of death. But it was Keith Windham who had gone through that door, not he. . . . Had he known that he was dying? . . . Every word of the few he had spoken had been about *him* . . .

Then through the haze of shock and grief penetrated the sound of a distant shot, and he remembered that there were other lives than his at stake.

'Go – go and hide yourselves!' he commanded. But the two Camerons shook their heads. 'Not until you are in the boat, Mac 'ic Ailein!'

'I will come, then,' said Ewen. He would rather have stayed, now; but he knelt again and kissed Keith's forehead. And that it should not be found on him, an equivocal possession, perhaps, he drew out his own letter to Alison, and slipped it, all sodden, into his pocket. Then he suffered the gillies to hurry him down to the boat, for already it was clear that the soldiers were crossing the river, and some twenty yards away a couple of ill-aimed bullets raised spurts of sand.

By the boat was waiting Lachlan, Lachlan who, directly he was recovered from the result of his first attempt by Loch Tarff, had once more set about the fulfilment of his vow, who had hung about Inverness through July and found no opportunity, lost track of his quarry when he went to Fort Augustus, picked it up again in Moidart, and had hardly let him out of his sight since. It was he who had removed the horse.

'Ewen, my brother, forgive me – forgive me!'

Ewen turned on him a terrible face. 'Never! You have killed my friend!'

'Never? Then as well have my life, too!' cried Lachlan. The reddened dirk, which a year ago he had been moved to fling into the loch, spun glinting through the moonlight and splashed into the sea, and its owner, turning, ran headlong towards the road and the oncoming patrol.

Soon the noise of shots and shouting could be heard no longer, only the creak of the oars in the rough rowlocks as young Angus and the fisherman pulled hard over the moonlit sea towards the French privateer. But Ewen sat in the sternsheets of the little boat with his face buried in his hands, and cared not that he went to safety.

The day would come when, pondering over his memories of those broken sentences, recalling the pistol lying on the sand, he would arrive at a glimpse of the truth, and guess that Lachlan's blade had saved Keith Windham from a decision too cruel, and that perhaps he had been glad to be so saved. But he would never realize – how should he? – that the tide which for a year had been carrying the Englishman, half ignorant, sometimes resisting, among unlooked-for reefs and breakers, away from the safe, the stagnant Dead Sea of his choice, had borne him to no unfitting anchorage in this swift death, devoid of thoughts of self. For Ewen saw Keith only as a loser through meeting him – a loser every way – whereas in truth he had been a gainer.

A hail came over the water; they were approaching the privateer. He tried to rouse himself from his stupor of grief and regret, and from the self-reproach which stabbed scarcely less deep because it was causeless. And as he did so the kind moonlight showed him his friend's ring upon his finger.

EPILOGUE
HARBOUR OF GRACE

THE fresh wind scouring the mouth of the Seine kept the fishing-boats from Honfleur lying well over, and at the foot of the cliffs of Ste Adresse the waves were shivering themselves in a joyful welter of foam. Long pennants of cloud streamed and vanished in the blue; all the shipping rocked at anchor, and Alison Cameron, crossing the market-place of Havre-de-Grâce with a basket on her arm, had to clutch at her black cloak lest it should be whirled off her shoulders.

She had reached the French port in time to see her father alive; in time, indeed, to give him nearly six weeks of the most devoted care. But in May he had died peacefully, ignorant of the catastrophe which had torn for ever the webs that he had helped to weave. Since he was ill, it had not been very difficult to keep from him the news of the downfall of Jacobite hopes and the fugitive state of the Prince, and to invent reasons for the absence of any news of Ewen Cameron. Of Hector's capture he had known before leaving Scotland. It was the thought of Ewen, to whose care he knew Alison now definitely committed, which had made his last hours easy. 'Your man will never let you want for aught, my lass,' he had said, near the end; and Alison had the strength to keep from him the anxiety which racked her.

And so one morning she found herself left alone in the lodging where her father had lain ill, a little house belonging to a youthful married couple, kind and sympathetic enough, and glad that the Scottish lady should stay on there, waiting for the husband who, Madame Grévérend was privately sure, would never come now, having without doubt been slain in the deserts of *l'Écosse*. And when, later on, a gossip would ask her why the young Scottish lady did not voyage back to those deserts to find her husband, or to procure news of him, or at least to have the solace of weeping on his tomb, Madame Grévérend would explain that the poor creature was so persuaded that her husband would in the end come to Havre-de-Grâce seeking her, that she feared to miss him if she went away.

'But she will wait for ever, one fears,' Madame Grévérend would finish; 'and she left without even a good-for-nothing like this to plague her!' And here she would snatch up her fat, curly-headed Philippe and kiss him. 'Yes, she has lost everything, poor lady, and she only five months married.'

But one has never lost everything. Alison still had that possession which Madame Grévérend could not understand, the certitude which had come to her in the cabin of the brig at Inverness. Sooner or later Ewen would come for her.

Yet it was hard, sometimes, to cling to that belief, when the weeks went by and there was not the slightest crumb of authentic news of him. All she had was negative; for there was in Havre-de-Grâce another Scots refugee, a Mr Buchanan who had served in the Duke of Perth's regiment, and he had convinced her, on evidence that seemed conclusive to a mind which only longed to believe it, that Ardroy had not been among the slain or massacred in the battle. Where, then, was he?

Her marketing finished, Alison took her way homewards through the bright windy weather, and came, down the little Rue des Vergers, to the small, sanded courtyard with the pear-tree where she dwelt above Monsieur and Madame Grévérend. In that sunlit space there was at the moment only the grey cat curled in a corner, a pair of pigeons promenading, and Philippe, seated easily upon his mother's doorstep, deliberately pouring sand on to his curls, as if in penitence for some misdeed, by means of an old teacup.

'My bairnie, don't do that!' called Alison, half laughing, half horrified. '*Fi donc, quelle saleté!*'

Philippe gave her a most roguish glance, scooped up and emptied upon his locks a sort of final bumper cupful, and then rose uncertainly to his fat legs and came to her, lifting a beaming, smeared face for a kiss. Alison wiped his countenance and gave him one.

'Are you all alone, Philippe?'

The child intimated that he was, and then entered unasked

upon a long explanation of the complicated reasons which had led him to make a garden of his head.

'I think you had better come up to my room with me, and let me brush out that horrid sand, my pretty,' said Alison, wondering what would happen if she held him upside down and shook him. '*Veux-tu bien?*'

He nodded, and Alison held out a hand. But neither of his were available, since one still clutched his teacup, and the other was tightly closed over some small object.

'What have you there?' asked the girl. It might so well be a beetle or a worm.

Philippe was coy about revealing his treasure, though he evidently desired to display it. But at last he opened a fat fist. '*De l'argent!*' he said exultingly, for though immature he was a true Norman. And indeed there lay in his pink palm a small coin.

There was something about that piece of money which caused Alison's heart to leap suddenly into her throat; and, to the infant's dismay, she snatched his treasure from his hand and looked at it closely. It was no coin of France; no coin of any realm at all, in fact, but a Scottish trade token of the town of Inverness.

'Who gave you this, Philippe?' she asked, looking almost frightened. For Mr Buchanan, who might otherwise have been the donor, had gone away three days ago.

But her plundered companion was plainly making preparations for one of the most resonant howls of his short life. 'There, there, darling,' said Alison hastily, going down on her knees and restoring him his token. 'I am not going to take it away. But who in God's name gave it to you?'

It required time for the little boy to master his emotion, but when this was done he embarked upon another tortuous narrative, from which a close attention could gather that a strange gentleman had come and asked for Madame Cameron and had presented him with this earnest of his regard.

'And where is the gentleman now?' asked Alison breathlessly.

Philippe turned his rotund person and pointed up the stairs with the teacup.

Next moment he was alone in the middle of the courtyard, alone with the pigeons and the cat and Madame Cameron's abandoned basket, and Alison was flying up those stairs to her room. But half-way she stopped, with her hand to her heart, for her own light footfalls had not prevented her from hearing those others going impatiently to and fro above her – unknown steps, belonging to a man with a halt in his walk.

No, of course she had been too sanguine. It was not Ewen. The tumult of her heart died down again to the old sad patience. Yet it must be someone from Scotland, someone from the Highlands, too, for the token proved that; and if he asked for her, it was because he came with news of Ewen, or of Hector.

And perhaps because at the bottom of her heart she trembled to think what that news might be, Alison turned and went down the stairs again and picked up her basket from the courtyard (and none too soon, for it had already riveted Philippe's attention as well as the cat's) and went a great deal more soberly up the stairs once more, and opened the door.

It was she who recovered speech the first, but scarcely coherent speech.

'Oh, Ewen, darling of my heart . . . you look so thin, so ill! And why are you lame? I thought it could not be you. . . . I knew you would come. . . . Sit down, for pity's sake!' She dragged him to a chair. 'Are you hungry – when did you eat? I must get you –'

But she was powerless in the arm he put about her, though the arm was trembling a little, and she fell on her knees beside the chair and cried into his coat; and then Ewen dried her eyes by a method which he had just discovered.

'I am neither thin, nor ill, nor lame, nor hungry; and I have all I want. Open your eyes and look at me like that again!'

His dear voice, at least, was not altered. 'I shall tell Madame Grévérend, when she returns, to make ready –'

'How concerned are women with food! I have no wish to eat at present; I only want to be sure that I am here,' said her husband, half laughing. 'If you go away to give orders, *m'eudail*, I may perhaps fancy I am back on the sea again, or . . . back on the sea,' he repeated rather hastily, turning his head a moment aside.

'You *are* here,' said Alison earnestly, as if he really needed the assurance; 'you are here, Ewen, heart's dearest, and I always knew that you would come!'

Long, long afterwards, that is to say, when Philippe and the pigeons had gone to roost, and the windy day had flamed itself out in a royal sunset, Alison, in her husband's arms, where she had been clasped for fully five minutes without stirring or speaking, fingered the back of his hand and said half-dreamily: 'How came you by this strange ring, dear heart?'

Ewen moved abruptly; something like a shudder ran through him. 'I will tell you some time,' he said hesitatingly, 'but not yet. Oh, Alison, I cannot speak of it yet. . . .'

Some dreadful remembrance of the defeat, she thought pitifully, then, seeing how pale he had become, slipped off his knee, and, bending over him, drew his head with a lovely gesture to her breast. And Ewen hid his eyes there like a child.

But leagues on leagues away, the tide from the Outer Isles was beginning to fill the silver cup of Morar; and he stood there once again, helpless and heartbroken, looking down at Lachlan's handiwork. Not even Alison, whose arms held him close, whose cheek was pressed on his hair, not even Alison could stand with him in that place, where Keith Windham had come to the last of their meetings, and the bitter grief of Angus's prediction had reached its real fulfilment.

Yet he must not sadden Alison on this, of all days: it was Keith who had given it to him.

He lifted his head from its resting-place. '*My dearest on earth,*' he said, but not as he had said it a year ago, for the gift he asked meant even more now, – '*my dearest on earth, give me your kiss!*'

THE GLEAM IN THE
NORTH

AUTHOR'S NOTE

In all that concerns Doctor Archibald
Cameron this story follows historical fact
very closely, and its final scenes embody
many of his actual words.

CONTENTS

Chapter 1

THE BROKEN CLAYMORE

1

'AND then,' said the childish voice, 'the clans charged ... but I expect you do not know what that means, Keithie; it means that they ran very fast against the English, waving their broadswords, and all with their dirks in their left hands under the targe; and they were so fierce and so brave that they broke through the line of English soldiers which were in front, and if there had not been so many more English, and they well-fed – but we were very hungry and had marched all night ...'

The little boy paused, leaving the sequel untold; but the pause itself told it. From the pronoun into which he had dropped, from his absorbed, exalted air, he might almost have been himself in the lost battle of which he was telling the story this afternoon, among the Highland heather, to a boy still younger. And in fact he was not relating to those small, inattentive ears any tale of old, unhappy, far-off things, nor of a battle long ago. Little more than six years had passed since these children's own father had lain badly wounded on the tragic moorland of Culloden – had indeed died there but for the devotion of his foster-brothers.

'And this,' concluded the story-teller, leaving the gap still unbridged, 'this is the hilt of a broadsword that was used in the battle.' He uncovered an object of a roundish shape wrapped in a handkerchief and lying on his knees. 'Cousin Ian Stewart gave it to me last week, and now I will let you see it ... You're not listening – you're not even *looking*, Keithie!'

The dark, pansy-like eyes of his little hearer were lifted to his.

'Yes, My was,' he replied in his clear treble. 'But somesing runned so fast down My's leg,' he added apologetically. 'It comed out of the *fraoch*.'

Not much of his small three-year-old person could be seen, so deep planted was it in the aforesaid heather. His brother Donald, on the contrary, was commandingly situated in a fallen pine-stem. The sun of late September, striking low through the birch trees, gilded his childish hair, ripe corn which gleamed as no cornfield ever did; he was so well-grown and sturdy that he might have passed for seven or eight, though in reality a good deal younger, and one could almost have imagined the winged helm of a Viking on those bright locks. But the little delicate face, surmounted by loose dark curls, which looked up at him from the fading heather, was that of a gently brooding angel – like that small seraph of Carpaccio's who bends so concernedly over his big lute. Between the two, tall, stately and melancholy, sat Luath, the great shaggy Highland deerhound; and behind was the glimmer of water.

The historian on the log suddenly got up, gripping his claymore hilt tight. It was big and heavy; his childish hand was lost inside the strong twining basketwork. Of the blade there remained but an inch or so. 'Come along, Keithie!'

Obediently the angel turned over as small children do when they rise from the ground, took his brother's outstretched hand and began to move away with him, lifting his little legs high to clear the tough heather stems.

'Not going home now, Donald?' he inquired after a moment, tiring, no doubt, of this prancing motion.

'We will go this way,' replied the elder boy somewhat disingenuously, well aware that he had turned his back on the house of Ardroy, his home, and was making straight for Loch na h-Iolaire, where the two were never allowed to go unaccompanied. 'I think that Father is fishing here somewhere.'

2

Conjecture or knowledge, Donald's statement was correct, though, as an excuse for theirs, his father's presence was scarcely sufficient, since nearly a quarter of a mile of water intervened between Ewen Cameron of Ardroy and his offspring. He could not even see his small sons, for he sat on the farther

side of the tree-covered islet in the middle of the loch, a young
auburn-haired giant with a determined mouth, patiently splicing
the broken joint of a fishing-rod.

More than four years had elapsed since Ardroy had returned
with his wife and his little son from exile after Culloden. As
long as Lochiel, his proscribed chief, was alive, he had never
contemplated such a return, but in those October days of 1748
when the noblest and most disinterested of all the gentlemen
who had worn the White Rose lay dying in Picardy of brain
fever (or, more truly, of a broken heart) he had in an interval
of consciousness laid that injunction on the kinsman who almost
felt that with Lochiel's his own existence was closing too. All
his life Lochiel's word had been law to the young man; a wish
uttered by those dying lips was a behest so sacred that no hesi-
tations could stand in the way of carrying it out. Ewen resigned
the commission which he bore in Lochiel's own regiment in the
French service, and breathed once more the air of the hills of
home, and saw again the old grey house and the mountain-
clasped loch which was even dearer. But he knew that he would
have to pay a price for his return.

And indeed he had come back to a life very different from
that which had been his before the year 1745 – to one full of
petty annoyances and restrictions, if not of actual persecution.
He was not himself attainted and thereby exempted, like some,
from the Act of Indemnity, or he could not have returned at
all; but he came back to find his religion proscribed, his arms
taken from him, and the wearing of his native dress made a
penal offence which at its second commission might be punished
with transportation. The feudal jurisdiction of the chiefs was
shattered for ever, and now the English had studded the Highlands with a series of military outposts, and thence (at a great
expenditure of shoe-leather) patrolled all but the wildest glens.
It was a maimed existence, a kind of exile at home; and though
indeed to a Highlander, with all of a Celt's inborn passion for
his native land, it had its compensations, and though he was
most happily married, Ewen Cameron knew many bitter hours.
He was only thirty-three – and looked less – and he was a
Jacobite and fighter born. Yet both he and his wife believed that

he was doing right in thus living quietly on his estate, for he could thereby stand, in some measure, between his tenants and the pressure of authority, and his two boys could grow up in the home of their forefathers. Keith, indeed, had first opened his eyes at Ardroy, and even Donald in England, whither, like other heroic Jacobite wives in similar circumstances, Lady Ardroy had journeyed from France for her confinement, in order that the heir should not be born on foreign soil.

Besides, Lochiel had counselled return.

Moreover, the disaster of Culloden had by no means entirely quenched Jacobite hopes. The Prince would come again, said the defeated among themselves, and matters go better ... next year, or the year after. Ewen, in France, had shared those hopes. But they were not so green now. The treaty of Aix-la-Chapelle had rendered French aid a thing no more possible; and indeed Jacobite claims had latterly meant to France merely a useful weapon with which to threaten her ancient foe across the Channel. Once he who was the hope of Scotland had been hunted day and night among these Western hills and islands, and the poorest had sheltered him without thought of consequences; now on the wide continent of Europe not a crowned head would receive him for fear of political complications. More than three years ago, therefore, poor, outcast and disillusioned, he who had been 'Bonnie Prince Charlie' had vanished into a plotter's limbo. Very few knew his hiding-places; and not one Highlander.

3

'My want to go home,' said little Keith, sighing. The two children were now standing, a few yards from the verge, looking over the Loch of the Eagle, where the fringing birches were beginning to yellow, and the quiet water was expecting the sunset.

Donald took no notice of this plaint; his eyes were intently fixed on something up on the red-brown slopes of Meall Achadh on the far side – was it a stag?

'Father not here,' began the smaller boy once more, rather wistfully. 'Go home to Mother now, Donald?'

'All in good time,' said Master Donald in a lordly fashion. 'Sit down again, if you are tired.'

'Not tired,' retorted little Keith, but his mouth began to droop. 'Want to go home – Luath goned!' He tugged at the hand which held him.

'Be quiet!' exclaimed his brother impatiently, intent on the distant stag – if stag it were. He loosed his hold of Keith's hand, and, putting down the claymore hilt, used both his own to shade his eyes, remembering the thrill, the rather awful thrill, of coming once upon an eight-pointer which severe weather had brought down almost to the house. This object was certainly moving; now a birch tree by the loch-side blocked his view of it. Donald himself moved a little farther to the left to avoid the birch branches, almost as breathless as if he had really been stalking the beast. But in a minute or two he could see no further sign of it on the distant hillside, and came back to his actual surroundings to find that his small brother was no longer beside him, but had trotted out to the very brink of the loch, in a place where Donald had always been told that the water was as deep as a kirk.

'Keith, come back at once!' he shouted in dismay. 'You know that you are not to go there!'

And then he missed the claymore hilt which he had laid down a yard or so away; and crying, 'How *dare* you take my sword!' flung himself after the truant.

But before he could reach it the small figure had turned an exultant face. 'My got yours toy!' And then he had it no longer, for with all his childish might he had thrown it from him into the water. There was a delightful splash. 'It's away!' announced Keithie, laughing gleefully.

Donald stood there arrested, his rosy face gone white as paper. For despite the small strength which had thrown the thing, the irreplaceable relic was indeed 'away' ... and since the loch was so deep there, and he could not swim ... Then the hot Highland blood came surging back to his heart, and, blind with a child's unthinking rage, he pounced on the malefactor. One

343

furious push, and he had sent his three-year-old brother to join
the claymore hilt in the place where Loch na h-Iolaire was as
deep as a kirk.

4

A child's scream – two screams – made Ewen Cameron throw
down his rod and spring to his feet. In that stillness of the heart
of the hills, and over water, sounds travelled undimmed, and
he had for a little time been well aware of childish voices at a
distance, and had known them, too, for those of his own boys.
But since it never occurred to him that the children were there
unattended, he was not perturbed; he would row over to them
presently.

But now ... He ran across the islet in a panic. The screams
prolonged themselves; he heard himself called. God! what had
happened? Then he saw.

On the shore of the loch, looking very small against the great
old pines behind him, stood a boy rigid with terror, screaming
in Gaelic and English for his father, for Angus, for anyone ...
and in the water not far from shore was something struggling,
rising, disappearing ... Ardroy jumped into the small boat in
which he had rowed to the island, and began to pull like a madman towards the shore, his head over his shoulder the while.
And thus he saw that there was something else in the loch also –
a long, narrow head forging quickly through the water towards
the scene of the accident, that place near land, indeed, but deep
enough to drown twenty children. Luath, bless him, thought the
young man, has gone in from a distance. Before he had rowed
many more strokes he himself dropped his oars, and, without
pausing even to strip off his coat, had plunged in himself. Even
then, strong swimmer though he was, he doubted if he should be
in time ... The dog had got there first, and had seized the child,
but was more occupied in trying to get him bodily out of the
loch than in keeping his head above water. But with a stroke or
two more Ardroy was up to them, only praying that he should
not have to struggle with Luath for possession. Mercifully the
deerhound obeyed his command to let go, and in another

moment Ewen Cameron was scrambling out of Loch na h-Iolaire, himself fully as terrified as either of the children, but clutching to him a sodden, choking little bundle, incoherent between fright and loch-water.

5

The old house of Ardroy stood some quarter of a mile from the loch, rather strangely turning its back upon it, but, since it thus looked south, capturing the sun for a good part of the day, even in midwinter. Comfortable and unpretentious, it had already seen some hundred and thirty autumns, had sometimes rung with youthful voices, and sometimes lacked them. Now once again it had a nursery, where at this moment, by a fire of peat and logs, a rosy-cheeked Highland girl was making preparations for washing two small persons who, after scrambling about all afternoon in the heather and bracken, would probably stand in need of soap and water.

And presently their mother came through the open door, dark-haired like her younger son, slight, oval-faced, almost a girl still, for she was but in her late twenties, and combining a kind of effortless dignity with a girlish sweetness of expression.

'Are the children not home yet, Morag?' she asked, using the Gaelic; and Morag answered her lady that surely they would not be long now, and it might be that the laird himself was bringing them, for he had gone up past the place where they were playing.

'Ah, there they are,' said Lady Ardroy, for she had heard her husband's step in the hall, and as she left the room his soft Highland voice floated up to her, even softer than its wont, for it seemed to be comforting someone. She looked over the stairs and gave an exclamation. Ardroy was dripping wet, all save his head, and in his arms, clinging to him with an occasional sob, was a pitiful little object with dark hair streaked over its face.

Ewen looked up at the same moment and saw her. 'All is well, dear heart,' he said quickly. 'Keithie has had a wee mishap, but here he is, safe and sound.'

He ran up the stairs and put the small wet thing, wrapped in

345

Donald's coat, into its mother's arms. 'Yes – the loch ... he fell in. No harm, I think; only frightened. Luath got to him first; I was on the island.'

Alison gave a gasp. She had seized her youngest almost as if she were rescuing him from the rescuer, and was covering the damp, forlorn little face with kisses. 'Darling, darling, you are safe with mother now! ... He must be put into a hot bath at once!' She ran with him into the nursery. 'Is the water heated, Morag?'

Ardroy, wet and gigantic, followed her in, and behind came the mute and coatless Donald, who stood a moment looking at the bustle, and then went and seated himself, very silent, on the window-seat. Close to the fire his mother was getting the little sodden garments off Keith, Morag was pouring out the hot water, his father, who could be of no use here, was contributing a damp patch to the nursery floor. But Keithie had ceased to cry now, and as he was put into the bath he even patted the water and raised a tiny splash.

And then, after he was immersed, he said to his mother, raising those irresistible velvety eyes, 'Naughty Donald, to putch Keithie into the water!'

'Oh, my darling, my peeriewinkle, you must not say things like that!' exclaimed Alison, rather shocked. 'There, we'll forget all about falling in; you are safe home now. Towel, Morag!'

'Donald putched Keithie into the water,' repeated the little naked boy from the folds of the towel. And again, with deeper reprobation in his tone, '*Naughty* Donald!'

Ardroy, anxiously and helplessly watching these operations, knelt down on one knee beside his wife and son and said gently, 'Donald should not have gone near the loch; that was naughty of him, but you must not tell a lie about it, Keithie!'

'*Did* putch My in!' reiterated the child, now wrapped in a warm blanket, and looking not unlike a chrysalis. 'Did – *did!*'

'Yes, I did,' said a sudden voice from behind. 'It's not a lie – I did push him in.' And with that Donald advanced from the window.

His kneeling father turned so suddenly that he almost over-balanced. 'You – you *pushed* your little brother into Loch na h-Iolaire!' he repeated, in a tone of utter incredulity, while Alison clutched the chrysalis to her, looking like a mother in a picture of the massacre of the innocents. 'You pushed him in – deliberately!' repeated Ardroy once more, getting to his feet.

The child faced him, fearless but not defiant, his golden head erect, his hands clenched at his sides.

'He threw my broadsword hilt in. It was wicked of him – wicked!' The voice shook a moment. 'But he is not telling a lie.'

For a second Ewen gazed, horrified, at his wife, then at his heir. 'I think you had better go downstairs to my room, Donald. When I have changed my clothes I will come and talk to you there. – You'll be getting Keithie to bed as soon as possible, I suppose, *mo chridhe*?'

'Donald ... Donald!' murmured his mother, looking at the culprit with all the sorrow and surprise of the world in her eyes.

'Naughty Donald,' chanted his brother with a flushed face. 'Naughty ... naughty ... naughty!'

'A great deal more than naughty,' thought the young father to himself, as he went to his bedroom and stripped off his wet clothes. 'Good God, how came he to do such a thing?'

In the hall Luath, wet too, rose and poked a cold nose into his hand. 'Yes,' said his master, 'you did your duty, good dog ... but my boy, how *could* he have acted so!'

He put that question squarely to the delinquent, who was waiting for him in the little room where Ardroy kept his books and rods and saw his tenantry. Donald's blue eyes met his frankly.

'I suppose because I was angry with Keithie for being so wicked,' he replied.

Ewen sat down, and, afraid lest his horror and surprise should make him too stern, drew the child towards him. 'But, surely, Donald, you are sorry and ashamed now? Think what might have happened!'

The fair head drooped a little – but not, evidently, in penitence. 'I am not sorry, Father, that I threw him in. He was wicked; he took my claymore hilt that was used at Culloden and threw it in. So it was right that he should be punished.'

'Great heavens!' exclaimed his parent, loosing his hold of him at this pronouncement, 'don't you think that your little brother is of more importance than a bit of an old broadsword?'

To which Donald made the devastating reply: 'No, Father, for I don't suppose that I can ever have the hilt again, because the loch is so deep there. But some day I may have another brother; Morag said so.'

Words were smitten from the laird of Ardroy, and for a moment he gazed speechless at this example of infantile logic. 'Donald,' he said at last, 'I begin to think you're a wee thing fey. Go to bed now; I'll speak to you again in the morning.'

'If you are going to punish me, Father,' said the boy, standing up very straight, and looking up at him with his clear, undaunted eyes, 'I would liefer you did it now.'

'I am afraid that you cannot have everything you wish, my son,' replied Ardroy rather grimly. 'Go to your bed now, and pray to God to show you how wicked you have been. I had rather you felt that than thought about getting your punishment over quickly. Indeed, if the sight of your little brother all but drowning through your act was not punishment ...' He stopped, for he remembered that Donald had at least screamed for help.

But the executor of vengeance stuck to his guns. 'It was Keithie who deserved punishment,' he murmured, but not very steadily.

'The child's bewitched!' said Ewen to himself, staring at him. Then he put a hand on his shoulder. 'Come now,' he said in a softer tone, 'get you to bed, and think of what you would be feeling like now if Keithie had been drowned, as he certainly would have been had I not happened to be on the island, for Luath could not have scrambled right out with him ... And you see what disobedience leads to, for if you had not taken Keithie to the loch he could not have thrown your hilt into it.'

This argument appeared to impress the logical mind of his son. 'Yes, Father,' he said in a more subdued tone. 'Yes, I am sorry that I was disobedient.'

And, though Ardroy at once divined a not very satisfactory

reason for this admission, he wisely did not probe into it. 'Go to bed now.'

'Am I to have any supper?'

'Supper's of small account,' replied Ewen rather absently, gazing at the golden-haired criminal. 'Yes ... I mean No – no supper.'

On that point at least he was able to come to a decision. And Donald seemed satisfied with its justice. He left the room gravely, without saying good night.

Later, bending with Alison over the little bed where Donald's victim was already nearly asleep, Ewen repeated his opinion that their elder son was fey. 'And what are we to do with him? He seems to think that he was completely justified in what he did! 'Tis ... 'tis unnatural!'

And he looked so perturbed that his wife smothered her own no less acute feelings on the subject and said consolingly, 'He must at least have done it in a blind rage, dear love.'

'I hope so, indeed. But he is so uncannily calm and judicial over it now. I don't know what to do. Ought I to thrash him?'

'You could not,' murmured Lady Ardroy. Like many large, strong men, Ewen Cameron was extraordinarily gentle with creatures that were neither. 'No, I will try whether I cannot make Donald see what a dreadful thing he did. Oh, Ewen, if you had not been there ...' Her lips trembled, and going down on her knees she laid her head against the little mound under the bedclothes.

Keithie half woke up and bestowed a sleepy smile upon her. In common with his impenitent brother he seemed to have recovered from his fright; it was the parents of both in whose cup the dregs of the adventure were left, very disturbing to the palate.

Chapter 2

LIEUTENANT HECTOR GRANT OF THE
RÉGIMENT D'ALBANIE

ALISON retired early that evening, to keep an eye upon her
youngest born after his immersion. But Ardroy did not go to
bed at his usual hour; indeed, he remained far beyond it, and
half past eleven found him pacing up and down the big living-
room, his hands behind his back. Now and again, as he turned
in his perambulation, there was to be seen the merest trace of
his memento of Culloden, the limp which, when he was really
tired, was clearly to be recognized for one.

Deeply shocked at this fratricidal tendency in his eldest son,
and puzzled how best to deal with it, the young man could not
get his mind off the incident. When he looked at Luath, lying
on the deerskin in front of the hearth, nose on paws and eyes
following his every movement, he felt almost ashamed that the
dog should have witnessed the crime which made Donald, at
his early age, a potential Cain!

At last, in desperation, he went to his own sanctum, seized an
account book and bore it back to the fireside. Anything to take
his mind off the afternoon's affair, were it only the ever-
recurring difficulty of making income and expenditure tally. For
Ewen had never received – had never wished to receive – a
single louis of the French gold buried at Loch Arkaig, though it
had been conveyed into Cameron territory by a Cameron, and
though another Cameron, together with the proscribed chief of
the Macphersons (still in hiding in Badenoch), was agent for its
clandestine distribution among the Jacobite clans. Ardroy had
told Doctor Archibald Cameron, Lochiel's brother, and his own
cousin and intimate, who had been the hero of its transportation and interment, that he did not need any subsidy; and John
Cameron of Fassefern, the other brother, representative in the
Highlands of the dead Chief's family now in France, was only

too relieved not to have another applicant clamouring for a
dole from that fast dwindling hoard.

And Ardroy himself was glad of his abstention, for by this
autumn of 1752 it was becoming clear that the money landed
from the French ships just after the battle of Culloden, too late
to be of any use in the campaign, had now succeeded in setting
clan against clan and kinsman against kinsman, in raising
jealousies and even – for there were ugly rumours abroad – in
breeding informers. Yes, it was dragon's teeth, after all, which
Archibald Cameron had with such devotion sowed on
Loch Arkaig side – seed which had sprung up, not in the
guise of armed men to fight for the Stuarts, but in that of
a crop of deadly poison. Even Ewen did not suspect how
deadly.

In the midst of the young laird's rather absent-minded calculations Luath suddenly raised his head and growled. Ardroy
laid down his papers and listened, but he could hear nothing.
The deerhound growled again, on a deep, threatening note, and
rose, the hair along his neck stiffening. His eyes were fixed on
the windows.

'Quiet!' said his master, and, rising also, went to one, drew
aside the curtains, and looked out. He could see nothing, and
yet he, too, felt that someone was there. With Luath, still growl-
ing, at his heels, he left the room, opened the door of the house,
and going through the porch, stood outside.

The cool, spacious calm of the Highland night enveloped him
in an instant; he saw Aldebaran brilliant in the south-east between two dark continents of cloud. Then footsteps came out of
the shadows, and a slim, cloaked figure slipped quickly past him
into the porch.

'*Est-il permis d'entrer, mon cher?*' it asked, low and half
laughing. 'Down, Luath – it's a friend, good dog!'

'Who is it?' had been surprised out of Ewen in the same
moment, as he turned.

'Sure, you know that!' said the voice. 'But shut your door,
Ardroy!'

The intruder was in the parlour now, in the lamplight, and as
Ewen hastened after him he flung his hat upon the table, and

351

advanced with both hands outstretched, a dark, slender, clear-featured young man of about five and twenty, wearing powder and a long green roquelaure.

'Hector, by all the powers!' exclaimed his involuntary host. 'What –'

'What brings me here? I'll tell you in a moment. How does Alison, and yourself, and the bairns? Faith, I'll hardly be knowing those last again, I expect.'

'Alison is very well,' replied Ewen to Alison's only brother. 'We are all well, thank God. And Alison will be vastly pleased to see you, as I am. But why this unannounced visit, my dear Hector – and why, if I may ask, this mysterious entrance by night? 'Tis mere chance that I am not abed like the rest of the house.'

'I had my reasons,' said Hector Grant cheerfully. 'Nay, I'm no deserter' (he was an officer in French service), 'but I thought it wiser to slip in unnoticed if I could. I'll tell you why anon, when I am less – you'll pardon me for mentioning it? – less sharp-set.'

'My sorrow!' exclaimed his host. 'Forgive me – I'll have food before you in a moment. Sit down, Eachainn, and I will tell Alison of your arrival.'

Hector caught at him. 'Don't rouse her now. The morn will be time enough, and I'm wanting a few words with you first.' He threw off his roquelaure. 'May I not come and forage with you, as we did – where was it ... at Manchester, I think – in the '45.'

'Come on then,' said his brother-in-law, a hand on his shoulder, and they each lit a candle and went, rather like schoolboys, to rifle the larder. And presently Ardroy was sitting at the table watching his midnight visitor give a very good account of a venison pie. This slim, vivacious, distinctly attractive young man might almost have passed for a Frenchman, and indeed his long residence in France had given him not a few Gallic tricks of gesture and expression. For Hector Grant had lived abroad since he entered French service at the age of sixteen – and before that too; only during the fateful year of the Rising had he spent any length of time in Britain. It was, indeed, his French commission which had saved him from the scaffold, for he had been one of the ill-fated garrison of Carlisle.

'Venison – ah, good to be back where one can have a shot at a deer again!' he presently observed with his mouth full. 'I envy you, *mon frère*.'

'You need not,' answered Ewen. 'You forget that I cannot have a shot at one; I have no means of doing it – no firearms, no, not the smallest fowling-piece. We have to snare our deer or use dogs.'

'*C'est vrai*; I had forgotten. But I cannot think how you submit to such a deprivation.'

'Submit?' asked Ardroy rather bitterly. 'There is no choice: every Highland gentleman of our party has to submit to it, unless he has "qualified" to the English Government.'

'And you still have not done that?'

Ewen flushed. 'My dear Hector, how should I take an oath of fidelity to the Elector of Hanover? Do you think I'm become a Whig?'

'Faith, no – unless you've mightily changed since we marched into England together, seven years ago come Hallowmas. But, Eoghain, besides the arms which you have been forced to give up, there'll surely be some which you have contrived to keep back, as has always been done in the past when these distasteful measures were imposed upon us?'

Ewen's face darkened. 'The English were cleverer this time. After the Act of '25 no one was made to call down a curse upon himself, his kin and all his undertakings, to invoke the death of a coward and burial without a prayer in a strange land if he broke his oath that he had not, and never would have in his possession, any sword or pistol or arm whatsoever, nor would use any part of the highland garb.'

Hector whistled. '*Ma foi*, you subscribed to that!'

'I had to,' answered Ewen shortly.

'I never realized that when I was here two years ago, but then my visit was so short. I did indeed know that the wearing of the tartan in any form was forbidden.'

'That,' observed Ardroy, 'bears harder in a way upon the poor folk than upon us gentry. I had other clothes, if not, I could buy some; but the crofters, what else had they but their hamespun plaids and philabegs and gowns? Is it any wonder that they resorted at first to all sorts of shifts and evasions of the law, and do still, wearing a piece of plain cloth merely wrapped round the waist, sewing up the kilt in the hope that it may pass for breeches, and the like?'

'But that is not the only side of it,' said the young Franco-Scot rather impatiently. 'You are eloquent on the money hardship inflicted on the country folk, but surely you do not yourself relish being deprived by an enemy of the garb which has always marked us as a race?'

He was young, impetuous, not remarkable for tact, and his brother-in-law had turned his head away without reply, so that Hector Grant could not see the gleam which had come into those very blue eyes of his, nor guess the passionate resentment which was always smouldering in Ardroy's heart over a measure which, in common with the poorest Highlander, he loathed with every fibre of his being, and which he would long ago have disobeyed but for the suffering which the consequences to him would have brought upon his wife and children.

'I should have thought –' young Grant was going on, when Ewen broke in, turning round and reaching for the claret, 'Have some more wine, Hector. Now, am I really not to wake Alison to tell her that you are here?'

Hector finished his glass. 'No, let her sleep, the darling! I'll have plenty of time to talk with her – that is, if you will keep me a few days, Ardroy?'

'My dear brother, why ask? My house is yours,' said Ewen warmly.

Hector made a little gesture of thanks. 'I'll engage not to wear the tartan,' he said smiling, 'nor my uniform, in case the English redcoats should mislike it.'

'That is kind of you. And, as I guess, you could not, having neither with you' ('*A moi*,' said Hector to this, like a fencer acknowledging a hit). 'I'll see about a bed for you now. There is one always ready for a guest, I believe.'

Again the young officer stayed him. ''Tis not much past midnight yet. And I want a word with you, Ewen, a serious word. I'd liefer indeed say it before I sleep under your roof, I think ... more especially since (for your family's sake) you have become ... prudent.'

Ardroy's face clouded a little. He hated the very name of 'prudence', and the thing too; but it was true that he had to exercise it. 'Say on,' he responded rather briefly.

'*Eh bien,*' began Hector, his eyes on the empty wineglass which he was twirling in his fingers, 'although it is quite true that I am come hither to see my sister and her children, there is someone else whom I am very anxious to have speech with.'

'And who's that?' asked Ewen a trifle uneasily. 'You are not come, I hope, on any business connected with the Loch Arkaig treasure? 'Tis not Cluny Macpherson whom you wish to see?'

Hector looked at him and smiled. 'I hope to see Cluny later – though not about the treasure. Just now it's a man much easier to come at, a man in Lochaber, that I'm seeking – yourself, in short.'

Ewen raised his eyebrows. 'You have not far to go, then.'

'I am not so sure of that,' responded young Grant cryptically. He paused a moment. 'Ewen, have you ever heard of Alexander Murray?'

'The brother of Lord Murray of Elibank, do you mean? Yes. What of him?'

'And Finlay MacPhair of Glenshian – young Glenshian – did you ever meet him in Paris?'

'No, I have never met him.'

'*N'importe.* Now listen, and I will tell you a great secret.'

He drew closer, and into Ardroy's ears he poured the somewhat vague but (to Ewen) alarming details of a plot to surprise St James's Palace and kidnap the whole English Royal Family, by means, chiefly, of young officers like himself in the French service, aided by Highlanders, of whom five hundred, he alleged, could be raised in London. The German Elector, his remaining son and his grandsons once out of the way, England would acquiesce with joy in the *fait accompli*, and welcome her true Prince, who was to be ready on the coast. The Highlands, of course, must be prepared to rise, and quickly, for Hector believed that an early date in November had been fixed for the attempt. The Scots whom he had just mentioned were in the plot; the Earl Marischal knew of it. And Hector himself, having already resolved to spend his leave in visiting his sister, had also, it was evident, conceived the idea of offering Ardroy a share in the enterprise, apparently hoping to induce him to go to London and enrol himself among the putative five hundred Highlanders.

'But, before we discuss that,' he finished, 'tell me what you think of the whole notion of this *coup de main*? Is it not excellent, and just what we ought to have carried out long ago, had we been wise?' And he leant back with a satisfied air as if he had no fear of the reply.

But there was no answering light on the clear, strong face opposite him. Cameron of Ardroy was looking very grave.

'You want to know what I think?' he asked slowly. 'Well, first I think that the scheme is mad, and could not succeed; and secondly, that it is unworthy, and does not deserve to.'

Hector sat up in his chair. *'Hé! qu'est-ce que tu me chantes là?'* he cried with a frown. 'Say that again!'

Ewen did not comply; instead he went on very earnestly: 'You surely do not hold with assassination, Hector! But no doubt you do not see the affair in that light ... you spoke of kidnapping, I think. O, for Heaven's sake, have nothing to do with a plot of that kind, which the Prince would never soil his hands with!'

'You are become very squeamish on a sudden,' observed his visitor, surveying him with an air at once crestfallen and deeply resentful. 'And somewhat behind the times, too, since you retired to these parts. The Prince not only knows but approves of the plan.'

His brother-in-law's face expressed scepticism. 'I think your enthusiasm misleads you, Hector. His Royal Highness has always refused to countenance schemes of the kind.'

'You are a trifle out of date, as I was forced to observe to you, my dear Ewen! I suppose His Royal Highness may change his mind. And, after all, it is five years or so since you have been able to know anything of his opinions. As it happens, it is in connection with this enterprise that he is sending MacPhair of

Lochdornie and Doctor Cameron to Scotland. They are to work the clans meanwhile, so that when the blow is struck in London by those responsible –'

But by now Ewen was interrupting him. 'Archie – Archie Cameron is connected with this plot! I'm sorry to appear to doubt you, Hector but – since at this point we had best be frank – I don't believe it.'

Hector's lips were compressed, his eyes glinting. He seemed to be making an effort to keep his temper. 'He'll tell you differently, *parbleu*, when you meet him!'

'When I meet him! He's not in Scotland.'

'He is, by this time! And I suppose, since he's your cousin, and you have always been intimate with him, that he'll come here, and mayhap you will accord him a more courteous welcome than you have me!' He pushed back his chair and got up.

Ewen did the same. 'I ask your pardon if I was uncivil,' he said with some stiffness. 'But I cannot be courteous over a scheme so ill-judged and so repugnant. Moreover Archibald Cameron will not come here. When he was over in '49 on the business of the Loch Arkaig gold he purposely kept away from Ardroy.'

'Purposely? Why? – Oh, ay, lest he should compromise you, I suppose!'

'Something of the sort,' answered Ewen without flinching.

'Yes, that's your chief preoccupation now, I see!' flared out Hector, hot as ginger. 'It were much better I had not come here either, but I'll go at once, lest *I* should commit that unpardonable sin!'

'Hector, Hector, do not be so hasty!' cried Ewen, angry enough himself, but still able to control his tongue. 'You asked me what I thought – I told you. Give me your cloak; sit down again! Let's leave this business till the morning, and we'll talk of it again then.'

'No, indeed we will not!' retorted the young plotter defiantly. 'I'll find some other roof to shelter me tonight – some humbler dwelling where the White Rose is still cherished. It grows no longer at Ardroy – I see that very plainly.' He flung the cloak round him with a swing. 'I'll bid you good night, *monsieur mon beau-frère*!'

Ewen had put his hands behind him; one was gripping the wrist of the other. He had turned a little pale. 'You can say what you please to me in this house,' he answered between his teeth, 'for you know that I cannot touch you. But if you still feel minded to repeat that about the White Rose to me tomorrow, somewhere off my land –'

'The White Rose,' broke in a gentle voice from the doorway. 'Who is speaking of – O *Hector*!'

It was Lady Ardroy, in her nightshift with a shawl about her. Both men stood looking at her and wondering how much she had heard.

'Hector, dear brother, what a surprise!' She ran across the big room to him. 'Have you but just arrived? Take off your cloak – how delightful this is!' With the words she threw her arms round his neck and kissed him warmly.

But there must have been something amiss in her brother's answering salute, as in her husband's silence. 'What is troubling you?' she asked, looking from one to the other, her hand still on Hector's shoulder. 'Is anything wrong? Is there ... ill news?'

Neither of the men answered her for a moment. 'Ewen considers it ill,' said Hector at last, curtly. 'But it does not touch him – nor you, my dear. So I'll say good night; I must be going on my way.'

'Going on your way – *tonight!*' There was almost stupefaction in his sister's tone. 'But 'tis long past midnight; you cannot go, Hector – and where are you bound at such an hour? Ewen, make him bide here!'

'Hector must please himself,' replied her husband coldly. 'But naturally I have no desire that he should continue his journey before morning.'

Alison gazed at him in dismay. Highland hospitality – and to a kinsman – offered in so half-hearted a fashion! 'Surely you have not been ... differing about anything?' (They had always been such good friends in the past.)

Again neither of them answered her at once, but they both looked a trifle like children detected in wrong-doing. 'You had better go back to bed, my heart,' said Ewen gently. 'Did you come down because you heard voices?'

'I came,' said Alison, her eyes suddenly clouding, 'because of Keithie – I don't know, but I fear he may be going to be ill.'

'You see, I had best go,' said her brother instantly, in a softer tone. 'If you have a child ill –'

'But that is neither here nor there,' replied Alison. 'O Hector, stay, stay!'

Of course the young soldier wanted to stay. But having announced in so fiery a manner that he was going, and having undeniably insulted the master of the house, how could he with dignity remain unless that master begged him to? And that Ardroy, evidently, was not minded to do.

'If Hector wishes to please you, Alison, he will no doubt bide here the night,' was all the olive-branch that he tendered. 'But I gather that he fears he will compromise us by his presence. If you can persuade him that his fear is groundless, pray do so.'

'No,' said Hector, not to Ewen but to Alison. 'No, best have no more words about it. It were wiser I did not sleep here to-night. I'll come on my return ... or perhaps tomorrow,' he added, melted by his sister's appealing face. 'I'll find a shelter, never fear. But things have changed somewhat of late in the Highlands.'

With which mysterious words he kissed Alison again, flung his cloak once more about him, and made for the door. Lady Ardroy followed him a little way, distressed and puzzled, then stopped; half her heart, no doubt, was upstairs. But Ewen left the room after the young officer, and found him already opening the front door.

'Do me the justice to admit that I am not turning you out,' said Ardroy rather sternly. 'It is your own doing; the house is open to you tonight ... and for as long afterwards as you wish, if you apologize –'

'I'll return when you apologize for calling me an assassin!' retorted Hector over his shoulder.

'You know I never called you so! Hector, I hate your going off in anger in this fashion, at dead of night – and how am I to know that you will not stumble into some ill affair or other with the redcoats or with broken men?'

Hector gave an unsteady laugh. 'If I do, you may be sure I shall not risk "compromising" you by asking for your assistance! Sleep quietly!' And, loosing that last arrow, he was lost in the darkness out of which he had come.

Ardroy stood on the edge of that darkness for a moment, swallowing down the anger which fought with his concern, for he had himself a temper as hot as Hector's own, though it was more difficult to rouse. Hector's last thrust was childish, but his previous stab about the White Rose had gone deep; did not Ewen himself sometimes lie awake at night contrasting past and present? ... Yet he knew well that the root of that flower was not dead at Ardroy, though scarce a blossom might show on it. It was not dead, else one had not so felt at every turn of daily life both the ghost of its wistful fragrance and the sting of its perennial thorns.

He went back with bent head, to find Alison saying in great distress, 'O dearest, what has happened between you and Hector? And Keithie is feverish; I am so afraid lest the cold water and the exposure ... for you know he's not very strong ...'

Ewen put his arm round her. 'Please God 'tis only a fever of cold he's taken ... And as for Hector – yes, I will tell you about it. He'll think better of it, I dare say, foolish boy, in the morning.' He put out the lights on the improvised supper-table; they went upstairs, and soon there was no sound in the dark room but an occasional sigh from the deerhound stretched out in front of the dying fire.

Chapter 3

A FRENCH SONG BY LOCH TREIG

By three o'clock next afternoon Ewen Cameron was riding fast to Maryburgh to fetch a doctor. Little Keith was really ill, and it was with a sickening pang at his own heart that Ardroy had tried to comfort the now extremely penitent Donald, whom he had found weeping bitterly because Keithie, flushed and panting, had refused the offer of some expiatory treasure or other, had indeed beaten him off pettishly when he attempted to put it into the hot little hand.

Ardroy had to try to comfort himself, too, as he went along Loch Lochy banks, where the incomparable tints of the Northern autumn were lighting their first fires in beech and bracken. Children had fever so easily; it might signify nothing, old Marsali had said. For himself, he had so little experience that he did not know; but Alison, he could see, was terribly anxious. He wished that his aunt, Miss Margaret Cameron, who had brought him up, and still lived with them, were not away visiting; she could have borne Alison company on this dark day. He wished that he himself could have stayed at home and sent a gillie for the doctor, but even one who spoke English might get involved in some difficulty with the military at Fort William, and the message never be delivered. It was safer to go himself.

There was also last night's unfortunate business with his brother-in-law to perturb him. High-spirited and impulsive as he was, Hector might repent and come back in a day or two, if only for his sister's sake. Ewen devoutly hoped that he would. For that same sister's sake he would forgive the young man his wounding words. It was worse to reflect that Hector had evidently mixed himself up in some way with this mad, reprehensible plot against the Elector. And he had averred that Archibald Cameron, of all men, had come or was coming to Scotland on the same enterprise.

Ewen involuntarily tightened his reins. That he did not

believe. His respect and affection for Archibald Cameron were scarcely less than those he had borne his elder brother Lochiel himself. Archie had probably come over again to confer with Cluny Macpherson about that accursed Loch Arkaig gold, very likely in order to take some of it back to France with him – a risky business, as always, but a perfectly justifiable one. It was true, as Ewen had told Hector, that Archie purposely avoided coming to Ardroy, though it lay not far from the shores of Loch Arkaig, yet if Doctor Cameron really were in Scotland again Ewen hoped that they should meet somehow. He had not seen his cousin for nearly three years.

On the other hand, if Archie had come over to work in any way for the Cause in the Highlands, there was certainly a good deal of ferment here at present, and a proportionately good chance of fishing in troubled waters. There were ceaseless annoyances of one kind or another; there were the evictions of Jacobite tenants in favour of Whigs ... above all, there was this black business of the Appin murder trial soon to open at Invera-ray, the Campbell stronghold, which everyone knew would end in the condemnation of an innocent man by the Campbell jury because the victim of the outrage had been a Campbell. Yes, it might be fruitful soil, but who was to organize a new rising; still more, who was to lead it? There was only one man whom the broken, often jealous clans would follow, and he was far away ... and some whispered that he was broken too.

Although he was not well mounted (for a good horse was a luxury which he could not afford himself nowadays) Ardroy, thus occupied in mind, found himself crossing the Spean, almost before he realized it, on that bridge of General Wade's erection which had been the scene of the first Jacobite exploit in the Rising, and of his own daring escape in the summer of '46. But he hardly gave a thought to either today. And, in order to examine one of his horse's legs, he pulled up at the change-house on the farther side without reflecting that it was the very spot where, six years ago, he had been made to halt, a prisoner with his feet tied together under a sorrel's belly.

While he was feeling the leg, suspecting incipient lameness, the keeper of the change-house came out; not a Cameron now, but a Campbell protégé, yet a decent fellow enough. Though on the winning side, he too was debarred from the use of the tartan – which was some consolation to a man on the losing.

'Good day to you, Ardroy,' he said, recognizing the stooping rider. 'You'll be for Maryburgh the day? Has the horse gone lame on you, then?'

'Hardly that yet,' answered Ewen, 'but I fear me there's a strain or something of the sort. Yes, I am going to Maryburgh, to fetch Doctor Kincaid. Can I do aught for you there, Mac-Nichol?'

'*Dhé!* ye'll not find the doctor at Maryburgh,' observed the other. 'He's away up Loch Treig side the day.'

'Loch Treig!' exclaimed Ewen, dismayed. 'How do you know that, man? – and are you very sure of it?'

MacNichol was very sure. His own wife was ill; the doctor had visited her that same morning, and instead of returning to Maryburgh had departed along the south bank of the Spean – the only practicable way – for a lonely farm on Loch Treig. It was of no use waiting at the change-house for his return, since he would naturally go back to Maryburgh along the shorter road by Corriechoille and Lianachan. There was nothing then to be done but ride after him. MacNichol did not know how far along Loch Treig was the farm to which the doctor had gone, but he did know that the latter had said its occupant was very ill, and that he might be obliged to spend the night there.

Ewen's heart sank lower and lower. It would be getting dusk by the time that he had covered the twelve or fourteen miles to the nearer end of that desolate loch. Suppose he somehow missed the doctor, or suppose the latter could not or would not start back for Ardroy so late? Yet at least it would be better than nothing to have speech with him, and to learn what was the proper treatment for that little coughing, shivering, bright-cheeked thing at home.

So he went by Spean side where it hurried in its gorges, where it swirled in wide pools; by the dangerous ford at Inch, past the falls where it hurled itself to a destruction which it never met; he rode between it and the long heights of Beinn Chlinaig and finally turned south with the lessening river itself. And after a while there opened before him a narrow, steel-coloured trough of loneliness and menace imprisoned between unfriendly heights – Loch Treig. On its eastern side Cnoc Dearg reared himself starkly; on the other Stob Choire an Easain Mhoir, even loftier, shut it in – kinsmen of Ben Nevis both. The track went low by the shore under Cnoc Dearg, for there was no place for it on his steep flanks.

As there was no habitation anywhere within sight, Ewen concluded that the farm to which Doctor Kincaid had gone was probably at Loch Treig head, at the farther end of the lake, where the mountains relaxed their grip – another five or six miles. He went on. The livid surface of the water by which he rode was not ruffled today by any wind; a heavy, sinister silence lay upon it, as on the dark, brooding heights which hemmed it about. One was shut in between them with that malevolent water. It hardly seemed surprising that after a mile and a half of its company Ewen's horse definitely went lame; the strain which he feared had developed – and no wonder. But he could not spare the time to lead him; he must push on at all costs.

The halting beast had carried him but a little way farther before he was aware of distant sounds like – yes, they *were* snatches of song. And soon he saw coming towards him through the September dusk the indistinct figure of a man walking with the uncertain gait of one who has been looking upon the wine-cup. And Ewen, thinking, 'That poor fool will either spend the night by the roadside or fall into the loch,' pulled up his horse to a walk, for the drunkard was staggering first to one side of the narrow road and then to the other, and he feared to knock him down.

As he did so he recognized the air which the reveller was singing ... But the words which belonged to that tune were neither Gaelic, Scots nor English, so how should they be sung here, by one of the loneliest lochs in the Highlands?

> *'Aux nouvell's que j'apporte*
> *Vos beaux yeux vont pleurer ...'*

What was a Frenchman doing here, singing 'Malbrouck'?

'Quittez vos habits roses,'

sang the voice, coming nearer:

> *'Mironton, mironton, mirontaine,*
> *Quittez vos habits roses,*
> *Et vos satins brochés.'*

Cnoc Dearg tossed the words mockingly to the other warder of
Loch Treig, and Ewen jumped off his horse. It was not perhaps,
after all, a Frenchman born who was singing that song in so
lamentable and ragged a fashion along this lonely track to
nowhere.

The lurching figure was already nearly up to him, and now
the singer seemed to become aware of the man and the horse in
his path, for he stopped in the middle of the refrain.

'Laissez-moi passer, s'il vous plaît,' he muttered indistinctly,
and tried to steady himself. He was hatless, and wore a green
roquelaure.

Ewen dropped his horse's bridle and seized him by the arm.

'Hector! What in the name of the Good Being are you doing
here in this state?'

Out of a very white face Hector Grant's eyes stared at him
totally without recognition. 'Let me pass, if you pl – please,'
he said again, but in English this time.

'You are not fit to be abroad,' said Ewen in disgust. The
revelation that Hector could ever be as drunk as this came as a
shock; he had always thought him a temperate youth, if ex-
citable ... but it was true that he had seen nothing of him for
the past two years. 'Where have you been – what, in God's
name, have you been doing?'

The young officer of the régiment d'Albanie did indeed cut a
sorry figure. His waistcoat hung open, his powdered hair was
disordered and streaked with wet, there was mud on his breeches
as well as on his boots.

'Answer me!' said Ewen sternly, giving him a little shake. 'I
am in haste.'

'So am I,' replied Hector, still more thickly. 'Let me pass, I
say, whoever you are. Let me pass, or I'll make you!'

'Don't you even know me?' demanded his brother-in-law indignantly.

'No, and have no wish to ... O God, my head!' And, Ardroy having removed his grasp, the reveller reeled backwards against the horse, putting both hands to his brow.

'You had best sit down for a moment,' counselled Ewen dryly, and with an arm round him guided him to the side of the path. Hector must be pretty far gone if he really did not know him, for it was still quite light enough for recognition. The best way to sober him would be to take him to the nearest burn tumbling down across the track and dip his fuddled head into it. But Ewen stood looking down at him in mingled disgust and perplexity, for now Hector had laid that head upon his knees and was groaning aloud.

As he sat hunched there the back of that same head was presented to Ardroy's unsympathetic gaze. Just above the black ribbon which tied Hector's queue the powder appeared all smirched, and of a curious rusty colour ... Ewen uttered a sudden exclamation, stooped, touched the patch, and looked at his fingers. Next moment he was down by the supposed tippler's side, his arm round him.

'Hector, have you had a blow on the head? How came you by it?' His voice was sharp with anxiety. 'My God, how much are you hurt – who did it?' But Hector did not answer; instead, as he sat there, his knees suddenly gave, and he lurched forward and sideways on to his mentor.

Penitent, and to spare, for having misjudged him, Ewen straightened him out, laid him down in the heather and bog-myrtle which bordered the track, brought water from the burn in his hat, dashed it in the young man's face, and turning his head on one side tried to examine the injury. He could not see much, only the hair matted with dried blood; it was even possibly the fact of its being gathered thus into a queue and tied with a stout ribbon which had saved him from more serious damage – perhaps, indeed, had saved his life. The wound, great or small, was certainly not bleeding now, so it must either have been inflicted some time ago, or have been slighter than its consequences seemed to indicate; and as Ewen bathed the reci-

pient's face he detected signs of reviving consciousness. After a
moment, indeed, the young soldier gave a little sigh, and, still
lying in Ardroy's arms, began to murmur something incoherent
about stopping someone at all costs; that he was losing time and
must push on. He even made a feeble effort to rise, which Ewen
easily frustrated.

'You cannot push on anywhere after a blow like that,' he said
gently. (Had he not had a presentiment of something like this
last night!) 'I'll make you as comfortable as I can with my
cloak, and when I come back from my errand to the head of
the loch I'm in hopes I'll have a doctor with me, and he can –
Don't you know me now, Hector?'

For the prostrate man was saying thickly, 'The doctor – do
you mean Doctor Cameron? No, no, he must not be brought
here – good God, he must not come this way now, any more
than Lochdornie! Don't you understand, that's what I am trying to do – to stop Lochdornie ... now that damned spy has
taken my papers!'

'What's that?' asked Ewen sharply. 'You were carrying
papers, and they have been taken from you?'

Hector wrested himself a little away. 'Who are you?' he
asked suspiciously, looking up at him with the strangest
eyes. 'Another Government agent? Papers ... no, I have no
papers! I have but come to Scotland to visit my sister, and she's
married to a gentleman of these parts ... Oh, you may be
easy – he'll have naught to do now with him they name the
young Pretender, so how should I be carrying treasonable
papers?'

Ewen bit his lip hard. The half-stunned brain was remembering yesterday night at Ardroy. But how could he be angry with
a speaker in this plight? Moreover, there was something extremely disquieting behind his utterances; he must be patient –
but quick too, for precious time was slipping by, and he might
somehow miss Doctor Kincaid in the oncoming darkness. If
Hector could only recognize him, instead of staring at him in
that hostile manner, with one hand plucking at the wet heather
in which he lay!

'Hector, don't you really know me?' he asked again, almost

pleadingly. 'It's Ewen – Ewen Cameron of Ardroy, Alison's husband!'

His sister's name seemed, luckily, to act as a magnet to Hector's scattered wits. They fastened on it. 'Alison – Alison's husband?' Suspicion turned to perplexity; he stared afresh. 'You're uncommonly like ... why, it *is* Ardroy!' he exclaimed after a moment's further scrutiny.

'Yes,' said Ewen, greatly relieved, 'it is Ardroy, and thankful to have come upon you. Now tell me what's wrong, and why you talk of stopping MacPhair of Lochdornie?'

Relief was on Hector's strained face too. He passed his hand once or twice over his eyes and became almost miraculously coherent. 'I was on my way to Ben Alder, to Cluny Macpherson ... I fell in with a man as I went along the Spean ... he must have been a Government spy. I could not shake him off. I had even to come out of my way with him – like this – lest he should guess where I was making for ... I stooped at last to drink of a burn, and I do not remember any more ... When I knew what had happened I found that he had taken everything ... and if Lochdornie makes for Badenoch or Lochaber now he'll be captured, for there was news of him in a letter I had on me – though it was mostly in cipher – and the redcoats will be on the alert ... He must be warned, for he is on his way hither – he must be warned at once, or all is lost!' Hector groaned, put a hand over his eyes again, and this time kept it there.

Ewen sat silent for a moment. What a terrible misfortune! 'You mentioned Archibald Cameron's name just now,' he said uneasily. 'What of *his* movements?'

'Doctor Cameron's in Knoidart,' answered Hector. 'He'll not be coming this way yet, I understand. No, 'tis Lochdornie you must –' And there he stopped, removed his hand and said in a different tone, 'But I am forgetting – you do not wish now to have aught to do with the Prince and his plans.'

'I never said that!' protested Ardroy. 'I said ... but no matter! I've given proofs enough of my loyalty, Hector!'

'Proofs? We have all given them!' returned the younger man impatiently. 'Show me that I wronged you last night! You have a horse there – ride back without a moment's delay to Glen Mallie and stop Lochdornie. I'll give you directions.'

He looked up at his brother-in-law in a silence so dead, so devoid of any sound from the sullen water of the loch, that the very mountains seemed to be holding their breaths to listen.

'I cannot turn back now,' said Ardroy in a slow voice. 'But when I have found the doctor –'

'Ah, never think of me!' cried Hector, misunderstanding. 'I'll do well enough here for the present. But to save Lochdornie you must turn back this instant! Surely some good angel sent you here, Ewen, to undo what I have done. Listen, you'll find him –' he clutched at Ardroy, 'somewhere in Glen Mallie, making towards Loch Arkaig. If he gets the length of the glen by dark it's like he'll spend the night in an old tumble-down croft there is on the side of Beinn Bhan – you'll know it, I dare say, for I believe 'tis the only one there. You'll be put to it to get there in time, I fear; yet you may meet him coming away ... But if once he crosses the Lochy ...' He made a despairing gesture. 'You'll do it, Ewen?' And his unhappy eyes searched the face above him hungrily.

But Ewen turned his head aside. 'I would go willingly, if ... Do you know why I am on this road at all, Hector?' His voice grew hoarse. 'My little son is very ill; I am riding after the only doctor for miles round – and he gone up Loch Treig I know not how far. How can I turn back to warn anyone until I have found him?'

'Then *I* must go,' said Hector wildly. ''Tis I have ruined Lochdornie's plans. But I shall go so slow ... and it is so far ... I shall never be in time.' He was struggling to his knees, only to be there for a second or two ere he relapsed into Ewen's arms. 'My head ... I can't stand ... it swims so! O God, why did I carry that letter on me!' And he burst into tears.

Ewen let him weep, staring out over the darkening loch where some bird flew wailing like a lost spirit, and where against the desolate heights opposite he seemed to see Keithie's flushed little face. Words spoken six years ago came back to him, when the speaker, himself in danger, was urging him to seek safety. 'God knows, my dear Ewen, I hold that neither wife, children nor home should stand in a man's way when duty and loyalty call him – and as you know, I have turned my back on all these.' He could hear Archibald Cameron's voice as if it were yesterday. Duty and loyalty – were they not calling now?

Hector had cast himself face downwards, and the scent of the bruised bog-myrtle came up strong and sweet. Ewen clenched his teeth; then he stooped and laid a hand on his shoulder.

'I will turn back,' he said almost inaudibly. 'Perhaps the child is better now ... If anyone passes, call out; it may be the doctor – you need him.' His voice stuck in his throat, but he contrived to add, 'And send him on to Ardroy.'

Hector raised his face and seized his brother-in-law's arm in an almost convulsive grip. 'You'll go – you'll go? God bless you, Ewen! And forgive me, forgive me! ... Had I not been so hasty last night ...'

'If Lochdornie be not in the croft I suppose I'll come on him farther up the glen,' said Ewen shortly. There were no words to spare for anything save the hard choice he was making. He stripped off his cloak and wrapped it round Hector as well as Hector's own; the night, fortunately, was not setting in cold, and when he passed Inverlair, as he returned, he would make shift to send someone to fetch the stranded wayfarer to shelter. Hector hardly seemed to hear him say this, for all his being was fixed on the question of Lochdornie and the warning, and he babbled gratitude and directions in a manner which suggested that his mind was drifting into mist once more.

But as Ewen pulled round his horse and threw himself into the saddle he could almost see Alison in the road to bar his return. How could he ever tell her what he had done! When he met her again he would perhaps be the murderer of his child and hers.

Soon his hoof-beats made a dwindling refrain by the dark water, and the wardens of Loch Treig tossed the sound to each other as they had tossed Hector's song. Sharp, sharp, sharp, said the echo, are the thorns of the White Rose, and the hearth where that flower has twined itself is never a safe one.

Chapter 4

THE MAN WITH A PRICE ON HIS HEAD

1

THE sky was clear with morning, and even decked for the sun's coming with a few rosy feathers of cloud, at once brighter and tenderer than those he leaves behind at evening. But the hollows of the hills were yet cold and drowsy after the night; the mountain grasses, tawny and speckled like the hairs on a deerhide, stood motionless; the rust of the bracken shone with moisture. And the tiny ruined croft up the braeside, behind the old thorn which had so long guarded it from ill, seemed to slumber even more soundly than the fern and the grasses. For the little habitation was dead; half the moss-grown thatch had fallen in, and the young rowan tree which now leant smotheringly over the roof could thrust its bright berries within if it chose.

None the less there was life inside that abandoned shell of a building, but life which, like that outside, was scarcely yet stirring. In the half of the croft which still kept its thatch a man was lying on his back, lightly asleep; from time to time he moved a trifle, and once he opened his eyes wide and then, passing a hand over them, stared up at the sky between the rowan boughs with a little frown, as of one who is not over pleased to see daylight. Then he drew the cloak which covered him a little farther up, turned on his side, and thrusting a hand into the heap of dried bracken beneath his head, closed them again. The face on that makeshift pillow was that of a man in the middle forties, handsome and kindly, and not at first sight the face of one whom adventure or dubious dealings would have led to seek shelter in so comfortless a bedchamber, and whose apparent reluctance to leave it suggested that he had not, perhaps, enjoyed even that shelter very long.

Presently, however, the sleeper opened his eyes again, raised his head as if listening, then laid it back in the fern and remained very still. Somewhere in the branches of the mountain ash above him a robin broke into its loud, sweet autumn song. But when it ceased a slow and rather dragging footfall could be heard, though dully, coming up the hill-side, and pausing at last outside the crazy half-shut door which was all that hid the present inmate of the ruin from the outer world. The latter, however, continued to lie without moving; perhaps he hoped thus to escape notice.

A pause, then the broken door, catching in the weeds of the threshold, was pushed open. A tall man, his stature exaggerated by the little entry to proportions almost gigantic, stood there against the flushed sky, breathing rather fast. With one hand he leant upon the jamb, with the other he wiped the sweat from his forehead. As he stood, the light behind him, his face was not clearly discernible, nor could he, coming suddenly into this half-dark place, make out more of the man in the corner than that there was a man there.

He peered forward. 'Thank God that I have found you,' he said in Gaelic. 'Give me a sign, and I will tell you why I have come.'

The man under the cloak raised himself on an elbow. 'I give you the sign of the Blackbird,' he said in the same tongue. It was the old Jacobite cant name for James Edward Stuart. 'And what do you give me, honest man?'

'I have no password,' answered the newcomer, entering. 'But in exchange for the blackbird,' he gave a rather weary little laugh – 'I give you the grouse, since it's that fowl you must emulate for a while, Lochdornie. You must lie close, and not come into Lochaber as yet; I am come in all haste to warn you of that.'

An exclamation interrupted him. The man in the corner was sitting up, throwing off the cloak which had served him for a blanket.

' 'Tis not Lochdornie – Lochdornie's in Knoidart. You have warned the wrong man, my dear Ewen!' He was on his feet now, smiling and holding out his hands in welcome.

'What! it's *you*, Archie!' exclaimed Ewen in surprise so great that he involuntarily recoiled for an instant. Then he seized the outstretched hands with alacrity. 'I did not know ... I thought it was Lochdornie I was seeking!'

'Are you disappointed, then, at the exchange?' asked Doctor Cameron with a half-quizzical smile. 'Even if you are, *Eoghain mhóir*, I am delighted to see *you*!'

'Disappointed – of course not! only puzzled,' answered Ewen, looking at him, indeed, with a light of pleasure on his tired face. 'Had I known it was you I should have come less un – have made even more haste,' he substituted. 'Then is Lochdornie here too?'

'No, he is in Knoidart, where I was to have gone. I don't know why we laid our first plans that way, for at the last moment we thought better of it, and changed places. Hence it comes that I am for Lochaber, instead of him. But what were you saying about a grouse and a warning? From whom are you bringing me a warning?'

'From my young brother-in-law, Hector Grant. He's of your regiment.' For Doctor Cameron was major in Lord Ogilvie's regiment in the French service wherein Hector also had a commission.

'He is, but I had no notion that he was in Scotland.'

'But he knows that you and Lochdornie are; and seems, unluckily, to have carried that piece of news about him in some letter which –'

'Sit down before you tell me, dear lad,' said his cousin, interrupting, 'for you look uncommon weary. ' 'Tis true I have no seat to offer you –'

'Yon fern will serve well enough,' said Ewen, going towards the heap of bracken and letting himself fall stiffly upon it. He *was* weary, for he had walked all night, and in consequence his injured leg was troubling him. Doctor Cameron sat down beside him.

'I came on Hector,' resumed Ardroy, 'last evening by Loch Treig side, staggering about like a drunken man from a blow on the head, and with his pockets rifled. It seems that while making for Cluny's hiding-place he fell in with some man whom he could not shake off – a Government spy, he thought afterwards. When I found him Hector was trying himself to warn

Lochdornie of the loss of the letter; but that was manifestly impossible, and he implored me to take his place. Luckily I was mounted ... on a lame horse,' he added with a shrug. 'So I have come, and glad I am to be in time.'

Archibald Cameron was looking grave. 'I wonder what was in that letter, and whom it was from?'

'Hector did not tell me. He had not too many words at his command; I had enough ado at first to get him to recognize me. The letter was, I gather, mostly in cipher, which is something; but cipher can be read. And since he was so insistent that a warning should be carried, and I turn –' He checked himself – 'Since he was so insistent you will pay heed, Archie, will you not, and avoid crossing the Lochy yet awhile?'

'Yes, indeed I will. I must not be captured if I can help it,' answered Doctor Cameron simply. 'But, my dear Ewen' – he laid a hand on his kinsman's arm, 'do not look so anxious over it! You have succeeded in warning me, and in preventing, perhaps, a great wreckage of hopes. The Prince owes you a fine debt for this, and some day he will be able to repay you.'

'I am already more than repaid,' said the young man, looking at him with sincere affection, 'if I have stayed you from running into special peril ... and I'm glad that 'twas for *you*, after all, that I came. But what of MacPhair of Lochdornie – should one take steps to warn him also?'

'He'll not be coming this way yet,' replied his cousin. 'We are to meet in a week, back in Glen Dessary, and since he is to await me there, there is no danger.'

'And what will you do meanwhile – where will you bestow yourself?'

'Oh, I'll skulk for a while here and in Glen Dessary, moving about. I am become quite an old hand at that game,' said Archibald Cameron cheerfully. 'And now, *'ille*, the sun's coming up, let us break our fast. I have some meal with me, and you must be hungry.' Rising, he went over to the other corner of the shelter.

Directly his back was turned Ewen leant his head against the rough wall behind him and closed his eyes, spent with the anxiety which had ridden with him to the point where the in-

creasing lameness of his horse had forced him to abandon the
beast and go on foot, and then had flitted by his side like a little
wraith, taking on the darling shape of the child who was causing
it. He heard Archie saying from the corner, 'And how's all with
you, Ewen? Mrs Alison and the children, are they well?'

'Alison is well. The children ...' He could get no further, for
with the words it came to him that by sunrise there was perhaps
but one child at Ardroy.

Archibald Cameron caught the break in his voice and turned
quickly, the little bag of meal in his hand. 'What's wrong, Ewen
– what is it?'

Ewen looked out of the doorway. The sun was up; a hare ran
across the grass. 'Little Keith is ... very ill. I must get back
home as quickly as I can; I will not stay to eat.'

Archie came quickly over to him, his face full of concern.
'Very ill – and yet you left home for my sake! Have you a
doctor there, Ewen?'

Ardroy shook his head. 'I was on my way to fetch one yesterday when I came upon Hector ... so I could not go on ... I
dare say Keithie is better by now. Children so easily get fever
that it may mean nothing,' he added, with a rather heartrending
air of reciting as a charm a creed in which he did not really
believe. 'That's true, is it not?' And as Doctor Cameron nodded,
but gravely, Ewen tried to smile, and said, getting to his feet,
'Well, I'll be starting back. Thank God that I was in time. And,
Archie, you swear that you will be prudent? It would break my
heart if you were captured.'

He held out his hand. His kinsman did not take it. Instead, he
put both of his on the broad shoulders.

'I need not ask you if you are willing to run a risk for your
child's sake. If you will have me under your roof, Ewen, I will
come back with you and do my best for little Keith. But if I
were taken at Ardroy it would be no light matter for you, so
you must weigh the question carefully.'

Ewen started away from him. 'No, no! – for it's you that
would be running the risk, Archie. No, I cannot accept such a
sacrifice – you must go back farther west. Ardroy might be
searched.'

'Why should it be? You must be in fairly good repute with the authorities by now. And I would not stay long, to endanger you. Ewen, Ewen, let me come to the bairn! I have not quite sunk the physician yet in the Jacobite agent.'

'It would be wrong of me,' said Ewen, wavering. 'I ought not. No, I will not have you.' Yet his eyes showed how much he longed to accept.

'You cannot prevent my coming after you, my dear boy, even if you do not take me with you, and it would certainly be more prudent if you introduced me quietly by a back door than if I presented myself at the front ... Which is it to be? ... Come now, let's eat a few mouthfuls of drammoch; we'll go all the faster for it.'

2

That evening there seemed to be bestowed on Loch na h-Iolaire a new and ethereal loveliness, when the hunter's moon had changed the orange of her rising to argent. Yet the two men who stood on its banks were not looking at the silvered beauty of the water but at each other.

'Yes, quite sure,' said the elder, who had just made his way there from the house. 'The wean was, I think, on the mend before I came; a trifle of treatment did the rest. He'll need a little care now for the next few days, that is all. A beautiful bairn, Ewen ... You can come back and see him now; he's sleeping finely.'

'It's hard to believe,' said Ewen in a low voice. 'But you *have* saved him, Archie; he was very ill when you got here this morning, I'm convinced. And now he is really going to recover?'

'Yes, please God,' answered Archibald Cameron. 'I could not find you at first to tell you; then I guessed, somehow, that you would be by the lochan.'

'I have been here all afternoon, since you turned me out of the room; yet I don't know why I came – above all to this very spot – for I have been hating Loch na h-Iolaire, for the first time in my life. It so nearly slew him.'

'Yet Loch na h-Iolaire is very beautiful this evening,' said his cousin, and he gave a little sigh, the sigh of the exile. 'Those were happy days, Ewen, when I used to come here, and Lochiel too, we've both fished in this water, and I remember Donald's catching a pike so large that you were, I believe, secretly alarmed at it. You were a small boy then, and I but two and twenty ...' He moved nearer to the brink. 'And what's that, pray, down there – hidden treasure?'

Ewen came and looked – the moon also. Through the crystal clear water something gleamed and wavered. It was the Culloden broadsword hilt, cause of all these last days' happenings.

'That thing, which was once a Stewart claymore, is really why you are here, Archie.'

But the more obvious cause lay asleep in the house of Ardroy clutching one of his mother's fingers, his curls dank and tumbled, his peach-bloom cheeks wan, dark circles under his long, unstirring lashes – but sleeping the sleep of recovery. Even his father, tiptoeing in ten minutes later, could not doubt that.

Without any false shame he knelt down by the little bed and bowed his head in his hands upon the edge. Alison, a trifle pale from the position which she was so rigidly keeping – since not for anything would she have withdrawn that prisoned finger, though it would have been quite easy – looked across at her husband kneeling there with a lovely light in her eyes. And the man to whom, as they both felt, they owed this miracle (though he disclaimed the debt) who had a brood of his own oversea, wore the air, as he gazed at the scene, of thinking that his own life would have been well risked to bring it about.

3

Since by nine o'clock that evening Dr Kincaid had not put in an appearance, it could be taken for granted that he was not coming at all. This made it seem doubtful whether he had seen Hector by the roadside, and though such an encounter was highly desirable for Hector's own sake, yet, if the doctor had missed him, it probably meant that the farmer at Inverlair had sent at once and got the injured man into shelter, as he had promised Ewen to do.

Alison was naturally distressed and increasingly anxious about her brother now that her acute anxiety over Keithie had subsided, and her husband undertook to send a messenger early next morning to get news of the stricken adventurer. But to-night nothing could be done to this end. So, while his wife remained by the child's side, Ardroy and his cousin sat together in his sanctum, and Ewen tried more fully to convey his gratitude. But once again Doctor Cameron would none of the thanks which he averred he had not deserved. Besides, it was rather good, he observed, to be at the old trade again.

Ewen looked thoughtfully at his kinsman as the latter leant back in his chair. Archibald Cameron had been greatly beloved in Lochaber where, after his medical studies in Edinburgh and Paris, he had settled down to doctor his brother Lochiel's people – poor and ignorant patients enough, most of them. Small wonder, however, if he regretted that lost life, quiet, strenuous and happy; whether he did or no it was the second time in a few hours, thought Ewen, that he had referred to it. Ewen could not help thinking also what strange and dangerous activities had been the Doctor's, man of peace though he was, since that July day in '45 when his brother the Chief had sent him to Borrodale to dissuade the Prince from going on with his enterprise. He had become the Prince's aide-de-camp, had taken part in that early and unsuccessful attack on Ruthven barracks during the march to Edinburgh, had been wounded at Falkirk, and shared Lochiel's perils after Culloden, adding to them his own numerous and perilous journeys as go-between for him with the lost and hunted Prince; it was he who conveyed the belated French gold from the sea-coast to Loch Arkaig and buried it there. Then had come (as for Ewen too) exile, and anxiety about employment; after Lochiel's death fresh cares, on behalf of his brother's young family as well as his own, and more than one hazardous return to the shores where his life was forfeit. If Archibald Cameron had been a soldier born and bred instead of a physician he could not have run more risks ...

'Why do you continue this dangerous work, Archie?' asked

Ewen suddenly. 'There are others who could do it who have not your family ties. Do you so relish it?'

Doctor Cameron turned his head, with its haunting likeness to Lochiel's. He looked as serene as usual. 'Why do I go on with it? Because the Prince bade me, and I can refuse him nothing.'

'But have you seen him recently?' asked Ewen in some excitement.

'This very month, at Menin in Flanders. He sent for me and MacPhair of Lochdornie and gave me this commission.'

'Menin! Is *that* where he lives now?'

Archibald Cameron shook his head. 'It was but a rendezvous. He does not live there.'

'Tell me of him, Archie!' urged the younger man. 'One hears no news ... and he never comes! Will he ever come again ... and could we do aught for him if he did?'

But Archibald Cameron, for all that he had been the Prince's companion on that fruitless journey to Spain after the 'Forty-five, for all that he was devoted to him, body and soul, could tell the inquirer very little. The Prince, he said, kept himself so close, changed his residence so often; and a cloud of mystery of his own devising surrounded him and his movements. It had been a joy, however, to see his face again; an even greater to be sent upon this hazardous mission by him. Yes, please God, his Royal Highness *would* come again to Scotland some day, but there was much to be done in preparation first.

Ewen listened rather sadly. Too many of his questions Archie was unable to answer, and at last the questioner turned to more immediate matters.

'Did the Prince send for anyone else save you and Lochdornie to meet him at Menin?'

'There was young Glenshian, the Chief's son – Finlay Mac-Phair ... Fionnlagh Ruadh, as they call him.'

'Two MacPhairs! I had not fancied you so intimate with those of that name, Archie!'

'Nor am I,' answered Archibald Cameron quickly. 'But one does not choose one's associates in a matter of this kind.'

'Or you would not have chosen them?' queried Ewen. Doctor

Cameron made no answer. 'Why not?' asked Ardroy with a tinge of uneasiness. 'I thought that MacPhair of Lochdornie was beyond suspicion. Of young Glenshian I know nothing.'

'So *is* Lochdornie beyond suspicion,' answered the elder man. He got up and sought on the mantelshelf for a pine chip to light the still unlighted pipe he was holding, lit the chip at a candle and then, without using it, threw it into the fire. 'But he does not think that I am,' he ended dryly.

'*Archie!* What do you mean?'

Doctor Cameron waited a moment, looking down into the fire. 'You remember that Lochdornie and I were both over in the '49 after the Loch Arkaig gold, and that with Cluny's assistance we contrived to take away quite a deal of it?'

'Yes.'

'Six thousand pounds of that went to Lady Lochiel and her family. Lochdornie – he's an honest man and a bonny fighter, but the notion was put into his head by ... by some third person – Lochdornie accused me of taking the money for myself.'

'You are jesting, man!' cried Ewen in a tone of horror. 'It's impossible – you are making a mock of me!'

'No, I am not,' answered his kinsman, with the composure which had only for a moment left him. He sat down again. 'That was why I went later to Rome, to the King, to clear myself.'

'And after that,' said Ewen, leaning forward in his chair, his eyes burning, 'you can come over and work side by side with MacPhair of Lochdornie! Why, in your place, I could not trust my fingers near my dirk!'

Doctor Cameron looked at him rather sadly. 'It's well for you, perhaps, that you are not a conspirator, Ewen. A man finds himself treading sometimes in miry ways and slippery on that road, and he's lucky who can come through without someone calling him a blackguard. Remember, Lochdornie's a Mac-Phair, and our clans have so often been at variance that there's some excuse for him. And indeed I can put up with a Mac-Phair's doubts of me so long as our Prince does not think that any of the gold has stuck to my fingers; and that he does not, thank God! Heigh-ho, my poor Jean and the children would be going about at this moment in Lille with stouter shoes to their feet if it had!' He smiled rather ruefully. 'Lochdornie and I sink our difference, and get on well enough for our joint purpose. At any rate, I do not have to suspect him; he's as loyal as the day ... and when all's said, he has never thought me more than mercenary. 'Tis for the Prince's sake, Ewen; *he* sent me, and I came.'

Ewen looked at him for a moment without speaking, and marvelled. To consent to work with a man who doubted one's honesty was in his eyes a pitch of devotion more wonderful than was Doctor Cameron's actual return to Scotland with a rope round his neck. He did not believe that his own pride would have permitted him to make so sharp a sacrifice.

'And to think that it was on Lochdornie's account – or so I believed at the time – that I turned back yesterday!' he said in a tone which suggested that he was not likely ever to repeat the action.

'No, you did it for the sake of our dear Prince,' said his cousin instantly. 'And wasn't that the best motive you could have had?'

Ardroy did not answer; he was frowning. 'Is young MacPhair of Glenshian in the Highlands too?'

'No, he remains in London. He is thought to be more useful there.'

'Why, what does he do there? But that brings to my mind Archie – what is this cock-and-bull story which Hector has got hold of, about a plot to kidnap the Elector and his family? He called it "kidnap", but I guessed the term to cover something worse. He coupled it, too, with the name of Alexander Murray of Elibank.'

'Hector is a very indiscreet young man,' said Doctor Cameron.

Ewen's face clouded still more. 'It is true, then, not an idle tale?'

'It is true,' said Doctor Cameron with evident reluctance, 'that there is such a scheme afoot.'

'And I refused to believe or at least approve it!' exclaimed Ewen. 'That indeed was why Hector left the house in anger. I swore that the Prince, who was so set against the idea of an enemy's being taken off, could not know of it, and that you of all men could not possibly have a share in it!'

'I have not, Ewen, and I don't approve. It is a mad scheme, and I doubt – I hope, rather – that it will never come to the ripening. It is quite another business which has brought me to Scotland, a business that for a while yet I'll not fully open, even to you.'

'I have no wish to hear more secrets,' retorted Ardroy with a sigh. 'I like them little enough when I do hear them. It's ill to learn of men who serve the same master and have notions so different. Yes, I must be glad that I don't have to tread those ways, even though I live here idly and do naught for the White Rose, as Hector pointed out to me the other night.'

He saw his cousin look at him with an expression which he could not read, save that it had sadness in it, and what seemed, too, a kind of envy. 'Ewen,' he said, and laid his hand on Ewen's knee, 'when the call came in '45 you gave everything you had, your home, your hopes of happiness, your blood. And you still have clean hands and a single heart. You bring those to the Cause today.'

'Archie, how dare you speak as if you had not the same!' began the younger man quite fiercely. 'You –'

'Don't eat me, lad! God be thanked, I have. But, as I told you, I am not without unfriends ... We'll not speak of that any more. And, Ewen, how can you say that you do naught for the White Rose now when only yesternight you threw aside what might have been your child's sole chance of life in order to warn the Prince's messenger? If that bonny bairn upstairs had died I'd never have been able to look you in the face again ... You have named him after poor Major Windham, as you said you should. I see you still have the Major's ring on your finger.'

Ewen looked down at the ring, with a crest not his own, which he always wore, a memento of the English enemy and friend to whom he owed it that he had not been shot, a helpless fugitive, after Culloden.

'Yes, Keithie is named after him. Strangely enough Windham, in his turn, though purely English, was named for a Scot,

382

so he once told me. Six years, Archie, and he lies sleeping there at Morar, yet it seems but yesterday that he died.' Ardroy's eyes darkened; they were full of pain. 'He lies there – and I stand here, because of him. I might well name Keithie after Keith Windham, for there had been no Keithie if Windham had not rushed between me and the muskets that day on Beinn Laoigh.'

'You have never chanced upon that brute Major Guthrie again, I suppose?'

The sorrow went out of the young man's face and was succeeded by a very grim expression. 'Pray that I do not, Archie, for if I do I shall kill him!'

'My dear Ewen ... do you then resent his treatment of you as much as that?'

'His treatment of me!' exclaimed Ewen, and his eyes began to get very blue. '*Dhé!* I never think of that now! It is what he brought about for Windham. Had it not been for his lies and insinuations, poor Lachlan would never have taken that terrible and misguided notion into his head, and – have done what he did.' For it was Lachlan MacMartin, Ewen's own foster-brother, who, misapprehending that part which the English officer had played in his chieftain's affairs, had fatally stabbed him just before Ewen's own escape to France, and had then thrown away his own life – a double tragedy for Ardroy.[1]

'So you charge Major Guthrie with being the real cause of Keith Windham's death?' said his cousin. ' 'Tis a serious accusation, Ewen; on what grounds do you base it?'

'Why, I know everything now,' replied Ewen. 'Soon after my return to Scotland I happened to fall in with one of Guthrie's subalterns, a Lieutenant Paton, who was in charge of the English post there was then at Glenfinnan. He recognized me, for he had been in Guthrie's camp on the Corryarrick road, and in the end I had the whole story, from which it was clear that Guthrie had talked about Windham's "betrayal" of me – false as hell though he knew the notion to be – so openly in those days after my capture that it became the subject of gossip among his redcoats too. And when Lachlan went prowling

1. See *The Flight of the Heron*, by the same writer.

round the camp in the darkness, as I learnt afterwards from his father that he did, he overheard that talk, and believed it. It was Guthrie, no other, who put the fatal dirk in Lachlan's hand ... And it is a curious thing, Archie,' went on the speaker, now pacing about the room, 'that, though I have not the two sights, as some men, I have for some time felt a strange presentiment that before long I shall meet someone connected with Keith Windham, and that the meeting will mean much to me. For Alison's sake, and the children's – and for my own too – I hope the man is not Major Guthrie.'

'I hope so, too,' returned Doctor Cameron gravely, knowing that at bottom, under so much that was gentle, patient and civilized, Ardroy kept the passionate and unforgiving temper of the Highlander. 'But is it not more like to be some relative of Major Windham's? Had he no kin – did he not leave a wife, for instance?'

His cousin's eyes softened again. 'I knew so little of his private affairs. I never heard him mention any of his family save his father, who died when he was a child.' He looked at the ring again, at its lion's head surrounded by a fetterlock, and began to twist it on his finger. 'I sometimes think that Windham would have been amused to see me as the father of two children – especially if he had been present at my interview with Donald last Monday.' His own mouth began to twitch at the remembrance. 'He used to laugh at me, I know, in the early days of our acquaintance. At Glenfinnan, for instance, and Kinlocheil ... about the guns we buried; and he remembered it, too, when he was dying. I wish he could have seen his namesake.'

'I expect,' said Archibald Cameron, 'that he knows, in some fashion or other, that you do not forget him.'

'Forget him! I never forget!' exclaimed Ewen, the Celt again. 'And that is why I pray God I do not meet the man who really has my friend's blood upon his hands.'

'If the Fates should bring you into collision, then I hope it may at least be in fair fight – in battle,' observed Doctor Cameron.

'What chance is there of that?' asked Ewen. 'Who's to lead

us now? We are poor, broken and scattered – and watched to
boot! When Donald's a man, perhaps ...' He gave a bitter sigh.
'But for all that I live here so tamely under the eyes of the
Sassenach, I swear to you, Archie, that I'd give all the rest of
my life for one year – one month – of war in which to try our
fortunes again, and drive them out of our glens to their own fat
fields for ever! I could die happy on the banks of Esk if I
thought they'd never cross it again, and the King was come
back to the land they have robbed him of! ... But it's a dream;
and 'tis small profit being a dreamer, without a sword, and with
no helpers but the people of dreams, or the *sidhe*, perhaps, to
charge beside one ... in a dream ...'

The exaltation and the fierce pain, flaring up like a sudden
fire in the whin, were reflected in Archibald Cameron's face
also. He, too, was on his feet.

'Ewen,' he said in an eager voice, 'Ewen, we may yet have an
ally better than the *sidhe*, if I can only prepare, as I am here to
do ... for that's my errand, – to make ready for another blow,
with that help.'

Ardroy was like a man transformed. 'Help! Whose? France
is a thrice-broken reed.'

'I'll not tell you yet. But, when the hour strikes, will you get
you a sword to your side again, and come?'

'Come! I'd come if I had nothing better than yon claymore
hilt in the loch – and if your helper were the Great Sorrow himself! Archie, when, when?'

'In the spring, perchance – if we are ready. No, you cannot
help me, Ewen; best go on living quietly here and give no cause
for suspicion. I shall hope to find my way to Crieff by Michaelmas, and there I shall meet a good many folk that I must needs
see, and after that Lochdornie and I can begin to work the clans
in earnest.'

Ewen nodded. Thousands of people, both Highland and
Lowland, met at the great annual cattle fair at Crieff, and under
cover of buying and selling much other business could be transacted.

'O God, I wish the spring were here!' he cried impatiently.

In his dreams that night it was come, for the birds were singing, and he had plunged into Loch na h-Iolaire after the
drowned hilt; and when he reached the surface again it was a
whole shining sword that he held. But, while he looked at it
with joy and pride, he heard a voice telling him that he would
never use it, and when he turned he saw, half behind him, a
young man whom he did not know, who put out a hand and
laid it on the steel, and the steel shivered into atoms at his
touch. Ewen tried in wrath to seize him, but there was no one
there, and he held only the fragment of a blade from that lost
battle on the moor. He woke; and in an hour had forgotten his
dream.

Chapter 5

KEITHIE HAS TOO MANY PHYSICIANS

1

STILL rather pale, and wrapped about in a voluminous shawl, little Keith was nevertheless to be seen next afternoon, sitting up in bed making two small round-bodied, stiff-legged animals of wood – known to him as 'deers' – walk across the quilt.

'First one goed in front, then the other goed in front, then they comed to the loch, and one putched the other in – spash!'

'Oh, Keithie, no!' begged the now repentant and shriven Donald, who was sitting beside him. 'Let's play at something else. Let the deer have a race to the bottom of the bed; I'll hold one, and yours shall win!'

'Can't. Mine deer is drownded now,' returned the inexorable Keith, and, to make the fact more evident, he suddenly plopped the animal into a bowl of milk which stood on the table by him. As his mother hurriedly removed it the door opened, and her husband and Doctor Cameron came in.

'Ought he to be sitting up like this, Doctor Archibald?' she asked. 'He seems so much better that I thought . . .'

Doctor Cameron came and took Donald's place. The small invalid eyed him a trifle suspiciously, and then gave him his shy, angelic smile.

'He *is* much better,' pronounced his physician after a moment. 'Still and on, he must have another dose of that draught.' He got up and poured out something into a glass. 'Here, my bairn – no, your mother had best give it you, perhaps.' For even a fledgling seraph may revolt at a really nauseating drink of herbs, which at its last administration had, indeed, been copiously diluted with his tears. So Doctor Cameron handed the glass to Alison.

With refusals, with grimaces, and finally with an adorable sudden submission Keithie drank off the potion. But

387

immediately after he had demolished the consolatory scrap of sugar which followed it, he pointed a minute and accusing finger at its compounder, and said, 'Naughty gentleman – naughty, to make Keithie sick!' with so much conviction that Alison began anxiously – 'Darling, do you really –'

It was precisely at that moment that the door was opened and 'Doctor Kincaid from Maryburgh' was announced.

The three adults in the room caught their breaths. None of them had ever imagined that Doctor Kincaid would come *now*. 'Tell the doctor that I will be with him in a moment,' said Alison to the servant visible in the doorway; and then in a hasty aside to Ewen, 'Of course he must not see –' she indicated Doctor Cameron on the other side of the bed.

But there was no time to carry out that precaution, for the girl, fresh from the wilds, and ignorant of the need for dissimulation, had brought Doctor Kincaid straight up to the sickroom, and there he was, already on the threshold, a little uncompromising, hard-featured man of fifty, overworked between the claims of Maryburgh, where he dwelt, of its neighbour Fort William, and of the countryside in general. There was no hope of his not seeing Doctor Cameron; still, the chances were heavily against his knowing and recognizing him. Yet who, save a doctor or a relative had a rightful place in this sick-room ... and a doctor was the one thing which they must not admit that guest to be.

So completely were the three taken by surprise that there was scarcely time to think. But Ewen instinctively got in front of his kinsman, while Alison went forward to greet the newcomer with the embarrassment which she could not completely hide, murmuring, 'Doctor Kincaid ... how good of you ... we did not expect ...'

'You are surprised to see me, madam?' asked he, coming forward. 'But I came on a brither o' yours the nicht before last in a sair plight by Loch Treig side, and he begged me to come to Ardroy as soon as possible. But I couldna come before; I'm fair run off ma legs.'

'How is my brother?' asked Alison anxiously. 'I heard of his mishap, but with the child so ill –'

'Ay, ye'd be thinking of yer wean first, nae doot. Aweel, the young fellow's nane too bad, having an unco stout skull, as I jalouse your good man must hae kent when he left him all his lane there.'

'But I arranged with the farmer at Inverlair –' began Ewen.

'Ou ay, they came fra Inverlair and fetched him, and there he bides,' said Doctor Kincaid. He swept a glance round the room. 'Ye're pretty throng here. Is yon the patient, sitting up in bed?'

'Well, Doctor, he seems, thank God, so much better,' murmured Alison in extenuation of this proceeding. As she led the physician to the bedside she saw with relief that Doctor Archibald had moved quietly to the window and was looking out; and she thought, 'After all, no one could *know* that he was a doctor!'

Doctor Kincaid examined the little boy, asked some questions, seemed surprised at the answers (from which answers it appeared that his directions had been anticipated), but said that the child was doing well. And since not even a middle-aged physician in a bad temper could resist the charm of small Keith, he gave a sort of smile when he had finished, and said kindly, 'There, my wee mannie, ye'll soon be rinning aboot again.'

The flower-like eyes were upraised to his. 'Then My not have no more nasty drink like that gentleman gived Keithie?' observed their owner, and again a small finger pointed accusingly to Archibald Cameron – to his back this time.

Doctor Kincaid also looked at that back. 'Ah,' he observed sharply, 'so yon gentleman has already been treating the bairn – and the measures ye have taken were of his suggesting? Pray, why did ye no' tell me that, madam?'

Ewen plunged to the rescue. He had been longing for Archie to leave the room, but supposed the latter thought that flight might arouse suspicion. 'My friend, Mr John Sinclair from Caithness, who is paying us a visit, having a certain knowledge of medicine, was good enough ... Let me make you known to each other – Doctor Kincaid, Mr Sinclair.'

'Mr Sinclair from Caithness' – Ewen had placed his domicile

as far away as possible – turned and bowed; there was a twinkle in his eye. But not in Doctor Kincaid's.

'Humph! it seems I wasna sae mickle needed, seeing ye hae gotten a leech to the bairn already! But the young man wi' the dunt on his heid begged me sae sair to come that I listened to him, though I micht hae spared ma pains!'

Alison and Ewen hastened in chorus to express their appreciation of his coming, and Ewen, with an appealing glance at his kinsman, began to move towards the door. One or other of the rival practitioners must certainly be got out of the room. And Archie himself now seemed to be of the same opinion.

'A leech? no, sir, the merest *amateur*, who, now that the real physician has come, will take himself off,' he said pleasantly.

'Nay, I'm through,' said Doctor Kincaid. 'Ye've left me nae mair to do.' And, as he seemed to be going to leave the room in 'Mr Sinclair's' company, Alison hastily appealed for more information about a detail of treatment, so that he had to stay behind. Doctor Cameron, followed by Donald, all eyes, slipped out. Ardroy and his wife, most desirous not to invite or answer any questions about their medically skilled guest, now became remarkably voluble on other subjects; and, as they went downstairs with Doctor Kincaid, pressed him to stay to a meal, hoping fervently that he would refuse – which, luckily, the doctor did.

But outside, as he put a foot into the stirrup, he said, pretty sourly, to Ewen, 'I'm glad the wean's better, Ardroy, but I'd hae been obleeged tae ye if ye hadna garred me come all these miles when ye already had a medical man in the hoose. There was nae need o' me, and I'm a gey busy man.'

'I am very sorry indeed, Doctor,' said Ewen, and could not but feel that the reproach was merited. 'The fact is that –' He was just on the point of exonerating himself by saying that Mr Sinclair had not yet arrived on Tuesday, nor did they know of his impending visit, but, thinking that plea possibly imprudent, said instead, 'I had no knowledge that Mr Sinclair was so skilled. We . . . have not met recently.'

'Humph,' remarked Doctor Kincaid, now astride his horse. 'A peety that he doesna practise; but maybe he does – in Caithness. At ony rate, he'll be able tae exercise his skill on your brither-in-law – if ye mean tae do ony mair for that young man. For ye'll pardon me if I say that ye havena done much as yet!'

Ewen's colour rose. To have left Hector in that state on a lonely road at nightfall – even despite the measures he had taken for his removal – did indeed show him in a strange and unpleasant light. But it was impossible to explain what had obliged him to do it, and the more than willingness of Hector to be so left. 'Can I have him brought hither from Inverlair without risk to himself?' he asked.

'Ay,' said Kincaid, 'that I think ye micht do if ye send some sort of conveyance – the morn, say, then ye'll hae him here Saturday. He'll no' walk this distance, naturally – nor ride it. And indeed if ye send for him he'll be better off here under the care of yer friend Sinclair, than lying in a farm sae mony miles fra Maryburgh; I havena been able to get to him syne. Forbye, Ardroy,' added the doctor, looking at him in a rather disturbing manner, 'the callant talked a wheen gibberish yon-nicht – and not Erse gibberish, neither!'

French, of course; Ewen had already witnessed that propensity! And he groaned inwardly, for what had Hector been saying in that tongue when light-headed? It was to be hoped, if he had forsaken 'Malbrouck' for more dangerous themes, that Doctor Kincaid was no French scholar; from the epithet which he had just applied to the language it sounded as though he were not. However, the physician then took a curt farewell, and he and his steed jogged away down the avenue, Ewen standing looking after him in perplexity. He did not like to leave Hector at Inverlair; yet if he fetched him here he might be drawing down pursuit on Archie – supposing that suspicion were to fall upon Hector himself by reason of his abstracted papers.

However, by the time he came in again Ewen had arrived at a compromise. Archie should leave the house at once, which might be more prudent in any case. (For though Doctor Kincaid would hardly go and lay information against him at Fort William ... what indeed had he to lay information about? ... he might easily get talking if he happened to be summoned

391

there professionally.) So, as it wanted yet five days to Archie's rendezvous with Lochdornie, and he must dispose himself somewhere, he should transfer himself to the cottage of Angus MacMartin, Ewen's young piper, up at Slochd nan Eun, on the farther side of the loch, whence, if necessary, it would be an easy matter to disappear into the mountains.

Doctor Cameron raised no objections to this plan, his small patient being now out of danger; he thought the change would be wise, too, on Ewen's own account. He stipulated only that he should not go until next morning, in case Keithie should take a turn for the worse. But the little boy passed an excellent night, so next morning early Ewen took his guest up the brae, and gave him over to the care of the little colony of MacMartins in the crofts at Slochd nan Eun, where he himself had once been a foster-child.

2

The day after, which was Saturday, Ewen's plan of exchanging one compromising visitor for another should have completed itself, but in the early afternoon, to his dismay, the cart which he had sent the previous day to Inverlair to fetch his damaged brother-in-law returned without him. Mr Grant was no longer at the farm; not, reported Angus MacMartin, who had been sent in charge of it, that he had wandered away light-headed, as Ewen immediately feared; no, the farmer had said that the gentleman was fully in his right mind, and had left a message that his friends were not to be concerned on his behalf, and that they would see him again before long.

A good deal perturbed, however, on Alison's account as well, Ewen went up to Slochd nan Eun to tell Doctor Cameron the news. He found his kinsman sitting over the peat fire with a book in his hand, though indeed the illumination of the low little dwelling had not been designed in the interests of study. Doctor Cameron thought it quite likely, though surprising, that Hector really had fully recovered, and added some medical details about certain blows on the head and how the disturbance which they caused was often merely temporary.

'Nevertheless,' he concluded, 'one would like to know what notion the boy's got now into that same hot pate of his. You young men –'

'Don't talk like a grandfather, Archie! You are only twelve years older than I!'

'I feel more your senior than that, lad! – How's the bairn?'

'He is leaving his bed this afternoon – since both you and your colleague from Maryburgh allowed it.'

Doctor Cameron laughed. Then he bit his lip, stooped forward to throw peat on the fire, and, under cover of the movement, pressed his other hand surreptitiously to his side. But Ewen saw him do it.

'What's wrong with you, Archie – are you not well today?'

'Quite well,' answered his cousin, leaning his elbows on his knees. 'But my old companion is troublesome this afternoon – the ball I got at Falkirk, you'll remember.'

'You'll not tell me that you are still carrying that in your body!' cried Ewen in tones of reprobation.

Archie was pale, even in the peat glow. 'How about the gash you took at Culloden Moor?' he retorted. 'You were limping from it that morning in Glen Mallie; I saw it, but I don't make it a matter for reproach, Eoghain! 'Tis impossible to have the bullet extracted, it's too awkwardly lodged, and I shall carry it to my grave with me ... and little regard it if it did not pester me at times. However, here I am comfortably by your good Angus's fire, not skulking in the heather, and cared for as if I were yourself.'

But Ewen went down from Slochd nan Eun with an impression of a man in more discomfort than he would acknowledge, and a fresh trouble to worry over. Yet how could he worry in the presence of Keithie, to whom he then paid a visit in the nursery – Keithie, who, now out of bed, sat upon his knee, and in an earnest voice told him a sorrowful tale of how the fairies, having mistaken his 'deers' for cows, had carried them off, as all Highland children knew was their reprehensible habit with cattle. And so he could not find them, for they were doubtless hidden in the fairy *dun*, and when they were restored they would not be real 'deers' any more, they would only look like them, as happened with cows stolen and restored by the *sidhe*. His father, holding the little pliant body close, and kissing him under the chin, said that more probably his deers were somewhere in the house, and that he would find them for him.

Which was the reason why, somewhat later, he went in search of Donald, and discovered him in his mother's room, watching her brush out her dark, rippling hair, which she had evidently been washing, for the room smelt faintly and deliciously of birch.

'Do you want me, my dear?' asked Alison, tossing back her locks.

'Do I not always want you, heart of mine? – As a matter of fact, I am here on an errand for Keithie. Do either you or Donald know anything of the present whereabouts of his "deers"? He tells me that the *daoine sidhe* have taken them.'

But they both denied any knowledge of the animals.

'Angus is going to make Keithie a much larger deer,' announced Donald, his hand in his father's. 'I asked him to. A stag – with horns. Father, have you ever heard the queer crackling sound that Mother's hair makes when she brushes it? Does yours?'

'I doubt it,' replied Ewen, and he looked first at Alison's slim, pretty figure as with arms upraised she began to braid her hair about her head, and then at her amused face in the glass. And in the mirror she caught his gaze and smiled back, with something of the bride about her still.

But in the glass Ewen saw her smile abruptly die out. Her eyes had wandered away from his, reflected there, to the window, and she stood, all at once, like a statue with uplifted arms.

'What –' he began ... and in the same moment she said breathlessly, 'Ewen – look!'

He took a step or two forward, and saw, about a quarter of a mile away on the far side of the avenue, a moving growth of scarlet: and more, two thinner streams of it, like poppies, spreading out to right and left to encircle the house. Alison's arms fell; the soft masses of her hair slipped in a coil to her shoulder. 'Soldiers!' shouted Donald, and gave a little skip of excitement.

For a second Ewen also stood like a statue. 'My God! and Archie half-disabled today! ... Have I the time to get up to him? Yes, this way.' He indicated the window at the far side of the room, which looked over the back premises. 'Listen, my heart, and you, too, Donald! If the soldiers cut me off, and I cannot get up to Slochd nan Eun to warn him – if I see that it is hopeless to attempt it, then I shall run from them. Likely enough they'll think I am the man they're after, and I shall lead them as long a chase as I can, in order to give Archie time to get away ... for some of the MacMartins may meanwhile take the alarm. Do you understand?'

'Oh, Ewen ...' said his wife, hesitating. He took her hands.

'And should I be caught ... nay, I think I'll *let* myself be caught in the end ... and they bring me to the house, you may feign to be agitated at the sight of me, but you must not know me for who I am; you must let them think that I am the man you are hiding. But you must not call me Doctor Cameron neither – you must not name me at all! If they take me off to Fort William, all the better. By the time they have got me there Archie will be miles away. Then all Colonel Leighton can do, when he recognizes me, will be to send me back again. Heaven grant, though,' he added, 'that the officer with these men does not know me! – Dearest love,' for Alison had turned rather white, 'remember that it was for Keithie's sake – for our sakes – that Archie came here at all! I must get him safely away if ... if it should cost more than that!'

'Yes,' said Alison a little faintly. 'Yes ... go – I will do as you say.'

He held her to him for an instant and the next was throwing up the sash of the far window. 'You understand too, Donald? And, Alison, I think you will have to tell a lie, and say that I myself am away from home. – One thing more' – Ewen paused with a leg over the window-sill – 'if I fail to warn Archie, which I'll contrive to let you know somehow, you must send another messenger, provided that messenger can get away without being followed.'

He hung by his hands a moment and dropped: a loud cackling of astonished hens announced his arrival below. Lady

395

Ardroy went back to the glass and began hastily to fasten up her hair.

'How near are they, Donald? – Run quickly to the kitchen and tell the servants to say, if they are asked, that the laird went away to Inverness ... yesterday ... and that if they see him they are to pretend not to know him. And then come back to me.'

Donald left the room like a stone from a catapult. This was great sport – and fancy a lie's being actually enjoined by those authorities who usually regarded the mere tendency to one as so reprehensible!

Chapter 6

'WHO IS THIS MAN?'

1

WHEN the officer in charge of the party of redcoats, having set his men close round the house of Ardroy, went in person to demand admittance, it was no servant, out of whom he might have surprised information, who answered his peremptory knocking, but (doubtless to his annoyance) the châtelaine herself.

Captain Jackson, however, saluted civilly enough. 'Mrs Cameron, I think?' for, being English, he saw no reason to give those ridiculous courtesy titles to the wives of petty landowners.

'Yes, sir,' responded Alison with dignity. 'I am Mrs Cameron. I saw you from above, and, since I have no notion why you have come, I descended in order to find out.'

'If I may enter, madam, I will tell you why I have come,' responded the officer promptly.

'By all means enter,' said Alison with even more of stateliness (hoping he would not notice that she was still out of breath with haste) and, waiting while he gave an order or two, preceded him into the parlour. Captain Jackson then became aware that a small boy had somehow slipped to her side.

He took a careful look round the large room, and meanwhile Alison, studying his thin, sallow face, decided that she had never seen this officer before, and hoped, for the success of the plan, that neither had he ever seen Ewen. Behind him, through the open parlour door, she perceived her hall full of scarlet coats and white cross-belts and breeches.

'I am here, madam,' now said the invader, fixing her with a meaning glance, 'as I think you can very well guess, in the King's name, with a warrant to search this house, in which there is every reason to believe that the owner is sheltering a rebel.'

'Mr Cameron is away, sir,' responded Alison. 'How, therefore, can he be sheltering anyone?'

'Away?' exclaimed Captain Jackson suspiciously. 'How is that? for he was certainly at home on Thursday!'

('The day of Doctor Kincaid's visit,' thought Alison. 'Then he *did* give the alarm!')

'Mr Cameron was here on Thursday,' repeated Captain Jackson with emphasis.

'I did not deny it,' said Alison, beginning to be nettled at his tone. 'Nevertheless he went away yesterday.'

'Whither?' was the next question rapped out at her. 'Whither, and for what purpose?'

Alison's own Highland temper began to rise now, and with the warming uprush came almost a relief in her own statement. 'Does "the King" really demand to know that, sir? He went to Inverness on affairs.'

By this time Captain Jackson had no doubt realized that he had to do with a lady of spirit. 'Perhaps, then, madam,' he suggested, 'Mr Cameron deputed the task of hiding the rebel to you? I think you would do it well. I must search the house thoroughly. Are any of the rooms locked?'

'Yes, one,' said Lady Ardroy. 'I will come with you and unlock it if you wish to see it.'

'No, you'll stay where you are, madam, if you please,' retorted the soldier. 'I will trouble you for your keys – all your keys. I do not wish to damage any of your property by breaking it open.'

Biting her lip, Alison went in silence to her writing-desk. Captain Jackson took the bunch without more ado, and a moment later Alison and her eldest son were alone ... locked in.

And when she heard the key turned on her the colour came flooding into her face, and she stood very erect, tapping with one foot upon the floor, in no peaceable mood.

'Mother,' said Donald, tugging at her skirt, 'the redcoat has not locked *this* door!' For Captain Jackson had either overlooked or chosen to disregard that, in the far corner of the room, which led into the kitchen domain.

Alison hesitated for a moment. No, better to stay here

quietly, as if she had no cause for anxiety; and better not as yet
to attempt to send another messenger to Slochd nan Eun who,
by blundering, might draw on Doctor Cameron just the danger
to be averted. So for twenty minutes or more she waited with
Donald in the living-room, wondering, calculating, praying for
patience, sometimes going to the windows and looking out,
hearing now and then heavy footsteps about the house and all
the sounds of a search which she knew would be fruitless, and
picturing the havoc which the invaders were doubtless making
of her household arrangements. Perhaps, in spite of Morag's
presence, they were frightening little Keith – a thought which
nearly broke her resolution of staying where she was.

Yet, as the minutes ticked away with the slowly fading daylight outside, and nothing happened, her spirits began to rise.
Ewen had evidently not been stopped; indeed, if he once got
safely beyond the policies it was unlikely that he would be. He
had probably reached Slochd nan Eun unmolested. Surely, too,
he would remain there until the soldiers had gone altogether?
And feeling at last some security on that score, Alison sat down
and took up a piece of sewing.

But she had not even threaded her needle before there was a
stir and a trampling outside the house, and she jumped up and
ran to the window. More soldiers ... and someone in the midst
of them, tightly held – her husband!

And in that moment Alison knew, and was ashamed of the
knowledge, that she must at the bottom of her heart have been
hoping that if anyone were captured ... No, no, she had not
hoped that! For Doctor Cameron's life was in jeopardy, while
nothing could happen to Ewen save unpleasantness. In expiation of that half-wish she braced herself to the dissimulation
which Ewen had enjoined. She drew the boy beside her away
from the window.

'The soldiers have caught your father, Donald, after all. Remember that you are to pretend not to know who he is, nor
what he is doing here.'

The little boy nodded with bright eyes, and held her hand
rather tightly.

'Will they do anything to me, Mother, for – saying what is not true?'

'No, darling, not this time. And if they take Father away to Fort William, it is only what he hopes they will do; and he will soon come back to us.'

By this time the door of the parlour was being unlocked, and in another moment Captain Jackson was striding into the room.

'Bring him in,' he commanded, half-turning, and the redcoats brought in a rather hot, dishevelled Ardroy, with a smear of blood down his chin, and with four soldiers, no less, holding him firmly by wrists and arms and shoulders. It was not difficult for Alison to show the agitation demanded; indeed there was for an instant the risk that it might exceed its legitimate bounds; but she had herself in hand again at once. Her husband gave her one glance and shook his head almost imperceptibly to show that he had not succeeded in his attempt. Then he looked away again and studied the antlers over the hearth while the sergeant in charge of him made his report, the gist of which was that the prisoner, coming unexpectedly upon them near the lake up there had led them the devil of a chase; indeed, had he not tripped and fallen, he might have escaped them altogether.

'Tripped!' thought Alison scornfully – as if Ewen with his perfect balance and stag's fleetness, ever tripped when he was running! He had thrown himself down for them to take, the fools! and that this really was the case she knew from the passing twitch of amusement at the corner of her husband's blood-stained mouth. But, seeing him standing there in the power of the *saighdearan deary* – oh, she wished he had not done it!

'Well, have you anything to say, "Mr Sinclair"?' demanded Captain Jackson, planting himself in front of the prize. And at the mention of that name both Ewen and his wife knew for certain that they owed this visitation to Doctor Kincaid.

'Not to you, sir. But I should wish to offer my apologies to Lady Ardroy,' said Ewen, with an inclination of the head in Alison's direction, 'for bringing about an ... an annoying incident in her house.'

Captain Jackson shrugged his shoulder. 'Very polite of you, egad! But, in that case, why have you come here in the first instance?' He moved away a little, got out a paper, and studied it. Then he looked up, frowning.

'Who are you?' he demanded.

'Does not your paper tell you that?' asked Ewen pleasantly.

Alison wondered if the officer thought that he was Lochdornie; but Lochdornie was, she believed, a man between fifty and sixty, and Doctor Cameron in the forties. Surely this officer could not take Ewen for either? Her heart began to lift a little. Captain Jackson, after looking, still with the frown, from Ewen to the paper, and from the paper to Ewen, suddenly folded it up and glared at her.

'Madam, who is this man?'

'If I have sheltered him, as you state, is it likely that I should tell you?' asked Alison quietly.

'Call the servants!' said Captain Jackson to a soldier near the door. 'No, wait a moment!' He turned again and pointed at Donald, standing at his mother's side, his eyes fixed on the captive, who, for his part, was now looking out of the window. 'You, boy, do you know who this man is?'

'Must you drag in a small child –' began Alison indignantly.

'If you will not answer, yes,' retorted the Englishman. 'And he is quite of an age to supplement your unwillingness, madam. Come, boy' – he advanced a little on Donald, 'don't be frightened; I am not going to hurt you. Just tell me now, have you ever seen this man before?'

The question appeared to Donald extremely amusing, and, since he was not at all frightened, but merely excited, he gave a little laugh.

'Oh yes, sir.'

'How often?'

His mother's hand on his shoulder gave him a warning pressure. 'I ... I could not count.'

'Six times – seven times? More? He comes here often, then?'

Donald considered. One could not say that Father *came* here; he *was* here. 'No, sir.'

'He does not come often, eh? How long has he been here this time?'

Donald, a little perplexed, glanced up at his mother. What

was he to say to this? But Captain Jackson now took steps to prevent his receiving any more assistance from that source. He stretched out a hand.

'No, thank you, Mrs Cameron! If you won't speak you shan't prompt either! Come here, boy.' He drew Donald, without roughness, away, and placed him more in the middle of the room, with his back to his mother. 'Have you ever heard this gentleman called "Sinclair"?' he asked. 'Now, tell the truth!'

Donald told it. 'No, never!' he replied, shaking his golden head.

'I thought as much! Well now, my boy, I'll make a guess at what you *have* heard him called, and you shall tell me if I guess right, eh?' And Captain Jackson, attempting heartiness, smiled somewhat sourly.

'I'll not promise,' said the child cautiously.

'The young devil has been primed!' said the soldier under his breath. Then he shot his query at him as suddenly as possible. 'His name is the same as yours – *Cameron!*'

Taken aback by this, Donald wrinkled his brows and said nothing.

'With "Doctor" in front of it – "Doctor Cameron"?' pursued the inquisitor. 'Now, have I not guessed right?'

'Oh no, sir,' said Donald, relieved.

Ewen was no longer looking out of the window, and he was frowning more than Captain Jackson had frowned. He had never foreseen Donald's being harried with questions. 'Do you imagine,' he broke in suddenly, 'that a man in my shoes is like to have his real name flung about in the hearing of a small child?'

Captain Jackson paid no heed to this remark. 'Now, my boy, you can remember the name quite well if you choose, of that I'm sure. If you don't choose ...' He paused suggestively.

'Take your hand off that child's shoulder!' commanded Ardroy in a voice so dangerous that, though he had not moved, his guards instinctively took a fresh grip of him.

'Oho!' said Captain Jackson, transferring his attention at once from the little boy, 'is that where the wind blows from? This young mule is a relative of yours?'

'Is that the only reason a man may have for objecting to see a small child bullied?' asked Ewen hotly. ' 'Tis not the only one in Scotland, I assure you, whatever you English may feel about the matter.'

But Captain Jackson declined to follow this red herring. 'It lies entirely with you, "Mr Sinclair", to prevent any further questioning.'

'No, it does not!' declared Ewen. 'I have told you once, sir, that a man in my position does not have his real name cried to all the winds of heaven. Lady Ardroy herself is ignorant of it: she took me in knowing only that I was in need of rest and shelter. I do not wish her to learn it, lest Mr Cameron, when he returns, be not best pleased to find whom she has been housing in his absence. But I will tell you my name at Fort William – if, indeed, your commanding officer there do not find it out first.'

This excursion into romance – a quite sudden inspiration on its author's part – really shook Captain Jackson for a moment, since he was well aware that there were divisions, and sharp ones, among the Jacobites. Yet from Doctor Kincaid's account Ewen Cameron himself, two days ago, had answered for 'Mr Sinclair'. As he stood undecided, enlightenment came to him from a most unexpected quarter.

'Father,' suddenly said a high, clear little voice, 'Father, has you finded them?'

'What's this?' The English officer swung round – indeed, every man in the room turned to look at the small figure which, quite unobserved, even by Alison, had strayed in through the open door. And before anyone had tried to stop him Keith had pattered forward and seized his father round the legs. 'My comed down to look for mine deers,' he announced, smiling up at him. 'Who is all these peoples?'

It was the last query about identity asked that evening. Ewen saw that the game was up, and, the soldiers who held him having, perhaps unconsciously, loosed their hold at this gentle and unexpected arrival, he stooped and caught up the wrecker of his gallant scheme. 'No, my wee bird, I have not found your deers ... I have been found myself,' he whispered, and could

403

not keep a smile from the lips which touched that velvet cheek.

But the implications of this unlooked-for greeting had now burst upon Captain Jackson with shattering force. Half-inarticulate with rage, he strode forward and shook his fist in the prisoner's face. 'You ... you liar! You are yourself Ewen Cameron!'

'Pray do not terrify this child also,' observed the culprit coolly, for Keithie, after one look at the angry soldier, had hidden his face on his father's shoulder. 'He is only three years old, and not worthy of your attentions!'

Captain Jackson fairly gibbered. 'You think that you have fooled me – you and your lady there! You'll soon find out at Fort William who is the fool! Put that child down!'

'Please make that red gentleman go away!' petitioned a small voice from the neighbourhood of Ardroy's neck.

'That's out of my power, I fear, my darling,' replied the young man. 'And you had better go to Mother now.' Since, with the child in his arms, not a soldier seemed disposed to hinder him, he walked calmly across the room and put Keithie into Alison's, whence he contemplated Captain Jackson with a severe and heavenly gaze.

'Well, now that this charming domestic interlude is over,' snapped that officer, 'perhaps, sir, you will vouchsafe some explanation of your conduct in leading my men this dance, and in striving to hide your identity in your own house in this ridiculous fashion? "When Mr Cameron returns", forsooth!'

Again Ewen, usually a punctiliously truthful person, was inspired to a flight of imagination. 'I admit that it was foolish of me,' he replied with every appearance of candour. 'But I saw you and your men coming, and having been "out", as you probably know, in the Forty-five, I thought it better to instruct my wife to say that I was from home, and left the house by a back window. I see now that I should have done better to show more courage, and to stay and face your visit out.'

During this explanation Captain Jackson, his hands behind his back, was regarding the self-styled coward very fixedly. 'Do you think that you can gull me into believing that you led my men that chase because of anything you did six or seven years

ago, Mr Ewen Cameron? No; you were playing the decoy –
and giving the man you are hiding here a chance to get
away!'

Ardroy shrugged his shoulders. 'Have it your own way, sir,'
he said indifferently. 'I know that a simple explanation of a
natural action is seldom believed.'

'No, only by simpletons!' retorted Captain Jackson. 'However, you can try its effect upon Lieutenant-Governor Leighton
at Fort William, for to Fort William you will go, Mr Cameron,
without delay. And do not imagine that I shall accompany you;
I have not finished looking for your friend from Caithness, and,
when you are no longer here to draw the pursuit, it may be that
I shall find him.'

It was true that Ewen had contemplated being taken to Fort
William, but not exactly in his own character and upon his own
account. This was a much less attractive prospect. However,
there was no help for it, and the only thing that mattered was
that Archie should get safely away. If only he could be certain
that he had! Surely the MacMartins ... His thoughts sped up
to Slochd nan Eun.

'Take two file of men, sergeant,' said Captain Jackson, 'and
set out with Mr Cameron at once. You can reach High Bridge
by nightfall, and lie there.'

At that Alison came forward; she had put down Keithie and
was holding him by the hand; he continued to regard the English
officer with the same unmitigated disapproval. 'Do you mean,
sir, that you are sending my husband to Fort William at once –
this very evening?'

'Yes, madam. I have really no choice,' replied the soldier,
who appeared to have regained control of his temper. 'But if he
will give me his word of honour to go peaceably, and make no
attempt to escape by the way, I need not order any harsh
measures for the journey. Will you do that, Mr Cameron?'

Ewen came back to his own situation, and to a longing to feel
Keithie in his arms again for a moment. 'Yes, sir, I pledge you
my word as a gentleman to give no trouble on the road. Indeed,
why should I?' he added. 'I am innocent.'

'But if Mr Cameron is to go at once,' objected Alison, 'pray allow me time to put together a few necessaries for him, since however short a while he stays at Fort William he will need them.'

Instant departure was not so urgent that Captain Jackson could reasonably refuse this request. 'Yes, you may do that, madam,' he replied a trifle stiffly, 'provided that you are not more than a quarter of an hour about the business; otherwise the party may be benighted before they can reach High Bridge.' And he went quite civilly to hold the door for her.

As Alison passed her husband she looked at him hard with a question in her eyes; she wanted to be sure. Again he gave an almost imperceptible shake of the head. She drew her brows together, and with a child on either side of her, the elder lagging and gazing half-frightened, half-admiringly, at his captive father, went out of the room. Captain Jackson did the same; but he left four men with muskets behind him.

Of these Ewen took no notice, but began walking slowly up and down the room dear to him by so many memories. Now that the moment of being taken from his home was upon him he did not like it. But he would soon be back, he told himself. How heavily would he be fined by the Government for this escapade? However little, it would mean a still harder struggle to make both ends meet. But no price was too high to pay for Archie's life – or for Keithie's. Both of them were tangled up somehow in this payment. He wondered too, with some uneasiness, how and why the redcoats whom he had allowed to capture him had been right up by Loch na h-Iolaire when he came upon them. *Dhé!* that had been a chase, too – he was young enough to have enjoyed it.

The door was opened again; there was Alison, with a little packet in her hand, and Captain Jackson behind her. 'You can take leave of your wife, Mr Cameron,' said he, motioning him to come to her at the door.

But only, it was evident, under his eyes and in his hearing. So nothing could be said about Archie; even Gaelic was not safe, for it was quite possible that the Englishman had picked up a few words. Under the officer's eyes, then, Ardroy took his wife in his arms and kissed her.

'I shall not be away for long, my dear. God bless you. Kiss the boys for me.'

To Alison Cameron it seemed incredible that he was really being taken from her with so little warning, when only a couple of hours ago he had been in her room asking about Keithie's lost toys. And, for all either of them yet knew, he might be sacrificing himself in vain. But she looked up into his eyes and said with meaning, 'I will try to do all you wish while you are away,' a wifely utterance to which Captain Jackson could hardly take exception.

And three minutes later, with no more intimate leave-taking than that, she was at the window watching her husband being marched away under the beeches of the avenue with his little guard. Before he vanished from sight he turned and waved his hand, with the air of one who meant to be back ere any of their leaves had fluttered down.

'I am sorry for this, madam,' said the voice of Captain Jackson behind her. 'But, if you'll forgive me for saying so, Mr Cameron has brought it upon himself. Now understand, if you please, that no one is to leave the house on any pretext; I have not finished yet. But you are free to go about your ordinary occupations, and I'll see that you are not molested – so long as my order is observed.'

For that Alison thanked him, and went upstairs to solace her loneliness by putting little Keith to bed. She had already tried to send Morag – the easiest to come at of the servants – up the brae, and had not found it feasible. And surely, surely Doctor Cameron must have taken the alarm by now and be away? Still, there was always her promise to Ewen – a promise which it began to seem impossible to carry out.

2

Yet, in a sense, that promise was already in process of being kept, though in a manner of which Alison was fortunately ignorant. At the very moment when she had finally succeeded in satisfying her younger son's critical inquiries about 'the gentleman downstairs that was so angry', her eldest born, whom she had last seen seated on the stairs gazing down through the rails with deep interest at the group of soldiers in the hall, was half-way between the house and Loch na h-Iolaire, his heart beating rapidly with excitement, triumph, and another less agreeable emotion.

Both in courage and intelligence Donald was old for his years. He knew that his mother had tried in vain to send Morag out of the house while she was making up the packet for Father. The resplendent idea had then come to him of himself carrying out Father's wish, and warning Doctor Cameron of the presence of the soldiers, of which he partially at least grasped the importance. On the whole, he thought he would not tell his mother until the deed was accomplished ... for it was just possible that if he mentioned his purpose beforehand she would forbid him to carry it through. As for getting out of the house, perhaps the soldiers at the various doors would not pay much attention to him, whom they probably considered just a little boy – though it was scarcely so that he thought of himself. Perhaps also they would not be aware that never in his life before had he been out so late alone. He could say that he had lost a ball in the shrubbery, and that would be true, for so he had, about a month ago; and even if it had not been true, lies seemed to be strangely permissible today. He could creep out of the shrubbery on the other side and then run, run all the way round the end of the loch and up the track which climbed the shoulder of Meall Achadh.

As it happened, Donald did not have to employ the plea about the lost ball, for in wandering round the back premises he came on a door which was not guarded at all. Its particular sentry was even then escorting his father towards Fort William, and by some oversight had not been replaced. So the small adventurer quite easily found himself among the outbuildings, deserted and silent, except for the voices of two invisible red-coats who were arguing about something round the corner of the stables. By them his light footfall went unheard, and a moment or two afterwards Donald was looking back in elation from the edge of the policies on the lighted windows of the house of Ardroy.

That was a good ten minutes ago. Now ... he was wishing that he had brought Luath with him ... It was such a strange darkness – not really dark, but an eerie kind of half-light. And the loch, which he was now approaching ... what an odd ghostly shine the water had between the trees! He had never seen it look like that before. This was, past all doubt, the hour of that dread Thing, the water-horse.

And Donald's feet began to falter a little in the path as he came nearer and nearer to the Loch of the Eagle, so friendly in the day, so very different now. No child in the Highlands but had heard many a story of water-horse and kelpie and *uruisg*, however much his elders might discourage such narratives. It was true that Father had told him there were no such things as these fabled inhabitants of loch and stream and mountain-side, but the awful fact remained that Morag had a second cousin in Kintail who had been carried off by an *each uisge*. On Loch Duich it was; seeing a beautiful horse come into his little enclosure he could not resist climbing on to its back; that was just what the water-horse wanted, for it rushed down to the loch with its rider, and Morag's second cousin was never seen again. Only, next day, his lungs floated ashore; all the rest of him had been eaten up. Not quite to know what one's 'lungs' were made it still more horrible.

At Donald's age one is not capable of formulating an axiom about the difficulty of proving a negative, but this evening's adventure brought the boy some instinctive perception of its truth. Father had never *seen* a water-horse, it was true ... but in the face of Morag's story ... Then there was another most disturbing thought to accompany him; what if something in the nature of an angel were suddenly to appear and throw him into the loch as a punishment for having pushed Keithie in and made him ill! There would be no Father on the island now to rescue *him*.

Donald's steps grew slower still. He was now almost skirting Loch na h-Iolaire in the little track through the heather and bracken, where the pine branches swayed and whispered and made the whole atmosphere, too, much darker and more alarming. If he had realized earlier the possibility of an avenger ...

Then he thought of those who had fought at the great battle
before he was born, of cousin Ian Stewart and the broken claymore, of his father, of the dead Chief whose name he bore, and
went onwards with a brave and beating heart. But there were
such strange sounds all round him – noises and cracklings which
he had never heard in the day, open-air little boy though he
was; and once he jumped violently as something shadowy and
slim ran across his very path. 'Only a weasel,' said the child to
himself, 'but a very large one!'

And then Donald's heart gave a bound and seemed to stop
altogether. Something much bigger than a weasel was coming,
though he could not see it. It was trampling through the undergrowth on his right. The *each uisge*, undoubtedly! There broke
from him a little sound too attenuated for a shriek, a small
puppy-like whimper of dismay.

'Who's there?' called out a man's voice sharply. 'Who's there
– answer me!'

At least, then, it was not a water-horse. 'I'm ... I'm Donald
Cameron of Ardroy,' replied the adventurer in quavering tones,
his eyes fixed on the dark, dim shape now visible, from the
waist upwards, among the surging waves of bracken. This did
not look like an avenging angel either; it seemed to be just a
man.

'Donald!' it exclaimed. 'What in the name of the Good
Being are you doing here at this hour? Don't be frightened,
child – 'tis your uncle Hector.' And the apparition pushed
through the fern and bent over him. 'Are you lost, my boy?'

Immensely relieved, Donald looked up at the young man. He
had not seen him for nearly two years, and his actual recollec-
tions of his appearance were hazy, but he had often heard of
the uncle who was a soldier of the King of France. Evidently,
too, Uncle Hector had lately been in some battle, for he wore
round his head a bandage which showed white in the dusk.

'No, Uncle Hector, I'm not lost. I am going up to Slochd nan
Eun to tell Doctor Cameron that there are some soldiers come
after him, and that he must go away quickly.'

'Doctor Cameron!' exclaimed his uncle in surprise. Then,
glancing round, he lowered his voice and dropped on one knee

beside the little boy. 'What on earth is *he* doing at Ardroy? I thought he never came here now. You are sure it was Doctor Cameron, Donald – and not Mr MacPhair of Lochdornie?'

'No, I know it was Doctor Cameron. He stayed in our house first; he came because – because Keithie was ill.' His head went down for a second. 'He made him well again. The other doctor from Maryburgh came too. Then Doctor Cameron went up to stay with Angus MacMartin. And if you please I must go to Slochd nan Eun at once.'

But his young uncle, though he had risen to his feet again, was still blocking the path and staring down at him, and saying as though he were speaking to himself, 'Then it was *he* who is just gone away from Slochd nan Eun with Angus, only they were so discreet they'd not name him to me! – No, my little hero, there's no need for you to go any farther. I have just come from Angus's cottage myself, and they told me the gentleman was gone some time since, because of the soldiers down at the house. And, by the way, are the soldiers still there?'

'Yes, and some of them have taken Father away to Fort William. They ran after him – he got out of a window – and they caught him and thought at first he was Doctor Cameron. Father wanted them to think that,' explained Donald with a sort of vicarious pride.

Hector Grant's brow grew black under the bandage. '*Mon Dieu, mon Dieu, quel malheur!* – I must see your mother, Donald. Go back, *laochain*, and try to get her to come up to me here by the loch. I'll take you a part of the way.'

'You are sure, Uncle Hector,' asked Donald anxiously, 'that Doctor Cameron is gone away?'

'Good child!' said Uncle Hector appreciatively. 'Yes, *foi de gentilhomme*, Donald, he is gone. There is no need for you to continue this nocturnal adventure. And I fancy that your mother will forgive me a good deal for putting a stop to it. Come along.'

Most willingly did Donald's hand slide into that of his uncle. If one can be quit of a rather terrifying enterprise with honour … It did not seem nearly so dark now, and the water-horse had gone back into the land of bedtime stories. But there was still

411

an obstacle to his protector's plan of which he must inform him.

'I don't think, Uncle Hector,' he said doubtfully, as they began to move away, 'that the soldiers will let Mother come out to see you. Nobody was to leave the house, they said. They did not see me come out. But perhaps they would let you go in?'

Uncle Hector stopped. 'They'll let me in fast enough, I warrant – but would they let me come out again? ... Perhaps after all I had better come no nearer. Can you go back from here alone, Donald – but indeed I see you can, since you have such a stout heart.' (The heart in question fell a little at this flattering deduction.) 'By the way, you say Keithie is better – is he quite recovered?'

'Keithie? He is out of bed today. Indeed,' said Keithie's senior rather scornfully, ' 'tis a pity he is, for he came downstairs by his lane when the soldiers were here and did a very silly thing.' And he explained in what Keithie's foolishness had consisted. 'So 'twas he that spoilt Father's fine plan ... which I knew all about!'

' "Fine plan" – I wonder what your mother thought of it?' once more commented Hector Grant half to himself. 'Well, Donald, give her a kiss for me, and tell her that I will contrive somehow to see her, when the soldiers have gone. Meanwhile I think I'll return to the safer hospitality of Meall Achadh. Now run home – she'll be anxious about you.'

He stooped and kissed the self-appointed messenger, and gave him an encouraging pat.

'Good night, Uncle Hector,' said Donald politely. 'I will tell Mother.' And he set off at a trot which soon carried him out of sight in the dusk.

'And now, what am I going to do?' asked Lieutenant Hector Grant in French of his surroundings. Something croaked in the rushes of Loch na h-Iolaire. *'Tu dis?'* he inquired, turning his head. 'Nay, jesting apart, this is a pretty coil that I have set on foot!'

Chapter 7

A GREAT MANY LIES

1

IT is undoubtedly easier to invite durance than to get free of it again. So Ewen found after his interview next day with old Lieutenant-Governor Leighton, now in command at Fort William, who was rather querulous, declaring with an injured air that, from what he had been told about Mr Cameron of Ardroy, he should not have expected such conduct from him. 'However,' he finished pessimistically, 'disloyalty that is bred in the bone will always out, I suppose; and once a Cameron always a Cameron.'

Since Ewen's captor and accuser, Captain Jackson, was still absent, the brief interview produced little of value either to Colonel Leighton or himself, and Ardroy spent a good deal of that Sunday pacing round and round his bare though by no means uncomfortable place of confinement, wishing fervently that he knew whether Archie had got away in safety. Never, never, if any ill befell him, would he forgive himself for having brought him to the house. The next day Colonel Leighton had him in for examination again, chiefly in order to confront him with Captain Jackson, now returned empty-handed from his raid, and it was Ewen's late visitor who took the more prominent part in the proceedings, either questioning the prisoner himself or prompting his elderly superior in a quite obvious manner. The reason for this procedure Ewen guessed to lie in the fact that Leighton was a newcomer at Fort William, having succeeded only a few months ago the astute Colonel Crauford, an adept at dealing with Highland difficulties, and one on whom Captain Jackson seemed to be desirous of modelling himself, if not his Colonel.

Ewen steadily denied having had any doubtful person in his house, 'Mr Sinclair', whose presence he could not entirely

413

explain away, being, as he had already stated, a friend on a visit, which visit had ended the day before the arrival of the military. He stuck to his story that when he himself had seen the soldiers approaching his courage had failed him, and he had dropped from a window and run from them.

'If that is so, Mr Cameron,' said the Lieutenant-Governor (echoing Captain Jackson), 'then you must either have had a guilty conscience or you were playing the decoy. And I suspect that it was the latter, since you do not look the sort of man who would get out of a window at the mere approach of danger.'

Ardroy supposed that this was a species of compliment. But he was feeling bored and rather disheartened at having landed himself in a captivity which promised to be longer than he had anticipated. He would not indeed regret it, he told himself, if he had saved Archie, but of that he was not perfectly sure, for though Captain Jackson had failed to capture him, yet a party from one of the scattered military posts might have done so, once the alarm was given. He looked over the heads of the two officers out of the window, whence he could get a glimpse of the waters of Loch Linnhe, shining and moving in the sun. The thought of being shut up in Fort William for an indefinite period was becoming increasingly distasteful. But it was ridiculous to suppose that they had grounds for keeping him more than a few days!

So he declared that appearances were deceitful, and again pointed out his exemplary behaviour since his return to Scotland. He desired no more, he said, than to go on living quietly upon his land. It was no doubt very tame and unheroic thus to plead for release, but what was the use of remaining confined here if he could avoid it? And for a while after that he sat there – having been provided with a chair – hardly listening to Colonel Leighton as he prosed away, with occasional interruptions from his subordinate, but wondering what Alison was doing at this moment, and whether Keithie were any the worse for his fateful excursion downstairs; and scarcely noticing that the Colonel had ceased another of his homilies about disloyalty to listen to a young officer who had come in with some message

– until his own name occurring in the communication drew his wandering attention.

The Colonel had become quite alert. 'Bring him up here at once,' he said to the newcomer, and, turning to the listless prisoner, added, 'Mr Cameron, here's a gentleman just come and given himself up to save you, so he says, from further molestation on his behalf.'

He had Ewen's attention now! For one horrible moment Ardroy felt quite sick. He had the wild half-thought that Archie ... but no, Archie was incapable of so wrong and misguided an action as throwing away his liberty and wrecking his mission merely to save him from imprisonment.

Then through the open door came the young officer again, and after him, with a bandage about his head and a smile upon his lips, Hector.

Ewen suppressed a gasp, but the colour which had left it came back to his face. He got up from his chair astounded, and not best pleased at this crazy deed. Hector Grant did not seem to find *his* situation dull; he had about him an air which it would have been unkind, though possible, to call a swagger; which air, however, dropped from him a little at the sight of his brother-in-law, in whose presence he had evidently not expected so soon to find himself. He glanced across at him, with a slightly deprecatory lift of the eyebrows, while Ardroy feared that he must be looking, as he felt, rather blank. It was well-meaning of the lad, but how could it possibly help matters?

Colonel Leighton, however, glanced hopefully at the voluntary captive. 'Well, sir, and so you have come to give yourself up. On what grounds, may I ask.'

'Because,' Hector answered him easily, 'I heard that my brother-in-law, Mr Cameron of Ardroy here present, had been arrested on the charge of having entertained a suspicious stranger at his house. Now as I was myself that supposed stranger –'

'Ah,' interrupted Colonel Leighton, shaking his head sagely, 'I knew I was right in my conviction that Mr Cameron was lying when he asserted that he had sheltered nobody! I knew that no one of his name was to be trusted.'

'He was not "sheltering" me, sir,' replied Hector coolly. 'And therefore I have come of my own free will to show you how baseless are your suspicions of him. For if a man cannot have his wife's brother to visit him without being haled off to prison –'

' "His wife's brother". Who are you, then? You have not yet told us,' remarked Captain Jackson.

'Lieutenant Hector Grant, of the régiment d'Albanie in the service of His Most Christian Majesty the King of France.'

'You have papers to prove that?'

'Not on me.'

'And why not?' asked the other soldier.

'Why should I carry my commission with me when I come to pay a private visit to my sister?' asked Hector. (Evidently thought Ewen, he was not going to admit the theft of any of his papers, though he himself suspected that the young man did, despite his denial, carry his commission with him. He wondered, and was sure that Hector was wondering too, whether the missing documents were not all the time in Colonel Leighton's hands.)

'And that was all your business in Scotland – to visit your sister?'

'Is that not sufficient?' asked the affectionate brother. 'I had not seen Lady Ardroy for a matter of two years, and she is my only near relative. After I had left the house I heard, as I say, that my presence (Heaven knows why) had thrown suspicion upon Mr Cameron, and I hastened –'

But here Captain Jackson interrupted him. 'If it was upon your behalf, Mr Grant, that Mr Cameron found it necessary to run so far and to tell so many lies on Saturday, then he must be greatly mortified at seeing you here now. I doubt if it was for you that he went through all that. But if, on the other hand, you *were* the cause of his performances, then your visit cannot have been so innocuous as you pretend.'

Hector was seen to frown. This officer was too sharp. He had outlined a nasty dilemma, and the young Highlander hardly knew upon which of its horns to impale himself and Ewen.

The Colonel now turned heavily upon Ardroy.

'*Is* this young man your brother-in-law, Mr Cameron?'

'Certainly he is, sir.'

'And he did stay at your house upon a visit?'

Awkward to answer, that, considering the nature of Hector's 'stay' and its exceeding brevity. Hector himself prudently looked out of a window. 'Yes, he did pay me a visit.'

'And when did he arrive?'

Ewen decided that on the whole truth was best. 'Last Monday evening.'

'I should be glad to know for what purpose he came.'

'You have heard, sir. He is, I repeat, my wife's brother.'

'But that fact, Mr Cameron,' said Colonel Leighton weightily, 'does not render him immune from suspicion, especially when one considers his profession. He is a Jacobite, or he would not be in the service of the King of France.'

'You know quite well, sir,' countered Ewen, 'that the King of France has by treaty abandoned the Jacobite cause.'

'*Was* it on Mr Grant's account that you behaved as you did on Saturday?' pressed the Colonel.

But Ewen replying that he did not feel himself bound to answer that question, the commanding officer turned to Hector again. 'On what day, Mr Grant, did you terminate your visit to Mr Cameron?'

'On the day that your men invaded his house – Saturday,' answered Hector, driven to this unfortunate statement by a desire to give colour to Ewen's 'performances' on that day.

'But Mr Cameron has just told us that "Mr Sinclair" left the previous day – Friday,' put in Captain Jackson quickly, and Hector bit his lip. Obviously, it had a very awkward side, this ignorance of what Ewen had already committed himself to.

Captain Jackson permitted himself a smile. 'At any rate, you were at Ardroy on Thursday, and saw Doctor Kincaid when he went to visit the sick child.'

This Hector was uncertain whether to deny or avow. He therefore said nothing.

'But since you are trying to make us believe that you are the mysterious "Mr Sinclair" from Caithness who was treating him,' pursued Captain Jackson, 'you must have seen Doctor Kincaid.'

'I see no reason why I should not have done what I could for my own nephew,' answered Hector, doubling off on a new track.

'Quite so,' agreed Captain Jackson. 'Then, since your visit was purely of a domestic character, one may well ask why Mr Cameron was at such pains on that occasion to pass you off, not as a relation, but as a friend from the North? ... And why were you then so much older, a man in the forties, instead of in the twenties, as you are today?'

'Was there so much difference in my appearance?' queried Hector innocently. 'I was fatigued; I had been sitting up all night with the sick child.'

'Pshaw – we are wasting time!' declared Captain Jackson. 'This is not "Mr Sinclair"!' And the Colonel echoed him with dignity. 'No, certainly not.'

'Is not Doctor Kincaid in the fort this morning, sir?' asked the Captain, leaning towards him.

'I believe he is. Go and request him to come here at once, if you please, Mr Burton,' said the Colonel to the subaltern who had brought Hector in. 'And then we shall settle this question once for all.'

By this time Ewen had resumed his seat. Hector, his hands behind his back, appeared to be whistling a soundless air between his teeth. It was impossible to say whether he were regretting his fruitless effort – for plainly it was going to be fruitless – but at all events he was showing a good front to the enemy.

Doctor Kincaid hurried in, with his usual air of being very busy. 'You sent for me, Colonel?'

'Yes, Doctor, if you please. Have you seen this young man before – not Mr Cameron of Ardroy here, but the other.'

'Perhaps Doctor Kincaid does not greatly care to look at me,' suggested Ewen.

The doctor threw him a glance. 'I had ma duty to do, Ardroy.' Then he looked, as desired, at the younger prisoner. 'Losh, I should think I had seen him before! God's name, young man,

418

you're gey hard in the heid! 'Tis the lad I found half-doited on Loch Treig side Tuesday nicht syne wi' a dunt in it of which yon's the sign!' He pointed to the bandage.

'Tuesday night, you say, Doctor?' asked Captain Jackson.

'Aye, Tuesday nicht, I mind well it was. I was away up Loch Treig the day to auld MacInnes there.'

Captain Jackson turned on Hector. 'Perhaps, Mr Grant,' he suggested, 'you were light-headed from this blow when you thought you were at Ardroy till Saturday.'

'And what's to prevent me having been carried there at my brother-in-law's orders?' queried Hector.

' 'Tis true that Ardroy spoke of doing that,' admitted Doctor Kincaid. 'He speired after the young man the day I was at his hoose. But yon was the Thursday.'

'Mr Cameron says that Mr Grant came to Ardroy on the Monday, and Mr Grant himself states that he stayed there until Saturday. Yet on Tuesday, Doctor, you find him twenty miles away with a broken head. And he has the effrontery to pretend that he was the "Mr Sinclair" whom you saw in the sick child's room at Ardroy on the Thursday!'

'Set him up!' exclaimed the doctor scornfully. 'The man I saw then, as I've told you, Colonel, was over forty, a tall, comely man, and fair-complexioned to boot. And I told you who that man was, in my opeenion – Doctor Erchibald Cameron, the Jacobite, himself – and for this callant to seek to pretend to me that *he* was yon "Sinclair" is fair flying in the face of such wits as Providence has gien me. Ye'd better keep him here for treatment of his ain!' And on that, scarce waiting for dismissal, Doctor Kincaid took himself off again.

'Doctor Kincaid's advice is sound, don't you think, Colonel?' observed Captain Jackson with some malice. 'And as the roads do not seem over safe for this young man, egad, 'twere best to keep him off them for a while.'

'Your fine redcoats don't seem able to make 'em safe, certainly,' retorted Mr Grant.

'Come, come,' said Colonel Leighton impatiently, 'we've had enough of bandying words. One thing is quite plain: Mr Cameron and his kinsman here are both in collusion to shield someone else, and that person has probably been correctly named by Doctor Kincaid. Have Mr Cameron taken back. You can put Mr Grant in the same room with him, for the present at any rate.'

2

'My dear Hector!' began Ardroy, half-laughing, half-sighing, when the door of that locality was shut on them.

'Oh, I know what you are going to say, Ewen!' Hector did not let him say it in consequence. 'Yes, I've done no good – I may even have done harm – but I could not stay a free man when I had brought all this trouble upon you ... as I have done – don't shake your head! But I had a faint hope that I could gull them into some sort of an exchange. At any rate, I have brought you all kinds of messages from Alison.'

'You saw her? How is Keithie? And – most important of all – did Archie get safely away?'

' 'Tis "Yes" to all of your questions. I did see Alison; Keithie, I understand, is as well as ever he was – and Doctor Cameron was clear away from the MacMartins before I myself arrived there on Saturday evening. Nor has he been captured since, or one would have heard it in the neighbourhood.' Here Hector looked at the windows. 'I wonder how much filing those bars would need?'

Ewen could not help laughing. 'You go too fast, Eachainn! I hope shortly to be invited to walk out of the door in the ordinary way, and against you – since I do not believe that they have your stolen papers – they can prove nothing. It was self-sacrificing of you in the extreme to come here and give yourself up, but my arrest, I feel sure, was due in the first instance to Doctor Kincaid's sense of duty, of which he made mention just now, and not to any information about Doctor Cameron rifled from your pockets.'

His hand at his chin, Hector looked at him. 'I wish I could believe that. Yet it is my doing, Ewen, for this reason: if I had not been so damnably ill-tempered at Ardroy the other evening I'd not have come upon that spy where I did next day, and have lost my papers; my loss was the direct cause of your going to warn Lochdornie and hence meeting Doctor Cameron in his stead; and if you not met him he could not have come back to Ardroy with you, and have been seen by that curst interfering physician of yours. You see I know all about that from Alison, with whom I contrived a meeting through your little hero of a son; I came upon him trotting up to Slochd nan Eun in the dark to carry a warning.'

'*Donald* went up to Slochd nan Eun! Did Alison choose *him* as the messenger?'

'Not a bit of it. 'Twas his own notion, stout little fellow. I found him by the loch and sent him back, since I knew that whoever was sheltering with Angus MacMartin was already gone. It was from Donald that I first learnt who it was. He's a brave child, Ewen, and I congratulate you on giving me such a nephew!'

And yet, thought Ewen all at once, it is really Donald who is the cause of everything; if he had not pushed Keith into the loch I should never have ridden for Doctor Kincaid and come upon Hector ... Nay, it goes further back: if Keithie had not first thrown in that treasure of Donald's ... Perhaps in justice I ought to blame my cousin Ian for giving it to him!

Hector meanwhile was looking round their joint prison. The room stood at the corner of the block of buildings in the fort nearest to the loch, and was actually blessed with a window in each of its outer walls. It was therefore unusually light and airy, and had a view across and down Loch Linnhe. In some ways, though it was less lofty, it had already reminded Ewen of the tower room at Fort Augustus where he had once gone through such mental anguish.

'This place might be worse,' now pronounced the newcomer. 'I doubt this room was not originally intended to keep prisoners in.' Going to one of the windows he shook the bars. 'Not very far to the ground, I should suppose, but there seems to be a considerable drop afterwards down that bastion wall on the loch side.'

But Ewen, scarcely heeding, was murmuring that he ought never to have brought Doctor Cameron to Ardroy.

Hector turned round from his investigations. 'Yet he's clear away now, Ewen, that's certain.'

'But the authorities must guess that he is in Scotland.'

' 'Tis no more than a guess; they do not know it. Even from that unlucky letter of mine I do not think they could be sure of it.'

'Hector, what *was* in that letter?' asked his fellow-captive. 'And why were you carrying it? On someone else's account, I suppose? It was very unfortunate that you were charged with it.'

Lieutenant Grant got rather red. He stuffed his hands into his breeches pockets and studied the floor for a moment. Then he lifted his head and said with an air of resignation, 'I may as well make a clean breast of it. Ever since my mishap I have been wondering how I could have been so misguided, but I had the best intentions, Ewen, as you'll hear. I wrote the letter myself.'

'Wrote it yourself! and carried it on you! To whom was it then?'

'To Cluny Macpherson.'

'But you were on your way to Cluny Macpherson – or so I understood!'

'Yes, I was. But you know, Ewen, how jealously the secret of his hiding-place in Badenoch is kept, and how devilish hard it is to come at him, even when one is accredited as a friend. I had no doubt but that from the information I had been given I should meet with some of his clan, but whether they would consent to guide me to his lair on Ben Alder was quite another matter. So, thinking over the problem that morning, it occurred to me that I would write him a short letter, in case I found diffi-culty in gaining access to his person. You will ask me why in Heaven's name I wrote it beforehand and carried it on me, but it was really my caution, Ewen, that was my undoing. I saw that it would not be wise to write it in a shape which any chance per-son could read, and that I must turn most of it into cipher. But I could not write my letter and then turn portions of it into cipher – a laborious process, as you know – sitting on a tussock of heather in a wind on Ben Alder, with an impatient gillie of Cluny's gibbering Erse at me. So I wrote down my information as shortly as I could and turned it into cipher before setting out, in order to have it ready to hand over should need arise. And I still believe that the cipher may defy reading, though when you came upon me by Loch Treig, knowing that the letter was gone from me, with the Doctor's and Lochdornie's names in it, I –' He made one of his half-French gestures.

'Yes,' said Ewen meditatively, 'as things turned out, your notion was not a fortunate one. Was the letter directed to Cluny?'

'No; that foolishness at least I did not commit, since I meant to give it, if at all, straight into the hands of one of his men.'

'That's something, certainly. And if the man who took it was a spy – and not an ordinary robber, which is always possible – I should say the letter had been sent straight to Edinburgh or to London.'

'Why not to the old fellow here? 'Tis true that if he had it he could not read the cipher, but that Captain Jackson might.'

'I think the letter was never brought here, because, if it had been, even though neither of them could read a word of it, they would know that it had been taken from you on Tuesday, and would hardly have wasted their time in allowing you to pretend that you were at Ardroy until Saturday, nor have sent for Doctor Kincaid to testify that you were not the "Mr Sinclair" whom he saw there, worse luck, on Thursday.'

'Unless they wished to give me more rope to hang myself in,' commented Hector, with a slight access of gloom. 'But as to that,' he added after a moment, more cheerfully, 'I'm more like to be shot as a deserter by the French than hanged as a conspirator by the English.'

'You should have thought of that before coming here and giving yourself up!' exclaimed Ewen. 'Are you serious, Hector?'

'No,' confessed Lieutenant Grant with a grin. 'Lord Ogilvie will see to it that he does not lose one of his best officers in that manner. I'll report before my leave's up, never fear. By the way, I *was* carrying my commission on me, as a safeguard, though I denied it; and the scoundrel who took my papers has that too, a bad meeting to him!'

'I thought you were lying to those officers just now,' observed Ardroy. 'But again, had your commission been brought here, I am sure that Captain Jackson could never have resisted the temptation of clapping it down in front of you when you denied that you had it.'

'I wonder,' remarked Hector rather irrelevantly, 'who has done the more lying of late, you or I? Nay, you, past a doubt, for you have had vastly more opportunity. And you don't enjoy it, more's the pity!'

Chapter 8

ON CHRISTMAS NIGHT

1

No more scope for lying, however, was to be afforded to either of the captives, nor were they invited to walk out of Fort William, though for a week, ten days, a fortnight, this was their waking hope every morning. But as this perennial plant daily bloomed and faded, Ewen began to think that Colonel Leighton was not, perhaps, so happy an exchange as some had fancied for the astute but determined Crauford, that he was keeping them there because he knew that he was incompetent and wanted to disguise the fact by a show of severity. Of course it was quite possible that he was only obeying orders from Edinburgh, or, as time went on, from London, but that they could not find out. 'At any rate,' declared Hector, 'he is stupid; *bête comme une oie*, a man one cannot reason with. I saw that at once.'

Stupid or clever, Colonel Leighton was the master of the situation. As the October days crawled by, shortening a little, so that one saw the glow from the sunset – when there was one – fall ever a little less far round on the wall, Lieutenant Grant's temper grew shorter also. What right had Colonel Leighton to keep him imprisoned here, an officer of a foreign power against whom he had no producible evidence? He kept sending messages to that effect, and getting the invariable reply that since the Lieutenant-Governor had only his word that he possessed this status, Mr Grant must produce his commission or something equivalent if he hoped to be believed. Long ago it had become plain that poor Hector's chivalrous attempt at a bargain was worse than useless, for his surrendering himself had not released his brother-in-law; its only effect was to have introduced another inmate into the cage, and one who was as restless as any squirrel.

November set in, cold and very windy, and with it came a sinister reminder that there are even worse fates than bondage. There lay in Fort William a prisoner, brought thither from Inveraray, tied on a horse, at the beginning of October, for whom the sands of captivity were running out. On the seventh of November, a day of tempest, an armed procession set out down the side of Loch Linnhe, and in the midst was James Stewart of Acharn. Next morning, in the same high wind, he was taken across Loch Leven and hanged at Ballachulish in Appin, the scene of the murder of Campbell of Glenure, meeting his unjust fate with composure and with the psalm destined ever after to be associated in that country with his name, the thirty-fifth. Presumably to impress them with the wisdom of submissive conduct, the two imprisoned Jacobites were given a full account of the proceedings, and Ewen, with his mother's Stewart blood on fire, chalked up one more count in the score against the Campbells.

November was to have seen that attempt on the liberty of George II over which Ewen and his brother-in-law had come to loggerheads that night at Ardroy. But no news of any such attempt filtered through to the captives. Ewen was very glad, and Hector, presumably, sorry. It was a subject not mentioned between them, although the breach which it had made was healed.

And so another five or six weeks trailed by. James Stewart's chain-encircled body, still guarded by soldiers, rattled and froze on the hillock by Ballachulish ferry, and Lieutenant Hector Grant of the régiment d'Albanie by this time much more nearly resembled a panther than a squirrel. He could think or talk of nothing but escape, and every day his denunciations of Ewen for his passivity became more fervid. He told him among other things that he was like a cow which stays in a byre merely because the farmer has put it there. In vain Ewen pointed out the small advantages to be reaped by escape, at least in his own case, since he could not possibly return to Ardroy; he would be rearrested at once. As Hector knew, he had twice written to a lawyer in Edinburgh to take up his case. 'Yes, but what answer have you had?' Hector would reply. 'You are over trusting,

Mac 'ic Ailein; that old Leighton of the devil never forwards your letters, 'tis clear. He probably uses them as curlpapers for his wig.' Yet when Ewen offered his assistance in carrying out the very unpromising plans for his own escape with which Hector constantly dallied, the young man would not hear of it, alleging that he had got Ardroy into sufficient trouble already.

But at last Ewen's own patience, not natural to him, but painfully acquired in the difficult years since his return from exile, was completely exhausted. For one thing, it fretted him more with every day that dawned that he knew nothing of Archie's doings, nor had he even learnt whence that aid was to come on which Doctor Cameron was building. So, one day about mid-December, when he and Hector had been discussing the various unsatisfactory plans for escape which the latter had concocted, he considerably startled that youth by saying, 'Let us fix on Christmas Day, then, for the garrison will be more or less drunk, and we may have some small chance of walking out in the manner you propose.' (For the great obstacle to evasion in the orthodox way, by sawing through the bars of a window and letting themselves down, was the by now established impossibility of procuring a file or anything like it.)

Hector leaped up from his chair. '*Enfin!* You mean it, Ewen – you are at last converted? *Dieu soit loué!* And you suggest Christmas Day. You do not think that Hogmanay would be better?'

'No, for the garrison is English. It is on the evening of Christmas Day that we must look for the effect of their potations.'

'Christmas Day be it, then! Now we can plan to better purpose!'

2

During those weary weeks Ewen had written as often as he was allowed to his wife, and had received replies from her, all correspondence of course passing through the hands of the authorities at Fort William, so that only personal and domestic news could be conveyed. But Alison had all along been determined to come and visit him, should his release be delayed, and wrote a few days after this that she believed she should succeed in getting permission to do so before Christmas.

'Faith, if she do not come before, 'twill be of little use, or so I hope, coming after,' declared her brother. 'Indeed, if one wished to throw dust in the eyes of that Leighton creature, it might have been well had she said that she was coming at the New Year.'

'But I, at least, desire to be here when she comes,' objected Ewen. In his heart of hearts he thought that the New Year would probably find them still in Fort William, since the success of their plan for Christmas Day depended upon so many factors out of their control. But he did not wish to dash Hector's optimism, and proceeded with his occupation of making a sketch map of Loch Linnhe and its neighbourhood from memory on a clean pocket-handkerchief, though in truth pencil and linen combined but ill for cartography.

And four days before Christmas Alison came. A message from the Lieutenant-Governor had previously apprised the captives of the event, and they trimmed each other's hair and shaved with great particularity. Lady Ardroy had written that she would bring them some Christmas fare; this, the two agreed, would prove a most useful viaticum for the subsequent journey.

She brought something else, more unexpected. The young and courteous officer who escorted her up himself carried the big basket of provisions, for, to the captives' amazement, Alison's two hands were otherwise engaged. One held the small hand of Keith, so wrapped about in furs that he looked a mere fluffy ball, the other rested on Donald's shoulder. The officer deposited the basket on the table and swiftly closed the door on the family reunion – but not before Alison was in her husband's arms. It was over three months since she had seen him marched away down the avenue at Ardroy.

And then, while Hector and his sister embraced, Ewen could attend to the claims of his offspring. 'Keithie, you look for all the world like a fat little bear!' he exclaimed, catching him up, to find him as smooth cheeked, as long lashed, as satisfying to feel in one's arms as ever. Nor was the small person at all abashed by his surroundings, remarking that he had seen a great many red gentlemen downstairs, and why was Father living with them? He would prefer him to come home. The fairies had restored his 'deers' unharmed, and he now had in addition a *damh-feidh* with horns, which he had put in the large, large basket so that Father could see it. Meanwhile Donald, who appeared grown, and did seem a trifle overawed by the place in which he found himself, rather shyly told him that Angus had recovered the claymore hilt from the Loch of the Eagle; and he too asked, not so cheerfully as Keith, even reproachfully, why his father did not return, as Mother had said he would.

But it was the prisoners who had most questions to put. Chief among Ewen's was, what had become of Doctor Cameron? To his disappointment, Alison knew nothing of his movements, and less still, as discreet inquiry on her husband's part elicited, of what success or failure he had met with in his mission. It was said that he had left the West altogether, owing to the persistent searches made for him.

'Then it is well known to the English that he is in the Highlands,' said Ewen despondently, 'and it is my fault!'

'No,' said Alison with decision, 'the knowledge seems too widespread for that. But enough of Doctor Archibald for the moment; I have to speak of something which concerns you both more nearly at this time – and it would be better to speak French, because of the children,' she added, plunging into that tongue, which they all three spoke with ease.

And, beckoning them close to her Lady Ardroy, to their no small astonishment, unfolded a plan of escape which it seemed had been devised in conjunction with young Ian Stewart of Invernacree, her husband's cousin, and the rest of his Stewart kin in Appin. If he and Hector could succeed in getting out of the fort, and would be on the shore of Loch Linnhe at a given spot and hour on the night of Christmas Day –

'*What* night?' exclaimed both her hearers together.

Alison looked a little startled. 'We had thought of Christmas night for it, because the garrison – What are you both laughing at?'

At that Hector laughed the more, and Ewen seized and kissed her.

'Because, *mo chridhe*, you or Ian must have the two sights, I think. That is precisely the night that Hector and I were already favouring, and for exactly the same reason. Go on!'

Flushed and eager, Alison went on. Under the fort a boat would be waiting, manned by Stewarts; this, with all possible speed would convey them down Loch Linnhe to Invernacree in Appin, where old Alexander Stewart, Ewen's maternal uncle, proposed that the fugitives should remain hid for a while. Some twenty miles would then lie between them and Fort William, while in any case the pursuit would probably be made in the first instance towards Ardroy.

To all the first part of the plan Ewen agreed without demur. The presence of a boat waiting for them would solve their greatest difficulty, how to leave the neighbourhood of the fort without taking the most easily traced way therefrom, by land. For the previous part of the programme, the actual breaking out of their prison, they must as before rely upon themselves – and upon the effects of the garrison's Christmas celebrations.

But to taking refuge with his uncle and cousin Ewen would not agree. 'If I succeed in getting free, darling, it's more than enough that I shall owe them (Hector must please himself; but he behoves to make haste to rejoin his regiment). But I am not going to risk bringing trouble on folk who are now at peace, particularly after what took place in Appin last spring, for which an Appin man has paid so dearly. My plan is to reach Edinburgh somehow, and there secure the legal aid for which I have been vainly trying by letter. And though there is not over-much chance of justice for a Jacobite, I would yet make an effort after it, and a free man has a better chance of this than a prisoner. The English know the justice of my case, or they would not have denied me the services of an advocate. After all, if all goes well, I shall be able to return to you and the bairns in quiet ... and be ready for the call to arms when it comes,' he added internally, for not even to Alison had he revealed what Archibald Cameron had told him.

After this Alison set the children to unpack the basket and to range its contents on the table. 'I must keep them occupied at a distance for a few moments,' she explained, as she came back. 'Now, first for your escape from this room. Since there are bars to your windows ... Hold out a hand, one of you!'

'Not ... a file!' exclaimed Hector, almost snatching from his sister the little key to freedom. 'Oh, you angel from heaven!'

Alison smiled. ''Twas Ian Stewart thought of that. There's something further. You may be wondering why I have not taken off my cloak all this while. If I had, you would certainly be thinking I had lost my figure.' And, smiling, she suddenly held her mantle wide.

'Faith, no,' admitted Hector, 'that's not the jimp waist I've been accustomed to see in you, my sister.'

'Wait, and you shall know the reason for it ... Look out of the window, the two of you, until I bid you turn.'

The two men obeyed. From the table came the chatter of the children, very busy over the basket. 'My want to see what's in that little pot!' 'Keithie, you'll drop that if you are not more careful; oh, here's another cheese!'

'Now,' said Alison's voice, 'lift up my cloak.'

Husband and brother turned round, and, deeply puzzled, each raised a side of it. In her arms Lady Ardroy held, all huddled together, the coils of a long, thin, strong rope.

'Take it – hide it quickly ... don't let the weans see it; Keithie might go talking of it before the soldiers below. I thought you might find it of service.'

Hector flung his arms about her. 'Of service! 'Tis what I have been praying for every day. Alison, you are a sister in ten thousand! Hide it under the mattress, Ewen, until we have an opportunity to dispose of it as this heroine has done – for our room might be searched if they grew suspicious. And, *ma foi*, if our jailers notice anything amiss with our figures they will but think we have grown fat upon your Christmas fare, darling!'

'Keithie help you make yours bed, Father?' asked the voice of one anxious to be helpful, as Ewen hastily carried out Hector's first suggestion; and the voice's owner trotted over to him and lifted an inquiring gaze. 'But why are you doing that now?'

Alison whisked him away. ' 'Tis extraordinary,' she remarked in French, 'how children always see what they should not!'

Nevertheless, some half-hour later, two men, each winding half a rope round their bodies beneath their clothes, would have given a good deal had those indiscreet and innocent eyes still been upon them. The room seemed so empty now; only among the provisions on the table stood, very stiffly, Keithie's ridiculous new wooden stag, with one of its birch-twig horns hanging down broken, Keithie at the last having left the animal there for his father's consolation. The recipient, however, found now that it came nearer than he liked to unmanning him.

3

One may arrange an escape with due regard for sheltering darkness and the festive preoccupation of one's jailers, may have accomplices in readiness, may join them undiscovered and get a certain distance away from one's prison – only to find that Nature is not in a mood to lend her assistance, that she has, in fact, definitely resolved to hinder one's flight. And in the Highlands at midwinter this lack of cooperation on her part may lead to serious consequences.

In other words, young Ian Stewart's boat, with its four rowers, was having an increasingly rough and toilsome journey down Loch Linnhe this Christmas night. The party had waited undetected in the boat on the upper reach of the loch near the fort, the same luck had attended their reception of the two fugitives, on whose descent from their window and down the counterscarp to the shore fortune had also smiled, and, amid mutual congratulations, rescuers and rescued had started on the twenty miles' homeward pull. The wind, as they knew, was dead against them, hence they could not help themselves by a sail, and the tide would shortly be against them also, but these were circumstances which had for some time been anticipated. What, however, was dismaying, though not at all beyond precedent on Loch Linnhe, was the rapidity with which this contrary wind was rising in strength, and the degree to which it was lashing up the waters of the loch to anger.

The boat itself was heavy and solid, and there was little risk of its being swamped, though now and again a wave would fling a scatter of spray over the bows. The real danger lay in the fact that its progress was being so retarded that dawn, even early day, might be upon them before they had covered nearly as much distance from Fort William as was desirable, seeing that with daylight they could be observed and reported upon from the shore. At the helm Ian Stewart, more and more uneasy, watched the pallid light spreading in the east, though the mist leant low upon the mountains of Ardgour to their right. In front, about a mile away, a single light in some small cottage on the shore indicated the Narrows, where the long spit of land from the Ardgour side pushed out till, in that one place, Loch Linnhe was only a quarter of a mile across instead of a mile and a quarter. Young Invernacree looked at the set faces of his men as they tugged at the oars, and turned to his cousin beside him.

'I had hoped to be through the Narrows before the tide made there, but I fear it is too late. You know with what force the flood rushes up through them at first, and with this wind and the men so spent I doubt we shall be able to pass for a while.'

Ewen nodded; he was beginning to have the same doubt. 'Then let us pull in near the Ardgour shore, out of the tide rip, until the first force of it is over. Shall I relieve one of your gillies? Ay, you'd best let me – look there!'

For the bow rower at that very moment was showing signs of collapsing over his oar. Before Ian Stewart could prevent the substitution, even had he wished, Ewen was clambering carefully forward past the other oarsmen in the rocking craft, all unconscious on what a journey that change of place was to launch him.

He got the exhausted rower off the thwart to the bottom of the boat, and seized the oar, finding himself glad to handle it after three months of enforced inaction. Slowly but rather more steadily now the boat drew near to comparative shelter, and away from the oncoming flood racing through the neck of the Narrows. Nevertheless, the water was still far from smooth, for gusts of wind came tearing over the low-lying point of the spit. Had they ceased rowing they would have been blown back, or, worse still, got broadside on to the wind. 'We had much better pull right in to land,' thought Ewen, 'lest another man should collapse.' And the thought had not long formulated itself before the leader of the expedition came to the same conclusion, and, after vainly trying to shout it to his cousin, sent down by word of mouth from man to man the information that he was going to make straight for the shore near the cottage and beach the boat there.

Ewen nodded his head vigorously to show his approval, and, since he was the bow oar and must jump ashore with the rope, reached about behind him with one hand until he found it, realizing as he did so that in such rough weather it would be no easy matter to perform this operation neatly. Preoccupied with seizing the right moment, and doubting whether, in the bluster of wind and waves, Ian could from the stern apprize him of this, he pulled on with the rest, glancing now and then over his shoulder to see how near they were getting to the dim grey beach with its line of foam. And the moment had come, for there was Ian waving his arm and shouting something which he could not catch, Hector also.

Rapidly shipping his oar, Ewen clutched the rope and jumped over the gunwale into cold and yeasty water above his knees, which sucked heavily at him as he waded hastily into shallower, trailing the rope with him. Braced for the strain, he was hauling in the slack of this when that – or rather those – fell upon him of which his kinsman's shout had been intended to warn him. Two men in great coats, appearing (so it seemed to him) from nowhere, had dashed into the water with offers of help. Bewildered at first, Ewen was beginning to thank them, when, to his extreme dismay, he caught the gleam of scarlet under their coats. 'No, no!' he shouted almost unconsciously, his one thought being that the whole boatload were delivering themselves into an ambush, for somehow he was aware that the door of the lighted cottage behind him had opened and was emitting more soldiers. Apart from Hector recaptured, he had a vision of his cousin Ian involved in very serious trouble. And obviously Ian's gillies had the same idea, for instead of pulling in to the shore they were now vigorously backing water to keep off. What their young laird was shouting to them was probably furious orders to go on and land; but the receding and tossing boat itself tore the rope alike through Ewen's hands and those of the soldiers from which he was now trying to snatch it. He himself made a desperate effort to reach the bows and scramble on board again, but it was too late; this could only be done now by swimming, and moreover one of the soldiers had by this time closed with him, and they were soon struggling up to mid-thigh in icy, swirling water.

At last Ewen tore himself from the man's clutches with a push which sent his assailant under, spluttering. In front of him was the boat which he could not reach, with Ian standing up in the stern gesticulating and shouting something of which the wind carried away every syllable, while Ardroy on his side shouted to the rowers to keep off, and that he would fend for himself. Then, the better to show his intention, he turned his back on the boat, his face to the shore on which he was left. The ducked redcoat had arisen, dripping like a merman and cursing like the proverbial trooper; his companion was dodging to and fro in a few inches of water, waiting to intercept the marooned fugitive on his emergence from the swirl on the beach. Two more were hurrying down from the open door of the cottage; and Ewen was unarmed, half-drenched and hampered by the breaking water in which he stood. It looked like prison again, most undoubtedly it looked like it! He set his teeth, and began to plunge stumblingly through the foam towards the shore but away from the reinforcements.

And some three-quarters of an hour later, rather to his own astonishment, he was crouching, wet, exhausted, but free, behind a boulder on the slope of Meall Breac, at the entrance to Glen Clovulin. How he had got there he hardly knew, but it seemed to have been by dodging, by running, and by one short encounter of the nature of a collision, in which it was not he who had proved the sufferer. He had been favoured by the bad light and by the high, broken ground, an outcrop of the height of Sgurr nan Eanchainne, for which he had made at full speed, and which, by falling again into a sort of gulley, had made something of a wall between him and his pursuers – who never, in fact, pursued him so far.

The wind was dropping now, and the mist crawling lower; he was safe enough from the soldiers at any rate. Presumably the boat had got through the Narrows; he had not had time to look. He could not help wondering what were the present feelings of his cousin Ian, who had undertaken this exploit, involving a good deal of risk, for him, a kinsman, and had in the end only carried off a young man with whom he had no ties of blood at all. Still, from Ewen's own point of view, this braeside, though windy and destitute of food, was greatly to be preferred to the room with the barred windows in Fort William. 'Better peace in a bush than peace in fetters,' as the Gaelic proverb had it. But what he really wanted was peace at Ardroy.

Chapter 9

THE WORM AT THE HEART

1

ALTHOUGH in the weeks to come it never occurred to Ewen – who was besides well able to look after himself – that he had been abandoned to his fate on Ardgour beach (he was only to wish sometimes that he had not been quite so precipitate in leaping ashore with the rope), Hector Grant was often to feel remorse for the safety which had been bestowed on him while his brother-in-law had been left to fend for himself.

It was true that the Stewarts had kept the boat hanging about on the other side of the Narrows as long as they dared, but no figure had appeared to claim their help, and young Invernacree avowed that he hardly hoped for it, because of the presence of the soldiers on the spit. Yet since, by the last he had seen of the drama on the shore, Ardroy appeared to be outdistancing his pursuers, Ian had every confidence that he would make his way down the farther side of Loch Linnhe into Morven, and thence across to Invernacree, for which, after relinquishing the hope of taking him off at Clovulin, the rowers had then made with what speed was left in them. At Invernacree Hector was sheltered for a night or two, during which he gave up his former project of crossing to Ireland, and so to France, for the desire to know what had happened to wreck the scheme for kidnapping the Elector was drawing him, in spite of the hazards, to London. And so here he was, this cold January evening, actually in the capital, a refuge much less safe, one would have thought, than his unlucky relative's in the wilds of Ardgour. But Hector was a young gentleman attracted rather than repelled by danger; indeed a habit of under-estimating the odds against him seemed to carry him through better, perhaps, than it sometimes carried others whom this trait of his was apt to involve in difficulties

437

not of their seeking. He argued that he was less likely to be looked for in London than anywhere else.

Perhaps this was true, but Lieutenant Grant, after a couple of days in the capital, found himself facing other problems which had not previously weighed upon him: first, the problem of getting back to France from England without papers of any kind; second, the problem of remaining in London without money, of which he had exceedingly little left; and third, the problem of his reception by his colonel, Lord Ogilvie, when he did rejoin his regiment, since from the moment when he had escaped from Colonel Leighton's clutches the blame for his continued absence could no longer be laid at that old gentleman's door. Indeed, Hector foresaw that the sooner he returned to France the less likely would he be to find a court-martial awaiting him there.

So it was, for him, a trifle dejectedly that he walked this evening along the Strand towards his lodging in Fleet Street, wondering whether after all he could contrive to slip through at the coast without the papers which he saw no means of obtaining. He had just come from the 'White Cock' tavern, a noted Jacobite resort, where converse with several English adherents of that cause had neither impressed him nor been of any service. No one seemed to be able to tell him exactly why the plot had failed to mature; they had all talked a great deal, to be sure, but were obviously the last persons to help him. The young soldier thought them a pack of *fainéants*; if he were only back in the Highlands, Ardroy, he could wager, would have got him over to France by some means or other.

He was nearing the sculptured gateway of Temple Bar when a beggar woman, who had been following him for some time, came abreast of him, and, shivering, redoubled her whining appeals for alms. More to be rid of her than from any charitable impulse, Hector put his hand into his pocket ... and so remained, staring with an expression of horror at the suppliant. His purse was gone. Little as he had possessed an hour ago, he now possessed nothing at all.

'I have been robbed, mother,' he stammered, and his face

must have convinced the woman that here was no feigned excuse, for, grumbling, she turned and went her way.

The late passers-by looked curiously at this young man who stood so rigid under the shadow of Temple Bar. All Hector knew was that he had had his purse at the 'White Cock' a short time ago, for he had paid his score from its meagre contents. Had he dropped it there, or had it been stolen from him since? He must go back at once to the tavern and inquire if it had been found. Then it occurred to him, and forcibly, that to go in and proclaim his loss would reveal him as a simpleton who could not look after his property in London, or might even seem as though he were accusing the *habitués* of the 'White Cock' of the theft. Either idea was abhorrent to his proud young soul.

He glanced up. The winter moon, half-eaten away, sailed eerily over the shrivelled harvest on the spikes of Temple Bar. Townley's head, he knew, was one of the two still left there, the commander of the doomed garrison of Carlisle. Hector's own might well have been there too. And although those grim relics seemed to be grinning down at him in the moonlight, and though the action was not overwise, the young Highlander took off his hat before he passed onwards.

Yes, London was a hostile and an alien town. He had not met one Scot there, not even him whom he had thought certainly to meet, young Finlay MacPhair of Glenshian, the old Chief's son, who had been in the plot. Did he know where to find him, he reflected now, he might bring himself to appeal in his present strait to a fellow Gael where he would not sue to those spiritless English Jacobites. And at the 'White Cock' they would know young Glenshian's direction.

Hector turned at that thought, and began quickly to retrace his steps, lifting his hat again, half-defiantly, as he passed the heads of the seven years' vigil, and soon came once more to the narrow entry off the Strand in which the 'White Cock' was situated. There were still some customers there, drinking and playing cards, and as he came down the little flight of steps inside the door an elderly Cumberland squire named Fetherstonhaugh, with whom he had played that evening, looked up and recognized him.

'Back again, Mr Grant? God's sake, you look as though you had received bad news! I trust it is not so?'

'There is nothing amiss with me, sir,' replied Hector, annoyed that his looks could so betray him. 'But I was foolish enough to go away without inquiring the direction of my compatriot, Mr Finlay MacPhair of Glenshian, and I have returned to ask if any gentleman here could oblige me with it.'

At first it seemed as if no one there could do this, until a little grave man, looking like an attorney, hearing what was toward, got up from an equally decorous game of picquet in the corner, and volunteered the information that Mr MacPhair lodged not far from there, in Beaufort Buildings, opposite Exeter Street, the second house on the right.

Hector could not suppress an exclamation. He lowered his voice. 'He lives in the Strand, as openly as that? Why, the English Government could put their hands on him there any day!'

'I suppose,' replied the little man, 'that they do not wish to do so. After all, bygones are bygones now, and Mr MacPhair, just because he was so promptly clapped into the Tower, never actually bore arms against the Elector. But he keeps himself close, and sees few people. Perhaps, however, as you come from the Highlands, he will receive you, sir.'

'Ay, I think he'll receive me,' quoth Hector a trifle absently. His ear had been caught by some conversation at a little distance in which the word 'purse' occurred. The conversation was punctuated with laughter, whose cause was evidently the exiguous nature of the purse's contents, and he distinctly heard a voice say, 'I'll wager 'tis his, the Scotchman's – they are all as poor as church mice. Ask him!'

'Egad, if he is so needy he will claim it in any –' began another voice, which was briefly recommended to lower itself, or 'the Scotchman' would hear. And in another moment a young gentleman, plainly trying to school his features to the requisite gravity, was standing before Hector saying, 'A purse has just been found, dropped doubtless by some gentleman or other, but as no one here claims it, it must be the property of one who has left. Is it by any chance yours, Mr Grant?'

And he displayed, hanging across his palm, Hector's very lean and rather shabby green silk purse.

The colour mounted hotly into the young Highlander's face. Do what he would he could not restrain a half-movement of his hand to take his property. But almost swifter than that involuntary movement – instantly checked – was the proud and angry impulse which guided his tongue.

'No, sir, I am not aware of having lost my purse,' he said very haughtily, and translated the tell-tale movement of his hand into one towards his pocket. He affected to search in that emptiness. 'No, I have mine, I thank you. It must be some other gentleman's.'

And, having thus made the great refusal, Hector, furiously angry but outwardly dignified, marched up the steps and out of the 'White Cock' as penniless as he had come in.

The door had scarcely closed behind him before Mr Fetherstonhaugh joined the group round the purse-holder, his jolly red face puzzled. 'I could have sworn that purse was Mr Grant's – at any rate I saw him pull forth just such another when he was here an hour ago.'

'But 'tis impossible it should be his,' said someone else. 'Who ever heard of a Scot refusing money – still less his own money!'

The depleted purse passed from hand to hand until one of the company, examining its interior more closely, extracted a worn twist of paper, opened it, and burst into a laugh. 'May I turn Whig if the impossible has not happened! The purse *is* his, sure enough; here's his name on an old bill from some French tradesman in Lille!'

'And the lad pretended that he had his purse in his pocket all the time!' exclaimed Squire Fetherstonhaugh. 'He must be crazy!'

'No, he must have overheard our comments, I'm afraid,' said a voice, not without compunction.

'Aye, that will be it,' said the elder man. 'You should be less free with your tongues, young gentlemen! I have a notion where Mr Grant lodges, and, if you'll make over the purse to me, damme if I don't send it to him tomorrow.'

'Take out the bill, then, sir,' advised one of the original

jesters, 'and he will be devilish puzzled to guess why it reached him.'

On the whole it was well that Hector did not know how fruitless was his pretence, as he walked away towards Fleet Street again with an added antipathy to London in his heart. What else could he have done, he asked himself, in the face of such insolent comment? And, after all, it was not a great sum which he had so magnificently waved from him, and the young French lady who had made the purse for him three years ago had almost passed from his memory. That somebody besides himself, the woman with whom he had found a lodging, would also be the poorer for his fine gesture, did not occur to him that night.

2

Ten o'clock next morning saw Lieutenant Grant outside Beaufort Buildings, and knocking, as directed, at the second house on the right-hand side. The woman who opened told him to go to the upper floor, as the Scotch gentleman lodged there. Up, therefore, Hector went, and, knocking again, brought out a young, shabbily dressed manservant.

'Can I see Mr MacPhair of Glenshian?'

'Himself is fery busy,' replied the man, frowning a little. He was obviously a Highlander too.

'Already?' asked Hector. 'I came early hoping to find him free of company.'

'Himself is not having company; he is writing letters.'

Hector drew himself up. 'Tell Mr MacPhair,' he said in Gaelic, 'that his acquaintance Lieutenant Hector Grant of the régiment d'Albanie is here, and earnestly desires to see him.'

At the sound of that tongue the frown left the gillie's face, he replied in the same medium that he would ask his master, and, after seeking and apparently receiving permission from within, opened wide the door of the apartment.

Hector, as he entered, received something of a shock. To judge from his surroundings, Finlay MacPhair, son and heir of a powerful chief, was by no means well-to-do, and he, or his

servant, was untidy in his habits. A small four-post bed with
dingy crimson hangings in one corner, together with an ash-
strewn hearth upon whose hobs sat a battered kettle and a
saucepan, showed that his bedchamber, living apartment and
kitchen were all one. In the middle of the room stood a large
table littered with a medley of objects – papers, cravats, a
couple of wigs, a plate, a cane, a pair of shoes. The owner himself, in a shabby flowered dressing-gown, sat at the clearer end
of this laden table mending a quill, a red-haired young man of a
haughty and not over agreeable cast of countenance. A half-
empty cup of coffee stood beside him. He rose as Hector came
in, but with an air a great deal more arrogant than courteous.

'At your service, sir; what can I do for you?'

'It's not from *him* I'll ever borrow money!' resolved Hector
instantly. But Finlay MacPhair's face had already changed.
'Why, 'tis Mr Grant of Lord Ogilvie's regiment! That stupid
fellow of mine misnamed you. Sit down, I pray you, and take a
morning with me. Away with that cold filth, Seumas!' he added
petulantly, indicating the coffee cup with aversion.

They took a dram together, and Hector was able to study his
host; a young man in the latter half of the twenties like himself,
well-built and upstanding. The open dressing-gown showed the
same mixture of poverty and pretension as the room, for Mr
Grant had now observed that over the unswept hearth with its
cooking pots hung a small full-length oil portrait of a man
whom he took to be old John MacPhair, the Chief himself, in
his younger days, much betartaned and beweaponed, with his
hand on an immensely long scroll which would no doubt on
closer view be found to detail his descent from the famed Red
Finlay of the Battles. In the same way the Chief's son wore a
very fine embroidered waistcoat over a shirt which had certainly been in the hands of an indifferent laundress.

'Well, Mr Grant,' said he, when the 'morning' had been
tossed off, 'and on what errand do you find yourself here? I
shall be very glad to be of assistance to you if it is within my
power.'

He put the question graciously, yet with all the air of a chief
receiving a not very important tacksman.

'I have had a misfortune, Mr MacPhair, which, if you'll
permit me, I will acquaint you with,' said Hector, disliking the
prospect of the recital even more than he had anticipated. And
he made it excessively brief. Last September a spy had
treacherously knocked him on the head in the Highlands, and
abstracted the pocket-book containing all his papers. Since then
he had been confined in Fort William. (Of the subsequent theft
of his money in London he was careful not to breathe a word.)

'Lost all your papers in the Highlands, and been shut up in
Fort William!' said Finlay MacPhair, his sandy eyebrows high.
'I might say you've not the luck, Mr Grant! And why, pray,
do you tell me all this?'

Hector, indeed, was almost wondering the same thing. He
swallowed hard.

'Because I don't know how the devil I'm to get out of
England without papers of some kind. Yet I must rejoin my
regiment at once. And it occurred to me –'

'*I* can't procure you papers, sir!' broke in young MacPhair,
short and sharp.

'No, naturally not,' agreed Hector, surprised at the sudden
acrimony of the tone. 'But I thought that maybe you knew
someone who –'

He stopped, still more astonished at the gaze which his contemporary in the dressing-gown had fixed upon him.

'You thought that I – *I* – knew someone who could procure
you papers!' repeated Finlay the Red, getting up and leaning
over the corner of the untidy table. 'What, pray, do you mean
by that, Mr Grant? Why the devil should you think such a
thing? I'd have you remember, if you please, that Lincoln's Inn
Fields are within convenient distance of this place ... and I
suppose you are familiar with the use of the small-sword!'

Hector, too, had leapt to his feet. He had apparently met
with a temper more inflammable than his own. Yet he could
imagine no reason for this sudden conflagration. He was too
much taken aback for adequate anger. 'Mr MacPhair, I've no
notion what I have done to offend you, so 'tis impossible for me
to apologize ... Not that I'm in the habit of apologizing to any
man, Highland or Lowland!' he added, with his head well back.

For a moment or so the two young Gaels faced each other like two mutually suspicious dogs. Then for the second time Finlay MacPhair's demeanour changed, and the odd expression went out of his eyes. 'I see now it's I that should apologize, Mr Grant, and to a fellow-Highlander I can do it. I misjudged you; I recognize that you did not intend in any way to insult me by hinting that I was in relations with the English Government, which was what I took your words to mean.' And he swept with a cold smile over Hector's protestation that he was innocent of any such intention. 'I fear I'm ever too quick upon the point of honour; but that's a fault you'll pardon, no doubt, for I'm sure you are as particular of yours as I of mine. Sit down again, if you please, and let us see whether our two heads cannot find some plan for you to get clear of England, without the *tracasserie* at the ports which you anticipate.'

Rather bewildered, Hector complied. And now his fiery host had become wonderfully friendly. He stood with his hands in his breeches pockets and said thoughtfully, 'Now, couldn't I be thinking of someone who would be of use to you? There are gentlemen in high place of Jacobite leanings, and some of the City aldermen are bitten that way. Unfortunately, I myself have to be so prodigious circumspect, lest I find myself in prison again ...'

'Nay, Mr MacPhair, I'd not have you endanger your liberty for me!' cried Hector on the instant. 'Once in the Tower is enough, I'm sure, for a lifetime.'

'Near two years there, when a man's but twenty, is enough for a brace of lifetimes,' the ex-captive assured him. 'Nay ... let me think, let me think!' He thought, walking to and fro meanwhile, the shabby dressing-gown swinging round the fine athletic figure which Hector noted with a tinge of envy. 'Yes,' he resumed after a moment, 'there's an old gentleman in Government service who is under some small obligation to me, and he chances to know Mr Pelham very well. I should have no scruples about approaching him; he'll remember me – and as I say, he is in my debt. I'll do it ... ay, I'll do it!' He threw himself into his chair again, and in the same impulsive manner pulled towards him out of the confusion a blank sheet of paper which, sliding along, revealed a half-written one beneath.

At that lower sheet young Glenshian looked and smiled. 'I was about writing to Secretary Edgar at Rome when you came, as you see.' He pushed the page towards his visitor, and Hector, who had no wish to supervise Mr MacPhair's correspondence, but could not well avert the eyes which he was thus specifically invited to cast upon it, did see a few scraps of Finlay Mac-Phair's ill-spelt if loyal remarks to that trusted servant of their exiled King's, something about 'constant resolucion to venture my owne person', 'sincer, true and reale sentiments', and a desire to be 'laid at his Majesty and Royal Emenency's feet'. But he could not think why he should be invited to peruse them.

The letter upon which he was now engaged on his compatriot's behalf Finlay did not offer to show the latter, though had Hector looked over the writer's shoulder he would have been more impressed with its wording than with the vagaries of its orthography, and would certainly have found its contents more arresting than those of the loyal epistle to Rome.

'Dear Grandpapa,' wrote Finlay MacPhair of Glenshian with a scratching quill to the old gentleman in Government service whom, since he was no relation of his, he must have known very well thus playfully to address, 'Dear Grandpapa, Get *our ffrind* to writ a pass for a Mr Hector Grant to go to France without delai. Hee's harmlesse, and my oblidging an oficer of Lord Ogilby's regt. in this maner will not faile to rayse my creditt with the party, which is a matter I must now pay particular atention tow. Besides, I am in hopes to make some litle use of him leater. And let me know, if you please, when we shall meet to talk of the afair I last wrot of, otherwise I must undow what I have begun. Excuse my ansiety, and beliv me most sincerly, with great estinne and affection, Your most oblidged humble servt, Alexander Jeanson.'

And this was addressed, in the same independent spelling, to 'The Honble Guin Voughan at his house in Golden Square,' but Hector did not see the direction, for the writer folded and sealed the letter in an outer sheet on which he wrote, 'To Mr Tamas Jones, at Mr Chelburn's, a Chimmist in Scherwood Street.'

'That is not the real name of my acquaintance, Mr Grant,' said the scribe with great frankness, handing him the missive. 'And yon is the address of an apothecary at whose shop you should leave this letter with as little delay as possible. Call there again by noon tomorrow, and I'll engage there'll be somewhat awaiting you that will do what you wish.'

Hector thanked him warmly, so genuinely grateful that he failed to perceive that he had not wronged the punctilious Mr MacPhair after all, for he did know someone who could procure useful papers for a Jacobite in difficulties. The benefactor, however, cut short his thanks by asking him a question which somewhat allayed his gratitude.

'I hope, Mr Grant,' he said, looking at him meaningly, 'that there was nothing of a compromising nature among the papers which were taken from you in the Highlands?'

Hector reddened, having all along desired to obscure that fact. He fenced.

'No papers lost in such a manner, Mr MacPhair, but must, I fear, be regarded as compromising.'

'But naturally,' replied young Glenshian somewhat impatiently. 'As you no doubt found when you were in Fort William. Did they question you much there about them?'

'No. My papers were not in their hands, as far as I know.'

'Then why were *you*?'

'Oh, 'tis a long story, not worth troubling you with. But the gist of it is that I gave myself up.'

He had succeeded in astonishing Mr MacPhair. 'Gave yourself up!' exclaimed the latter. 'In God's name, what for? Gave yourself up at Fort William! I fear the knock on your head must have been a severe one!'

'Perhaps it was,' said Hector shortly. 'At any rate I accomplished nothing by doing it, and on Christmas Day I escaped.'

'My dear Mr Grant, you astonish me more and more! I took it that you had been released. And after escaping you come to London, of all places!'

'It was on my way to France,' said the adventurer, sulkily. And he then added, in a not very placatory manner, 'If you wish to give me to understand that on this account you prefer to withdraw the letter you have written, here it is!' He drew it out of his pocket.

Finlay MacPhair waved his hand. 'Not for worlds, not for worlds! It is the more needed; and your escape shall make no difference, even though it was unknown to me when I penned that request. But I should like to know, Mr Grant, why you gave yourself up. You must have had some extraordinary reason for so extraordinary a proceeding.' And, as Hector hesitated, foreseeing to what a truthful answer might lead, he added, in a tone which very plainly showed offence, 'I have surely earned the right to a little more frankness on your part, Mr Grant!'

The claim could not be gainsaid. Hector resigned himself, and in as few words as possible gave that reason. Even then he somehow contrived to keep out Doctor Cameron's name.

Glenshian threw himself back in his chair, and looked at the narrator under lowered lids. 'So you played this heroic role because you considered that you had compromised your brother-in-law by the loss of your papers. Then there *was* something compromising in them?'

'No, not to him ... I see I had best explain the whole matter,' said Hector in an annoyed voice, and being tired of cross-examination came out bluntly and baldly with everything – the loss of his prematurely written letter to Cluny Macpherson (mostly unintelligible, he hoped, owing to its cipher), Ardroy's going back to warn Lochdornie, his finding instead Doctor Cameron and bringing him to his house, the search there and Ewen's arrest. To all this the young chief listened with the most unstirring attention, his hand over his mouth, and those curiously pale hazel eyes of his fixed immovably on the speaker.

'*Dhé*, that's a tale!' said he slowly at the end. 'And this letter of yours, with its mention of the arrival of Lochdornie and Doctor Cameron – you never discovered what had become of it?'

'No. But I am pretty sure, as I say,' replied Hector, 'that it never found its way to Fort William. I was, I confess, in despair lest harm should come to either of them through its loss, but I cannot think that any has. 'Tis now more than three months since it was stolen from me, and by this time the Government has probably learnt from other sources of their presence in Scotland.'

Frowning over his own confession, and remembering too at that moment how Alison that day at Fort William had spoken of searches made by the military after the Doctor, he did not see the sharp glance which was cast at him.

'Ay, 'tis very probable they know it,' said Mr MacPhair dryly. 'What part your lost letter may have played in their knowledge ...' He shrugged his shoulders. 'And indeed,' he went on, with an air of disapproval, 'I cannot anyways commend this mission of my kinsman Lochdornie's and Doctor Cameron's. Had the Prince taken my advice on the matter when he made it known to me – as, considering my large interests and influence in the Western Highlands, he had done well to – they would not have been sent upon so risky an undertaking. However, since it has been set on foot, I hope my cousin Lochdornie will find means to report to me on his proceedings there; which indeed,' added the future Chief, 'it is no less than his duty to do. And yet I have had no word from him. It would be well did I hear from the Doctor also. I only trust he may not be engaged in damping down the ardour of the clans, as he did three years ago.'

'Doctor Cameron damp down the clans!' exclaimed Hector, thinking he had not heard aright. 'My dear Mr MacPhair, he's more like, surely to inflame them with too little cause ... And how should the Prince have selected him for this mission if that were his habit?'

Finlay shrugged his shoulders. 'Archie Cameron has always had the Prince's ear since the day when Lochiel sent him to Arisaig to dissuade His Royal Highness from his enterprise. Moreover, 'twas to the Doctor's own interest to come to Scotland again. There's always the treasure of Loch Arkaig, about which he knows even more than Cluny – more than any man alive.' The half-sneering expression habitual to his face leapt into full life as he went on, 'That gold is like honey to a bee in his case. He dipped pretty deeply into it, did the immaculate Doctor Archibald, when we were in Lochaber together in the '49!'

'But not upon his own account!' cried Hector. 'Not for himself, Mr MacPhair! That I'll never believe!'

'Your sister's married to a man that's akin to the Doctor, you told me,' was Glenshian's retort to this. 'Unfortunately, I was there with Archibald Cameron at the time ... Well, there's many a man that's true enough to the Cause, but can't keep his fingers from the Cause's money. I don't blame him overmuch, with that throng family of young children to support. I've known what it is to be so near starving myself, Mr Grant, that I have had to sell my shoe-buckles for bread – 'twas when I was released from the Tower. So I'm aware why Archie Cameron finds it suits him to go back to the Highlands at any cost.'

Hector stared at him, incredulous, yet conscious of a certain inner discomfort. For it was quite true that young Glenshian had accompanied Doctor Cameron and his own kinsman Lochdornie to the Highlands in 1749, and rumours had run among the Scottish exiles over the water that since that date the two latter were scarcely on speaking terms. But when Hector had learnt that these two were going over again together, he had supposed the report much exaggerated. Still, he who spoke with such conviction was the future Chief of Glenshian, and deeper, surely, in the innermost councils of Jacobitism than he, a mere landless French officer.

'Mr Grant, I am going to ask you a favour in my turn,' here said Finlay the Red, with an air of having dealt conclusively with the last subject. 'I expect you know Captain Samuel Cameron of your regiment?'

'Crookshanks, as we call him?' answered Hector a little absently, being engaged in dissipating the momentary cloud of humility by the reflection that as one Highland gentleman he was the equal of any other, Chief or no. 'The brother of Cameron of Glenevis – that's the man you mean?'

'That is the man. They say that one good turn deserves another; will you then take him a letter from me? I'm wanting a messenger this while back, and since you are returning to the regiment, here is my chance, if you will oblige me?'

Only too pleased to confer some obligation, as a species of set-off against his own, Hector replied that he would be delighted, so Finlay once more seized paper and took up his pen. For a few seconds he nibbled the quill reflectively, the fraction of a smile at the corner of his mouth; then he dashed off a few lines, sealed the missive carefully, and handed it to its bearer. 'You'll not, I hope, be robbed again, Mr Grant!' he observed, and yet, despite the little laugh which accompanied the words, Hector felt that after what had passed he could not well take offence at them. He accepted the gibe and the letter with meekness, and prepared to take his leave. Young Glenshian rose too.

'Your visit, Mr Grant,' he said agreeably, 'has been of this advantage to me, that I know now from a first-hand source that my kinsman and Doctor Cameron did really make their appearance in the Highlands this autumn. In the absence of news from either of them I have sometimes wondered whether the plan had not fallen through at the last. Though even at that,' he added, smiling, 'the evidence is scarcely first hand, since you did not actually set eyes on either of them.'

'But my brother-in-law, with whom I was imprisoned —' began Hector.

'Ay, I forgot — a foolish remark of mine that! I'll pass the testimony as first hand,' said Finlay lightly. 'But where, I wonder, did the Doctor go after he had evaded capture at your brother-in-law's house?'

'That I never knew,' responded Hector. 'In Fort William neither Ardroy nor I had much opportunity for learning such things.'

'He'll have made for Loch Arkaig as usual, I expect,' commented young MacPhair. He looked at the table. 'Mr Grant, you'll take another dram before you leave?'

'No, thank you, Mr MacPhair,' replied Hector with a heightened colour. If he could not swallow Mr MacPhair's insinuations against Doctor Cameron's honesty, neither would he swallow his whisky. He went and took up his hat, young Glenshian watching him with that curl of the lip so natural to him that he appeared always to be disdaining his company.

And then Hector remembered the question which, during these days in London, no Englishman had satisfactorily answered for him. Striving to banish the resentment from his voice and look, he said, 'May I venture to ask a question in my turn, Mr MacPhair? Pray do not answer if it be too indiscreet. But, as I have told you, it was the proposed scheme for ... a certain course of action in London which brought me over the sea last September. Why did that scheme come to naught?'

Mr MacPhair did not seem to find the question indiscreet, nor did he pause to consider his answer. 'Why, for the same reason that the Rising failed in '46,' he replied with prompt scorn. 'Because your English Jacobite is a man of fine promises and no performance, and as timid as a hare! The very day was fixed – the tenth of November – and nothing was done. However, perhaps you'll yet hear something to rejoice you before the summer is out. Well, a good journey to you, Mr Grant; commend me to my friends over there. I am very glad to have been of service to you.'

In his worn dressing-gown, surrounded by that clamorous disorder, Fionnlagh Ruadh nevertheless dismissed his visitor with an air so much *de haut en bas* that a sudden heavy strain was thrown on the cord of Hector's gratitude. He bowed, biting his lip a little.

'I hope I may be able to repay you one day, Mr MacPhair,' he said formally, and thought, 'May the Devil fly with me to the hottest corner of hell if I don't ... somehow!'

'Seumas,' called the young chief, raising his voice, 'show this gentleman downstairs.'

And the gillie, who was peeling potatoes on the landing, hastened to obey. Hector was chagrined that he could not slip a vail into the bony hand, but, not having a penny himself, how could he?

'Arrogant, touchy, and vain as a peacock!' was his summary of his late host as he walked away from the Strand in the direction of the 'chimmist' in Sherwood Street. But the peacock had done him a real service, and in mere gratitude he ought to try to forget that today's impression of Finlay MacPhair of Glenshian had not been a pleasant one.

In any case it was soon swept away by the mingled relief and mortification caused by a small packet awaiting him at his lodging, which, on being opened, was found to contain his

purse. Then they had known of his loss all the time at the
'White Cock' – or guessed! He had only made himself more of
a laughing-stock by refusing to receive his property!

3

When Seumas returned to his potato-peeling, his master, on the
other side of the door, was already resuming his correspondence. But not the letter to Secretary Edgar which he had
shown to Hector. From a locked drawer he extracted another
sheet of paper, headed simply 'Information', and underneath
the few lines already there he wrote:

'Pickle has this day spoken with one from the Highlands who
says that Doctor Cameron and MacPhair of Lochdornie were
certainly there at the end of September, and Doctor Cameron
was then come into Lochaber, by which it may be seen that the
information sent by Pickle in November last was very exact.
But where the Doctor then went the informant did not know.
It would not dow for Pickle to goe himself into those parts, for
the Doctor distrusts him, hee knowing too much about the
Doctor, and besids the risque is too great, Pickle being of such
consequence there; but if hee had more mony at his disposal he
cou'd employ it very well in finding a person who would goe,
and undertakes hee'd find out more in a day than any government trusty in a week, or souldier in a moneth; or Pickle would
be apt to corespond with persons not suspected by the disaffected, who cou'd be on the Watch for these men, if it were
made worth their while. But Pickle's jants have already cost
him a deal of mony, and hee has never receaved more than his
bare exspences, and is at this moment in debte to severall persons in this town, in spite of the great promasis made to him,
and the great services he hath already performed, both in regard to afairs in the Highlands, and among the Pretender's
party in England. If something be not paid imediatly Pickle is
not dispos'd to –'

He broke off, hastily covering the paper. 'Damn you, Seumas,
what do you want?'

The gillie might have entered upon a stage cue. 'If I am to buy flesh for dinner –' he began timidly in his native tongue.

His master sprang up in wrath. 'Do you tell me that you have spent all I gave you? Death without a priest to you! Here, take this, and see you make it last longer!'

Pulling a small handful of silver out of his breeches pocket, he flung a few coins towards him, and as Seumas meekly stooped to pick them up from the floor, sat down again and counted over the rest, his brow darkening.

He really was poor – still. Yet, for all his pretence to Hector, no one stood in less danger than he of being again confined by the English Government, and well he knew it. But though that Government left him at large to continue his services it paid them chiefly in promises; and it is galling to have sold your soul, to betray your kin, your comrades, and, as far as in you lies, your Prince, and to get so few of the thirty pieces in return. Perhaps the paymasters thought but poorly of what they obtained from the informer.

Did the letter-writer himself suspect that, as he sat there now, his chin on his hand, and that scowl darkening his face? It did not seem likely, for no services that Finlay MacPhair of Glenshian could render, however base, would ever appear to him other than great and valuable. Behind those strange light eyes was no place for remorse or shame; the almost crazy vanity which dwelt there left them no entrance to his spirit.

Chapter 10

'AN ENEMY HATH DONE THIS'

1

THE snow gave no signs of ceasing. It had never been blinding, it had never swirled in wreaths against one, yet this steady and gentle fall, only beginning about midday, had contrived to obliterate landmarks to a surprising degree, and to make progress increasingly difficult. When Ewen had started this morning he had not anticipated a snowstorm, though the sky looked heavy, and even now the fall was not enough to stop him, but he found his surroundings getting darker than was pleasant, and began to think that he might possibly be benighted before he reached the little clachan for which he was bound.

Although it was the second week in February, Ardroy was still west of Loch Linnhe – in Sunart, in fact. At first, indeed, when, leaving his hiding-place on Meall Breac, he had wandered from croft to croft, seeking shelter at each for no more than a night or two, he had known that it would be folly on his part to attempt to cross the loch, since all the way southward from Fort William the soldiers must be on the look-out for him. Yet he had not gone far up Glen Clovulin when he heard that those whom he had so unluckily encountered that morning at Ardgour were a party on their way from Mingary Castle to relieve the guard quartered at Ballachulish over the body of James Stewart, in order that it should not be taken down for burial. They could not possibly have known at that time of his and Hector's escape; perhaps, even, in their ignorance, they might not have molested the boat's crew had they landed.

But five weeks had elapsed since that episode, and it might be assumed that even Fort William was no longer keeping a strict look-out for the fugitives. Ewen was therefore working his way towards the Morven district, whence, crossing Loch Linnhe into Appin, he intended to seek his uncle's house at

455

Invernacree, and once more get into touch with his own kin. To Alison, his first care, he had long ago dispatched a reliable messenger with tidings of his well-being, but his own wandering existence these last weeks had cut him off from any news of her, since she could never know where any envoy of hers would find him.

Pulling his cloak – which from old habit he wore more or less plaid-fashion – closer about him, Ewen stopped now for a moment and took stock of his present whereabouts. The glen which he followed, with its gently receding mountains, was here fairly wide, so wide in fact that in this small, close-falling snow and fading light he could not see across to its other side. He could not even see far ahead, so that it was not easy to guess how much of its length he still had to travel. 'I believe I'd be wiser to turn back and lie the night at Duncan MacColl's,' he thought, for, if he was where he believed, the little farm of Cuiluaine at which, MacColl being an Appin man and a Jacobite, he had already found shelter in his wanderings, must lie about two miles behind him up the slope of the farther side of the glen. He listened for the sound of the stream in the bottom, thinking that by its distance from the track he could roughly calculate his position. Even in that silence he could hardly hear it, so he concluded that he must be come to that part of the valley where the low ground was dangerously boggy, though the track, fortunately, did not traverse it, but kept to higher ground. He was therefore still a good way from the mouth of the glen.

But while he thus listened and calculated he heard, in that dead and breathless silence, not only the faint far-off murmur of water, but the murmur of human voices also. Hardly believing this, he went on a few steps and then paused again to listen. Yes, he could distinctly hear voices, but not those of persons talking in an ordinary way, but the speakers seemed rather to be repeating something in antiphon, and the language had the lilt of Gaelic. Once more Ardroy went forward, puzzled as to the whereabouts of the voices, but now recognizing the matter of their recitation, for there had floated to him unmistakable fragments about the snare of the hunter, the terror by night, and the arrow by day. A snow-sprinkled crag suddenly loomed up before him, and going round it he perceived, somewhat dimly at first, who they were that repeated Gaelic psalms in the darkening and inhospitable landscape.

A little below the track, on the flatter ground which was also the brink of the bog, rose two shapes which he made out to be those of an old man and a boy, standing very close together with their backs to him. A small lantern threw a feeble patch of light over the whitened grass on which it stood; beside it lay a couple of shepherd's crooks and two bundles.

Ewen was too much amazed to shout to the two figures, and the snow must have muffled his approach down the slope. The recitation went on uninterrupted:

' *"There shall no evil happen unto thee,"* ' said the old man's voice, gentle and steady.

' *"Neither shall any plague come nigh thy dwelling,"* ' repeated the younger, more doubtfully.

' *"For he shall give his angels charge over thee."* '

' *"To keep thee in all –"* ' The lad who had turned his head, broke off with a shrill cry, 'Sir, sir, he has come – the angel!'

' *"To keep thee in all thy ways,"* ' finished the old man serenely. Then he too looked up and saw Ewen standing a little above them, tall, and white all over the front of him with snow.

'I told you, Callum, that it would be so,' he said, looking at the boy; and then, courteously, to Ewen, and in the unmistakable accents of a gentleman, 'You come very opportunely, sir, to an old man and a child, if it be that you are not lost yourself, as we are?'

Ewen came down to their level, and, in spite of the falling snow, removed his bonnet. 'I think I can direct you to shelter, sir. Do you know that you are in danger of becoming bogged also?'

'I was beginning to fear it,' said the old man, and now there was a sound of weariness, though none of apprehension, in his voice. 'We are on our way to Duncan MacColl's at Cuiluaine, and have lost the path in the snow. If it would not be delaying you overmuch, perhaps you would have the charity to put us into it again.'

457

'You are quite near the track, sir,' replied Ardroy. 'But I will accompany you to Cuiluaine. Will you take my arm? The shortest way, and perhaps the safest, to regain the path, is up this slope.'

The old man took the proffered support, while the boy Callum, who had never removed his soft, frightened gaze from the figure of the 'angel', caught a fold of Ewen's wet cloak and kissed it, and the rescuer began to guide both wayfarers up the whitened hillside.

'But, sir,' protested the old traveller, breathing a little hard, when they were all back upon the path, 'we are perhaps taking you out of your own road?'

They were, indeed, since Ewen's face was set in the opposite direction. But there was no question about it; he could not leave the two, so old and so young, to find their doubtful way to Cuiluaine alone. 'I shall be glad enough to lie at Mr MacColl's myself tonight,' he answered. 'I was almost on the point of turning back when I heard your voices. Do I go too fast for you, sir?'

'Not at all; and I hope I do not tire this strong arm of yours? We were just coming in our psalm a while ago to "*And they shall bear thee in their hands, that thou hurt not thy foot against a stone*".' He turned round with a smile to the boy following behind. 'You see how minutely it is fulfilled, Callum! – Are you of these parts, sir?'

'No,' answered Ewen. 'I am a Cameron from Lochaber.'

'Ah,' observed the old man, 'if you are a Cameron, as well as being the Lord's angel to us, then you will be of the persecuted Church?'

'An Episcopalian, do you mean, sir? Yes,' answered Ewen. 'But not an angel.'

'*Angelos*, as you are no doubt aware, Mr Cameron, means no more in the original Greek than a messenger.' He gave the young man the glimpse of a beautiful smile. 'But let us finish the psalm together as we go. You have the Gaelic, of course, for if we say it in English, Callum will not be able to join with us.'

And, going slowly, but now more securely, on the firmer ground, they said the remaining four verses together. To Ewen, remembering how as a child he had wondered what it would be like to 'go upon the lion and the adder', and whether those creatures would resent the process, the whole episode was so strange as to be dreamlike. Who was this saintly traveller, so frail looking and so old, who ventured himself with a boy of sixteen or so through bogs and snow in a Highland February?

Ere they reached Duncan MacColl's little farm up the other side of the glen he had learnt his identity. His charge was a Mr Oliphant, formerly an Episcopal minister in Perthshire, who had been moved by the abandoned condition of 'these poor sheep' in the Western Highlands to come out of his retirement (or rather, his concealment, for he had been ejected from his own parish) to visit them and administer the Sacraments. He was doing this at the risk of his liberty, it might be said of his life, for transportation would certainly kill him – and of his health in any case, it seemed to Ewen, for, indomitable and unperturbed though he seemed in spirit, he was not of an age for this winter travelling on foot. When he had learnt his name Ewen was a little surprised at Mr Oliphant having the Gaelic so fluently, but it appeared that his mother was Highland, and that for half his life he had ministered to Highlanders.

The light from the little farmhouse window on the hillside above them, at first a mere glow-worm, cheered them through the cold snowy gloom which was now full about the three. Nearer, they saw that the door, too, stood open, half-blocked by a stalwart figure, for Duncan MacColl was expecting Mr Oliphant, and in considerable anxiety at his delay. He greeted the old man with joy; he would have sent out long before this to search for him, he said, but that he had no one of an age to send – he was a widower with a host of small children – and was at last on the point of setting forth himself.

'But now, thank God, you are come, sir – and you could not have found a better helper and guide than Mr Cameron of Ardroy,' he said warmly, ushering them all three into the living-room and the cheerful blaze. 'Come ben, sirs, and you, little hero!'

' 'Twas not I found Mr Cameron,' said Mr Oliphant, with his fine, sweet smile. 'He was sent to us in our distress.'

'Indeed, I think it must have been so,' agreed MacColl. 'Will you not all sit down and warm yourselves, and let the girl here dry your cloaks? You'll be wise to take a dram at once.' He fussed over the old priest as a woman might have done, and, indeed, when Ewen saw Mr Oliphant in the light he thought there could hardly be anyone less fitted for a rough journey in this inclement weather than this snowy-haired old man with the face of a scholar and a saint.

But there was for the moment no one but the boy Callum with them in the kitchen when Mr Oliphant turned round from the fire to which he had been holding out his half-frozen hands.

'*Angelos*, will you take an old man's blessing?'

'I was about to ask for it, sir,' said Ewen, bending his head; and the transparent hand was lifted.

So Ardroy had a private benediction of his own, as well as that in which the house and all its inmates were included, when Mr Oliphant read prayers that night.

Ewen was up betimes next morning, to find the snow gone from the ground, and a clear sky behind the white mountain-tops.

'Ay, I was surprised to see that fall,' observed Duncan Mac-Coll. 'We have had so strangely mild a winter; there were strawberries, they say, in bloom in Lochiel's garden at Achna-carry near Christmas Day – though God knows they can have had little tending. Did ye hear that in Lochaber, Mr Cameron? 'Twas a kind of a portent.'

'I wish it may be a good one,' said Ewen, his thoughts swinging regretfully back to forfeited Achnacarry and his boyish rambles there. 'By the way, you have no news, I suppose, of someone who owns a very close connection with that name and place – you know whom I mean?'

' "Mr Chalmers"?' queried the farmer, using the name by which Dr Cameron often passed. 'No, I have heard nothing more since I saw you a few weeks syne, Mr Cameron, until last Wednesday, when there was a cousin of mine passed this way

and said there was a rumour that the Doctor was in Ardnamurchan again of late.'

'Do you tell me so?' exclaimed Ewen. 'To think that all this
time that I have been in Ardgour and Sunart I have never
heard a whisper of it, though I know he was there before
Christmas. Yet it is possible that he has returned, mayhap to his
kinsman Dungallon.' For Doctor Cameron's wife was a
Cameron of Dungallon, and there were plenty of the name in
Ardnamurchan.

'I think it will likely be no more than a rumour,' said Mr
MacColl. 'Forbye, from what he told me last night, there will
soon be another man in Ardnamurchan who'll need to walk
warily there, though not for the same reason.'

'You mean Mr Oliphant? Yes, I know that he is set on going
there, despite the presence of the garrison at Mingary Castle.
And 'tis an uncommon rough journey for a man of his age and
complexion. He should have someone with him besides that lad.
Could not some grown man be found to accompany him?'

Duncan MacColl shook his head. 'Not here, Mr Cameron. I
would offer to go myself, but that I have the whole work of the
farm on my hands just now, for my herdsman is ill. Yet it's
true; he needs a stronger arm than young Callum's.'

Ewen stood in the doorway reflecting, a tribe of shy, fair
children peeping at him from odd corners unnoticed. The idea
which had come to him needed weighing. He did greatly long
to get back across Loch Linnhe, and if he offered himself as Mr
Oliphant's escort he would be turning his back upon Appin and
all that it meant, even if it were but for a short time. On the
other hand, supposing Archie were in Ardnamurchan after all
... As so often, two half-motives coalesced to make a whole.
And when Mr Oliphant had breakfasted he made his proposal.

'But, my dear Mr Cameron, you admitted last night that you
were already on your way towards Appin!'

Ewen replied that this morning, because of some news which
Mr MacColl had just given him, he was, on the contrary,
desirous of going into Ardnamurchan. 'And if you would allow
me to be your escort, sir,' he added, 'I should account it a
privilege.'

And he meant what he said. There clung to this gentle and heroic old man, going on this entirely voluntary and hazardous mission, that air of another sphere which either attracts or repels. Both from instinct and from training it strongly attracted Ardroy, who felt also that for once in his life he could render a real service to the Church of his baptism, continually persecuted since the Revolution and now, since Culloden, driven forth utterly into the wilderness – and become the dearer for it.

'You make a sacrifice, however, Mr Cameron,' said the old priest, looking at him with eyes as keen as they had ever been. 'Be sure that it will be repaid to you in some manner.'

'I want no repayment, sir, other than that of your company. To what part of Ardnamurchan do you propose to go?'

Mr Oliphant told him that his plan was to visit, in that remote and most westerly peninsula of Scotland (and indeed of Britain) the hamlet of Kilmory on the north and of Kilchoan on the south. But Ewen and Duncan MacColl succeeded in dissuading him from going to the latter because of its dangerous proximity to Mingary Castle with its garrison. The inhabitants of Kilchoan could surely, they argued, be informed of his presence at Kilmory, and come thither, with due precautions against being observed.

' 'Tis a strange thing,' broke out Ewen during this discussion, 'that the Episcopalian people of England, whose established Church is Episcopal, and whose prayer-book we use, should acquiesce in this attempt to stamp out the sister Church in Scotland!'

'Mr Cameron,' said Duncan MacColl impressively, 'when the One whom I will not name enters into an Englishman he makes him not only wicked but downright foolish! I've not been in England myself, but I've remarked it. Now in this country that One works otherwise, and there's more sense in a Scot's misdoings.'

There was a twinkle in Mr Oliphant's eyes at this dictum, for like most of the best saints he had a strong sense of humour. 'I'm glad that you can find matter for patriotism even in the Devil's proceedings, Mr MacColl!'

2

So they set out on their journey together, the young man and
the old, on this tolerably fine February day, and travelled over
bad tracks and worse roads towards Ardnamurchan. The boy
Callum was originally only to have gone as far as Acharacle,
where Mr Oliphant hoped to find another guide, but now there
was no need for him to come even as far as this, and he returned from Cuiluaine to his father's croft, to tell for the rest
of his life the story of a rescue in the snow by an archangel.

The distance which the two wayfarers had to traverse was
not great, but, besides the bad going, Ewen was so afraid of
pushing on too quickly for Mr Oliphant's strength that he
probably went slower than they need have done. However,
after a night spent with some very poor people who gave them
of their best and refused the least payment, they came with
twilight on the second day to Kilmory of Ardnamurchan and
the thatched dwellings of fisher-folk who looked perpetually
upon mountainous islands rising from an ever-changing sea,
and knew scarcely a word of English. By them Mr Oliphant
was received as if he had come straight from heaven, and the
tall gentleman, his escort, the *duine uasal mór*, with the respect
due to a celestial centurion. And word went instantly round to
all the scattered crofts, to Swordle, to Ockle, to Plocaig, to
Sanna, and in particular to Kilchoan on the southern shore.

Next day Mr Oliphant was hard at work, baptizing, cate-
chizing, visiting. It was pathetic to see the eagerness and
reverence of these poor and faithful people, who once had been
under the care of a zealous Episcopal minister, now torn from
them, so that they were left shepherdless, save when the Presbyterian intruder, as they considered him, came there on his rare
visits to this portion of his vast parish; and his ministrations
they naturally did not wish to attend. So now they came
streaming in from all the hamlets and crofts in the neighbourhood; and from Kilchoan came even a couple of Coll fishermen, Episcopalians, whose boat was in harbour there.

But these, like all from the Mull side, came with caution,

lest the garrison at Mingary Castle should hear of unusual gatherings at Kilmory and come to investigate the cause, which would certainly result in the penal laws being set in motion against Mr Oliphant, and perhaps against his hearers, who far exceeded the scanty number of five which was permissible at one service. Fortunately, it appeared that the soldiers had for the moment something else to occupy them than hunting out Episcopalians. The colonel of the garrison had been missing since the previous day, when he had gone out alone, taking a gun, and had not returned. The inhabitants of Kilmory said uncompromisingly that if he never came back it would be a good day for them, for he was a very evil and cruel man whom the soldiers themselves hated. But they had this consolation in his temporary disappearance, that the military, if they were still searching for him, would hardly trouble Kilmory or the coast round it, where there was nothing to be shot save gulls.

Nevertheless, when Mr Oliphant held a service that afternoon in the largest of the cottages, it was thought well to place a few outposts, and Ewen, though he would have liked to hear the old man preach, offered to be one of these. So about sunset he found himself walking to and fro on the high ground above the hamlet, whence he could survey the beginning of the road which dipped and wound away southwards over the moorland towards Mingary Castle and Kilchoan. But northward the island peaks soared all blue and purple out of the sea like mountains of chalcedony and amethyst, headland upon headland stretched against the foam, and the eye travelled over the broken crests of that wild land of Moidart, pressing after each other as wave follows wave, to the lovely bay where the Prince had landed seven and a half long years before, and whence he had sailed away ... into silence. Farther still the coast swept round to an unseen spot, both bitter and sacred in memory, where Ewen's murdered English friend slept under some of the whitest sand in the world.

And miles away to the north-west lay his own home and the Eagle's Loch. Ewen sighed. When should he see his wife and children again? Soon now, please God. But spring, too, would soon be come, and with the spring his sword was promised – if the time were ripe. But would it be? He knew nothing, the dwellers in these remote parts knew less, and, from what he had already heard from them, his hopes of finding Archibald Cameron in Ardnamurchan and learning of the prospects of an uprising were little likely to be fulfilled.

With the fall of twilight the momentary afterglow faded rapidly, and the strange, jagged heights of Skye began to withdraw into the magic region whence they had emerged. Voices came up from the hamlet, and the sentry saw that the service must be over, for men and women were streaming away. They would reassemble in the morning, for next day early Mr Oliphant was to celebrate the Eucharist.

Ewen's watch was ended. As he turned to go, still gazing, half-unconsciously, towards Loch nan Uamh, he struck his foot against some slight obstacle. Glancing down, he saw that it was a little shrivelled bush – scarcely even a bush – no more than eighteen inches high. There was nothing on its meagre stem but very fine, thickly set thorns; not even a rag of the delicately cut leaves which, with those thorns and its delicious, haunting fragrance, mark off the little wild rose of Scotland, the burnet rose, from every other, and especially from its scentless sister of English hedgerows in June. Ewen stood looking down at it. Yes, this rose was ill to pluck, and ill to wear ... but no other grew with so brave a gesture in the waste, and none had that heart-entangling scent.

3

Next morning had come. There was not a sound from the men and women kneeling in the cold light upon the sand and grass; nothing but the indrawn breath of the sea, now and then a gull's cry, and that old, clear, steady voice. It was at the Epistle that some intense quality in it first riveted Ewen's attention: *'and forgiving one another, if any man have a quarrel against you; even as Christ forgave you, so also do ye'*. Had not these simple, reverent people much to forgive their oppressors?

The altar stood in the doorway of a cottage; it was only the rough table of common use covered with a coarse, clean cloth.

A fisherman's lantern had been placed at either end, for it was not yet very light. Mr Oliphant wore the usual preacher's black gown and a stole, nothing else of priestly vestment: there were no accessories of any kind, nothing but what was poor and bare and even makeshift – nothing but the Rite itself.

Just before the consecration the sun rose. And when, with the rest, Ewen knelt in the sand before that rude, transfigured threshold, he thought of Bethlehem; and then of Gennesaret. And afterwards, looking round at the little congregation, fisher-folk and crofters all, he wondered when these deprived and faithful souls would taste that Bread again. Not for years, per-haps. And when would he, scarcely in better case – and in whose company?

He was to remember this strange and peaceful Eucharist when that day came and brought one still stranger.

Ardroy could not help Mr Oliphant in his ministrations, so he went out fishing with some of the men on that sea which for once had none of the violence of winter. Gleams of sunshine chased each other on the peaks of Rum, and all the day seemed to keep the serenity of its opening. That evening, his last there, Mr Oliphant preached on the Gospel for the day, on the parable of the tares, and this time Ewen was among the con-gregation. Yes, one had to be denied the exercise of one's re-ligion truly to value it, to listen hungrily as he found himself listening. He had not so listened to Mr Hay's discourses, good man though he was, in the days when Episcopalian worship was tolerated.

Next morning, after a moving scene of leave-taking, the old priest left Kilmory under Ewen's escort. Many of his temporary flock would have desired to come part of the way with him, but it was judged wiser not to risk attracting attention. Mr Oliphant now meaning to visit Salen, on Loch Sunart, and Strontian, Ardroy intended to go with him as far as Salen; and he had a further plan, which he developed as he walked, that after he had visited Sunart and Ardgour Mr Oliphant should follow him into Appin, staying with Mr Stewart of Invernacree, where, all Stewarts of that region being, as their religious and political opponents put it, 'madly devoted to the Episcopal clergy' he would be sure of a most ready welcome.

They were discussing this plan as they went along the side of Loch Mudle, where the road led above the little lake in wild, deer-haunted country. The water had a pleasant air this morning, grey winter's day though it was, and the travellers stopped to look at it.

'To tell truth,' said Mr Oliphant, 'I was not aware that Ardnamurchan possessed any loch of this size. It minds me a little of –'

He stopped, for Ewen had gripped his arm. 'Forgive me, sir; but I heard just then a sound not unlike a groan. Could it be?'

They both listened intently. For a while there was nothing but the silence which, in very lonely places, seems itself to have the quality of noise. Then the sound came again, faint and despairing, and this time Mr Oliphant too heard it. It was not easy to be sure of its direction, but it appeared to come from the tree-covered slope above them, so Ewen sprang up this and began to search among the leafless bushes, helped after a moment or two by catching sight of a gleam of scarlet. That colour told him what he was going to find. He climbed a little higher, parted the stems, took one look at the figure sprawled in a tangle of faded bracken, and called down to his companion.

'Mr Oliphant – here he is ... and it must be the missing officer from Mingary Castle.' Then he pushed his way through and knelt down by the unfortunate man.

It seemed a marvel that he was still alive. One arm was shattered, the white facings of his uniform were pierced and blood-stained, and half his face – not a young face – was a mask of blood. Yet he was semi-conscious, his eyes were partly open, and between the faint moans which had drawn attention to him he uttered again and again the word 'water'. From the condition of the fern round him it looked as if he had tried to drag himself along to the tiny streamlet which could just be heard whispering down at a little distance. But he had never got there.

'Is this murder, think you?' asked Mr Oliphant in a horrified voice. 'Ah, you have some brandy with you; thank God for that!'

But Ewen had by now caught sight of something lying a little way off. 'No, sir, not murder; nor has he been gored by a stag, as I thought at first. 'Tis a burst fowling-piece has done it – there it lies. And he has been here, poor wretch, nearly two days!'

They wetted the dried, blackened lips with brandy and tried to get a little down the injured man's throat, but he seemed unable to swallow, and Mr Oliphant feared that the spirit might choke him. 'Try water first, Mr Cameron,' he suggested, 'if you can contrive to bring some in your hands from the burn there.'

Holding his hollowed palms carefully together, Ewen brought it.

'We must, by some means or other, inform the garrison of Mingary at once,' said the old priest, carefully supporting the ghastly head. 'I wish we had Callum with us; speed is of the first importance. Shall I lower his head a little?'

'Yes, it would be better. But I can reach Mingary as quickly as the lad would have done,' said Ewen, without giving a thought to the undesirability of approaching that stronghold. 'I'm spilling this; he's past drinking, I fear. Certainly if help is not soon –' He gave a sudden violent exclamation under his breath, and, letting all the rest of the water drain away, sank back on his heels staring as though he had come on some unclean sight. For under the trickles of water and brandy the dried blood had become washed or smeared off the distorted face, sufficiently at least to make it recognizable to a man who, even in the mists of fever, and seven years ago, had during twenty-four hours seen more than enough of it.

'What is wrong, then?' asked Mr Oliphant, but he did not glance up from the head on his arm, for he had began cautiously to try the effect of brandy again.

Ewen did not answer for a moment. He was rubbing one wet hand upon a ground as though to cleanse it from some foul contact.

'I doubt it is worth going for help,' he said at last in a half-strangled voice. 'If one had it, the best thing would be to finish this business ... with a dirk.'

'I suppose you are jesting, Mr Cameron,' said the old man in a tone which showed that he did not like the jest. 'How far do you think it is to Mingary Castle?'

'The distance does not concern me,' answered Ewen. 'I am not going there.'

And at that Mr Oliphant looked up and saw his face. It was not a pleasant sight.

'What – what has come to you?' he exclaimed. 'You said a moment ago that if assistance were not brought –'

'I had not seen then what we were handling,' said Ewen fiercely. He got to his feet. 'One does not fetch assistance to ... vermin!'

'You are proposing that we should leave this unfortunate man here to die!'

Ewen looked down at him, breathing hard. 'I will finish him off if you prefer it. 'Tis the best thing that can happen to him and to all the inhabitants of Ardnamurchan. You have heard what his reputation is.' And turning away he began blindly to break a twig off the nearest birch tree.

Mr Oliphant still knelt there for another second or two, silent, perhaps from shock. Then he gently laid down the head which he was supporting, came round the prostrate scarlet figure and over to his metamorphosed companion.

'Mr Cameron, it is not the welfare of Ardnamurchan which you have in your mind. This man has done you some injury in the past – is it not so?'

Ewen was twisting and breaking the birch twig as though it were some sentient thing which he hated.

'But for God's mercy he had made a traitor of me,' he said in a suffocated voice. 'Yet that I could forgive ... since he failed. But he has my friend's blood on his hands.'

There was a silence, save for the faint moaning behind them.

'And for that,' said Mr Oliphant sternly, 'you will take his blood on yours?'

'I have always meant to, if I got the chance,' answered Ewen, with dreadful implacability. 'I would it had been in fair fight – this is not what I had desired. But I am certainly not going to save his worse than worthless life at the expense, perhaps, of your liberty and mine ... I am not going to save it in any case. He slew my best friend.'

'You made mention just now, Mr Cameron, of God's mercy.'

'Ay, so I did,' said Ewen defiantly. 'But God has other attributes too. This,' he looked for a moment over his shoulder, 'this, I think, is His justice.'

'That is possible! but you are not God. You are a man who only yesterday received the greatest of His earthly gifts with, as I believed, a humble and thankful heart. Today you, who so lately drank of the cup of salvation, refuse a cup of cold water to a dying enemy.'

Ewen said nothing; what was there to say? He stood looking down through the trees on to the loch, his mouth set like a vice.

'Are you going to Mingary, my son?' asked Mr Oliphant after another brief and pregnant silence.

'No, I am not.'

'Very well then, I must go.' But his voice was not as steady as heretofore when he added, 'I would to God that it were you!'

In the grim white face before him the blue eyes darkened and blazed. Ardroy caught hold of the old man's arm. 'There's one thing that's certain, Mr Oliphant, and that is, that *you* are not going to enter the lion's den for the sake of that scoundrel!'

'The lion's den? Is that what is keeping you back – a natural distaste for endangering yourself? I thought it had been something less of man's weakness ... and more of the devil!'

'So it is,' retorted Ewen stormily. 'You know quite well that I am not *afraid* to go to Mingary Castle!'

'Then why will you not let me go? I am only an old, unprofitable man whose words are not heeded. If I do not come out again what matter? It is true, I shall not get there near as quick as you, and every minute' – he glanced back – 'the faint chance of life is slipping further away. But one of us has to go, Mr Cameron. Will you loose my arm?' His worn face was infinitely sad.

Ewen did not comply with his request. He had his left hand pressed to his mouth, in truth, his teeth were fixed in the back of it – some help, if a strange one, to mastery of the wild passions which were rending him, and to keeping back, also, the hot tears which stung behind his eyes.

He heard Mr Oliphant say under his breath, in accents of the most poignant sorrow, '*Then appeared the tares also*. Such tall, such noble wheat! Truly the Enemy hath done this!' He understood, but he did not waver. He *would* not go for help.

'Mr Cameron, time is very short. Let me go! Do not lay this death on my conscience too. Loose me, in the name of Him Whom you are defying!'

Ewen dropped the speaker's arm, dropped his own hand. It was bleeding. He turned a tempest-ridden face on Mr Oliphant.

'It shall not be the better man of us two who goes to Mingary,' he said violently. 'I will go – you force me to it! And even though he be carrion by the time help comes, will you be satisfied?'

Mr Oliphant's look seemed to pierce him. 'By the time you get to Mingary, Highlander though you are, your vengeance will be satisfied.'

'As to that –' Ewen shrugged his shoulders. 'But you, how will you ever reach Salen alone?'

'Salen? I shall not start for Salen until help has come; I shall stay here.' And as Ewen began a fierce exclamation he added, 'How can I, a priest, leave him lying at the gate and go away?'

'And then they will take you? – No, I will not go to Mingary ... I will not go unless you give me your word to withdraw yourself as soon as you hear the soldiers coming. That might serve, since I shall not say that any is with him, and they will not think of searching.'

Mr Oliphant considered a moment. 'Yes, I will promise that if it will ease your mind. And later, if God will, we may meet again on the Salen road, you overtaking me. Now go, and the Lord Christ go with you ... *angelos!*'

For an instant his hand rested, as if in blessing, on Ewen's breast. The young man snatched it up, put it to his lips, and without a word plunged down the slope to the track below, so torn with rage and shame and wild resentment that he could hardly see what he was doing.

But once on the level he clenched his hands and broke into

the long, loping Highland trot which he could keep up, if need were, for miles. He might, in Mr Oliphant's eyes, be no better than a murderer and a savage, he might in his own be so weak of will that a few words from an old man whom he scarcely knew could turn him from his long-cherished purpose, he might be so cursed by fate as to have met his enemy in circumstances which had snatched from him his rightful revenge – but at least, if he were forced to play the rescuer, he would keep his word about it. Out of this brief but devastating hurricane of passion that intention seemed to be the only thing left to him – that and the physical capacity to run and run towards the black keep of Mingary Castle which he so little desired to enter.

Chapter 11

THE CASTLE ON THE SHORE

THE ancient stronghold of the MacIans of Ardnamurchan, where James IV had held his court, which had repulsed Lachlan Maclean with his Spanish auxiliaries from the wrecked Armada galleon, and had surrendered to Colkitto's threat of burning in Montrose's wars; which had known Argyll's seven weeks' siege and Clanranald's relief, stood on the very verge of the shore gazing over at Mull. At high tide the sea lapped its walls – or at least the rocks on which those walls were built – save on the side where a portion of the fortress had its footing on the mainland. It looked very grim and grey this winter morning, and the runner, drawing breath at last, felt exceedingly little inclination to approach it.

And yet air, flag, garrison, were all unstirring; Mingary seemed a fortress of the dead, staring across dull water at a misty shore. No one was visible save the sentry on the bridge crossing the fosse which guarded the keep on the landward, its most vulnerable side. As Ewen approached, the man brought his musket to the ready and challenged him in the accents of the Lowlands.

Ardroy made his announcement from a distance of some yards. 'I am come to tell you that your missing colonel is found. He is lying in sore straits on the slopes of Loch Mudle, and if you want him alive you must send without a moment's delay to fetch him.'

The sentry shook his head. 'I canna tak messages. Ye maun come ben and see an officer.'

'I cannot wait to do that,' replied Ewen impatiently. 'I am in great haste. I tell you your colonel is very badly hurt; his fowling-piece must have burst and injured him.'

'Man, ye suld ken that I couldna leave ma post if King Geordie himsel' was deein',' said the sentry reproachfully, and suddenly uplifting his voice, bellowed to someone within,

473

'Sairgeant, sairgeant!' and motioned vehemently to Ewen to pass him.

Most unwillingly Ardroy crossed the bridge, and at the end of the long narrow entry into the fortress found himself confronted by a stout sergeant who listened, with no great show of emotion, to his tale. 'I'll fetch the captain – he'll wish tae see ye, sir.'

The wish was by no means reciprocal; and Ewen cursed inwardly at the recognition of his social status, from which he had hoped that his shabby clothes, worn for so long in bad weather, would have protected him.

'I am in great haste,' he asserted once more. 'Surely you could give the captain my message?'

But even as the last word left his lips two officers, talking together, suddenly appeared from he knew not where under the archway. Yet once again Ewen made his announcement, and this time it had an immediate effect. A few questions were asked him, he described the spot in detail, hasty orders were given for a party to set forth instantly with a litter and restoratives, and then the captain asked Ewen if he would be good enough to guide them to the place, which after a second or two of hesitation he agreed to do. Indeed, provided he were not asked questions of too searching a nature on the way, the arrangement would suit him well.

But he was not destined to profit by it. He had noticed the other officer, a young lieutenant whose face seemed vaguely familiar, looking at him closely; now, when this latter could gain the attention of his superior, he drew him aside and whispered to him.

The captain swung round to Ewen again, looking at him with a gaze which the Highlander did not at all appreciate. 'By the way, you have not told us your name, sir?' he remarked. 'We are so much in your debt that we should be glad to learn it.'

Ewen helped himself to that of the good tenant of Cuiluaine. He was, he announced, a MacColl, originally of Appin.

'Well, Mr MacColl,' said the captain, 'obliged as we are to you for your information, I don't think we will trouble you to accompany us to Loch Mudle.'

'Then I'll bid you good day,' responded Ewen, making as if to go. But he had known instantly that the subaltern's whisper meant he would not be allowed to walk out of Mingary Castle.

The officer took a step forward. 'Not so fast, if you please. I'll ask you to await our return here, Mr MacColl.'

'In God's name, why?' demanded Ewen, playing astonishment. But he was not really astonished; this was what came of running into a hornet's nest!

'That I shall be able to tell you when I return,' said the officer. 'For one thing, I think you have made a mistake in your name. Sergeant, a guard!'

'My name! What is wrong with my name? You are not proposing to keep me here illegally when I have just saved your colonel's life for you!'

'Believe me, I regret it, Mr ... Mr MacColl,' returned the captain suavely. 'I doubt if there is much illegality about it; but, since there is such great need of haste at the moment, we cannot possibly discuss the matter now. Sergeant, have this gentleman safely bestowed.'

'And how do you suppose that you are going to find your injured officer without me?' asked Ewen sarcastically, as a guard came trooping under the archway.

'Easily, if the details you have furnished are correct. And I shall be the first to apologize to you, Mr MacColl, for this detention ... if there is cause for apology. Come, Burton.' He swung on his heel and hurried off.

Resistance were foolish. Grinding his teeth, Ewen went whither he was taken, and three minutes later found himself in a dusky place with oozing stone walls and a floor of solid rock. There was a barred window just out of his reach, a worm-eaten table, a rough bench and a broken pitcher – nothing else. As Mingary Castle was of thirteenth-century construction, this spot might well have been even more disagreeable, but Ewen in his present temper would have found a boudoir intolerable if he could not leave it at will. He was furiously angry – angry even with Mr Oliphant. One might have known that this would happen! Here he was, caged up again, and all for rendering, as much against his will as a good action had ever been done in the history of the world, a service to a man whom he hated and had sworn to kill! He sat down upon the bench and cursed aloud.

When he ceased it was to become conscious of fresh details of his prison, notably the rustiness of the iron bars across the window, and to hear, faint but distinct, the sound of waves not very far away. He might be here for weeks in this seagirt hole! ... Or Guthrie, if he recovered sufficiently, might recognize what he had done for him, and let him go out of gratitude.

That would be the most intolerable consequence of all – that Guthrie should know he had played the Good Samaritan! Ewen jumped up. Out of this place he would be before Guthrie was brought into it! He felt capable of tearing down the stones with his nails, of wrenching the iron bars of the window out of their sockets with his bare hands.

But ... that was not necessary! In his pocket, surely, was still the file which had won his and Hector's freedom from Fort William. What great good fortune that no orders had been given to search him! Without a moment's delay he pushed the crazy table under the window, and, mounted rather precariously upon it, began to file feverishly at the middle bar.

Ardroy had worked away for perhaps a hour, his hands red with rust, hoping that no one would hear the noise of scraping, when it came to him where he had seen the face of the subaltern who had whispered about him to the captain. It was the lieutenant who had brought up Hector the day that youth had surrendered himself at Fort William. He had without doubt recognized the other ex-captive. There was more need of haste than ever; his case was worse than he had supposed, and even if Guthrie, distasteful as the notion was, should be smitten with gratitude, he would hardly dare to let an already escaped prisoner go free.

By three o'clock the first bar was through. It was half-worn away, or it would not have yielded to the file in the time. The second was eaten too, and when in about three-quarters of an hour that also parted, and could be wrenched aside, by cautiously thrusting his head out Ewen was able to ascertain where he was – only a matter of ten feet or so above the basaltic rock on which the castle was built. At the base of this rock leapt the waves, not an encouraging sight; but if, as he judged, it was now high tide or thereabouts, he guessed that by half-tide the rock, and indeed a good part of the little bay to the west of the castle, would be clear of these invaders. He thought this probable because to his left he could see that a stone causeway, now slapped by the waves, had been constructed for use when the tide was low.

Ardroy drew his head in again and resumed his filing, debating, while he worked, where he should aim for when he got out. He certainly must not immediately go back in the direction whence he had come. Then should he make across the peninsula to its northern shore, or should he strike out for its extreme end?

Suddenly he thought of the two Coll fishermen in Kilchoan bay. If they had not yet sailed for their island he might induce them to take him in their boat back up Loch Sunart, and, even if they were gone, he could perhaps find someone else at Kilchoan willing to do this for him. It would be a good plan to get clear off the peninsula before he had the whole garrison of Mingary searching for him. It might no doubt be better, for the purpose of getting away unseen from the castle, to wait until nightfall, but by then, who knew, the sawn bars might be discovered, and he removed to another dungeon. Moreover, the detestable Guthrie, living or dead, would have been brought in, and be under the same roof with him. He must be gone before either of these things could happen.

And at length the last bar, a very thin one, gave. The daylight was now beginning to fade a trifle, and the waves were no longer washing against the rock below; as Ewen had anticipated, a considerable segment of the little bay was free of water altogether. Once down on the shore he had only to cross this and climb the low, grassy cliff at some convenient spot, and he would be well away from Mingary, even, perhaps, out of sight of it. It seemed, indeed, a good deal to hope that before he got as far as that he should not have been seen and shot at, but he reflected that only a very few of the garrison could possibly have observed his entrance or know of his being made prisoner, that a number, including two officers at least, had gone off to Loch Mudle, and that the rest would surely not fire without reason at an unknown individual making his way, not too fast, along the shingle below them.

It required, in the end, more muscular effort to pull himself from the shaky table entirely up to the level of the little window and to get himself through this, than to lower himself the other side. At last, with a good deal of strain and wriggling, he was through, dropped on to the shelf of rock at the bottom of the masonry, and crouched there a moment or two, holding his breath, for men's voices and laughter had all at once drifted ominously to his ears. But he could not make out whence they came, and in any case must go on.

There was a place on the side of the shelf nearest to the sea which was much wider, and which seemed to overhang the shore; but this end of it Ewen naturally avoided, creeping along in the opposite direction pressed as close as possible to the grey stones of the keep. But soon he could do this no longer, for the shelf had narrowed until it ceased altogether; on which, finding foothold with some difficulty, he clambered down the rock itself to the beach.

But when the fugitive was there he instantly stood motionless, for he saw, only too clearly, what the overhanging shelf had hidden from him. Above him towered Mingary, with who knew what observers on its battlements, but between him and the sea, at no great distance, was worse – a party of about a dozen soldiers uproariously washing their feet in a pool left by the tide. It was their voices which he had heard on the ledge.

One moment of sharp dismay and Ardroy turned, quick as a fox, and began to tiptoe away over the shingle. If he could only reach the low cliff over there unobserved, he would soon be up that. He did not think that he had been seen; his impression was that the men mostly had their backs turned in his direction, or were absorbed in their chilly ablutions. And their talk and guffaws might cover the scrunch of the shingle under his feet.

But to get away from so many eyes without being seen by any was too much to ask for. A minute later cries of 'Halt, you there

– halt and tell your business!' reached him, and he knew that measures were on foot to enforce the command. Ewen did not look back; he took to his heels, a pretty certain means, he knew, of ensuring a bullet's being sent after him. But he was too desperately set upon escape to weigh that risk. Instant pursuit, of course, there would be; he heard the cries with which it started, and the sound of men scrambling to their feet over stones – yet not a single shot.

Two facts, indeed, were in the Highlander's favour, though he knew it not; no redcoat had committed so unheard-of a folly as to burden himself with his musket when off duty, and not a single man of the party at the pool happened to be fully shod when he took the alarm. Those with one boot paused to pull on the other, those with none, less cautious or more zealous, began the chase as they were – and, over shingle and edges of bare rock, did not get very far. Meanwhile, therefore, Ewen had quite a respectable start, and made the very best of it. In a few minutes he had reached the slope, part grass, part rock, part bare earth, and had hurled himself up it. For one instant he thought that a patch of earth over which he had to pull himself was going to give way and slide with his weight, but his muscles carried him to a securer spot before this could happen. And, once on the top, he found a stretch of rough but not precipitous going between him and the hamlet of Kilchoan, which now seemed his best goal. To turn the other way was to pass the fortress again.

A glance showed him that no one had yet topped the cliff. He ran like a deer through heather stems and bog-myrtle, up slopes and down them, and when his track was crossed by a tangled hollow with a burn at the bottom he plunged gratefully down, for it meant cover, and he could work along it unseen for a little. When he was obliged to come up again on the other side he saw with thankfulness the forms of only three pursuers running stumblingly towards the ravine which they had yet to cross, and he took fresh breath and sped still faster over the moorland.

Soon, as he went, Kilchoan bay with its string of white cottages round the shore was fully visible, under the remains of a smouldering sunset. He could see only one sailing-boat at anchor; was that the Macleans', the Coll men's? In another three minutes he was near enough to see figures moving about in her. Perhaps she was about to sail with the ebb. He came, still running very fast, though the pace was distressing him, through a little cluster of fishermen's huts at the edge of the strand. 'Is that boat out yonder from Coll?' he shouted to an old man at his door, and understood the ancient to pipe after him as he passed that it was, and just upon sailing.

Ewen pulled up breathless. 'I want a boat ... take me to her!' But he could see without being told that there was no boat within easy reach. He threw a look behind him; two scarlet-clad forms were doggedly pounding along towards the cottages, and would be on the shore in another couple of minutes. He must do without a boat. Shouting and waving to the Coll men, who seemed to have been attracted by what was going on, he ran out along a wet spit of rock and, pausing only to remove his shoes, plunged into the water.

The sea was as calm as a summer's day and colder than anything he had ever imagined. The yellow-bladdered fingers of the low-tide seaweed slid gropingly round him, but in a moment he was clear of them, and, gasping for breath, was striking out furiously for the fishing-boat ... Then he was underneath her counter, and the Macleans, with exclamations which showed that they recognized him, were helping him over the side. And as by now the two persistent soldiers could be heard shouting, with gesticulations, for a boat, there was no need for the dripping fugitive to explain from whom he was escaping.

'Will you take me with you?' he got out, panting. It was folly now even to suggest their putting about and passing Mingary to go up Loch Sunart, as he had once thought of doing.

'Ay, will we,' said the elder Maclean. 'Ye'll please give my brother a hand with the sails, then.' He ran forward to the anchor.

The pursuers had not even got hold of a boat before the little fishing vessel was moving up the top of the Sound of Mull towards the open sea and the flat mass of the isle of Coll, vaguely discernible about eight miles away; while Ewen, after making fast the last halyard, had sunk drenched and exhausted on a thwart.

An hour and a half later he was sitting on a heap of nets in the bows of the *Ròn*, the Seal, clad in an odd assortment of garments. His own were hanging up to dry. For a February night in these latitudes the air was remarkably warm, as he had already noticed, thinking, not of himself, but of the old man to whom he had lent his arm for so many miles. But surely Mr Oliphant had gained some kind of shelter for the night ... only Ewen prayed that shelter were not Mingary Castle.

Though darkness would soon shroud the little boat from Mingary, the Macleans were not willing to put about because, other considerations apart, they were carrying meal to their families in Coll, where it was needed immediately; and Ewen had to acquiesce in this reluctance, feeling, as he did, that they had already rendered him a much greater service than he could have expected of them, in thus taking him off under the very eyes of the redcoats.

The *Ròn* rolled before the following wind, and the sail flapped; the younger Maclean was singing under his breath some air of the Outer Isles full of cadences at once monotonous and unexpected. A hidden moon was tingeing the heavy clouds over Mull, and at last Ewen had time to think. But thought was tumbled and broken, like those clouds. He had met his enemy, after all these years, and ... well, what had he done with him? Saved him, or tried to, at another's bidding, and with a reluctance which amounted to abhorrence. Small credit could he take to himself for that deed!

The wind freshened, and seemed to be changing too; it ran cool over Ewen's damp hair. The *Ròn* was feeling the Atlantic swell; blessed little boat, which had cheated his pursuers! And where was now his heat of baffled revenge – a mere cinder in his breast. Certainly it burnt with flame no longer; quenched, perhaps, as the half-fantastic thought whispered, by the cold waves of Kilchoan bay. And was he glad of it, or did he miss the purpose which had lain buried in his heart so long, the purpose which he had avowed to Archibald Cameron that evening at

Ardroy, but which he could never again take out and finger over, like a treasure? Ewen did not know. Half to console himself for its loss, he reminded himself that he too had had a score, and a heavy one, against that wretched man moaning his life away above the wintry loch, and that he could never have been quite certain that his vengeance was entirely on his dead friend's account. He could not have paid Keith Windham's score without paying his own as well.

Time passed; Ardroy lay still without moving, half-propped against the gunwale, his head on his arm, seeing more clearly, with every wave that heaved, dimly frothing, past the boat's nose, from what Mr Oliphant had saved him; beginning indeed to have shuddering glimpses of a deep and very dark place in himself full of horrible things. Well did the Gaelic name the Enemy 'the One from the Abyss'! . . . But that very deliverance had parted him from the old man, it might be for ever, and he could not say to him now what he longed to say. Perhaps he would never be able to.

'Will you sleep, sir?' came a voice in his ear. One of the Macleans was bending over him. 'We'll not make Coll till morning now; the wind's gone round, and we must take a long tack to the northward. I have brought a sail to cover you.'

Ewen looked up. The moon was gone, the clouds too; the sky was velvet dark, and sown with myriad points of light. 'Thank you, Maclean; yes, I'll sleep awhile.'

And to himself he said, as he stretched himself on the brine-scented nets, 'Thank God – and a saint of His – that I can!'

Chapter 12

AFTER SUNSET

1

'My dear Ewen,' said old Invernacree, and he reached across and replenished his nephew's glass, 'my dear Ewen, have you not had your fill of wandering, that you cannot bide with us a few days?'

But Ewen shook his head. 'I would that I could, for I have, indeed, had my fill of wandering – near three months of it. But I must push on to Edinburgh tomorrow, to consult an advocate, as I told you, sir.'

Mid-March had come and passed ere he finally sat at his uncle's board, not sorry to see silver and napery again, and to look forward to a comfortable bed. There had been difficulties and delays innumerable over leaving the island of Coll – the want of a boat, stormy weather. Indeed, Ardroy had only crossed Loch Linnhe that morning early, before it was clear of the mountain mists, glad beyond measure to see 'green Appin' again at last, and the old white house, his mother's early home, standing high among its ancient oaks with his own kin in it. And now, supper being over, he was alone with his uncle, the ladies having withdrawn – the middle-aged daughter, by his first wife, who kept house for the twice-widowed Alexander Stewart of Invernacree, and the pretty girl who was Ian's own sister. Ian himself, to Ewen's regret, was from home.

The candlelight fell on Ewen's auburn head and air of content and shabby clothes – no others in the house would fit him – and on Invernacree's silver hair and deeply furrowed face. To Ewen it had seemed almost more strange, these last few years, to see his uncle, so essentially a Highlander and a Jacobite of the old breed, in Lowland garb and without a scrap of tartan, than to see himself thus clad. Looking thoughtfully at him now, he saw how greatly the death of his elder son at Culloden Moor had aged him. But at the moment there was content on the old man's face also, though tempered by his nephew's refusal to contemplate a longer stay.

'Yes, I fear I must lose no more time,' resumed Ewen. 'I had thought to be in Edinburgh, as you know, soon after Christmas, and now it is close upon Lady Day.'

'Ay,' said Invernacree. 'Ay, I doubted from what he told me at the time that Ian somehow mismanaged that affair at the Narrows – either he or that young Frenchified brother-in-law of yours whom he brought here in your stead.'

'No, sir, I assure you that he did not!' protested his nephew warmly. 'Neither Ian nor Hector was a whit to blame for what happened. If there was a blunder it was mine. I owe Ian more than I can easily repay, and if Hector had had his wish, we should have broken out of Fort William long before we did.'

'But it was young Grant, nevertheless, who brought trouble upon you in the first instance; he told me so himself.'

Ewen could not repress a smile. 'Hector is indiscreet,' he said, thinking of someone else who had remarked that of him. 'Yet I suppose he told you the whole story, so that you have not truly been without news of me for centuries, as my cousins have just been complaining.'

'Why, we have had much more recent news of you than Hector Grant's,' exclaimed his uncle. 'They must have been teasing you, the jades, for they cannot have forgotten who brought it. Can you guess who it was, Ewen?'

'I think so. Mr Oliphant did make his way here, then, sir?' Ewen's face had lit up.

'He did,' said the old man with an air of satisfaction. 'We had the privilege of his presence under this roof for a se'nnight, and he left unmolested at the end of it for Ballachulish. It was from him that we learnt of the truly Christian deed of charity to an enemy which was the cause of your separation from him. But he feared – and justly, it seems – that you might have become a prisoner in Mingary Castle on account of it.'

Ewen had coloured vividly and turned his head away. 'I escaped the same day from Mingary,' he said hurriedly. And then, after a second or two, 'Mr Oliphant should have told you how unwillingly I was brought to that act – how, had it not been for his persuasion, I should not have done it at all.'

'Then, my dear Ewen, I honour you the more for having done it,' was his uncle's reply. 'But Mr Oliphant said not a word of that. A saintly man; there are many here in Appin will long remember with thankfulness his stay among us, which, under God, we owe to you. He left a letter for you, which I was near forgetting; my memory, Ewen, grows old too. If you will come into my room I will give it to you now.' He rose, helping himself up by the table. 'Fill your glass, nephew!'

Ewen rose and lifted it. 'The King!' said Alexander Stewart, and they drank. In that house there was no need to pass their glasses over water-jug or finger-bowl, since, King George of England existing to all who ever broke bread there merely as the Elector of Hanover, there was no other King than James the Third and Eighth to avoid pledging by that consecrated subterfuge.

A tall, upright old man, though moving stiffly, Invernacree opened the door of his own study for his nephew. 'Sit there, Ewen, under your mother's picture. It is good to see you there; and I like to remember,' he added, looking him up and down, 'that Stewart blood went to the making of that braw body of yours. I sometimes think that you are the finest piece of manhood ever I set eyes on.'

'My dear uncle,' murmured the subject of this encomium, considerably embarrassed.

'You must forgive an old man who has lost a son not unlike you – No matter; sit down, *Eoghain mhóir*, while I fetch you good Mr Oliphant's letter. He, I assure you, could not say enough of you and what you had done for him.'

'I cannot say enough of what he did for me,' murmured Ewen as he took the letter and put it in his pocket. 'And in truth I went with him into Ardnamurchan half in hopes of meeting Doctor Cameron there, in which I was disappointed. Do you know aught of the Doctor's recent movements, Uncle Alexander?'

'Nothing whatever. He did not come into Appin, and I have no notion where he may be now. Ian, though he alleged some other motive, has gone, I believe, to try to learn some news; the boy is made very restless by the rumours which go about. But rumours will not help us. I doubt our sun went down upon Culloden Moor, Ewen.'

'A man might have thought,' objected his nephew, 'that the sun of the Stuart cause went down at Worcester fight; yet nine years afterwards Charles Stuart was riding triumphantly into London. 'Tis not yet nine years since Culloden.'

Old Alexander Stewart shook his head. 'The Lord's hand is heavy on His people. I never read, in the two first psalms for the sixteenth morning of the month, of the heathen coming into the Lord's inheritance, and the wild boar out of the wood rooting up the Lord's vine, and much more, only too appropriate, without thinking of that sixteenth of April seven years ago – and with good reason. You know,' he went on, looking into the fire, 'that when Alan's body was found, there was a little psalter in his pocket, and it was doubled open at the 79th psalm, as if he had been reading it while he waited there on the moor in the wind and the sleet. There was his blood across the page.'

'No, you never told me that, Uncle Alexander,' said Ewen gently.

'Ay, it was so; they brought the book to me afterwards. I put it away for a long time, though it was the last thing I had of his, but now I have the custom of reading the daily psalms out of it ... to show that I gave him willingly to his God and his Prince – No, I am never likely to forget the Culloden psalms.'

He was silent, sitting perfectly still, so that the leaping flames might have been casting their flicker on the chin and brow of a statue. His nephew looked at him with a great pity and affection.

'I have sometimes wondered,' began Invernacree again, 'whether the Almighty does not wish us to learn that His Will is changed, and that for our many unfaithfulnesses He does not purpose at this time to restore the kingdom unto Israel.'

With the older school of Jacobites religious and political principles were so much one that it was perfectly natural to them to speak of one hope in terms of the other, and his language held no incongruity for Ewen. In moments of depression he had himself harboured the same doubt and had given voice to it, as that evening with Archibald Cameron – but he was too young and vigorous to have it as an abiding thought, and he tried to comfort the old man now, pointing out that a new door had opened, from what Doctor Cameron had told him; that if France would not and could not help there were others willing to do so.

'Yes,' admitted his uncle, 'it may be that all this long delay is but to try our faith. But I can recall Killiecrankie, the victory that brought no gain; I fought at Sheriffmuir nearly forty years ago, and I remember the failure at Glenshiel the year you were born – the failure which drove your father into exile. If this spring do not bring the assistance which I hear vaguely spoken of on all sides since Doctor Cameron's arrival, then our sun has truly set; we shall never see the White Rose bloom again. The hope of it is perhaps no more than the rainbow which spans the loch here so constantly between storms, or those streamers which you see in the northern sky at night – we have been seeing them of late, very bright. But they mean nothing ... if it be not ill weather next day. They come too late – after sunset.'

'But before dawn!' suggested Ewen.

'If you like, my dear boy, if you like, yes. You are young, and may yet see a dawn. Get you to bed now, and do not let an old man's faithlessness make you despond ... Good-night, and God bless you!'

Up in the room which had been his mother's as a girl, and which he always occupied when he visited Invernacree, Ewen broke the seal of Mr Oliphant's letter.

'My dear son,' wrote the old man, 'I think you will guess how often I have thought of you and blessed you and prayed for you, even as David prayed, "Deliver my darling from the power of the dog." And I am sure that you were delivered, if not without scathe; and I hope, my dear son, that you had not to pay by an unjust captivity for your good deed, which *was* good even though it were done in the spirit of the man who said "I go not," and went. For you will remember that, for all his first refusing, it was he who was justified, and not the other.

'The unfortunate officer, your enemy, was still alive when

the soldiers reached the place. I had written upon a piece of paper, which I then placed in his pocket, these words: "If you recover, you owe it to a man whom you greatly injured." I would not mention your name lest it brought harm upon you, and I thought, too, that you would not have wished it. But I wrote what I did for the man's own sake; it was right that he should know it – if indeed he would ever know anything again in this world. I had concealed myself, as I promised you, and I was not searched for. Moreover, I found help and shelter upon my road to Salen; yet I greatly missed my son's strong arm and his heartening company. But I reflected that, even as he had been sent to me in my necessity, so he had been sent elsewhere in another's.

'Yet I have the hope, *angelos*, that before long you will reach this house of your good uncle's, which has been so kind a haven to me, and where it has been my delight to speak of you.

'The Lord bless and keep you, and lead you back safely to your own!'

Ewen put the letter carefully away in his breast, and going to the window stood looking out into the clear March night. The five-mile width of Loch Linnhe, shining faintly, lay before him; dark mountains lifted themselves on the farther side whence he had come, Shuna's island bulk lay to the right, and the castle on the islet down below stood warden over the inlet of Laich. Away to the left a warm yellow moon was entangled in trees. But it was not under her rays that the water shone. Over the mountains facing him, though it was after ten at night, the sky was irradiated with a soft, white glow. As Ewen stood there it grew in intensity and widened; a faint, perfectly straight shaft of the same unearthly light shot up into the sky, then another. But Ardroy was thinking of other things: of the old priest's letter; of how his presentiment about meeting one who had to do with Keith Windham had been fulfilled; and of how strangely – it was not a new thought now – he had resembled his own small son in his desire that vengeance should be meted out to the evil-doer who had wrought him such an injury. 'He was wicked – it was right that he should be punished!' had been

Donald's cry of justification on that September evening. The idea still had power to raise in Ewen some of the rueful dismay which had swept over him when it had first presented itself, one morning when he was pacing the sandy shores of Coll, half-deafened by the green Atlantic surges, and praying for the wind to change ... But all reflections were merged now into an impatience to begin tomorrow's journey to Edinburgh, the next milestone on the road which was to bring him back to his wife and home. He turned away from the window, and began to make ready for bed.

Yet when, after blowing out his candle, he went for a last look over the loch, he gave a smothered exclamation. The moon was gone, vanquished, and the whole of the sky from north-west to north-east was pulsing with light, with great eddying rivers and pools of that magic radiance. The miraculous glow was no longer a background to the dark mountains of Morven, nor did it now send forth those straight pencils of light; it streamed and billowed, as it seemed for miles, right over the house-top; and it was never still for an instant. It shimmered across the sky like ethereal banners, for ever changing their shape; like the swirling draperies of a throng of dancers – as the Gaelic indeed names the Northern Lights; like reflections flickering through the curtain of space from some mighty effulgence behind it. Ewen had often seen the Aurora Borealis, but he could not remember ever having seen it so fine at this time of year. For a while he lay and watched from his bed what he could see of those bright and soundless evolutions; they were a commentary on his uncle's words this evening; but he was too tired, and the bed, after three months of hard and varied lying, too seductive, for him to stay awake and ponder the matter.

When he woke some hours later and turned over, the night was quite dark; all the wonderful white dance of flame in the heavens was gone as if it had never been.

2

Next day Ewen set out from Invernacree on his journey to
Edinburgh, a gillie of his uncle's carrying his modest valise –
not his, in truth, but one of Ian's. He meant to go on foot
through Benderloch to the ferry on the curve of Loch Etive at
Bonawe, and there, in the little inn on the farther side, hoped to
hire a horse. If he failed in this he would have to trudge on for
another twelve or thirteen miles to the next hostelry at Dalmally, beyond the Pass of Brander and Loch Awe.

The proud mass of Ben Cruachan, monarch of all the heights
around, with a wreath of cloud veiling the snow upon his summit, frowned at the Cameron as he came along the northern
shore of beautiful Etive towards the heart of Lorne. Ewen dismissed the gillie, took his valise and was rowed across the wind-
rippled blue water.

'Is it true that the innkeeper here has horses for hire?' he
asked, as he paid the ferryman on the farther side.

'Ay, he has, though but the one now. The beast will not be
hired out the day, however, for I saw him no later than noon.'

The tiny inn under the three wind-bent pines looked as if it
could scarcely provide a decent meal, still less a horse, yet,
somewhat to Ewen's surprise, there was a very well-appointed
chaise standing outside it. But there seemed something wrong
with this equipage, for one of the horses was out of the shafts,
and the middle-aged postilion was talking earnestly to an
elegantly dressed young man, presumably the traveller. Various
ragged underlings of the hostelry, possessing no knowledge of
English, vociferated round them.

Ewen called one of these, told him he wanted a saddle-horse,
and entered the inn to pay for its hire. He had some difficulty in
finding the innkeeper, and the man had finally to be summoned.

'You have a saddle-horse for hire, I believe,' said Ardroy.
'For how many stages are you willing to let it out?'

The Highlander seemed embarrassed. 'I fear that I cannot let
you have it at all, sir. I have but the one horse for hire, and the
young gentleman out there, who is returning from Dunstaffnage

Castle to Edinburgh, requires it for his chaise, for one of his own horses has suddenly gone lame.'

With instant resentment Ewen thought, 'From Dunstaffnage? A Campbell, of course, who thinks all belongs to him in Lorne! I would like to show him that he is wrong ... But *I* need the horse, to carry me,' he said aloud, with an unwonted haughtiness, 'and this sprig of Clan Diarmaid must make shift with his remaining horse, and go the slower.'

'He is not a Campbell, sir,' returned the innkeeper quickly. 'It is a Sassenach, a young English lord returning from a visit to Dunstaffnage.'

Ewen was slightly mollified. Even an Englishman was preferable, on the whole, to a Campbell. 'Perhaps,' he suggested, 'if he is told that this horse of yours is the only means of my getting on my way he will have the grace to relinquish it.'

Like the innkeeper he had used the Gaelic. The sentence was scarcely finished when a voice behind him made him start, he did not know why. 'It seems that there is now some difficulty about this horse of yours,' it said, addressing the landlord with some impatience, 'but I am unable to understand what your people say. Why cannot I hire the horse, since it is for hire?'

Ewen had turned, and saw a very handsome youth clad in what he, somewhat cut off of late from such vanities, guessed to be the latest mode. 'I am myself the difficulty, I fear, sir,' he said civilly. 'I had hoped to hire the horse to ride as far, at least, as Dalmally.'

'The horse iss for the saddle,' explained the innkeeper to the young Englishman. 'Though, inteet, he iss going fery well in harness too.' He looked from one client to the other in evident perplexity.

'In that case it would seem that I must ride postilion,' observed Ardroy with a recrudescence of annoyance.

The young traveller – English nobleman, if the innkeeper were correct – came forward to the elder. He was not only extremely good-looking, but had a delightfully frank and boyish expression; and, indeed, he was not very much more than a boy. 'Sir, could we not come to some arrangement, if we take the same road, and if I have unwittingly disappointed you of a

491

horse? There is plenty of room in my chaise if you would do me the honour of driving in it.'

The offer was made so spontaneously, and speed was so desirable, that Ewen was tempted by it.

'You are too kind, sir,' he said, hesitating. 'I should be incommoding you.'

'Not in the least, I assure you,' declared the agreeable young traveller. 'There is ample room, for I left my man behind in Edinburgh, and it would be a pleasure to have a companion. My name is Aveling – Viscount Aveling.'

'And mine is Cameron,' replied Ewen; but he did not add 'of Ardroy'. It flashed through his mind as ironical that a young English Whig – for Lord Aveling must be of Whig sympathies, or he would not have been visiting Campbell of Dunstaffnage – should propose to take the road with a man who not three months ago had escaped from Government hands at Fort William.

'Then you will give me the honour of your company, sir?' asked the young man eagerly. 'Otherwise I shall feel bound to surrender the horse to you, and I will not disguise that I am anxious to reach Edinburgh with as little delay as possible.' He said this with something of a joyous air, as though some good fortune awaited him at his journey's end. 'I hope to lie tonight at Dalmally,' he went on, 'and I think that even on horseback you would hardly go beyond that, for the next stage is, I am told, a long one.'

'No, that is quite true,' admitted Ewen, 'and so, my lord, I will with gratitude take advantage of your very obliging proposal. And if we are to be fellow travellers, may I not propose in my turn that before taking the road in company you should join me in a bottle of claret?'

As they went together to the little eating-room he reflected that the boy was exceptionally trusting. 'He knows nothing of me – no more than I know of him, if it comes to that.' Then for a moment he wondered whether he were acting unfairly by this friendly youth in taking advantage of his offer, but to explain his own position, and perhaps thereby deprive himself of the means of proceeding quickly, was to be overscrupulous.

So they sat down to some indifferent claret, and over it this suddenly blossoming acquaintance ripened as quickly to a very unlooked-for harvest. Lord Aveling seemed to Ardroy a really charming and attractive young man, unspoilt, so far as he could judge, by the fashionable world of routs and coffee-houses in which he probably moved – for it transpired after a while that he was the only son of the Earl of Stowe, whose name was known even in the Highlands. It appeared, also, that he was really visiting Edinburgh, and had only gone to Dunstaffnage on a short stay, from which he was now returning. He had never been in Scotland before, he said, and, but for a very particular circumstance, would not have come now, because the country, and especially the Highlands, held a most painful association for him, he having lost a brother there in the late rebellion.

Ewen said that he was sorry to hear it. 'He was a soldier, I presume?'

The young man nodded. His bright face had saddened, and, looking down, he said as though to himself, 'I am ashamed now that I did not attempt the pilgrimage when I was at Dunstaffnage – I suppose, sir,' he went on rather hesitatingly, 'that you do not chance to know a wild spot on the coast, farther north, called Morar?'

Ewen put down his wine-glass very suddenly, the colour leaving his face. He tried to speak and could not. But his companion went on without waiting for an answer, 'It was there that my brother met his death, Mr Cameron. And he was not killed in fair fight, he was murdered. That is why I do not like the Highlands ... yet I wish time had permitted of my going to Morar.'

A moment Ewen stared as though the handsome speaker were himself a ghost. Keith Windham's brother – could it be true? The tiny inn-parlour was gone, and he was kneeling again in the moonlight on that bloodstained sand. He did not know that he had put his hand over his eyes.

And then the voice that was – he knew it now – so like Keith's, was asking him breathlessly, fiercely, 'Where did you get that ring – my God, where did you get it?'

Ewen dropped his hand and looked up almost dazedly at the young Englishman, who was on his feet, leaning over the table, with a face as white as his own, and eyes suddenly grown hard and accusing.

'He gave it to me ... it was in my arms that he died at Morar ... the victim of a terrible mistake.'

'A mistake, you say? He was killed, then, in the place of another?'

'No, no – not that kind of mistake. My unfortunate foster-brother –'

'Your foster-brother was the murderer! And by whose orders? Yours?'

Ewen gave a strangled cry, and leapt to his own feet, and faced this stern, almost unrecognizable young accuser.

'God forgive you for the suggestion! I wished that day that Lachlan's dirk had been in my own breast! Major Windham was my friend, Lord Aveling, my saviour ... and yet he came to his death through me – And you are his brother! I felt ... yes, that was it – you have his voice.'

'I am his brother of the half-blood,' said the young Viscount, standing very still and looking hard at him. 'My mother was his mother too ... And so you wear his ring. But if you have not his blood upon your hands, what do you mean by saying that he came to his death through you?'

Ewen caught his breath. 'His blood on *my* hands! If it is on anyone's – besides poor deluded Lachlan's – it is on those of another British officer who –' he stopped suddenly and then went on, '– who is probably gone to his account by this time.'

'And you are prepared to swear –'

'Great God, should I have worn his ring all these years if what you think were true? He drew it off his finger – 'twas the last thing he did – and put it into my hand. I will swear it –' he glanced down in search of the dirk which he might not wear, and made a little gesture of desperation. 'I cannot; I have no weapon.'

'Let that pass; I will take your word,' said the young Englishman, speaking with difficulty. 'I can see that what you say is true, and I ask your pardon for my suspicions.' No one, indeed, could well have doubted that it was grief, not guilt, which had made the face of this Highland gentleman so drawn. 'But,' added Lord Aveling after a moment, 'I should be greatly your debtor if you could bring yourself to tell me a little more. All we heard was that while on patrol-duty on the western coast in the August of '46 my unfortunate brother was murdered by a Highlander, either a Cameron or a MacDonald, and was buried where he died. It was impossible, in the then unsettled state of the country, to have his body exhumed and brought to England. And now, I suppose, if this place be as wild as we have heard, his very grave is forgotten?'

'No, it is not forgotten,' answered Ewen, in a much quieter voice. 'I have been there twice – I was there last year. There is a stone I had put ... He did not love the Highlands overmuch, yet 'tis a peaceful and a beautiful spot, Lord Aveling, and though the wind blows sometimes the sand is very white there, and when the moon is full ...' He broke off, and stood with his deep-set blue eyes steady and fixed, the young man staring at him a trifle awed, since he had heard of the second sight, and the speaker was a Highlander.

But Ardroy was seeing the past, not the future, and after a moment sat down again at the table and covered his face with his hands. His half-drained glass rolled over, and the claret stain widened on the coarse cloth. Keith Windham's brother stood looking down at him until, an instant or two later, there came a knock at the door, when he went to it, and dismissed the intruder, the postilion anxious for his lordship to start.

When he came back Ardroy had removed his hands and regained control of himself.

'Since we have met so strangely, you would perhaps desire me to tell you the whole story, my lord?'

And sitting there, sometimes gazing with a strange expression at the stain on the cloth, sometimes looking as if he saw nothing, Ewen told it to the young man in detail.

Chapter 13

THE RELUCTANT VILLAIN

1

LORD AVELING'S elderly postilion may well have wondered when, at last, the two gentlemen came out to take their places in the chaise, why they both looked so grave and pale; yet, since he had been fidgeting over the delay, to see them come at all was welcome. He whipped up the horses, and soon the travellers, not much regarding it, had had their last glimpse of lovely Etive, had crossed the tumbling Awe, and began to enter the Pass of Brander. Close above them were the mighty flanks of Cruachan; on the right the still, black water, bewitched into strange immobility before it rushed into Loch Etive, but streaked with long threads of white as they approached its birthplace in Loch Awe.

The emotions of the inn had left both Ewen and Lord Aveling rather silent, but at last the younger man said, indicating the view from his window:

'As you say, Mr Cameron, my poor brother did not like the Highlands. I, too, find them, with exceptions, uncongenial. This gloomy defile, for instance, and the great mountain beneath which we are travelling, are to me oppressive.'

'Others, and Highlanders to boot, have found Ben Cruachan oppressive, my lord,' returned Ewen with meaning. 'For were you not told at Dunstaffnage that the name of this fine mountain above us has been adopted by the Campbells as their war-cry?'

Lord Aveling looked at him. 'Your clan is no friend to the Campbells, I think.'

Ewen smiled a trifle bitterly. He wondered whether Lord Aveling had heard that enmity in his voice, or had learnt of it otherwise.

'Forgive me if I seem impertinent in asking of your affairs,

496

Mr Cameron,' went on the young man, 'and believe me that they are of interest to me because of your connection with my poor brother. I understand from what you have told me that you left the country after the battle of Culloden; did you find the Highlands much changed upon your return?'

He was obviously inspired only with a friendly interest, and Ardroy, though never very prone to talk about his own concerns, found himself, to his surprise, engaged upon it almost naturally with this unknown young Englishman, his junior, he guessed, by ten years or so. Yet how could he help it? the boy had Keith Windham's voice.

'And so it has been possible for you to settle down quietly,' commented Lord Aveling. 'I am very pleased to hear it. Not all of your name have been so wise – but then your clan is fairly numerous, is it not? For instance, that Doctor Cameron who is such a thorn in the side of the Government ... ah, you know him, perhaps?' For Ewen had not been able to suppress a slight movement.

'Doctor Cameron? I ... I met him in the Rising,' he answered carelessly. Better not to say how intimate was that knowledge, or the young man would probably shut up like an oyster, and he was not averse from hearing his views on Archie.

'It seems,' went on the youth, 'that he is one of the Pre – the Prince's chief agents. However, he has evidently come to the end of his tether in that capacity – or so I heard from ... from Edinburgh this morning.'

'Indeed?' remarked Ewen a little uneasily.

'Yes; I was told that the Lord Justice-Clerk had just received information as to his whereabouts, and, having communicated it to General Churchill, had issued a warrant, which the General immediately sent to the commander of the military post at Inver – Inversnaid, I think the name was. Probably, therefore, Doctor Cameron is captured by now.'

'Inversnaid,' repeated Ewen, after a second or two in which his hand had furtively tightened itself on his knee; 'Inversnaid – that's on the upper end of Loch Lomond. There *is* a barracks near it.'

'On Loch Lomond, you say, sir? I fear my knowledge of the

geography of Scotland is but small, yet I remember that Inversnaid, or something very much like it, was the name ... The prospect of this long lake upon our right – Loch Awe, is it not? – is very fine, Mr Cameron!'

'Yes, very fine indeed,' agreed his companion perfunctorily. 'But – excuse me, Lord Aveling – did your correspondent say ... I mean, was Doctor Cameron reported to be near Loch Lomond?' A growing dismay was fettering his tongue, while his brain, on the contrary, had started to go round like a wheel, revolving possibilities. Could Archie really be in that neighbourhood?

'Loch Lomond was not mentioned in my letter,' replied the young man. 'He was said to be in Glen Something-or-other, of which I don't recall the name. You have so many glens in your country,' he added with an apologetic smile.

What glen could it be? Those running up respectively from Loch Lomond or Loch Katrine? But Archie would never 'skulk' so near Inversnaid as that. If that warrant had really been dispatched from Edinburgh (for the whole thing might only be a rumour) then all one could hope for was that the information on which it had been issued was incorrect. Ewen stole a glance at his fellow-traveller.

'I'll hazard, my lord,' said he, trying to speak carelessly, 'that the place was either Glenfalloch or Glengyle.'

Lord Aveling turned his head from contemplating the twilight beauties of Loch Awe; he looked faintly surprised. 'No, it was neither of those, I am sure,' he replied; and Ewen felt that he was upon the point of adding, 'Why, may I ask, are you so anxious to know?' But he did not.

'If I could but get a sight of that letter!' thought Ewen. 'If he only received it this morning it is probably still in his pocket, not in his baggage. I wish he would bring it forth!' Yes, the letter was probably there, concealed from his longing eyes only by one or two thicknesses of cloth. How could he induce Lord Aveling, who so little guessed of what vital interest the name was to him, to read through his letter again? It would never do to avow that interest openly, because the young Englishman would then certainly refuse, by gratifying his curiosity, to lend himself to the conveyance of a warning to one whom he must regard as a dangerous enemy of the Government. For to warn Archie was now beginning to be Ewen's one desire ... if he could only learn where to find him.

But then he thought despairingly, 'Even if I knew that, and could set off this moment, how could I possibly get there in time?' For if, as Lord Aveling had seemed to imply, the warrant had already left Edinburgh for Inversnaid by the time his letter was dispatched to Dunstaffnage, then, by this morning, when he received it there, so much farther from the capital than was Inversnaid, all was over ... Unless, indeed, by God's mercy, this unnamed glen had been searched and found empty, as it was rumoured had happened to not a few places in the last six months.

'You have no doubt destroyed your letter, my lord?' he suggested desperately after a while – desperately and, as he felt, clumsily.

He saw the colour leap into the young man's cheek – and no wonder! The question was a most unwarrantable impertinence. He would reply 'And what affair is that of yours?' and there would be nothing to do save to beg his pardon.

But no; the youth said – and he actually smiled, 'No, Mr Cameron, I have not done that. Indeed, I fancy 'twill be long before that letter is torn up.' He turned his head away quickly, and once more looked out of the chaise window, but Ewen had the impression that the smile was still upon his lips. He was somewhat puzzled; it could hardly be that the news of Doctor Cameron's possible arrest was so agreeable to the young traveller that he meant always to preserve the letter which announced it. There must be some other reason; perhaps the missive contained some private news which had pleased him. At any rate, it still existed, and, as it was in his possession, why would he not consult it? Was it, after all, packed away in his valise?

'I wonder what glen it could have been,' hazarded Ardroy with a reflective air. 'I thought I knew all the glens in that neighbourhood' (which was false, for he had never been there).

Lord Aveling's left hand – the nearest to his companion – made a quick undecided movement to his breast, and Ewen held his breath. He was going at last to bring out the letter and look! But no ... for some unimaginable reason he was not! The hand fell again, its owner murmuring something about not remembering the name, and immediately beginning, rather pointedly, to talk about something else.

It was useless to go on harping on the matter, even though the letter was indubitably in the young man's pocket. Perhaps, in any case, he himself was allowing its contents to assume quite undue proportions in his mind. There had been so many of these false alarms and unfruitful attempts to seize Archie – that much, at least, he had learnt at Invernacree – and a mere visitor to Edinburgh, an English traveller new to Scotland, was not the person most likely to possess the really accurate knowledge which alone could cause alarm. It was some rumour of the dispatch of a warrant which Lord Aveling's correspondent had passed on to him, some gossip which was circulating in Edinburgh, nothing more.

2

So, by the time they came with lighted lamps to Dalmally, and the little inn in the strath where they were to spend the night, Ewen, by way of revulsion, was almost ready to laugh at himself and his fears. Even if the news about the issue of the warrant were true, the information which had caused it was palpably false. As if Archie would lie hid, as Lord Aveling's correspondent reported, within reach of Inversnaid barracks! Again, if it had been true, then, having regard to the time which had elapsed, and the extraordinary swiftness with which news was wont to travel from mouth to mouth in the Highlands, the news of Doctor Cameron's capture in Perthshire would certainly be known here at Dalmally, almost on the borders. And a few careful questions put to the innkeeper soon after their arrival, out of Lord Aveling's hearing, showed Ardroy that it was not. He sat down to supper with that young man in a somewhat happier frame of mind.

The most esteemed bedroom of the inn had been put at the disposal of the guests. There happened to be two beds in it, and for persons of the same sex travelling together – or even not travelling – to share a room was so usual that the landlord did not even apologize for the necessity; he was only overheard to congratulate himself that he could offer the superior amenities of his best bedchamber to these two gentlemen.

But the gentlemen in question did not congratulate themselves when they saw it.

'Did you say that you once shared a room with my poor brother?' inquired Lord Aveling when their mails had been brought in and they were alone together in that uninviting apartment.

'Hardly a room,' answered Ewen. 'It was but a little hut, where one slept upon bracken.'

'I believe that I should prefer bracken to this bed,' observed his lordship, looking with distaste at the dingy sheets which he had uncovered. 'I shall not venture myself completely into it. Yet, by Gad, I'm sleepy enough.' He yawned. 'I wager I shall sleep as well, perhaps better, than I have done of late at Dunstaffnage Castle, where one heard the sea-wind blowing so strong of nights.'

'Yes, and I dare venture you found Edinburgh none too quiet neither,' observed Ewen idly, surveying his equally dubious sheets, and resolving to follow his companion's example.

'Oh down at General Churchill's quarters 'twas peaceful enough,' returned Lord Aveling, stifling another yawn, 'for the Abbey stands – but there,' he added, beginning to take off his coat, 'you must know better than I what is the situation of Holyrood House.'

Ewen's pulse quickened. 'So it was General Churchill whom you were visiting in Edinburgh, my lord?'

'Yes,' replied the young man. 'I thought I had already mentioned it.' And then he began to redden; even in the meagre candle-light the colour could be seen mounting hotly to his face. 'He is an old acquaintance of my father's.'

Ewen remained motionless, one arm out of his coat; but he was not speculating as to why the young nobleman had so curiously flushed. The thought had shot through him like an arrow: if he has been visiting the Commander-in-Chief, then his news about the warrant out for Archie is no hearsay, it is cold and deadly truth ... and probably the letter which he received this morning announcing the fact was from General Churchill himself.

Talking amiably between yawns, Lord Aveling proceeded to remove his wig and coat. Ewen watched him almost without realizing that he was watching, so overcome was he with the revelation of the identity of the youth's correspondent. And in the same half-tranced state he saw his fellow-traveller bend rather hurriedly over the coat, which he had flung on a chair, extract something from an inner pocket and thrust it under his pillow. The Commander-in-Chief's letter, no doubt, which he seemed so oddly to guard from sight.

Ewen came to life again, finishing taking off his own coat, and removed his boots, in silence. Meanwhile Lord Aveling had fetched a case of pistols from his valise, and, taking out a couple of small, handsomely mounted weapons, placed them on the rickety chair beside his bed. 'We are not like to use these, I hope, Mr Cameron, but there they are, to serve whichever of us wakes first and finds a housebreaker in the room.'

A moment or two afterwards, apologizing for what he termed his unmannerly drowsiness, he had blown out his candle, thrown himself upon his bed, pulled a long travelling cloak over himself, and was asleep almost at once. Ardroy took up his candle meaning to blow it out too, but for a moment he stood there looking across his own bed at what he could see of the sleeper – no more, really, than the back of a fair, close-cropped head half-sunk in the pillow, and one slim, silk-clad foot and ankle projecting beyond the cloak. If Keith could see them together now, him and this rather charming and ingenuous young half-brother of his! Ewen blew out the light, and sat down on the side of his bed, his back to his fellow-traveller, and stared out through the greyish square of the uncurtained window.

Had he but known that General Churchill himself was the boy's informant, he would certainly have forced him somehow to look at his letter again, if not in the chaise, then at supper, and to tell him the name of that glen. But it was not yet too late. The letter was still there – here, rather, in this room, and only a few feet away. He had only to wake Lord Aveling and say, 'Show me the line, the word, in your letter which concerns Doctor Cameron, for I'll take no denial!'

And then? Was the young Englishman going to accede quietly to that demand? Naturally not. There would be an unseemly, an unchivalrous struggle, ending, no doubt, in his overpowering the boy and reading the letter by force. Meanwhile, the house would probably be roused, and all chance of his slipping away undetected on the task of warning Archie gone.

There was, it could not be denied, another method ... the only prudent one ...

'No, that I *cannot* do!' said Ardroy to himself. He took his head in his hands for a moment, then got up, fetched his cloak and, lying down and covering himself up, tried to compose himself to sleep.

The attempt was foredoomed to failure, for he could think of only one thing: Archie, betrayed but ignorant of his betrayal, and the soldiers already on their way from Inversnaid to surprise and drag him off. And here he, his cousin and friend, who had always professed so much affection for him, and into whose hands the knowledge of this attempt had so surprisingly come, lay peaceably sleeping while the tragedy drew nearer and nearer, and would not, on account of a scruple, put out one of those hands to learn the final clue – an act which, with luck, could be carried through in a few moments, and which could harm no one ... But no, he was going to allow Archibald Cameron, his dead Chief's brother, to go unwarned to capture because a gentleman did not clandestinely read another's letters.

Ewen lay there in torment. Through the window close to his bed he could see a wild white sky, where the thin clouds drove like wraiths before a phantom pursuer, though there was no sound of wind at all. It was so light a night that even in the room he could probably see to do *that* without the aid of a candle; so light that outside, if he succeeded in getting away unhindered with one of the horses, the same witchlike sky would enable him to find his way without too much difficulty along the road to Tyndrum and Perthshire. He saw himself riding, riding hard ...

What nonsense! Was he not almost convinced that the information on which the warrant had been issued was false, and that Doctor Cameron would not lie in any place within reach of Inversnaid? ... so why indulge this overmastering desire to see the name of the alleged place? And, said the same voice, you are sure also that any action would be too late now, for the warrant sent express to Loch Lomond some days ago must either have been carried out by this time or have failed of its purpose. In either case the dishonourable and repugnant act which you propose is futile ... And if the boy wakes while you are engaged upon it, what will you say to him?

Ewen turned over on his other side, not to see that tempting sky. But could one be *sure* that the danger was not real, was not still within his power to avert? And was not the true dishonour to let a friend go to his doom because one was afraid of a slight stain on one's own reputation? He wondered if Keith Windham, in his place, would have hesitated – Yes, any gentleman would hesitate. It was ignominious, a mean thing to do. But not a crime. It was not for himself. Had one the right to cherish selfish scruples when so much was at stake for another man? No! ... For Archie's sake, then!

He rose very softly from his bed and put on the clothes he had laid aside, but not his boots. Then, standing up, he took his bearing in the dim room, where Aveling's breathing showed how soundly he was asleep. The first step was to find out where the young man had put the letter. Ewen had seen him take something from his coat and slip it under his pillow: probably this was a letter-case or something of the kind and contained the carefully guarded epistle. This was unfortunate, because it would be much more difficult to extricate it without waking him, though, for some obscure reason, the thought of withdrawing it from that hiding-place was less distasteful – perhaps because attended with more risk – than that of searching the pockets of the discarded coat.

Ewen could see now, if not very distinctly, the position of everything in the room, which was important, lest he should stumble over any object and make a noise. The key was in the locked door; he tiptoed over and removed it to his own pocket, since above all things the lad, if he woke, must not be allowed to rouse the inn. Being light on his feet, for all his stature, Ardroy accomplished this without a sound. The next step was to remove the pistols, lest the youth, thinking, not unnaturally, that he was being robbed, should try to use them. Ewen lifted them from the chair and slipped them also into his pockets. And still the sleeper showed no signs of waking.

Then, tingling with repugnance, but quite resolved and unrelenting, Ewen stood over him – he could only see him as a dark mass – and began carefully to slide his hand under the paler mass which was the pillow. Every fibre in his body and brain revolted from what he was doing, but he went on with it; it was for Archie. He wondered, as his fingers gently sought about there, what he should do or say if the young Englishman woke. Try to explain? Hold him down? Half-measures would be of no use ... What a weight a man's head was! Yes, Keith's had lain heavy on his arm that night, but Keith had been dying ... His groping fingers encountered something at last, and with infinite precautions he slipped it out at the top of the pillow and tiptoed away to the window with his prize.

It was a small leather letter-case which he held. Ardroy hastily pulled out the contents, rather dismayed to find how little he could make of them in the dusk. There came out first some bank-notes, which he stuffed back as though his fingers had encountered a snake; then some papers which might have been bills, and lastly three letters, of which, peer at them as he might, he could not distinguish a word.

This was extremely daunting. Either he would be obliged to light the candle, which he particularly wished to avoid doing, or he must take all three letters down to the stable with him, and trust to find a lantern there to read them by. But that would indeed be theft, and unnecessary theft. He only wanted one line – one word – in one letter, General Churchill's.

Annoyed, he took up his candlestick. The problem was where to put it, so that the light might not wake the sleeper. On the floor, he decided, between the window and his own bed, whose bulk would shield the flame. He did so, and knelt down on one knee by it. What a disconcertingly sharp sound flint and steel made; he had to strike more than once, too, for the tinder would not catch. At last the candle sprang into flame, and, kneeling there behind his bed, holding his breath, Ardroy examined the letters.

The first he took up was some weeks old, and bore a London address, so he did not examine it further; the second, in a small fine writing, was dated from 'The Abbey, March 16th', and signed – Ewen turned hurriedly to the end – yes, signed 'Churchill'.

But not 'William' or 'James' or whatever the General's name was ... no – *'Georgina'*.

Ewen stared at the signature, horror-struck. This was infinitely worse than bank-notes, worse, even, than a real snake would have been. Now he knew why its recipient was reluctant to bring forth, in the close proximity of the chaise, this letter so palpably in a lady's hand, and – as the present reader could not avoid seeing – thick-studded with maidenly endearments. That was why Lord Aveling had coloured so, had repudiated the idea of destroying the epistle. Obviously he was not of the stuff of the complacent *jeune homme à bonnes fortunes*. His shy delicacy in the matter made the present thief's task tenfold more odious. But having gone so far he could not draw back, and the writer, be she never so fond, was also General Churchill's daughter ... or niece, perhaps? No, at the bottom of the first sheet – there were two separate ones, of a large size – was a reference to 'Papa', presumably the Commander-in-Chief.

But where in all this was the name for the sake of which he had embarked upon the repulsive business? Ewen could not see it anywhere, as, hot with embarrassment, he picked his way among expressions not meant for the eyes of any third person, which seemed, too, to show that Lord Aveling was a recently accepted suitor. But the shamed reader of these lovers' confidences did not want to have any knowledge of the sort thrust upon him. Not yet finding what he wanted he put down this letter and took up the third; no, that was from London, and

signed 'Your affectionate Father, Stowe'. So with an inward
sigh he went back to the love-letter, wishing with all his soul
that the enamoured Miss Georgina Churchill did not write so
fine a hand and so long an epistle.

And, just as he thought that he was coming to the place, he
heard a creak from Aveling's bed.

'Great Heavens, what's wrong? What are you at there, Mr
Cameron – are you ill?' And then a further movement and an
ejaculation, 'Who the devil has taken my pistols from this
chair?'

Ewen was still on one knee beyond his bed, feverishly scanning the letter held below its level. 'It was I who removed them.
I was afraid,' he said with perfect truth, 'that you might wake,
and, seeing a light, use them by error.' And he went on searching – ah, thank God, here he was coming to it at last!

*'I must tell you that Papa had a message last night from the
Lord Justice-Clerk informing him that Doctor Cameron –'*

The word 'warrant' swam for a second before his eyes, but he
could get no farther, for now he was to pay the price of his
villainy. Young Aveling, who must have thrust his hand instinctively under his pillow, had by this time discovered his
second, his greater loss, and with one movement had thrown off
his covering and was on his feet, his voice shaking with rage.
'You have stolen my wallet! Give it back to me at once, you
damned lying, treacherous thief!'

Ewen rose quickly to his own feet and threw the little case on
to his bed, which was still between them. 'You will find your
money all there, my lord.' Then, very swiftly, he picked up the
candle, put it on the window-sill behind him, found the passage
again and tried to go on with his reading of it. But he knew that
he would have the young man upon him in a moment, and so he
had.

'Money! It's not the money! You have my letters, my most
private letters ...' And uttering a cry of rage he precipitated
himself round the bottom of Ewen's bed.

But Ewen, despite his preoccupation, could be just as quick.
The young Englishman found himself confronted by the barrel
of one of his own pistols. 'You shall have this letter in one

moment if you wait,' said its abductor coolly. 'But if you desire it intact do not try to take it from me.'

'*Wait!*' ejaculated the boy, half-choking. Alight with fury – for instinct no doubt told him which of the three letters the robber held – he did a surprising thing: disregarding entirely the levelled pistol, he dropped suddenly to his knees, and, seizing his enemy by the leg, tried to throw him off his balance – and nearly succeeded. For a second Ardroy staggered; then he recovered himself.

'You young fool!' he exclaimed angrily; clapped the pistol on the window-ledge behind him, stuffed Miss Georgina Churchill's letter into his pocket, stooped, seized the young man's arms, tore their grip apart, and brought him, struggling and panting, to his feet. 'You young fool, I want to give you your letter unharmed, and how can I, if you persist in attacking me?'

'Unharmed!' echoed the young man, with tears of rage in his eyes. He was helpless in that grip, and knew it now. 'You call it unharmed, when you have read it!'

'I regret the necessity even more than you,' retorted Ardroy. 'But you would not tell me what I needed to know. If you will go back to your bed, and give me your word of honour not to stir thence for a couple of moments, you shall have your letter again at the end of them.'

'My word of honour – to you!' flashed the captive. 'You false Highland thief, I should think you never heard the term in your life before! Give me back the letter which you have contaminated by reading – at once!'

Ewen did not relish his language, but what right had he to resent it? 'You shall have the letter back on the condition I have named,' he answered sternly. 'If you oblige me to hold you like this ... no, 'tis of no use, you cannot break away ... God knows when you'll get it back. And if you attempt to cry for help' (for he thought he saw a determination of the kind pass over the handsome, distorted features) 'I'll gag you! You may be sure I should never have embarked upon this odious business if I had not meant to carry it through!'

'"Odious"!' his captive caught up the word. 'You are a spy and a thief, and you pretend to dislike your trade!'

Ewen did not trouble to deny the charge. He felt that no stone which his victim could fling at him was too sharp. 'Will you give me your word?' he asked again, more gently. 'I do not wish to hurt you ... and I have not read your letter through. I was but searching in it for what I need.'

But that avowal only raised the young lover's fury afresh. 'Damn you for a scoundrelly pickpocket!' he said between his teeth, and began to struggle anew until he was mastered once more, and his arms pinned to his sides. And thus, very white, he asked in a voice like a dagger:

'Did you turn out my brother Keith's pockets before, or after, you murdered him?'

As a weapon of assault the query had more success than all his physical efforts. This stone was too sharp. Ewen caught his breath, and his grip loosened a little.

'I deserve everything that you have said to me, Lord Aveling, but not that! Your brother was my friend.'

'And did you read *his* most private correspondence when he was asleep? Give me my letter, or I'll rouse the house – somehow!'

The matter had come to something of an *impasse*. Ewen was no nearer to his goal, for as long as he had to hold this young and struggling piece of indignation he could not finish reading the passage in the letter. He decided that he should have to take a still more brutal step. At any rate, nothing could make his victim think worse of him than he did already.

'If you do not go back and sit quietly upon your bed,' he said, with a rather ominous quietness himself, 'I shall hold you with one hand, and thrust one sheet of your letter in the candle-flame with the other!'

'You may do it – for I'll not take it back now!' flashed out the boy instantly.

'But if you give me your word to do as I say,' went on Ewen, as though he had not spoken, 'I will restore you a sheet of it now as earnest for the return of the rest, when I have finished reading the one sentence which concerns me – Now, which is it to be, Lord Aveling?'

In that extremely close proximity their eyes met. The young man saw no relenting in those blue ones fixed on his, hard as only blue eyes can be at need. And Ewen – Ewen did not like to think to what desperate measures he might have to resort if the card he had just played were in truth not high enough ...

But the trick was won. Despite his frenzied interjection, the young lover wanted his property too much to see it reduced to ashes before him. He choked back something like a sob. 'I'll never believe in fair words ... and a moving story again! ... Yes, I will do it. Give me the sheet of my letter.'

'You pledge your word not to molest or attempt to stop me, nor to give any kind of alarm?'

'Before I do, I suppose I may know whether you intend to cut my throat, as you –' But, frantic as the youth was, Ewen's face became so grim that he did not finish.

'I'll not lay a finger on you further.'

'Then I pledge you my word – the word of an Englishman!' said the boy haughtily.

'And I keep mine – as a Highlander,' retorted Ewen. He loosed him at once, selected that sheet of Miss Churchill's letter which he did not require, and handed it to its owner in silence. The youth thrust it passionately inside his shirt, went back to his own bed, and, shivering with rage and exhaustion, sat down and hid his face in his hands.

Ewen, his back half-turned, found the passage again.

'*Papa had a message last night from the Lord Justice-Clerk informing him that Doctor Cameron was said to be at the house of Stewart of Glenbuckie, and a warrant was immediately dispatched to the post at Inversnaid.*'

Glenbuckie ... Glenbuckie ... in what connection had he heard of that place before? Glenbuckie was ... good God, was it possible that he did not really know with sufficient exactitude ... that he had committed this shameful violence for nothing? The sweat started out all over Ewen's body, and he prayed desperately for an illuminating flash of memory. Well had that poor boy huddled there spoken of the many glens there were in Scotland!

Then the knowledge returned to him, bearing with it a tragic recollection from the early days of the Rising, when the notor-iety given to Stewart of Glenbuckie's name by the mysterious death of its then bearer, in Buchanan of Arnprior's house, had resulted in one's learning the whereabouts of the glen from which he came. Yes, Glenbuckie was somewhere in the Bal-quhidder district – a glen running directly southward from the farther end of Loch Voil, he believed ... a long way and a difficult. And, his mind already calculating distances and route, Ewen read the passage again. There was a little more, for Miss Georgina Churchill had been at the pains to tell her lover that the person who had sent this information to the Lord Justice-Clerk was someone who claimed to have recently met and spoken with Doctor Cameron ... Ewen sat down and pulled on his boots.

For the last few moments he had almost forgotten Aveling. Putting the pistol in his pocket again he went over to him. 'Here is the other sheet of the letter, my lord. You will not accept my apologies, I know, but I make them to you none the less, and sincerely – and also for borrowing the horse from Bonawe, which I propose to do as far as Tyndrum, where I hope you will find him when you arrive. If I can, I will leave your pistols there also. If not, I will pay for them.'

The young Englishman jumped up and snatched his letter. 'You'll pay for everything one day, by God – in Newgate, or wherever in this barbarous country of yours they bestow their Highland robbers! And I'll have you indicted for my brother's murder as well as for assaulting me in order to assist an attainted rebel! Since you are his confederate, you shall swing with Doctor Cameron at Tyburn!'

But Ewen was already unlocking the door of the room. His great dread was that the young man, strung up by rage and dis-illusionment to what in a woman would have been hysteria point, might forget his promise and proceed unwittingly to rouse the inn. He did not want to use the pistols in order to get clear of the premises, so he slipped as quickly as possible out of the room and locked the door on the outside, hearing, not without remorse, sounds from within which suggested that the boy had flung himself upon the bed and was weeping aloud.

So ended, in dishonour and brutality, this encounter with his dead friend's brother, who had acted so generously towards him, and to whom he had felt so strongly attracted. A moment only that thought flashed bitingly through Ewen's brain; it was no time to indulge in regret or to think of consequences to himself – his immediate task was to warn Archie. To his crimes of treachery and violence he must, therefore, if he could, add that of horse-stealing.

And even as Ardroy cautiously lifted the latch of the stable door at Dalmally, away in the little rebuilt barracks near Inversnaid, on Loch Lomond, Captain Craven of Beauclerk's regiment was reading the belated dispatch from the Commander-in-Chief at Edinburgh which he had been roused from his bed to receive.

'Too late to do anything tonight,' was his comment. Then his eyes fell upon the date which it bore. 'Gad, man,' he said to the wearied messenger, 'I should have received this warrant yesterday! The bird may be flown by tomorrow. What in God's name delayed you so?'

Chapter 14

IN TIME – AND TOO LATE

1

THE fitful sun of the March afternoon came flooding straight through the open door of Mr Stewart of Glenbuckie's house into the hall, which was also the living-room, and through this same open door little Peggy Stewart, the room's sole occupant, had she not been otherwise engaged, could have looked out across the drop in front of the high-standing house to the tossing slopes beyond the Calair burn. But Peggy had earlier begged from her mother, who had been baking today, a piece of dough, and, following the probably immemorial custom of children, had fashioned out of it, after countless remodellings, an object bearing some resemblance to the human form, with two currants for eyes. And while she sat there, regarding her handiwork with the fond yet critical gaze of the artist, before taking it to the kitchen to be baked, there suddenly appeared without warning, in the oblong pale of sunlight which was the doorway, the figure of a large, very tall man. This stalwart apparition put out a hand to knock, and then, as if disconcerted at finding the door open, withdrew it.

Miss Peggy, who was no shyer than she need be, rose from her little stool near the spinning-wheel and advanced into the sunlight. And to a man who had ridden all night on a stolen horse, and had since, tortured by the feeling that every delay was the final and fatal one, stumbled and fought his way over the steep and unfamiliar mountain paths on the western slopes of Ben More and Stobinian, to such a man the appearance at Stewart of Glenbuckie's door of a chubby little girl of six, dressed in a miniature tight-waisted gown of blue which almost touched the floor, and clasping in one hand what he took to be an inchoate kind of doll, was vaguely reassuring.

'Is this the house of Mr Duncan Stewart?' he asked.

513

Gazing up at this tall stranger with her limpid blue eyes the child nodded.

'Is he within, my dear?'

Miss Peggy Stewart shook her curly head. 'My papa is from home.'

'And ... have you a gentleman staying here?'

'He is not here either. Only Mother is here.'

Instantly Ewen's thoughts swung round to the worst. They had both been arrested, then, Stewart as well as Archie. The noticeable quiet of the house was due to its emptiness – only a woman and a child left there. He was too late, as he had expected all along. He put his head mutely against the support of the door, and so was found an instant later by Mrs Stewart, who, hearing voices, had come from the kitchen.

'Is aught amiss, sir? Are you ill?'

Ardroy raised his head and uncovered. But this lady did not sound or look like a woman whose husband had recently been torn from her. Hope stirred again. 'Madam, have the soldiers been here after ... any person?'

Mrs Stewart's calm, fair face took on a look of surprise. 'No, sir, I am glad to say. But will you not enter?'

At this bidding Ewen walked, or rather stalked, over the threshold; he was stiff. 'Thank God for that!' he said fervently. 'But they may be here at any moment.' He bethought him, and closed the door behind him. 'There is a warrant out for ... that person.'

Mrs Stewart lowered her voice. 'Then it is fortunate that he is not in the house.'

'He is away, with your husband?'

'No, sir. Mr Stewart is in Perth on affairs. I do not know where "Mr Chalmers" has gone this afternoon, but he will return before dark.'

'He must at all costs be prevented from doing that, madam,' said Ewen earnestly, while Peggy tugged at her mother's skirts whispering, with equal earnestness, something about her 'bread mannie' and the oven. 'If he comes back here, he will be running into a trap. I cannot understand why the warrant has not already been executed, but, since it has not, let us take advantage of the mercy of heaven – My own name, by the way, madam, is Cameron, and I am "Mr Chalmers's" near kinsman. He must be found and stopped before he reaches this house!'

'Certainly he should be,' agreed Mrs Stewart. 'Unfortunately – be quiet, my child – unfortunately, I do not know in which direction he has gone, whether down the glen or up it.'

'Mr Chalmers was going to Balquhidder,' observed Peggy with composure. 'He told me; he said tell Mother, but I forgot – Mother, please put my bread mannie in the oven!'

The two adults looked down anxiously at the source of this information.

'Are you sure, Peggy, that that is where Mr Chalmers has gone? – Yes, darling,' added her mother hastily, 'I will have your bread mannie put in at once if this gentleman will excuse me.' She gave Ewen a look which seemed to say, 'I am not usually so weak and indulgent, but it is politic in this case, for if she cries we shall get no more out of her.'

Yet, as it happened, indulgence got no more either, for there seemed no more for Peggy to tell when she was asked, and so Ewen stood on the threshold of Mrs Stewart's spotless kitchen and watched with troubled eyes the consignment of Peggy's masterpiece to the oven. And, with his own boys in mind, he found time to wonder at that world set apart, that fairy world in which children dwell, and to think how happily and uncomprehendingly they move amid the tragedies and anxieties of the other, touching them at every point, and often by sheer contrast heightening them, but usually unaffected by the contact ...

Then Mrs Stewart came out, saying over her shoulder to someone within, 'Janet, keep the child with you for a while. Mr Cameron, you'll take some refreshment before you start?'

But Ewen refused, hungry and spent though he was, for he would not spare the time. Mrs Stewart, however, returned swiftly to the kitchen, and was heard giving orders for bread and meat to be made ready for him to take with him.

'Now I'll give you directions,' she said, hurrying out again. 'Yet, Mr Cameron, I cannot think that this is true about a warrant, for had there been any soldiers on the march from

Loch Lomond side the country people would most certainly have sent messengers on ahead to warn us. For I have heard my husband say that since the garrison at Inversnaid makes a practice of selling meal and tobacco to the Highlanders, and there is a canteen in one of the barrack rooms itself, many a piece of news leaks out to us that way. For this is all, as you know, what the English call a "disaffected" region, and "Mr Chalmers" has been with us for some time quite unmolested.'

'Yet in this case extraordinary precautions may have been taken against any tidings reaching you,' urged Ewen. 'And I have seen a letter from a member of General Churchill's household which stated that a warrant had been issued on the fifteenth – six days ago. It was in fact that letter which brought me here, for I did not know my cousin's whereabouts. But they certainly know it in Edinburgh. Someone has informed against him, Mrs Stewart.'

She was plainly shocked. 'Oh, sir, that's impossible! No one in these parts would do such a thing!'

But Ardroy shook his head. 'It may not have been a man from this district, but it has been done – and by someone who had speech with the Doctor recently. It remains now to circumvent the traitor. Supposing the child to have been mistaken, have you any trusty person whom you can send in the opposite direction, or in any other where you think "Mr Chalmers" likely to have gone?'

'Only the gardener; but I will send him at once up the glen. Yet if Peggy is right, 'tis you will meet the Doctor, though I know not how far you'll have to go, nor whether you had best –' She stopped and drew her brows together. 'Nay, I believe he ever takes the track through the wood when he goes to Balquhidder, for the path down the open glen gives no shelter in case of danger. It will be best for you to go by the wood. You saw the burn, no doubt, as you came up to the house? Follow it a space down the glen till it goes into the wood, and go in with it. The track then runs by the water till it mounts higher than the burn; but you cannot miss it. And I must tell you,' she finished, 'that Mr Chalmers is wearing a black wig, which changes him very much; and commonly, unless he forgets, he makes to walk with a stoop to reduce his height. But you'll be knowing his appearance well, perhaps?'

'Very well indeed,' said Ewen, checking a sigh. 'God grant I meet him! I am to begin by following the burn, then?' He repeated her simple instructions and went towards the door. Every moment he expected it to be flung wide by a redcoat.

But he opened it, and there was nothing but the pale unclouded sun, almost balanced now on one of the crests opposite, the sharp sweet hill air, and a murmur of wind in the pines below the house. On the threshold Mrs Stewart tendered him the packet of bread and meat, and a small voice from a lesser altitude was also heard offering him, as sustentation, 'my bread mannie'. It was true that this gift, withdrawn from too brief a sojourn in the oven, was far from being bread, but Ewen gravely accepted the amorphous and sticky object and wrapped it in his handkerchief. He could not refuse this fair-haired child whose tidings might be destined to prove the salvation of Archibald Cameron, and he stooped and kissed her. The little figure waving an adieu was the last thing he saw as he walked quickly away from the house towards the wood which clung about the downward course of the Calair.

2

As Mrs Stewart had said, the track through the wood was quite easy to find and follow. Ewen hurried along it at a very fast pace, since the farther from Stewart's house he could encounter Archie the better. And yet, it *might* be a wild goose chase into which he had flung himself; it might be for the sake of a mere rumour that he, Ewen Cameron of Ardroy, had assaulted the future Earl of Stowe and stolen, or rather borrowed, a horse. The pistols he had certainly stolen, for he had not left them, as he had the horse, at the inn at Tyndrum, but had kept them with him, and might be glad of them yet. For though, contrary to all his expectations, he was in time to warn Archie (if only he could come upon him) he could not feel at ease about the warrant, even though its execution was so strangely delayed, or believe that machinery of the kind, once set in motion, would cease to revolve.

So he hastened on; the path, fairly wide here, having quitted the stream, was full of holes crammed with damp, dead leaves; through the bare oaks and ashes and the twisted pine boughs on his left he saw the sun disappear behind the heights opposite. As its rays were withdrawn the air grew at once colder, and an uneasy wind began to move overhead; it left the oaks indifferent, but the pines responded to its harper's touch. Ardroy had lived his life too much in the open air and in all weathers to be much mentally affected by wind, yet the sound tuned with his anxious thoughts almost without his being aware of it.

So far he had not met or even seen a single person, but now, as he heard steps approaching, his pulse quickened. He was wrong – it was not Archie, for there came into sight an elderly man bent under a load of sticks which he had evidently been gathering in the wood. No word issued from him as they passed each other, but he turned, sticks and all, and stared after the stranger. Meanwhile Ewen hastened on; he must, he thought, have come a considerable way by now, and for the first time he began to wonder what he should do if he got to Balquhidder itself without encountering his cousin, and to regret that he had not asked Mrs Stewart's advice about such a contingency.

It was while he was turning over this difficulty in his mind that he came round a bend in the woodland path and perceived, at the foot of a tree, a man with one knee on the ground, examining something at its foot. Was it? ... it looked like ... Yes! He broke into a run, and was upon Doctor Cameron before the latter had time to do more than rise to his feet and utter an amazed:

'Ewen! *Ewen!* ... It can't be! How, and why –'

And not till that moment did it occur to Ewen that all this had happened before, in different surroundings. 'I am come to warn you – once again, Archie!' he said, seizing him by the arms in his earnestness. 'You must come no farther – you must not return to Stewart's house. There's a warrant out against you from Edinburgh, and soldiers coming from Inversnaid. Your hiding-place has been betrayed.'

'Betrayed!' said Archibald Cameron in incredulous tones. 'Dear lad, you must be mistaken. There's but six or seven people know that I am in these parts, and I could answer for everyone of them.'

Ewen was not shaken. It was like Archie not to believe in treachery. 'You may think that,' he replied, 'but it has been done. I have the fact on too good authority to doubt it. I have seen Mrs Stewart, and told her, and have come to intercept you. You must not go back there.'

Archie slid his arm into his. 'But first, my dear Ewen, I must learn whence you come and how? I know that you escaped from Fort William before the New Year but —'

'I'll tell you everything in proper time,' broke in his kinsman, 'but in the name of good sense let us find a more concealed place to talk in than this path! — What is occupying you by this tree, pray?' For at the mention of leaving the path Doctor Cameron's gaze had strayed back to the spot over which he had been stooping. Ewen could see nothing there but some bright-coloured toadstools.

'It is, I think, a rare fungus,' said Archie meditatively. 'I should like — well, why not?' He stooped and picked one, and then allowed Ewen to draw him away into the undergrowth, just there waist-high or more, and find a spot under an oak, where, if they chose to sit or crouch, they would be invisible from the track.

But for the moment they stood beneath the oak tree looking at each other, the elder man still holding the little orange toadstool between his fingers. Even though the black tie-wig, in place of the brown one he usually wore, or of his own fair, slightly greying hair, did change Archibald Cameron, even though Ewen's gaze, scanning his face closely, did seem to find there a hint of a fresh line or two about the kindly mouth, he looked much the same as when Ardroy had last set eyes on him in the dark little croft up at Slochd nan Eun. And, as he might have done then, he wanted most to know of Ewen's affairs.

But Ewen took him to task. 'Are you fey, Archie, that you waste time over questions of no moment, and won't believe what I tell you? Someone has betrayed you and sent information to Edinburgh which has been acted upon. To come by the knowledge of this and of your whereabouts I have made a life-long enemy of a man I liked, committed an assault on him, stolen a horse, and, worse than all, read a private letter by stealth. You must at least pay some heed to me, and pay it at once!'

His concern was too acute to be ignored any longer. 'Forgive me. *laochain*,' said the elder man. 'What do you wish me to do?'

'Move your quarters instantly. It means capture to return to Duncan Stewart's.'

Archie was attentive enough now. 'I doubt if there is anyone else in the neighbourhood who is anxious for my presence.'

'But it would be infinitely better to leave the neighbourhood altogether,' urged his cousin.

Doctor Cameron considered. 'I might lie for a while in the braes of Balquhidder on the far side of the loch – 'tis solitary enough there. But if the soldiers are coming from Inversnaid it would be well to avoid that direction, and better to make at right angles through this wood and up the slopes of Beinn an-t-Shithein ... Yet, Ewen, 'tis sore hearing and hard believing that anyone can have informed of me. From whom was this letter which you –'

The sound of a shot, followed by a scream, both quite near, killed the question on his lips, and drove the blood from Ewen's heart, if not from the speaker's own. In a moment more, as they both stood mute and tense, a patter of light running feet and the pound of heavier ones could be heard, and along the path which they had left came flying, with terror on her face, a little bare-foot girl of about twelve, closely pursued by a soldier, musket in hand, who was shouting after her to stop.

Both men started indignantly to make their way out of the undergrowth towards the pair, but Ewen turned fiercely on his companion.

'Archie, are you quite mad?' he whispered. 'Stay there – and down with you!' He gave him a rough push, and himself crashed through the bushes and burst out on to the path just in front of the runners. The little girl, sobbing with fright, almost collided with him; he seized her, swung her behind him, and angrily faced the panting soldier. 'Put down that musket, you ruffian! This is not the Slave Coast!'

The man's face was almost the colour of his coat from his exertions, but, at least, there was no evil intent written there. 'I were only trying ... to stop the varmint!' he explained, very much out of breath. 'She's sent on ahead by some rebels in a farm ... we marched by a while since ... to carry a warning belike ... I've bin a-chasing of her up and down hills for the last half-hour. Orders it was ... I wouldn't lay a finger on a child ... got two of me own ... only fired to frighten her into stopping – Hold her, or she'll be off again!'

But there did not seem much likelihood of that. The little girl was on her knees in a heap behind the Highlander, her hands over her ears. He stooped over her.

'You are not hurt, my child, are you?' he asked in the Gaelic. 'Then get you home again; you have done your work. You need not be frightened any more; the redcoat will not harm you.' And he took out a piece of money and closed her fingers over it.

'What are you saying to her – what are you giving her money for?' demanded the soldier suspiciously. 'I believe you'll be in league with the rebels yourself!'

'I should scarce tell her to go home if I were,' answered Ewen with an indifference which he was far from feeling. Good God, if next moment a picket should appear and search the bushes – or if Archie did not now remain motionless beneath them! 'I do not know what you mean,' he continued, 'about a warning, but between us we have stopped the child, and the sixpence I have given her will make her forget her fright the quicker – Off with you!' he repeated to the girl.

Ewen's words had no doubt conveyed to the child a sense that she had accomplished her mission, though the eyes under the elf-locks of rusty hair were still fixed on him, and her whole eager, thin little face asked a wordless question to which he dared not make a further reply. Then, without a sign, she sprang up and slipped into the undergrowth, apparently to avoid the proximity of the redcoat, emerged from it on the other side of him, and ran back the way she had come.

Her late pursuer turned and looked after her, while Ewen's finger closed round one of Lord Aveling's pistols in his pocket. What was the soldier going to do next? If he took a dozen steps off the path to his right he must see Archie crouched there; and if he did that he would have to be shot in cold blood. If he even stayed where he was much longer he would have to be accounted for somehow, since his mere presence would prevent the Jacobite from getting away unobserved. And get away he must, at once.

'Where's your main body?' asked Ardroy suddenly.

The soldier turned round again. 'D'ye think I'm quite a fool that you ask me that?' he retorted scornfully. 'If you're one of the disaffected yourself, as I suspect you are, from speaking Erse so glibly, you'll soon find that out.' And swinging suddenly round again, he went off at a trot on the way he had come.

'Why, the Duke of Argyll himself speaks Erse on occasions!' Ewen called after him mockingly. But there was no mockery in his heart, only the most sickening apprehension. He was right, only too right, about the warrant, and the child had been sent on ahead to carry a warning, just as Mrs Stewart had said would probably happen. Had Mrs Stewart herself sent her? No, the man said she had come from a farm.

Directly the redcoat was out of sight Ardroy hurled himself into his cousin's lair. Doctor Cameron was already on his feet.

'You heard, Archie? There's not a moment to lose! He'll be back with a party, very like, from the child running this way ... though how she knew ...'

'Yes, we must make for the side of Beinn an-t-Shithein,' said Archibald Cameron without comment. 'That is to say I must. You –'

'Do you suppose I am going to leave you? Lead, and I'll follow you.'

'There's no path,' observed the Doctor. 'Perhaps 'tis as well; we'll not be so easy to track.'

For ten minutes or so Ewen followed his cousin uphill through the wood, sometimes pushing through tangle of various kinds, sometimes stooping almost double, sometimes running, and once or twice getting severely scratched by holly bushes. But they were not yet in sight of its upper edge when Doctor Cameron came to an abrupt stop and held up his hand.

'Listen! I thought I heard voices ahead.'

The wind, which had risen a good deal in the last half-hour, and now tossed the branches overhead, made it difficult to be sure of this. Ewen knelt and put his ear to the ground.

'I hear something, undoubtedly.' He got up and looked at Archie anxiously. 'If we should prove to be cut off from the hillside, is there any place in the wood where we could lie hid – a cave, or even a heap of boulders?'

'There is nothing that I know of. – Ewen, where are you going?'

'Only a little farther on, to reconnoitre. Oh, I'll be careful, I promise you. Meanwhile stay you there!' And he was off before Archie could detain him.

It took him but five minutes or so of careful stalking to be certain that there were soldiers between them and the slopes which they were hoping to gain. There were also, without doubt, soldiers somewhere in the lower part of the wood near the stream. If they could neither leave the wood, nor hide in it, Archie must infallibly be taken.

Ewen slid round the beech-trunk against which he was pressed, meaning to retrace his steps immediately to the spot where he had left his kinsman, but for a moment he stood there motionless, with a horrible premonition at his heart. O God, it could not be that this was the end for Archie! A sort of blindness seemed to pass over his vision, and when it cleared he found his eyes fixed on something farther down the slope of the wood, a little to his left, something that he must have been looking at already without recognizing it for what it was – a small thatched roof.

It seemed like a miracle, an answer to prayer at the least. Ewen slipped back with all speed to the Doctor.

'Yes, we are cut off,' he whispered, 'and we cannot go back. But, Archie, there's some kind of little building farther down the wood. I saw but its roof, yet it may serve us better than nothing. Let us go and look at it.'

They hurried down the slope again. Here the dead leaves were dry, and rustled underfoot, but the need of haste overrode that of silent going. And in a few minutes they both stood looking at Ewen's discovery, a small log hut. It stood on a level piece of the wood, with a little clearing of some ten yards square in front of it, but on its other sides bushes and stout hollies pressed close up to it.

'I never before heard of any hut in this wood,' commented Archie in surprise, 'but there it is, certainly! Perhaps the Good People have put it there for us.'

If they had, it could not have been recently, for, as Ewen saw with relief, the logs of which it was constructed were so weathered and mossed that it was not at first very distinguishable from its surroundings. But it was in good repair, and, on going round to the front, the fugitives saw that it actually had a solid, well-fitting door – which, indeed, they found difficult to push open, though it was not secured in any way. To Ewen it seemed of good augury that it opened inwards. Some logs, years old, lay about near the entrance.

'I don't know that we are wise to hide here,' murmured Ardroy, 'but there seems no choice.' And they went in.

Within it was dark, for the hut had no windows. Finding that there was no means of securing the door on the inside save a crazy latch, Ewen suggested bringing in some of the stray logs and piling them against the door; so he and Archie hurriedly staggered in with several, and proceeded to lay some against the bottom, and to rear others against it at an angle in order to wedge it.

'But we cannot stand a regular siege in here, Ewen,' objected the Doctor, looking round their dim shelter.

'No; but if the soldiers find the door immovably fixed they may think it is so fastened up that no one could have got into the hut, and we meanwhile lying as close as weasels within they'll likely go away again – that is, if they come at all. Please God, however, they'll pass the place without seeing it, as we nearly did. Or they may never search this quarter of the wood at all.'

'Yes, I think they'll have to break the door to matchwood

before they get it open now,' opined Archie. 'My sorrow, but it's dark in here!'

Indeed, the only light now came from the hole in the thatch intended to let out the smoke, which hole also let in the rain, so that the ground beneath, in the middle of the hut, was more puddle than anything else. It seemed as if the place had been occupied by a woodcutter, for, in addition to the felled logs outside, there was a big but extremely rusty axe propped against the wall in one corner, by the side of the rough bench built into the latter; axe and bench were, with the exception of the blackened stones of the fireplace (some of which they had added to the logs against the door) the only objects there.

So, having now no occupation but waiting upon Fate, the cousins sat down in the gloom upon this bench; and it was then that Ewen realized that he was nearly famished, and ate his provisions. Archie would not share with him.

'And now, tell me –' each said to the other; and indeed there was much to tell, though they dared not utter more than a few sentences at a time, and those in a low voice, and must then stop to listen with all their ears.

And Ewen learnt that Archie had come to these parts because Lochaber and the West were getting too hot to hold him, owing to the constant searches which were carried out for him; he was, he admitted, all but captured in Strontian when he went to Dungallon's house. That was when Ewen was in Fort William. But here, up till now, he had been unmolested, and who had given notice of his presence he could not imagine.

'And the assistance you hoped for,' asked Ewen, 'is it to come soon?'

He heard his kinsman sigh. 'I'm as much in the dark about it yet, Ewen ... as you and I are at this moment. I begin to wonder whether Frederick of Prussia –'

Ewen gave a stifled exclamation. '*Prussia!* It is Prussia then –'

'You did not know? Prussia, and perhaps Sweden, if certain conditions were fulfilled. But how have you not learnt that?'

'You forget; you did not tell me that night at Ardroy, and since then I have either been a close prisoner or skulking in the wilds. One night in Appin did not teach me much, especially as my cousin Ian was away ... And so troops are to land?'

'They were to. 'Twas inspiring news at first, to me and to those I visited. But time has gone on, and on ...' Archie paused. 'I am totally without information now, Ewen. My communications with Lochdornie are cut off, though I believe he is still in Scotland. But I doubt if he knows any more than I do. I verily think that if May comes and brings nothing I shall return to the Prince. Talk of what is promised is windy fare to give to longing hearts when the fulfilment tarries thus.'

A little chill ran through his listener. He had never heard Archibald Cameron so plainly dispirited. For himself, he knew too little to proffer any encouragement; and his uncle's words about the sunset of the Cause recurred to him. But he had not subscribed to them, nor did he now; it was too natural to hope. Even when months ago he had bitterly asked of the man at his side who was to lead them, he had not despaired, in his heart, of the coming of a day when they might be led. But, evidently, it was not to be yet ... and here was poor Archie, risking his life to bring good tidings, and at last, after months of hardship and peril, himself doubting if the tidings were true.

'Yes, many thousands of men were, I believe, promised,' resumed Doctor Cameron, 'when the ground should be prepared. But the preparing of it has not been easy when the weeks slipped away and I could hold out naught more definite than the hopes I had brought with me in September – Not that I blame the Prince one whit for that!' he added quickly. And they both fell, and this time quite naturally, into one of the prudent silences which had continually punctuated this conversation in the semi-darkness.

It was a longer silence than usual. Ewen's thoughts went circling away. Had Archie, with all his devotion, merely been beating the air all these months?

'I hope Mrs Stewart has not been molested,' said Archie's voice after a while. 'But I begin to believe that the soldiers have abandoned the search, or, at least, that they are not going to search this part of the wood.'

Ewen nodded. 'I begin to think that it is so. I wonder how

soon we might with safety leave this place, or whether we had best spend the night here.'

'I've no idea what time it may be,' said his cousin. He pulled out his watch and was peering at it when Ardroy gripped his other wrist. 'Did you hear anything?' he asked in the lowest of whispers.

His watch in his hand, Doctor Cameron sat as still as he. With its ticking there mingled a distant sound of snapping sticks, of something pushing through bushes just as they had done in their approach to the hut. The sounds came nearer, accompanied by voices. Ewen's grip grew tighter, and the Doctor put back his watch.

'Ay, it is a hut!' called out a man's voice. 'Come on, cully — damn these hollies! I warrant he's in here! Come on, I tell you, or he may bolt for it!'

'I'm coming as quick as I can,' shouted another voice. The cracklings and tramplings increased in volume. Ewen slipped his hand into his pocket, took out one of Lord Aveling's elegant pistols, and closed his cousin's fingers over it.

Chapter 15

' 'TWAS THERE THAT WE PARTED –'

1

ARCHIE shook his head with a little smile which said that resistance would be of no use; that their only hope lay in keeping perfectly quiet. But Ewen would not take the weapon back.

The men outside could be heard fumbling over the door for the means of opening it, which, naturally, they could not find.

'Curse it, there's no way to open this door!' Kicks and blows were bestowed upon it. 'Come out of it, rebel!'

'If ye're in there!' added the other voice with a snigger.

'There ain't no means of knowing that till we get the door open,' said the first voice.

'If there was a lock we could blow it open, but there ain't none.'

'Do you stay and watch the place, then, and I'll be off and fetch the captain; he ain't far off now.'

'And while you're doing that the rebel will burst out and murder me and be off! Maybe, too, there's more than this Doctor Cameron in there!'

'You're a good-plucked one, ain't you!' observed the first voice scornfully. 'You go for Captain Craven then; and I'll warrant no one comes out of this hut without getting something from this that'll stop his going far!' By the sound, he smacked the butt of his musket.

'Good! I'll not be long, then, I promise you.' The speaker could be heard to run off, and the man who remained, either to keep up his courage or to advertise his presence, began to whistle.

Ewen and his cousin looked into each other's eyes, fearing even to whisper, and each read the same answer to the same question. If they attempted to break out and run for it before the captain and the main body came up, it was beyond question

528

that, since they could not suddenly throw open the door, but must first pull down their barricade, at the cost of time and noise, the man outside, forewarned by their movements, could shoot one or both as they dashed out. Moreover, wounded or unwounded, they would undoubtedly be in worse case in the open, the alarm once given by a shot, than if they remained perfectly silent, 'as close as weasels', in their hiding-place. There was always a chance that the officer, when he came, would pooh-pooh the idea of anyone's being inside the deserted-looking little structure and would not have the door broken open ... even, perhaps, a chance that he would not bring his men here at all.

But it was a hard thing to do, to sit there and wait to be surrounded.

It was too hard for Ewen. After four or five minutes he put his lips to Archie's ear. 'I am going to open the door and rush out on him,' he breathed. 'I have another pistol. He will probably chase me, and then you can get away.' He had brought off that same manoeuvre so successfully once – why not again?

But Archie clutched his arm firmly. 'No, you shall not do it! And in any case ... I think it is too late!' For the musician outside had ceased in the middle of a bar, and next instant was to be heard shouting, 'This way, sir – in the clearing here!'

Then there was the tramp of a good many feet, coming at the double. Oh, what did it matter in that moment to Ewen if the Cause were once more sinking in a bog of false hopes! For the safety of the man beside him, whom he loved, he would have bartered any levies that ever were to sail from Prussia or Sweden. But the issue was not in his hands ...

'Why were we so crazy as to come in here!' he murmured under his breath. 'O God, that I had never seen this hut!'

Archibald Cameron had loosed his arm. He still held the pistol, but in a manner which suggested that he did not mean to use it. From the orders which they could hear being given the hut was now surrounded. The door was then pushed at hard from without, but as before, when it had been attempted, it would not budge an inch.

'Did you hear any sound within while you kept watch, Hayter?' asked the officer's voice.

'No, sir, I can't say that I did.'

'Yet the door is evidently made fast from within. It is difficult to see how that can be unless someone is still inside. There is no window or other opening, is there, out of which a man could have got after fastening the door.'

'No, sir,' was shouted, apparently from the back of the hut.

'Forbye the hole there'll be in the thatch for letting out the reek, sir,' suggested another voice, and a Scottish voice at that.

'But a man would hardly get out that way,' answered the officer. 'No, there's nothing for it but to break in the door.'

Two or three musket butts were vigorously applied with this intention, but in another moment the officer's voice was heard ordering the men to stop, and in the silence which ensued could be heard saying, 'Aye, an excellent notion! Then we shall know for certain, and save time and trouble. One of you give him a back.'

The two motionless men on the bench inside looked dumbly at each other. What was going to happen now? A scrambling sound was heard against the log wall of the hut, and Archie pointed mutely upwards. They were sending a man to climb up and look in through the hole left for the smoke.

Ewen ground his teeth. They had neither of them thought of that simple possibility. The game was up, then; they could do nothing against such a survey. His cousin, however, possibly from previous experience in 'skulking', advised in dumb show one precaution: pulling Ewen's sleeve to attract his attention, he bowed his head until it rested on his folded arms, thrusting his hands at the same moment out of sight. For a moment Ewen thought that the object of this posture was to escape actual identification, not very probable anyhow in the semi-darkness; then he realized that its purpose was that the lighter hue of their faces and hands should not be discernible to the observer. For a second or two he dallied with an idea which promised him a grim satisfaction – that of firing upwards at the blur of a face which would shortly, he supposed, peer in at that fatal aperture in the thatch. But to do that would merely be to advertise their presence. So he followed Archibald Cameron's example, and they sat there, rigid and huddled upon themselves, trusting that in the bad light they would, after all, be invisible. And if so, then, to judge from the officer's words, the latter would be convinced of the emptiness of the hut and would draw off the party without breaking in the door. O God, if it might be so, if it might be so!

The scrambling sound had reached the thatch now. Half of Ewen's mind was praying for Archie's life, the other wrestling with a perverse inclination to glance up. And, queerly mingled with that impulse, came a memory of his childish interpretation of the text, 'Thou, God, seest me', when he used to picture a gigantic Eye, looking down through his bedroom ceiling ... Eternities of waiting seemed to spread out, and then, abruptly, to collapse like a shut fan with the jubilant shout from above: 'He's here, Captain, and there's two of them! I can see them plain!'

By the sound, the speaker slid down with the words from his post, and, almost simultaneously too, came another blow on the door, and the ritual command, 'Open in the King's name!'

The cousins both lifted their heads now, and Archie, hopeful to the last, laid a finger on his lips. The order was repeated; then, as if uncontrollably, blows began to rain on the door.

'Come out and surrender yourselves!' called the officer's voice sternly, and another shouted, 'Use that log there, ye fools — 'tis heavier than the butts!' and yet another cried excitedly, 'What if we was to fire the thatch, sir?'

And at that, quite suddenly, the battle madness of the Highlands, the *mire chatha*, came upon Ewen Cameron, and he went berserk. This was to be a trapped beast, an otter at bay ... an otter, any beast shows fight then! Did the redcoats anticipate coming in unhindered to take them, or that they, Highlanders both, would tamely suffer themselves to be burnt out? He sprang up. Archie had got up too, and was holding out his hand to him and saying, through the hail of blows upon wood which almost drowned his words, 'My dearest lad, I hope they'll let *you* go free!'

From his kinsman's next action this seemed unlikely in the

extreme. Thrusting the second pistol at Doctor Cameron with 'Take this too – I'll need both hands!' Ewen seized the great rusty axe from the corner and flung himself against the barri-caded portal just as one of the up-ended logs which wedged it slipped and fell, dislodged by the blows under which the door was quivering, and set against it the living prop of his own shoulder.

'Ewen, Ewen,' besought his companion in great distress, "'tis useless – worse than useless! My time has come!' But Ardroy did not even seem to hear him, leaning with all the might of his strong body against the door, his right hand gripping the axe, his left arm outspread across the wood trying to get a hold on the logs of the wall beyond the hinges.

Suddenly a crackling sound above showed that the suggestion just made had been carried out, and the roof-thatch fired, probably by a brand flung upwards. The thatch, however, was damp and burnt sullenly; yet in a moment or two some eddies of smoke, caught by the wind, drifted in through the aperture. Then the flame caught, perhaps, a drier patch, and a sudden thick wave of smoke, acrid and stifling, drove downwards in the gloom as though looking for the fugitives. But already the door was beginning to splinter in several places. The assailants seemed to guess that it was buttressed now with the body of one of the besieged. 'Stand away from that door, you within there,' shouted the officer, 'or I fire!'

'Fire, then, and be damned to you!' said Ewen under his breath. 'Get back, Archie, *get back!*'

But, instead of a bullet, there came stabbing through one of the newly made little breaches in the door, like a snake, a tongue of steel, bayonet or sword. It caught Ewen just behind and below the shoulder pressed against the door; a trifle more to one side and it might have gone through the armpit into the lung. As it was, it slid along his shoulder blade. Involuntarily Ardroy sprang away from the door, as involuntarily dropping the axe and clapping his right hand to the seat of the hot, searing pain.

'Are you hurt?' exclaimed his cousin. 'O Ewen, for God's sake –'

'They are not going to take you as easily as they think!' said

Ewen between his teeth; and, with the blood running down his back under his shirt, he pounced on the fallen axe again. The door shivered all over, and by the time he had recovered his weapon he saw that it was giving, and that nothing could save it. He pushed Archie, still imploring him to desist, roughly away. 'Keep out of sight, for God's sake!' he whispered hoarsely, and, gripping the axe with both hands, stood back a little the better to swing it, and also to avoid having the door collapse upon him.

In another moment it fell inwards with a bang and a noise of rending hinges, and there was revealed, as in a frame, the group of scarlet-clad figures with their eager faces, the glitter of weapons, the tree-trunks beyond. And to those soldiers who had rushed to the dark entrance Cameron of Ardroy also was visible, against the gloom and smoke within, towering with the axe ready, his eyes shining with a light more daunting even than the weapon he held. They hesitated and drew back.

The officer whipped out his sword and came forward.

'Put down that axe, you madman, and surrender Archibald Cameron to the law!'

'Archibald Cameron is not here!' shouted back Ewen. 'But you come in at your peril!'

None the less, whether he trusted in his own superior quickness with his slighter weapon, or thought that the rebel would not dare to use his, Captain Craven advanced. And neither of these hypotheses would have saved him ... though he was saved (luckily for Ewen). For the Highlander in his transport had forgotten the small proportions of the place in which he stood, and his own height and reach of arm. The smashing two-handed blow which he aimed at the Englishman never touched him; with a thud which shook the doorway the axe buried itself in the lintel above it; and as Ewen with a curse tried to wrench it out, the haft, old and rotten, came away in his hand, leaving the head imbedded above the doorway, and himself weaponless.

As he saw the axe sweeping down towards him the young officer had naturally sprung back, and now, before Ewen had time to recover himself, the sergeant rushed past his superior and seized Ardroy round the body, trying to drag him out. As they struggled with each other – all danger from the axe being now over – another man slipped in, got behind the pair, and raised his clubbed musket. Archie sprang at the invader and grabbed at his arm, and though he only half-caught it, his act did diminish the fierce impact of the blow, and probably saved Ewen from having his head split open. As it was, the musket butt felled him instantly; his knees gave, and with a stifled cry he toppled over in the sergeant's hold, his weight bringing the soldier down with him.

But the redcoat got up again at once, while Ewen, with blood upon his hair, lay face downwards across the fallen door, the useless axe shaft still clutched in one hand; and it was over his motionless body that Archibald Cameron was brought out of his last refuge.

2

'Inversnaid,' said Ewen to himself in a thick voice. 'Inversnaid on Loch Lomond – that is where I must go. Which is the way, if you please?'

He had asked the question, it seemed to him, of so many people whom he had passed, and not one had answered him. Sometimes, it was true, these people bore a strong resemblance to trees and bushes, but that was only their cunning, because they did not want to tell him the way to Inversnaid. He was not quite sure who he himself was, either, nor indeed what he was doing here, wandering in this bare, starlit wood, stumbling over roots and stones. But at least he understood why Ewen Cameron had thought him drunk, when he had only received a blow on the head – poor Hector!

'Poor Hector!' he repeated, putting up a hand to it. It was bandaged, as he could feel. Who had done that? Doctor Kincaid? But he could not see Loch Treig anywhere; this was a wood, and the wood people refused to tell him the way to Inversnaid.

It was not very dark in the wood, however, for it was a clear, windy night, and the starlight easily penetrated the stripped boughs of it; only under the pines were there pools of shadow.

It was now some time since Ewen had discovered that he was lying out in the open, under a tree, and no longer sitting in the little hut which he faintly remembered, where Archie and he had been together one day; some time since he had got with difficulty to his feet, had lurched to that very hut, and, holding on tight to the doorway, had looked in at its black emptiness, and wondered why the door lay on the ground. Yet it was while he stood propped there that the name of Inversnaid had come to him with an urgency which he could not interpret, and he had turned at once in what he felt was the direction of Loch Lomond. He was in no state to realize that it was much less the absence of a warrant against him than the impossibility of transporting him, in his then inert condition, over miles of the roughest country to Inversnaid which had saved him, in spite of the resistance which he had offered, from being taken there as a prisoner himself.

Ah, here was a tree or bush of some kind, covered with red flowers – holding a lantern – very odd, that! No, two of them, both with lights. The first was a female bush – a rose tree, by the look; one must be polite to it. He tried to doff his hat, but he had none. 'Madam, will you tell me the shortest way to Inversnaid?'

The kind bush replied that she would take him there; and then she drew an arm through hers, while the other lantern-bearing tree did the same. And so, at last, he found someone to help him on his journey.

'He's clean crazed, James,' said Mrs Stewart, showing an anxious face above her red and green flowered shawl as she looked round the lurching figure which she was guiding at the man who was performing the same office on the other side. 'I don't know what we are going to do with him now that we have found him.'

'Pit him tae bed and gar him bide quiet,' responded the practical James. 'Haud up, sir; ye maun lift yer feet a wheen higher, if ye please.'

'I remember now, the blade came off the axe,' said Ewen suddenly, his eyes fixed as though he were seeing something ahead. He had been silent for some time, though talkative at first. 'If it had not, I should have killed that officer, and some of the other redcoats too, perhaps.'

'Ay, I mak nae doot o' it,' agreed James Stoddart soothingly, and they went on again, while behind the three pattered the little barefoot girl whom the soldier had chased that afternoon. It was she who, having hung about in the wood instead of going home, had played Mercury, and had given Mrs Stewart, already horrified by the news of Doctor Cameron's capture, the further tidings that the other gentleman had been left lying as if he were dead, at the spot of the disaster. Yet, though she had been afraid to go near him, she reported having seen him move. On that Mrs Stewart had summoned the only person likely to be of use, James Stoddart, her gardener and factotum, and had set out for the hut in the wood.

'I doubt this is not the way to Loch Lomond,' said Ewen, stopping dead all at once. 'Madam, you are misleading me, and that is worse than not answering.' He looked down at Mrs Stewart rather threateningly.

'Man,' said James Stoddart stoutly, 'dinna haver, but trust the leddy! She kens whaur tae tak ye. Come on noo, we're gey near the place.' (And this was true, in the sense which he gave to the phrase, for Ewen's previous wanderings in the wood had all the time been leading him back in the direction of the house above the Calair.)

'Come, Mr Cameron,' added Mrs Stewart gently.

'My name is Grant,' retorted Ewen with some irritation. 'Hector Grant, an officer in the French service.' And under his breath he promptly began to sing snatches of 'Malbrouck'.

But when he got to *'Ne sait quand reviendra'*, he broke off 'Yes, he's gone, and God knows when he will return ... *"Madame à sa tour monte,"* it says. Will you go up into your tower, madam, to look out for him? But there was a man who looked in – through the roof. That is not in the song.' He wrinkled his brows, and added, like a pettish child, 'When shall we be through this wood? I am so weary of it!'

Yet for the rest of the night he walked in it, always trying to find the way to Loch Lomond, long after Mrs Stewart and James Stoddart had somehow got him into the house, and into the bed which Archie Cameron had occupied but the night before. And not until she had him lying there, still babbling faintly of doors and axes and eyes in the roof and Inversnaid and Loch Treig, and also of a stolen horse and some letter or other, and once or twice of his brother-in-law Ewen Cameron, did Mrs Stewart, just outside the room, bring forth her pocket-handkerchief.

'The Doctor betrayed and taken, this gentleman that tried to save him clean broke in his wits – O James, what a weary day's work! And to think that but this morning I was baking, and the bread never came forth better! Had I the second sight, as I might have, being Highland –'

'If ye had it, mem,' broke in James Stoddart '– not that I believe any has it; 'tis an idle and mischievous supersteetion – ye and the laird wad ne're have ta'en the Doctor intil the hoose, and y'd hae been spared a' this stramash.'

But Mrs Stewart was already drying her eyes. 'If it comes to that,' she retorted with spirit, 'a body might think it wiser never to have been born, and that would be a poor choice.'

'There's ae man will be wishing the nich he hadna been, I'm thinkin',' observed the gardener uncompromisingly, 'and that's Doctor Cameron.'

'Doctor Cameron will be wishing no such thing,' returned his mistress. 'He's a brave man, and used to running risks, though he'll be grieving indeed for the blow his taking is to the Prince. Ah me, what will the laird say when he hears the news!'

'Humph,' said her downright companion, 'the Doctor will be grieving for mair than Prince Charlie. He kens weel they'll hang him, the English.'

'Nonsense, James,' retorted Mrs Stewart. 'The English have not sufficient cause nor evidence against him. He has done nothing they can lay their fingers on. But no doubt they'll put him in prison, and for long enough, I fear.'

'Nay, ye'll see, mem, he'll not bide lang in prison,' predicted James Stoddart, shaking his head with a certain gloomy satisfaction. And yet, Presbyterian and Lowlander though he was, he was perfectly staunch to his master's political creed, and no tortures would have drawn any admissions from him. 'A kind and bonny gentleman too, the Doctor,' he went on, 'but for a' he never said aught as he went aboot his business in these pairts, whatever it was, he kenned fine what wad happen him if the redcoats catched him. I saw it whiles in his ee.'

'You have too much imagination, James Stoddart,' said Mrs Stewart a trifle severely – and most unjustly. Turning from him she tiptoed back into the room for a moment. 'I think the poor gentleman is quieting down at last,' she reported, returning. 'I shall go to bed for a while. Do you sit with him and give him a drink if he asks for it – and for God's sake hold your tongue on the subject of the Doctor's being hanged!'

'I've nae need tae hauld it,' responded the irrepressible James. 'If the gentleman didna ken it too, and ower weel, wadna he hae keepit his skin hale on his back and his heid frae yon muckle dunt it's gotten?'

Chapter 16

THE DOOR IN ARLINGTON STREET

1

THE trees of St James's Park this May afternoon made a bright green canopy over the hooped and powdered beauties who sailed below, over the gentlemen in their wide-skirted coats and embroidered satin waistcoats, the lap-dogs, the sedan-chairs, the attendant black boys and footmen, and also, since spring leaves flutter equally above the light heart and the heavy, over a tall, quietly dressed young man in a brown tie-wig who was making his way, with the air of looking for someone, among the loungers in the Birdcage Walk. Of the glances, which despite his plain attire, more than one fine lady bestowed upon him he was completely unconscious; he was too unhappy.

The weeks of Ewen's convalescence at Glenbuckie had been bad, but this was worse – to come to London directly one was physically fit for it, only to find that no scheme of real value was on foot to save Archibald Cameron from the fate which seemed to be awaiting him. Taken from Inversnaid to Stirling, and from Stirling to Edinburgh Castle, Doctor Cameron had been brought thence with a strong escort to London, arriving in the capital on the sixteenth of April, the very anniversary of Culloden. He had been examined the next day before the Privy Council at Whitehall, but it was common knowledge that they had got from him neither admissions nor disclosures, and he had been taken back a close prisoner to the Tower. That was nearly a month ago.

At first, indeed, his bandaged head on the pillow which had been Archie's, Ewen had known little about past or present. Mrs Stewart, aided by Peggy (so Peggy herself was convinced), had nursed him devotedly, and the task had perhaps helped her to forget her own anxiety on her husband's account, for Duncan Stewart had been arrested as he was returning from Perth.

Luckily, however, for Ewen, once Mr Stewart's person was secured his house had not been searched. But a considerable harvest of suspects had been reaped, as Ewen was to find when he came perfectly to himself, for his own cousin John Cameron of Fassefern, Lochiel's and Archie's brother, had been imprisoned, and Cameron of Glenevis as well, and there was glee in Whig circles, where it was recognized what a blow to a dying cause was Archibald Cameron's capture. Of Lochdornie there was no news, but a warrant had been issued against him.

Ewen himself, who had arrived in London but the day previously, had now come to St James's Park merely to search for a Scottish Jacobite gentleman of his acquaintance, one Mr Galbraith, who, on inheriting a small estate from an English relative, had settled in England and had a house in Westminster. Had he not been told that Mr Galbraith was walking here with a friend Ewen would not have chosen so gay a promenade. It was the first time that he had ever been in London, and though he was not unaccustomed to cities, knowing Paris well, not to speak of Edinburgh, he seemed to feel here, and to resent, an unusual atmosphere of well-to-do assurance and privilege. Even the trees had not to struggle out with difficulty in this place, as in the North.

None too soon for his wishes, he caught sight of the elderly Mr Galbraith at a distance, talking earnestly to a tall, thin gentleman with a stoop. Just before the Highlander reached them this gentleman took his leave, and Mr Galbraith came on alone, his head bent, his hands holding his cane behind his back, so deep in thought that he almost ran into Ewen.

'I beg your pardon, sir ... why, it is Mr Cameron of Ardroy!' He held out his hand. 'What are you doing in London? I am very glad to see you again, however, very glad!'

Ewen glanced round. No one was within earshot. 'I have come to try what I can do for my unfortunate kinsman in the Tower. It must be possible to do something! You have studied the law, Galbraith; you can tell me of what worth is any evidence which can be brought against him at his trial.'

'At his trial!' repeated Mr Galbraith with an intonation

which Ewen found strange. But then some noisy beaux went past, and he stopped, took Ewen's arm, and piloted him to a more secluded spot where a hawthorn-tree invited to a seat on the bench below it. But they did not sit down.

'Doctor Cameron will not be so fortunate as to have a trial,' resumed Mr Galbraith. 'You have not heard that – but no, I have only just heard it myself this afternoon. I was even now discussing it with a friend from the Temple.'

'No trial!' stammered Ewen. 'But, Mr Galbraith, in Great Britain an accused man must have a trial ... it is illegal ... it –'

'It is perfectly legal in this case,' said Mr Galbraith gravely. 'Have you forgotten that Doctor Cameron's attainder of 1746 has never been reversed? He will be brought up quite soon now, it is thought, for sentence to be pronounced ... and the sentence will probably take its course.'

A gust of wind shook down some hawthorn petals between them. Ewen's eyes followed them to the ground.

'You mean to say,' and he found a difficulty in speaking, 'that he will be put to death on a charge seven years old for a course of action on account of which so many have since made their peace and been amnestied?'

'But *he* has never made his peace nor been amnestied. He was exempted from the Act of Indemnity, as you know, because he did not surrender himself in time. Surely if he is your kinsman you must always have known that, Ardroy?'

'I knew, naturally, that he was exempted from the Act. But to proceed to this extremity is iniquitous,' said Ewen hotly, '– unworthy even of the Elector and his parasites? To deny a man a fair trial –'

Mr Galbraith put his hand on his arm. 'My dear Ardroy, remember where you are, and be careful of your language! You will not help your kinsman by getting yourself arrested. Come home with me now, and we will talk the matter over quietly.'

They left St James's Park and its throngs in silence. The beauty of the trees in the sunlight was hateful to Ewen; the sunlight itself was hateful, and these laughing, careless men and women in their bright clothes more hateful still. They were of the same race, too, as the Crown lawyers who were going to do this heartless thing under a show of legality.

And yet, for all the resentment in his heart, through which throbbed the long-memoried and vengeful Celtic blood, there was also a voice there to which he did not wish to listen, appealing to the innate sense of justice which had come to him from some other strain, telling him that the English could hardly be blamed for using this weapon ready to their hand if they considered Archibald Cameron so dangerous a foe to their peace. And again another, as sombre and hollow as the wind in a lonely corrie, whispering that this was what he had always feared.

In Mr Galbraith's comfortable, dark-panelled house in Westminster Ardroy talked little; he listened. No, said his compatriot, there had not been a great deal of interest shown when Doctor Cameron was brought to London in April, so many people being out of town with the Duke, horse-racing at Newmarket. Should popular feeling be sufficiently aroused it was possible that pressure might be brought to bear on the Government. As to why the authorities preferred to rely upon the old sentence of attainder rather than to try Doctor Cameron for treason, it was said very secretly – and here Mr Galbraith, in his own library, dropped his voice and glanced round – it was said that the Government had sufficient evidence to hang him if he were brought to trial, but did not wish to use it because to do so would probably reveal the source through which it was acquired.

'I should not have thought their hands so clean that they need hold back for that!' commented Ewen scornfully.

His host shook his head. 'That is not the reason for their reluctance – yet, mind you, Ardroy, this is but a theory, and whispered only in corners at that! The Government are said to have the evidence from an informer whose identity they do not wish known. Whoever he may be, he is either too highly placed or too useful to expose.'

Disgust and wrath fought together in his hearer. 'An informer! Pah! But, yes, there has been treachery; I know that well. I wish I had the wringing of the scoundrel's neck; but he is, I think, some man up in Perthshire – in Scotland at any rate. And the Government are so tender of him that they do not wish his identity disclosed! If Doctor Cameron is sacrificed I think it will not be impossible to find him, protected or no! But that's for ... later on. Now, Mr Galbraith, what do you think of the chances of a rescue from the Tower?'

'I think nothing of them,' said the Scot emphatically. 'A rescue is impossible; an escape only feasible by some such stratagem as Lady Nithsdale employed to save her husband after the 'Fifteen, and such a stratagem has a very small chance of succeeding the second time. No, the only hope is that, for whatever reason, the Government should see fit to commute the sentence which is, I fear, sure to be pronounced ... You'll stay and sup with me, I hope, Ardroy, for I have some friends bidden with whom I should like to make you acquainted. Tomorrow evening, if you will allow me, I shall take you to the "White Cock" in the Strand, and present you to some of those who frequent it. It may be,' said Mr Galbraith somewhat doubtfully, 'that in the multitude of counsellors there is wisdom ...'

2

It was late, after eleven o'clock, when Ewen left Mr Galbraith's house in Westminster and started to walk back to Half Moon Street, off Piccadilly, where he lodged over a vintner's. All the time he wished that he were walking eastwards, towards the Tower. But what would be the use? He could not gain admission if he were.

The hand of Care lay fast upon his shoulder, and to dull the pressure he turned his thoughts, as he walked, to the one bright spot in the last few weeks – Alison's visit to Glenbuckie. Unknown to him, Mrs Stewart had contrived to get word of his condition to Ardroy, and the convalescent woke one day to feel his wife's lips upon his brow. He had made much more noticeable progress towards recovery after that.

There were other patches of sunlight, too, in those heavy days; little Peggy Stewart had made one of them. More than once, in the early part of his illness, he had wakened to find beside him a small, sedate and very attentive watcher whose legs dangled from the chair in which she was installed, and who said, when he opened his eyes, 'I will tell Mamma that you are awake, sir,' and slipped importantly down from her sentry-post. Later had come conversation: 'Have *you* a little girl, sir?' and the comment, made with great decision, when the small damsel heard of two boys, that she thought a little girl would be better. Another time it was, 'You never eated my bread mannie! Mamma found it in your pocket.' 'I am very sorry, Peggy,' Ewen had meekly replied. 'I am sure it would have been very good.' Peggy also expressed regret that his hair had been cutted off; and this was the first intimation which Ewen received that his fevered head had been shorn, and that when he was restored to the outer world he would in consequence have to wear a wig – as, indeed, most men did.

Alison on her arrival, like Peggy, had lamented that operation, and when her husband, making a jest which for him held a pang, suggested that he might take the opportunity of wearing a black wig in order to change his appearance, Alison had cried out in horror. She did not desire his appearance changed ... and then, understanding the reason of his speech, was all for anything that would serve to disguise him, particularly when she found, to her dismay, that he was set upon going to London directly the journey was possible for him, entirely abandoning his long-cherished idea of engaging an advocate for himself at Edinburgh. To that course, in the end, she became at last partially reconciled, and longed to accompany him, separated from him so long as she had been, and feeling that he would not be fit to look after himself for a while yet. But the great obstacle to this plan had been, not the children, since Aunt Margaret was back at Ardroy now, but the stark, bare obstacle which wrecks so many desires – want of money. Alison had brought her husband all that she could raise at the moment, but it would barely suffice for his own outfit, journey and maintenance in London. So she must stay behind. 'And besides,' as she said bravely, 'what could I do towards saving the Doctor, Ewen? I am not his wife, and cannot play the part of Lady Nithsdale.'

Lady Nithsdale! Here, within three miles of the Tower, those words of Alison's came back to him, and Mr Galbraith's of this afternoon, who had said that part would never again be played with success. Had it any chance of prospering, then that brave woman, Jean Cameron, who was Archie's wife, was of the stuff to play it. But she was in France.

Ewen could not throw off the shadow which dogged him. Why, why had he ever persuaded his cousin to shelter in the woodcutter's hut? Indeed, if the fairies had put it there, as Archie had suggested, it had been for no good purpose. He saw it again, accursed little place, as he walked up St James's Street in surroundings so widely different, glancing back at the Palace front as he crossed to the farther side. And it occurred to him how strange it was that he should be walking about London perfectly unmolested, when if the authorities here knew of his doings at Fort William and Glenbuckie, or if he were to meet Lord Aveling coming out of one of the clubs or coffee-houses which abounded in this region – as well he might, though not perhaps at so late an hour as this ... But he felt beyond troubling over his own fate.

As yet the Highlander hardly knew his way about London, and at the junction of Bennet Street with Arlington Street made a mistake, turned to the left instead of to the right, and, being deep in thought, went on without at once realizing that he was in a cul-de-sac. Then, brought up by the houses at the end, he stopped, wondering where he had got to. As he tried to take his bearings the door of a house on the opposite side, almost in the angle, opened a little way, and a gentleman muffled in a cloak slipped very quietly, almost stealthily, out. A man who must have been waiting for him outside stepped forward and took the burning torch out of its holder by the door to light him home – though Arlington Street itself was sufficiently well lit. The two crossed near Ewen, whom perhaps they did not notice, and made for the little street up which he had just come. Ewen turned quickly and looked after them. For the cloaked gentleman had spoken to his attendant in Gaelic, bidding him, somewhat sharply, hold the torch more steady.

The two were Highlanders then! Ewen stifled the half-impulse to follow and accost them which the sound of that beloved tongue had raised in him. After all they were no concern of his, and he certainly did not know the speaker, who was young and wore his reddish hair unpowdered, for his hat cocked at a rakish angle suffered the torchlight to gleam for an instant upon it.

Some Highlander, Jacobite or Whig – more probably the latter who knew intimately a man of position, to judge from the elegant new brick house from which he had emerged. Well, God knew he only wished that *he* had a friend with influence, living in this street, which looked as if it housed people of importance.

3

Next evening, a rainy one, Mr Galbraith took Ewen, as he had promised, to the 'White Cock' in the Strand to introduce him to some of its *habitués*. The Highlander was struck with the discreet and unassuming appearance of this Jacobite resort – which some said should be called *en toutes lettres* 'The White Cockade' – the narrow passage in which it was situated, the disarming and rather inconvenient short flight of steps which led into its interior. But if its accessories were discreet there did not seem to be much of that quality about its customers. Already Ardroy had been a little astonished at the openness with which Jacobite sentiments were displayed in London. But was this merely vain display? had the tendency roots, and was it likely in the present instance to bear fruit? Somehow, as he talked with the men to whom his fellow-countryman presented him, he began to doubt it.

He had been there perhaps three-quarters of an hour or more when the door at the top of the steps, opening once again, admitted a man who removed his wet cloak to his arm and stood a moment looking round with a certain air of hesitation, as one searching for an acquaintance, or even, perhaps, a trifle unsure of his reception. Then he threw back his head in a gesture which was not unfamiliar to Ewen, who happened to be watching him, and came down the steps.

Ardroy got up. It could not be! Yet, unlikely as it seemed, it *was* Hector! Ardroy hurried forward, and Hector's eyes fell upon him.

'Ewen! you here in London!' There was not only astonishment but unmistakable relief in Lieutenant Grant's tone. Ewen was even more surprised to see him, but not particularly relieved. What on earth had brought Hector to London again – or had he never rejoined his regiment last January?

'I'll tell you in a moment why I am in England,' said the young officer hurriedly. 'What incredible good fortune that you should be here! Come with me to my lodging – 'tis not far off.'

'First, however, let me present you –' began Ewen; but Hector broke in, 'Another time – not tonight, another time!' and began to ascend the steps again.

Puzzled, Ewen said that he must excuse himself to his friend Mr Galbraith, and going back he did so. By the time he got up the steps Hector himself was outside. His face in the light of the lamp over the doorway had a strange wretchedness, or so Ewen thought.

'Hector, is aught amiss with you?'

'*Amiss?*' queried his brother-in-law with a sort of laugh. 'I'm ruined unless ... But come to my lodging and you shall hear.' Seizing Ardroy by the arm he thereupon hurried him off through the rain. No, he had not got into trouble over his outstayed leave, and he had only arrived in London that morning.

'And God be praised that I have met with you, Ewen – though I cannot think why you are here.'

'Surely you can guess that,' said Ardroy. 'Because of Archibald Cameron. I thought it must be the same with you.'

'So it is,' answered Hector, with what sounded like a groan. 'Here we are – beware the stair, 'tis very ill lit.' He guided his kinsman into an upstairs room, fumbled with tinder and steel, and lit a lamp so carelessly that the flame flared high and smoky without his noticing it. 'Archibald Cameron – ay, my God, Archibald Cameron!' he said, and turned away.

'Don't take it so much to heart, Eachainn,' said Ewen kindly, laying a hand on his shoulder. ' 'Tis not quite hopeless yet.'

'God! you don't know yet what it is I'm taking to heart!'

exclaimed Hector with startling bitterness. 'Oh, I'm grieved to the soul over the Doctor...but unless I can disprove the slander about his capture I am ruined, as I told you, and may as well blow my brains out!'

Ewen stared at him in astonishment. 'My dear Hector, what slander? Ruined! What in Heaven's name are you talking about?'

Hector seized his wrist. 'You have not heard it then? Nor have they, I suppose, at the "White Cock" or they would have turned me out *sans façon*. I tell you I was in a sweat of fear when I went in; but thank God that I did go, since by it I found you, and there's no man in the world I'd sooner have at my back ... more by token since you know the circumstances.'

'But those are just what I don't know!' exclaimed Ardroy, more and more bewildered. 'See, Hector, calm yourself a little and tell me what you are talking about. Has it anything to do with Archie?'

'Everything in the world. They are saying over there in Lille, in the regiment – the Doctor's own regiment and mine – that 'twas an officer in French service who betrayed him, and some think that the officer is –' He stopped, his mouth twitching, his eyes distracted, and made a sort of gesture of pointing to himself.

'Good God!' ejaculated Ewen in horror. '*You!* On what possible –'

'On what grounds? Because of the fatal letter which I lost that day on Loch Treig side, the letter which, you remember, we agreed at Fort William had probably never reached the authorities or done any harm at all – which in any case was taken from me by treachery and violence. But they hint, so I am told, that it was written in order to convey information, and that I *gave* it to the spy! O my God, that men should whisper such a thing of me, and that I cannot kill them for it!' Hector smote his hands together, and began to pace about the little room like a wild animal.

But Ewen stood a moment half-stupefied. Too well he knew, at least from hearsay, of mutual accusations among Jacobites of divergent views. But in Hector's own regiment, among his fellow-officers ... Then he recovered himself.

'Hector,' he said with emphasis, 'that story is sheer nonsense! 'Twas a much more recent piece of information than any contained in your letter which led to Archie's capture.'

'How do you know?' asked the young man, swinging round with a tragic face. 'How do you know that?'

'Because I – but I'll tell you the whole story in a moment. 'First do you tell me –'

'Ewen,' interrupted his brother-in-law vehemently, 'if you'll only clear me I give you leave, with all my heart, to dirk me afterwards if you like.'

Ewen could not keep back a smile. 'The inducement is not overwhelming. But, Hector,' he added, as a sudden unwelcome idea smote him, and he in his turn gripped the young officer by the arm, 'I hope to God that you have not deserted – have not come over without leave?'

'No, no, Lord Ogilvie gave me leave. He does not believe the rumour, thank God! He thought it best that I should come; I had already called out a lieutenant in my company ... unfortunately he got wind of it and stopped the meeting. He thought that if I came over I might be able to find out who really was responsible for the Doctor's capture and thus clear myself. And it goes without saying that if there is any scheme on foot for Doctor Cameron's release or rescue you may count on me *de tout mon cœur*.'

'Alas, I fear that there is none at present,' said Ewen sadly. 'Yet, as regards his capture, though I cannot give you the name of the man responsible, I can prove that it was not you. But, Hector, who can have put about this slander? Who started it?'

Hector shook his head. 'I could not find out – how does one discover a thing like that? Nor has anyone dared to tax me with it directly; 'twas more hints, sneers, looks, avoidance of me. And those of your name in the regiment were naturally among the foremost.'

'You must,' said Ewen, considering, 'have been too free with your tongue over your unlucky loss of that letter last autumn.'

'Too free with my tongue! I never breathed a word about it to a soul over there, not even to Lord Ogilvie. I was far too much ashamed.'

'And did you not tell anyone when you were in Scotland?'

'Save you, no one.'

' 'Tis very strange. Well, tell me what chanced after our sudden parting that dark morning at Ardgour, and how you succeeded in getting over to France.'

Hector told him.

'*Dhé!*' exclaimed his brother-in-law at the end, 'so 'twas young Glenshian who helped you to papers! How the devil did he contrive to do it?'

'Faith, I don't know overwell. He gave me a letter to someone whom I never saw, with a feigned name at that. I was grateful enough to the future Chief, though there is something about the man which I find it hard to stomach. You have never met him, I think. Now, Ewen, keep me in suspense no longer!'

'Stay one moment,' said Ardroy slowly. 'You told young Glenshian – you could not help yourself – of the loss of your necessary papers; perhaps you told him of the loss of the letter too?'

A flush fell over Hector's face and his jaw fell a trifle. He thumped the table. 'You're right; I did! But he, surely, could not have spread –'

'No, no, I do not suppose that for an instant! It was only that you said you had told nobody save me.'

'Nobody over the water nor in Scotland. I vow I had forgotten Finlay MacPhair in London. He was so anxious to know whether I had lost any compromising document. But that he could have put about such a libel is out of the question. I fear, however, that he may have mentioned my misfortune to some third person ... But now for your proof, Ewen, which is to clear me! And tell me, too, how soon you got back from Ardgour, and all that has befallen you of late. You look, now that I see you closer ... have you been ill by any chance?'

Chapter 17

FORESEEN AND UNFORESEEN

1

IT had been arranged that Hector should come to Ewen's lodging early next morning, and that they should both go to wait upon Mr Galbraith. Ewen therefore remained in his room writing a letter to Alison, but when it was already three-quarters of an hour past the time appointed, and still the young man did not arrive, Ardroy began to get uneasy about him. When an hour and a quarter had elapsed he was walking about his room really anxious. What had the boy been doing? Should he go to the Strand in search of him? But then he might so easily miss him on the way. When another twenty minutes had ticked itself away among the sun, moon and stars of Mrs Wilson's great clock, he strode into his bedroom for his hat. He could wait no longer; he must go and look for the truant.

And then he heard his landlady's voice explaining to some-one that she thought Mr Cameron must by now have gone out.

'No, I have not,' said Ewen, appearing on the threshold of his bedroom. 'Is that you at last, Hector? What on earth has delayed you so?'

'I'll tell you in a moment,' said young Grant rather hoarsely. 'I have made what haste I could.' And indeed his brow was damp, and he sank down in a chair in the sitting-room as if exhausted. Ewen asked him if he were ill, for he was clearly under the sway of some emotion or other; and, when Hector shook his head, said, 'Then 'tis this business of the slander on you. Have you discovered something?'

'No, no, it is not that,' said Hector. And then he got it out with a jerk. 'Ewen, Doctor Cameron was this morning condemned to death, without trial.'

A club seemed to strike Ewen's head – like that musket butt in the wood. Yet this news was expected.

'How did you hear it?' he asked after a moment's silence.

'I ... O Ewen, I would have given anything to get to you in time, but I swear that it was only by chance that I was on the spot, and then it was too late. I tried to send a messenger. In truth it should have been you, not I, but it was not my fault!'

A light broke on Ardroy. 'You mean that you actually heard him sentenced?'

Hector nodded, and went on in the same apologetic tone, 'It was all chance and hurry. Had your lodging not been so far away –'

'You have seen Archie this morning! Where was he brought up for sentence, then?'

'At the Court of King's Bench in Westminster Hall.'

Ewen sat down at the table. 'Tell me about it. – No, I do not blame you, Hector; why should I? Yet I would have given much ...' He clenched his hand a second on the edge of the table. 'Tell me everything.'

So Hector told him. The story began with his going for an early walk along the riverside, and finding himself, when he got to Westminster, in the presence of a considerable crowd, which, as he then discovered to his surprise, was waiting in the hopes of getting a glimpse of that Jacobite as he was brought by coach from the Tower to have sentence passed upon him. 'After the first astonishment my thoughts were all of you, Ewen,' said Hector earnestly, 'and I was for coming at once to fetch you. But it appeared that the Court was already assembled, and that the prisoner might arrive at any moment. I tried to get a hackney coach – I could not; I tried to send a messenger – no one would stir. Then I thought, "If I cannot warn Ewen, who, after all, has probably heard of this from another source, I will at least do my best to get a sight of the Doctor, to tell him how he seems." I had no hope of entering Westminster Hall, since the press was so great; and moreover those who went in appeared to have tickets of admission. And the crowd moved and pushed to such an extent that I began to fear I should not get the slightest glimpse of Doctor Cameron when he came; and, after a while, indeed, I found myself penned with one or two others into an angle of the building where I could see nothing. However, there was in this angle a small door, and when the man nearest it, in a fit of annoyance, began to beat upon it, it was suddenly opened by an official, who grumblingly consented to find places for four or five of the nearest – and this he did.'

'And so you heard – or saw?'

'I did both, though with difficulty, being at the back of the court, which was crammed with persons like myself, and suffocatingly hot. The proceedings were quite short. The Doctor was extremely composed, neither defiant nor a whit overwhelmed; he appeared, too, in good health. Nor did he attempt to deny that he was the person named in the Act of Attainder.'

'Did he make no defence – had he not an advocate?'

'No. The only defence which he made was to say that he could not have acted otherwise than he did, having to follow Lochiel, his brother and Chief, that in the troubles he had always set his face against reprisals or harsh treatment, of which he gave some instances, and that his own character would bear investigation in the same light. Then came that barbarous sentence for high treason, pronounced by one of the three judges present – the Lord Chief Justice, I think it was – and, Ewen, it was not imagination on my part that he laid particular emphasis on those words respecting the hanging, "but not till you are dead", glowering at the Doctor as he uttered them. Many people remarked it, and were talking about it afterwards. But Doctor Cameron was perfectly calm, and merely made a civil bow at the end; after that, however, he asked earnestly that the execution of the sentence, which had been fixed for this day fortnight, might be deferred a little in order to enable him to see his wife, to whom he had already had permission to write bidding her come to him from France. And he added that she and their seven children were all dependent upon him, and that it would be worse than death to him not to see her again. So the Court decided to instruct the Attorney-General that the sentence should not be carried out until a week later, on the seventh of June, in order to permit of this. Then the Doctor was removed, and everyone fought their way out again; and I came away feeling that if I really believed my rashness and carelessness last September were the cause of Archibald Cameron's standing there ... and where I suppose he may stand in three weeks' time – even though no one accused me of it I would blow my brains out tonight!'

'Be reassured, Hector, they are not the cause!' said Ardroy in an emotional voice. But his face was very haggard. ' 'Tis I am the person most immediately responsible, for it was I who found that accursed hut in the wood at Glenbuckie and persuaded him to lie hid in it ... Yes, I expected this news, but that makes it no easier to bear – Hector, he must be saved somehow, even if it should mean both our lives!'

'I am quite ready to give mine,' answered young Grant simply. 'It would be the best means, too, of clearing my honour; far the best. But we cannot strike a bargain with the English Government, Ewen, that they should hang us in his place. And I hear that the Tower is a very strong prison.'

'Let us go to Westminster and see Mr Galbraith,' said his brother-in-law.

They walked for some distance in silence, and when they were nearing the top of St James's Street Ewen pulled at his companion's arm.

'Let us go this way,' he said abruptly, and they turned down Arlington Street. 'Just from curiosity, I have a desire to know who lives in a certain new house in the bottom corner there.'

Hector, usually so alert, seemed too dulled by his recent experience to exhibit either surprise or curiosity at this proceeding. They walked to the end of Arlington Street.

'Yes, that is the house,' observed Ewen after a moment's scrutiny. 'Now to find out who lives in it.'

'Why?' asked Hector. And, rousing himself to a rather perfunctory attempt at jocularity, he added, 'Remember that you are in company with Alison's brother, Ardroy, if it's the name of some fair lady whom you saw go into that house which you are seeking.'

' 'Twas a man whom I saw come out of it,' replied Ewen briefly, and, noticing a respectable-looking old gentleman in spectacles advancing down Arlington Street at that moment, he accosted him with a request to be told who lived at Number Seventeen.

'Dear me,' said the old gentleman, pushing his spectacles into place, and peering up at the tall speaker, 'you must, indeed, be a stranger to this part of the town, sir, not to know that Number Seventeen is the house of Mr Henry Pelham the chief minister, brother to my Lord Newcastle.'

'I am a stranger,' admitted Ewen. 'Thank you, sir.' He lifted his hat again, and the old gentleman, returning the courtesy, trotted off.

'Mr Pelham the minister?' remarked Hector with reviving interest. 'And whom pray, did you see coming out of Mr Pelham's house?'

'That is just what it might be useful to discover,' replied Ewen musingly, 'now that one knows how important a personage lives there.'

'But I suppose that a good many people must come out of it,' objected the young officer. 'Why does the particular man whom you happened to see so greatly interest you?'

'Because he was a Highlander, and it was close upon midnight. And as a Highlander – though, naturally, a Whig – if one could interest him on a fellow-Highlander's behalf ... and he an intimate of Mr Pelham's –'

'How did you know that he was a Highlander, since I take it that he was not wearing the Highland dress?'

'Because I heard him rate his servant in Erse.'

'That's proof enough,' admitted Hector. 'Would you know him again if you saw him?'

'I think so. However, the chances are against my having the good fortune to do so.' Ewen began to walk on. 'I wonder what Mr Galbraith will have to say about this morning's affair.' And he sighed heavily; there was always much to be said – it was rather, what was to be done.

2

Darkness had fallen for some time when Ewen neared his lodging in Half Moon Street again; in fact it was nearly eleven o'clock. But when he was almost at the door he realized that to enter was out of the question. He must do something active with his body, and the only form of activity open to him was to walk – to walk anywhere. So, not knowing or caring where he was going, he turned away again.

His brain was swimming with talk – talk with Hector, talk at Mr Galbraith's, talk at the 'White Cock', where the three of them had supped. There it had been confidently announced that public opinion would be so stirred over Doctor Cameron's hard case that the Government would be obliged to commute the sentence, for already its severity seemed like to be the one topic throughout London. It was reported that many Whigs of high standing were perturbed about it and the effect which it might have upon public opinion, coming so long after the rising of '45, and having regard to the blameless private character of the condemned man. It was even said – the wish having perhaps engendered the idea – that sentence had only been passed in order that the Elector might exercise his prerogative of mercy, and by pardoning Doctor Cameron, perhaps at the eleventh hour, gain over wavering Jacobites by his magnanimity. But one or two others, less optimistic, had asked with some bitterness whether the party were strong or numerous enough now to be worth impressing in this way.

For fully half an hour Ewen tramped round streets and squares until, hearing a church clock strike, he pulled himself out of the swarm of unhappy thoughts which went with him for all his fast walking, saw that it was between half past eleven and midnight, and for the first time began to consider where he might be.

He had really become so oblivious of his surroundings as he went that it was quite a surprise to find himself now in a deserted, narrow, and not particularly reputable-looking street. Surely a few minutes ago – yet on the other hand, for all the attention he had been paying, it might have been a quarter of an hour – he had been in a square of large, imposing mansions. Had he merely imagined this; were grief and anxiety really depriving him of his senses? He turned in some bewilderment and looked back the way he had come. London was a confusing town.

It was a light spring night, and he could see that beyond the end of this narrow street, there *were* much larger houses, mansions even. He was right. But he also saw something which kept him rooted there – two men, armed with weapons of some kind, stealing out of a passage about fifty yards away, and hastening to the end of the street where it debouched into the square. When they got there they drew back into the mouth of an entry and stood half-crouching, as if waiting.

Surprise and curiosity kept Ewen staring; then he realized that these men were probably lurking there with a purpose far from innocent. And even as he started back towards the entry this purpose was revealed, for the bulk of a sedan-chair, with its porters, came suddenly into view, crossing the end of the street, on its way, no doubt, to one of the great houses in the square; and instantly the two men darted towards it, flourishing their weapons, which had the appearance of bludgeons.

Ewen quickened his pace to a run, ran in fact with all his might to the succour of the sedan-chair, which very probably contained a lady. He was certainly needed by its occupant, of whichever sex, for the two chairmen, calling loudly for the watch, had taken ingloriously to their heels at the approach of danger. Before Ewen came up one of the footpads had already lifted the roof of the chair, opened the door, and was pulling forth no female in distress, but a protesting elderly gentleman in flowered brocade, stout and a trifle short. Yet he was a valiant elderly gentleman, for, the moment he succeeded in freeing his right arm, out flashed his sword. But the next instant his weapon was shivered by a cudgel blow, and he himself seized by the cravat.

That, however, was the exact instant also at which another sword, with a longer and a younger man behind it, came upon the assailants from the rear. Apparently they had not heard Ardroy's hurrying footfalls, nor his shouts to them to desist.

Now one of them turned to face him; but his stand was very short. He dropped his cudgel with a howl and ran back down the narrow street. His fellow, of a more tenacious breed, still held on to the cravat of the unfortunate gentleman, trying to wrest out the diamond brooch which secured the lace at his throat. Ewen could have run his sword through the aggressor from side to side, but, being afraid of wounding the gentleman as well, took the course of crooking his left arm round the man's neck from behind, more than half-choking him. The assailant's hands loosed the cravat with remarkable celerity and tore instead at the garotting arm round his own throat. The rescuer then flung him away, and, as the footpad rolled in the gutter, turned in some concern to the victim of the attack, who by this time was hastily rearranging his assaulted cravat.

'My dear sir,' began the latter in a breathless voice, desisting and holding out both his hands, 'my dear sir, I can never thank you enough ... most noble conduct ... most noble! I am your debtor for life! No, thank you, I am shaken, but little the worse. If you will have the further goodness to lend me your arm to my house – 'tis but a few paces distant – and then I must insist on your entering that I may thank my preserver more fittingly. I sincerely trust,' he finished earnestly, 'that you are yourself unharmed?'

Ewen assured him that this was the case, and, sheathing the sword which in England there was no embargo upon his wearing, offered his arm. By this time the second footpad had also vanished.

'The outrageousness,' went on the rescued gentleman, 'the insolence, of such an attack within a few yards of my own door! Those rascally chairmen – I wonder were they in collusion? I vow I'll never take a hired chair again ... There come the watch – too late as usual! My dear sir, what should have befallen me without your most timely assistance Heaven alone knows!'

They were by this time mounting the steps of a large house in the square, whose domestics, even if they had not heard the disturbance in the street, must have been on the look-out for their master's entrance, for he had given but the slightest tap with the massive knocker before the door swung open, revealing a spacious, pillared hall and a couple of lackeys. Almost before he knew it, Ewen was inside, having no great desire to enter, but realizing that it would be churlish to refuse.

'A most disgraceful attack has just been made upon me, Jenkins,' said the master of the house, to a resplendent functionary who then hurried forward. 'Here, at the very corner of the square. Had it not been for this gentleman's gallantry in coming to my assistance – If that is the watch come to ask for particulars,' as another knock was heard at the hall door, 'tell them to come again in the morning; I'll not see them now.'

'Yes, my lord,' said the resplendent menial respectfully. 'Your lordship was actually *attacked*!' His tone expressed the acme of horror. 'May I ask, has your lordship suffered any hurt?'

'None at all, none at all, thanks to this gentleman. All my lady's company is gone, I suppose? Has she retired? No? I am glad of it. Now, my dear sir,' he went on, laying his hand on Ewen's arm, 'allow me the pleasure of presenting you to my wife, who will wish to add her thanks to mine.' He steered his rescuer towards the great staircase, adding as he did so, 'By the way, I fancy I have not yet told you who I am – the Earl of Stowe, henceforward very much yours to command.'

Chapter 18

CROSSING SWORDS

IF a man ever wished himself well out of a situation in which, as it happened, his own prowess had landed him, it was Ewen Cameron of Ardroy when that announcement fell upon his ears. What fatality had induced him to succour and be brought home by the father of the very man whom he had treated so scurvily two months ago, and who had sworn to be revenged upon him? Obviously the wisest course was to excuse himself and withdraw before he could meet that injured young gentleman.

But already Lord Stowe was motioning him with a courteous gesture to ascend the imposing staircase. Without great incivility he could not withdraw now, nor, it seemed to him, without great cowardice to boot. And if he must encounter Lord Aveling again, this place and these circumstances were certainly more favourable than any which he could have devised for himself. Moreover, Aveling might not be in London at this moment. Above all, Ewen's was a stubborn courage as well as, on occasions, a hot-brained one; he never relished running away. He therefore went on up the wide shallow staircase, and was looked down upon with haughty disapproval by Aveling's ancestors.

Outside a door the Earl paused. 'May I know the name of my preserver?'

'I beg your pardon, my lord,' returned Ewen. 'I forgot that I had not made myself known to you. My name is Ewen Cameron of Ardroy, at your service.'

Now, what had Lord Stowe heard of Ewen Cameron of Ardroy? If anything at all, nothing of good, that was certain. The bearer of that name lifted his head with a touch of defiance, for its utterance had certainly brought about a change in his host's expression.

'A kinsman of the unfortunate Doctor Cameron's, perhaps?' he inquired.

'Yes. He is my cousin – and my friend,' answered Ewen uncompromisingly.

'Ah,' observed Lord Stowe with a not unsympathetic intonation, 'a sad business, his! But come, Mr Cameron.' And, opening the heavy inlaid door, he ushered him into an enormous room of green and gold, where every candle round the painted walls burned, but burned low, and where the disposition of the furniture spoke of a gathering now dispersed. But the most important person still remained. On a sofa, in an attitude of incomparable grace, languor and assurance, with a little book poised lazily between her long fingers, half-sat, half-reclined the most beautiful woman whom Ewen had ever seen. And then only, in the suddenness of these events and introductions, did he realize that he was in the presence of Keith Windham's mother as well as of Lord Aveling's.

As the door shut Lady Stowe half-turned her head, and said in silver tones, 'You are returned at last, my lord. Do I see that you bring a guest?'

'I do, my love,' replied her husband, 'and one to whom we owe a very great debt indeed.' And Ewen was led forward across the acres of carpet to that gilt sofa, and kissed the cool, fragrant hand extended to him, but faintly conscious of embarrassment at the praises of his courage which the Earl was pouring forth, and with all thoughts of an avenging Aveling dissipated. It was of Lady Stowe's elder son, his dead friend, whom he thought as he looked at that proud and lovely face. Not that there was any likeness. But surely this could not have been Keith Windham's mother; she seemed no older, at least by candle-light, than he when he died seven years ago!

Then Ewen found himself in a chair, with the Countess saying flattering things to him, rallying him gently, too, in those seductive tones.

'You are a Scot, sir, a kinsman of that unfortunate gentleman who is in all our minds just now, and yet you come to the rescue of an Englishman and a Whig!'

'It was an Englishman and a Whig, Lady Stowe, who once saved me from a far greater danger,' replied Ewen. He said it

561

of set purpose, for he wished to discover if she knew what her elder son had been to him.

Apparently Lady Stowe did not, nor was she curious to learn to what he referred, for she merely said: 'Indeed; that is gratifying!' and, in fact, before the subject could be enlarged upon from either side, Lord Stowe was remarking to the guest by way of conversation suitable to his nationality, 'My son has recently been visiting Scotland for the first time.'

The menace of Aveling returned to Ewen's memory. By the tense it seemed as if that young gentleman had now returned from the North.

'You are from the Highlands, I suppose, Mr Cameron,' went on the Earl pleasantly. 'My son visited them also for a short while, going to Dunstaffnage Castle in Lorne. Do you happen to know it?'

Ewen intimated that he did, from the outside. And now a voice was crying out to him to end the difficult situation in which he stood (though neither his host nor his hostess was aware of it) by offering of his own will some explanation of the episode at Dalmally. For, with this mention of Lord Aveling in the Highlands, not to acknowledge that they had made each other's acquaintance there seemed so unnatural and secretive as to throw an even worse light upon his behaviour towards him. At the very least it made him appear ashamed of it. He pulled himself together for the plunge.

'I must tell you, my lord –' he was beginning, when his voice was withered on his lips by an extraordinary grating, screeching sound which, without warning, rent the air of the great drawing-room. Startled as at some supernatural intervention, Ewen glanced hastily round in search of its source.

'Do not be alarmed, Mr Cameron,' came Lady Stowe's cool tones through the disturbance. ' 'Tis only that my macaw has waked up ... but I apologize for the noise he makes.'

And then the Highlander beheld, in a corner not very far away, a gilded cage, and therein a large bird of the most gorgeous plumage, with a formidable curved beak and a tail of fire and azure, who was pouring forth what sounded like a stream of imprecations.

'For heaven's sake!' cried the Earl, jumping to his feet. 'I thought you had given up having that creature in this room, my lady! Is there no means to make him stop?' For the deafening scolding went on without intermission.

Lady Stowe leant forward. 'If you will have the goodness to cover him up,' she said with complete calm, 'he will be quiet.'

Both men looked round helplessly for something with which to carry out this suggestion; Ewen, too, had got to his feet. 'Cover him up with what, pray?' asked Lord Stowe indignantly. 'Good Gad, this is insupportable!' And, slightly red in the face, he tugged at the nearest bell-pull. Meanwhile the infernal screeching continued unceasingly, except for one short moment when the macaw made a vicious grab at the Earl's lace-bordered handkerchief, with which he was exasperatedly flapping the bars of the cage in an endeavour to silence its inmate.

A footman appeared. 'Remove this bird at once!' shouted his master angrily. (He was obliged to shout.) The man hesitated.

'Montezuma will bite him, and he knows it,' observed Lady Stowe, raising her voice but slightly. 'Send Sambo, John.'

The man bowed and withdrew with alacrity. 'This is worse than footpads!' declared the Earl, with his hands to his ears. 'I cannot sufficiently apologize, Mr Cameron!' – he had almost to bawl the words. 'Really, my lady, if I could wring your pet's neck without getting bitten, I would!'

'I know it, my love,' returned her ladyship, with her slow, charming smile. 'And so, I am sure, would poor Mr Cameron.'

Then black Sambo appeared in his scarlet turban and jutting white plume. Smiling broadly, he strutted off with the great gilt cage, whose occupant continued to scream, but made no onslaught upon those dusky fingers.

'I really cannot sufficiently apologize,' began the Earl once more to his half-deafened guest, 'for my wife's fancy –'

'What?' called a young, laughing voice from the door, 'has Montezuma been misbehaving again?' Someone had come in just as the exiled and vociferating fowl was borne out. 'But for that noise, I had thought you gone to bed by this time. You promised, my dear mother, that he –' But here the speaker

realized that there was a stranger in his family circle, pulled out
a handkerchief, flicked some probably imaginary grains of
powder off his gleaming coat, and advanced across the wilderness of the carpet to the three by the sofa, a veritable Prince
Charming in peach-coloured satin and a deal of lace. And
Ewen, watching his fate advance upon him in the person of this
smiling and elegant young man, silently cursed the departed
macaw with a mortification a thousand times deeper than the
Earl's. But for that ridiculous contretemps he might either have
made his confession, or escaped meeting his late victim, or
both.

But there was no escape now. Lord Aveling, still smiling, got
within a yard or two of the group when he saw who the stranger
was. He stopped; the smile died, his face froze, and the hand
with the filmy handkerchief fell, gripping the Mechlin.

Lord Stowe must have been blind had he not noticed the
startling change on the countenance of his heir. But, if not
blind, he was possibly short-sighted, for he did not by any
means appear to read its full significance.

'You are surprised to see a guest here so late, Aveling, I perceive,' he said mildly, 'but you will be still more surprised when
you learn the reason for this gentleman's presence tonight.'

'I've no doubt at all that I shall,' said Lord Aveling under his
breath. He had never removed his eyes from Ewen; they seemed
to say, almost as clear as speech, 'You cannot have had the insolence to make your way in here to apologize!'

'I was this evening,' went on Lord Stowe with empressement,
'the victim of a murderous attack – perhaps you have already
heard of it from the servants.'

'An attack!' repeated Lord Aveling, at last turning his gaze
upon his parent. 'On whose part – this gentleman's?'

'Good Gad, Aveling, what can you be thinking of?' ex-
claimed his father, shocked. 'This gentleman, Mr Cameron of
Ardroy, had the great goodness to risk his own person for mine
– Mr Cameron, this is my son, Lord Aveling.'

Ewen bowed, not very deeply.

'An introduction is not necessary, my lord,' observed Lord
Aveling. 'We met not long ago in Scotland, Mr Cameron and

I.' And with that he turned his back carelessly on the guest and went over to the sofa to speak to his mother.

Lord Stowe looked as if he could hardly believe his ears or eyes, partly at this announcement, partly at the sight of his son's uncivil behaviour. 'You met in Scotland!' he repeated after a moment, in tones of amazement.

'I was just on the point of making that fact known to your lordship,' said Ewen, 'when the bird interrupted me.' He was white with chagrin. 'Lord Aveling and I did, indeed, meet as he was returning from Dunstaffnage Castle.'

'Yes,' cut in the young man, turning round again, 'and owing to a difficulty over posthorses I had the privilege – as I see I must now consider it – of offering Mr Cameron a seat in my chaise as far as Dalmally.'

'My dear Aveling, why did you not tell us this before?' asked Lady Stowe.

'How could I guess that it would be of any interest to you to learn that I gave a lift to a stranger in the wilds of Scotland? It would have seemed, my dear mother, to be laying too much stress upon a deed of charity. Moreover, I can affirm, with my hand upon my heart, that Mr Cameron of Ardroy is the last person in the world whom I expected to find in this house.'

His manner, if controlled, was patently full of some ironical meaning which, though clear enough to Ardroy, was puzzling to his parents, who, having no clue to it, may have received the impression that he was a trifle the worse for wine. The Countess said, with a smiling authority, 'Then it behoves you all the more, Francis, to hear how Mr Cameron beat off the footpads who assailed your father's chair this evening at the corner of the square.'

'English footpads?' queried the young man, and he looked meaningly for an instant at the rescuer.

'Why, what else?' asked his father. 'Two footpads armed with cudgels. I had the narrowest escape of being robbed, if not of being murdered.'

'I can quite believe that you had, sir,' observed Lord Aveling, looking at Ewen again.

But Ewen had by now resolved that he was not going to

suffer these stabs any longer, nor was he disposed to hear the account of his prowess given a second time, and to the mocking accompaniment which he knew that it would receive. He therefore took advantage of the check to Lord Stowe's imminent narrative, brought about by these (to him) unintelligible remarks of his son's, firmly to excuse himself on the score of the lateness of the hour. Either Lord Aveling would allow him to leave the house without further words, or he would not; in any case, it was probable that he desired such words to take place without witnesses. The fact that he had not previously mentioned to his family their encounter and its disastrous end seemed to point to the fact that his young pride had been too bitterly wounded for him to speak of it, even in the hope of obtaining revenge. It might be very different now that his enemy was delivered so neatly into his hands.

'You must promise to visit us again, Mr Cameron,' said the Countess with the utmost graciousness, and Lord Stowe said the same, adding that if there were any way in which he could serve him he had but to name it. Ewen thought rather sardonically how surprised the Earl would be if he responded by a request that he should prevent his son from landing him in Newgate, but he merely murmured polite thanks as the Earl conducted him to the door of the drawing-room. It seemed as though he were going to pay his rescuer the further compliment of descending the stairs with him, but in this design he had reckoned without his son, who, as Ewen was perfectly aware, had followed behind them, awaiting his opportunity.

'I will escort Mr Cameron down the stairs, my lord,' he said easily, slipping in front of his father. 'You must remember that we are old acquaintances.'

He sounded perfectly civil and pleasant now, and after a barely perceptible hesitation the Earl relinquished the guest to his care, shook hands with great warmth, repeating his assurance of undying gratitude and a perpetual warm welcome at Stowe House. Then the door closed, and Ewen and Lord Aveling were alone together.

'Will you come into the library downstairs?' asked the young man, somewhat in the tone he might have used to a mason come about repairs, and with as little apparent doubt of the response.

'Yes,' answered Ardroy with equal coldness, 'I will,' and followed him down the great staircase.

In the marble-pillared hall a footman stepped forward. 'Take lights into the library,' commanded the young lord, and while he and Ewen waited for this to be done, without speaking, or even looking at each other, Ewen, gazing up at a portrait of some judicial ancestor in wig and ermine (not inappropriate to the present circumstances) thought, 'What is to prevent my opening the door into the square and leaving the house?' What indeed? Something much stronger than the desire to do so.

But in another moment the lackey was preceding them with a couple of branched candlesticks into a room lined with books. He made as though to light the sconces too, but Lord Aveling checked him impatiently, and the man merely set the lights on the big, polished table in the centre and withdrew. The son of the house waited until his footsteps had died away on the marble outside.

'Now, Mr Cameron!' he said.

Ewen had always known that to come to London was to invite the Fates to present him with the reckoning for his behaviour at Dalmally. Well, if it had to be, it was preferable to have it presented by the victim himself rather than by some emissary of the justice which he had invoked. And, however this unpleasant interview was to end, he might perhaps during its course succeed in convincing Lord Aveling of the sincerity of his regrets for that lamentable episode.

'I suppose, my lord,' he now answered gravely, 'that you must say what you please to me. I admit that I have little right to resent it.'

The admission, unfortunately, appeared to inflame the young nobleman the more. 'You are vastly kind, Mr Cameron, upon my soul! You lay aside resentment, forsooth! I fear I cannot rise to that height, and let me tell you, therefore, that what I find almost more blackguardly than your infamous conduct at Dalmally is the *coup* you have brought off tonight, in –'

'The *coup* I have brought off!' exclaimed Ewen in bewilderment. 'My lord, what –'

Aveling swept on '– in forcing an entrance to this house, and ingratiating yourself with my parents, having put my father under a fancied obligation by a trick so transparent that, if he were not the most good-natured man alive, he would have seen through it at once.'

At this totally unexpected interpretation of the sedan-chair incident a good deal of Ewen's coolness left him.

'You cannot really think that the attack on Lord Stowe was planned – that I was responsible for it!'

'How else am I to account for your being there so pat?' inquired the young man. 'You hired the ruffians and then came in as a deliverer. It has been done before now. And having succeeded in laying Lord Stowe under an obligation you know that I cannot well –' He broke off, his rage getting the better of him. 'But the insolence, the inexpressible insolence of your daring to enter this house after what has happened!'

'Since I did *not* plan the attack, Lord Aveling,' said Ewen firmly, 'I had no notion whom I was rescuing. Nor did Lord Stowe tell me his name until he was on the point of taking me upstairs. It was too late to withdraw then.'

'As I am henceforward unable to believe a word that you say, sir,' retorted the young man, 'it is of small use your pretending ignorance of my father's identity.'

'Yet perhaps you are still able to recognize logic when you hear it,' rejoined Ewen with some sharpness, his own temper beginning to stir. 'Had I known that the gentleman in the sedan-chair was Lord Stowe – which, if I had planned the attack, I must have known – the merest prudence would have kept me from entering a house in which I was so like to meet you.'

'Yes,' said Aveling with a bitter little smile, 'you would have done better to part sooner from my father after this pretended rescue!'

'And yet,' said the Highlander, looking at him with a touch of wistfulness in his level gaze, 'as chance has brought us together again, is it too much to hope, my lord, that you will at least endeavour to accept my most sincere and humble apologies for what my great necessity forced me to do that evening?'

'Apologies?' said Viscount Aveling. 'No, by heaven, there are no apologies humble enough for what you did!'

'Then I am ready to give you satisfaction in the way usual between gentlemen,' said Ewen gravely.

The young man shook his powdered head. 'Between gentlemen, yes. But a gentleman does not accept satisfaction of that kind from a highwayman; he has him punished, as I swore I would you. But you doubtless think that by gaining the Earl's goodwill you have put that out of my power? Let me assure you, Mr Highwayman, that you have not; the law is still the law!'

'I doubt if the law can touch me for what I did,' answered Ewen.

'Not for theft, horse-stealing and assault? Then this must indeed be an uncivilized country! ... And behind those crimes remains always the question of how my brother really met his end.'

'That I have already told you, Lord Aveling.'

'Yes; and I was fool enough to believe you! I am wiser now; I know of what you are capable, Mr Ewen Cameron!'

Ewen turned away from the furious young man, who still maintained his position by the door. He was at a loss what to do next. There was no common ground on which they could meet, though once there had seemed so much; but he himself had shorn it away. One of the candles in the massive silver-branched candlesticks which had been deposited upon the table was guttering badly, and, in the strange way in which a portion of the mind will attend to trifles at moments of crisis, he took up the snuffers which lay there in readiness and mended the wick with scarcely the least consciousness of what he was doing.

His action had an unexpected result. Lord Aveling started a few paces forward, pointing at the hand which had performed this service. 'And you still have the effrontery to wear the ring which you took from poor Keith!'

Ewen laid down the snuffers. 'I have the effrontery, since

you call it so, to wear the ring he gave me; and I shall wear it until my own dying day.'

The words though they were very quietly uttered, rang like a challenge; and as a challenge the young man took them up.

'Will you?' he asked. 'I think not. Here in this house, above all, I have no liking to see my poor brother's property on your finger. You will kindly surrender it to his family.'

'Although I take you to be jesting, my lord,' began Ewen very coldly.

'Jesting!' flashed out Aveling. 'No, by God! You will give me back Keith Windham's signet ring, or –'

'Or?' questioned Ewen.

'Or I'll have it taken from you by the lackeys!'

'Then you will hardly be in a position to throw my theft of your property in my face!' retorted Ardroy.

'I had not stolen my pistols and my horse,' riposted Lord Aveling.

'Nor have I stolen my friend's ring. He gave it to me, and I give it up to nobody!'

'I dispute your statement!' cried the young man with passion. 'You took that ring, whether you are guilty of my brother's death or no. You are very capable of such an act; I know that now. Give it up to me, or I shall do what I say. My father has retired by now; do not imagine that he can protect you!'

'As to that, my lord, you must follow your own instincts,' said Ewen scornfully, 'but you'll not get my friend's dying gift from me by threats – no, nor by performances either,' he added, as he saw Lord Aveling move towards the bell-pull.

'Yes, you think they are but threats, and that you can treat them with contempt,' said the young man between his teeth. 'I'll show you in one moment that they are not! I have only to pull this bell, and in two or three minutes a so-called Highland gentleman will go sprawling down the steps of Stowe House. You will not be able to bully half a dozen footmen as you bullied me!'

Ewen stood perfectly motionless, but he had paled. It was quite true that this irate, beautifully dressed young man had the power to carry out this new threat. Of the two he fancied he would almost have preferred the menace which Lord Aveling had uttered at Dalmally, that he would bring his assailant to Newgate. But he put the hand with the ring into his breast and said again, 'I can only repeat that you must follow your instincts, my lord. I follow mine; and you do not get this ring from me unless you take it by force!'

Aveling put his hand to the embroidered Chinese bell-pull hanging by the mantelpiece. Ewen looked at him. It needed a great effort of self-control on his part not to seize the young man and tear it out of his hand before he pulled it, as he could easily have done. And, in view of events in the bedroom at Dalmally, still only too fresh in his mind, this abstention evidently struck the angry Aveling as strange.

'I observe,' he said tauntingly, still holding the strip of silk, 'that you are not so ready to assault me now, Mr Cameron, when you know that you would instantly have to pay for it!'

'It was in someone else's interests that I used violence on you then, my lord. I have no one else's to serve now,' said Ewen sadly.

Lord Aveling dropped the bell-pull. 'You mean Doctor Cameron. No, you did not benefit him much. You were too late, I imagine.'

'I was just too late.'

'And if you had not been,' remarked the young man, 'I should not, perhaps, have heard him sentenced this morning.'

Ewen gave a little exclamation, 'You were at the King's Bench this morning, my lord? You were there – you heard it all? But they cannot, they cannot, mean to carry out so cruel and iniquitous a sentence!'

Suddenly and oddly reflective, Lord Aveling gazed at him, the tassel of the abandoned bell-pull still moving slowly to and fro across the wall. 'I would have given wellnigh all I possess to be in your place, my lord,' went on Ardroy, his own dangerous and unpleasant situation clean forgotten, 'to see how he looked ... though I have heard how well he bore himself. But if the judges knew what manner of man he was, how generous, how kind, how humane, they would not have condemned him on that seven years' old attainder.'

Francis Delahaye, Lord Aveling, was a very young man, and he had also been in an extreme of justifiable rage. But even that fury, now past its high-water mark, had not entirely swamped his native intelligence and sensitiveness, which were above the ordinary. He continued to look at Ewen without saying anything, as one in the grip of a perfectly new idea. Then, instead of putting his hand again to the bell-pull, he slowly walked away from its neighbourhood with his head bent, leaving the door unguarded and his threat unfulfilled.

But Ewen neither took advantage of these facts nor looked to see what his adversary was doing. The full wretchedness of the morning was back upon him; Archie had only three weeks to live. And if only he had not made an enemy of this young man, Lord Stowe, so grateful to his rescuer, might have been induced to use his influence on Archie's behalf. But it was hopeless to think of that now.

It was at this moment, during the silence which had fallen, that steps which sounded too authoritative to be those of a servant could be heard approaching along the marble corridor outside. Lord Aveling, at any rate, could assign them to their owner, for he came back from whatever portion of the library he had wandered to, murmuring with a frown, 'My father!' On that the door opened, and the Earl came in. His expression was perturbed.

'I waited for your reappearance, Aveling,' he said to his son; 'then I was informed that Mr Cameron had not left the house, and that you were both closeted in here. And your manner to him had been so strange that I decided to come in person to find out what was amiss.'

There was dignity about Lord Stowe now; he was no longer a somewhat fussy little gentleman deafened by a macaw, but a nobleman of position. His son seemed undecided whether to speak or no. Ewen spoke.

'An explanation is certainly owing to you, my lord, and by me rather than by Lord Aveling. His manner to me a while ago was, I regret to say, quite justified by something which occurred between us in Scotland.'

572

'And which, if you please,' put in Aveling like lightning, 'I wish to remain between us, Mr Cameron.'

'That is very unfortunate,' observed Lord Stowe gravely, looking from one to the other. 'As you know, I am under a great obligation to Mr Cameron.'

'From his past experience of me, my lord, Lord Aveling doubts that,' observed Ewen quietly.

'Doubts it! Good Gad, Aveling, are you suggesting that I was drunk or dreaming this evening?'

'No, my lord,' said his son slowly. He was examining his ruffles with some absorption. 'Since I gave voice to my doubt, I have ... revised my opinion. I do not question your very real debt to Mr Cameron.'

'I should hope not,' said the Earl with some severity. 'And, as I said before, I am extremely anxious to repay it. If I can do this by composing the difference which has arisen between you –'

'No, you can't do that, my dear father,' said the young man with vivacity. 'Leave that out of the question now, if you will, and ask Mr Cameron in what way you can best repay that debt. I believe I could give a very good guess at what he will reply.'

Ewen gave a start and looked at the speaker, upon whose lips hung something like a smile. How did Lord Aveling know – or did he not know? Such intuition savoured almost of the supernatural.

'Well, Mr Cameron, what is it?' inquired the Earl. 'In what can I attempt to serve you? You have but to name the matter.'

But Ewen was so bewildered at this *volte-face* in his enemy, not to mention his uncanny perspicacity, that he remained momentarily tongue-tied.

'Mr Cameron's request is not, I believe, for himself at all,' said Lord Aveling softly. 'There is a person upon whose behalf he has done and risked a good deal. I think he wishes, if possible, to enlist you on the same side.'

'I take it,' said his father, 'that you are referring to the unfortunate gentleman, Mr Cameron's kinsman, who was today condemned to death. Am I right, Mr Cameron?'

Ewen bent his head. 'I ask too much, perhaps, my lord.' He lifted it again, and speech came to him, and he pleaded earnestly for commutation of the sentence, almost as though the decision had lain in Lord Stowe's hands. 'And surely, my lord,' he finished, 'clemency in this case must prove to the advantage, not to the disadvantage, of the Government.'

The Earl had listened with courtesy and attention. 'I will certainly think over what you have said, Mr Cameron,' he promised, 'and if I can convince myself, from what I hear elsewhere, that a recommendation to mercy is advisable, I will take steps in the proper quarters. Come and see me again tomorrow afternoon, if you will give yourself the trouble. – Aveling, you wish me, I gather, to leave you to settle your own difference with Mr Cameron?'

'If you please, my lord.' He smiled a little, and opened the door for his father to pass out.

'Why did you do that? How, in God's name, did you know?' cried Ewen directly it was shut again.

The dark mahogany panels behind him threw up Lord Aveling's slight, shimmering figure. 'It was not so difficult to read your mind, Mr Cameron. I wish I could think that among my friends I numbered one with ... the same notions that you have. As to my own mind ... well, perhaps Doctor Cameron made an impression on me this morning other than I had expected, so that, to tell truth, I half-wished that you *had* been in time with the information which you stole from me.'

Ewen sat down at the table and took his head between his fists. Once more Keith Windham's ring glittered in the candlelight.

'We heard a rumour in Edinburgh,' went on Aveling, 'that there was one man and one man only with Doctor Cameron when he was taken, and that he resisted desperately, and was left behind too badly hurt to be taken away by the soldiers. I begin to have a suspicion who that man was ...'

Ewen was silent.

'– Although you said that you arrived too late ... But I do not wish to press you to incriminate yourself.'

574

'Yes, you have enough against me without seeking any more,' answered Ardroy without raising his head.

'I think that I have wiped out that score,' said Aveling reflectively. 'Indeed, that I have overpaid it.' He was silent for a second or two, and then went on with a very young eagerness, 'Mr Cameron, I am going to ask a favour of you, which may not displease you either. Will you, as a matter of form, cross swords with me – over the table if you prefer it – so that we may each feel that we have offered satisfaction to the other? I was too angry to know what I was saying when I refused your offer of it just now. See, I will shift the candlesticks a little. Will you do it?'

Ewen got up, rather moved. 'I shall be very glad to do it, my lord.' He drew his plain steel-hilted sword; out came the young man's elegant damascened weapon; the glittering blades went up to the salute, and then kissed for a second above the mahogany.

'Thank you, sir,' said Aveling, stepping back with a bow, and sheathing again. 'Will you forgive me now for what I said about my brother? I am well content that you should keep his ring, and I am sure that the giver would have been pleased that you refused to surrender it, even to save yourself from what I had the bad taste to threaten you with.'

Sword in hand, Ewen bowed; words, somehow, would not come. So much that was racking had happened this day, and he was not long over a convalescence. The young, delicate face looking gravely and rather sweetly at him across the table swam for a second in the candle-light, and when he tried to return his sword to the scabbard he fumbled over the process.

'I can see that you are much fatigued, Mr Cameron,' said Lord Aveling, coming round the table. 'Will you take a glass of wine with me before you go?'

Chapter 19

KEITH WINDHAM'S MOTHER

1

'A GENTLEMAN to see you, sir,' said the voice, not of Ewen's landlady, Mrs Wilson, but of the impish boy from the vintner's shop below. And, coming nearer, he added confidentially, 'He ain't given no name, but he's mighty fine – a lord, belike!'

'Where is he, then – show him in at once!' ordered Ewen, picturing Mr Galbraith, the only person, save Hector, likely to call at this morning hour, left standing at the top of the stairs. And yet what should make the soberly attired Galbraith 'mighty fine' at this time of day?

But the impish boy's diagnosis was exactly correct; the young gentleman who entered *was* fine – though not so fine as last night – and he *was* a lord. Ewen went forward amazed; despite the peaceful termination to last night's encounter, Viscount Aveling was the last person he should have expected to walk into his humble apartment.

'I am not intruding, I hope, Mr Cameron, visiting you thus early?' inquired the young man in the voice which was so like his dead brother's. 'I wished to make sure that you would keep your promise of waiting upon my father this afternoon, for he is genuinely anxious to afford you any assistance in his power. Yet I feared that you might be kept away by the memory of my ... my exceedingly inhospitable behaviour last night.'

All the frank and boyish charm which had formed the essence of Ewen's first impression of him was back – more than back.

'I assure you, my lord,' replied Ewen warmly, 'that any memories of that sort were drowned in the glass of wine we took together. I shall most gratefully wait upon Lord Stowe at any hour convenient to him. But will you not be seated? It is exceedingly good of you to have come upon this errand.'

Lord Aveling laid down his tasselled cane upon the table, and lifting the full skirts of his murrey-coloured coat out of the way, complied.

'I do not think that Lord Stowe can promise much, Mr Cameron,' he said, 'and it may be that any step will take time. But I believe that strong feeling is being aroused by the sentence, which is a hopeful sign. My father was himself present when judgement was given, and was much impressed, as I was, by Doctor Cameron's bearing.'

'Everyone seems to have been at the Court of King's Bench but I,' said Ewen sadly.

'Yet surely,' objected the young man, 'it would have been very painful for you, Mr Cameron, to hear the details of that sentence, which sound so barbarous and cold-blooded when enumerated beforehand; and I must own that the Lord Chief Justice hurled them, as it were, at the unfortunate gentleman with what seemed more like animus on his part than a due judicial severity.'

'Yes, I have already been told that,' said Ewen. 'Yet I should have seen my kinsman had I been present, even though I could not have had speech with him – that, I knew, would be too much to expect in the case of a State prisoner. It is I, alas,' he added with a sudden impulse towards confidence, 'who am, in a measure at least, responsible for his capture.'

'My dear Mr Cameron,' exclaimed young Aveling with vivacity, 'considering how you ... moved heaven and earth to warn him, and that you, if I guess rightly, were the man struck down defending him, how can you say that?'

'Because it was I who suggested our taking refuge in the fatal hut in which he was captured,' answered Ewen with a sigh. 'I should like to hear him say that he forgives me for that: but I must be content with knowing in my heart that he does.'

Lord Aveling was looking grave. 'You have touched, Mr Cameron, on the other reason which brought me here. It seems to me that you are going openly about London without a thought of your own safety. But you must be a marked man if any note were made, at the time of Doctor Cameron's capture, of your personal appearance – of your uncommon height, for instance. Have you taken any precautions against recognition?'

'What precautions could I take?' asked Ewen simply. 'I can only hope that no such note was made. After all, *I* am of no importance to the Government, and, as it happened, I did not even touch a single soldier. My weapon broke – or rather, came to pieces.'

'I should call that fortunate,' observed his visitor with the same gravity.

'I suppose it was, since I must have been overpowered in the end; there were too many of them ... I think I *am* singularly fortunate,' he added with the same simplicity. 'Last night, for instance, Lord Aveling ... I am still at a loss to know why you changed your mind, and did not carry out your threat, and showed besides so much generosity to me, and helped instead of hindering me with my request to Lord Stowe.'

The blood showed easily on Aveling's almost girl-like complexion. He rose and resumed his cane, saying meanwhile, 'If you do not guess why you turned my purpose – but no, why should you? 'twould be out of keeping – I'll tell you some day.' And here he hesitated, half-turned, turned back again, then, fingering with deep interest the tassels of his cane, said in a lower tone: 'You have a secret of mine, Mr Cameron. I hope I can rely upon you ... to preserve it as such?'

'A secret of yours, my lord?' exclaimed Ewen in surprise. Then a flush spread over his face also, and he became more embarrassed than his visitor. 'You mean – that letter! Lord Aveling, if I were to spend the rest of my life apologizing –'

'I do not desire you to do that, sir,' interrupted the young lover, now poking with his cane at one of Mrs Wilson's chairs, to the considerable detriment of its worn covering. 'We have closed that chapter. Nevertheless –' He stopped.

'Then at least believe me,' put in Ewen earnestly, 'that anything I may have had the misfortune to read is as though I had never seen it!'

The young man ceased stabbing the chair. 'I thank you, Mr Cameron, and I have no hesitation in relying upon that assurance. Nevertheless, since you are shortly to wait upon my father, it is as well that you should know that, though the lady has consented to my unworthy suit, my parents, that is to say, my mother ...' Again he stopped.

Ewen bowed. 'You honour me with your confidence, my lord.' (And indeed, as he felt, the way in which he had earned it was sufficiently singular.)

'My mother,' went on Lord Aveling after a second or two, 'has, I know, other views for me. I doubt if she suspects this attachment; but of my father's I am not so sure; yet he may very well give his consent to the match. And as for me –' here he threw back his head and looked at Ewen, if not in the face, yet very nearly, 'as for me, my heart is immutably fixed, though at present I find it more politic to say nothing as yet of pledges which I am firmly resolved never to relinquish until they are exchanged for more solemn vows at the altar!'

Ewen bowed again, rather touched at this lofty declaration, which promised well for the happiness of Miss Georgina Churchill. 'There is no conceivable reason, my lord, why any member of your family should suppose me aware of this attachment.'

'No, that is true,' said his visitor; 'and you must forgive me for troubling you at such a time with my affairs. And now, if you will excuse me, I will take my leave. Do not fail to wait upon my father, Mr Cameron; and if you should get into trouble with the authorities over your doings in that glen whose name I still cannot remember,' he added with a half-shy, half-mocking smile, 'send for your humble servant!' And he bowed himself out of the door; the room was the darker for his going.

When Ewen had recovered from the surprise of this visit he went out in search of Hector, who was sufficiently amazed at the tale of his brother-in-law's doings on the previous night. 'But the fact remains,' was his summing up, 'that you have made an exceedingly useful friend in the Earl of Stowe, not to speak of the young lord.'

'And your own investigations as to the source of that slander, Hector, how are they going?'

Hector frowned. 'Not at all. And 'tis a ticklish matter to investigate – to ask men, for instance, if they have suspicions of you?'

'That I can well believe. Promise me that you will do nothing rash; that you will take no serious step without consulting me. Don't, for God's sake, get involved in a dispute just now, Hector! You must forgive me for lecturing you, but you know that you have a hot temper!'

'Yes,' agreed Hector Grant with surprising meekness, 'I know that I have. And you know it too, Ewen – none better. I will be careful.'

On Ewen's return to Half Moon Street, Mrs Wilson was prompt to call his attention to an elegant coroneted note lying on his table.

'A blackamoor boy brought it soon after you was gone out, sir – one of them the quality has.'

The note was from the Countess of Stowe, Stowe House seeming to favour the vintner's abode today.

'Dear Mr Cameron,' ran the delicate writing, 'I understand that you will be having an interview with Lord Stowe this afternoon. Pray do not depart without giving me the pleasure of your company. My son has told me something of you which makes me greatly desire to see you as soon as possible. Be good enough, ere you depart, to ask to be conducted to my boudoir.'

How strange it was, how strange! He might have been going to meet Keith in that boudoir, instead of telling his mother about the circumstances of their friendship and his death. For that, of course, was why Lady Stowe wished to have speech with him.

2

The Earl of Stowe received the Highlander in his own study that afternoon. He was extremely gracious, made many references to his rescue and to his gratitude, announced that, after reflection, he had come to the conclusion that the Government would certainly do well to spare the life of so amiable and humane a gentleman as Doctor Cameron appeared to be, and that he should use his utmost endeavours to persuade them to do so. He could not, naturally, say what success would attend his efforts, and he warned his visitor not to be too sanguine.

Yet a great deal of public interest and sympathy was undoubtedly being aroused by the case. For his part, he had been
very favourably impressed by the Jacobite's appearance, and by
his manly and decent bearing on a most trying occasion.

'You, I understand, Mr Cameron, were not able to be present
in the King's Bench when he was sentenced. My son made a
suggestion to me with regard to that, after seeing you this
morning. I fancy, from what he said, that you would be gratified if I could procure you an order to visit Doctor Cameron in
the Tower?'

'Gratified!' exclaimed Ewen, in a tone which left no doubt
of the fact. 'My lord, you would be repaying my trifle of
assistance last night a hundred times over! Does your lordship
mean that?'

'Certainly I do,' replied his lordship, 'and I think that it is a
matter within my power, since I know Lord Cornwallis somewhat well. Today is Friday; I will try to procure you an order
for next Monday. But if it is granted you would, I fear, have to
submit to a search on entering the Tower, for I understand that
they are keeping Doctor Cameron very strictly.'

Ewen intimated that that process would not deter him, and,
thanking the Earl almost with tears in his eyes, prepared to
withdraw, a little uncertain about his next step. Was Lord
Stowe, for instance, aware that the Countess also wished to see
his visitor? Yes, fortunately, for he was saying so.

'... And you will excuse me if I do not myself take you to
my lady. An enemy who, I trust, will not attack you for many
years yet is threatening me today, and just at present I am
using this foot as little as possible.' It was with a wry smile that
the Earl hobbled to the bell-pull.

A large portrait of Aveling as a ravishingly beautiful child,
playing with a spaniel, hung over the fireplace in Lady Stowe's
boudoir; another of him as a young man was on the wall
opposite to the door, while a miniature of a boy who could
only have been he stood conspicuously on a table among
various delicate trifles in porcelain or ivory. All these Ewen
saw while looking eagerly round for some memento of his dead

friend, of which he could find no trace. Then a door at the other end of the warm, perfumed room opened, and the mistress of the place came in, regally tall, in dove-grey lutestring, the black ribbon, with its single dangling pearl, which clasped her slender throat, defining the still perfect contour of her little chin – a famous toast who could afford to dress simply, even when she had a mind to a fresh conquest.

'Mr Cameron, this is kind of you,' she said, as he bent over her hand. Save Alison's he had heard no sweeter voice. 'It is even generous, for I fear that your reception by my son last night was not what it should have been, considering the debt we all owe you.'

Wondering not a little what explanation Lord Aveling had subsequently given his mother of his behaviour, Ewen replied that the difference which had unfortunately arisen between them in Scotland had quite justified Lord Aveling's coldness, but that they had afterwards come to a complete understanding.

'So my lord told me,' said the Countess, 'and indeed my son also. But he was mysterious, as young men delight to be. I know not whether you disagreed over the weather, or politics, or over the usual subject – a woman.' Here she flashed a smiling glance at him. 'But I see, Mr Cameron, that you are not going to tell me ... therefore it was the last. I hope she was worth it?'

'If it had been a woman,' replied her visitor, 'surely your son's choice, Lady Stowe, would have been such as you would have approved. However, our difference was over something quite other. You will remember that I do not share Lord Aveling's political allegiances.'

Lady Stowe smiled. 'I suppose I must be content with that, and put away the suspicion that you fell out over ... sharing an allegiance which was not political!'

'As to that, my lady,' said Ewen, 'I give you my word of honour.' Entirely wrong as she was in her diagnosis, the remembrance of that love-letter made him very wishful to leave the dangerous proximity of Miss Georgina Churchill, lest by any look or word he should betray the secret he had so discreditably learnt and so faithfully sworn to keep.

'But you are standing all this while,' exclaimed Lady Stowe.

'Be seated, I pray. Have you seen my lord, and is he able to do what you wish?'

'His lordship has been most kind, and promised to use his influence,' said Ewen as he obeyed – extremely relieved at the change of subject. 'And knowing that influence to be great, I have proportionate hopes.'

'You must command me too, if there is anything that I can do,' said the Countess softly. 'The Princess Amelia might be approached, for instance; no stone must be left unturned. But fortunately there is a good while yet. Do you know many people in London, Mr Cameron?'

Ewen replied that he did not, that he had never been there before, though he knew Paris well.

'Ah, there you have the advantage of me, sir,' observed his hostess. 'I have never been to Paris; it must by all accounts be a prodigious fine city. Do you know the Ambassador, the Earl of Albermarle?'

'No, my lady – not as an ambassador, at least. He was in command at Fort Augustus when I was a prisoner there in the summer of '46. But I never saw him.'

He wanted to talk about Keith Windham, not to exchange banalities about Paris and diplomats, and hoped that a reference to the Rising might bring about this consummation. In a measure, it did. Lady Stowe turned her powdered head away for a moment.

'Yes, I remember,' she said in a low voice. 'It was the Earl who gave my unfortunate elder son the commission which led to his death. Aveling has told me the story which he had from you – no, no need to repeat it, Mr Cameron, for the recital must be painful to you also. And to a mother ... you can guess ... her first-born, murdered –' She was unable to continue; she put a frail handkerchief, with a scent like some dream of lilies, for an instant to her mouth, and Ewen could see that her beautiful eyes were full of tears.

And he pictured Alison (or, for the matter of that, himself) bereaved by violent means of Donald. ... He began to say, with deep feeling, how good of her it was to receive him, seeing that he had been, in a sense, the cause of Major Windham's death, and once again the moonlit sands of Morar blotted out for a second what was before his eyes.

'I was ... wholly devoted to him,' went on Keith's mother, in the same sweet, shaken voice; 'so proud of his career ... so – But that must not make me unjust. It was to be, no doubt ... And I am very glad to have you here, Mr Cameron, the last person who saw my dear son alive.'

And she looked at him with a wonderfully soft and welcoming glance, considering what painful memories the sight of him might be supposed to call up. Who was Ewen, the least personally vain of men, and absorbed besides in far other reflections, to guess that Lady Stowe, like old Invernacree, had found him the finest piece of manhood she had ever seen, and that she was wondering whether the charm which had never yet failed her with the opposite sex would avail to bring to her feet this tall Highlander, already bound by a sentimental tie – though not exactly the tie which a lady desirous of forgetting her years would have chosen.

She put away her handkerchief. 'But it is wrong and selfish, do you not think, Mr Cameron, to dwell too much on painful memories? I am sure my dear Keith would not wish to see us sad. He is happy in Heaven, and it is our duty to make the best of this sometimes uncheerful world. – I am holding a small rout upon the Thursday in next week; will you give me the pleasure of your company at it?'

Ewen was conscious of the kind of jolt caused when a hitherto decorously travelling chaise goes unexpectedly over a large stone.

'I fear I shall be too much occupied, my lady,' he stammered. 'I thank you, but I must devote all my time to –'

'Now, do not say to conspiring,' she admonished him, smiling. 'As a good Whig I shall have to denounce you if you do!'

'If it be conspiracy to try to procure the commutation of Doctor Cameron's sentence,' answered Ewen, 'then his lordship is conspiring also.'

'Very true,' admitted Lady Stowe. 'We will not, then, call it by that name. But, Mr Cameron, you cannot spend all your time writing or presenting petitions. What do you say to coming to a small card-party of my intimate friends, on Monday? You can hardly hope to be accomplishing anything so soon as that?'

Ewen bowed. 'I am deeply grateful to your ladyship, but I am in hopes of an order to visit Doctor Cameron in the Tower on that day, and since I do not know for what hour the permission will be granted –'

'Mr Cameron, you are as full of engagements as any London beau! And an order for the Tower! How are you going to promise me to come and take a hand at quadrille on Monday?'

'His lordship has been so good as to promise to try to obtain one.'

Lady Stowe made a *moue*. 'I vow I shall ask Lord Cornwallis not to grant it! Nay, I was but jesting. Yet you are vastly tiresome, sir. If you should not get the order will you promise me to come and take a hand at quadrille on Monday?'

'I am a poor man, Lady Stowe, with a wife and children, and cannot afford to play quadrille,' replied Ewen bluntly.

His hostess stared at him. 'You are married ... and have children!'

'I have been married these seven years,' said Ewen in a tone of some annoyance. Lady Stowe was, he knew, old enough to be his mother, but that was no reason why she should think, or pretend to think him a boy.

The Countess began to laugh. 'I cry you mercy, sir, for having supposed you a bachelor, since it seems to displease you. Tell me of your wife and children.'

'There is little to tell,' responded Ewen. At least, there seemed little to tell this fine lady.

'Seven years,' said her ladyship reflectively. 'Then you were married soon after the Re – the Rising?'

'No, during it,' replied her guest. 'About five weeks before the battle of Culloden – But I am sure that this cannot interest you, my lady.'

'On the contrary,' said Lady Stowe, smiling her sweet, slow smile. 'And your wife – how romantical! Tell me, did she seek and find you upon the battlefield ... for something tells me that you were left there for dead?'

'My wife was then in France,' replied Ardroy rather shortly.

'But you *were* left upon the battlefield?' pursued Lady Stowe, looking at him with fresh interest.

'Yes, I was,' admitted Ewen, with a good deal of unwillingness. 'But you must forgive me for saying once more that I do not see of what interest it can be to your ladyship whether I was or no.'

'O Mr Cameron, do not snub me so!' cried the Countess. Secretly she was charmed; what man in the whole of London would have spoken to her with such uncompromising directness? 'I protest I meant nothing uncomplimentary in the assumption – rather the reverse!'

'Few men who were so left were lucky enough to come off with their lives,' remarked Ewen grimly.

'Why? Ah, I remember hearing that it was very cold in the north then. Did you suffer from the severity of the weather?'

'I suppose I did,' admitted Ardroy, 'though I knew little about it at the time. And it was not, for the most part, the weather which killed our wounded ... But I am occupying too much of your ladyship's time, and if you will permit me I will take my leave.' And he rose from his chair with that intention.

But Lady Stowe remained sitting there, looking up at him. 'Have you taken a vow never to speak of your past life, Mr Cameron? For I protest that you are singularly uncommunicative, which is, I believe, a trait of your countrymen from the Lowlands. That provokes a woman, you know, for she is naturally all curiosity about persons in whom she is interested. And in your case, too, there is the link with my poor Keith. Did you tell *him* nothing?'

'It was about him, not myself, that I came to talk,' was almost upon Ewen's lips; but he kept the remark unuttered. If Keith's mother wanted to know more of his past history he supposed he must gratify the desire; moreover, he was afraid that he had taken up a churlish attitude towards this gracious and beautiful lady. He had not yet got over the jolt.

So he tried to make amends. 'I fear that I am being extremely uncivil, and that you will think me very much of a barbarian, Lady Stowe. Anything that you care to hear about me I am very ready to tell you; and in exchange you will perhaps (if I do not ask too much) tell me something of Major Windham. I knew so little of his past life.'

The Countess of Stowe studied him as he stood there in her boudoir, nothing of the barbarian about him save, perhaps, his stalwart height. He would evidently come to see her to talk about her dead son, though he would not come to a rout or a tea-party. Very well then. And for how many occasions could she make her reminiscences of Keith last out? There must not be too many served up at each meeting. And would those deep blue eyes look at her again with that appealing gaze? On such a strong face that fleeting expression held an irresistible charm ... but then so had his very different air when she tried to make him speak of what he had no mind to. Like a true connoisseur Lady Stowe decided to cut short the present interview in order to have the pleasure of looking forward to others. She glanced at the cupid-supported clock on the mantelpiece, gave an exclamation and rose.

'I had forgotten the time ... I must go and dress ... Then it is a bargain, Mr Cameron? You'll come again and hear of my poor boy? Come at any time when you are not conspiring, and I will give orders that you shall be instantly admitted – that is, if I am without company. You shall not, since you do not wish it, find yourself in the midst of any gatherings. Nor indeed,' she added with a faint sigh, 'could we then speak of my dear Keith.' And with that, swaying ever so little towards him, she gave him her hand.

No, thought Ewen as he went down the great staircase, but they might have spoken of him this afternoon a great deal more than they had done. Lady Stowe had told him nothing, yet the shock of Keith's death, even to a mother's heart, must be a little softened after seven years. And what could it have mattered to her whether or no *he* had been left out all night on the battlefield, and whether he were married or single? He concluded that fashionable ladies were strange creatures, and wondered what Alison would have made of the Countess of Stowe.

Not far from the steps of Stowe House, when Ewen got into the square, there was waiting an extremely respectable elderly man who somehow gave the impression of being in livery, though he was not. As Ardroy came towards him he stepped forward, and, saluting him in the manner of an upper servant, asked very respectfully for the favour of a few words with him.

'Certainly,' said Ewen. 'What is it that you wish to speak to me about?'

'I understand, sir,' said the man, 'that you are the gentleman that was with Major Windham when he was killed, and was telling my lady his mother how it happened. I'm only a servant, sir, but if you would have the goodness ... I taught him to ride, sir, held him on his first pony, in the days when I was with Colonel Philip Windham his father, and I was that fond of him, sir, and he always so good to me! 'Twas he got me the place in his lordship's household that I have still; and if, sir, you could spare me a moment to tell me of his end among those murdering Highlanders ... ?' His voice was shaking, and his face, the usually set, controlled face of a superior and well-trained servant, all quivering with emotion.

Ewen was touched; moreover no chance of learning more of the friend about whom he really knew so little was to be lost. 'Come back with me to my lodging,' he said, 'and I will tell you anything you desire to know.'

The man protested at first, but, on Ewen's insisting, followed him at a respectful distance to Half Moon Street. So yet another inmate of Stowe House came to the vintner's that day. The name of this one was Masters, and Ewen, bidding him sit down, told him the whole story.

'It must have been a terrible grief to Lady Stowe,' he ended sympathetically, and was surprised to see a remarkable transformation pass over the old servant's saddened face.

'Did her ladyship give you that impression, sir? Nay, I can
see that she did.' He hesitated, his hand over his mouth, and
then broke out: 'I must say it – in justice to *him* I must say it –
and I'm not in her service, but in my lord's – Mr Cameron, she
never cared the snap of a finger for Mr Keith, and when he was
a boy it used near to break his heart, for he worshipped her,
lovely as she was. But 'twas my young lord she cared for, when
he came, and rightly, for he is a very sweet-natured young
gentleman. Yet she had Mr Keith's devotion before her second
marriage, when he was her only son, and she took no heed of it
– she neglected him. I could tell you stories, sir ... but 'tis
better not, and he's dead now, my Mr Keith, and few enough
people in his life to appreciate him as they should have done.
But if *you* did, sir, that's a great thing for me to think of ... and
your being with him at the end, too ... Might I look at that
ring of his you spoke of, sir, if not asking too great a favour?
Oh, thank you, thank you, sir!'

For Ewen had taken off Keith Windham's signet ring and put
it into the old man's hand. Then he went to the window and
stood looking out.

He could not but believe the old servant. What he had told
him interpreted the whole of this afternoon's interview. Lady
Stowe had avoided speaking of Keith to him at any length not
from grief, but from indifference. He could hardly credit it,
yet it must have been so – unless perchance it was from remorse. Well, now he knew what he thought of ladies of fashion.
Poor Keith, poor Keith!

'Masters,' he said at last, without looking round, 'since you
knew him well I will ask you to tell me something of Major
Windham's young days – but not now. I hope, by the way, that
he and Lord Aveling were upon good terms?'

'Very good, very good indeed,' the old man hastened to
assure him. 'My young lord admired Mr Keith, I think; and Mr
Keith was fond of him, there's no doubt, though he teased him
at times for being, as he said, as pretty as a girl. But my young
lord took it in good part. 'Twas he, young as he was then, that
wanted to have Mr Keith's body brought to England for burial,

but her ladyship would not. May I give you back this ring, sir, and thank you for allowing me ...' He faltered, and, holding out the ring with one hand, sought hastily with the other for his handkerchief.

Chapter 20

'LOCHABER NO MORE'

So smart a coach drawing up on Tower Hill this fine May morning soon drew a little crowd of idlers, mostly small boys, some shouting their conviction that it contained the Lord Mayor, against others who upheld that the Prince of Wales would emerge from it. But the two gentlemen who presently stepped out did not fulfil either expectation.

'I have brought you to this spot, Mr Cameron,' said the younger of the two in a lowered voice, 'that you may see for yourself how vain are any dreams of a rescue from that!'

And Ewen, standing, as he knew, on perhaps the most blood-drenched spot in English history, gazed at the great fortress-prison whence most of those who had died here had come forth to the axe. And at the sight of it his heart sank, though he knew Edinburgh Castle on its eagle's nest, and how the Bastille upreared its sinister bulk in the Faubourg St Antoine at Paris.

'It is a bitter kindness, Lord Aveling, but it is a kindness, and I thank you.'

The young man motioned to him to enter the coach again, and they drove down to the entrance under the Lion Tower, where he would leave him.

It was indeed a kind thought of the young lord's, not only to bring him, on his father's behalf, the permit from Lord Cornwallis to visit Doctor Cameron, but also to carry him to the Tower in his own coach. Yet as Ardroy, showing the precious paper with the Constable's signature, followed his conductor over the moat and under the archway of the Middle Tower, he felt how powerless after all were the very real friendship of the Earl of Stowe and his son, and all their prestige. Archibald Cameron was in a place whence it would take more than aristocratic influence to free him.

At the third, the Byward Tower, his guide halted and informed him that he must be searched here, and led him to a room for that purpose. The officials were extremely civil and considerate, but they did their work thoroughly, taking from him every object about him and in his pocket, save his handkerchief; his sword as a matter of course, his money, a little notebook of accounts and a pencil, even his watch. All, naturally, would be restored to him as he came out. Ewen rather wondered that he was allowed to retain his full complement of clothes, but he did not feel in spirits to make a jest of the affair.

And then he heard, to his surprise, that Doctor Cameron was confined in the Deputy-Lieutenant's own quarters, and that therefore he had little farther to go. Soon he found himself in a house within the fortress – in reality the lodgings of the Lieutenant of the Tower, who occupied the rank next the Constable's in this hierarchy; but neither he nor the Constable resided there. On one side this house looked out to the river, and on the other to the Parade, Tower Green and the Chapel of St Peter, and Ewen was told that it was by no means unusual for State prisoners to be confined in its precincts; several of the Jacobite lords had been imprisoned here.

Then he was suddenly in the presence of the Deputy-Lieutenant himself, General Charles Rainsford. The soldier was as considerate as the rest, and even more courteous. His affability chilled Ewen to the core. Had the authorities seemed hostile or anxious ... but no, they knew that once they were on their guard no one escaped or was rescued from the Tower of London.

'You will find Doctor Cameron well, I think, sir,' volunteered the Deputy-Lieutenant. 'My orders are so strict that I cannot allow him out of doors, even attended by a warder, to take the air, but as he has two rooms assigned to him he walks a good deal in the larger, and by that means keeps his health.'

'Does he know that I am to visit him?'

'He does, and has expressed the greatest pleasure at it.'

'Mrs Cameron is not yet arrived in London, I think?'

'No, but the Doctor expects her shortly.'

And on that the visitor was entrusted to a warder, and went with him up the shallow oaken stairs. They stopped before a door guarded by a private of the regiment of Guards, and when it was opened Ewen found himself in a long, narrowish room, almost a gallery, at whose farther end a figure which had evidently been pacing up and down its length had turned expectantly. They each hurried to the other, and, for the first time in their lives, embraced.

Ewen could never remember what were the first words which passed between them, but after a while he knew that Archie and he were standing together in the embrasure of one of the windows, and that Archie was holding him by the arms and saying, in a voice of great contentment, 'Ever since I heard that you were coming I have been asking myself how in the name of fortune you contrived to get permission!'

'It was fortune herself contrived it,' answered his cousin, laughing a trifle unsteadily. ' 'Tis indeed a fairy story of luck; I will tell you of it presently. But first,' and he looked at him searchingly, 'are you well, Archie? They told me you were, but are you?'

'Ay, I am wonderfully well,' said the Doctor cheerfully; 'and more, I am happy, which you don't ask me. I have done my duty, as well as I can, to my Prince; I am to have my Jean's company for more than a week; none of the Privy Council nor any of the Government is a whit the wiser for aught I have told them. And for the resolution which God has given me to die without enlightening them – and, I hope, with becoming firmness – I thank Him every day upon my knees. You cannot think how well content I am, Ewen, now that there is no hope left to torment me.'

Ewen could not look at him then. Yet it was obviously true; one had only to hear the ring of quiet sincerity in Archibald Cameron's voice to know that this attitude was no pose. That was the wonder, almost the terror of it.

'But there is hope, there is hope!' said Ewen, more to himself than to Archie. 'Meanwhile, is there not anything you want?'

'Yes, one thing I do stand in need of, and have displayed a good deal of impatience, I fear, because it is denied me, and that is paper and pen. You have not such a thing as a bit of old pencil about you, 'ille?'

'I haven't a thing about me save my pocket-handkerchief,' answered Ewen regretfully. 'They took good care of that out-bye. And why have they denied you writing materials? Oh, if I had but known, I might have smuggled in the pencil I had when I came, and some paper, perhaps in my hat.'

'As to that, I must be patient,' said Archie with a little smile. 'And, indeed, I am no hand at composition; yet there are some matters that I desire to set down. Perhaps I'll contrive it still. Come, let me show you my other apartment, for I'd have you know that I am honoured with a suite of them, and the other is indeed the more comfortable for a sederunt, though I please myself with the glimpse of the river from this room. 'Tis low tide, I think.'

Ewen, following his gaze, saw without seeing the glitter of water, the tops of masts, a gay pennon or two and a gull balancing on the wind. Then Archie put his hand on his arm and drew him into a smaller room, not ill-furnished, looking in the opposite direction, and they sat down on the window-seat.

'Yes,' said the Doctor, 'I fare very differently here from poor Alexander. I have been thinking much of late of him and his sufferings – God rest him!'

It was long since Ewen had heard any reference to that third of the Lochiel brothers who, by turning Roman Catholic and Jesuit, had cut himself off from his family, but who had been the first to die for the White Rose, a martyr to the horrible conditions on board the ship which brought him as a prisoner to London. 'Yes,' went on Archie, 'this is a Paradise compared to the place where Alexander was confined.'

Indeed, looking through the window by which they sat, one saw that May can come even to a prison. The pear trees on the wall below, which General Rainsford's predecessor had planted not so many years before, had lost their fair blossom by now, but below them was a little border of wallflowers, and Tower Green, at a short distance, deserved its name. On the spot, too, where the child queen had laid down her paper diadem after her nine days' reign a little boy and girl were playing with a kitten.

'And your head, Ewen?' asked his cousin after a moment's silence. 'How long was it before you recovered from the effects of that blow? I was greatly afraid at the time that your skull was fractured.'

'It was you, then, who bound up my head? I thought it must have been. Oh, Archie, and by that the soldiers must have known for certain who you were! You should not have done it!'

'Tut – the redcoats knew that already! And I could not accomplish much in the way of surgery, my dear Ewen; I had not the necessaries. As you may guess, I have not had a patient since – you'll be my last. So take off that wig, in which you seem to me so unfamiliar, and let me see the spot where the musket-butt caught you.'

'There's naught to see, I am sure, and not much to feel,' said Ewen, complying. 'My head is uncommon hard, as I proved once before. I was laid by for some weeks, that was all,' he went on, as the cool, skilful fingers felt about among his close-cropped hair. 'Just when I naturally was a-fire to get to London after you. But now, when I am here, there seems nothing that one can do. And, Archie, 'tis I have brought you to this place!'

Doctor Cameron had ended his examination and now faced him with, 'My dear Ewen, I can, indeed, feel small trace of the blow. Yet it is clear that it must have severely shaken your wits, if you can utter such a piece of nonsense as that!'

' 'Tis no nonsense,' protested Ewen sadly. 'Was it not I who discovered that thrice-unlucky hut and persuaded you to go into it?'

'And I suppose it was you who surrounded the wood with soldiers from Inversnaid ... you might have brought them from somewhere nearer, for 'twas a most pestilent long tramp back there that night! Nay, you'll be telling me next that 'twas you sent the information to Edinburgh –'

'God! when I can find the man who did –' began Ewen, in a blaze at once.

'Ah, my dear Ewen,' said his kinsman soothingly, 'leave him alone! To find him will not undo his work, whoever he is, and I have wasted many hours over the problem and am none the wiser. I had better have spent the time thinking of my own shortcomings. "Fret not thyself at the ungodly" – 'tis sound advice, believe me. I can forgive him; he may have thought he was doing a service. It will cost me more of a struggle to forgive the man who slandered me over the Loch Arkaig gold ... but I think I shall succeed even in that before the seventh of June.'

'Who was that man?' demanded Ewen instantly, and all the more fiercely because he winced to hear that date on Archie's lips.

The Doctor shook his head with a smile. 'Is it like I should tell you when you ask in that manner? 'Tis a man whom you have never met, I think, so let it pass.'

'Is he known to me by name, however?'

'How can I tell,' replied Doctor Cameron shrewdly, 'unless I pronounce his name and see? But come, let's talk of other folk better worth attention; there are so many I should be glad to have tidings of. How is Mrs Alison, and the boys, especially my wee patient? And have you any news, since we parted, of your fellow-prisoner in Fort William?'

'Poor Hector's over here in London, and in great distress,' began Ewen without reflecting, 'for there's an ill rumour abroad, in Lille at least, accusing him –' And there he stopped, biting his lip. He ought not to have brought up that subject in Archie's hearing, blundering fool that he was!

'Accusing him of what, lad?'

So Ewen had to tell him. He hurried over the tale as much as he could, and, seeing how shocked and grieved Archie appeared, laid stress on the fact that, if ever Hector were really brought to book, he himself was in a position to disprove his connection with the capture of the Jacobite.

'But I would give much to know who set the story about,' he ended, 'for there are only two persons whom he told of the loss of that letter, myself and the man who helped him to return to his regiment in January, young Finlay MacPhair of Glenshian, and it is almost incredible that *he* should have spread such a report.'

But the end of that sentence left Ardroy's lips very slowly, in fact the last words were scarcely uttered at all. He was staring at his companion. Over Archie's face, at the mention of Finlay MacPhair, there had flitted something too indefinable to merit a name. But in another moment Ewen had reached out and caught him by the wrist.

'Archie, look at me – no, look at me!' For Doctor Cameron had turned his head away almost simultaneously and was now gazing out of the window, and asking whether Ewen had seen the two bairns out there playing with the little cat?

Ewen uttered an impatient sound and gripped the wrist harder. 'Deny it if you dare!' he said threateningly. 'I have named *your* slanderer too!'

'Dear lad –'

'Yes or no?' demanded Ewen, as he might have demanded it of his worst enemy.

The Doctor was plainly rather chagrined as he faced him. 'I am sorry that I have not better control of my features – Now, for God's sake, Ewen –' for Ardroy, releasing his wrist, had got to his feet. 'Ewen, I implore you not to take advantage of a secret which you have surprised out of me!'

But Ardroy was in one of his slow white rages. 'The man who was associated with you when you risked your life for that accursed money in '49 was viper enough to traduce you over it! It was he, then, who poisoned his cousin Lochdornie's mind against you! God's curse on him till the Judgement Day! And I warrant his dirty lie did not stop short with Lochdornie – did it now, Archie?'

Doctor Cameron, distressed, did not answer that. 'Oh, my dear Ewen, if I could persuade you to leave this question alone. What does it matter now?'

'Your good name matters to me as much as my own,' said Ewen, towering and relentless.

'But 'tis all past history now, Ewen, and the slander will die with my death ... Ewen, Ewen, promise me that you'll not go stirring up old scores with that young man! I cannot say I love him, but he is powerless to harm me any more now, and, as I say, I hope to forgive him without reservation. My dear lad, you will only cause me more distress than the lie itself, if I am to spend the short time which remains to me thinking of you quarrelling on my behalf with young Glenshian!'

Ewen had begun to stride up and down the little room, fighting with his resentment. 'Very good then,' he said after a moment, coming and sitting down again, 'I will not give you that distress; it is a promise. Moreover – perhaps this will reassure you a little,' he added with a wrathful snatch of a laugh, 'the man is not in London now, I believe.'

'Then let's cease to waste time over him,' said Doctor Cameron with evident relief. 'And you have not told me yet, as you promised, how you procured this order to see me.'

Trying to put away the thought of Glenshian, Ewen told him. 'Had I not good fortune – though indeed, at first, when I found myself in Stowe House, I thought it was the worst kind of ill-luck which had befallen me. The Earl and his son were both at the King's Bench that day, too, which prejudiced them, it is clear, in your favour. – By the way,' he added with some hesitation, 'was it a surprise to you that you had no trial?'

'No,' replied his cousin. 'I always suspected that the Government would make use of the old sentence of attainder if ever they caught me.'

'Yes, perhaps it was inevitable,' murmured Ewen, but he was thinking – though he did not mean to speak – of the unknown informer protected by the Government, whose identity, according to Jacobite belief, a trial would have revealed.

'Yes, I was not long before their lordships in the King's Bench,' went on Archie. 'The Privy Council examination at Whitehall a month before was a more lengthy affair, but, I fear, very unsatisfactory to those honourable gentlemen. My memory was grown so extraordinarily bad,' he added, with a twinkle in his eye.

'All the world knows that you told them nothing of the slightest importance,' said Ewen admiringly. 'Was that how you contrived to outwit them?'

'If you can call it outwitting. I think no man on earth could possibly have forgotten so many things as I made out to have done. And I admit that in the end their lordships lost patience with me, and told me squarely that, as I seemed resolved not to give any direct answers, which they assigned to a desire to screen others, they did not think it proper to ask me any further questions.' The remembrance seemed to entertain him. 'But before that came to pass my Lord Newcastle (saving his presence) had become like a very bubblyjock for fury and disappointment because he thought that I was about to tell them that I had met the Prince quite recently in Paris. (I had met him recently, but 'twas not in Paris.) They made great preparations for noting the date, and when I told them that it was in 1748 the Duke positively bawled at me that it was "the height of insolence, insolence not to be borne with", till I had hard work to keep my countenance. It is sad – and no doubt blameworthy – to rouse such emotions in the great!' And Archibald Cameron laughed a little laugh of genuine amusement.

'You know, Archie,' said Ewen earnestly, '– or more probably you do not know – that popular feeling is very strongly stirred about you, and that remonstrances are preparing on all sides. And when Mrs Cameron comes, if she has any intention of petitioning –'

'I expect she will desire to – poor Jean! Can I commend her to you a little, *'ille*?'

'You do not need to. I was about to ask you where she is likely to lodge? Near the Tower, no doubt?'

'I will tell her to leave her direction at the Tower gates, that you can learn it if necessary; and give me yours, that I may tell her of it. She may be lonely, poor soul; I doubt she will be allowed to stay here with me all day. And afterwards ...'

It was Ewen who looked out at Tower Green this time, but more fixedly than Archie had done. 'Afterwards,' he said in a moment, 'if there is to be no "afterwards" you mean, I will take Mrs Cameron –' He stopped, wrenched his fingers together for a second, and said with great difficulty, 'I cannot speak of that "afterwards", Archie – I don't know how you can ... Oh, if one could but push time back, and be again as we used to be eight years ago! The sunshine out there makes me think of that fine spring in Lochaber, before Lochiel and you had staked everything on the sword that was drawn in summer at Glenfinnan. But even Donald – even Alexander – did not pay as you are going to pay – though indeed there's hope still,' he added quickly.

Doctor Cameron laid his hand on his. 'But I am not unhappy, Eoghain,' he said gently. 'Eight years ago I had done nothing for my Prince. I do not know that I would change.'

Hector Grant was having his supper when Ewen walked in upon him that evening.

'At last,' said Ardroy, throwing his hat upon a chair. 'This is the second time that I have tried to find you today.'

'And I have been seeking you,' retorted Hector. 'Where were you?'

'I have been in the Tower,' answered Ewen, and went and stood with his back turned and an elbow on the mantelpiece, and for a while said no more. After a moment Hector rose and put a hand on his shoulder, also without a word.

'I see no hope of rescue, even by guile. I see no way in which any man's life can be given for his,' said Ewen after a long pause. 'Nothing but a reprieve can save him. But I do not think that he is hoping for one.'

'I am,' said the sanguine Hector, who had recovered from his emotion of the morning of the sentence. 'The Government must soon be aware how widespread is the feeling in favour of it.'

There was another silence.

'Go on with your supper,' said Ewen. 'I have a piece of news for you meanwhile. From something which I learnt from Archie I think it may well have been young Glenshian who put about that slander on you concerning his capture.'

Hector showed no disposition to continue his forsaken meal. '*Dieu du ciel*, what makes you think that?'

'Because he was the man who vilified Archie himself over the matter of the Loch Arkaig treasure – but I don't suppose you know of that dirty and cowardly action. Archie did not tell me that it was he; I surprised it out of him. Yet, by the same token, Finlay MacPhair is quite capable of having traduced you.'

Hector frowned. 'Yes; and now that I come to think of it, he repeated that story about Doctor Cameron to me last January.'

'To you!' exclaimed Ewen in amazement. 'Why have you never told me?'

'It has only once come into my mind since we have been in London, and then I thought it would needlessly distress you.'

'Archie has made me promise that I'll not make it an occasion of quarrel with Glenshian,' said Ewen, looking not at all like a man who had given so pacific an undertaking. 'Otherwise I would challenge him directly he returns to town, and make him withdraw his slander publicly.'

'But I have not promised to abstain from making *my* injury a cause of quarrel,' quoth Hector in tones of anticipation. 'When Mr MacPhair of Glenshian is returned, will you come with me, Ewen, and we will ask him a question or two?'

But Ewen, instead of replying, suddenly sat down at Hector's supper-table and covered his face with his hands.

Chapter 21

FINLAY MACPHAIR IS BOTH UNLUCKY
AND FORTUNATE

1

WHEREVER Ewen went during the next few days the hard case
of Doctor Cameron seemed to be the all-absorbing topic of
conversation, and that among persons of no Jacobite leanings at
all. Mrs Wilson, when she encountered her lodger, could talk of
nothing else, and reported the general feeling of her compeers
to be much roused. At the 'Half Moon', the public-house at the
corner of the street, she heard that quite violent speeches had
been made. Indeed, she herself all but wept when speaking of
the condemned man, with that strange inconsistency of people
easily moved to sympathy, who would nevertheless flock in
thousands to see an execution, and who doubtless would so
flock to Tyburn on the appointed day to see the carrying out of
the sentence against which they so loudly protested.

Had, therefore, a name been mentioned, it would probably
have been with tears of sensibility that Mrs Wilson conducted
to Ewen's little parlour, one day at the end of the week, a lady,
very quietly dressed, who said, on hearing that Mr Cameron
was out, that she would await his return. Mrs Wilson would
have liked to indulge in visions of some romance or intrigue,
but that the lady, who was somewhat heavily veiled, seemed
neither lovely nor very young. Ardroy, when he came in a
little later and was informed of her presence, was at no loss to
guess who it was, and when he entered his room and found her
sitting by the window with her cheek on her hand, he took up
the other listless hand and kissed it in silence.

The lady drew a long breath and clutched the strong, warm
fingers tightly; then she rose and threw back her veil. Under the
bonnet her face appeared, lacking the pretty colouring which
was its only real claim to beauty, but trying to smile – the brave

face of Jean Cameron, whom Ewen had known well in the past, surrounded by her brood, happy in the Highlands before the troubles, less happy, but always courageous, in poverty and exile after them.

'Oh, Ardroy ... !' She bit her lip to fight down emotion. 'Oh, Ardroy, I have just come from him. He ... he looks well, does he not?' And Ewen nodded. 'He says that he has not been so well for years. You know he suffered from ague all the winter, two years ago, but now ... And they seem so kind and well-disposed ... in that place.' She seemed to shrink from naming the Tower.

'Yes, he is in very good hands there,' answered Ewen; and felt a shock run through him at the other interpretation which might be wrested from his speech.

'And you think, do you not, that there is ...' But Mrs Cameron could not bring out the little word which meant so much, and she bit her lip again, and harder.

'I think that there is a great deal of hope, madam,' said Ewen gently, in his grave, soft voice. 'And now that you have come, there is even more than there was, for if you have any purpose of petitioning, all popular feeling will be with you.'

'Yes, I thought ... I have been drawing up an appeal ...' She sought in her reticule. 'Perhaps you would look at what I have roughly written – 'tis here at the end.' And into his hand she put a little paper-covered book. Opening it where it naturally opened, Ewen saw that it was a record of household accounts, and that on a page opposite the daily entries made at Lille, sometimes in English, sometimes in French, for 'bread', or 'coffee', *pain de sucre*, or 'stuffe for Margret's gowne', figured alien and tremendous terms, 'Majesty' and 'life' and 'pardon'.

'I thought that when I had made a fair copy I would present the petition to the Elector at Kensington Palace on Sunday.'

'Yes,' said Ewen. 'But you will need an escort. May I have the great honour?'

Mrs Cameron gave a little exclamation of pleasure, soon checked. 'Archie tells me that you have got into serious trouble with the Government on his account. You should not show yourself in so public a place, and with me.'

'No one would dream of looking for me at Kensington Palace. Moreover, I have someone to answer for me now,' said Ewen, smiling down at her. And he told her about Lord Stowe.

2

When, that afternoon, Ewen had taken Jean Cameron back to her lodging in Tower Street he went to the 'White Cock', where he had arranged to meet Hector Grant. But that young man was to be seen walking to and fro in the Strand itself, outside the passage, evidently waiting for him.

'Don't go in there, Ewen,' he said eagerly, 'till I have at least told you my news. Young Glenshian is back in town – if he ever left it!'

'Are you sure?'

'I have seen his gillie. I met him by chance about an hour ago. He said that his master had been ill, though I could not make out from him whether he had really been away from London or no. At any rate, the man, who recognized me, admitted that Glenshian was able to receive visitors. It seems that he is recovering from a fever of cold which settled upon his lungs. So now I can perhaps find out the part which Finlay MacPhair has played in this slander upon me, for I am no nearer the truth than when I arrived here. Will you come with me? I think you have a score to settle too.'

'I promised not to settle it,' answered Ardroy. 'And you, Hector, do not yet know that you have one.'

'Oh, I'll be prudent,' promised the young soldier. 'I will move cautiously in the matter, I assure you, for Fionnlagh Ruadh is not over peaceable himself. But I must at least put the question to him, and what time better than the present, if you are at liberty?'

Ewen said that he was, and would accompany him, though he was not himself anxious to meet Archie's traducer, since he might not have his way with him. But it seemed unwise to let Hector go alone, and his presence might conceivably keep the bit a shade tighter in that young gentleman's mouth.

At the house in Beaufort Buildings Hector was prepared to

find his way unannounced to the upper floor, but the woman this time said that she would take the two gentlemen up, since Mr MacPhair's servant was out, and she thought his master as well. Indeed, she seemed sure of the latter's absence, for she threw open the door with barely a knock, advanced into the room, and was consequently brought up short.

'I beg your pardon, sir,' she said in half-abashed tones. 'I quite thought you was out. Two gentlemen from Scotland to see you.'

And there was visible, in a room less disorderly than Hector remembered, Mr Finlay MacPhair sitting by a small fire fully dressed, with a large flowered shawl about his shoulders, and a book in his hand.

He turned his red head quickly. 'I thought I had given orders –' he began with a frown – and then seemed by an effort to accept the inevitable. 'Visitors from Scotland are always welcome,' said he, and rose, holding the shawl together. 'Why, 'tis rather a visitor from France! Is it not Mr Hector Grant?'

Hector bowed. 'And my brother-in-law, Mr Cameron of Ardroy. Ewen, let me present you to Mr MacPhair of Glenshian.'

'The gentleman, I think, who went to prison in order to shield Doctor Cameron last autumn?' said Glenshian, and held out his hand. 'I am honoured to make your acquaintance, sir – very greatly honoured. Be seated, if you please, gentlemen, and forgive my being happed up in this fashion. I am still somewhat of a sick man after a recent illness.'

Mr MacPhair was easy and fluent, and apparently more concerned with apologies for his shawl than observant, which was perhaps as well, for the man whose acquaintance he professed to be so proud to make was gazing at him in what would have been a disconcerting manner had young Glenshian been fully aware of it.

Hector took a chair and said that he was sorry to hear of Mr MacPhair's indisposition. Ewen also seated himself, more slowly, but he said nothing. The cloaked gentleman who had come so secretly out of Mr Pelham's house that May night was

605

here before him, and he was no Whig, but Finlay MacPhair, the son and heir of a great Chief whose clansmen had fought for the Cause. What had he been doing in Arlington Street?

'Yes,' said young Glenshian, going to a cupboard, 'I had the ill-luck to take a cold at the Carnival ball in Paris (for I was over there, on the King's affairs, in the spring) which ended in a *fluxion de poitrine*, and left me with somewhat of a cough and a general weakness. I doubt I shall not be my own man again for a while. – Now, gentlemen, before you tell me why I am thus honoured by your company, you'll pledge me, I hope, in this excellent Bordeaux – But where the devil has Seumas put the glasses?'

His guests, however, both refused the offer of the Bordeaux with so much decision and unanimity that Finlay, raising his eyebrows, left the cupboard and came and sat down.

'Not even to drink the King's health?' he observed. 'Well, gentlemen, if you will not drink, let us get to business – unless this is a mere visit of ceremony?'

'No, 'tis not a visit of ceremony, Mr MacPhair,' answered Ewen gravely. 'Mr Grant has a question to ask of you, which you will greatly oblige him by answering; and I, too, find that I have one which, by your leave, I should like to put when you have answered his.'

'This sounds, I declare, like an examination before the Privy Council,' remarked young Glenshian, his lip drawing up a little. 'Pray proceed then, sirs, each in your turn! You'll allow me, I hope, the liberty of not replying if I so wish?'

'Nay, Mr MacPhair, do not imagine that we come as in-quisitors,' said Hector with unwonted suavity. 'It will be of your courtesy only that you reply.'

'Ask, then!' said Finlay, fixing his piercing light eyes upon him.

Even Hector hesitated for a second, choosing his words. 'Mr MacPhair, while eternally grateful to you for your assistance in procuring my return to France last January –' He paused again, seeing in those eyes something akin to the sudden violent resentment with which their owner had at first greeted the sub-ject on that occasion, then went on: 'I should nevertheless be glad of your assurance that you did not, by pure inadvertence, let it be somewhat freely known that I had lost, along with my other papers in the Highlands, the compromising cipher letter of which I told you?'

There was no outburst from Glenshian, but all and more of his native arrogance in his reply. 'Certainly I did not,' he said contemptuously. 'Why should I speak of your private affairs, Mr Grant? They are nothing to me!'

Hector bit his lip. 'I thank you for the assurance, Mr Mac-Phair. Yet that letter was hardly a private affair, and ... the knowledge of the loss of it has undoubtedly gone about, and has much damaged my reputation, especially in my regiment.'

'Well, I am very sorry to hear that, Mr Grant,' responded his host, pulling the shawl about him and crossing his legs. 'But you must forgive me if I say that to lose a paper of that nature could hardly be expected to enhance it!'

At the half-amused, half-hortatory tone Ewen fully expected Hector to flare up. But that young man remained surprisingly controlled, and answered, though with rather pinched lips, 'Yet the strange thing is, that I told no one save Mr Cameron and yourself that I *had* lost it!'

Fionnlagh Ruadh turned his dangerous gaze on Mr Cameron. 'I suppose he has satisfied you that he is not the culprit?' he asked, again in that half-humorous tone. To this Hector vouchsafed no reply, and apparently Glenshian did not expect one, for he went on, 'But surely, Mr Grant, if a letter such as you told me of were sent, upon capture, to the English Government, as is natural, you could scarcely expect them to be so tender of your reputation as not to let it be known upon whom it was captured?'

'Ay, but was it sent to the Government?' demanded Hector.

Glenshian's haughty head went back. 'And pray how do you expect *me* to know that?'

Ewen leant forward. It *was* the same man; after this prolonged scrutiny he felt sure of it. 'That is indeed an idle question, Hector,' he observed. 'And Mr MacPhair has assured you that he had no hand in spreading the knowledge of your misfortune, which assurance no doubt you accept. I think the moment has come for me to ask my question, if he will be good enough to answer it.'

'I hope yours is less offensive than the last!' rapped out Glenshian.

'I am afraid it is not very pleasant,' admitted Ardroy, 'and I must crave your indulgence for putting it ... I should wish to learn how it is, Mr MacPhair, that you know Mr Pelham so well as to leave his house in Arlington Street between eleven and twelve at night?'

Oddly enough, it was Hector, not young Glenshian, who appeared the most affected by this shot. 'What!' he exclaimed, 'do you mean to say that Mr MacPhair was the man you saw that night?'

But Mr MacPhair himself was frowning at his questioner in an angry and puzzled astonishment which seemed genuine enough, 'Mr Pelham, sir?' he said sharply '– whom do you mean? You cannot, I imagine, refer to Mr Pelham the minister of state?'

'Yes,' said Ewen unperturbed, 'I do – Mr Henry Pelham, my Lord Newcastle's brother. And as you leave his house so late at night, I conclude that you must know him very well.'

Now young Glenshian pushed back his chair, his eyes glittering. 'You are crazy as well as infernally insulting, Mr Cameron of Ardroy! I do not know Mr Pelham even by sight.'

'Then why were you coming out of his house that night?' pursued Ardroy. 'You were speaking Erse to your servant, who was carrying a link. I happened to be passing, and by its light I saw enough of your face and hair to recognize you. Perhaps you had quite legitimate business with Mr Pelham, but it would be less disquieting if we knew what it was.'

The young Chief had jumped to his feet, the shawl sliding to the ground; his expression was sufficiently menacing. Hector, all attention, had sprung up too, and was now at Ewen's side.

'Do you imagine,' said Glenshian between his teeth, 'that we are in Lochaber, Mr Cameron, and that you can safely come the bully over me, the two of you? I thought the late Lochiel had tried to civilize his clan; it seems he had not much success!

I tell you that I do not know Mr Pelham, and have never been inside his house – and God damn you to hell,' he added in an access of fury, 'how dare you put such a question to me?'

'Because,' answered Ewen unmoved, 'I desire to find out who *was* the man that came out of Mr Pelham's house on the night of the fifteenth of May, a red-haired, Erse-speaking man as like you, Mr MacPhair, as one pea is like another.'

'I'd like to know,' broke in Finlay bitterly, 'why, if you see a red-headed Highlander coming out of an English minister's door, you must jump to the conclusion not only that he is a Jacobite playing fast and loose with his principles, but that it is the future chief of Glenshian, a man who has lain near two years in the Tower for Jacobitism? *Dhé*, if it were not so amazing in its impudence –'

'You mean that I am to consider myself mistaken?'

'I do indeed, Mr Cameron; and before you leave this room you'll apologize for your assumption in any words I choose to dictate! Faith, I am not sure that an apology, even the humblest, is adequate!'

And here – if the assumption in question were mistaken – Ewen agreed with him.

'I am quite ready to apologize, Mr MacPhair,' he said, 'if you'll prove to me that I was wrong. On my soul, I am only too anxious that you should. Or if you will convince me that your clandestine business with the Elector's chief minister was such as an honourable man of our party might fairly have.'

'And who made you a judge over me?' cried Finlay the Red, and his left hand went to his side, gripping at nothing, for he was not wearing his sword. Then he flung out the other in a fiery gesture. 'I'll have that apology, by Heaven! You'll be only too ready to offer it when you hear my secret!'

'If you tell me that your errand to Mr Pelham's house –' began Ewen.

'God's name!' broke out the angry MacPhair, 'am I to shout it at you that I never went there! *He* went, I don't doubt, and you saw him coming out. I suppose therefore that I should not have been so hot with you just now. You'll pardon me for that when you hear ... and perhaps you'll pardon me if I sit down again. I am still weakly.' Indeed he was palish, and there was moisture on his brow. 'Be seated again, gentlemen, and I will tell you both why Mr Cameron thought he saw me coming out of the minister's house one night – a night, too, when, if he had inquired, he would have found that I was not in London.'

The visitors somewhat doubtfully reseated themselves, Hector frowning tensely on their host, but content to leave the weight of the business for the moment on Ardroy's shoulders, where Mr MacPhair himself seemed to have put it.

'The explanation,' said Glenshian, coughing a little, and picking up his shawl, 'is – that I have, to my sorrow, a double.'

'A double!' exclaimed Ewen, raising his eyebrows. 'Do you mean a man who resembles you?'

'Ay, a man who so resembles me that even my close acquaintance have been deceived. He dogs my path, Mr Cameron, and I get the credit of his ill-deeds. He can even imitate my hand of write.'

'But who – who is he?'

Young Glenshian shrugged his shoulders. 'Some by-blow of my father's, I must believe. And that, no doubt (since I never heard of the Chief's recognizing him nor doing aught for him), has led him to take this method of revenge, by bringing discredit, when he can, upon my good name. 'Tis not, as you may guess, a pleasant secret for a man of honour to unveil, and I must be glad that I am dealing with gentlemen.'

'You hardly called us that a while ago,' retorted Ewen, knitting his brows. *Had* he been mistaken that night, in the quick, passing glare of the torch? If he had been, then he was wronging young Glenshian even more deeply than young Glenshian had wronged Archie.

Hector's voice, silent for some time, broke in. 'Is it not possible, Mr MacPhair,' it said, 'that this discreditable double of yours counts for something in *my* affair?'

'And how could that be?' asked Finlay with a shade of contempt. 'I hold no communication with him; he has not access to my papers.'

'Your *papers*!' said Hector like lightning. 'If he had had access – you mean that he might know something of my loss?

– By Heaven, Mr MacPhair, I believe you *have* communicated the circumstances of it to someone!'

For a second a very strange look had slid over Glenshian's features. He drew himself up under the shawl. 'Allow me to say, Mr Grant, that I am heartily tired of this inquisition about the damned letter over which you make such a pother. I wish I had never been so weak as to listen to your woeful tale. But I can hold my tongue with any man on earth, and my friends would tell you that I am incapable of setting about anything resembling a slander.'

Ewen could not let it pass. He had sworn not to make it a subject of quarrel, but he could not let it pass. 'If you search your memory, Mr MacPhair,' he said meaningly, 'I am afraid that you will find that is not true. I have it on the best authority that it was you who put about the slander concerning Doctor Cameron and the Loch Arkaig treasure.'

'Slander?' queried Finlay with an undisguised sneer. 'My dear Mr Cameron, the fact that the unfortunate gentleman is shortly to suffer for his loyalty, which we must all deplore, does not make my statement a slander! And, upon my soul, your presumption in coming here to take me to task, first for one supposed action, then for another, is ...' He seemed unable to find a word to satisfy him. 'But, by the God above us, if we were alone in the Highlands, or somewhere quiet ...' He did not finish, but gritted his teeth.

'I am not going to quarrel with you over it,' said Ewen very sternly, '– at least, not now. Perhaps some day we may argue as to the ethics of your conduct – in the Highlands or elsewhere. For the moment I'll say no more than that the action of traducing an innocent and scrupulously honourable man of your own party is worthy of this unnamed shadow of yours in whom you invite me to believe.'

'But surely, Ewen,' broke in Hector, suddenly pushing back his chair, 'you are not taken in by that cock-and-bull story of a double! Why, a child –' He stopped, and involuntarily glanced behind him, as a mild crash announced that his abrupt movement had overturned some small article of furniture, and, on seeing that this was a little table with some books upon it, he got up with a muttered apology to set it on its legs again, having no wish to give Mr MacPhair a chance to reflect upon his breeding. 'Such a tale might deceive a child,' he went on meanwhile, picking up the fallen books and some papers which had accompanied them to the floor, 'but not a grown –' He gave a great gasp, and was silent.

Ewen, whose attention had been withdrawn from Hector's little mishap to the remarkable agitation which it had caused in their host, looked round once more to see the reason for the sudden cessation of his brother-in-law's remarks. Hector was standing rigid, staring at a paper which he held, as if he could not believe his senses. And Glenshian, Glenshian the invalid, was flinging himself like a wild beast out of his chair. 'Give me that!' he shouted. 'My private papers ... how dare you –'

Ewen got quickly between them. 'What is it – what is it, Hector?'

Hector looked at him with a livid, dazed face. 'My stolen letter's *here*, in his own possession! ... it fell out from these books ... *he had it all the time!* Stand aside, Ewen, and let me get at him! No, he's not worth steel, I'll wring the treacherous neck of him!'

'Will you?' rang out Glenshian's voice, breathless yet mocking, behind Ardroy. 'You'll lose a little blood first, I fancy!' He had snatched up his sword from somewhere, got between the winged chair in which he had been sitting and the corner of the hearth, and was awaiting them, a flush on his pale face and his lips drawn back over his teeth – a real wolf at bay. 'I suppose you'll need to come on both at once to give each other courage!'

Ewen gripped at Hector's shoulder, but fury had lent that young man the agility of an eel. He slipped past Ardroy and his sword came out with a swish. 'Keep the door, you, lest we be interrupted!' he cried, pushed aside the chair, and next moment was thrusting frantically at the man backed against the wall.

Himself shocked and revolted, Ewen rushed to the door and locked it, but ran back at once crying, 'Hector, stop! this is madness!' To have Hector either wounded by or wounding young Glenshian here, in a brawl in a London house, would be disastrous; moreover, by the vigour of his assault, it looked as if more than wounding was in Mr Grant's mind, and that would be more disastrous still. Ardroy's protest went entirely disregarded; he might not have been there. Glaring at each other, the two combatants thrust and parried without pause, steel clicking upon steel with a celerity rarely heard in a school of arms. But Glenshian was already panting, and the sweat was running in little rivers down his face. '*Stop*, in God's name!' cried Ewen again; 'the man's ill, remember, Hector!'

For all response the young officer unexpectedly cut over his opponent's blade, and all but got him in the chest; and Ewen in despair tugged out his own sword with the intention of beating up both blades. But that was not easy to do without exposing one of the duellists to a thrust from the other; and if – another method – he seized Hector, the nearer, by the shoulder and dragged him away, Glenshian would almost certainly rush at his adversary and run him through during the operation. So Ewen dropped his own sword and snatched up the heavy shawl which had fallen from the convalescent's shoulders; then, waiting his opportunity, flung it unfolded over its owner's head, seized his brother-in-law by the collar and swung him away staggering, and rushing in, at no small risk to himself, upon the entangled young man against the wall, who, almost screaming with rage, was just freeing himself, he seized him round the body, pinning his arms to his sides so that his still-held sword was useless.

Behind him Hector, cursing *him* now, was evidently preparing to come on again, and Ewen was by no means sure that he might not find his excited point in his own back. But from Finlay MacPhair there was a most unlooked-for end of resistance. His objurgations ceased, his head fell back and his knees gave; the sword in his hand went clattering to the uncarpeted floor. He would have followed it had not Ewen held him up. Hector, breathing hard, came to a standstill.

'Where have you wounded him?' demanded Ewen.

'I haven't touched the filthy carrion,' answered Hector, inexpressibly sulky. 'You prevented me, curse you! Why the devil –'

'Then it is merely exhaustion,' said Ewen. 'Here, help me lift him to the bed, or that chair; he's swooning.'

'Shamming, more like,' said Hector disgustedly. 'Put him on the floor; I'd say throw him out of the window but that ... Oh, very well.'

He came to lend a hand, for big and powerful as Ewen was, the now completely unconscious Glenshian was neither small nor light. They carried him with little ceremony to the bed in the corner and dumped him on it. Ewen leant over him for a moment, shrugged his shoulders and left him there, merely observing, 'He said he had not recovered of his illness.'

'Luckily for him,' was Hector's comment.

The two stood looking at each other in the middle of the room.

'I cannot believe it!' said Hector, out of breath and still a trifle livid. 'But here's the letter.' He pulled it out of his pocket. 'I knew my own writing in an instant. But what would he want with it – and how did it get into his hands?'

'We do not know yet what he wanted with it,' answered Ewen gropingly. 'As to the way in which it came to his hands – he may have got it from Mr Pelham.'

'You don't believe that tale of a double, of course?'

'Not now.' Ewen put his hand over his eyes. 'Oh, Hector, as you say, 'tis incredible! It's like a dark, dark passage ... one cannot see where it leads. A MacPhair of Glenshian!'

'I am going to see if there are more papers of the sort,' said Hector, beginning to rummage feverishly among the books which he had tumbled to the floor. Ewen came to his assistance. But the little pile of volumes – most of them French, and indecent – had evidently not been used as a hiding-place, nor indeed would they have made a good one. A few bills had been pushed underneath or between them, and with the bills, by some extraordinary inadvertence, Hector's stolen letter.

'Look at your letter again,' suggested Ardroy, 'and see if it bears traces of what hands it has been in.'

Hector studied it anew. 'Yes, the names have been deciphered, sometimes with queries. And on the back, see, are some words in pencil. "You will please to return this when you have finished with it." But they are not signed.'

'The question is,' said Ewen reflectively, 'whether Mr Pelham handed over the letter to Glenshian, for whatever purpose, or whether Glenshian sent it to him in the first instance.'

'Yes, that is the question. And how, in the latter case, did it first come into Glenshian's hands?'

Dark and slippery paths indeed, such as Archie had hinted at last autumn! Ewen looked round the room. There was a writing-desk in one corner. Should they break it open? The key, no doubt, was on that limp, unstirring figure on the bed, but Ewen, at least, could not bring himself to search for it there. Hector was apparently less troubled with scruples or repugnance. He went and stooped over it, and came back not with the keys, but with a pocket-book, and pulled the contents out on to the table.

'More bills,' said he. 'A paper of accounts ... an assignation, or what looks like it ... a letter in cipher, addressed to Mr Alexander Jeanson (who is he? 'tis probably an alias) and – hallo, here's a letter from Lille!'

He caught it up, ran his eyes over it, uttered a sound as if he had been stabbed to the heart, and handed it to Ewen.

Ewen read: 'Lille, February 15th, 1753. I shall punctually attend to the recommendation which you sent me by the young gentleman from Troy, and should it come to pass that my namesake is taken, I'll contrive that the loss which that gentleman has sustained shall serve as a cloak to cover Pickle, to whom commend me. C.S.'

'I don't understand,' said Ewen, puzzled. 'Who signs "C.S." – is it a pretended letter from the Prince? Who is "Pickle", and who is "the young gentleman from Troy"?'

'Myself,' answered Hector in a suffocated voice. 'Is not my name a Trojan one? And "C.S." – I know his writing; he has but reversed his initials, and see the reference to "my namesake's" capture – is that fox Samuel Cameron, of my regiment, to whom, to oblige Glenshian there, I took a letter in January ... the very letter, probably, that told him of my loss, which Glenshian had just learnt from me! Was there ever such in-

615

famy – double infamy!' He glared at the bed. 'And he made me his catspaw – made me myself the instrument of what may yet be my ruin, I think I'll –'

But Ewen, as white as a sheet, was gripping his arms with vice-like strength.

'Hector, let's go, let's go! A terrible thought has just come to me, and if I stay I, too, shall be tempted to run my sword through him! God preserve us both from murdering a senseless man! Come, come quickly!'

'But what ails you – what is it, your thought?'

Ewen shuddered, and began to drag at him. 'Come!' He glanced at the bed in a kind of horror. 'I saw him move; he is coming to himself.'

He unlocked the door, still in the same nervous haste, and only just in time to avert suspicion, for steps were hurrying up the stair. A thin, pale young man, who seemed a servant, stopped at the top on seeing the two gentlemen in the doorway.

Hector kept his head. 'We were just about to seek assistance for your master, Seumas,' he said in Gaelic. 'He has had some kind of fainting fit, and we have laid him on his bed.'

The gillie uttered an inarticulate cry and rushed past them. Exclamations of grief and of endearment, in the same tongue, floated out through the open door.

'We need not stay to listen to that!' said Hector scornfully. 'And the dog will recover to do fresh mischief. But when he does –'

'I think he has done the worst he can ever do,' said Ewen almost inaudibly, as they went down the stairs, and he put a shaking hand to his head as though he had received a physical shock.

'That was his gillie,' whispered young Grant when they were outside. 'Did you recognize him as the man who held the torch that night?'

'Instantly,' answered Ardroy, who had a strange look, as of a man sleep-walking. 'But it needed not that. That was not the first time his master had come out of that door! ... Oh, Hector, Hector, now I know, I think, on whose account it was that Archie had no trial. For whether Finlay MacPhair himself, or the unknown man who sent the information to Edinburgh from Glenbuckie, be the "Pickle" whom Samuel Cameron – of Archie's own clan and regiment – has slandered you to shield, there's not a doubt that the centre of the black business is Finlay – a MacPhair and a Chief's son! God help us all! is there no faith or loyalty left ... save in the Tower?'

Chapter 22

'STONE-DEAD HATH NO FELLOW'

1

'AVELING,' said the Earl of Stowe with determination, one morning eight days later, 'I have decided to go about this matter today to one of the Secretaries of State, Jardyne for choice.'

'But, my lord,' protested his son in astonishment, 'you cannot – you are quite unfit to leave the house.'

For the enemy whose approach Lord Stowe had announced to Ewen Cameron a fortnight ago, if still kept more or less at bay, had not yet withdrawn from the assault; and his lordship was still confined to his bedroom, where he sat at this moment in a dressing-gown, one swathed foot supported on a rest.

'My dear child,' said Lord Stowe, 'consider the situation! Here we are at the second of June, and in five days, unless a miracle be performed for him, that unfortunate gentleman suffers at Tyburn. For all my promises to Mr Cameron, and for all the representations which I have made to those in authority, I have accomplished nothing on his kinsman's behalf. Nor can I see any sign of the petitions delivered to His Majesty and the two princesses at the beginning of this week having had any effect whatsoever. I must make yet another effort, for when a man's life is at stake, what is a gouty toe? Call Rogers, let him dress me, and I will be carried down to my coach, and go to see Mr Jardyne.'

Lord Aveling looked at his father with real admiration; and, indeed, who shall say that heroism is confined to the young and heroic? Then he rang the bell for Rogers, and to that horrified elderly valet Lord Stowe conveyed his self-sacrificing intention.

Meanwhile Aveling went to visit his mother, whom he found at her toilet-table, her woman in attendance.

'Your father is completely crazy,' she said, on hearing the news. 'I have no patience with such foolishness! Why should

618

he so put himself about for this Doctor Cameron, who is less than nothing to him? If the Government mean to hang and quarter him they will, and no amount of inflammation to my lord's toe will save him – Willis, give me the hare's foot and the last pot of rouge that I commanded, the new kind. I am a thought too pale today.'

'I do not think,' said her son, studying his mother's delicate profile as she leant forward to the mirror and put the last touches to her complexion – he was never admitted at any unbecoming stage of her toilet, and all fashionable people rouged as a matter of course – 'I do not think that the Earl is doing this entirely on Doctor Cameron's account. He considers, as you know, that he owes a heavy debt to Mr Ewen Cameron, and to use his influence on his kinsman's behalf is the manner in which he undertook to discharge it.'

Lady Stowe dabbed with the hare's foot a moment before saying anything, and when she spoke her tone was a curious one. 'I, too, made an offer to that young man – that I would tell him anything he wished to know about your poor brother, and that he should be admitted for that purpose at any hour when I was not receiving. I cannot learn that he has ever tried to avail himself of the opportunity.'

'No doubt he has been very much occupied,' suggested Lord Aveling. 'It was probably he who escorted Mrs Cameron when she went to deliver her petition to His Majesty last Sunday at Kensington, and fainted, poor lady, ere she could present it.'

The Countess laid down the hare's foot and surveyed the result. 'To be frank, I think that unfortunate woman must be making herself a great nuisance to the Royal Family. The King, the Princess Amelia, and the Princess Dowager of Wales all battered with petitions! I do not wonder that she has been shut up in the Tower with her husband, to prevent her from troubling any more people of position in that way.'

'Shut up in the Tower!' exclaimed Aveling. 'I had not heard that.'

'It may be only a rumour,' admitted his mother. 'If it be true, then perhaps we shall see Mr Cameron here again ... I wish you would tell me, Aveling, what you quarrelled about in

Scotland?' And she darted a sudden glance at him.

Francis Lord Aveling shook his head smiling. 'About nothing that you could possibly imagine! And we are excellent friends now.'

'For your half-brother's sake, I suppose,' observed Lady Stowe, taking up a gold pouncet box and sniffing the essence in it.

'I am not sure that that is the reason.'

'Well, whatever be the attraction, you can tell your new friend, when next you see him, that if he is tired of escorting females in distress about London, my invitation still remains open.' Lady Stowe rose, and sweeping away towards the long mirror at a little distance, examined the fall of her sacque. Then, a tiny spot of colour burning under the rouge, she said carelessly, 'Do bring him again, Francis! I vow his Highland strangeness diverts me.'

Only Mrs Willis, her woman, noticed that her ladyship's right hand was clenched hard round the pouncet box which she still held.

The heroic, no doubt, must pay for their admirable deeds; nevertheless, the consciousness of their heroism is probably sustaining during the latter process. Besides, this particular piece of heroism had not been in vain. When, about an hour and a half later, Lord Aveling heard the rumble of his father's returning coach, he hurried down to find the courageous noble-man being assisted from it, and hardly suppressing his cries of anguish.

'No, no – not like that! Jenkins, don't be so damned clumsy! Yes, that's better. My God, what an infernal invention is gout! Is that you, Aveling? I am going straight to bed; come and see me in a quarter of an hour.'

But when he entered the bedchamber Lord Aveling found his parent disposed in an easy chair as before.

'No, I was sure I could not endure the pressure of the bed-clothes. The foot is better thus. Oh – h – h, damn it, don't speak, there's a good fellow!'

The young man went and looked out of the window at the

swaying green in the square garden. More and more did he respect his progenitor. Yet it must be worse to hang ... and the rest ... in beautiful summer weather too.

' 'Tis easier now, for the moment,' said the sufferer's voice. 'Come and sit down by me, Francis – only, for God's sake, nowhere near my foot! At any rate, I have got something out of this inferno ... I only wonder that it never occurred to me before, when I might have spared myself these torments. Jardyne put the case in a nutshell. "Why", asked he, "do you come to me? Go to the Duke of Argyll. If he will but intercede for Doctor Cameron's life, he will not be refused. He is our first man in Scotland, and it is not our interest to deny him a favour when he thinks proper to ask for it!" So you see, Aveling, that if only the Duke can be got to make intercession for Doctor Cameron the thing is done! Now, why did no one ever think of applying to him before, for there is no doubt that Jardyne is right?'

And father and son looked at each other.

'It must be done at once,' said Lord Stowe. 'The Duke, I think, is in town.'

'But who is to do it?'

'Why, the person best qualified – the poor gentleman's wife.'

Aveling nodded. 'But what if it be true, as my mother seems to have heard, that Mrs Cameron has been shut up in the Tower with her husband? What then?'

'Shut up in the Tower!' exclaimed the Earl. 'Oh, surely not!' He turned his head. 'What is it, Rogers?'

'I understand, my lord, from the footman, that Mr Cameron is below, inquiring for my Lord Aveling.'

'Mr Cameron? I'll see him at once,' quoth Aveling, getting up. 'This is very opportune; I can tell him this hopeful news of yours, my lord.'

'Yes; and tell him to urge the poor lady to appeal to the Duke without wasting an hour ... don't for Heaven's sake come near this foot, boy! ... Tell him that I will give her an introduction to His Grace. Egad, I'll be writing now to the Duke to ask for an audience for her, while you interview Mr Cameron.'

621

'I'll tell him, too, sir, at what cost you gained this promising notion,' said the young man, smiling at his father as he left the bedchamber.

Downstairs, in the library which had witnessed their reconciliation, Ewen Cameron was standing, staring at the marble caryatides of the hearth so fixedly that he hardly seemed to hear the door open. Aveling went up to him and laid a hand on his shoulder.

'I have some hopeful news for you, my dear Mr Cameron.'

Ewen turned. Aveling thought him looking very pale and harassed. 'I have need of it, my lord.'

'In spite of his gout, my father has just been to see one of the Secretaries of State – no, no,' he added quickly, for such a light had dawned upon the Highlander's face that out of consideration he hastened to quench it – ' 'tis no *promise* of anything, but an excellent piece of advice. Mr Secretary Jardyne says that if his Grace of Argyll would intercede for Doctor Cameron's life the Government would undoubtedly grant his request. Neither my father nor I can imagine why we never thought of that course earlier.'

A strange hot wave of colour passed over Ardroy's face, leaving it more haggard looking than before.

'Then I suppose it must be done,' he said in a sombre voice. 'Do you know why I am here, Lord Aveling? – 'tis a sufficiently strange coincidence to be met with this recommendation. I came to ask what his lordship thought of the prospects of an application to the Duke of Argyll!'

'Why,' cried the younger man, 'this is indeed extraordinary, that you, also, should have thought of making application in that quarter!'

'Not I! I doubt if I should ever have thought of it,' responded Ewen, frowning. 'The notion is Mrs Cameron's.'

'Excellent!' cried Lord Aveling, 'because she is the one person to carry it out, as my father and I were just agreeing. If she will go, he will give her –'

'She cannot go,' broke in Ardroy. 'That is the difficulty. She is herself a prisoner in the Tower now, at her own request in order that she may be with her husband for ... for the few days that remain. The only way, it seems, in which this request could be complied with was to make her as close a prisoner as he is. It was done the night before last. This morning I received a distracted letter from her; evidently this thought of appealing to the Duke to use his influence had come to her there – too late for her to carry it out.' He paused; his hands clenched and unclenched themselves. 'So ... she has asked me to be her deputy.'

'Well, after all,' said Aveling reflectively, 'you are a near kinsman of her husband's, are you not, which would lend you quite sufficient standing. My father will give you an introduction to the Duke; indeed, I believe he is now writing to him on Mrs Cameron's behalf.'

'Yes, I suppose I must do it,' said Ewen between his teeth. He was gazing at an impassive caryatid again.

'You will not carry so much less weight than poor Mrs Cameron,' observed Aveling consolingly. 'Of course – to put it brutally – there is much appeal in a woman's tears, but on the other hand you will be able to plead more logically, more –'

'Plead!' exclaimed Ewen, facing round with flashing eyes. 'Ay, that's it, *plead* – beg mercy from a Campbell!'

Aveling stared at him, startled at his look and tone. 'What is the obstacle? Ah, I remember, your clans are not friendly. But if Doctor Cameron can countenance –'

'He knows nothing about it,' said Ewen sharply.

'And his wife, not being a Cameron born, does not understand your natural repugnance.'

'She does,' answered Ewen starkly, 'for she *is* a Cameron born. She knows what it means to me, but she implores me ... and could I, in any case, hold back if I thought there were the faintest chance of success? And now you tell me that one of the Secretaries of State actually counsels it. God pity me, that I must go through with it, then, and kneel to MacCailein Mor for Archibald Cameron's sake! I'd not do it for my own!'

The blank-eyed busts which topped the bookshelves in Lord Stowe's sleepy, decorous library must have listened in amazement to this unchaining of Highland clan feeling, a phenomenon quite new to them, for even Lord Aveling was taken aback by the bitter transformation it had worked in a man already wrought upon by grief and protracted anxiety.

'Let *me* go, then, Cameron!' he cried. 'God knows I am sorry enough for your cousin, and I have no objection to appealing to the Duke of Argyll. I would do my very utmost, I promise you ... Or, perhaps, you could find some other substitute?'

'You are goodness itself,' said Ewen in a softened tone. 'No, I am the man, since Jean Cameron cannot go. It may be,' he added in a rather strangled voice, 'that, just because I am a Cameron and an enemy, MacCailein Mor may be moved to do a magnanimous act ... O God, he *must* do it, for all other hopes are breaking ... and there is so little time left!'

2

It was with that despairing cry in his ears that Aveling had hastened upstairs to his father's room and held council with him. As a result of this conclave Lord Stowe wrote a fresh letter to the Duke of Argyll, saying that he was anxious to wait upon his Grace with a friend whom he was desirous of presenting to him (he did not mention the friend's name, lest by chance the audience should be refused), but that as he was himself confined to his room with gout he would send his son in his stead, if the Duke would allow. The same afternoon the Duke replied very civilly by messenger that he would receive Lord Aveling and his friend at eleven o'clock on Monday morning. The Sabbath, he explained, he kept strictly as a day set apart from all worldly matters.

So two days were lost; but, as Aveling assured that friend, the Duke's influence was so great that he could no doubt have Doctor Cameron reprieved on the very steps of the scaffold. And to those the Jacobite would not come till Thursday.

Nor did Ardroy have to go to the Duke of Argyll with his hat in his hand and a letter of recommendation, like a lackey seeking a place (as he had pictured himself) since he went under the auspices of the Earl of Stowe, and accompanied by that nobleman's heir.

'I shall present you,' said Aveling to him as they went, 'and then take my leave at the first opportunity. Is not that what you would prefer?'

'As you will,' replied Ewen; and then, forcing a smile, 'Yes, I believe I should prefer it. You are always consideration itself, my dear lord.'

That was almost all that passed between them till they came to Argyll House. And waiting in the portico, into which there drifted a faint perfume of late lilacs from the Duke's garden, Ewen thought, 'When next I stand here, the die will have been cast, one way or the other.' His heart began to beat violently, and when the door was flung open he was so pale that his companion looked at him with some uneasiness.

But as he stepped over MacCailein Mor's threshold Ardroy had gathered up his forces, and regained at least his outward composure. The two were ushered into a large and lofty room, sparsely but massively furnished, at the end of which hung a great blue velvet curtain suggesting another room beyond. Over the hearth voyaged the lymphad, the proud galley of Lorne, a sinister device to many a clan of the West. Ewen averted his eyes from it. How long, he wondered, would he on whose ancestral banners it had fluttered keep the suppliant waiting? ... but fortunately he neither knew as yet what name that suppliant bore, nor, indeed, that he came to sue.

But the Duke was punctual to the moment. A large clock by the wall with a heavy pendulum of gilt and crystal struck the hour, and the echo of its chimes had not died away before the velvet curtain parted in the middle, held back by an announcing lackey.

'His Grace the Duke of Argyll!'

And he who was sometimes called the King of Scotland came through – a man of seventy, upright, dignified, and rather cold, plainly but richly dressed, with a heavy full-bottomed wig framing a delicate-featured face of much intelligence – a man who had long wielded great authority, though he had only succeeded his brother the second Duke a decade ago. For more than forty years Archibald Campbell, once Lord Islay, had been the mainstay of the English Government in the North; and all this was written, without ostentation, in his air.

Lord Aveling, who had never seen the Duke at close quarters, was impressed, and wondered what the Highlander by his side was feeling, but abstained from looking at him.

'My Lord Aveling, I think?' said Argyll pleasantly, and the young man bowed. 'I am sorry to hear that the Earl of Stowe is indisposed; it gives me, however, the chance of making your acquaintance.'

He came forward with a little smile and held out his hand. 'Pray present me also to this gentleman, whose name I have not the honour of knowing.'

And all at once young Lord Aveling, used as he was to all the demands of society, knew nervousness – though not for himself. Something of it was apparent in his voice as he replied, 'This, your Grace, is Mr Ewen Cameron of Ardroy, a near kinsman of the gentleman now under sentence in the Tower.'

What age had left of the Duke's eyebrows lifted. A line appeared on either side of his mouth. 'And what does Mr Ewen Cameron' – there was the faintest stress on the patronymic – 'want of me?'

And his gaze, not hostile, not piercing, but unmistakably the gaze of command, rested on Aveling's tall companion.

'Your Grace,' began Ewen; but it seemed to him that his voice was frozen in his throat. It was not awe which enchained it, for he was not in the least overawed, but realization of this man's power for life or death, and of his personality. He was MacCailein Mor, the Chief of the hated, swarming and triumphant race of Campbell ... and he seemed to be feigning ignorance of why he, the Cameron, was there to wait upon him, so that he might have the reason, which he could well have guessed, put by the petitioner into words. The moment was as bitter as death to Ardroy, and he hoped that Lord Aveling *would* leave them alone together. But he finished his sentence.

'Your Grace, I am come on behalf of Mrs Cameron, and by her express desire, she now having made herself close prisoner with her husband, and being therefore unable to wait upon you herself.'

'You come as the emissary of a lady, sir?' inquired the Duke smoothly. 'Your errand must have my best attention then. But we stand all this while. Pray be seated, gentlemen. He waved them towards chairs.

'If your Grace will excuse me,' put in Lord Aveling, 'I will withdraw. I came but to present Mr Cameron in my father's stead.'

'Both of you deputies, in fact,' said Argyll, looking from one to the other, and again he smiled the little smile which did not reach his eyes. 'I am sorry to lose your company, my lord, but I know that you young men (if you'll forgive me for calling you one) have better things to occupy you than talking affairs with an old one. Mr Cameron and I will then bid you farewell, with regret. Commend me, if you please, to his lordship, and convey to him my condolences on his indisposition.' He shook hands again with every appearance of cordiality, a footman appeared, and Aveling was gone.

The Duke turned with equal courtesy to the visitor who remained.

'And now Mr Cameron – Cameron of Ardroy, is it not ... Ardroy near Loch Arkaig, if I am not mistaken? Pray be seated, and let me know in what I can serve you on Mrs Cameron's behalf? The chance to do so is not a pleasure of frequent occurrence where one of your name is concerned.'

'If your Grace will permit me, I had rather stand,' said Ewen somewhat hoarsely. 'I am come, as I am sure you can guess, as a suppliant.'

'Is that so?' remarked the Duke, looking long and steadily at him. His face betrayed nothing. 'You will forgive me, perhaps, if I myself sit, for I am old and weary.' And he seated himself slowly in a high-backed chair. 'You come, you say, as a suppliant, and I am to see in you the representative of Mrs Cameron?'

'If you please, my Lord Duke – of a woman who turns to you, in her mortal distress, as her last hope.'

'I think,' said the Duke of Argyll in a soft voice, 'that with a Highland gentleman such as yourself I prefer to be MacCailein Mor.'

Ewen swallowed hard. It had come to him that he could only get through his mission if he forgot that fact.

'Because for one thing,' went on Argyll, 'if you are a kinsman of Doctor Cameron's you are equally a kinsman of his brother, the late Lochiel, and of the boy who is Lochiel now.'

'Yes, I am a kinsman of all three,' said Ewen in a low voice. Archibald Campbell was trying, was he, to fancy that in some sort he had the Chief of the Clan Cameron before him, about to beg for mercy? 'A kinsman by marriage. And do not think, MacCailein Mor,' – he gave him the title since he wished it, and had every right to it – 'do not think that Doctor Cameron himself knows of his wife's appeal to you!'

'No? But let us be clear, Mr Cameron, on what score she ... you ... which am I to say? – is appealing to me. You have not yet informed me.'

Ewen's lip gave a little curl as he drew himself up. The Campbell knew perfectly well the nature of that appeal. He himself did not look much like a suppliant, as he stood there facing the Duke, nor did he feel like one, but he did his best to keep his tone that of a petitioner. 'Mrs Cameron desires to throw herself at your Grace's feet, as at those of the foremost man in Scotland, whose wish is paramount with the Government in all things Scottish, to beg, to implore you to use your great influence to have the sentence on her husband commuted.'

'Commuted,' said Argyll after a moment. 'Commuted to what?'

'To imprisonment, to transportation – to anything save an undeserved death.'

The Duke leant forward, his fine hands, half-hidden by their ruffles, grasping the lion-headed arms of his chair. 'Undeserved, do you say, Mr Cameron? A man comes from abroad, with every circumstance of secrecy, not once or twice only, but constantly, during a period of seven years, to work against the established government in the North, to foment disaffection by any means in his power, to promise foreign intervention in aid of it – all this in a country just settling down after a most dis-

astrous upheaval, in which he, too, bore a prominent part ...
and you call his death undeserved!'

'Having regard to Doctor Cameron's private character,' replied Ardroy firmly, 'I do. Your Grace must know – what on
all sides is acknowledged to be the case – how blameless a
reputation he bears and how humane, and how strenuously,
before the troubles, he upheld all Lochiel's efforts for the
betterment of the clan. It was largely due to him, too, that
Glasgow did not fare worse during the hostilities, and that
Kirkintilloch was spared, and Mr Campbell of Shawfield's
house and property protected. Doctor Cameron's is not the case
of an ordinary plotter, my lord.'

'In what manner can any plotter be extraordinary, Mr
Cameron, save perchance in the amount of harm he does?'
asked the Duke. 'In that certainly Doctor Cameron has been
singular. Since the year 1747 his comings and goings, or his
supposed comings and goings, have kept Lochaber and the
West in a continual ferment. In his private character he may be
all that you urge and more, yet he has proved the veritable
stormy petrel of the Highlands, and the sentence on him is so
well deserved that if I were to crawl on all fours to the English
Government they would not remit it.'

'You underrate your power, MacCailein Mor,' said Ewen in a
low voice. O God, did he mean that, or was he merely holding
out for more fervid, more grovelling entreaties? 'You underrate
your power,' he repeated. 'And you would show more than
your power, your ... generosity ... by intervening on behalf
of a man whose ancestors and your –'

'No doubt,' broke in Argyll before the sentence was completed. 'But that would be somewhat of a selfish luxury. I have
to consider my country, not my own reputation for magnanimity.'

Ewen seized upon this passionately. 'My lord, my lord, you
would be considering your country! The best interests of this
Government are surely not served by the carrying out of this
extraordinarily harsh sentence, which your Grace must be
aware is agitating all London! There is no doubt whatever –
and in your heart you must know it – that an act of mercy on

the part of the present dynasty would do far more towards establishing it in popular esteem than the depriving one Jacobite of life on a seven-year-old attainder could possibly do.'

'When I spoke of my country, Mr Cameron,' said the Duke with emphasis, 'I meant my native land, Scotland, whose welfare and good settlement I had at heart before you were born. Now you desire that I should induce the English Government to commute Doctor Cameron's sentence in order that he may have the opportunity of going back to injure her again.' And as Ewen tried to protest he went on more strongly: 'No, Mr Cameron, if I advise His Majesty's ministers to commute the sentence to one of perpetual imprisonment, that is only to make of Doctor Cameron a constant centre of intrigue and trouble, ending after some years in his escape, as George Kelly escaped in the end (for there are plenty of crypto-Jacobites in London who will conspire though they will not fight). If transportation is substituted for imprisonment, then he may escape and return to Scotland more easily still. No, I cannot now go back upon the work and convictions of a lifetime, and deliberately plant again in my country's breast the thorn which by good fortune has just been plucked from it.'

'You said a while ago,' murmured Ewen with stiff, cold lips, the great room grown a little misty and unreal about him, 'you said that the Government would not grant you this boon though you crawled to them – and yet one of its first officials has stated that such a request would not be denied for a moment if you made it. Now you say that it goes against your conscience to make it. Which is it, my Lord Duke?'

Argyll got up from his chair.

'You are a very bold young man, Mr Cameron of Ardroy! Are you trying to bring me to book?' The look which flickered over his pale, dignified features was nearer amusement than irritation. 'I do not think that Mrs Cameron would have taken that line. Believe me, it is not a wise one!'

'I will take any line that ... that pleases your Grace!' declared Ewen, desperate. Was *he* throwing away what Jean Cameron might have won? 'Do you wish me, who, though I am not of Lochiel, have a strain of the blood and am a cadet of the clan, do you wish me to kneel to you? I will, here and now, if you will ask for Archibald Cameron's life!'

'There is no need for you to assume that uncomfortable position, Mr Cameron,' replied the Duke drily. 'Spiritually you are already upon your knees. And I am sorry if the floor is hard ... since I cannot for a moment entertain your request ... It is a harsh saying, no doubt, but a very true one, when matters of this kind are in question (and it was an Englishman who uttered it) – "Stone-dead hath no fellow". I am grieved that I must endorse it in the case of Doctor Cameron, for I consider that the Government is more than justified in carrying out this long overdue sentence – a sentence better merited, indeed, today than it was even at the time of its infliction – and for the sake of Scotland's welfare I cannot advise them to do otherwise.'

Ewen put his hand up to his throat. Otherwise he did not move. Those were the accents of finality; to entreat further was only to batter oneself against a rock, to lower Archie himself in the eyes of the Campbell. Would Jean Cameron now have wept, implored, clung round the knees of MacCailein Mor? Surely not.

'It is not,' went on Argyll, walking slowly to and fro with his hands behind his back, 'it is not as though Doctor Cameron had shown the slightest sign of real repentance for his ill-doings, the slightest intention of future amendment. His answers before the Privy Council in April were inspired by the most obstinate intention of concealing every fact he knew under cover of having "forgotten" it, and when last month, immediately after sentence had been passed upon him, he, in a conversation with Mr Sharpe, the Solicitor to the Treasury, seemed to lament his unhappy position, and to say that if His Majesty extended his clemency to him he would strive to lead his fellow-clansmen into less treasonable paths, there was not one word of the only course which could conceivably merit such clemency – the making of disclosures.'

Through the silence the slow swing of the pendulum of the great gilt clock behind Ewen seemed to emphasize how fast the sands were slipping in the glass of Archibald Cameron's life. Ardroy clenched one hand round the wrist of the other; his eyes were fixed, not on the Duke, who had come to a standstill, but on the shaft of yellowish light which penetrated the aperture between the curtains. So *that* was the one chance, a mocking rift of hope like that blade of thin sunlight, a spar in the tumbling sea which one must let drive by, and drown without clutching ...

' "Disclosures",' he said at last; and there was nothing in his voice to show what he thought of the word or the thing. 'You mean, my lord Duke, that if Doctor Cameron were to become a second Murray of Broughton, that if he would tell all he knows –'

The Duke held up his hand quickly. 'Pray, Mr Cameron, do not associate *me* with any suggestion so affronting to a High-lander! I merely mention that Mr Sharpe, as I remember, seemed much disappointed – for the Government are well aware that there is some new scheme afoot. You must draw what conclusion you can from that. For myself, I think the bargain would scarce be worth the Government's while ... Yet, out of a perhaps misplaced humanity, I will go so far as to point out that that door, which was once open, may, for aught I know, be open still.'

Open still – open still; the crystal pendulum swung on – but that was not what it was saying.

'Your Grace is very good ...' Ewen heard his own voice, and wondered at its cold steadiness, since his heart felt neither cold nor steady. 'But that is not a door at which a Cameron of Lochiel could ever knock. I will detain you no longer, Mac-Cailein Mor.'

He supposed that Argyll must have summoned a footman, for soon after that he passed once more through the pillars of the portico. And once outside, in the brief summer shower, laden with the scent of lilacs, which was now making sweet the June dust, all the leaping flame of repressed feeling sank to extinction, and in its place there was nothing but ice about his heart. He had failed; the last hope of all was gone. On Thurs-day –

And now he must write to Jean Cameron and tell her.

Chapter 23

CONSTANT AS STEEL

AND after that came the death in life of those intervening two days, which seemed a whole lifetime on the rack, and yet a river hurrying with implacable haste to the sea.

There was no hope for Archibald Cameron now, except the faint possibility of that eleventh hour reprieve to which a few still pinned their faith. At one moment Ewen would feel that the intensity of his desire alone must call this into being; the next, that he had always known the sentence would take its course. Lord Stowe, grave and disappointed, advised him not to trust to a miracle. It was remarkable that Aveling, young and generous-hearted though he was, gave the same advice, and would not take the easier path of trying to buoy up his friend's spirits with an anticipation which he did not share. But Lady Stowe, with whom Ewen had an interview, not of his seeking, on the Tuesday, proclaimed her conviction that the execution would not take place, and hinted at the influence which she herself had brought to bear on certain members of the Government. Hector Grant was in a frenzy, dashing hither and thither, sure that something could still be done, and talking wildly of a rescue at Tyburn itself, of kidnapping Lord Newcastle or Henry Pelham and holding them to ransom, and other schemes equally impossible.

But by noon on Wednesday Ewen had abandoned all dreams, sober and extravagant alike. His faint hope of seeing Archie once more was dead too; even the Earl of Stowe's influence could not procure him another interview. And in the afternoon he shut himself up in his lodging, and would see no one, not even Hector. He could talk about tomorrow's tragedy no longer, and, like a wounded animal which seeks solitude, only asked to be left alone. How desperately hard it was to meet a friend's fate with composure and resignation – how much less hard to face one's own! He knew, for he himself had once been

633

almost as near the scaffold as Archibald Cameron was now.

He had sat for he knew not how long that afternoon immured in the close little parlour, with the window fast shut since the moment when he had overheard two men in the street below arranging to go to Tyburn on the morrow, and one of them, who was a trifle drunk, offering the other some only too vivid reminiscences of the execution of the Scottish Jacobites in 1746. Ewen had sprung up, and, calling upon his Maker, had slammed down the window with such violence that he had nearly shattered it. Then, after walking to and fro for a while like a man demented, he had flung himself down on the settle, and was still sitting there, his head in his hands, when a timid tap at the door announced Mrs Wilson.

'I'd not disturb you, sir,' she whispered sympathetically, 'but that there's a messenger below from the Tower in a hackney coach, and he brings this.' She held out a letter.

Ewen lifted his head from his hands.

'From the Tower?' he repeated, looking at her stupidly. Surely she did not mean that?

But, opening the letter, he saw the heading; saw, too, that it came from the Deputy-Lieutenant.

'Dear Sir,' it ran –

'Doctor Cameron having very earnestly desired to see you once more, and I myself having come to the conclusion that it were better Mrs Cameron did not pass the night here, but left before the gates were shut, and that some friend should be present to take her away, I have obtained leave from the Constable for you to visit the prisoner and also to perform this office; and have therefore sent the bearer in a hackney-coach to bring you back with all speed, as the gates must infallibly be closed at six o'clock this evening.

'Your obedient humble servant,
'CHARLES RAINSFORD.'

Ewen drew a long breath. 'I will come at once,' he said.

Nearly all the way, jolting in the coach with the warder, or whatever he was, Ardroy was turning over and over a once entertained but long abandoned idea of changing clothes with Archie. The same obstacle brought him up again – his own unusual stature, though Archie was of a good height himself. Yet this unexpected summons did so clearly seem as though Fate were holding out a last opportunity of rescue – but what opportunity? Ewen's former visit had shown him how impregnable were the Tower walls, how closely guarded the gates. Tonight every soul there would be doubly alert. And if Archie were by now in irons there was no hope of any kind ... there was little enough in any case.

To his surprise, when he came to the Byward Tower, they did not offer to search him, and he was told, also, that Doctor Cameron had been moved from the Lieutenant's house and was there, in the Byward Tower itself. Ewen asked the reason.

'It was thought safer, sir. My Lords Kilmarnock and Balmerino were lodged here in '46, though my Lord Kilmarnock, too, was at first in the Lieutenant's house.'

'And Mrs Cameron, is she in this tower with her husband?'

'No, sir; she remains in the Lieutenant's house until she leaves, before the gates are shut.'

He could see Archie alone, then, and he could not but be glad of that.

It had indeed a very different setting, this last meeting, and one which better fitted the circumstances than the former. Unlike the pleasant apartments with their glimpses of the outer world, this place was heavily charged with an atmosphere of finality, for the roof curved cage-like above the large, circular stone-vaulted room with its narrow windows. In the middle was a table with a couple of chairs; and at this table Archie was sitting with a book open before him; but his eyes were on the door. He was not in irons.

They clasped hands in silence as the door swung to and clashed home. Only then did Ewen see that they were not alone, for some distance away a wooden-faced warder sat stiffly on a chair against the wall.

'Cannot that man leave us for a little?' murmured Ewen.

'No,' said his cousin. 'I must have a shadow now until – until there's no more need of watching me. This good fellow must even sleep here tonight. But we can speak French or Erse; he'll not understand either.'

Ewen was bitterly disappointed. If there were a witness present they had not the faintest chance of changing clothes. He said as much in his native tongue.

'My dear Ewen,' replied Archibald Cameron smiling, 'Nature, when she gave you that frame, never intended you for such a role – and in any case it is quite impracticable. Come, sit down and let us talk. You see there is another chair.'

It seemed of a tragic incongruity to sit quietly talking at a table, but Ewen obeyed. Talk he could not, at first. But Archie began to speak with perfect calm of his last arrangements, such as they were; he had given his wife, he said, what he had been able to set down from time to time of his wishes and sentiments, by means of a bit of blunt pencil which he had contrived to get hold of after all.

'Four or five scraps of paper they are,' he concluded. 'I could not come by more, but I have signed my name to every one of them, that they may be known for authentic.'

Only once did he betray emotion; it was in speaking of his young children in exile, and their future, so desperately uncertain when he was gone.

'I have no money to leave them,' he said sadly. 'Had that gold from Loch Arkaig really stayed in my hands they would not be penniless now, poor bairns! But I have been very much pleased,' he went on, 'with a letter which my wife showed me from my eldest boy – you remember John, Ewen; he always had a great admiration for you. I have for some time observed in him a sense of loyalty and honour much beyond what might have been expected from a boy of his years, and in this letter of which I speak he expresses not only his conviction of my inviolable fidelity to the Cause, but a desire that I should rather sacrifice my life than save it upon dishonourable terms. I have great hopes of his future, even though the principles of uprightness and loyalty be not over-popular nowadays.'

Ewen saw that great velvet curtain in the Duke of Argyll's house, with the shaft of light slipping through ... Did Archie know of that appeal? He certainly did not know of the chance of life which Ewen himself had rejected on his behalf, for that Ewen had not communicated to Mrs Cameron when he wrote.

'Did the Privy Council,' he asked somewhat hesitatingly, 'ever hold out a promise of mercy if you would make disclosures?'

Archie nodded. 'Yes. And I believe that hopes of my doing so must have been cherished for some time after my examination, since Mr Sharpe, the Solicitor to the Treasury, certainly had them as late as the seventeenth of May, when I was sentenced. Tell me, Ewen,' he added, looking at him hard, '– for Jean has confessed to me the step which she worked upon you to take – had his Grace of Argyll the same hopes?'

'You know of that?' exclaimed Ewen, half-apprehensive, half-relieved. 'You know – and you forgive me for going to him?'

'My dear lad, there's no question of forgiveness. I ought to thank you from the bottom of my heart for undertaking what I know must have been a very repugnant task. Moreover, as I am neither a saint nor a hermit, but an ordinary man like the next, I'll not deny that a span of forty-six years sometimes seems a little short to me. If MacCailein Mor could by honourable means have prolonged it, I should not have relished accepting the boon from his hands, but I should not have refused it.'

Ewen turned very pale. 'Archie ... you make me feel like your executioner! You might have had your life, perhaps – but I – in effect I refused it for you! I ... But it's not too late.' He half-rose from his chair.

Archie caught at his arm. 'Ah, *loachain*, I guess why you refused it for me. Should I think that you know me less well than my poor John? I'd have liked to have had the refusing of it to MacCailein Mor myself, on the terms which I can divine that he offered.'

'To do him justice, he offered nothing. At the end indeed he spoke of ... of a possible door. You can guess what it was. He would have naught to do with it himself. Yet –' Ewen turned his head away. What an inhuman, sterile deity seemed, after all, that abstraction called honour! 'Oh, Archie, if it were possible to accept! ... It was not so hard then to turn one's back on the chance; I did it without weighing the matter. I knew you would not consent. But it is much harder now.' And at last he looked at his cousin, with eyes which, half-ashamedly, implored, as if somehow, somehow ...

Archibald Cameron smiled and gave his head a little shake. 'You will be glad by this time tomorrow. What welcome do you think Murray of Broughton's former friends give him nowadays? And would you set the door of Ardroy wide for me, Ewen, were I to save my skin as he did? You know you would not! – But enough of this talk. There has been no choice in the matter. I *could* not bring myself to betray either my companions or my Prince's plans.'

'Yet you yourself have been betrayed!' came instinctively to Ewen's lips.

Archie's face clouded a little. 'I am glad to think that I do not know the informer, whether the thing was done of his own free-will or at another's instigation. It is easier to forgive, thus.'

This time it was Ewen who was determined that Archie should read nothing upon his face, and he set it immovably. Of what use to burden his spirit, so soon to be gone, with the hatred and suspicion which lay so heavy on his own since the encounter with young Glenshian?

Moreover – luckily perhaps – Archie here pulled out his watch. 'Good Mr Falconar, the Scots nonjuring clergyman who has been visiting me, and will attend me to Tyburn tomorrow, is to bring me the Sacrament at five o'clock. I would have wished to take it tomorrow morning before I set out, but then Jean could not have received it with me, nor you, if you wish to do so?'

'Will it be here?'

'Yes.' The Doctor pointed to where a little table, covered with a white cloth, stood against the wall, with two or three footstools ranged before it. 'And Jean herself will be brought hither. But I have said farewell to her already ... Ewen, be patient with her – though, indeed, she has the bravest heart of any woman living.'

'You do not need to urge that,' said Ardroy.

'I know that I do not. It is you who are to take her away from the Tower, too, God bless you!'

'Shall I ... take her back to Lille?'

'It is not necessary; that is arranged for.' Archie got up suddenly; Ewen had a glimpse of his face, and knew that he was thinking of the fatherless children to whom she would return.

He sat there, rapidly and quite unconsciously fluttering over the leaves of the book lying on the table, and then said in a voice which he could scarcely command, 'Archie, is there nothing else that I can do for you?'

Doctor Cameron came and sat down again. 'There is something. But perhaps it is too hard to ask.'

'If it be anything which concerns me alone it is not too hard.'

'Then ... I would ask you to be there tomorrow.'

Ewen recoiled. 'I ... I did not dream that you would ask *that*!'

'You would rather stay away?'

'*Archie* – what do you think I am made of?'

Archibald Cameron looked at him rather wistfully. 'I thought – but it was, I see, a selfish thought – that I should like to see one face of a friend there, at the last. I have heard that a Tyburn crowd, accustomed to thieves and murderers, is ... not a pleasant one; and I have been warned that there will be very many people there.'

'They will not be hostile, Archie; that I can stake my soul on. You do not know the sympathetic and indignant feeling there is abroad. But, if you wish it, I will be there; nay, if it is your wish, I will make it mine too ... Yet even you will not ask me to remain until the end of all?' he added imploringly.

'No,' said his cousin gravely but serenely, 'not until that. Yet I think the end, thank God, will matter very little to me. In spite of the terms of the sentence and of Lord Chief Justice Lee, I have a good hope that I will not be cut down until I am quite dead ... Ewen, Ewen, think it's yourself that's going to the gallows (as you nearly did once) and not I! You would not play the child over your own fate, I know that well!' For Ewen had his head on his arms, and his nails were digging into the table. He did not answer.

'I could wish it were not Tyburn,' Archibald Cameron went on, as if to himself. 'My lords Kilmarnock and Balmerino were luckier to suffer on Tower Hill, and by the axe. Yet I must not complain, being but a commoner; indeed, I should think of the great Marquis of Montrose, who was hanged likewise – and from a very lofty ladder too. And I thank my God I was always easier ashamed than frightened ... Ewen, Mr Falconar will be here in a few minutes. Do you wish to make some preparation before you take communion with me?'

Ewen roused himself, and mechanically knelt down by the table where he had been sitting, put his hands before his face and tried to say a prayer. But it was impossible. His whole soul was too pulsing with revolt to bow itself before that mystery of divine self-humiliation and pain and joy; he could not even say 'Lord, I am not worthy'; his heart was nothing but a burning stone.

Nevertheless he still knelt there, rising only when he heard the bolts withdrawn, and there came in, first a very tall, thin man in lay dress, who walked with a limp, and then, on the arm of Rainsford himself, Mrs Cameron. The Deputy-Lieutenant considerately dismissed the warder and himself took the man's place, and, almost before Ewen, dazed with pain, had realized it, the service was beginning. Archibald Cameron, his hand in his wife's, knelt at some distance from the improvised altar; Ewen a little way behind them. And, save that it was not dark, but a June evening, the bare masonry of the place might almost have suggested an Eucharist in the catacombs; but Ewen did not think of that. He seemed to be able to think of nothing, though he did perceive that Mr Falconar, who appeared to be greatly moved was using, not the English Communion Office, but the proscribed Scottish Liturgy of 1637.

When the moment of communion approached, the two in front of him rose, and Archie glanced round at him, but Ewen shook his head, and so Doctor Cameron led his wife to one of the footstools and knelt beside her. But when Ewen saw them kneeling there without him, the ties of human affection drew

him more strongly than his nonjuring training, with its strict
doctrine of the Eucharist and his own fear of unworthy reception, held him back. So he got up after all, and knelt humbly
on the floor by Archie's side; and drinking of the cup after him
whose viaticum it truly was, felt for the moment wonderfully
comforted, and that the Giver of that feast, first instituted as
it was in circumstances of betrayal and imminent death, had
pardoned the hard and rebellious heart in him. And he remembered, too, that peaceful Eucharist by the winter sea in Kilmory
of Ardnamurchan, and wished that Mr Oliphant were here.
Then he went back to the table where he had sat with Archie,
and knelt down again there with his head against the edge, for
a long time.

At last he looked up. The service was over; Mr Falconar was
gone. Archie, with his back to him, had his wife in his arms.
Ewen thought that if he also went, the two might have a
moment or two together – save for the presence of the Deputy-
Lieutenant, who, considerate as ever, was looking out of one
of the little windows. But he could not go without a last word.
He got to his feet, approached a little way, and said his cousin's
name.

Doctor Cameron put his wife into a chair and turned; and
Ewen held out his hand.

'I shall not see you again to have speech with,' he said in
Gaelic. His very hands felt numb in Archie's clasp. 'I wish I
could die with you,' he whispered passionately.

Archie held his hands tightly. 'Dear lad, what then would
Alison do, wanting you, and your boys, and your tenants? You
have work here; mine is over.'

'Gentlemen,' came Rainsford's voice from behind, 'there remains but eleven minutes ere the gates are closed.'

Time, the inexorable, had dwindled to this! Ewen caught his
breath. 'Good-bye,' he said after a second struggle. 'Good-bye,
faithful and true! Greet Lochiel for me. I will keep the promise
I have made you. Look for me there – give me a sign.' He
embraced Archie and went out quickly, for the door was ajar,
with the armed sentries close outside. Only Mrs Cameron and
General Rainsford remained behind.

But outside, beyond the sentries, was still Mr Falconar, with his handkerchief to his eyes. As for Ewen, he leant against the wall to wait for Mrs Cameron and folded his arms tightly across his breast, as if by that constraint he could bridle a heart which felt as though it were breaking. Perhaps he shut his eyes; at any rate, he was roused by a touch on his arm. It was Mr Falconar, still painfully agitated.

'Sir, I shall spend this night praying less, I think, for *him* than for strength to carry me through this terrible business tomorrow without faltering.'

'You mean the attending Doctor Cameron to the scaffold,' asked Ewen in a voice which sounded completely indifferent.

'Yes,' said the clergyman. 'I declare to you, sir, that I do not know how I am to come through it. Doctor Cameron's composure shames me, who am supposed to uphold it. My great fear is lest any unworthy weakness of mine should shake his calm in his last moments – though that hardly seems possible.'

Ewen was sorry for him. 'You cannot withdraw now, I suppose, for he must have a minister with him.'

'It is usual, I understand; but *he* does not need one, sir. He has not left it until the eleventh hour, like some, to make his peace with God. I must carry out as much of my office as he requires, but he does not need me to pray for him on the scaffold, priest though I be. I shall ask his prayers. I would ask yours, too, sir, that I do not by any weakness add to his burden tomorrow.'

Ewen looked at him with a compassion which was shot through by a strange spasm of envy. This man, who dreaded it so, would see Archie once more at close quarters, be able to address him, hear his voice, go with him to the very brink ...

Then through the half-open door came the Deputy-Lieutenant with Mrs Cameron again on his arm. She looked half-fainting, yet she walked quite steadily. Mr Falconar being now nearest the door, General Rainsford put her into his charge, and called hastily for the warder to take up his post again within. In a kind of dream Ewen watched the clergyman and the all but widow go down the stairs. His heart ached for her, little and brave and forlorn, her dress slipping slowly from one worn stone step to the next.

He had started to follow her, and had descended a step or two, when he was aware of a voice calling hurriedly but softly to him from above. He went back again, wondering.

It was the Deputy-Lieutenant who had called after him, and now met him at the top of the stairway. 'Doctor Cameron has remembered something which he had intended to give his wife; but it was you whom he wished called back, if possible.' He pulled out his watch. 'Four minutes, no longer, Mr Cameron!'

So he *was* to have speech with Archie once more. And, the warder being still outside, and the Deputy-Lieutenant not seeming to purpose coming in again, for that brief fraction of time they would be alone. Had Archie made a pretext to that end?

He was standing in the middle of the room with something in his hand. 'I forgot to give these to Jean, as I intended, for my eldest son.' And he held out to Ewen two shabby shoe-buckles of steel. 'Bid Jean tell him from me,' he said earnestly, 'that I send him these, and not my silver ones; and that if I had gold ones I would not send him the gold, but these, which I wore when skulking. For steel being hard and of small value is an emblem of constancy and disinterestedness; and so I would have him always to be constant and disinterested in the service of his King and country, and never to be either bribed or frightened from his duty. – Will you tell her that, Ewen?'

No, he had not been sent for under a pretext. Ewen took the buckles. 'She shall have them; and I will faithfully repeat your message.' Then he was mute; it seemed as if Archie were gone already, as if the immeasurable gulf already severed them. Archibald Cameron saw the dumb misery on his face and put his hand on his arm.

'Don't look like that, my dearest Ewen! I thank God I am ready to be offered, and you need have no apprehension for me tomorrow. It is poor Falconar I shall be sorry for.'

'Indeed,' said Ewen, finding his voice again, 'he seems most painfully apprehensive; he was speaking to me just now. I fear, as he does, that his presence will be no support to you. I was about to ask him whether he could not procure another clergyman to take his place, but so few in London are nonjurors, and I suppose you would –'

He never finished. The colour came surging over his drawn face, as a wild arrow of an idea sped winging into his brain. 'Archie,' he said breathlessly in Gaelic, 'if a layman might ... if it could be contrived ... could not ... could not *I* take his place tomorrow?'

In the Doctor's face also the colour came and went for a moment. 'My dear Ewen ... if it is like to prove a trial to Falconar, how would you –'

'I'd rather stand with you in the cart than see you stand there from a distance, and be unable to get at you,' said Ewen with great earnestness. 'I should be near you – I could speak to you. Mr Falconar says you have no need of his ministrations. And I would not break down, I swear to you! Archie, would you be willing?'

'Willing!' exclaimed Archie in the same low voice. 'I would give one of the few hours left me for your company! But it asks too much of you, Eoghain.'

'Not so much as to stand in the crowd and watch you like a stranger,' reiterated Ewen. 'And – my God, the four minutes must be nearly gone! – 'tis as if Providence had planned it, for Mr Falconar is little under my height, and lame of a leg as I am at times. If I wore his dark clothes – 'tis a pity he goes in lay dress, but that cannot be helped – and perhaps his wig, who would look at my face? And the clergyman always drives by himself to Tyburn, does he not?'

'I believe so,' said Doctor Cameron, considering, 'and in a closed carriage. You would not be seen on the way, since you would not travel publicly and slowly, as I shall.'

'I only wish I could, with you! But, Mr Falconar apart, would you not rather have some clergyman?' And, as Archie shook his head, Ardroy asked hastily, knowing that his time must be almost up, 'Is there anything which I must do ... *there*? – To be sure I can ask Mr Falconar that.'

'I suppose it is usual to read a prayer. I should like the commendatory prayer from the Prayer Book ... and I'd a thousand times rather you read that for me than poor Mr Falconar.'

'Mr Cameron,' said Rainsford, impatiently appearing at the door, 'you must come instantly, if you please, or I shall be obliged to detain you as a prisoner also – but not here with Doctor Cameron. You have but just time to join Mrs Cameron in the coach.'

'I have your leave, then, if I can contrive it?' whispered Ewen.

Archibald Cameron bent his head. 'Good-bye,' he said in English. 'Remember my message.'

And this time Ewen hurried from the room with but the briefest farewell glance, so afraid was he of being detained and prevented from carrying through his scheme.

By running down the stairs he reached the carriage just before it started. Mr Falconar, hat in hand, was at the door of it, Mrs Cameron invisible within.

'Give me your direction, sir,' said Ardroy hastily to the clergyman. 'I must see you when I have escorted Mrs Cameron home: 'tis of the utmost importance.' ('Yes, he is much of a height with me,' said something in his mind.)

Mr Falconar gave it. 'I shall await you this evening,' he said, and Ewen scrambled into the already moving coach.

But now, as they drove out under the archway of the Lion Tower, he must put aside his own plan, his own grief, and think of one who was losing even more than he. Jean Cameron was sitting upright in the corner, her hands clasped, looking straight in front of her, and alarming him not a little by her rigidity. Suddenly she said, without looking at him:

'He is not afraid.'

'No, madam,' answered Ewen, 'no man was ever less afraid.'

The pure in heart shall see God,' she murmured to herself. And a moment afterwards, somewhat to Ardroy's relief, she broke into wild weeping.

Chapter 24

'THE SALLY-PORT TO ETERNITY'

THURSDAY, the seventh of June, 1753, dawned just as those would have wished who were intending to make its forenoon a holiday – sunny and clear-skied, yet not without the promise of a cloud or two later on, whose shadow might be grateful if one had been standing for some hours in the heat. For many of the spectators would begin their pilgrimage to Tyburn very early in the day, in order to secure good places, since, though the great triangular gallows could be seen from almost any distance, the scaffold beside it, for what came after the gallows, was disappointingly low. Moreover, it was a thousand pities not to hear a last speech or confession, if such were made, and that was impossible unless one were fairly near the cart in which the victim stood before being turned off. So hundreds set off between six and seven o'clock, and hundreds, even thousands, more came streaming without intermission along the Oxford road all morning; and the later they came the more they grumbled at the inferior positions which they were necessarily obliged to take up; yet they grumbled with a certain holiday good nature. For though disgraceful scenes did take place at Tyburn, some at least of those who in this eighteenth century came to see a fellow-creature half-hanged and then disembowelled were quite well-to-do citizens who were conscious of nothing callous or unnatural in their conduct. An execution, being public, was a spectacle, and a free spectacle to boot; moreover, today's was a special occasion, not a mere hanging for coining, or murder, or a six-shilling theft. Of those there were plenty, with a dozen or more turned off at a time; but Tyburn had not seen an execution for high treason for many years, the Jacobite rebels from Carlisle having all met their deaths on Kennington Common.

And Ewen Cameron, as he sat in Mr Falconar's clothes in the shut carriage, which, with some difficulty at the last, had brought him to Tyburn a little before noon, was appalled at the density and magnitude of the crowd, and almost more at the noise proceeding from it.

Mr Falconar had only agreed to the substitution with many tergiversations and much misgiving. He was afraid that he was turning his back upon his duty; he was afraid that the fraud might be discovered by one of the Tower officials, if the coach appointed to take him to Tyburn had to follow in its slow course the sledge on which the condemned Jacobite would be drawn there, a transit which would begin at ten and take a couple of hours or more. But while Ewen was closeted with the clergyman there had come a message from the Deputy-Sheriff of Middlesex, in charge of the execution, to say that, owing to the crowds which were anticipated on the morrow, the carriage was to fetch Mr Falconar from his house at a later hour, and to go to Tyburn by a less frequented route. So Ewen did not follow Archibald Cameron in his sorry and yet perhaps triumphal procession through the streets of London.

But he was come now, by a less protracted pilgrimage, to the same heart-quelling goal; and he was come there first. He had not alighted nor ever looked out. There was a sheriff's man on the box beside the driver who would tell him, he said, at what moment his services would be required.

'Till then I should advise your reverence to stay quietly in the carriage,' he was remarking now. 'There's nothing to be gained by standing about, unless you'd wish to get used to the sight of the gallows, and seeing as you ain't in parson's dress, some mightn't know you was the parson.'

'I will stay in the coach,' said Ewen.

'You haven't never attended a criminal here before, sir, I should suppose?'

'No.' That was true, too, of the man whom he was impersonating.

The good natured underling went away from the step, but came back a moment later. 'No sign of 'em,' he reported. 'The prisoner's long in coming, but that we expected, the streets being so thick with people. But we hear he's had a very quiet journey, no abuse and nothing thrown, indeed some folk in tears.'

'Thank God for that,' said Ewen; and the sheriff's officer removed himself.

Faces surged past the windows, faces young and old, stupid, excited, curious or grave. Some looked in; once a drunken man tried the handle of the door; and the babel of sound went on, like an evil sea. Ewen sat back in the corner and wondered, as he had wondered nearly all night, whether he had undertaken more than he had strength for. He tried to pray, for himself as well as Archie, and could not. Not only was yesterday evening's rebellion back upon him in all its force, but in addition he was beset by a paralysing and most horrible sensation which he had never known in his life. He seemed himself to be standing on the edge of some vast battlement, about to be pushed off into naked, empty, yawning space that went down and down for ever, blackness upon blackness. In this nothingness there was no God, no force of any kind, not even an evil force ... certainly there was no God, or he could not allow what was going to take place here, when a life like Archibald Cameron's would be flung into that void, and those other lives twined with his wantonly maimed. Of what use to be brave, loyal, kind and faithful – of what use to be pure in heart, when there was no God to grant the promised vision, no God to see? Archie was going to be butchered ... to what end?

A louder hum, swelling to a roar, and penetrating the shut windows as if they had been paper, warned him that the prisoner's cortège was at last in sight. And as it seemed to be the only way of summoning up that composure which he would soon so desperately need, Ewen tried, as his cousin had yesterday suggested to him, to imagine that it was he who was facing this tearing of soul from body. The attempt did steady him, and by the time – it was a good deal longer than he expected – that the sheriff's man appeared at the window again he was tolerably sure of himself. And he had the comfort of knowing that Archie – unless he had undergone a great change since yesterday – was not a prey to this numbing horror.

'The Doctor's just gone up into the cart, sir, so now, if you please ...'

And with that Ewen stepped out from the coach into the brilliant sunshine and the clamour of thousands of voices and the sight of the gaunt erection almost above his head and of the cart with a drooping-necked horse standing beneath it. In the cart, with his arms tied to his sides above the elbows, stood Archie ... and another figure. It was then about half past twelve.

'You go up them steps, sir, at the back of the cart,' said the sheriff's man, pointing. 'Way there, if you please, for the clergy-man!' he shouted in a stentorian voice. 'Make way there, good people!'

There was already a lane, but half-closed up. It opened a little as an excited murmur of 'Here's the parson!' surged along it; showed a disposition to close again as several voices cried, 'That's no parson!' but opened again as others asseverated, ''Tis a Roman Catholic priest – or a Presbyterian – let him pass!' And the speakers good-naturedly pressed themselves and their neighbours back to make sufficient space.

Ewen made his way to the steps. They were awkward to mount; and when he reached the last two there was Archie, in what would have been the most natural way in the world had his arms been free, trying to extend a hand to him.

'So you are come!' he said, and the warmth of greeting in his voice and the smile he gave him was payment enough to Ewen for what he still had to go through.

Doctor Cameron was newly attired for his death, smarter than Ardroy had often seen him, in a new wig, a light-coloured coat, scarlet waistcoat and breeches, and white silk stockings. Ewen looked at him with a mute question in his eyes.

'I am very well,' said his cousin serenely, 'save that I am a little fatigued with my journey. But, blessed be God, I am now come to the end of it. This is a kind of new birthday to me, and there are many more witnesses than there were at my first.'

Still rather dizzily, Ewen looked round at the sight which he was never to forget – the sea of lifted faces, indistinguishable from their mere number, the thousands of heads all turned in the same direction, the countless eyes all fixed upon this one spot. There was even a tall wooden erection to seat the better class. Near the cart in which he now stood with Archie were two or three mounted officials, one of whom was having trouble with his spirited horse; not far away was the low wheelless sledge on which the Doctor had made his journey, the hangman sitting in front of him with a naked knife; each of its four horses had a plume upon its head. And on a small scaffold nearer still, its thin flame orange and wavering in the sunny breeze, burnt a little fire. Ewen knew its purpose. By it was a long block, an axe, and a great knife. Archibald Cameron's glance rested on them at the same moment with an unconcern which was the more astonishing in that it contained not the slightest trace of bravado.

At this juncture the gentleman on the restive horse tried to attract Ewen's attention in order to say something to him, but the noise of the multitude made it impossible for his words to be heard, though he beckoned in an authoritative manner for silence; he then tried to bring his horse nearer, but it would not obey. The rider thereupon dismounted and came to the side of the cart.

'I wished but to ask you, sir,' he began courteously, looking up at Ewen, '– the Reverend Mr Falconar, is it not? – how long you are like to be over your office?'

But it was Archibald Cameron who answered – to save *him* embarrassment, Ewen was sure. 'I require but very little time, sir; for it is but disagreeable being here, and I am as impatient to be gone as you are.'

'Believe me, I am not at all impatient, Doctor Cameron,' replied the gentleman, with much consideration in his tone. 'I will see to it that you have as much time allowed you as you have a mind to.'

'You are Mr Rayner, the under-sheriff?' queried Archie. 'I was not sure. Then, Mr Rayner, as I do not intend to address the populace, for speaking was never my talent, may I have the favour of a few words with you?'

'Assuredly, sir,' replied Mr Rayner. 'And, for the better convenience of both of us, I will come up to you.'

And in a few seconds he had joined them in the straw-strewn cart. At this the clamour of the nearer portion of the crowd considerably increased, and it was plain from their cries that they imagined a reprieve had come at this last moment, and were not displeased at its arrival.

But Mr Rayner had no such document in his pocket. Ewen heard the brief conversation which ensued as a man hears talk in a foreign tongue; though every word of it was audible to him it seemed remote and quite unreal.

'Although I do not intend to speak to the people, Mr Rayner,' said Archibald Cameron very composedly, 'I have written a paper, as best I could by means of a bit of old pencil, and have given it to my wife with directions that you should have a copy of it, since it contains the sentiments which, had I made a speech from this place, I should have expressed as my dying convictions.'

'If Mrs Cameron will deliver the paper to me,' replied Mr Rayner, 'I will take order that it is printed and published, as is customary in the case of a dying speech.'

The Doctor inclined his head. 'I thank you, sir,' he said with much gentleness, 'for your civility and concern towards a man so unhappy as I,' he paused a moment '– as I appear to be. But, believe me, this day which has brought me to the end of life is a joyful one. I should wish it known that I die in the religion of the Episcopal Church of Scotland, which I have always professed, though not always practised. I know that I am a sinner, but I have no doubt of God's mercy and forgiveness, even as I forgive all my enemies, especially those who have brought about my death.'

'You have the sympathy of a great many persons, sir,' said Mr Rayner in a low voice. And after a second or two's pause he added, 'There is nothing further that you wish to say – no last request to make?'

'Yes, there is one,' answered the dying Jacobite; and Ewen saw him glance, but with no trace of flinching, at the little scaffold. 'It is that you would defer, as long as the law will admit, the execution of the latter part of the sentence. I think you know what I mean,' he added.

'I know so well,' replied the under-sheriff gravely, 'that I give you my solemn word of honour that it shall be deferred for at least half an hour. That much I can do for you, and I will.'

And, with a bow, he went down from the cart. His last words had lifted a great and sickening apprehension from Ewen's heart ... and, who knows, from Archibald Cameron's also.

'I think there's nothing now to wait for,' said Archie, and he suddenly looked rather weary, though he showed no other sign of the strain upon nerves which, however heroically commanded, were only human. 'And oh, my dearest Ewen,' – he dropped his voice until it was almost inaudible – 'take my last and best thanks for coming and facing this with me – and for me!'

'But I have done nothing,' said Ewen in a dead voice.

'Nothing? You have come to the threshold with me. What can any friend do more? – And now I must go through.'

'But ... you wished me to read a prayer with you, did you not? I think I can do it, and it would perhaps ... seem more fitting.' In his heart, still a thrall to that dark horror of nothingness, Ewen thought what a mockery the act would be. And yet ... would it?

'If you can,' said Archie gently. 'We'll say it together. You have a Prayer Book?'

Ewen took Mr Falconar's out of his pocket. And while the quiet horse in the shafts shook his bridle once or twice as if impatient, and the flame on the scaffold, replenished, shot up higher, Ewen read with very fair steadiness, and Archie repeated after him, the commendatory prayer for a sick person on the point of departure. Around the cart many bared their heads and were silent, though in the distance the noise of innumerable voices still continued, as unceasing as the ocean's.

'O Almighty God, with whom do live the spirits of just men made perfect, after they are delivered from their earthly prison. We humbly commend the soul of this Thy servant, our dear brother, into Thy hands, as into the hands of a faithful Creator and merciful Saviour ...'

And, as Ewen went on, the poignancy, even the irony of that prayer, read as it was over a man in full health and in the prime of life, was softened by the perfect courage and readiness of him who joined in it. The black void was neither black nor void any longer; and for a moment this parting under Tyburn's beams almost seemed like some mere transient farewell, some valediction on the brink of an earthly sea, some handclasp ere crossing one of their own Highland lochs when, as so often, the mist was hanging low on the farther shore ...

He finished. 'Amen,' said Archibald Cameron in a low voice. He looked up for a moment into the June blue, where the swallows were wheeling. ' "Lord, into Thy hands I commend my spirit." – Ewen, you had best go now. And do not fear for me – you heard what Mr Rayner promised?'

Ewen gazed at him with shining eyes. 'I know now that there is a God, and that you are going to Him! May He give me grace to follow you some day.'

Then Archie held out his hands as far as he could, they kissed each other, and Ewen turned away.

Yet on the narrow steps leading from the cart he all but stumbled. And above him he heard the sound of his cousin's voice for the last time. It still held the same extraordinary and unfeigned composure, even cheerfulness, in its tones.

'Take care how you go. I think you don't know the way as well as I do!'

The press was now so enormous that though Ewen was able to reach the carriage again it was found impossible to drive away. So he was there, on his knees, when Archibald Cameron died, though he saw nothing of it. Afterwards he was glad that he had been so near him at his passing, even glad that the long groan of the multitude round the scaffold told him the very moment. And before, at last, a way could be made for the coach, he knew by the length of time itself that Mr Rayner had kept his word, and that the brave and gentle heart cast into the fire had been taken from no living breast.

EPILOGUE

'KEITHIE wants to swim too!'

'Keithie cannot, and let us have no greeting over it, now,' said the handsome elderly lady who, coming at the end of the long, fine day to take the air by the side of Loch na h-Iolaire before sunset, had just been annexed by her younger great-nephew. Little Keith, in Morag's guardianship, had been enviously watching his brother's progress through the clear, very still water, but Donald was back now, and dressed, in the boat wherein Angus MacMartin, his instructor, had rowed him out a little way from shore.

'When Donald putched Keithie into the loch,' proceeded the small speaker, looking up earnestly at Miss Cameron, 'Keithie swimmed and swimmed till Father came. Donald couldn't swim then. Didn't Keithie swim when you putched him in, Donald?' he inquired, raising his voice to carry to the boat. Nine months older than on the disastrous day to which he so uncompromisingly referred, Keith no longer used the possessive case of the personal pronoun to designate himself.

Donald, preferring to ignore this query entirely, cupped his hands together and shouted with all the strength of his healthy young lungs, 'Angus says that you can come into the boat now, Keithie, if Aunt Margaret will allow it, and sail your wee ship. Will you come too, Aunt Margaret?',

'No thank you, Donald, I will not,' replied his great-aunt with much firmness and in her ordinary voice. 'I prefer something stable under my feet – Keithie!' she clutched at his impatient little form, 'bide still! Do you want to fall in again?'

'Keithie didn't fall in,' corrected the child, raising his eyes of velvet. 'Donald pu –'

'Now, don't say again that your brother pushed you,' admonished Miss Cameron. 'It may be true, but you'd do better to forget it. You know that Donald is very sorry for having

654

done it; and you yourself were very naughty to throw in his claymore hilt.'

'Yes,' admitted small Keith, and his features took on an angelic expression of penitence. 'Keithie was very naughty.' He sighed. 'But good now,' he added with a more satisfied air, and, as if to prove his statement, stooped, his hand still in Miss Cameron's, picked up something at his feet, and held it out towards his brother in the boat, which Angus was now rowing in to shore. 'Donald, Donald, you can throw my wee ship into the loch because I throwed –'

The elder boy, standing in the bows, gave a sound like a snort. 'You know well that your ship floats!' he retorted indignantly. ' 'Tis not the same thing at all!'

'But the ship goes ... goes like this sometimes,' explained Keith eagerly, illustrating with the little painted vessel itself the topsy-turvy position which he had not vocabulary enough to describe.

'Come now,' interrupted Aunt Margaret, who was always direct, yet not the less esteemed by her great-nephews on that account, 'are you going with Angus or no, Keithie?'

'Wait, mem, if you please, till I make the boatie fast,' said the careful Angus. At three and twenty he was as reliable with his chieftain's children, or with anything that was his, as any veteran. He brought the boat into the bank and knelt to pass the rope round the root of a birch-tree.

'I shall sail my wee ship round and round and round the island,' proclaimed Keith, skipping up and down. 'I shall sail –'

'Preserve us, who's yonder!' broke in Miss Cameron, her eyes caught all at once by the figures of a man and a woman under the trees on the southern shore of the loch. They were standing very close together, looking at each other; very still, and very silent too, else in the windless calm their voices must have floated over the water. The westering sun smote upon an auburn head ...

'It's Father – he's come home at last!' cried Donald, and was out of the boat like a flash and tearing along the path towards them.

Angus jerked himself upright. 'Indeed, indeed it's himself!'

said he in an awed and joyful voice. 'Blessings be on the day!'

'Take the bairn and go,' commanded Miss Cameron, and in a second the young piper had tossed Keithie to his shoulder and was off to his master.

The sunset had been angry; now it was smoothed to serenity – a sea of the palest chrysoprase, with little islands of gold which had once glowed fiery rose, and far-stretching harbours clasped between promontories of pearl.

'I shall never forget it,' said Ewen to the two women, the old and the young, who stood with him where the Loch of the Eagle reflected that dying glory. 'No one who was there will ever forget it: he went to his death as a man goes to a banquet. All London was talking of it, friends and foes alike – and now Scotland. See, when I came through Edinburgh this letter from London had already been published in a journal there.' He pulled out a newspaper and pointed, and the two ladies read:

'Doctor Cameron suffered last Thursday like a brave man, a Christian and a gentleman. In short I cannot express what I have heard of his behaviour. It was reckoned by the thousands that saw him more than human, and has left such an impression on the minds of all as will not soon be forgot. His merit is confessed by all parties, and his death can hardly be called *untimely*, as his behaviour rendered his last day worth an age of common life.'

'We have had another Montrose in our kinsman,' said Miss Cameron proudly. 'But it does not surprise me. Did his body suffer the same fate as the great Marquis's?'

'No, Aunt Margaret. It was not quartered, and though his head was struck off, it was not exposed on Temple Bar, but buried in the coffin.'

And he was silent, thinking of that midnight scene in the vault of the Chapel of the Savoy, where, in the presence of a little half-clandestine gathering of mourners and sympathizers, the mangled body of the last Jacobite martyr had been laid to rest. Again, he saw the torchlight run glimmering over the inscription on the coffin-lid, heard Hector sobbing like a woman, and bowed his own head before the overwhelming conviction which possessed him, that the determination to have vengeance on the informer which flourished so greenly in his heart was but a mean, a shrivelled, a dishonouring wreath to lay upon the grave of one who died with such noble and unvindictive fortitude. Archie's life was too precious to be paid for in such coin. The traitor must go untouched by his hand; and the renunciation should be *his* tribute to the dear and honoured memory of Archibald Cameron.

Not that he forgave ... though Archie had forgiven ...

Ewen came back to the present. Miss Cameron was drying her eyes. Alison's face was hidden against his breast. He held her close, and laid his cheek for an instant on her head, for he could feel rather than hear her little sobbing breaths, and he guessed that she was saying to herself, 'Ewen, Ewen, what if it had been you!'

Then he saw Donald, preceded by Luath the deerhound, come bounding along the path under the birch-trees. In the boy's hand was the hilt of the broken claymore from Culloden Moor. 'I went to the house to fetch this, Father!' he cried, holding it aloft. 'I told you that Angus dived and brought it up again. And I've had a notion,' he went on fast and excitedly, 'that it could be mended, and have a new blade put to it ... Why is Mother crying?'

Holding Alison closer than ever, Ardroy took the broken blade and looked at it as if he were seeing more than what he held.

'No,' he said after a pause, 'I think it can never be mended now. It never could have been ... I do not know, Donald, but that you'll have to get a new kind of sword when you are a man.'

He gazed over his wife's dark head at the sunset, fading, fading ... How Archie had loved this land of mist and wind and clear shining which he had left like a malefactor and a hero! And these lochs and hills would doubtless yet breed more of his temper, but never a one who united to his courage and loyalty so much simple goodness – never a one.

THE JACOBITE TRILOGY

All the colour was gone from the sunset now, save the faintest opal tones, like the last cadence of a song. The four of them turned from the lochside, and began to go homewards under that June sky of the North which knows no real night and the child with the broken sword led the way.

THE END

Several of the chief characters in this book appear also in its predecessor, *The Flight of the Heron* and its sequel, *The Dark Mile*.

THE DARK
MILE

AUTHOR'S NOTE

Several of the chief characters in this book appear also in its two predecessors, *The Flight of the Heron* and *The Gleam in the North*, also published in this series.

David Maitland is not an historical character, though the role assigned to him before the story opens was actually played by some man whose identity and motives have never been established.

CONTENTS

THE THIRTEENTH CHIEF

1

ITS own peculiarly vehement and gusty wind was curvetting about Edinburgh this October afternoon of 1754, forerunner and abettor of the brief but, whole-hearted squalls of rain which now and then were let loose upon the defenceless city, and sent every pedestrian running to the nearest doorway. Yet between these cloudbursts it was fine enough, and during one of these sunny intervals a young man in black, holding on to his hat, walked quickly up the slope of the Canongate. His long stride accorded well with his fine height and build, and though his mourning was new and very deep, there was no trace of recent bereavement in his air. Indeed – despite the difficulty with his hat – he held his head with a sort of natural arrogance, and his glance at his surroundings in general was something that of a newly-crowned monarch surveying his territory and subjects. For only six weeks had elapsed since the earth had been shovelled down upon his old father's coffin in the roofless chapel of Holyrood, and the son who bore him no particular affection was come at twenty-nine into his inheritance as thirteenth Chief of Glenshian ... into possession of a ruined castle, an empty treasury, and immense prestige in the Western Highlands. But he already possessed some very singular assets of his own.

Just where the High Street, having succeeded the Canongate, gave way in its turn to the Lawnmarket, this Highland gentleman came to an abrupt and apparently unpremeditated halt in front of a small shop-window. It was rather a dingy window with bulging panes, evidently, from its contents, the property of a vendor of almanacs and broad-sheets; but the new Chief's attention was pretty plainly engaged by a roughly-executed wood engraving which was propped, unframed, against a pile of books in the very centre of the window. There was nothing about this to distinguish it from any other equally bad print of the time; one could only say that it was a stock representation of a man of early middle age. But the inscription ran, 'A True Effigies of Doctor Archibald Cameron, who lately suffered Death at Tyburn for High Treason.'

At this 'effigies' the young man in black stood looking with a frown, and a deepening frown. Regret, no doubt, was heavy upon him (since he too was a partisan of the White Rose) and a natural if vain, desire for vengeance upon the English Government which, only a year and four months before, had sent his fellow-Jacobite and compatriot to the scaffold.

It would have required a more than human insight to discover what was really causing that scowl; more insight, certainly, than was possessed by the middle-aged, down-at-heels and partially drunken Edinburgh chairman who was lounging at the entrance of the close by the shop, and looking at the tall, stationary figure with a gaze half sodden and half cunning. Once, indeed, he detached himself from the dark and greasy wall of the entry as though to accost it; then, muttering something inaudible, relapsed once more against his support.

Yet, for all that, he was to speak to the gentleman in black; the Fates would have it so, desiring no doubt to show that they at least could read the mind of Finlay MacPhair of Glenshian. Nevertheless it would not have come about but for this day's inclement weather. For while the young Chief, his hand at his chin, yet stood looking at the dead Jacobite's portrait, the heavens without warning opened afresh, and there descended such an unmitigated flood of water that no one, save an amphibian, would willingly have endured it. Mr MacPhair in his new blacks uttered an exclamation, took hold of the handle of the shop door, discovered that it was fastened, cursed strongly, and turning, hurled himself into the mouth of the adjacent close, almost colliding with the lounger already there.

'A bit o' a shooer!' observed the latter in a wheezy voice. He looked as if neither internally nor externally was he over-familiar with the fluid of which the cataract was composed.

Mr MacPhair gave him a contemptuous glance and said nothing. The rain flashed in sheets past the entry and drummed and bounced upon the cobbles.

'Sae ye were keekin' at the puir Doctor's picter in the windy,' commented the chairman, who, unlike most of his kind, was plainly a Lowlander. 'Dod, yon was a fearfu' end, a fearfu' end! Mony's the time Ah hae regretted it – mony's the time Ah hae been near greetin' ower it.'

'You must be uncommon tenderhearted,' observed Finlay MacPhair indifferently, and, looking out, cursed the downpour with precision.

'Nae mair than anither!' returned his companion in an injured tone. 'Nae mair than yerself, sir! Hendry Shand is no' gi'en ta greetin'. But Ah'd hae ye ken that there's whiles sic a thing as remorrse – aye, remorrse.' He sighed windily. 'The worrm, the Guid Buik tells o' ... Ye'll be ower young, Ah'm thinkin', tae ken it yersel'.'

'I may run the risk of knowing it very soon,' returned Glenshian meaningly. 'If I have to throttle you to stop your havers, for instance. Damn this rain!'

'Ma havers!' exclaimed the chairman with deep indignation. 'Havers! – me that's been stane-dumb a' this while, and never tellt a soul aboot the letter – '

'Continue your reticence, then,' said the Highlander, very much bored. 'I have no wish to hear your reminiscences.'

This word, with which he immediately grappled, seemed to offend the toper still more deeply. 'Remis – remishenshes ... They're nathing o' the sort! What for suld the Lord Justice-Clerk hae gi'en me a gowden guinea when Ah brocht him yon letter, gin it had been a matter o' remyshish – '

But the tall gentleman in black was no longer bored, no longer even on the other side of the alley. He was beside the speaker, gripping his shoulder. 'What's that you said about the Lord Justice-Clerk? For what letter, pray, did he give you a guinea?'

The other tried to shuffle off the hand. 'But that wad be

665

tellin',' he murmured, with a sly glance. 'Forbye, sir, ye said ye werena wishfu' for tae hear aboot ma remorrse. And indeed Ah hae nane the noo, for Ah've refleckit that Ah was but a puir body that was ready tae oblige the gentleman and earn a piece of siller.' He wriggled anew. 'Ye'll please tae let me gang, sir!'

For all answer his captor laid hold of his other shoulder, and thus held Hendry Shand's unsavoury person pinned against the wall. The rain, winged by a momentary gust, blew in upon them both unheeded. 'Since you have chattered of your remorse and of Doctor Cameron's death, you'll tell me before you leave this place of what letter you were speaking, and why Lord Tinwald gave you a guinea for it. And you shall thereby earn two . . . if you tell the truth . . . and it's worth it,' added the young Chief in a couple of afterthoughts.

In the semi-darkness Hendry Shand's eyes glistened. Finlay MacPhair saw the phenomenon, released him, pulled out a purse and, extracting two gold coins, held them up. Mr Shand moistened his lips at that fair sight. But, half drunk as he was, he had not mislaid his native caution as completely as had at first appeared.

'And wha's tae judge if it's warth it?' he inquired. 'And why sud ye be sae wishfu' – ' He broke off. 'Are ye for Geordie or Jamie? Ah'd like fine tae ken that first.'

'You cannot know who I am that you ask that,' replied the young man with hauteur. 'I am MacPhair of Glenshian.'

'Gude hae maircy on us!' ejaculated Hendry. 'Ye'll be the new Chief, then! The auld yin was for Jamie, they say, although he never stirred for him himsel'. Aiblins then ye were a frien' o' puir Doctor Cameron's?'

Finlay MacPhair bent his head. 'I knew him well. And I am aware that he was informed against, and so captured. If the letter you took to Lord Tinwald had to do with that matter' – his voice sank until it was almost drowned by the rain '–and it had, had it not? – and if you will tell me who gave it to you, you shall know what it means to be for the rest of your days in the good graces of the Chief of Glenshian.'

There was a pause, filled by the drip of the now slackening

rain from overfilled gutters. Hendry passed his hand once or twice over his mouth, his eyes fixed on him who made this promise. 'Aye,' he said slowly, 'and what guid will that dae me when Ah hae ma craig yerked by the next Whig, or lie shiverin' i' the Tolbooth? What for did Ah no' haud ma tongue a wee while langer!'

The coins jingled in Glenshian's impatient hand, and when the chairman spoke again his voice betrayed weakening.

'Forbye Ah canna tell ye, the name, for Ah never lairnt it.'

'Nonsense!' said the young man roughly. 'You are playing with me. I warn you 'tis no good holding out for more than I have offered.'

'Gin ye were tae dress me in jewels,' replied Mr Shand earnestly and inappropriately, 'Ah cudna tell ye what Ah dinna ken masel'. But Ah can tell ye what like the man was,' he added.

There was another pause. 'I doubt 'twill not be worth the two guineas, then,' said Glenshian, in a tone which showed his disappointment. 'But I'll give you one.'

'For ae guinea Ah'll tell ye naething,' responded Hendry with firmness. He seemed a good deal less drunk than he had been. 'But – hear ye noo! – for twa Ah'll tell ye what was intill the letter, for Ah ken that. And aiblins when Ah describe the gentleman tae ye, ye'll find that ye ken him yersel'.'

'It was a gentleman, then?'

'For sure it was a gentleman like yersel'.'

'Very good then,' said the new Chief, 'the two guineas are yours. But' – he glanced round – 'this is not a very suitable spot for you to earn them in. Is there not a more private place near?'

'Aye, there's ma ain wee bit hoose up the close – though 'tis hardly fit for the likes o' yersel', Chief of Glenshian. But you an' me wad be oor lane there.'

'Take me to it,' said Finlay MacPhair without hesitation.

2

Although it necessitated a change of scene to an environment even less pleasing than the unclean and draughty alleyway, Hendry Shand's was not a long story. Late one evening in the March of the previous year he had, it seemed, been accosted by a gentleman – whom he described – and offered a crown if he would take a letter to the house of Lord Tinwald, the Lord Justice-Clerk. At first Hendry had thought that the gentleman was ill, for he was as pale as a corpse and his hand shook, but afterwards came to the conclusion that he was merely agitated. On Hendry's asking if he should say whom the letter was from, and suggesting that the name, however, was probably inside it, the gentleman shook his head, and replied that the name was of no moment, though the letter was, and urged him to make haste.

'Aweel,' continued Hendry now, as he sat upon his frowsty bed in the one tiny dark room which constituted his 'hoose' and gave himself to the pleasures of narration, 'aweel, Ah set ma best fit foremost and gaed doun the street. Syne Ah thocht Ah heard ma gentleman cry efter me, "Come back, come back!", but Ah'd nae mind tae lose the croun he'd gi'en me, sae Ah took tae me heels. A' the way Ah was wonderin' what micht be i' the letter – for ye maun mind Ah hadna the least notion – an' it may be that as Ah rinned Ah held the letter a wee bit ower tight in ma hand, for a' on a sudden. Ah heard the seal gie a crack. Syne Ah stoppit, and losh, the letter was open!'

'In short, you opened it,' observed the listener.

'Na, na,' denied Hendry; but an eyelid fluttered for a second. 'Never say that, Chief o' Glenshian! But, seein' the bit letter was open, hadna Ah the richt tae lairn what for Ah was earnin' a siller croun? ... Aweel, ye can jalouse what was intill the letter – it sent the Doctor ootbye i' the windy tae the gallows.'

Mr MacPhair drew a long breath. 'You remember the wording?'

'Ay, certes. "*If ye wish tae tak Doctor Cameron, send wi'oot delay tae the hoose o' Duncan Stewart o' Glenbuckie in Balquhidder, where the writer saw him no' ten days syne.*" '

'That was all? And there was no name of any kind – not even initials?'

'No' a letter! Ye may be sure Ah keekit inside an' oot. There wasna a scratch ... Aweel, Ah cam tae Lord Tinwald's hoose, an' Ah thocht tae masel', Gin this letter is sae important, the Lord Justice-Clerk may gie me anither croun tae lie beside ma gentleman's. Sae Ah tellt his man there wad aiblins be an answer, "though Ah dinna ken for sure", Ah says, "for though the bit seal is broken, Ar canna read ae ward o' write". (Yon was a guid lee, but it was better tae say that.) Syne the auld judge sent for me, and Ah cud see he was far uplifted; and he speired what like was the man who gied me the letter. Ah tellt him, a douce sort o' man, yin that Ahd'd never seen afore in ma life. Then he gied me na croun, but a hale gowden guinea ... And when Ah heard that Doctor Cameron was ta'en by the redcoats i' Glenbuckie, and a' the Whigs in Enbra was sae cock-a-hoop, Ah had a mind tae gang tae Lord Tinwald and speir if the bit letter wasna worth mair, but Ah thocht better o' it, for Ah micht hae fand masel' i' the Tolbooth for meddlin' wi' affairs o' State ... And unless ye keep a shut mouth, Chief o' Glenshian, Ah micht find masel' there yet!'

And he looked anxiously at the listener in the dirty wooden chair.

'It's for you to keep that,' said the young man, leaning forward. 'This is to be kept a secret betwixt you and me, Mr Shand; and you shall not find yourself the worse of that, I promise you. You have not condescended much to me upon the particulars of your gentleman's appearance, but I suppose that you would know him again if you saw him?'

'Ma certie Ah wad that.'

'And you could write a letter?'

'Aye ... mebbe Ah cud.'

'If it were made worth your while, I presume? What I propose, then, is that if you see this gentleman again you shall use every endeavour to find out who he is and where he lives. You will then communicate these facts to me, by word of mouth if I be still in Edinburgh, by writing if I have taken my departure for the Highlands, as I am about to do. Do you understand?'

'Aye.'

'You undertake to do that then? I will pay you well for it.' The guineas jingled.

'Ah'd like fine tae ken first what ye intend tae dae wi' the gentleman gin Ah find him for ye?'

'I shall do him no harm. I merely wish to have a conversation with him, by which he will not suffer; on the contrary. 'Tis not vengeance that I am after, man! What's done is done, and Doctor Cameron cannot be brought to life again. Is it a bargain?'

'There's aye two sides tae a bargain,' observed Mr Shand, wriggling on the bed. 'What wad Ah get, noo, for a' this wark an' the fash of sendin' a letter tae ye in the Hielands?'

'You shall have three guineas for it,' responded his visitor. 'That's paying you well – overpaying you, in fact.'

Once more Hendry was seen slightly to lick his lips. 'Yon will be as well as the twa ye're tae gie me the noo?'

Glenshian hesitated a moment. 'Yes,' he said at last reluctantly. 'You shall have the three guineas in addition, making five in all. Three more guineas when I receive the gentleman's name and his direction.'

Hendry licked his lips openly this time. 'Five guineas!' he repeated below his breath. 'Ye swear that, Mr MacPhair?'

'My word is my bond,' responded Mr MacPhair haughtily. 'Nevertheless, I swear it.' He pulled out a pocket-book, scribbled something and tore out a leaf. 'Here is where I lodge in Edinburgh; should I be gone for the Highlands, you'll address your letter to me at Invershian.'

His agent did not immediately take the paper. 'Ah'll need ye tae be swearin' too that ye'll never tell the gentleman, if ye get this bit crack wi' him that ye're ettlin' after, wha 'twas that fand him for ye?'

The young Chief rose. 'I am willing to swear that too, and by the sword of Red Finlay of the Battles, my ancestor. A MacPhair who breaks that oath is like to die within the year. Take this paper, hold your tongue, and be diligent. Here's your two guineas.'

Hendry held out his dirty palm, bit the coins severally, stowed them away in some recess inside his shabby coat, then seized the unwilling hand of his visitor and dissolved into maudlin tears.

'Ah'll scarce tak bite nor sup nor sleep o' nichts till Ah find him for ye, Chief o' Glenshian,' he hiccoughed. 'Ah'll hunt like the tod efter him – wi' the Lord's assistance – and ye sall ken his name near as soon as Ah lairn it masel'...Ye're awa? Ah'll unsnib the dure for ye, sir. Gude bless ye, Gude bless ye in a' yer undertakin's!'

3

The rain had quite ceased, and a tremulous sunlight was now gilding the pools and the wet pebbles beyond the archway as MacPhair of Glenshian, with this benediction upon his head, closed the door of Mr Shand's retreat behind him. People had even come into the streets again, for, as he then emerged into the mouth of the close, he was aware of a figure standing where he had stood a little while ago, in front of the shop window. But this figure was a woman's.

For one brief second Finlay MacPhair studied her from the mouth of the wynd. He was looking at a gentlewoman of about thirty, whose bare hands were loosely clasped in front of her, and who was undoubtedly gazing at the print of Doctor Cameron; from his position in a line with the window Mr MacPhair could even seen the deeply sorrowful expression on her face, and guessed that her eyes were brimming with unshed tears. If sad, she was uncommonly pretty. But was that a wedding ring upon her left hand, or was it not?

He stepped out from the archway, and was aware that the lady never so much as moved an eyelash, so absorbed was she in her mournful gazing. The young Chief knew a stab of pique; he drew up his fine figure and cast a glance, as he passed, at the lady's back. So doing, he saw an excellent opportunity of breaking in upon that unflattering reverie, for on the stones between her and the gutter lay a forlorn little grey glove. He picked it up and approached the fair owner.

'Madam,' he said in the most courtly tones, 'I think this glove must be your property.'

Startled out of her preoccupation, the lady half turned. 'My glove, sir . . . have I dropped one?'

'I believe so. Allow me the privilege of restoring it,' said Glenshian with a smile. He put it into her hand, took the opportunity of directing an appraising stare under her bonnet, then swept her a low bow, replaced his hat, and walked slowly away.

A few seconds later, while the lady, holding her recovered glove, was still looking after the figure of its rescuer, who by now had crossed the Lawnmarket and was walking down the other side, the door of the shop opened and a very tall and broad-shouldered man was stooping his head to come out of it.

'So you finished with your mantua-maker sooner than you expected, my dear,' he observed with a smile. 'And whom, by the way, were you talking to just now? I did not see.'

'I have no notion,' replied the lady. ' 'Twas merely a gentleman who was kind enough to restore the glove I had dropped. There he goes!'

The newcomer turned and looked, and instantly the most remarkable change came over him. At first he stood as still as death, staring after the departing figure of Finlay MacPhair; the next moment he had taken a couple of steps forward and was at his wife's side.

'Let me have that glove, Alison,' he said in a suffocated voice – 'the one he gave back to you!'

Overcome with amazement, Alison Cameron made but a half movement to comply. Her husband took the glove from her hand and went instantly and dropped it, as one drops something repellent, into the rain-swelled gutter in the middle of the street, where, in company with cabbage-stalks and other refuse, it began to voyage along the Lawnmarket.

'Ewen, what ails you?' exclaimed its owner, looking up in alarm. 'My poor glove was not poisoned ... and now you have left me with but the one!'

'Anything MacPhair of Glenshian touches is poisoned!' answered Ewen Cameron between his teeth. 'And to think he dare come within a mile of that portrait!' He indicated the window; and then, making an effort to curb the fury which had so suddenly risen in him, said more quietly, as he drew his wife's arm through his, 'Come with me, *m'eudail*, and I will buy you another pair of gloves for your little cold hands.'

Chapter 1

WHAT THE MOON SAW

June 15th, 1755

'IF the moon looks through the roof she will see us all in bed!' a
little boy had gleefully announced this evening, sitting up suddenly in that retreat. ' – *Can* the moon look through the
roof?'

Nobody knows for certain, though it is commonly held that
she cannot. Yet, even if she has that power, and high as she was
riding on this clear June night above the old house of Invernacree in Appin, she would not have seen all its inmates in bed.
The child who had spoken of her, yes, and his elder brother,
both very soundly and rosily slumbering; these she would
indeed have seen; and in their respective apartments their great-
uncle, old Alexander Stewart of Invernacree, to whom these,
his dead sister's grandchildren, were paying a visit; and his two
daughters, Grizel and Jacqueline, between whom there lay
twenty-five years' difference in age, seeing that Invernacree had
married twice; and Morag Cameron, the children's nurse, who
had come with them from their own home of Ardroy, in Lochaber, while their mother lay in of the daughter whose presence
would be such a surprise to Donald and little Keithie when they
returned. All the servants likewise would the moon have seen
laid out on their truckle beds or pallets – all save a young maid
who was awake with the toothache, and wishing she had access
to the skill of the wise woman at home.

But in one of the larger bedrooms there were two persons –
two men – who had not even begun to undress, though it was
fully an hour since they had come upstairs. The younger was
sitting on the edge of the old four-poster bed, with an arm
round one of the columns at the foot; it might be presumed that
he usually occupied this bed himself, and so he did; for he was

675

Ian Stewart, the son of the house. He was of the dark type of Highlander, lithe and dark-haired, with deep blue eyes under black lashes, lean and sensitive in feature and looking about five and twenty. The other, of larger build altogether, unusually finely made in fact, fair complexioned and some ten years his senior, was his first cousin and very good friend, Ewen Cameron of Ardroy, the father of the two little boys in the green bedchamber, come to fetch them both home again. He was now leaning over the back of a high chair, gazing at his kinsman with eyes more markedly blue than his, because they were not so dark.

'Yes, my father is set upon my marrying soon,' said the young man on the bed with a sigh. 'One can well understand it, Ewen; he is old, and desires to see a grandson before he dies. But if Alan had lived – '

'No, there would not then have been the same necessity,' agreed Ardroy. Alan Stewart, the elder brother, had been killed, unmarried, at Culloden, nine years before. 'Yet, Ian, you have taken no vow against wedlock, have you? Or is there someone . . .?'

Ian Stewart ran his finger round and round a detail of the acanthus carving on the bedpost. 'There is no one,' he confessed. 'Indeed I wish there were. My father would not then have to look about for a suitable match – for which the choice is none so wide neither, since I naturally cannot marry a lady from a Whig family.'

'And has Uncle Alexander found anyone?'

'Two,' said Ian with a little grimace. 'Miss MacLaren, and Maclean of Garroch's second daughter – the eldest is promised. I have no objection to either of them . . . save that I do not desire to marry either. I want someone of my own choice. Now do not, Ewen, tell me that arranged matches generally turn out very well, as I can see that you are upon the point of doing, for you have no right to possess an opinion on that subject, you who had the luck to marry the woman you chose for yourself and waited for!'

Ewen Cameron smiled and, coming round, threw himself into

the chair on which he had been leaning. 'I was not going to say anything of the sort. I wish I could help you, Ian; and I am sure that Alison would if she could. She'd not be a true woman if she did not hanker after the chance.'

'If only I had the means to travel a little!' said his cousin regretfully. 'Still and on, to go from place to place looking for a wife as one might search for a brood mare would not content me neither. A spaewife once told me that I should love a woman who would be other than she seemed – not a very pleasant prophecy, was it? – But enough of my affairs. Tell me, Ewen, how are matters between you and the new Chief of Glenshian since he succeeded his father last autumn, and is now become almost your neighbour?'

Very likely Ewen Cameron of Ardroy could prevent his sentiments from appearing on his face if he so wished – he looked as though he could – but with his present companion there was evidently no need to hide the signs of a most uncompromising antipathy to the individual just named. His bright blue eyes seemed to change colour till they were the match of his cousin's dark blue ones; his already decided chin appeared still more decided. 'I am glad to say that I have not seen even his shadow near Ardroy, and I think it will be many a long day before Finlay MacPhair of Glenshian comes near my house. I know too much about him.'

Ian looked at him curiously. 'But is he aware of that?'

'Very well aware of it. I sometimes wonder that in the couple of years which have passed since I was enlightened as to his true character he has neither made overtures to me nor – ' Ewan paused.

'Nor what?'

' – Nor found means to send a gillie behind me some dark night with a *sgian dubh*. We were both in Edinburgh last autumn – in fact I saw him, though he did not see me.' Ardroy seemed to be going to add something else, but apparently changed his mind. 'However, I know now that he will not touch me, and I have sworn not to touch him. It is checkmate.'

Ian had got off the bed. 'Ewen,' he said, and his tone was

grave, 'are you jesting? Do you indeed go in danger of that man, because if so – '

'No, no,' said Ardroy lightly. 'I was not meaning that about the gillie; my tongue ran away with me.'

'Then 'tis the first time I have ever known it do so,' retorted his cousin, surveying him doubtfully. 'And what is the discreditable secret that you know about Glenshian?'

Ewen put his elbow on the arm of the chair and shaded his brow with his hand. 'There is nothing to be gained by sharing it.' His voice had grown all at once very sombre. Ian stood still and looked at him.

'Oh, very well,' he said at length, a trifle piqued. 'I have no wish to pry into your relations with Glenshian, though they seem devilish uncomfortable ones. And why you should have sworn not to defend yourself against him passes my comprehension. I always thought you had more common sense than most.'

'I did not swear that,' answered Ewen after a pause. 'I made a vow, two years ago, that it was not for me to take vengeance.' He dropped his hand now, and young Stewart could see that he was very pale. 'I cannot explain why I took such an oath ... perhaps I was fey with grief ... but I have never regretted it, and even if I should regret it in the future, still I must hold by it.'

'Two years ago,' 'fey with grief' – Ian realized to what his cousin must be referring, to the execution of his kinsman, Archibald Cameron, which had been so great a sorrow to him and which he had risked his life to avert. His own slight resentment vanished; he laid a hand for a moment on Ewen's shoulder, and then went past him and, drawing the window-curtains aside, looked out. Yet he wondered what could possibly be Finlay MacPhair's connection with the tragedy – no, he must have misunderstood Ewen; there could be none. And he would not reopen so painful a subject.

'I hope we do not disturb Uncle Alexander by our talk,' observed Ewen, rousing himself. 'Is not this room of yours next to his?'

'My father grows a little hard of hearing,' said Ian in reply. He dropped the curtain. 'And the wind blows tonight. Speaking of my father's deafness, by the way, I think that was the reason why I overheard you telling him something about your brother-in-law, Hector Grant – that he had come into an inheritance; or was I mistaken?'

'No, you were not mistaken,' answered his cousin, and rose suddenly to his towering height. 'Hector has been left a small property in Glenmoriston by some remote kinsman of his father's, and he will soon be coming over from his regiment in France to visit it. Indeed, Alison wonders whether he will not resign his commission and settle in Glenmoriston.'

'Oh, indeed,' said Ian dryly. 'But Mr Grant will find the existence of a Highland laird but a poor thing after his life as an officer in France. Would he not be better advised to think twice before taking such a plunge?'

Ewen swung round on him. 'I never knew that you disliked Hector!' he exclaimed in a tone of surprise.

'My dear Ewen, I don't. But I cannot think him, somehow, suited to the Highlands.'

'He's as Highland as yourself, *laochain*; his mother was a Macrae.'

'Maybe. But a lifetime spent in France has given him . . . too much French polish for my taste.'

'Is that your objection?' said Ewen, laughing. 'I had not noticed the defect myself; and to a "lifetime", why, he is only about two years older than you. He is younger than my wife.'

Ian made a gesture to dismiss Mr Hector Grant. 'Talking of Lady Ardroy, is the daughter like you or like her, Ewen? Your boys, I think, favour you both, one apiece.'

'You had better come with me when I return and see for yourself,' answered his cousin. 'I shall insist upon Uncle Alexander sparing you for a night or two. You have not visited us, I think, since you gave Donald that claymore hilt which Keithie threw into the loch, two years ago last autumn. Now, if you'll forgive me, I am going to bed!'

On that announcement his host remorsefully snatched up a

candle to light him to his room, excusing himself for having selfishly, as he declared, called him into his, by the fact that he saw him so rarely.

But, coming back, Ian Stewart did not follow his kinsman's example and go to bed. He sat down on the window-seat, where the curtain was already drawn aside, and gazed for a long time at the silver road which led across Loch Linnhe to the mountains beyond. The Celt in him had gone dreaming; dreaming as a girl is supposed to dream of the ideal lover. But *his* romance had never come to him, and soon it would be too late for it. He must mate, since it was his duty to beget children to come after him, without ever knowing that high rapture of which the poet sang, and the moonlight, and the flight of wild swans over the pool. There would be no Deirdre or white-breasted Bronwen for him, only a decorous young housewife, a MacLaren or a Maclean, whom he would respect and cherish, and to whom he would be faithful. In time, perhaps would come affection too. Well, perhaps that was better in the end than passion, but youth was slipping away, and he had never known youth's prerogative, to give, and hazard everything in the giving. His marriage would be as tepid an affair as that impassive moon now looking at him over the mountains of Ardgour.

Yet under that same roof, up in her little turret room, Ian's young sister Jacqueline was smiling in her sleep, having heard something that evening which had pleased her. For her sentiments about Lieutenant – now Captain – Hector Grant differed entirely from her brother's. In her dreams she did not seek the ideal lover, for it seemed to her that she had already met him, here in her father's house, more than two years ago. She had been but seventeen then. If, on his way to his recent inheritance in Glenmoriston, he should come this way again? ... She was dreaming that he had.

And away in northern France, where the same moon was silvering the steep-pitched roofs of Lille, a handsome young man in uniform was going home to his quarters, after a game of cards, with pockets somewhat lightened. But what did that matter? He was almost a man of substance now – no longer, at any rate, a mere landless Jacobite. In the deserted streets, whence all good burghers had long ago departed, and where his footfalls woke such echoes on the cobbles, he began to whistle a Scots air. And who knows whether, when at last he reached his couch, he was not visited by the image of a girl in far away Appin? But the moon could not be sure of this, for she sank to rest before he did.

She missed, therefore, by the hour of her setting, the conclusion of a novel and most interesting experiment in cattle-lifting not far from Ewen Cameron's home at Ardroy in Lochaber.

Chapter 2

ON HIS VERY HEARTHSTONE

June 17th

'Eh, Alison, my lass, she's going to be a beauty!' declared Miss Margert Cameron, indicating a red and puckered object in which only the eye of faith or of close kinship could discern any such promise. Both these requirements, however, were fulfilled by the keen gaze of Miss Cameron, the infant's great-aunt who had brought up Ewen Cameron himself from a child.

'You really think so?' asked Alison Cameron, as propped up in bed, she stooped her pretty becapped head with a smile over the sleeping baby in the crook of her arm. 'I am afraid that Donald and Keithie may not be of that opinion when they return tomorrow. It was tomorrow that Ewen said, was it not, Aunt Margaret?'

'Tomorrow it was, my dear. Now, shall I open your window a wee, since 'tis such a fine afternoon?' Erect, silver-haired and comely, she went to the window for that purpose, and gave an exclamation. 'Preserve us, there's about half a score of gillies or what not down below there! Now, might they but wear the tartan again, one could tell whose they were.'

She continued to look out, uttering various surmises as to the identity of the invaders, until bent old Marsali, who had the entrée, came into the bedchamber.

'There's a gentleman below asking for Mac 'ic Ailein, and he from home,' she announced in the Gaelic and unemotionally.

'A gentleman? Who is it?' inquired Miss Cameron with interest.

'By what he says, it will be MacPhair of Glenshian.'

Alison uttered a little exclamation, and her arm tightened round Miss Cameron the younger.

'Glenshian!' exclaimed the older lady. 'And what's Glenshian wanting here?'

'He's wanting the laird on an affair of business,' replied the old woman. 'Then he asked could he see Lady Ardroy.'

'The idea!' exclaimed Miss Cameron. 'I will come down, Marsali, and find out what he desires. Am I sufficiently *à la mode*, think you, Alison? This is the first time the present Glenshian has set foot in this house, and I must not disgrace its master.'

Alison beckoned her to the bed. 'Aunt Margaret,' she said in a rather troubled voice, 'I do not know how much you know, but Ewen and Glenshian are ... not good friends. I wonder what has brought him?'

'Not good friends? Since when? – Aye, I have fancied something of the sort. Then 'tis as well that Ewen is away,' deduced Miss Cameron briskly. 'Glenshian can't but be polite to an old woman, and he a young man too.'

'But you say he has brought a number of gillies with him!'

'Isn't he but nine months or so Chief, and likes to swagger about with his tail on? Never fash yourself for that, Alison, my doo,' replied Aunt Margaret, and, after setting her cap carefully to rights at the mirror, she left the bedchamber.

As she entered the big living-room below, a tall, red-haired young man turned round from his contemplation either of the antlers over the hearth or, possibly, of the worn escutcheon on the stone, where the motto *Fideliter* could more clearly be read than the half-defaced bearings of the shield. For a second or two he stared at the elderly lady as if surprised; then he bowed politely in response to her rustling curtsey.

'Good day to you, sir,' said Aunt Margaret pleasantly. 'My nephew Ardroy is from home, as I expect you'll have been told already, and his wife lies upstairs with a newborn bairn, so the task of welcoming you here falls upon me. I am Miss Cameron. Will you not be seated?'

'When you are, madam,' replied the Chief of Glenshian politely, and waited until Miss Cameron had disposed herself. Then he sat down at no great distance and looked at her, drawing his light eyebrows together in a contraction that was half puzzled, half annoyed.

'Ardroy will be sorry to miss you,' observed Miss Cameron after a moment. 'We do not expect him back before the morrow.'

'Aye, that makes my errand the more awkward,' responded the visitor, fingering his chin.

'Perhaps your errand can wait, sir?' suggested Aunt Margaret. 'Though I would not wish to give you the trouble of bringing yourself and your tail' – she gave a glance through the window – 'these many miles again. Can I not give my nephew a message?'

Finlay MacPhair shook his head. 'My business is not an agreeable one for a gentleman to come upon to another gentleman,' he remarked.

'Then perhaps,' suggested Miss Cameron, quite unperturbed, 'you'll find it easier to transact with a lady?'

'Not at all,' said the new Chief, frowning. 'Not at all. 'Tis no matter for a woman.'

'Improper, do you mean?' queried his hostess. 'I am old, Glenshian – nearly sixty-five. You may risk scandalizing me.'

Mr MacPhair gave an impatient movement. 'Has Ardroy no factor with whom I could deal?' he demanded.

'I'm all the factor he's ever had in the past,' replied Aunt Margaret with perfect truth. 'He's his own grieve now. See now, if it's some matters of affairs, I'm sure he'll be pleased to wait upon you at Invershian when he returns from Appin.'

The young man's lips curled in a sarcastic smile. 'I doubt it, madam. And that would not serve, neither; the business cannot be transacted anywhere but here.'

'Then you'll e'en have to put yourself to the trouble of coming again, sir, or stay until Ardroy returns. This house is at your disposal.'

'That's out of the question,' said the visitor rather rudely.

The very tiniest stiffening was apparent in Miss Cameron's upright figure as she sat there. 'If you will kindly enlighten me as to what you propose, sir, we will see about that,' quoth she.

'Madam,' returned Mr MacPhair with emphasis, 'I will enlighten you. You have lived in the Highlands, I daresay, for – '

'For well over half a century,' filled in Miss Cameron.

'And you will not be a stranger to the fact that Lochaber has always been noted for cattle-lifting.'

'Aye, nearly as noted as Glenshian,' agreed the lady, smiling.

The Chief of that region could not have relished the quite justified retort, but he could affect not to show that he felt it. 'All that,' he pursued, 'is supposed – *supposed* – to be old history now, but ... I'm wanting two of my best steers this week past, and I have but just come upon proof of where they went to. I regret to have to say it, madam ... but you'll find them amongst Ardroy's cattle!'

Miss Cameron jumped up, a sparkle in her eye. 'You accuse –'

The young man also rose. 'No, no, madam,' he protested with apparent sincerity. 'I should be loth to bring such an accusation against a gentleman. But what laird in these parts knows precisely what his tenants will be about when his back is turned ... and you say Ardroy is from home now. Yet, since the steers are branded – '

'Aye,' broke in Miss Cameron with vivacity, 'that alone proves, my good sir, that you are talking nonsense – and very offensive nonsense too! Had the cattle come here by straying or even by reiving, you would have had them back by now, branded as you say they are.'

'Yet I have not had them back.'

'Then they never came here.'

Glenshian looked at her loftily. 'I have the best of reasons for knowing that they did ... I should like to see Ardroy's herdsman.'

'I have no authority to allow that in his absence,' replied Miss Cameron. 'I perceive,' she went on with warmth, 'that you're almost upon saying that I went and lifted your steers myself one dark night, and have them hidden – in my bed-chamber belike! You may go and look, sir. But warrant you to interfere with Ardroy's dependents I cannot.'

'Then,' said the visitor still more loftily, 'I regret, but I shall have to do it without your warrant, madam. I am not going back without my steers.'

'You'll go back without much reputation for civility, Mr MacPhair!' retorted the lady. 'But as you have brought some sort of an army with you, and we are only women in this house . . .' She made a gesture. 'Forbye, are you sure you did not know all the while that Ardroy was from home?'

To this suggestion Glenshian deigned no answer. He said, looking black, 'There are men on Ardroy's land, at any rate – the men who drove off my cattle.'

'And do you think, sir, that they are going to help you find those phantom beasts?'

'Someone is going to help me find them. I have come for that!'

And like two duellists, the young man and the old woman faced each other. Miss Cameron made the first lunge.

'Very good then,' she said after a moment. 'Take your tail that's out there, and go up the braeside, Glenshian, and look for your steers. But if you think that one of Ardroy's gillies will lift a finger to help you without orders from him you are sore mistaken! In the latter end you and your gathering will likely all spend the night in a bog!' And she followed up this attack by a second. 'Here's another point for your consideration: God know's what sort of faces my nephew's tenants, and particularly the MacMartins, will show you when you go marching over his land and driving his cattle!'

'You will pleased to send word in advance, madam, upon what errand I am come.'

'And have the look of countenancing it! I shall do nothing of the sort!'

To the ears of the disputants, both now thoroughly roused – and the younger and stronger aware, too, that this damned old lady had him at something of a disadvantage by her refusal of support – there came in the momentary silence the rumble of carriage-wheels. Miss Cameron, if her older hearing did not perceive it quite as quickly, was, however, at once aware, from the way he turned his head, that the intruder had heard something or other.

'That's maybe Ardroy returning before he's expected,' she

remarked casually, though she did not think it was. 'You will be able to make your request to him in person, which will no doubt be more agreeable to a gentleman like yourself than trying to bully an old woman.'

'Request,' said Finlay MacPhair, throwing back his head. 'I'd have you know, madam – '

But, then, out of the corner of his eye, he perceived a chaise pass the window, and did not finish the sentence.

'Losh, it *is* Ardroy and the bairns!' exclaimed Miss Cameron in genuine surprise. 'What brings him back before his time?' She went to the parlour door (the vehicle having meanwhile passed out of sight, and being presumably by now in the act of discharging its occupants; and called, 'Ewen, come away ben at once; here's a visitor to see you!'

And so, a moment or two later, Ewen Cameron entered to find the enemy who, as he had declared only two nights ago, was not likely ever to trouble his house, standing in a very haughty manner almost upon its hearthstone. He had not seen Finlay MacPhair face to face – though he had seen his back – since the revelation of his treachery, two years ago, in the Chief's London lodging, when he himself had interposed between his sword and Hector Grant's.[1] He stopped, speechless, in the doorway.

'You are surprised to see me, Ardroy?' said the visitor, showing no embarrassed consciousness at all of their last meeting. 'But when you hear why I am come, I can't but think that you will put fewer obstacles in my path than your good aunt here has seen fit to do.'

'I wonder!' thought Aunt Margaret. Her nephew's dour expression suggested that there was one path at least in which he would place no obstacles, and that was Mr MacPhair's homeward one. His lips were so firmly closed that, to her, it seemed as if he were only keeping back with difficulty the utterance of this sentiment; but the traditions of Highland hospitality were too strong for him to give way to his visible desire.

'In what then can I serve you, Glenshian?' he asked in the

1. See *The Gleam in the North*.

most frigid tones, laying his hat and riding-whip upon the table as he spoke.

And Finlay the Red answered him with much directness: 'By restoring to me the cattle which your tenants have lifted from me.'

A quick flush dyed Ewen's fair skin. 'I think I cannot have heard you aright, sir. My tenants do not lift cattle ... from anyone!'

The young Chief smiled a half-pitying smile. 'Not with your knowledge, perhaps; I do not suggest that. But, as I was just remarking to Miss Cameron, who knows what goes on behind the laird's back?'

'In the case of a man with so many dependents as yourself, that question may perhaps be asked,' retorted Ewen. 'But I, with my mere handful' – there was no humility, rather the reverse, in his tone – 'I flatter myself that I know their employments pretty well.'

Glenshian sniggered. 'I would not be too ready to claim that knowledge if I were in your place, Ardroy. In the end it might prove awkward for you.'

But, before her nephew could reply to this innuendo, Aunt Margaret, already standing at the door, had slipped out of the room. Although by nature she relished a fight, it seemed to her that Ewen would prefer to have out this preposterous business unhampered by the presence of a woman. Moreover, she must prepare Alison for the onslaught of her small sons. The sound of their excited voices and of racing feet was even now audible upstairs, and the hall door had just opened to admit a man in riding costume whom she recognized, without much surprise, as young Invernacree.

'Is that Ian Stewart? she asked, and, Ian coming forward to salute her, she went on, in a voice which, despite herself, showed signs of trouble, 'MacPhair of Glenshian is here, making a great pother about a couple of steers which he swears Ewen's people have lifted from him. Whether you'd best go in on them or not I don't know. Ewen looks very angry, but I suppose they'll not come to blows – at least, I hope not.'

Ian hesitated a moment; then he remembered something which Ewen had let fall about a dark night and a *sgian dubh*. 'I can always leave the room if necessary,' he answered, and opening the parlour door, went in, on the sound of a voice which was not cousin's, to catch the words, '. . . if you refuse to put it to the proof!'

By the inflection it was the end of a sentence, and then he saw the speaker, standing at the far end of the room, young arrogant-looking, red-haired and tall. Ewen (still taller) who faced his visitor, swung round for a second as the door opened, saw his kinsman, then turned back and said, rather as if he were hurling a missile at the man on the hearthstone:

'Very good, then! It *shall* be put to the proof – and here is a witness. Ian, let me present to you Mr MacPhair of Glenshian, who has come here to accuse me of stealing two of his cattle. Glenshian, this is my cousin, Mr Stewart the younger of Invernacree.'

Chapter 3

BRANDED

IAN STEWART knew his kinsman well enough to divine that he
was in a towering rage, though a stranger might not have
guessed it. Across the room the red-haired young man returned
his own bow by a slight inclination of the head.

'Your servant, Mr Stewart – Perhaps hardly an unbiassed
witness, Ardroy, in view of that kinship; but let that pass. Truth
will always out.'

Ian heard his cousin give an exclamation under his breath. 'Is
it possible that you are learning that at last?' he asked.

The new Chief moved forward a little from his stand by the
hearth. 'You'll not advance your cause by being offensive, Ewen
Cameron!' he retorted, his eyes lighting up. 'There's one thing
you have certainly no need to learn, and that's the advantage of
having some relative or other at your heels in your dealings
with me! This time, however, I trust that your intervention will
not be required to save me from assassination by your henchman, as it was in the case of Mr Grant. I owe you thanks for
that intervention, if for nothing else.'

A brief but tingling silence succeeded this speech, to Ian so
startling that he almost thought his ears could not have conveyed its purport aright. But one glance at Ewen's face and pose
convinced him that battle was now joined between him and the
speaker over a matter more serious than a few supposedly
stolen cattle.

'Since you have brought up what occurred at our last
meeting, Mr MacPhair,' said Ardroy with extreme grimness
' – though I should have thought you would have preferred it to
remain in oblivion – we had best go into it thoroughly. If you
wish, I will ask Mr Stewart to withdraw.'

'By no means,' responded Finlay the Red, folding his arms. 'For I do not know what account you may have given him of that occasion.' He turned to Ian. 'Your kinsman here, Mr Stewart, most unwarrantably invaded my premises in London, and his satellite, Mr Hector Grant, took from me, at the point of the sword, a treacherous paper of his own writing which, since it came by good chance into my hands, I had been able to hinder from fulfilling its black purpose. I – '

He got no further, Ewen had stridden forward, overriding him. 'Don't listen to him, Ian! God's name, this impudence surpasses everything – who stole that letter, Finlay MacPhair, who deciphered it and sent it to the English Government, who – '

' 'Tis much more to the point,' broke in Glenshian with an unpleasant smile, 'to ask who wrote it, full of secret information as it was, and handed it over, under pretext of having been robbed, to a Government agent in the Highlands? Mr Stewart had better know the answer to that. It was the same Mr Hector Grant who was so anxious to get his damning property into his own hands again that he was ready to cut my throat for it!'

'That's a foul lie!' cried Ewen passionately. 'Hector Grant's letter was written and intended for the eyes of Cluny Macpherson and no man else.'

'And had no direction upon it!' sneered Glenshian. 'A curious kind of "letter". 'Twar nothing else but a paper of information, and if I had not rescued it – '

' "Rescued it!" ' burst out Ardroy, unable to contain himself. 'You "rescued" it from your ally, Mr Pelham, I suppose! Did you also "rescue" the letter from that dirty traitor, Samuel Cameron, which was in your pocket that day? You did not save him from being drummed out of the regiment for his complicity. And the noblest blood that has been shed in England this many a year ... do you ever look at your hands, Glenshian?'

At that unmistakeable insinuation the much perturbed Ian expected the Chief either to spring at his accuser's throat or to crumple up entirely. He himself felt both bewildered and re-volted, for he knew Ewen Cameron too well to suppose that he would ever make random accusations of such terrible gravity, especially against a fellow Jacobite. But Finlay MacPhair, though his face seemed suddenly drained of colour, neither sprang nor flinched. He again moved forward a little until he was quite near the table, and, drawing himself up to his full six feet of height said, with surprising coolness:

'If by that hyperbole you mean the late Dr Cameron's blood, then I can only assume that your affection for that unfortunate gentleman has unsettled your intellects, and that I need not therefore take with you the course I should pursue with any other man who had made such a suggestion to me.' Here his hand fell upon Ewen's riding-whip, which was now lying within his reach, and he fingered it significantly, looking the while at its owner, who stood with clenched hands well within range of a slash across the face. Ian, afraid to move for fear of precipitating such a catastrophe, nevertheless braced his muscles to fling himself upon the assailant the moment he should grasp the handle.

But Finlay MacPhair went on contemptuously, 'You were once good enough to assure me that some day in the Highlands we should settle accounts over the question of the late Dr Cameron's connection with the Loch Arkaig treasure. But I don't think I am disposed ever to go out with a man who has not yet disproved that he is . . . a cattle-thief!'

The word came out with all the sting of the lash which had not been lifted from the table. Ewen took a step backward and gripped one hand hard round the wrist of the other. With an immense effort he succeeded in answering quietly, though he was exceedingly pale, and his eyes sparkled like blue diamonds.

'I have already undertaken to disprove that. If you will wait a moment, I will go and give the necessary orders.' And, turning abruptly on his heels, he went out of the room. Ian followed him.

'Ewen,' he burst out, 'that man – he's insufferable! What are you going to do now?'

There was sweat on Ardroy's brow. He put up his hand and wiped it off. 'Give orders instantly to have all my cattle driven in and go through the tally,' he answered, gritting his teeth together. 'God give me patience! ... And I have not seen Alison yet ... I'd best not, I think, till this business is over, and he's out of my house.' And he flung through the porch, almost into the midst of Glenshian's waiting gillies, and Ian heard him calling, 'Angus – where is Angus MacMartin?'

2

An immense, blood-red and ominous sunset was towering in the west, high over the heads of antlike men and their dwarf cattle, ere the business of disproving the Chief of Glenshian's accusation was finished. Yet a warm brown dusk was already beginning to rest upon the great spaces of bloomless heather, seeming, indeed, rather to be breathed out by the ground itself, just as from Ardroy's own little loch, Loch na h-Iolaire, the Loch of the Eagle, there was already rising a ghostly film of mist. Ewen's shaggy cattle, thus unusually driven down and herded together in this comparatively level stretch not far from the loch, lowed uneasily, pushed at each other with their spreading horns, or looked about from under their tawny fringes in mild perplexity. Hours of the hardest and hottest work had gone to their collecting, not because they were so numerous, but because they were so scattered in their grazing.

'There still want three,' said Ewen, glancing at the list in his hand. He and Ian stood on the edge of the herd, with never a glance behind them, where on a little knoll Glenshian sat with gillie at his back. The only person who occasionally turned his eyes that way was eight-year-old Donald, who, heated from his assistance in the chase, now stood by his father's side and perpetually counted the cattle, reaching a different total every time.

'Those will be the three,' said Ewen, 'which gave Duncan the slip up there. But he sent a couple of men after them.'

'And there they come, I fancy,' observed Ian, pointing to a

small group of cattle and two men who were making their way slowly round the end of the loch. 'But your list is incorrect, Ewen, or else the beasts have been miscounted, for there are five steers there instead of three.' He said this in all innocence, suddenly realized the possible significance of what he had seen, and ejaculated under his breath, 'It's not possible!'

As for the laird of Ardroy beside him, he might have become one of the pines by the loch, he was so still. Nearer and nearer came the five steers, in a leisurely, lurching fashion, and the sunset glowed upon their lion-coloured pelts and touched their enormous horns with light. They were all of the same breed, indistinguishable save to the eyes of a herdsman. 'They *must* all be Ewen's!' thought Ian. 'Someone has miscounted.'

Ardroy roused himself and beckoned.

'What is the meaning of this, Duncan?' he asked hoarsely. 'Why have I two more beasts than the tally shows?'

Duncan looked at his master with eyes at once shrewed and visionary. 'Witchcraft, Mac 'ic Ailein,' he replied. 'Four days ago you had them not. Yet they may have strayed into the herd.'

'They have been stolen!' said Ardroy in a fierce, ashamed voice. 'They could never have strayed so far from Mac 'ic Fhionnlaigh's land. Stolen by one of my men – in effect, then, stolen by me! And I so certain –'

'Father,' broke in Donald's little voice by his side, 'here is the gentleman coming down to speak to you.'

And Ewen Cameron turned to meet the bitter chagrin and humiliation he saw falling upon him. Glenshian, descending leisurely from his mound, walked towards him through the rustling heather-stems, his hair glowing like fire beneath the red canopy spread above them all.

'It was well I had patience until the end,' he observed with a very disagreeable smile. 'Yet, as I said, truth will out. Here come two of my best steers, Ardroy – well hidden away they were, no doubt.'

'Prove your ownership!' said Ewen, short and sharp.

'Seumas!' called the Chief over his shoulder. The gillie went forward, seized one of the beasts by a horn, tugged it nearer, pushed it sideways, and, lifting the shaggy hair on one flank, disclosed a large 'G' roughly branded there. In the same dead silence he repeated the performance with another. A long breath went up from the assemblage of hot and weary men, and Glenshian's gillies began to talk excitedly together. Ardroy's were silent. And the colour on their master's face was not from the sunset.

'You'll allow my men, I suppose, to take my stolen property home?' queried Fionnlagh Ruadh. 'And, since you were so insistent that you knew all about your people's doings, Ardroy, I must conclude that this petty theft – one can hardly dignify it with the name of a *creach* – had your connivance.'

This he said so that all could hear; stepping closer, he added in a lower tone, 'Your own glove will be the better of a wash in the gutter now!'

He swung on his heel, went to his horse, which a gillie brought forward from the mound, gave an order, and mounted. With sulky, puzzled faces the Camerons watched the two alien steers being separated from the rest and driven off after him. Ian and little Donald saw Ewen himself, as if stung by a gadfly, go striding away from all of them, under that yet tremendous sunset which might have been painted for the setting of some great tragedy rather than of this ignominious little exposure.

Ian took his small relative's hand. 'Come home, Donald; we'll not wait for your father.'

And Donald, knitting his brows, came obediently. He asked questions, of course, which young Invernacree did his best to answer, in spite of his own bewilderment. What an odious and inexplicable scene! . . . Poor Ewen!

'Cousin Ian, Cousin Ian, our house is on fire!'

For they were now come in sight of the House of Ardroy, and its western windows did flame and glitter as if a conflagration raged within.

' 'Tis only the reflection of the sunset, *laochain*', answered the young man. ('Or else the house is angry, like its owner, at the affront put upon him.') But he did not pass on this fancy to the astonished and excited little boy at his side.

3

The burnt out sunset was only a memory, for even the tall candles were dwindled down nearly to their sockets that night ere Ian put to his cousin the question which had been secretly tearing at him all evening. For up till now they had spoken of nothing but the problem of the stolen cattle.

'Ewen, is it true about Finlay MacPhair – that he has Doctor Cameron's blood at his door?'

Ewen's eyes met his. The angry mortification still alight in their blue depths gave way to another emotion.

'It is quite true. I will tell you how I know it. First of all, it was common talk among the Jacobites in London that Archie would never be brought to trial because the English Government would have had to produce evidence whose source they did not wish to reveal – in other words they had some valuable spy whose usefulness they did not intend to curtail by disclosing his identity. Next, with my own eyes I saw Finlay MacPhair coming secretly one night out of the house of Mr Henry Pelham, my Lord Newcastle's brother – he who died last year. When I charged Glenshian with this, in Hector's presence, he denied it absolutely, and told us some fairy tale about a "double". Upon that we discovered in his lodging the very letter whose loss had caused some most damaging reflections on Hector's honour – the cipher letter which he had written to Cluny Macpherson and which was stolen from him in the Highlands the previous autumn, when Archie came over, by some man who was either an agent of the Government's or of Glenshian's himself.'

'That, I suppose,' commented Ian, 'was the letter which Glenshian pretended this afternoon contained intelligence really meant for the Government, because it was not openly directed to Cluny?'

'Yes. You see how he twisted that unlucky business, cunning as he is, in order to carry the war into the enemy's country. I need not tell you that you might as well suspect me of purposely giving information as Hector Grant – To resume, on finding this

letter of his in Finlay's possession Hector drew his sword upon
him; I contrived to separate them before either had injured the
other. Glenshian, who was recovering from an illness, swooned
from the exertion, and Hector, going through his pockets in
search of further evidence, found undeniable testimony that it
was actually through his agency that he had been slandered.
Finlay had taken steps to try to put the blame, or part of it, for
Archie's capture upon poor Hector's shoulders. Why should he
have done that, if it were not to ease his own?'

One candle expired guttering in an overflow of wax. Neither
of the men at the table even noticed it.

'You mean to say, then, it was Finlay MacPhair of Glenshian
who betrayed Archibald Cameron to death?' said the younger
in accents of horror. 'Ewen, I can scarce believe it! And if it be
so, why in God's name have you not warned everyone against
him – why have you so kept your knowledge to yourself? I
know you too well to suppose that it was from fear of any
consequence to yourself; moreover, if Glenshian knows that
you know – and indeed you have now charged him with it to
his face – you go always in danger of some measure of
retaliation on his part, as you hinted a few nights ago at
Invernacree.'

'It looks somewhat as though that retaliation had already
begun,' agreed Ewen with a wry smile. 'Your question is very
natural, Ian. But it is a different matter to be convinced of
Finlay's responsibility, as I am in my very bones, and to possess
sufficient proof to warrant my accusing him directly to the
King, or even to Secretary Edgar. I have warned a few friends,
privately. But my only proofs are that I saw him coming out of
Mr Pelham's door, and that Hector's deciphered letter – and
Samuel Cameron's – were in his possession. Moreover, as I told
you after Archie's execution, the man who sent to the authorities intelligence of his actual whereabouts in Glenbuckie is still
to find. He was probably in collusion with Glenshian, or even in
his pay – but I have no proof of that whatever. Yet Finlay's was
the hand – I shall believe that to my dying day – though this
unknown man was the dagger in it.'

Ian sighed. A lost cause, indeed, whose adherents could so shamelessly betray a comrade . . .

'What was it,' he asked dully, after a moment, 'that Glenshian said to you, as he was going away, about a glove and the gutter?'

Ewen pushed back his chair and rose. 'Oh, that! In Edinburgh last autumn he picked up a glove which Alison had dropped and returned it to her. I took it from her and threw it into the gutter. He must have seen me do it. . . I thought he had not . . . though I should have done it just the same . . . Well, 'tis all one . . . and perhaps he is even with me now.'

Chapter 4

THE LADY FROM THE LOCH

THE tide was running out very strongly from Loch Leven at Ballachulish two evenings later, and the passage across the ferry was consequently prolonged, so hard did the rowers have to strain to keep the ferry-boat even moderately in her course. Between the necessity of coaxing his mare to stand quiet for longer than usual in this craft, and the memory of the day before yesterday's scene at Ardroy, which continued to play itself over in his brain, Ian Stewart had little thought to spare for the sunset across Loch Linnhe, which was transmuting to red gold the sentinel heights at the entrance to Glencoe. If he noticed it at all, it was but to be reminded of that, even more splendid, by the Loch of the Eagle, and what it had witnessed.

One could not disembark on the Appin side of the passage without seeing what dangled from the gibbet on the hillock there; a thing which had once been a man, and a Stewart too – chained bones which testified to Campbell vengeance for a murdered Campbell. Today Ian hardly looked up, but took the road by the gate of Ballachulish House and under the flanks of Lettermore, past the very spot where Campbell of Glenure had fallen, without thought of that three-year-old tragedy. Another tragedy was engaging his mind – Archibald Cameron's – and the incredible part which Finlay MacPhair seemed to have played therein. Really it was less abhorrent to think that Ewen had been mistaken, that his strong affection for his dead kinsman had led him into fixing the guilt of his judicial murder on a man who had indeed behaved in an equivocal fashion, but who, in his position and with his traditions, surely could not have deliberately betrayed a comrade. Besides, as even Ewen had admitted, there was always the actual informer to account for. If Finlay's hands were smeared, his were dripping.

The cousins had not spoken again of that black business. The whole of yesterday had been spent in trying to find the man who had so smirched his young laird's honour by cattle-stealing, but all attempts had proved fruitless, and had only tended to injure the good feelings which existed between Ardroy and his dependents. Ian's belief that the culprit must have been tracked by one of Glenshian's people was shaken by the universal denials, not only of the theft, but of any smallest knowledge of it. The mystery of the stolen steers raged like a plague through the house as well; it seemed as if no one could talk of anything else – save, naturally, Ewen's infant daughter, whom Ian had been allowed to see, and even, to his secret terror, to hold. It was a thoroughly uncomfortable, even unhappy day, and had, Ian feared, sown seeds of mistrust and ill-feeling between Ewen and his tenantry whose harvest might not easily be rooted up. Finlay MacPhair could hardly have planned a better revenge, upon a petty scale, than this which Fate had planned for him.

But had the planning been entirely Fate's? Ian went so far as to wonder whether the Chief of Glenshian could possibly have bribed some very poor gillie of Ewen's to steal the animals, so that he, as owner, could come to Ardroy with the triumphant foreknowledge that he should find them there? Surely no Cameron or MacMartin would have lent himself to such a transaction! And yet . . . it had all fallen out so pat.

Immersed in these speculations, Ian rode on at a good pace. Duror of Appin was behind him; he would be home before long. The sunset had withered slowly, but now the mountains across Loch Linnhe were once more cloaking themselves in the grape-hued mystery of twilight. Young Invernacree, who loved them, and had something of the poet in him, came for a moment out of his absorption, some Gaelic verses about the high hilltops recurring to his memory; and then poetry and cattle-lifting were alike driven out of his mind by a distant sound ahead of him resembling that of horses galloping at a rate very unusual on this rough road, accompanied by a rumbling noise such as a heavy vehicle might make. He rounded a corner and saw that his ears had heard aright. Swaying and banging, a coach was fleeing away in front of him along the loch-bordered road – and fleeing was really the word for its progress behind its obviously runaway horses. Ian decided that he must already have heard the hoofs of these before they had broken into their mad gallop, but had been too preoccupied to realize the fact. Now ... he struck spurs into his mare and sent her forward after the receding vehicle.

It was instinctive, his pursuit, though even in its course he knew that he could do little good. The ill-fated coach had had too much start of him. He could not see the postillion for its bulk, and wondered whether the latter had lost his seat, and that this accounted for the coach's wild career; but in that case he must have come upon him by the roadside. Now he saw a man's head emerge for a moment from the left-hand window, the farthest from the loch and go back again; then a hand sought for the handle of the door and opened it.

'Is he going to jump out? Uncommon dangerous!' thought the pursuer. 'And is he alone in there, or is there another occupant?' For the man was with one hand keeping the door open, no easy task at that rate of progress; yet, as his head and shoulders remained within, it almost seemed as if he were occupied with some other person in the interior of the conveyance. And then, before he could jump – if such were his intention – the end came, and in a more catastrophic manner than the rider behind had anticipated. For the road again made a slight bend, and, to Ian's horror, the rocking coach, instead of following it round the curve, plunged straight ahead. The horseman utter a shout of dismay as he saw the vehicle go clear over the brink; it lurched, half stopped, then toppled over on to its side on the stones of the shore. There was a splash as it struck the shallow water – luckily the tide was out. Nor was the actual drop from the road, mercifully, more than a very few feet.

But, before it actually went over, the man who had been trying to get out had succeeded in doing so – half scrambling, half thrown – and was now picking himself up out of the road. The postillion – he was there after all – had stuck to the horses, and by the time Ian arrived he was cutting the traces of one, which was lying struggling. The other had wrenched itself free and was making off. Seeing that the gentleman on the road was, if not altogether unhurt, at least able to get to his feet, Ian, as he swung himself off his own mount, was for making to the assistance of the postillion. But he found his arm gripped, and a hoarse, desperate voice said in his ear:

'Help me, for God's sake! There's a lady – my daughter, inside the coach ... drowning perhaps ...'

Horrified, Ian ran down to the shore. A lady in there – how was one going to get her out? The upper wheels of the coach as it lay on its side reared themselves at about the level of his head; one could only see the underneath of the vehicle, and its great springs.

'I'll climb up, sir,' he said to the traveller, now at his elbow. He perceived him to be spare, middle-aged, rather harsh-featured, with a grey wig somewhat awry from his tumble.

Young and agile, Ian swung himself up and clambered on to the side of the coach, now become a roof, and stood there like a mariner boarding a derelict. In the accident the door had slammed itself to. Ian stooped, wrenched it open and looked in.

Down at the bottom of the species of large, ill-lighted box thus presented to his gaze, amid fallen cushions and wraps – and a glimmer of water also – there was a lady in a blue cloak. She lay on her side without stirring – yet surely there had not been time or water enough to drown her! She must have been thrown against something hard and have struck her head as the coach went over. But which was the quickest and best method of getting her out?

A distracted voice below was saying, 'Is she hurt? Help me up ... get her out, man! Why, the coach is half in the water!' And there was the elderly traveller trying vainly to emulate his own gymnastic feat.

'Stay where you are, sir,' said the young man hastily. 'I will pass her down to you. Postillion, leave that horse to shift for itself now, and come up here to me.'

'Do as the gentleman bids you, James,' said his employer, and the postillion left the now freed horse, which, subdued by its recent experience, got to its hind legs and remained there trembling. Ian had thought at first that by bending in through the window, with the man to hold him, he could haul the lady out, but he soon saw that she was too far away from his reach in this position. One of them must get down into the box and lift her up to the other; he had only been deterred from doing this at once by the fear that he should trample on her. However, he must risk that. He tugged off his riding boots, and taking a careful view of what lay beneath him, lowered himself through the door and felt about with his stockinged feet until he encountered something flat and solid upon which to rest his weight. He did not know what it was; it was enough that he stood neither upon the lady nor the broken glass of the undermost window. Water lapped cold about his ankles as he removed his arms from the doorway.

And there at his feet was the girl, as pale as the swansdown collar of her cloak. Ian stooped and very gently lifted her by the shoulders; her head fell limply back. He touched her face; it was not even wet. Thank God, her mouth and nose had not, then, been under water, though he could feel that parts of her clothing were saturated. Laying an inexpert hand upon her pulse he found it beating, as it seemed to him, regularly enough. But it was not too easy, in that confined space, and with uncertain footing, to raise the injured lady and hold her up to the postillion leaning ready to receive her at the aperture above, and Ian was afraid that the man might let her slip; however, he himself supported most of her weight from below. At last the postillion had her safe and drew her through; the rescuer scrambled after her to the upper side of the coach, and together they lowered her into the arms of the agitated gentleman waiting to receive her.

A moment or two later young Invernacree, somewhat breathless, was once again looking down on the girl. Now, however, she lay on the pebbles of the foreshore, half supported in the arms of her father, who had taken off her bonnet and was gazing with deep distress at the cut, scarcely more than a scratch, which its removal had disclosed above one shapely eyebrow. Ian went and dipped his handkerchief in the loch and the traveller, accepting it, wiped away the blood.

'I think the wound is but slight, sir,' said Ian earnestly. 'A splinter of broken glass, perhaps. But we will get the lady at once to shelter. My father's house is a bare mile from here. There is no vehicle obtainable, but surely the postillion and I could carry her upon a cloak; and on the way there is a small farmhouse whence I could despatch a messenger to warn my sister to have a bed ready, and where I could arrange also to have your missing horse sought for.'

The traveller thanked him warmly, promising only that he himself would assist the man to carry his daughter, in order that the rescuer should ride on ahead as messenger. But, on attempting this arrangement, it appeared that the gentleman's own fall from the coach had not been entirely innocuous, and that a slight wrench to one knee, of which in his devouring anxiety he had hardly been aware, would prevent that modification being carried out. He, and not Ian, must therefore ride the latter's mare; yet, having mounted, he did not push on ahead, preferring to ride behind, leading the remaining carriage-horse, as Ian and the postillion slowly carried his daughter along. It was a strange little procession, greeted with sympathetic outcries at the farmhouse when they stopped to exchange the cloak for a more convenient hurdle, and to send on a messenger to Miss Stewart.

When at last they came up the avenue at Invernacree, there was Grizel in the open doorway, with Jacqueline behind her, capable Grizel, skilled in leechcraft and nursing. She already had a bed prepared. Ian and the postillion carried the hurdle with its light burden up the stairs, the gentleman following them. The young lady was laid upon the bed, and Ian, descending again, gave orders that a man should ride at once for the doctor. Then he returned to the landing to wait for the young lady's father to emerge, and to conduct him downstairs. His own father, he had ascertained, was out.

He had not waited long before the bedroom door opened and the traveller came forth.

'I think you were right about that cut, sir,' he said. 'I thank God it is so little. But she is still senseless. Can one have a doctor here?'

'I have already sent a man on horseback for one, sir,' said Ian, looking sympathetically at this poor father's haggard face. 'Meanwhile, will you not come downstairs, and let me offer you a glass of wine or eau-de-vie after your accident?'

The gentleman thanked him and they went down. Old Invernacree, evidently just come into the house, was standing in the hall.

'I was out, and have but this moment heard of your mishap, sir,' he said courteously. 'I hope your daughter is not severely hurt. Will you please to come in here?' And he opened the door of his study.

The stranger sank into a chair and rested his brow on his hands, and there was silence for a moment or two. A servant brought in brandy; Ian took it from him and advanced to the guest's elbow.

'May I pour you out a glass of eau-de-vie, Mr – sir?' he corrected himself.

'Thank you, I should be glad of it.' The traveller raised his head. 'My name is Campbell – Campbell of Cairns.'

Ian's hand shook suddenly, and he poured a little stream of brandy on to the salver which held the glass. He heard his father draw his breath sharply, and saw that, standing there, he had put a hand to the table as if to steady himself. Mr Campbell of Cairns, between past shock and present anxiety, noticed nothing; with a murmured word of thanks he drained the glass and a little colour came into his thin, hard face.

'I thank you, sir,' he said, looking up at Ian. 'When my brain is a trifle clearer . . . I have a great deal, I know, to thank you for. I think I heard the name of Stewart used. Am I right?'

'Yes, our name is Stewart, Mr Campbell,' said the old laird, standing very still and regarding him fixedly. 'Stewart of Invernacree. This is my remaining son, Ian. My firstborn fell on Drummossie Moor.'

'Like many another brave man,' murmured Mr Campbell. At that moment the door opened, and he turned his head and got up. It was Grizel.

'Madam, what news of my daughter?'

'I think, sir,' said Miss Stewart, 'that you may be easy. She has come to herself. We may expect the doctor – if he is at home – before nightfall.'

'She has come to herself? Then I will go to her,' exclaimed Mr Campbell. 'That is, unless you think it inadvisable?'

'No,' said Grizel, 'I think you might well see her for a few moments, sir, for she has asked for you and is anxious for your safety.' And on that, with a murmured apology to his host, the anxious father followed her out.

'Ian,' said old Invernacree when the door was shut, 'do you realize who that man is?'

'Yes,' answered his son very gravely. 'But even Alan in his grave would not have us refuse him and his daughter shelter.'

'No,' acquiesced the old man. He seemed to have aged ten years in the last few minutes. 'No, that is the worst of it! ... O God, give me charity!'

Once more the door opened; this time it was Jacqueline who came in, looking even prettier than usual in her excitement. 'Father, Ian, the young lady has recovered her senses! Did you pull her out of the coach, Ian – and was it running away all the while – and who are they?'

It was her father who answered the last query.

'That is the man, Jacqueline,' he said, with a deep and steady sternness, 'who commanded the Campbell militia at the battle of Culloden; and they, as you know, were the troops who shot down your brother Alan.'

2

Supper that night at Invernacree was an uncomfortable meal, at least for all the Stewarts at the board, though it was not in old Invernacree to show a grudging hospitality. As for Mr Campbell of Cairns, his anxiety for his daughter and his own recent escape from serious accident, joined to the probability that he was not himself aware that Alexander Stewart regarded him as having the blood of his eldest son upon his hands, protected him in some measure from the full realization of the prevalent malaise, though naturally he could not suppose that one of his name would ever be very welcome under the roof of a Stewart, more especially of one who had lost a son at Culloden. Whatever he perceived, however, or did not perceive, he excused himself soon after the meal and retired to bed, while the old laird withdrew with a clouded face into his own study, whither no one liked to follow him. Grizel returned to the bedside of her patient, and Ian and Jacqueline were left alone together, she to inquire of every particular of the accident, and he to deplore the strange and unfortunate chance which had thrown Campbell of Cairns and his daughter, of all people, upon their kindness.

'Not that one could hold *her* responsible for anything, Ian,' observed Jacqueline almost pleadingly. 'She can have been little more than a child when Alan was killed.'

'No, naturally not,' agreed her brother. 'Yet I wish, chiefly for our father's sake, that it had been anyone – any Campbell even – but Campbell of Cairns!'

Jacqueline sighed. She herself had been but ten years old when the Cause went down in the sleet and the wind. She remembered her brother Alan well, of course, but nine years seems a long space of time to a girl not yet twenty. Ian had never replaced Alan in her father's heart – she knew that – but he had in hers.

'She is very beautiful, this Miss Campbell,' she remarked after a moment.

'Is she?' asked Ian indifferently. 'I had not time to observe it.'

He was not speaking the truth. If there had not indeed been time in the overturned coach to see whether the huddled girl he had lifted out were plain or comely, he had not helped to carry Miss Campbell all the way to Invernacree without observing the face upon which he had looked during that slow transit. And even viewed upside down, even with a handkerchief bound about the forehead and half obscuring the beautiful pencilling of the eyebrows, that face was one which a man would not willingly take his eyes from. Young Invernacree, therefore, was quite aware that the lady of the coach was lovely; and quite unmoved by the fact. She was a Campbell.

The invalid, reported Grizel next morning at breakfast, had passed a very fair night; the headache from which she had suffered yesterday was gone, nor was the slight cut on her forehead troubling her. But the doctor had decreed last night that she was not to leave her bed for a couple of days, nor to take her departure from Invernacree for a week or more.

'We shall be very pleased, shall we not, Grizel, to keep the young lady for as long as it suits her to remain?' said the laird at breakfast, with no trace of hostility in his tone. Nor was the speech due to the presence of the young lady's parent, since Mr Campbell was breakfasting in his own room.

'But what about her father, sir?' queried Ian.

Invernacree's fine old face grew dark. 'God forbid that I should turn even the slayer of my son from my door when he is in need of succour. Since Campbell of Cairns has broken bread beneath my roof, I cannot hasten his departure, but I can hope that he will soon take it of his own motion, for last night I seemed to see Alan's wraith behind him at every turn.'

'If Mr Campbell had shot poor Alan with his own hand our father could not feel it more acutely,' observed Grizel with a troubled face a little later, when she found herself alone with her half-brother and sister. 'I cannot quite so regard the matter; it was the fortune of war that he and not another should have commanded the Campbell militia and thus – '

'Was it the fortune of war which made the Campbells prostitute themselves to the service of the Hanoverian?' demanded

Ian, suddenly fierce. 'No, it was another kind of fortune, that which they have always known where to find – the profitable, the winning side in every quarrel!'

'My sorrow!' sighed Grizel. 'I know that as well as you, Ian. Yet Cairns seems a decent man enough, and it's likely has regrets now.'

'Grizel is over douce,' pronounced Jacqueline, twining her arm in her brother's. 'For my part, I shall be very glad when Mr Campbell is gone, but I have no desire to see his daughter drive away. She has a face like ... like moonlight on the loch yonder.'

'Your enthusiasm has betrayed you into a very unsuitable metaphor,' said Ian coldly, and somehow his arm disengaged itself from the girl's. 'I cannot but feel with my father in this matter, and wish them both gone as soon as may be.'

And half of Ian's inhospitable wish found itself fulfilled with more promptitude than he had dared to hope. Whether Mr Campbell made the urgent business of which he spoke an excuse, or whether it really was as pressing as he asserted, at any rate he alleged himself bound to depart next morning. He was well satisfied with his daughter's condition, and ready to leave her behind under Miss Stewart's care with full confidence and, as he added with much feeling, with deep gratitude. He departed in a postchaise, his coach, though now fished up from its ignominious position on the shore of Loch Linnhe, being still lamentably wet and muddy and having a broken window.

His host omitted no courtesy at his departure, but the courtesy was stern and strained, and Campbell of Cairns' own leave-taking was not free from embarrassment. He, or one of his sons, was, however, to return to fetch his daughter in about a week's time.

Chapter 5

WOULD SHE WERE GONE!

THE sun was coming into the bedroom, and Olivia Campbell, lying on her couch near the window, watched it with delight – the sun and the sweet air from the hills. Their presence seemed to dispel the last traces of that haunting memory of darkness and confinement which had hovered over her during the last few days. It had quite lifted now, and she could laugh at it, and say, as she had said to kind Miss Stewart, that nothing less romantic or more ridiculous could happen to any girl than the accident which had brought her to Invernacree. To be imprisoned in an overturned coach with the possibility of being drowned, before she could be extricated, in six inches or so of loch water! And how *had* she been extricated – how had Mr Ian Stewart, the actual rescuer, as she had heard from her father – how had this agile young man contrived to extract her from the bottom of her prison without trampling upon her?

Grizel indeed scarcely knew, for her brother had not been expansive on the subject; she could only be thankful that her patient had been extracted. 'You were in real danger, dear Miss Campbell, seeing that you were unconscious.' 'But in such a ludicrous kind of danger,' Olivia had responded, laughing. 'Not, indeed, that I wish to underrate your brother's skill in getting me out of it!'

Olivia had laughed a good deal in her two and twenty years of life, for she had a happy disposition and a keen sense of the ridiculous. People said that her widowed father loved her, his only daughter, better than any of his four tall sons, whom, like most men, young or old, she could generally charm into doing what she wanted. Wilful she was, more than a little, but at the core of too fine a temper to misuse her power very seriously, and exercising it much too spontaneously to be vain of it. So loth was her father to part with her that, though she had arrived sometime ago at full marriageable age, he neither made plans for a match nor smiled on those gentlemen who were so willing to make the plans for themselves. Olivia did not smile upon them either with any permanency, being wont to say that the only man who always pleased her was that friend of her father's, Mr Maitland of Strathmory, whom she had known from a child. But she was safe in saying that, for there were three very solid obstacles in the way of her ever uniting herself to that kind and personable gentleman – he was forty-five at least, was a Jacobite, and had a living if bedridden wife, not to speak of a son, just grown to manhood. Olivia called him God-father, though he had no right to that title, nor indeed any kind of relationship with her. Just occasionally it had occurred to her to wonder how Mr Maitland, holding such very different politi-cal views from her father – having, in fact, been 'out' in the Forty-five, could be on such friendly terms with him. But it was quite a couple of years now since he had paid them a visit at Cairns.

It was perhaps not surprising that she should suddenly think of her Jacobite friend, here, in a Jacobite, even an ultra-Jaco-bite, household. Before the Rising, so she had been told, re-lations between the Whigs and the adherents of the White Rose had been much easier, a case of live and let live; but the events of 1745 and 1746 had wiped out that tolerance and hardened the line of cleavage. And Olivia knew, of course, that, as a field officer commanding at Culloden, her father could not be wel-come in a house whose men had certainly fought on the op-posite side. That its eldest son had fallen there she fortunately did not know. But no trace of political animosity had coloured the kindness and care of the two Miss Stewarts, and it was only when she looked at the very unflattering oil painting of the ill-fated 'Pretender's son' over her mantelpiece that Olivia remem-bered where she was.

She glanced round the bedroom now in search of something to occupy her. It was not often that she was left thus alone.

711

Grizel had lent her a book, but she was tired of reading – tired, too, of lying on this couch, when she felt perfectly well. She slipped off it and went and sat down by the open window.

How delicious the air was! And, absurd though she might find her adventure, it had not been free from genuine peril. That rocking, swaying coach ... Yes, indeed there had been a possibility that she might not now be breathing this air, feeling the warm sunlight on her throat, looking at those distant blue and purple mountains ... nor watching with pleased eyes the dove which suddenly alighted on the sill outside and began to walk about there.

It was this bird which induced Olivia to lean out. 'You pretty creature!' she said impulsively, and put forth a cautious hand, hoping to stroke its sleek neck. But, though the pet dove was indifferent to her presence just inside the window, the stretching out of that strange hand alarmed it, and it flew off. Olivia leant out still farther to see where it had gone to, and thus became aware of a young man almost immediately below her, who was engaged in fastening up against the wall of the house a detached spray of something or other. And this young man, though his face was a little turned upwards, did not see her. His brow wore a slight frown as he worked, and between his lips was a piece of twine.

And so Olivia looked down upon her rescuer's countenance as he had looked upon hers – though not in this case exactly upside down nor for nearly so long a period. In fact it was only for a moment or so. Some instinct caused Ian to look up, and he instantly beheld Miss Campbell gazing down upon him. A blush sprang into the lady's cheek, and she made a movement to withdraw. Ian stepped backwards; he could not doff his hat, since he was already bareheaded. But he removed the string from his mouth, bowed, and said rather formally:

'Good morning, madam. I am glad to see you recovered.'

'I ... I was trying to stroke that dove,' said Olivia, with a natural idea of accounting for her situation at the window. 'But it flew away.' (It was to be hoped that Mr Stewart did not know the number of seconds which had elapsed since its flight, but he probably did.) 'I think I see it in the cedar trees yonder.'

'My sister Jacqueline could catch it for you,' Ian assured her gravely. 'It will not come to me. I will find her.'

'No, no, Mr Stewart,' said Olivia in haste. 'I do not want the bird. I want ... when shall I have the opportunity of thanking you for what you did for me?'

'Thanking me!' exclaimed the young man, looking up at her more fully. 'Miss Campbell, you have nothing to thank me for: I fear my sisters have been exaggerating a very simple and natural action, and one that in no way warrants gratitude.'

'But I think differently,' replied Miss Campbell in a soft voice – she had at all times a very pleasing one. And from the window she gave young Invernacree a glimpse of the charm of her smile, which, though he knew it not, was reported in the neighbourhood of Cairns – and further than that – to have the power to coax a man's heart out of his breast. Then she withdrew from the window rather suddenly, for Grizel had just come into the room behind her.

'I have been talking to your brother, in the most romantical fashion, out of the window,' confessed Olivia, laughing, 'When, dear Miss Stewart, will you allow me to go downstairs and thank him in proper form for his rescue of me?'

Grizel looked at her standing there. For a Campbell, she was dark; tall and of a beautiful shape, and held herself like a princess. She wore on her simple grey gown a plain muslin kerchief; but the gown had little green paniers too. Good, homely Grizel thought it very pretty. She smiled back.

'The doctor said that you might leave your room on the third day. Tomorrow, then, if you sleep well tonight.'

Olivia Campbell slept well enough when the time came. Strange to say, Mr Stewart the younger did not. The recollection of a glance, a smile, sent down from a window, had been with him all the rest of the day, and he resented the impression which he could not shake off. There she had stood in that grey gown, grey like the dove's plumage – but she did not at all remind him of a dove – and had given him that smile which seemed to smite down from the window into his very vitals.

713

'The girl's a finished coquette!' he said indignantly to himself. 'Thank God she will soon be gone!'

But, saints above, she was lovely – lovely beyond a dream! Yet he did not thank God for that.

Miss Campbell's leaving her room next day was something of an event. Alexander Stewart, forewarned of her approach, met her at the foot of the stairs, made the most paternal inquiries after her health, and gave her his arm to the drawing-room, where Jacqueline awaited her with a cordial, and an English spaniel which she had never seen before – it was Ian's – greeted her, after the manner of its kind, as a dear and seldom-seen friend.

After a little while dinner was announced. The spaniel's owner came into the dining-room and duly kissed her hand. She sat upon her host's right, Grizel upon his left, young Invernacree at the bottom of the table. The light from the window was behind him, and Olivia observed how well his head was set upon his shoulders. They ate roast muir-fowl, but the old laird had broth. The spaniel sat by her side throughout the meal, and gazed up at her with eloquent but sycophantic eyes. Young Mr Stewart did not say much. Was he shy, or sulky?

Olivia herself was neither, and Jacqueline, who already thought her the most beautiful being she should ever behold, was equally enraptured with her conversation. Even Invernacree, who was not accustomed to hearing brilliant talk from ladies, though at first a trifle mistrustful, ended by being subjugated by it too. After dinner the convalescent was allowed to take a turn in the garden, the old laird with his stick on one side, Jacqueline on the other, Grizel and Ian more or less in attendance. Miss Campbell was delighted with the view over Loch Linnhe, and asked the names of all the mountains she could see. Ian had to supply the names of some which his father's old eyes could not quite distinguish; he did so with a polite readiness, but nothing more. But the old man was pleased with her enthusiasm for Appin, and forgot what blood it was which coursed through the veins of the little hand lying so lightly upon his arm. He was sorry to deliver her over to his eldest daughter, who then bore her off to her bedchamber again.

Without Miss Campbell's presence, something seemed lacking at supper that night; old Invernacree went so far as to put the lack into words. Ian neither agreed nor dissented; and his spaniel lay heavily on his feet under the table. But his light burnt late that night, and he read himself almost into a state of stupor before he ventured to get into bed.

2

It is true that, in consequence of this precaution, Ian slept; but he woke early. Only three days more, however, and he would no longer be forced to look at that pale, sparkling face, that mouth with the curve which took his breath away, the arch of these slender eyebrows, black as a raven's feather, nor the wonderful grey eyes beneath them. She would be gone from Invernacree for ever, and this haunting fear – it was hardly less – would ebb back from his heart, and all would be as before .. ; Yes, and he could go and begin his wooing of Maclean of Garroch's second daughter.

The young man groaned, and flung himself out of bed. He must be bewitched. He plunged his face into cold water, threw on his clothes, and, early as it was, went out of the sleeping house and down to the edge of the loch with some idea of having a swim. But when he was there the intention abandoned him, and he walked for a long time to and fro on the pebbles, his hands clutched behind him. The tide was coming up Loch Linnhe, sucking gently sideways over the stones, little patches of mist were wreathing away before the sun, a gull or two was crying, and all at once, quite near the shore, Ian was aware of a dark, sleek, rounded head in the water – a young seal's. And into his mind sprang a medley of seal legends which as a child he had drunk in from his nurse, a woman of the Outer Isles, where seals were human creatures under spells, princes and princesses, the children of the King of Lochlann, who yet married sometimes with ordinary mortals; for if a man saw a seal-woman in her shape as she truly was (and three times a year she must assume it) he went mad for love of her, Ian stopped his pacing and threw a stone at the sleek head, which vanished instantly.

Ian was late for breakfast, an offence in the laird's eyes. Apologizing, he said that he had gone down to the loch betimes to have a swim, and had walked farther than he had realized. He forgot to add that he had not fulfilled his intention, so that Jacqueline was caused to wonder why his neatly tied-back hair was so evidently bone dry. She thought he looked rather strange, almost ill, but she knew better than to remark upon this.

After breakfast Ian went off to one of the farms. As he returned through the garden he saw Miss Campbell sitting in a chair, which had apparently been brought out for that purpose, by some old stone balustrading, whence there was a good view down over the loch. He had to pass near her to reach the house, to pass near or to turn back altogether; and this latter he could have done without being seen, for she was not looking his way. But he did not. It was uncouth, uncivil, to avoid her; was a Stewart to show himself lacking in breeding, and before a Campbell? He approached.

Olivia heard his step, and turned her beautiful head – like a lily on its stalk, the young man was thinking even then.

'Good morning, Mr Stewart. I am a shocking late riser, whereas you, no doubt, have been about much earlier.'

He had, indeed, and she was the cause of it. Ian said, 'You are under the doctor's orders, Miss Campbell. I hope he would not disapprove of your sitting in the open air on such a morning.'

'I regard myself,' returned Miss Campbell cheerfully, 'as now emancipated from the doctor's care. And your kindest and best of sisters, Mr Stewart, in whose judgement I have the greatest faith, permits it. I even have a book to read while she and Miss Jacqueline are about their household duties, so you see that I intend remaining here for some time.'

'Nevertheless, I fear that we shall have rain before long,' said

716

Ian doubtfully, looking westwards at the mountains beyond the loch.

'Let us not anticipate calamity,' answered Olivia gaily. 'Yet, since you are looking in that direction, Mr Stewart, will you not be my dominie, and rehearse me the names of the peaks over yonder which I tried to learn yesterday. I desire to know if I remember them aright.' She looked up and sent him a little smile, like a flower only half unfolded; but the same shaft sped through the young man again, and, tingling as though from some actual physical impact, he sat down upon the balustrade beside her and obeyed.

From that he found himself talking of the region in general. Miss Campbell spoke of the peaks of Jura, an island which Ian did not know. Her brothers, she said, had climbed some of those heights; no doubt Mr Stewart was familiar in the same way with some of the crests at which they were looking. 'If I were not a woman,' she said, pointing over the loch, 'I should like to stand on that summit yonder. Have you ever stood there, Mr Stewart?'

'No, never,' confessed Ian. 'I have not often been on the farther side of Loch Linnhe. But I think my brother Alan once – ' He pulled himself up, his colour changing, then went on rather lamely, 'My brother Alan once climbed Ben Mheon.'

'Oh, I did not know you had a brother.'

'Nor have I . . . now,' said Ian, looking away. 'He is dead.'

'Indeed, I am sorry,' came Olivia Campbell's voice after a moment, with real sympathy in its soft tones. 'Recently?'

Ian had a savage longing to go on, 'And it is your father who is responsible for his death,' not exactly from a desire to shock and wound the girl beside him, but to remind himself that he had no business to sit here talking idly with Campbell of Cairns' daughter because she had smiled at him. Yet, instead of flinging that reproach at her he found himself, to his surprise, bestowing something of a confidence.

'No, not recently. Nine years ago. He was my elder – the heir, and my father's darling. If he had lived – ' Again he broke off. Often and often as he had thought how different things would have been for him if Alan were not lying with all the dead of the clan in the great grave on Culloden Moor, there came at the moment a new realization of what the difference might have been, so startling that he got up from the balustrade. The thought was mad, traitorous! Even had he been still the younger son . . .

'The rain will really be here in a moment or two,' he said in a strained voice. 'It is sweeping fast over Loch Linnhe. Indeed you should go indoors – allow me to carry your shawl.'

'Mr Stewart,' said Olivia, looking up at him with compassionate eyes, I regret very much if I have trespassed upon memories – '

'No, no!' he broke in. 'You have done nothing . . . And here comes Grizel to hasten you. Pray take my arm.'

He offered it, catching up her wraps with the other hand, as Grizel came running over the grass at the first drops of the shower.

That evening Miss Campbell was with them until eight o'clock, but no longer, so that, as yesterday, supper seemed a dullish meal. And yet Ian had a shamed sense of safety. When he could not see the King of Lochlann's daughter he could not, surely, be bewitched by her.

But when he went to bed he found this a most fallacious doctrine. He was in the toils of something which he shrank from putting a name to. Was it only a little more than a week ago, when Ewen Cameron was here, that he had sat at this window and reflected how rapture had passed him by, and he must make a mere humdrum marriage? *This* was not rapture, God knew – it was enslavement, sorcery . . . and all to no purpose. He must forget the spell-weaver as fast as possible, for she could never be his wife.

He descended next morning, after a wretched night, to find Miss Campbell at breakfast with the rest of his family. During the meal it transpired that she had already heard that one of her brothers was coming to fetch her away the day after tomorrow. Lamentations from Grizel and Jacqueline, and polite regrets from the old laird. Ian alone said nothing. What was he to say, he who was so much relieved at the idea?

718

But was he relieved?

At any rate, since Miss Campbell was leaving so soon, he might safely show her some civility. He thought of offering to accompany her and Jacqueline to some spot whence they would have a good prospect, but the morning, which early had been fine, deteriorated with that blighting rapidity characteristic of the Western Highlands, and by the afternoon the steady drizzle had become torrents of rain, loch and mountains were blotted out, and Grizel had a fire burning in the drawing-room.

And there, about four o'clock, Ian somehow found himself playing chess with their guest, while Jacqueline looked on and Grizel sewed at a little distance. Miss Campbell proved to be a moderately good player; Ian was usually something more than that. Yet since, against his will, he paid more attention to the fair hand which moved the pieces than to the pieces themselves, it was not wonderful that in the end he was badly beaten.

'I verily believe,' said Olivia laughingly to Jacqueline, 'that your brother has allowed himself to be defeated out of chivalry. Else he could never have overlooked the disgraceful blunder which I made some twenty minutes ago.'

'I thought you were laying a trap for me,' retorted Ian with a smile. 'But indeed I have no pretensions to being a great chess player. I but learnt in order to please my father.'

'And I to tease mine,' averred Olivia. 'He used to say that all women played chess (when they played at all) without judgement, and I thought to disprove it.'

'I am sure,' said Jacqueline admiringly, 'that he cannot say so now!'

Miss Campbell laughed her low, captivating laugh. 'Now he says that they play without *true* judgement, so I have not done much to convert him from his opinion!'

And for a moment there was merriment round the fire. The rain lashing against the windows only made this warm, cheerful seclusion the more desirable, in the pleasant and homely room with the faded carpet whose red and yellow roses Ian could remember as long as he remembered anything, except perhaps the twin ivory elephants which his grandfather had brought, so he had always understood, from the mysterious land of China itself. He could see them now in the cabinet behind Miss Campbell's head, as he sat opposite her in her gown of green silk with a silver shine in its folds. All these years, and the familiar old room had never known its proud destiny – to enclose *her*; nor the battered old knights and castles theirs – to be touched by those beautiful fingers ... The spell snapped, as like a bitter, searing wind there blew into Ian's soul the remembrance of the identity of the father at whose prejudices the girl here by the hearth was gently laughing, and he and his sisters with her – the man of that greatly hated race whose action had cut off their brother Alan from that very fireside, to lie for ever out in the cold and the rain. With darkening eyes he rose from his seat opposite her, and to give some colour to the movement, threw another log on to the fire. Perhaps the chill which had swept over his spirit, as well as the fact that he was thinking of something else, was the reason why he threw on so many. The flames shot up hot and crackling.

'Why, Ian,' said Grizel in surprise, 'you'll roast us all! I am sure Miss Campbell, near the fire as she is, will be incommoded by such a blaze.'

'I beg your pardon,' said her brother mechanically, glancing round for a second at the guest. 'I was not thinking what I was about.' No more did he seem to be thinking of it now, when he remedied his absentmindedness by taking hold of the last log which he had thrown on and pulling it off again, not without cost to himself.

'Mr Stewart, did you not burn your hand then?' exclaimed Olivia Campbell, leaning forwards. 'Oh, why did you not leave that log where it was!'

'It had not caught fire,' replied Ian carelessly, pointing with his left hand to the piece of birch. The right was already thrust deep into his pocket, for, though the log in question was not alight, the flame through which he had plunged that member had licked his wrist and scorched his sleeve.

'Yes, but something has caught fire,' said Grizel, putting down her work. 'I can smell singeing. Ian, how could you be so foolish! Let me see what you have done to yourself!'

'Nonsense,' said her brother. ''Tis only my sleeve. I felt nothing.' He came and resumed his place at the little table opposite Olivia. 'Miss Campbell, will you allow me the opportunity of my revenge, or am I too unworthy a foe?'

But Miss Campbell seemed in distress ... and how lovely in it! 'Mr Stewart, I implore you to allow your sister to look at your hand!' And as Ian, shaking his head with a smile, and saying again that it was nothing, began to replace his pieces on the board with his left hand, she leant over and said in a pleading tone, 'Do not refuse me this favour!'

Ian set his king firmly where his queen should have stood. What a fool he had been to cause all this pother – and, incidentally, this pain to himself! His wrist was smarting like hell. But he answered with polite nonchalance, 'When we have had our game, Miss Campbell, with pleasure.'

'Jacqueline,' said Grizel, rising from her chair, 'pray go up to the cupboard in my room and bring what I have there in readiness for burns. -- If you will not seek a leech, Ian, the leech must e'en come to you.'

'No doubt,' observed Ian with a resigned air, as Jacqueline fled from the room. 'You have had experience, Miss Campbell, of what it is to fall into the clutches of a female Aesculapius. If you want to make Grizel happy, contrive to scratch yourself, however slightly. I have sometimes done it with that object, when I was a boy.'

He continued to arrange his side of the chessboard, still with his king and queen reversed; but Olivia made no effort to set hers. He *had* burnt himself, she could tell. How obstinate and crazy and generally incalculable men could be!

Miss Stewart seemed to share this unspoken opinion. 'I have no patience with you!' she declared, suddenly coming and standing over her brother, and looking as if a very little more would cause her to withdraw his other hand from its seclusion in his coat pocket. 'And what is that child about? I suppose I must needs go myself.' She went, and the chess players were left alone.

721

'You have not set your pieces, I see, Miss Campbell,' observed Ian in a business-like tone. 'Or is it that you will not play with me again?'

'I certainly cannot play with you until you have had your hand dressed,' said Olivia gravely.

'But I can make the moves equally well with my left. Or, for the matter of that, and to prove to you that it is unhurt, with my right.' And he plucked his other hand out of his pocket and laid it in the table by the chessboard. 'You see, all this to-do is about nothing, but, as I say, Grizel dearly loves – '

He got no further. Two swift, cool hands had his imprisoned as it lay there, and fingers, with incredible gentleness in their touch, were pushing the scorched cuff away from his red and blistered wrist. 'Mr Stewart, look at that!' said an accusing voice. 'Now, was it worth it!'

('If you will keep your fingers there, yes, it was worth it, a thousand times worth!') thought Ian. They were snowflakes ... snowdrops ... and what were the grey eyes – soft now, not sparkling – which looked at him so reproachfully? It was not the pain of the burn which made his head swim as he ventured to meet them, and the chessmen dance wildly for a second or two in the firelight. *Ah, beautiful and kind, and for ever impossible to love, you shall not know that it is my heart which you have between those healing hands of yours!*

'... But you see how little damage has been done,' he said, and knew not how dazedly he spoke. He tried to summon up resolution to draw his hand away. And there was a moment's silence; only the fire crackled, and, without, the wind flung itself against the glass. Then Grizel came in, and Jacqueline after her.

Ian rose to his feet at once. He did not intend any ministrations to be carried out in here. 'I'll come with you as meek as a sheep,' he said quickly, 'if Miss Campbell will but excuse me. Jacqueline, will you not stay with our guest?' And he followed his elder sister out.

'Do you think my brother's hand is much burnt, Miss Campbell?' asked Jacqueline a little anxiously.

Olivia was thoughtfully fingering a chessman. 'It was not his hand; it was his wrist. I wish he had not been so rash. If I may say so, one would not have expected it of him.'

'But one is never quite sure what Ian may not do,' explained Jacqueline, sitting down in Ian's place. 'He appears so composed, and then suddenly he is not composed. – But when I say that one is not sure what he may not do, pray do not think I mean that he would ever do anything dishonourable – that he would, for instance, ever forsake a friend.'

'I hope we should none of us do that,' said Miss Campbell.

'No, indeed! Yet I meant something more than that ... I do not know how to put it.'

'You mean perhaps, Miss Stewart, that he would never forsake a cause,' suggested Olivia, leaning forward with her elbows on the table. 'I do not forget that you are all Jacobites. – Perhaps you mean also that he would never forgive an enemy?'

'I don't know,' said little Jacqueline, looking troubled. 'We ought all to forgive our enemies, ought we not? – But perhaps I do mean that.'

'Yet I hope Mr Stewart will forgive me for that burn,' said Olivia with a whimsical little smile. 'You must intercede for me, Miss Jacqueline!'

'Oh, dear Miss Campbell, the burn was Grizel's fault, I think, not yours!'

'Then I hope he will forgive me for having called attention to the injury, for it was undoubtedly I who did that in the first place, and he was not best pleased, I think.'

'Men,' pronounced nineteen-year-old Jacqueline with a great air of experience, 'are very strange creatures in that respect. For if you neglect to notice their injuries they do not like that neither.'

'In short,' said Olivia laughing, 'we women are the only sensible sex. (Yet men say that *we* are not over faithful to our friends.) Come, let us put away the chessmen, for something tells me that your brother will not come back, although he challenged me to another game.'

And in this prediction Miss Campbell found herself perfectly correct.

Chapter 6

THE FIELD OF DAISIES

IF Ian slept ill that night he could, and did, attribute it to the
smart of his burnt wrist. But he knew in his heart that that was
not the cause.

The last day of Miss Campbell's sojourn at Invernacree was
going, he saw, to be gloriously fine. The last day; yes, tomorrow would see her leave his father's roof for ever. If,
therefore, he could only get safely through today, all would be
well. The best thing would be to invent some excuse which
would keep him out of doors most of the time, and at a distance; and after some casting about he succeeded.

But he had forgotten that his father had appointed this morning for going into the half-yearly accounts of the estate with
him, and this there was no escaping. All morning Ian added,
subtracted, verified and discussed; but in this unromantic pursuit he had less time to think of Miss Campbell, and at all events
could not be in her company. His arithmetic, however, was not
beyond reproach. At the end of their joint computations the
laird began to talk of the sum which he intended in the future to
apportion to his son when he married, for though he would not
at first have a separate establishment he would need more
money, and with economy Invernacree thought that he could
allow him this.

Ian thanked him in a voice which even to himself sounded
choked, and his father asked if by ill-chance he had taken a
fever of cold, as well as burning his hand so foolishly yesterday
(for inquiries at supper, not to speak of the presence of a bandage, had disclosed that fact to Mr Stewart; and in truth Ian
had not found writing too pleasant this morning). The young
man repudiated this suggestion.

'Indeed, I hope you are not indisposed,' said Invernacree, 'for it is so fine a day that I think a row upon the loch this afternoon might benefit as well as interest Miss Campbell, and Grizel thinks so too.'

'Dougal Livingstone and his brother are both available,' replied his son.

'I think,' pronounced the laird, 'that it would show more courtesy if you were to row Miss Campbell and your sisters yourself. Or at least (if the consequence of your folly last night incapacitates you) that you should accompany them.'

'Since when,' asked Ian, 'have you laid store, sir, by showing courtesy to a Campbell?'

Displeasure sat upon the old man's brow. 'One does not war with women, Ian. I cannot think that I have ever trained you in such a notion. And Miss Campbell is our guest.'

She has bewitched you, too, thought Ian. Aloud he said submissively, 'No, sir, you are in the right of it. I shall be pleased to row Miss Campbell and my sisters on the loch this afternoon.'

And even as he said it he knew that what he desired was to row Miss Campbell without his sisters. He caught his breath. But that could never be . . . mercifully.

'By the way,' said his father, reverting to business, 'you will have to go to Glasgow for me in a few weeks' time to see Buchanan about that affair I spoke of, and one or two others. I am too old for the journey now. – Where is that paper of memoranda I had under my hand a moment since?'

2

Dougal Livingstone and his brother were the rowers after all, and Ian, steering, was unable therefore to feast his miserable eyes upon the King of Lochlann's daughter, where she sat beside him in the stern, as well as he could have done had he faced her on a thwart. On the other hand she was so close to him that his miserable body was only too conscious of the fact.

The boat slipped over the hardly rippled lock, stained in the distance by the reflected mountains with hues that had vanished when the spot was reached, leaving the water as clear and colourless as before. Jacqueline chattered, the rowers at Olivia's request sang a *iorram*, Grizel told legends of this place and that. All illusion, like this tormenting nearness on the other side of the helm – like the mirage on the water, pretence of what was not and could never be ... When he moved the tiller from him his hand all but brushed her; when a stray whisper of breeze caught a ribbon of hers it sent it across his face or knee ...

'Ian,' said Jacqueline, suddenly leaning forwards and pointing, 'why should we not land on Eilean Soa and show Miss Campbell the cairn where the ancient king was buried with his treasure—'

Land, and be released from this torturing and intoxicating proximity? No ... yes ... which?

His decision was not awaited. 'Oh, let us land!' cried Olivia. 'Of all things I love a buried treasure!'

' 'Tis not there now,' observed the practical Grizel.

'We need not go round the point to the flat shore,' pursued Jacqueline. 'You know the place this side, with the solitary pine tree. I have often got ashore there.'

'It might be difficult for Miss Campbell,' said her brother doubtfully.

'Why, Mr Stewart, are you suggesting that I am less nimble than your sister!' cried the guest. 'I am no town lady, and I insist on being put ashore where Miss Jacqueline is accustomed to land.'

Ian yielded, and steered for the nearer side of the island, since to anyone young the place presented no difficulty. A slight spring up to an embedded piece of granite and a tiny scramble thereafter, aided by the tough stems of the tall island heather, and one was there. He got out, and, knee-deep in the heather a little above her, assisted Miss Campbell, half hoping that she would slip, so that he could catch her; but she showed no sign of such a thing.

It was Ian who slipped, or nearly, though it was not his fault.

For, having put one foot on the lump of granite to extend a hand to Grizel in the boat below, he felt the stone, to his astonishment, beginning to give beneath him, and sprang back, clutching the heather, just in time to watch it slowly leave its place, slide down, and disappear sedately into the water.

'I had no notion that I was so heavy!' called Olivia's laughing voice from above him. 'I am glad you did not follow it, Mr Stewart!'

'So am I,' observed Grizel from the boat. 'But, Ian, can we land here now?'

'You cannot,' replied her brother. 'Go round the point to the beach. Miss Campbell and I will walk across and meet you there.'

There was nothing else to be done, so the boat pushed off again and Ian was left alone with Olivia Campbell – alone, though but for a few minutes, in a world apart. His desire was equally to hasten to the other side of the little island . . . and to loiter here; not to speak or listen to her . . . and to detain her for hours. In this state of mind he preceded her from the landing-place, mechanically holding back a bramble or a branch when necessary, but really not conscious of what he was walking on, grass, rock or heather – till all at once he heard her cry:

'Oh, Mr Stewart, how beautiful . . . and how very unexpected!'

And because she had stopped, he stopped too, and found that they were both in a little abandoned meadow full of moondaisies, all swaying and nodding towards them in welcome. But in a few minutes the boat would have rounded the little green headland on their left, and he would never be alone with her again . . . thank God, thank God!

And was that why he took her hand in a cold, unsteady clasp, and without a word raised it to his lips and kissed the palm of it with a long, forsaken kiss? The touch of her fingers was like cool well-water to the burning lips of fever. She did not pull them away. But Ian dropped her hand, and stood looking at her among the knee-high daisies of Eilean Soa so wildly, so desperately, that for a second Olivia Campbell all but recoiled. She

727

did not, however; she said gently. 'The sun is very hot, Mr Stewart; will you not put on your hat?'

'Do you think I have sunstroke?' Ian spoke so low that she could scarcely catch the words. 'You know it is not that! ... You are going away tomorrow?'

'Yes,' answered Olivia gravely. 'Tomorrow, when my brother comes for me.' There was pity in her beautiful eyes; that made it harder still. 'I did not mean to do this to you– indeed I did not! ... There is the boat coming to shore, I will wait here.'

He still looked at her, for as long as it took a tiny breeze to run from side to side over the daisy heads and set them quivering. Then he turned, and strode through the flowers towards the shore.

But Olivia stood without moving, pressing her hands tightly together. No, indeed she had not meant to do this! And how had she done it – she had seen him so little, talked with him so seldom! In vain to ask that question of the thousand flower-faces in their white and golden dance; if they knew they would not tell her.

'Oh dear,' said Olivia, 'I *wish* it had not happened!'

And this was strange, for conquests were not distasteful to her.

But Ian continued to stride on, through a tangle of grasses, to the flat strand where the boat had already grounded.

'You have left Miss Campbell behind, I see,' observed Jacqueline as she sprang to land. 'Whatever can those flowers be among which she is standing?'

'I do now know,' said Ian. 'Are there any flowers?'

'Dear brother, you must be blind! One can see them from here – hundreds of them!' And she ran off.

Ian helped his elder sister out. 'If you will forgive me,' he said in a low voice, 'I will stay here by the boat while you go to the cairn with Miss Campbell. I ... my burnt wrist is paining me somewhat; I should be poor company.'

'Dear Ian ...' said Grizel, looking at him in perturbation. He was so oddly pale beneath his sunburn. 'Shall I stay with you? Why should your wrist ...'

'Because I wrenched it,' he lied, 'when that stone gave way.

728

The pain will go off in a little, but I think I will stay here. Go after Jacqueline and explain.'

She looked at him again dubiously and obeyed; and Ian, after a careless word or two to the rowers, walked to a rock a little way off, sat down there and was very still. If only he could have left the island, and gone home by himself. But he could not take the boat and abandon the ladies, even for a time; and though the swim to land was not beyond his powers it would have seemed the most extraordinary proceeding, calling for investigation, and above all things he wished no one of his family to know what had befallen him.

For there could be no doubt of it – he loved Olivia Campbell to distraction, and fight against the avowal of that passion as he had done, he was glad in his heart that she knew it. He thought not to have betrayed his love, because of the long and bitter racial feud almost as much as because of the blood which cried from the ground between them, but she was too generous, too noble, to make of that avowal a subject for triumph or for mockery. She might soon forget his mad and wordless confession – he hoped she would – but she would never misuse it.

And now, a supreme effort, it only remained during the homewards voyage to behave as naturally as he could, and to lay any blame for his recent defection upon yesterday's now fortunate injury. Olivia, in her divine kindness and comprehension, would support him in that pretence.

Even if the young man were already attributing to the enchantress all sorts of noble qualities of whose existence he could not possibly have been aware, he was right as far as the homewards voyage was concerned. Miss Campbell made it as easy for him as she could, contriving somehow to change places with Grizel so that the latter, and not she, sat next the tiller; and encouraging Jacqueline to talk, to tell her again, for instance, about the empty cairn and what it had once contained.

'But the burial chamber was so small,' she objected at one point. 'I should have thought a king would have been taller! Were they dwarfs in those days?'

'It was only the burnt bones of the king – or his ashes, I

729

forget which – that they found,' explained Jacqueline, looking a little surprised, for she had distinctly heard Grizel already informing the visitor of this fact. 'Isn't that so, Ian? – Ian, what are you dreaming about there?'

'You were talking of ancient kings,' answered her brother slowly, his eyes fixed on the point for which he was steering, 'and I was thinking of one, that is all. Yes, I believe that nothing but ashes was found in the cairn. None of us, after all, kings or king's daughters, can leave behind more of ourselves than that.'

'What a horrid speech!' cried Jacqueline; and Grizel, also disliking the macabre trend which he had given to the conversation, observed dryly, 'You certainly made an effort to reduce yourself to that condition yesterday evening,' and began to talk about the prospects of a fine sunset. And at last, as all ordeals must, the voyage came to an end.

A surprise awaited them all at Invernacree, where they were informed that Miss Campbell's brother had already arrived, in order to be able to make an early start with his sister next morning. He had come to the house to pay his respects, finding no one, not even the laird himself, at home, and had, the domestic understood, taken up his quarters at the tiny inn down by the loch.

'But Mr Campbell must not remain there!' exclaimed Grizel on hearing this news. 'Ian shall go and bid him come up to the house for the night – will you not, Ian?'

Without waiting to find his father Ian went off. He had no desire at all for the company of a male Campbell, and his father, he was sure, would have still less; yet he knew that Invernacree would not be satisfied to leave the traveller to the mercies of the inn, more especially when his sister was already staying beneath his roof. And after all, thought the young man, nothing mattered very much tonight. His outburst had by now numbed him; he felt nothing. Tomorrow the world would come to an end for him ... if it had not already done so over there on Eilean Soa among the daisies.

He found at the inn Mr Colin Campbell, a tall, fair young man of about his own age, who at first refused to put the laird of Invernacree to the trouble of receiving him for one night, and was stiff even when, unable to do anything else, he finally yielded. The two of them walked together up to the house, neither finding much to say to the other.

And through the evening, while Ian watched Olivia in a kind of dream, still numbed, but every now and again waking to a stab of pain, as though the blood was beginning to run once more in a frozen limb, it seemed to him not unfortunate, perhaps, that Colin Campbell was here, for the atmosphere was changed by it. The presence of that typical son of Clan Diarmaid seemed to draw Olivia so much further away from them, back into the circle to which she belonged; it showed things as they really were. It was better so.

She left early next morning with her brother in their father's coach, which by now had been repaired. Ian had no word alone with her. But as old Invernacree was about to hand her in she said, 'I shall never ride in this carriage again, sir, without the most grateful thoughts of what I owe to you and ... your family.'

For a moment her gaze went past him to that member of it for whom no doubt her thanks were specially intended, where he stood by Jacqueline's side, saying nothing and not, apparently, looking at anyone.

'My dear young lady,' replied the old man, with an air at once courteous and paternal, 'anything which my family has been able to do for you is their good fortune. God bless you, and may you have a better journey than the last!'

Their good fortune! Ian could have laughed out loud. If his father only knew!

Mr Colin Campbell, a little less stiff than last night, but still not at ease, got into the coach and slammed the door, the postillion chirruped to the horses, and that fatal vehicle drew away from the old white house among the oak trees. Grizel and Jacqueline stood on the steps for some time, Jacqueline waving a handkerchief, to which, as the coach turned just outside the gate, there was an answering flicker of white. But Ian had not stayed to see that.

So she was gone, the enchanted, the enchanting. Up in his own room he had only to shut his eyes, and he was back in the flowery meadow where he had kissed her hand. His heart still lay there among the daisy stems, in the place where the King of Lochlann's daughter had stood. But now that she was gone from Appin he had a half hope that it might creep back to his breast, even if it should never be the same heart again, but remain what it seemed now, as much ashes as any in the ancient tomb on Eilean Soa.

Chapter 7

AN EXPLANATION AT THE GOATS' WHEY

IN his house in the Trongate, in the pleasant and prosperous little city of Glasgow, Mr John Buchanan, Invernacree's 'doer' for nearly forty years, sat, a little more than six weeks later, on one side of a table and looked at Invernacree's son, on the other, with a smile compounded of shrewdness and benevolence, as befitted a family lawyer of long standing. He had the round legal face, not the long; it was smooth and fresh, with no trace of eyebrows remaining, and he did not wear spectacles.

'You'll find those all in order, Mr Ian,' he said, indicating the packet of documents which he had just handed over. 'Or rather the laird will. He still keeps the reins pretty closely in his own hands, I see.'

'There is, thank God, no reason why he should not,' observed Ian.

'Quite so, quite so,' agreed Mr Buchanan. 'And indeed it seems but a few years ago that you were a wee bit wean in petticoats. Yet you are twenty-five years of age now, I'm thinking.'

'Twenty-six,' said his visitor.

'D'ye hear that now, Gib?' remarked the lawyer to the large sphinx of a tabby which sat like an immense paperweight upon his table. 'Twenty-six! To think of it! And when shall I have the pleasure of drawing up your marriage contract, young man?'

'Oh, before very long, I expect,' responded Ian in as colourless a voice as he could muster. 'Then I am to tell my father that he will hear from you later on the subject of that wadset?'

'If you please. But, speaking of your prospective marriage, my dear young gentleman, who is the fortunate lady to be?'

733

Ian ran his hand down Gib's massive back, feeling the muscles under the fur ripple in the opposite direction at his touch. 'I have to ask her, sir, before I can tell you that ... It seems to me that I remember this cat of yours as long as I remember you.'

'I wonder does he remember you – eh, Gib, ye rascal, do ye? And to think you are twenty-six! Aye, 'tis time that ye thought of matrimony now that ye have taken poor Alan's place.'

Ian made no comment. 'I see you have a map upon the wall there,' he said. 'I shall make bold to study it for a moment, if I may.'

'Ye surely know your way home, Mr Ian?'

'Yes, I know my way home,' said the young man, getting up and going over to the map. Nevertheless he looked minutely at it, and there was something in his face as he did so which suggested that he was making calculations. 'Thank you, sir, 'twas only curiosity. Maps have ever interested me.'

He came back to the table. The cat Gib stood up, arched his back, stretched himself prodigiously, uttered a small sound and sat down again, fixing upon Ian a gaze of such apparent omniscience as almost to be perturbing. Then the topaz orbs blinked; with a twitch of the end of his tail the sage appeared to dismiss the matter from his mind, and lay solidly down again, folding his paws inward. But Ian had a momentary conviction, quite difficult to shake off, that Gib knew, if his owner did not, why he had just been studying the map.

As he walked away from Mr Buchanan's house, past the colonnades of the Trongate, with their cave-like little shops beneath, the papers entrusted to him safely inside his coat, his thoughts were busy with another paper – and that, not to mince matters, a stolen one – which lay nearer to his heart than they did, and was the sole cause of his consulting the lawyer's map just now.

About a week after Miss Olivia Campbell's departure from Invernacree, at the end of June, had come a letter from her to Grizel, which, among expressions of undying gratitude to the writer's dear Miss Stewart for her kindness and her skill, had contained the information that when the summer was a little more advanced she herself was, in deference to her father's wishes, going up into the hills of Central Perthshire to take that sovereign specific, goats' milk. 'Papa is of the opinion that my health – which is in truth perfectly sound, and never was better – would be re-established by a course of the whey. At any rate he so urges it, in order to counteract the possible effects of the coach accident, that I have not the heart to stand out against him; and so, my dear Miss Grizel, you may picture me next month up to Kilrain with my faithful Elspeth in attendance, drinking the whey as though I were some gouty old gentleman doing his annual cure. I trust there will be none of them there at the time, for they would surely think the presence of such a blooming young woman absurd, as I do. I promise you I shall be vastly bored.'

It was for days a matter of puzzled conjecture to Grizel how she could so completely have mislaid that letter, though she knew that she had left it about for a short time. So did Ian, who, though he was never going to see Miss Campbell again, nor would ever write to her or receive a word from her, pounced upon that sheet of paper over which her hand had travelled and which seemed to carry the very sound of her voice, secreted it, and unblushingly declared his complete ignorance of its where-abouts. To such hopeless folly had he come who was shortly to woo Miss Margaret Maclean.

Miss Campbell's letter, since he always carried it upon him, went with Ian to Glasgow when, in August, Invernacree sent him thither to see his lawyer, as he had projected some time before. And it was in Glasgow that temptation came down upon Ian like a river in spate. Olivia Campbell was at Kilrain, not thirty miles away, out of his homeward path, it was true, but not so greatly out of it. He had hoped never to see her again, never to go within distance of the spell which she had cast upon him. Now – he felt he could not live unless he did. The reason he gave himself for yielding to temptation was this: he had allowed her (since he could not help himself) to see his passion, but he had not told her why he could never contemplate asking for her hand. It was almost an affront to have acted so . . . but he had lost his wits that day on Eilean Soa.

He did not pretend that he had found them again now. He knew that it was mad to go to Kilrain, and could lead to nothing but fresh suffering for himself. Yet he would welcome that . . . And he must make his explanation, justify his silence – or so he told himself. To another voice which said that he could equally well, and far more prudently, write this explanation, he shut his ears. He had little desire to combat the flood setting towards Kilrain; he was only too glad to be carried along by it. By the time he paid his second and last visit to Mr Buchanan this afternoon his mind was made up, and he had consulted the map upon the lawyer's wall with entire composure. The detour might have been part of his original plan.

For all that, he had not left the green orchards of Glasgow behind him next morning, his face set north-eastwards, when his blood began to run faster. He knew his self-offered excuse for what it was; he was going to see Olivia Campbell because he could not keep away. And even how she would receive him weighed upon him but little, for she could not prevent him from resting his eyes once more upon her loveliness, though the moment of vision might be short. He could never have gone to Cairns to see her, whether she were like to refuse him admittance or to welcome him; but up in those hills which were neither Campbell nor Stewart territory, she could not entirely forbid his presence. And he fell to imagining the meeting, as, leaving the Clyde behind, he rode by glen or loch side, sometimes mounting, sometimes descending. Every stream which sang along his course or barred it seemed to utter her name, so liquidly sweet to the ear that he could forget the patronymic which followed it.

He halted at three o'clock to bait and rest his horse, for there was no haste, even though he should not reach Kilrain before dusk. It was even better so; he could more easily make inquiries as to Miss Campbell's whereabouts in the clachan without the risk of coming upon her unawares. He hardly knew what he should find at Kilrain, save goats.

And it *was* dusk when he came there, up the stony, winding road. It was not too ill a track, for little Kilrain lay upon a minor highroad; otherwise, perhaps, it would scarcely have gained its reputation for 'the whey'. A curled young moon, and a star too, shone in the green sky over the rounded summit of Meall na Creige, and there was no wind to stir the pines which fringed that crest. All in the little village seemed within, if not abed, but a light or two still showed at the end by which Ian had entered. Had they not, he would willingly have slept on the hillside, but the sound of his horse's hoofs on the stones brought an old man to the door of one of the nearest cottages, and of him young Invernacree, representing himself as a benighted traveller, asked if there were an inn to which he could betake himself.

The old man replied in the negative, but offered to take him in himself, adding that he and his daughter were accustomed to do this for the gentry who came there for their health. Asked if there were any of these now visiting Kilrain for that purpose, he at first said that there were none – which was to Ian as though the moon had been struck suddenly out of the sky – but his daughter, correcting him, declared that there was a young lady, a bonny young lady, staying with her woman a little way higher up the hill.

From the tiny room assigned to him Ian could see up the slope, and gazed at the one faintly illumined window at some quarter mile of distance which he imagined – probably wrongly – to be Miss Campbell's until the light went out there, and the moon, as if waiting for this extinction, sank into the black arms of the pine-trees on the ridge; and all was as quiet in Kilrain as if a very imprudent and unhappy young man had not come to it.

2

Though Olivia Campbell had written to her late hostess of her probable exceeding boredom when 'at the goats' milk', it was only because she felt the absurdity of going there. It was fashionable to pretend to ennui, but in reality she hardly knew the meaning of the word, either in its French form or in its English.

Least of all did she know it this morning as she knelt by the little mountain pool which an eager burn, slackened in its course by a sudden outward thrust of the slope, had amused itself by forming on this kind of escarpment. She was watching the antics of a couple of kids who, in the intervals of staring at her across that mirror, sprang about in the most ridiculous gymnastics or butted each other with infantile fury. Olivia knelt there in a blue gown and a large shady hat and laughed; securely seated on a big stone, with a cloak folded beneath her, Mrs Elspeth MacUre, who had been her nurse, knitted busily, and from time to time relaxed into a smile. And it was fine weather; fine with that loveliness-waking magic of the Western Highlands, which can wipe clean from the memory the days of mist and rain and storm, long and many though they be. Highlanders both, the two by the pool were not unmindful of this, though Mrs MacUre, who was of a stout habit, had already remarked rather ungratefully upon the heat.

'You'll fall in, you wee thing!' warned Olivia, addressing one of the kids. 'And I doubt you can swim. Are you prepared to wade in after this featherbrain if necessary, Elspeth?'

Mrs MacUre shook her head with decision, but replied not in words. She was counting stitches.

'I see a man coming up the path who can act rescuer if one is needed,' said Olivia in a lower voice. 'But do not be so rash, creature,' she went on, addressing the kid in Gaelic, as if she thought it could better understand that tongue ... 'Although,' she added with a little quick intake of the breath, 'he who comes is something skilful in rescue ... especially from water!' And, the colour leaping into her face, she rose to her feet. 'Mr Stewart, how ... how come you here?'

Hat in hand, Ian stood on the other side of the pool. Everything in the scene was painted on his brain with pigments that would never fade, he thought – the azure pool, the crystal burn that fed it, the glowing heather, miles upon miles of surging mountains, clouds like ships in full sail, and soaring, limitless sky – and yet he only saw one figure, Olivia's.

738

'Kilrain lay upon my road yesterday,' he replied, repeating what he had carefully rehearsed, 'but I was belated in my arrival last night. And I bethought me this morning that you had written to Grizel of your intention of being here in August; and so I resolved that, if you permitted it, I would pay my respects to you.'

If she had been alone, would she have sent him about his business, he wondered. And how much was she conscious of what had been virtually their last meeting, among the moon-daisies? He could not tell. She turned to her attendant, who was still knitting, and said with a smile, 'Elspeth, this is Mr Stewart of Invernacree, to whom I owe my rescue from that horrible coach, as you know. Pray, Mr Stewart, come round to this side of the lochan and let Mrs MacUre have a good look at you!'

Ian came round the pool – a very ordinary little Highland tarn, but more wonderful to him than all the stretch of the long sea-loch by which he dwelt, because she was upon its brink. Mrs MacUre, rose and curtsied to him. Even she shared in the enchantment, though to be sure he could have wished her away. And yet – she had perhaps her uses.

'And so you are travelling, Mr Stewart,' remarked Miss Campbell. 'You have very fine weather for your journey. May one ask whither you are bound – for Perth perhaps?'

'No, I am upon my way home,' confessed Ian. 'I have been to Glasgow upon affairs.'

'To Glasgow?' said the girl, and he saw those delicate eyebrows of hers lift a trifle. She recognized then that his homeward road had been by no means of the most direct. Indeed she showed her realization of it next moment by adding, with a spice of mischief, 'You too have perhaps been ordered to the goats' milk, Mr Stewart, for your health?'

Before Mrs MacUre Ian would not take up the challenge. He replied soberly, 'No, Madam, that is not the case. I had a fancy to see Kilrain, that is all, and came this way, but it was almost dark last night when I reached it.'

'Well, now you see it!' said Olivia, waving her hand towards the great sweep of view. 'This is the prospect for which you have, I imagine – though indeed I am no geographer – come a good many miles out of your way!'

'And is there no other?' asked Ian, venturing to look at her directly. 'Cannot one see more of the place from the pinewood yonder, for instance?'

On her answer to that simple question hung balanced, it seemed to him in some crazy fashion, the very continuance of the mountains in their solid majesty, the very preservation of the sun in the sky. He held his breath lest all should go crashing . . . And though Olivia could scarcely have guessed at that exaggerated conviction of his, at any rate she weighed his suggestion before rejecting it – and did not reject it.

'One might perhaps see a little farther down the valley from the other side of the wood,' she conceded. 'Shall we walk up that way? I will come back to you here, Elspeth; but if you find the sun too hot, do you return to the cottage.'

Ian did not know what Mrs MacUre said to this proposal, nor did he care. The sun still shone, and the hills were secure. Miss Campbell, when she could easily have avoided it, had granted him an interview alone; that was all that mattered.

3

They walked up the winding path towards the wood, a path so narrow that two could not go abreast. But Ian went by Olivia's side through the heather. She asked news of all at Invernacree, and he answered in a dream. She was graver than she had been by the pool; yet surely she could not be greatly displeased, or she would not have vouchsafed what she was vouchsafing.

To go into the pinewood out of the sunshine was like leaving the fair land of what might have been for the region of what really was. It was so much darker and colder here, and the pine stems stood stark and straight, like signposts pointing a man to his duty. Yet the sun did enter, in places, and the wood was beautiful, if with an austere beauty. And when they had walked a little way into its aisles Olivia Campbell stopped and said seriously: 'Mr Stewart, why have you come to Kilrain?'

He said, equally gravely, and quite calmly – at first: 'You know why; it is because I could not keep away, knowing that you were here. If I died for it I had to see you again – once again. But there is another reason too. You must know, since that day on Eilean Soa, that I worship you; yet I allowed you to depart next morning without explaining why I could never give you the proof of that worship ... even though it should mean nothing to you ... why I could not ask for what I had, doubtless, no chance of obtaining – your hand in marriage.'

Olivia stood with her eyes cast down; she neither flushed nor paled; she appeared to be thinking. Then suddenly she walked on a little way, and Ian did not follow her. He was not here to plead with her, but to tell her, alas, why he never could plead. He stayed where he was under the stern, dark trees and watched her move slowly away. She crossed a glint of sunlight; her blue gown flashed with colour; then she was beyond the bright barrier. And there she came to a standstill, turned her head, and made a little sign for him to come to her. Ian came.

'I thank you for the honour you wished to do me, Mr Stewart,' she said gently, looking at him much as she had looked that day on the island. 'And I thank you for coming all this way to tell me that it was impossible.'

'I hoped you would forgive me for that,' said Ian anxiously.

'Perhaps,' said Olivia, looking away from him, 'my forgiveness may depend a little upon the reason for your ... abstention. You have not yet given me that reason, you know!' There was the faintest glimmer of a smile round her enchanting mouth. 'I presume it is the very ordinary one that you are already affianced.'

'Ah no,' said Ian, 'it is something more – '

'More irrevocable than that? You are married then – secretly, perhaps?'

He shook his head. 'Miss Campbell, don't play with me! Does not your own heart tell you that one of my name and allegiance could never wed one of yours, especially –'

'Is that it?' cried Olivia, and her eyes sparkled, with what emotion the young man could not quite divine. 'Surely we have

741

buried the old clan hatreds now; and shall bury those between
Whig and Jacobite in time! Can it really be that you regard me
as someone outcast because my forbears and yours, a hundred
years ago – '

'How could I regard you as anything of the sort!' broke in
Ian passionately. 'You are everything that is lovely and desirable, and I would give the sun out of the sky, if I had it, and
walk in twilight all my days if only you were beside me! But
there's a river between us deeper than you know; there's no
bridge can cross it, and no power can turn its course. I can only
say farewell to you, and hope that God will bless some man
with you who is worthy of you ... if there be such a man ...
worthier at least than I should have been.' He snatched up her
hand and bent to kiss it; bent still further, and flinging himself
on his knees, pressed the hand for a moment to his hot forehead.

'Mr Stewart, what have I done?' asked Olivia, looking down
upon him in a very perturbed fashion. 'What is there between
us, more than our names and our politics? For what am I to
blame?'

'You? For nothing, for nothing!' answered the young man in
a stifled voice. 'But there is my brother Alan's blood between
us. He fell on Culloden Moor, and it was the Campbells –'

Olivia gave an exclamation. 'Culloden! He died *there*! I did
not know. And you mean that because my father ...' She did
not finish.

'Yes, that is what I mean,' said Ian. He had loosed her hand,
and now got to his feet again; he was very pale.

She too was pale, and put the hand he had released over her
eyes. 'But,' she said rather pitifully after a moment, 'my father
only did his duty, and it was not ... not by his very hand that
your brother fell.'

'Not by his hand, perhaps. But by his orders, by his act. There
is no difference. I would to God I could see it otherwise! You
are Highland too – you must see that it is not possible.'

Yes, Olivia Campbell was Highland too. Yet she did not
assent to this doctrine. She said, shivering slightly, 'This

wood is very cold. I think we will go out into the sun again.'

All the way out of the wood the young man beside her struggled with the desire to snatch her suddenly into his arms. All the fire, the melancholy of the Celtic nature, its passion for the hopeless and the intangible, its willingness to lose everything for a dream, and that not always a worthy dream, all surged up in him as he walked beside his Deirdre, his Bronwen, found at last, when he had thought the chance of it was over – and found in vain. Yet it was just that inheritance which kept him from a ravished kiss.

So they came in silence to the edge of the wood, and saw the sunshine spread over all the scene beyond it like a veil of gold.

'Where are you lodging, Mr Stewart?'

He told her.

'You are remaining at Kilrain tonight?'

'No,' he said with an effort. 'Now that I have seen you I shall continue my journey to Appin this afternoon.'

'I should like to have spoken with you again about this matter,' said Olivia faintly. 'There are considerations ... I cannot bear your thinking of my father in this way ... If I had not such a headache I think I could make you see it differently.' She put her hand once more to her head, and it was quite plain that she was not acting a part.

But if he stayed, if he stayed! ... Oh, could he be held to blame when she directly asked him to remain? And did he care if he were blamed? He offered his arm, his heart leaping so wildly that he almost felt its pulsations must quiver down to his finger-tips.

'Allow me to take you back to your lodging,' he said quietly. 'And, to avoid the sun, let us descend the hill inside the wood, if it is possible.'

Murmuring some excuse for her 'foolishness', Olivia accepted his arm, and, going back a few paces, they turned and went down the slope through the solemn pine boles. So there she was, walking beside him in the twilight, as he had said. But the sun of heaven was not his, to cast from the sky; he could do nothing, nothing ...

Chapter 8

THE ONLY SAFETY

1 *Aug 13th–14th*

STRANGE that it should often take an obstacle in the stream's path to show the stream which way it is flowing! This, at least, was what had happened to Olivia Campbell, and it was the matter which she sat deeply pondering at her bedroom window that evening, while the stars strove faintly overhead against the long-drawn Northern daylight.

She could not tell herself that she loved Ian Stewart, but she did recognize that she had been devoting a good deal of thought to him these last few weeks. And now she had been informed that she must not do so any more. Human nature being what it is, there could hardly have been given her a more specific reason for ensuring that she should.

But he – he was in earnest, and she had lost what she had never known that she possessed. She would never see him again after tomorrow . . . unless tomorrow she could persuade him to view differently that tragic gulf which in his eyes separated them. In her heart she doubted her power to do that, although he had agreed to stay until she could see him again. Besides, why was she about to try to make him see it differently? The attempt, thus formally arranged for, had the appearance of an endeavour to persuade him to make her an offer of marriage after all; and, since she had no intention of accepting such an offer, why should she try to provoke it? It would be no satisfaction to refuse him.

Olivia got up and began to move about her tiny low-ceiled room, her hands clasped together and her chin resting upon them. She somewhat prided herself upon being clearsighted. *Why* was it that she was loth to let him go? Surely it could not be some unworthy form of coquetry or pique. What was it, then, since she did not love him?

With that question still unanswered she sought the stuffy little box-bed in the wall which was all that the cottage – and many a dwelling better than a cottage – had to offer. But she could not sleep; and in this confined space the sudden headache of the morning, which had been perfectly genuine and had continued most of the afternoon, came on again. Her own hot forehead, when she put her hand on it, recalled young Invernacree's when he had pressed that same hand to his brow; and the remembrance brought back the hopeless passion in his voice as he had knelt there in the wood, renouncing her . . . But why should she think of that again now, and so insistently that she could see once more the top of his dark head bowed over her hand, even the very way in which his hair-ribbon was knotted, and feel a longing to lay her other hand in consolation on that bent head? Good God, had she really been conscious of such a feeling at the time, or was it a mere trick of memory? For what was hopeless passion to her, when she did not share it? She had met it before; and after a while felt glad to be rid of the tribute.

But this particular tribute she did not want to be rid of: that was the conclusion of the whole matter. It was not a conclusion which made for peaceful or refreshing sleep.

Its effects, indeed, were apparent next morning, for Mrs MacUre observed that she doubted Miss Olivia was getting as much benefit from the whey as her Papa would wish, and added, 'Did ye not sleep well, my dear?'

'Not very well,' confessed Olivia. 'It was so hot in my little room. But I shall be myself again when I am in the fresh air.'

'Would ye not do better to stay in the house the morn?' suggested her attendant. ' 'Tis going to be a hot day again. But at any rate ye'll need to stay until ye have drunk your whey.'

Olivia assented, knowing that Mr Stewart would not arrive to wait upon her until after that hour.

The rite over, she brought out a piece of embroidery and sat down to watch for him. Elspeth and she had the cottage to themselves, Mr Campbell having hired it in its entirety, which had enabled Mrs MacUre to bring it to a state of cleanliness not known for many years. The sun climbed a little higher; the goats could be heard bleating as they were driven to pasture; a few people went by; still Ian did not come. A panic seized Olivia; suppose he had not kept to the compact, if compact it could be called, which they had made yesterday? She flung down her embroidery, looked out of the window several times, took up a book and dropped it again after a page or two.

'Ye're unco restless, Miss Olivia,' observed Elspeth MacUre, who was in and out of the room enough to observe this fact. 'If ye're ettlin' to go out, why not go out now? 'Twill be hotter by and by.'

'I think I will not go just yet,' murmured her charge. To herself she said, 'But, upon my soul, if he does not arrive within the next five minutes, I will . . . and he can come and search for me!'

But in that case he might fail to find her, or, worse, he might not even try, but ride away discouraged.

'This is too tiresome!' she exclaimed aloud.

'What's tiresome, my dear? And who's keeping you in the house if ye're set on going out? I'm sure 'tis not your old Elspeth. She's ready to put on her bonnet the moment ye give the word.'

Olivia looked at her in mute despair. The five minutes had already fled away and another three been added to them. Save that convention forbade, even here, she would have gone to the cottage where Mr Stewart was lodging, not exactly to hasten him, but to ease her mind of this ghastly suspicion of a misunderstanding somewhere. But of course even she, who was somewhat of a law unto herself, could not outrage decorum so far as that. Should she send Elspeth? But that would be to reveal . . . too much.

The middle portion of a man's figure – more was never visible of any passer-by – came past the minute window. Olivia's heart leapt up; higher still when there came a knock at the door, which opened directly into the living-room. Elspeth hastened to open it, and there he stood, slim and strong against the sunlight, and doffed his hat. His hair was not as dark as she had thought – not so dark as her own – for the sun struck a gleam of brown from it . . .

'I called to inquire for Miss Campbell, whether she is recovered of her indisposition of yesterday?' came his voice.

'Miss Campbell is quite recovered,' called Olivia gaily from the corner of the room. 'Will you not come in, Mr Stewart?'

2

In the clear air above Meall na Creige a speck was hovering – a large hawk, perhaps even an eagle. Olivia looked up at it fixedly, because if there are tears in your eyes there is in this attitude a more reasonable hope of their not descending your cheeks.

It was all in vain: in vain that she stood here alone with Ian Stewart by the great lichened shoulder of rock on the other slope of the glen, surveying this fair sunlit world; in vain that she knew he loved her, and that she . . . that she was conscious without looking at him of that reserved and sensitive profile of his. The phantom of a young man whom she had never known stood there with them, a cold, shadowy presence, the green Stewart tartan on his breast all reddened with Campbell musket balls, and, since she was Highland too, she knew in her heart that the dead Alan's only brother, now the heir, could never go back to his father and his clan and announce that he had asked in marriage the daughter of the man whose command had winged those bullets. Nor was it merely the ban of his family and his race which was ranged against her; Ian's own fidelity to conviction, despite the way in which it racked him, was unshaken – she saw that; and though he had come to Kilrain with no other aim but that of seeing her, such a concession to his own weakness would never happen again. All was over before it had begun.

Olivia would not weep; she called to her all her pride of clan and of womanhood. Allow a man . . . any man – a Stewart least

of all – to see ... The bird above the mountain soared unexpectedly out of sight. Yet she must still look hard at something;
and, her hearing assisting her in the quest, her eyes fell upon a
horseman going at a walk upon the road below. He seemed, as
far as one could tell from a distance, to be gazing up at her and
her companion; then – yes, surely, he was trying to attract their
attention! Could it be news of some kind from Cairns?

'Mr Stewart,' she said rather breathlessly, 'do you see a man
down there on a grey horse who ... why, I believe he is dismounting and coming up to us!'

Until she spoke Ian had not been conscious of the rider, nor,
indeed, of anything much in his surroundings. Now he looked
down the heathery incline and saw the dismounted horseman
starting quickly up it. And very soon, to his surprise, and by no
means to his gratification, he heard Olivia say animatedly,
'Why, it is my dear Mr Maitland! Whatever can he be doing
here?'

In spite of his renewed act of renunciation Ian felt a sharp
pang as he heard these words. Who was this Mr Maitland of
whom Miss Campbell could speak in these terms, and whose advent could cause her, even at this moment, so much evident
pleasure? The newcomer had the figure of a young man, and he
mounted the hillside with all the speed and agility of one, but
before he had arrived at their level Ian saw that his face was
that of a man of five and forty or so – and a very attractive face
it was too, even if its beauty was almost too ethereal for mas-
culine taste. (But it occurred to Ian that a woman might not
think so.) A very sweet smile dawned upon it now as, just a trifle
out of breath with haste, he arrived at the rocky shoulder.

'My dearest Olivia!' he said, and kissed her hand. 'I feared I
should not find you. I went first to your lodging at the cottage,
and was fortunate in happening upon your good Elspeth there,
otherwise – '

'But how did you know that I was here at all – and still more,
why are *you* here?' asked Olivia, laughing, and slipping her
hand in a most intimate manner into the newcomer's arm.

'I knew that you were here from a letter of your father's, and

I am here because Kilrain lies on my way to Lochaber, whither I am bound on affairs,' the gentleman replied, putting his other hand over the one reposing on his arm.

'What good luck!' cried Olivia gaily. 'But, dear me, what a centre of travel this little spot is becoming! For here is Mr Ian Stewart of Invernacree, of whose prowess and kindness I wrote you. He also was passing through the clachan. Mr Stewart, let me present you to my oldest friend, Mr Maitland of Strathmory, whom I sometimes call my godfather.'

Ian came forward and bowed. Mr Maitland held out his hand.

'Indeed I have heard of you, sir, from Miss Campbell; and if I may, as so old a friend of hers, I should like to add my thanks to those of her family!'

His manner and his look a good deal disarmed Ian. And, after all, Olivia could hardly contemplate marriage with a man of twice her age whom she called, even occasionally, her godfather!

There was some further talk up by the rock. Mr Maitland wished to know if the young lady were really in need of a sojourn 'at the whey'; he had hoped that it was only a whim of her father's, to which Olivia emphatically responded that his hope was justified. She seemed to Ian quite to have shaken off the sadness consequent upon their recent interview, in the pleasure of seeing this elderly friend of hers. It was no doubt just as well . . .

Presently they were all going down the side of the hill together, for Mr Maitland announced that he must push on at once. Miss Campbell asked him where he was going and on what business, but the traveller returned no definite answer.

'Well, my dear Olivia,' said he when they reached his busily grazing horse, 'I hope that the rest of your stay will be agreeable and beneficial to you. It has been a great pleasure to have had this glimpse of you; I am only sorry that it must be so short.'

'You might have had a glimpse before this, and a longer one,' replied Miss Campbell with a little pout. 'Do you know that you have not visited us at Cairns since some time early in '53 – more than two years ago!'

749

'Is it really so long!' exclaimed the gentleman. 'I certainly deserve censure for that.' He began to alter a stirrup leather, and then to examine his horse's girths, and Ian, who, since he happened to be at the animal's head, had put an instinctive hand upon his bridle, was struck by the swift change which came over his face. As he turned away from the girl it was as though a mask had slipped off it, and, when he raised himself from his examination, Ian's impression of sudden metamorphosis was even strengthened. Why, the man looked tragically harassed, as well as ill! Ian was startled by it. Then Mr Maitland turned round again to Olivia, and she too must have observed some change, for Ian heard her say, 'I don't think you look very well, Mr Maitland. 'Tis you should be staying here, not I!'

'A touch of tertian fever, my dear, which I had a few days ago,' replied he carelessly. ' 'Tis nothing – save perhaps a sign of advancing years. So, by your leave, I'll not let myself be overtaken by the night!' He kissed her hand again (Ian wondering whether he were not accustomed, at any rate in the absence of strangers, to kiss her cheek or brow), gave her a message to her father, mounted, saluted Ian and was off.

Ian looked after him and his vanishing grey horse. He too ought to be riding along that road. Why prolong this pain? He said: 'I think my own mare must be reshod by now, a thing I found she needed; but the smith was indisposed this morning and could not shoe her.' It was in fact the discovery of this necessity and of the difficulty in remedying it – for, in more brutal language, the blacksmith was drunk – which had caused his delay in coming to Olivia's cottage. 'May I escort you back to your lodging before I set out?' he added.

Olivia assented, and they began to walk back along the road.

'There is a path,' said Ian after a moment or two, indicating one on their left which began to mount from the road. 'I fear this is rough walking for you, and the path would be somewhat shorter too, probably.'

'Do you wish it to be, I wonder?' murmured Miss Campbell to herself. But she did not say it aloud,

It was a wider path than some, and they went along it side by side. For a while it pushed by great bushes of broom, whose golden glory was now departed; ahead was a little wood, a mere copse of oak and hazel.

'Do you know, Mr Stewart,' said Olivia suddenly, as Ian held aside a branch for her to pass, 'that the gentleman who has just left us is a living argument against the conviction which ... which you hold, for Mr David Maitland has been a friend of my father's for as long as I can remember; yet he is a Jacobite.'

'There are Jacobites and Jacobites, Miss Campbell.'

'But Mr Maitland is not one of your theoretical Jacobites,' returned Olivia with vivacity. 'He was "out" in the Forty-five; he fought at Falkirk. I believe he only escaped proscription through the good offices of my father. And yet you see,' she ended with a little sigh, 'he is our intimate friend.'

'It was not a friend that I wished to be,' said Ian in a voice unlike his own. The sentiment, or something else, produced a silence between them, during which they reached the coppice; and the path, dipping slightly, brought them to the banks of a little woodland stream which it immediately crossed by means of stepping stones. They came to a halt.

'And so,' said Olivia slowly, looking at the sparkle of the water, 'you will not in future be able to think of me as a friend?'

Ian caught his breath. 'I hope that I shall be able to avoid thinking of you at all,' he said harshly, a man in pain not always measuring his words. Olivia bit her lip and turned her head away; then, not answering, she placed her foot on the first of the stepping-stones. It rocked a little, even beneath her light weight. The next moment she was caught by both elbows and steadied.

'Step on to the flat stone in the middle,' came Ian's voice. She obeyed, and he instantly released her.

'The stone was loose,' she said, excusing herself. 'Indeed I can usually cross a burn without falling in.'

Her companion was standing in the shallow water beside her. 'I do not doubt it. But, lest there be other loose stones ...' He offered his hand.

751

Olivia took it, and next moment was safely on the opposite bank. Before she could make a remark of any kind Ian, still holding her hand, began to speak again, the words tumbling out, and checking, too, like the watercourse at their feet.

'Forgive me ... forgive me for saying that! It is not true. I shall always think of you, I am afraid. It would be too much to expect you to think of me, sometimes ... just from kindness ... as one thinks of the very unhappy ... Perhaps I should know it – but perhaps it would be better if I did not ... And if you will forgive me, I will leave you, now that you are over the burn; there is your way back plain ... I cannot walk any farther with you ... there is term to what one can endure – and so I will go back the other way.'

He looked indeed absolutely exhausted, as a man might do after prolonged torture. Olivia's hand was still in his; after the first, she had not attempted to withdraw it. She tried to say 'Good-bye then', but no words came. And whether Ian drew her unconsciously towards him by that captive hand, or whether she as unconsciously came, or both, next moment her head was on his breast, and remained there.

Then with his other hand the young man gently turned her face up to his, and she did not resist; she only shut her eyes. So, in the oak copse by the stream, Stewart and Campbell kissed each other without a word; and equally without a word did Ian's clasp relax. Olivia heard footsteps splashing quickly through water ... She put her hands over her face, in a gesture of possession, not of concealment. The air should not so soon obliterate that gift – that gift which she had returned. When she removed them she was alone.

But the world was changed – how changed! She walked home in a different one, whether a gladder or a sorrier, she hardly knew. Mrs MacUre, after looking at her once or twice, forbore to ask what had become of her escort.

3

Twenty minutes after he had kissed Olivia Campbell, Ian was standing in dismay before the little forge in the village, to find that the blacksmith had not yet recovered from the effects of his drunken bout of the previous day, that the mare had not in consequence been reshod, but that her shoes, most un-fortunately, had been removed in readiness by the smith's boy, and could not be put on again. So he could not ride her away with the old shoes, as he had intended. There was no other saddle horse in Kilrain, nor could he get home on foot. The smith's wife, saddened and apologetic, was, however, sure that by sundown her man would have sufficiently recovered. If the gentleman would have a little more patience . . .

The gentleman flung away distracted. If he stayed he was lost. With that honey of Olivia's kiss still on his lips, the touch of her tingling in his veins, nothing but flight would save him. If he went near her again now all his defences would go down with a crash, and he saw himself imploring her to marry him out of hand, by a mere Scots marriage before witnesses, anything . . . There was no hope for him but to leave this sweet and fatal place at once. Yet because of this ridiculous and vulgar con-tretemps of a drunken blacksmith he was pinned here.

Patience! as if he would not have given his right hand to stay! Was Fate plotting against him to drive him into dishonour? For Olivia Campbell could not be indifferent to him, or she would never have allowed him, as she had, that moment by the stream which made his head turn when he thought of it. *Now*, if he asked her to be his wife, would it, in her eyes, be out of the question? He knew that it would not.

There was nothing to do but to go striding away up into the hills, too far away to run the risk of coming upon Olivia, till such time as that sun which had seen her lay her head against his heart should put an end, behind the shoulder of Meall na Creige, to this wretched and ecstatic day.

He did walk, for hours, in the peace of the high hills, but still the sun rode the heavens, though by Ian's watch it was time to turn. And at last he came once more in sight of Kilrain. The smoke of evening was beginning to rise from the thatched roofs as he descended, steering his course at random. By now he was very tired, for he had scarcely slept the night before, and emotion, joined to fasting (since he had not dined that day) can exhaust even a vigorous young man of six and twenty. And with fatigue a sort of trance came upon him, and he recognized without surprise that his returning steps had somehow led him into the little copse of the morning. It seemed appropriate. That surely was the very spot where he had stood with her when the wonder of the world had happened to him – yes, there were the stepping-stones.

'*Olivia*,' said the burn, hurrying gently along. '*Olivia* . . . *O . . . liv . . . i . . . a . . .*'

Ian threw himself down for a moment, to listen to that cool and gliding music.

Strange! He must actually have fallen asleep! Yes, he did remember, now, changing his posture and stretching himself out under an oak tree for a few minutes' rest. But by the change in the light it must have been much more than a few minutes' sleep. It had been long enough to hold a dream, also, one of those particularly vivid and sudden dreams which come with daylight slumber and partake of day's reality. Ian lay still a moment recalling it, for it was sweet.

He had dreamt that Olivia was standing there, looking at him, and he had tried to speak to her, to ask her for some memento, since he had none. But the chains of sleep held him fast, and he could not utter the words; he could not even open his eyes; yet he knew that she was there. Nevertheless, being in his dream the King of Lochlann's daughter out of the old tales as well as Olivia Campbell, she gave him as a token that grey, mottled skin of the seal, her other self, the possession of which enabled her at will to go back to the sea from whence she came. And the gift meant that she renounced her right – for him.

Ian lay still a moment longer, smiling rather bitterly. Of what odd elements were dreams compounded! It was time to relinquish them, to face reality, and to ride away. With a heavy

sigh he raised himself on to his right elbow ... and remained
there motionless, the blood rushing into his face. Between the
fingers and the palm of that open right hand lay a freshly
plucked sprig of bog-myrtle – bog-myrtle, the only too familiar
badge of Clan Campbell.

A little later, between sunset and moonrise, Ian checked his
mare for a last look at Kilrain before the drop of the road
should hide it from his view. Like to like – the sprig of gall was
in the folds of Olivia's letter over his heart. He stayed a moment
wrenched with longing; then tugged the mare round again, and
rode on down the slope.

Chapter 9

OTHER PEOPLE'S LOVE AFFAIRS

To every lover his own love affair is naturally the only one in the world. Yet while Ian Stewart, surrounded by goats, was dallying with the foreman's daughter up in the hills, a young man rather older than himself, whose existence he had temporarily forgotten, was approaching Invernacree with intent to pay his addresses to Ian's sister. And because of Ian's absence, he was going to find his path at first a good deal smoother than it might otherwise have been.

Of Captain Hector Grant, of the régiment d'Albanie in the service of His Most Christian Majesty of France, Ian himself had not long ago said that he was too French for his taste. Hector had indeed a slightly French air, and French manners – what wonder, since most of his life had been spent upon Gallic soil? In the uniform which he had left behind the former was probably even more apparent. Yet, as his brother-in-law Ewen Cameron had pointed out, he was Highland to the backbone for all that. Did not, indeed, the three motives which had now brought him to Scotland prove that fact? He was on his way to take possession of his recently-inherited Highland property, to satisfy his desire for vengeance upon another Highlander who had injured him, and to discover whether a certain Highland girl in Appin remembered him as well as he remembered her. And if he found Miss Jacqueline Stewart, that pretty, shy thing, ready to welcome him, and if her eyes still held the smile he had seen there more than two years ago – well, he was no longer, as then, a penniless French officer unable to think of marriage. She was a very charming girl, Miss Jacqueline; and Hector had had plenty of opportunity of comparing her with the French demoiselles. Mercifully, perhaps, his poverty had prevented him from marrying one of these, so that he was still free to woo a Highland lass.

And thus he came within sight of the tree-surrounded house of Invernacree, which had sheltered him after he had escaped with Ewen Cameron of Ardroy from captivity in Fort William on the Christmas Day of 1752.[1] It was only fitting, therefore, that he should pay his respects to old Alexander Stewart, and renew acquaintance with the son of the house, who – mainly, of course, on his cousin Ardroy's account – had so materially assisted in that escape. At the very outset fortune gave him a favourable omen, for as he rode up to the gate he perceived, under the oaks of the avenue, two ladies walking towards the house – the two Miss Stewarts, there was no question. Better, of course, had it been the younger alone – but that would come later! Hector stooped from the saddle, opened the gate and rode through.

The sound of the gate falling to again caught the ladies' ears; they both turned their heads and stopped. Mr Grant rode on a few paces, swung out of the saddle and advanced, hat in hand. And on Jacqueline Stewart's face, for one brief moment at least, was sufficient warranty for his welcome.

2

Two days later Hector Grant was still at Invernacree, and in those two days, thanks to an intensive system of wooing pursued under favourable circumstances – though Hector was not sure that old Invernacree would prove altogether tractable to handle when it came to the point – had achieved, as far as Jacqueline herself was concerned, the position of accepted suitor. In this he had been greatly assisted by the fine weather, since one cannot sit or walk with a lady in a garden – a locality very favourable to courtship – during persistent rain; in such the lady, at least, is condemned to the house, where love-making is more liable to interruption.

Now the sun which shone upon the pair was, naturally, the same which had shone for Ian in his more clandestine com-

1. See *The Gleam in the North*

merce with Miss Olivia Campbell among the rocks and the heather of Kilrain. Yet that ill-starred lover, when, returning home on the third day, he left his horse in the stable and crossed the garden on his way to the house, was by no means pleased to perceive the result of this equality of solar benefits; indeed, he stopped dead, astounded, scandalized, and then angry at what, himself unseen, he saw taking place.

Upon the seat encircling the trunk of the cedar-tree in the middle of the lawn was sitting his sister Jacqueline; she held an arm outstretched, and upon the wrist thereof perched, like a hawk, one of her doves. A handsome young man, whom Ian instantly recognized, with one knee upon the brown carpet of cedar needles, was laughingly tendering his arm also towards the bird; he appeared to be trying to tempt it away. The hands of these two arms were very near each other, their owners' heads not far apart.

And somehow Ian felt that he would have been less stirred to anger if he had come upon the intruder wholly upon his knees to Jacqueline, making an impassioned declaration in due form, or if Jacqueline's dove had not been so inextricably, so sacredly bound up in his mind with his own bright vision of Olivia leaning out of her window here, the day her smile had enslaved him. After that, this scene was sacrilege!

'Curse his impudence!' he said under his breath, and advanced.

The dove saw him first and flew off its mistress's wrist; the culprits, looking for the reason of its flight, became aware of a third person. Hector sprang to his feet.

'Good afternoon, Mr Stewart! If it were my place to do so, I would say, "Welcome home!" ' And, not in the least abashed, he came forward, holding out his hand.

Ian bowed rather stiffly as a preliminary to taking it, which he could not in common civility refuse to do. ('No,' he thought, 'it is not your place to welcome me, Mr Grant, and never will be!') Aloud he said, 'Your servant, sir! Good-day, Jacqueline; are you teaching Mr Grant to be a bird fancier?'

She, at least, was rosy in the face which she put up for his kiss.

But it was in no placid frame of mind that Ian went off to see his father, and to give an account of his mission to Glasgow. It was hard to return from renouncing the love of one's life to find a love affair – minor, of course – going on in one's own home; it was doubly hard when the suitor was a man whose name had been a source of irritation for the last two years. For that name was connected with the fiasco which had left his cousin Ewen, that December morning, stranded on Ardgour beach in great danger of recapture, a fiasco which his father had never ceased to make a source of reproach to him, though indeed the consequences to Ewen had not been lastingly serious, nor did Ewen himself bear his cousin the slightest grudge for a mishap which the latter could hardly have foreseen. But old Alexander Stewart, who had a great affection for his nephew Ardroy, had more than once muttered, 'Ah, your poor brother Alan would have seen in time what was going to happen!' It was all part and parcel of the feeling which Ian knew to exist in his father's mind, that he was no worthy substitute for his slain elder brother. Yes, it was bitter to come back to that knowledge, when it was partly to his position as Alan's successor that he had sacrificed his heart's happiness.

His father, however, greeted him affectionately enough, listened to his account of his interviews with the lawyer, received the papers and looked through them, remarking only that Ian had stayed longer than he expected in Glasgow, and surmising that Mr Buchanan had been busy.

'Yes,' replied Ian unblushingly, 'he was somewhat throng with clients, and I had to wait his leisure, which delayed me.' Here he tempered falsehood with truth by adding, 'The mare, too, unexpectedly needed reshoeing, and a drunken blacksmith delayed me still further.'

'Reshoeing! You should have looked to that before setting out. I must speak to them in the stables about it,' said Invernacree vexed. 'And I imagine a drunken smith can hardly have shod her well! Where did you come upon him?'

'Oh, in some clachan on the way,' replied Ian hastily, wishing he had not introduced the subject; and thereupon remarked upon the arrival of Mr Hector Grant, partly, also, in order to see what his father thought of the attentions paid by the guest to his younger daughter. But the old man did not appear to be aware of them, and on the whole Ian was glad, not wishing in reality, to discuss the subject of love-making.

He went out of the study to the privacy of his own room, and there took out of his pocketbook an object which the utmost care had not preserved from withering. Nothing droops more quickly than the bog-myrtle; yet it retains in death its sweet, half-bitter fragrance. So it was, so it always would be with the memory of those enchanted hours at Kilrain, ending, indeed, in frustration and parting, but yet with a talisman, a sign, magically given.

For how the sprig of gall came to be in his hand, unless Olivia had laid it there when he was asleep, Ian could not conceive. He rejected the idea that someone had done it as a jest – for who would have played such a prank? He could not in his sleep have reached out and clutched it, for there was none growing near; he had searched the spot. But there was a patch some way farther down the stream; and it *was* the Campbell emblem. Never before, he imagined, had a Stewart cherished the gall; never before had one of his name been so besotted as to put a withered fragment of it to his lips as he did now, though he knew not even whether his love had laid it in his hand, nor what had been her meaning if she had. But it was the Campbell emblem, and she was a Campbell . . . O God, if only she were not!

3

And now Captain Hector Grant's courtship began to prosper less conspicuously, for the home-coming of young Invernacree cast a perceptible blight upon its hitherto very rapid growth. It was not only that his physical presence was inconvenient, seeing that he was much more likely to come unexpectedly upon the lovers than was the old laird or Grizel, but it also reacted mentally upon Jacqueline herself, who began to close up as the anemone touched by a rash finger furls the pretty fringe which the tide had set waving in the pool. She was very fond of Ian, and sensitive to a disapproval which she felt the more, perhaps, that it was unexpressed. Hector cursed to himself, but he was unable to do much save see all he could of his lady, and as little as possible of her brother. He wondered how much longer he could with decency prolong his visit. Ian Stewart's covert hostility, which he could not quite understand, was additionally trying because he himself was in Ian's debt over the old Fort William business. And he had not yet approached the laird on the subject of his younger daughter – did not even know whether he suspected anything of his feelings. Suppose it was Invernacree's son who first enlightened the old man; that would be awkward in the extreme! Endowed with all the sensitive pride of a Highlander, Hector was uneasy lest he should have placed himself in a false position, and that in the house of another Highlander. And on the third afternoon after Ian's return he spoke of his perplexities to Jacqueline herself, driven to it by the knowledge that her brother was actually closeted with Invernacree at the very moment – at least, he had seen Ian go into the old man's study a little while ago, and, as far as he knew, he had not come out again. He and Jacqueline were seated in the window-seat of the drawing-room, and he was holding a skein of green silk for her to wind. But when he made the suggestion of asking her father for her hand without further delay the girl ceased winding, and looked intensely troubled.

'But I did not wish my father ... anyone ... to know just yet!' she objected.

'My darling! Yet your brother guesses, I think. I should have spoken to your father already,' said Hector, slipping the skein off his hands.

'But,' said Jacqueline, looking down at it, 'I hoped ... it is so short a time that you have been here ... O, pray, Mr Grant ...'

'Mr Grant!'

'Hector, then,' she said in a small voice, her fingers all the while doing a good deal of damage to the skein.

He captured the little ravagers. ' "O pray, Hector" – what

761

then?' he asked smiling. ' "O pray, Hector" – silence! But, my heart's treasure, what if your brother has forestalled me!'

'He cannot – he would not do such a thing! Ian is too fond of me!'

'*Cela n'empêche pas le moins du monde,*' her lover assured her, in the tongue which was almost as natural to him as his own. 'All the more reason, on the contrary, that he should. He does not love *me* with any great affection, I am sure, and he will be the less anxious to lose you. I should have been beforehand with your father. Directly I can be sure that your brother has left his room I shall ask for an interview and make a formal demand for – this.' He lifted the little hand to his lips as he spoke.

'Yes, I suppose you must,' murmured Jacqueline, still looking down. 'But if my father should refuse – ' she came to a stop, and when she raised her eyes they had become homes of tragedy.

'He'll not refuse,' returned Captain Grant with much assurance. 'But if he should, I'll get round him somehow. I will procure Ewen Cameron, for instance, to plead my cause.'

'That would be a good notion,' said the girl, brightening. 'My father thinks a great deal of Cousin Ewen ... But you say that Ian is with him now. Suppose they were already speaking of ... us!'

'That, *mon amour,*' observed the young man, 'as I was saying, is just what I am afraid of.'

But before he could enlarge upon this possibility they were somewhat apologetically interrupted by Grizel, who needed Jacqueline's presence on household affairs.

Chapter 10

FATHER AND SON

THE couple on the window-seat, however, need not have been
apprehensive. A delicate matter was indeed under discussion at
the moment in Alexander Stewart's study, but it did not affect
them. Indeed their affairs were miles away from the mind of the
young man who stood there, somewhat like a criminal before a
judge, and tried to fend off for a while longer the necessity to
which, willing or unwilling, he would in the end have to yield.

'But if I understand you rightly,' his father was saying, 'you
practically refuse to continue the prosecution of your suit to
Miss Margaret Maclean. Or do I not, by good fortune, understand you rightly?'

Ian moistened his dry lips. 'One cannot prosecute what is not
yet begun.'

'Don't quibble with me, sir! In essence it is begun. Before you
went to Glasgow you assured me that the match was not disagreeable to you, and that upon your return you would pay
your address to the lady. Acting on your promise, when I met
Garroch at Ballachulish one day in your absence – '

'Good God!' cried his unfortunate son, 'you have not already
opened the matter to him?'

'And why not, pray?' demanded Invernacree. 'Was I to suppose the word of a son of mine to be a mere tuft of bog-cotton,
blowing hither and thither in the wind? I was more than
justified in sounding Garroch on the subject; 'twas the proper
path to pursue, and he expressed much satisfaction at the
prospect of the alliance. But if you are not man enough to win
the lady for yourself – ' He paused, perhaps expecting his taunt,
by drawing blood, to rouse some angry reaction in this
strangely reluctant and impassive suitor. But instead of dis-

playing any healthy resentment (though indeed a slight quiver appeared to go through him) Ian Stewart turned his back and went and gazed out of the window in silence; and after a second or two put a hand over his eyes.

Whatever emotions of dismay or ruth were in the old laird's soul as he looked at the figure of all the son that was left to him, and whatever momentary compassion showed for an instant on his face, there was no faltering in his voice as he pursued mercilessly:

'If, as I say, you are not man enough, you must employ an ambassador. Shall I offer myself?'

Ian turned round. Against the faded grey paint of the folded shutters his face looked grey too, but Alexander Stewart's eyes were old. 'Father ... I will go ... but not yet – not yet! Give me a little time, for pity's sake!' The desperation in his voice was unmistakable.

'Time!' exclaimed the old man harshly, though his heart fluttered at the note. 'You have had time enough, my son. You assured me that you knew your duty – which ought, if you have the common instincts of humanity, to be something more than a duty. I am not proposing to you an ill-favoured or misshapen bride; I should be the last to wish such a one to become the mother of your sons. Miss Maclean is a modest and comely girl of good family. And you have been at liberty to choose elsewhere if you had so desired, and your choice had my approval. What more do you wish?'

'Or what less?' muttered Ian.

'Come nearer to me, if you please,' said Invernacree irritably. 'I cannot hear what you say, and you give the impression of trying to escape into the garden. Come and sit down here, and let us discuss this matter in a reasonable spirit.'

Ian obeyed in silence. He sat down at the library table not far from his father, who was ensconced restlessly in a big chair near the empty hearth; but by leaning his elbow on the table's edge the young man was able easily to raise a hand at need to shade his face. 'There is nothing to discuss, sir,' he said dully. 'I am ready to fulfil your wishes and my duty.'

'Ready! You are not ready!' burst out the old man impatiently. 'Why say you are? Your unreadiness is what I am complaining of.'

'I am ready if you will give me a little longer,' declared his son.

Alexander Stewart smote his hand upon the arm of his chair. 'Delay, delay! A very gallant suitor to keep a lady waiting! Ian, procrastination always has a motive, however secret. You will kindly tell me, before we go further, what it is you hope to gain by yours.'

'To gain? Nothing – nothing in the world,' answered Ian a trifle wildly. 'I only ask you not to press me to attempt what I cannot . . . yet. In a couple of months, perhaps . . .'

'A couple of months! And why, pray, will you find it easier to ask for the hand of Miss Maclean in a couple of months?'

Ian shaded his eyes with his hand and said nothing. He did not know that he *would* find it easier; and how could he explain? Through the open window came the murmur of Jacqueline's doves, which would always now bring back Olivia's face to him. The wind of Kilrain played again about his temples; under his feet was the hillside heather, and in his arms . . .

Suddenly and most unexpectedly he felt his father's hand upon his shoulder. 'Ian, my son' – Invernacree's old voice was charged with the feelings which he had been combating all the time – 'my only son, I would to God I had your confidence! I have nothing to complain of in your conduct hitherto. Can you not tell me what is at the bottom of this strange reluctance of yours? Are you – I can scarcely think of it of you, yet I suppose it is possible – are you entangled with some girl, and asking me for time in the hope that you will shortly be free? I beg you to tell me frankly if it is so; you will not find me unduly harsh.'

'No, I am not entangled with any girl,' said Ian quietly. 'I shall never be freer than I am now.'

A pause. Ian heard Invernacree sigh. 'I should like to know what you meant by that?'

Ian did not supply the interpretation.

765

'Do you mean, my boy, that you are in love, though not engaged in an intrigue, with some woman?'

His father's voice was so unusually gentle; besides, how could he say, No? Ian said, 'Yes, I do mean that.'

The words fell like stones; and Invernacree asked, as slowly, 'Does she know it?'

'Yes.'

'Is it impossible for you to marry her? I would not stand in the way of your happiness, Ian, if I could avoid it.'

'And what about Miss Maclean, to whom you have practically affianced me?' asked his son, dropping his hand. 'But it *is* impossible – quite impossible . . . and you would be the first to say so.'

'Why should I?' asked his father, still gently. He could see now how ravaged the boy's face looked. 'I could speak to Garroch of a prior attachment, unknown to me when I made my proposal. – But I suppose the lady is already married, or promised. Is that so?'

Ian shook his head. 'Let us put her out of mind, as I have, or am trying to. That I have not yet fully succeeded is my reason for begging a little delay before . . . before trying my fortune elsewhere.'

The unintentional turn of the phrase inevitably brought upon him the question, 'She refused your suit, then?'

A wintry sort of smile dawned round the young man's mouth. 'No, sir. I never pressed it.'

'Yet you say that you love her? This is a strange business. You do not, I expect, wish to tell me her name, and I suppose I must not ask it. 'Tis, perhaps, some lady whom you met while you were in Glasgow recently?'

'I did meet her while I was away, yes,' admitted Ian after a moment's hesitation. He glanced up. His father was looking at him so wistfully that, against his better judgement, against his own instincts, he was moved to add, 'You will not be the happier for knowing her name, sir, but that you may not feel I am withholding my confidence from you, I will tell you. It is Miss Campbell of Cairns.'

And with that, not wishing to see the change which his avowal would work on that old face, he got up and looked steadily at the clock on the mantelshelf, already feeling a traitor, to what he did not quite know, for having delivered up his secret.

And to one to whom it had dealt a shattering blow. The old laird had fallen back in his chair, his hand at his throat, 'God, God, what have I done to deserve this!'

In Ian's heart two streams of pity were coursing at the same time – for his father and for himself. He had surrendered his heart's desire that no real stroke might fall upon that silvery head; it was he himself who was bleeding from it. 'Father,' he said, kneeling beside him, 'you need have no fear! We shall never meet again, Miss Campbell and I. It was impossible, and I knew it; no one of our house could wed the daughter of Campbell of Cairns. I shall never of my own will set eyes upon her again. You can trust me, sir! It is over.'

He gripped the old man's shrunken wrist in his eagerness, and looked into his eyes. Alexander Stewart still drew his breath as one who has been plunged into some icy current. 'It was an evil day when Fate brought her here ... I might have known it. She was fair enough to bewitch any man ... Ian, Ian, you say this now, yet you ask for delay. If I should die before your two months' grace is up, what then?'

Ian winced, but he had to allay his father's fear without showing that the doubt hurt him. 'It would make no difference,' he said unsteadily. 'If in my own heart I did not feel the impossibility of making her my wife, should I have thrust her out of it ... to break it, I think, as I am doing, solely for my duty to you ... and Alan, and our house, and the clan? You have called me not man enough to win a bride – if it were not for that *here* which forbids me,' he struck his breast, 'I had ridden off with her to the Lowlands and lived with her in a shepherd's hut sooner than let her go! No, you need not fear to come back after death, father, and find a Campbell bride in this house!'

The passion with which he had spoken shook him, shook his

father also. Alexander Stewart lifted a trembling hand and laid it on the dark head beside him. 'Bless you, my poor boy ... I'll not press you ... You shall have time. I will write to Maclean; I'll find something to say, too, that will not betray your – '

The door opened very suddenly. Ian jumped up. It was Grizel looking in, with a question in her face.

'One moment, my dear,' said her father hastily. 'Come again in a few minutes, if you will. Ian and I are just discussing something of importance.'

If Invernacree had allowed his daughter to enter, and his interview with Ian had broken off upon that note of concord, subsequent events might have fallen otherwise. As it was it slackened the thread of it. The laird rose from his chair and took a turn up and down the room, while Ian stood with bent head by the hearth; then the old man stopped on the far side of the writing table and mechanically began to shift some piles of papers, looking at his son the while.

'I am deeply sorry for you, Ian. I only hope that time will bring healing, especially as you had known Miss Campbell for so short a space. By the way, what did you mean when you said that you had met her when you were in Glasgow?'

Ian raised his head. What a foolish admission that had been! Still, he had already bared his secret. 'I did meet her when I was away. It was then that I made the resolve I have told you of ... Need we speak of the matter any more, sir?'

But his father was going on. 'I could not quite understand why you found it necessary to spend so long in Glasgow. What was Miss Campbell doing there? And, by the way, how could she be there? I distinctly remember Grizel receiving a letter from her saying that she was going to the goats' whey at Kilrain about this time. It must have been her "fetch" that you saw in Glasgow, my poor boy,' concluded Invernacree, essaying a mild pleasantry.

'It was not her fetch,' answered Ian steadily. 'Nor was it in Glasgow that I met her – I never said so. It was at Kilrain.'

'At Kilrain! But you would not pass that way. Do you mean to tell me that you went to Kilrain of set purpose?'

'I did,' answered Ian. 'I went there in order to see her. It was there that I took farewell of her.'

'And you told me the other day,' said his father, a little colour coming into his cheeks, 'that Mr Buchanan had kept you waiting in Glasgow! You went half a day's journey out of your way after Miss Campbell, and spent – how long? – in her company?'

'Does that matter?' asked Ian wearily. ' 'Tis all over and done with now.'

'Do you think,' inquired his father, roused and stern, 'that you can put deceit behind you as easily as that? And what else, may I ask, have you put behind as "over and done with"?'

'What do you mean?' asked the young man, roused also.

'Who else was at Kilrain – who saw you there? If you have given cause for scandal – if you have compromised Miss Campbell – '

' – You fear that I might have to marry her!' finished Ian bitterly. 'Then I wish to God that I had compromised her! Unfortunately I cannot think that I did!'

The wrath which could still burn in the old Highlander lit up like fire among summer heather. 'You wish you *had* compromised her! I see what all your protestations are worth, all your fair speeches about my ghost and the barrier in your own heart! You have shown me the truth – '

Ian started forward. 'Father – no, as God is my witness! I do mean every word that I have spoken. Cannot you understand – you were young once – I said good-bye to her for ever . . . but it was cruelly hard, and is still . . .'

Alexander Stewart had become dry and cold now. 'We had better look at this dispassionately. Apart from your lying to me, your action may have a consequence which you would evidently welcome only too eagerly. For Campbell of Cairns, thickskinned like all his race, would probably raise no particular objection to his daughter marrying a Stewart – indeed, if matters turn out as you evidently hope, he would have to swallow any such objection. What if he holds that you have fatally injured her reputation – what then?'

Ian gave no intelligible reply. He had turned his back and laid his head against the hands which gripped the mantelshelf.

'Answer me what I have already asked you! Who else was at Kilrain?'

'Miss Campbell's woman – no one else.'

'How long were you there?'

'Two days.'

'And two nights?'

'Yes.'

'And you mean to tell me that there was no one else at Kilrain then, taking the whey? It is a fashionable enough occupation for gouty, scandalmongering old men!'

'There was no one else.'

'And no traveller passed through the clachan? It lies on a highroad, I believe.'

'One traveller passed.'

'He did not see you together, I hope?'

'Your hope is not justified.'

'He *did* see you? But – please God – he did not know either of you?'

Ian was silent.

'Answer me that, if you please – and try not to lie again!'

Ian suppressed all retort. 'He knew Miss Campbell – well, it seemed, and she him. He had known her since she was a child.'

'My God! A friend of the family – of her father's?'

'Apparently.'

'Then if he did his duty he would go straight and tell Cairns what he had seen!'

'As it happened,' said Ian, with infinitely more coolness than he was feeling, 'he was on his way into Lochaber. In any case he did not appear at all perturbed about Miss Campbell.'

' "He did not appear",' repeated his father scornfully. 'How can you tell what was in a stranger's mind, and what he would report? Your madness has – but there, what use to speak of it? I will give you credit for meaning what you said just now about having put away the idea of marrying Miss Campbell – you

770

could not be a Stewart and my son, with a brother lying under the sod of Culloden, without meaning it – but your disastrous folly has rendered all that unavailing. But the day that you are forced to marry Olivia Campbell, if it disgracefully comes to that, will see me carried to my grave . . . and I think you will not greatly care!'

Ian turned round; he was the colour of chalk. 'I will never marry Olivia Campbell – not if Cairns begged me to! – Father, I have done more than cut off my right hand that I might not fail in my duty to you and to the blood in my veins . . . and you can say such a thing as that about your death!'

'You have shaken my confidence too severely,' was the old man's unmoved reply. 'You may have done what you say, and I do not doubt your sincerity at the time, but – '

'In short, you don't trust me!' said Ian, flaring up. 'I have trampled my life's happiness under my feet – for you – and this is all the thanks I get for it! 'Tis true I never looked for thanks . . . but reproaches and distrust are a little too much to swallow quietly. – I think we had best bring this interview to an end!' And, seething with indignation, but impelled, too, by a fear of saying to his father what he would afterwards regret, he crossed quickly to the door and went out of the room, out of the house altogether.

Chapter 11

IAN STEWART LISTENS TO THE DEVIL

1 *Aug. 19th (continued)*

BEREFT of Jacqueline, Mr Hector Grant had meanwhile sat
down again upon the window-seat in the drawing-room, wishing, for once, that he had someone to advise him – Ewen
Cameron, for instance. But unfortunately Ewen was not
immediately available.

Jacqueline, sweet, half-timid creature, had left her silks
behind. The young officer took up and began to play with one
of the balls which she had been winding. His thoughts ran to the
little estate in Glenmoriston which his kinsman had left to him.
He had never seen it; nonetheless he began to imagine the house
– with Jacqueline in it ... The silken ball slid presently from his
fingers and bounced lightly upon the floor; Hector stooped to
recover it, and, just as he came upright again, was aware of a
man's figure going rapidly past the window – young Invernacree's for sure. So the interview in the study was over; he
could go in and have his.

Hector got up, and then sat down again. Was it wise to rush
in upon the old laird just now? How if he were to go instead
after young Stewart, and find out from him whether the
moment was propitious or no; even, perhaps, whether he and
his father had already discussed the situation? It occurred to
Captain Grant, for the first time, that quite possibly the covert
hostility in the young man's demeanour was due to that very
fact – that he, a suitor, had not spoken of his intentions in the
proper quarter. Ian Stewart might conceivably be thinking that
the visitor was only amusing himself with his sister. In that case
he could not bear a grudge against the suitor for revealing to
him that he was in earnest, and for tacitly asking his assistance
in proving it.

772

Yet even then there came to the impulsive and light-hearted young man a whimsical idea of letting chance direct his course. The ball of green silk was still in his hand; if he could roll it exactly on to a particular rose of the carpet he would go after young Invernacree; if not, he would seek the laird. To lay the matter still more upon the knees of the immortals Hector shut his eyes, and, slightly stooping, bowled his silken projectile gently along the floor, reflecting that, thus self-handicapped, it was very unlikely that he should judge either his goal or the necessary pace correctly.

He opened his eyes and received a shock. On the very heart of the faded rose stood a little sphere of vivid green. Hector did not know whether to be pleased or sorry. But having settled to abide by this test, he left the ball where it was and went out of the house in quest of Ian Stewart.

2

When he left his father's presence Ian had gone striding up the hillside behind the house so fast that, mountaineer though he was, his breath began to give out – but not his anger and his sense of injury. Finally, he came to a standstill under a clump of pines on a little plateau, and flung himself down upon a long-fallen trunk. The hills of Appin, softly contoured and warmly coloured, looked at him kindly, the line of strath below was green and pleasant, and between the trees he could see the pointed turrets of his home. But the young man's heart was too hot to feel a sense of peace or graciousness in anything. His father had been unjust and cruel; and his own great and difficult sacrifice, made so largely for his sake, was to go for nothing – because of Kilrain. And the magic of those few short hours with Olivia Campbell, already more bitter than sweet, was now, and always would be, bitter only. Ian hid his face in his hands.

Someone was coming up the slope. Ian rose hastily to his feet, and turning his back, pretended to be absorbed in examination of the trees above him. Meanwhile, the steps came nearer; their author was whistling a little tune between his teeth. And at the sound of it Ian faced round as if he had been stung, because he knew the air for French, and only one man hereabouts was likely to be whistling it. What the devil did Hector Grant mean by intruding himself on him at this moment of all others?

'Ah, 'tis you, Mr Stewart,' exclaimed the whistler as he arrived on the level of the little plateau. 'I was taking a stroll in this direction, and saw someone up here.' For Hector had decided that it might be wiser to conceal the fact that he had not come upon his quarry by accident, but as the result of inquiries.

'Yes, I was looking at these old trees,' said Ian shortly.

Hector perceived that his brow was overclouded. Nor did his manner diffuse geniality. Evidently the interview in the study had not been a pleasant one, whether the subject were timber or ... Jacqueline. He began to doubt whether the green silk ball had sent him in pursuit of young Invernacree at a propitious moment; and indeed, had he but known it, that ball had done him no good turn by causing him to stoop after it just after Ian passed the window, for had he seen the latter's face he would have thought more than twice before coming after him. However, here he was, and must go on with the business.

He seized upon the topic just introduced. 'Are they in danger, then, these trees – are you proposing to fell them?'

'Not immediately,' was the reply.

'I am glad of that,' responded the young officer. 'One does not see pines like these everywhere in the Highlands. But you of Appin are fortunate in your trees. How well, for instance, these oaks set off your house down there.' He turned and threw a glance at it.

'You think so?' inquired Ian, indifferently. Why did Captain Grant not continue his walk, if he had really been taking one, instead of standing here making conversation?

Now Hector did not at all relish this curt manner, and decided to learn the reason for it. 'Mr Stewart,' he asked, looking his contemporary straight in the face, 'have I offended you in any way?' In view of the object of his mission he went so far as to add immediately, 'I regret it very much if I have.'

'Offended me?' returned Ian, lifting his straight black brows. 'No, not that I am aware of. Why should you think so?'

'Because you are pretty short with me this afternoon,' returned Hector with truth. 'And, to be candid,' he hesitated a moment, 'my own conscience is not quite clear.'

'I am sorry to hear that,' replied Ian, folding his arms and leaning against the pine stem. But he did not sound sorry, he sounded bored, and Hector was piqued.

'I should be obliged if you could give me a few moments of your time, sir,' he said stiffly.

'Willingly,' answered Ian at once, but without changing his attitude. 'Only I am not, you know, qualified as a confessor – if you are a Catholic, that is.'

'You must know that I am not a Catholic,' retorted Hector with some warmth, scenting the erection of an imaginary barrier between himself and Jacqueline. 'From your acquaintance with my sister, who is your cousin Ardroy's wife, you must be aware that we are Episcopalians!'

'I beg your pardon,' said Ian, his manner suddenly as mild as milk. 'But I did not know what you might not have become after so long a residence in France.'

'I have never become anything but what I always was – a Highlander. Yes, and one thing besides. That is what I wish to speak to you about. Perhaps you can guess what I mean?'

'Not in the least,' said Ian with annoying lack of curiosity. 'Unless you mean that you have turned Whig or something of the sort.' He put up a hand to hide a yawn. 'In that case it would be better to confess to my father.'

'It would indeed be better to tell Mr Stewart what I have to tell, though it is certainly not a change in my politics,' agreed Hector, gathering momentum. 'Aye, I ought already to have told him – that is where I fear I have acted other than I should ... You have perhaps been speaking of the matter in your recent interview?'

Lightning came from the cloud at that. 'Interview? What do you know of any interview of mine?' flashed Ian, starting forward from the pine-tree. The merest reference to that scene flicked him on the raw. 'You were not present at it, so far as I know!'

Hector was brought up short. ' "So far as you know!" ' he repeated frowning. 'Pray, Mr Stewart, what do you mean by that expression?'

'Whatever you please,' replied Ian, resuming his pose against the tree. 'But, since you have somehow discovered that I have had a conversation with my father this afternoon, let me assure you that, from first to last, your name was not mentioned in it.'

It is certain that Hector Grant, the least pacifically-minded of young men, merited at this moment a good deal of commendation for keeping his temper in the face of provocation. But it was not his cue to quarrel with Ian Stewart if he could avoid it, so with an effort he passed over this suggestive speech, and said, 'May I be permitted to ask without offence, was there no mention neither of your sister, Miss Jacqueline Stewart!'

'Why should there be?' retorted Ian impatiently. 'And if there were, why should I be supposed to remember it and be interrogated upon the point?'

'I had no intention of interrogating you,' said Hector, biting his lip for a second. 'I only wished to ascertain ... but, in short Mr Stewart, I think you must be aware that I intend to ask in form for the hand of your younger sister.'

It was out now, and there was a silence under the pine-tree – charged, for all that the sun shone there and a bee was droning near, with a hostility almost sinister. Ian had not thought the affair between Jacqueline and the young soldier serious, but, on thus learning that it apparently was, an immense and unreasoning resentment surged up in him. His own love had suffered shipwreck at his own hand; why should another's immediately prosper; why should he help to give his little sister to a man whom he did not particularly like? The devil, moreover, suddenly showed his sore and tormented soul how he could prevent it.

He began with one hand to finger the crest of a tall stem of bracken beside him, though his eyes never moved from the figure of Hector Grant, standing before him against the back-

776

ground of space and hills. And at last he said slowly, 'Yes, I was afraid that that was the case.'

'Afraid?' interjected Hector. 'Why "afraid"?'

'However,' went on Ian with the same unwinking gaze, and a curious evenness of tone, 'since you have not yet approached my father on the matter there is no great harm done.'

'But I am going to approach him!' exclaimed the other.

The head of the fern bent and broke. 'I cannot prevent you, naturally. But I advise you not to do so.'

'And why, pray?' cried Hector, with one of his occasional half-French gestures. 'Are you so sure that Invernacree will refuse? I love your sister sincerely, I have every reason to believe that the feeling is returned, I have the means to support a wife, a home to take her to – '

Ian struck. 'And what sort of a name to give her?' he asked in a voice of steel. 'No sister of mine marries a man of whom it can be said that he once gave or sold information to a spy of the English Government!'

Hector Grant reeled back as though a thunderbolt had fallen between them; and he blanched slowly to the colour of ashes, as the guilty might blanch. 'Where . . . How did you hear that lie?' he gasped.

'Why, from a fellow-Jacobite – from Finlay MacPhair of Glenshian,' answered Ian, the devil still looking out of his eyes. 'So it is a lie, is it? Ardroy said it was. But then you are his brother-in-law; you were that before your transaction with the spy. Let me tell you, however, that you shall never be mine after it!'

Hector's pallor was now less that of ashes than of white-hot fury. He came right up to Ian where he stood under the pine-tree, with the scrap of bracken crushed in his hand. 'Glenshian, my worst enemy, told you that, and you believed it! Ewen told you that it was a lie, and yet you believe it! . . . No, no, you *pretend* to believe it, thinking to keep your sister from me! You are a damned dirty scoundrel, not worthy of the name you carry!' And he struck Ian with the back of his hand across the face.

3

For long after his son had flung indignantly out of the room old Invernacree had sat at his writing table, turning over papers with shaking hands, and then, when he was a little recovered from his agitation, really trying to give his mind to them in order to fend off other thoughts. But the effort, though he kept it up doggedly, was vain, and by the time the last ray of sun had slid from his southern window he was sitting there motionless, thinking – and thinking of his own first wooing, so many years ago. Yes, he had been too harsh with Ian; the boy had done his best. And, if he had gone after the enchantress, he had cut loose in the end. Ian himself had seen that the marriage was out of the question. Surely he could trust him not to go back upon his word, surely he could! Surely if, at Kilrain, Ian had not acted as he averred, he would have kept silence about the whole matter instead of admitting the meeting, as he had done. He had been too hard with his son over the small measure of deceit which he had employed; and he must tell him so.

Half abstractedly, as he reached this decision, Alexander Stewart observed the figure of a man coming hastily across the lawn from the stile which gave on to the hill path. For a moment he thought that it might be Ian's; then he saw that it was young Grant, and that he seemed to be in considerable haste.

A moment or two later there was a knock at the study door, and Invernacree's, 'Come in,' brought the young man in question with the same air of haste about him.

'Is anything amiss, Mr Grant?' asked Invernacree in some surprise, for there was discomposure as well in his visitor's mien.

'I am sorry to say, sir,' replied Hector, 'that I have just received news from the factor of my little estate in Glenmoriston which necessitates my immediate presence there.'

'But you will not set off this evening, surely?' asked Alexander Stewart, glancing at the clock.

'I fear that I must, sir. There is full time at least to cross the

ferry at Ballachulish, even if I get no farther, and that will be so
much gained in the morning. I deeply regret the necessity of so
sudden a departure, but I must pack my valise without a
moment's delay, and, if I may, order my horse to be brought
round while I make my adieux to the ladies.'

There was no doubt that the haste was genuine. 'I am very
sorry indeed, Captain Grant, to lose you thus suddenly,' said the
old laird courteously. 'The news from your factor is not, I fear,
of a very welcome order?'

'It is ... disturbing,' admitted Captain Grant, but did not
particularize further. He was fidgeting as he stood there.

'You met the messenger somewhere on the road, I suppose?
But where is my son? Does he know of this?'

'Mr Stewart,' said the young officer quickly, 'was with me
when I ... received the news a while ago. He will meet me later;
I think he intends to set me on my road a little.'

'That is well,' said the old man, nodding his head. 'Go pack
your effects then, Mr Grant, since you must. I will give orders
about your horse, and Grizel shall have some refreshment set
ready for you.'

'I fear I'll not have time to partake of any, sir,' said Hector
even more hurriedly. 'But I beg you to receive my deep apologies for this unceremonious departure.'

'Needs must, Captain Grant, I suppose, when affairs drive
one. I trust it is not the devil in this case,' said Invernacree
smiling, and going much nearer to the truth than he knew. 'I
will see you again when you are ready, and speed your departure. I wonder where my daughters are.' He went to the door
of his room, calling, 'Grizel, Grizel!' and next moment, when
Grizel appeared at the door of the drawing-room, announced,
'Here's Mr Grant must leave us at once, unfortunately. Tell
your sister – '

Hector stayed to hear no more but ran up the stairs. At the
top he met Jacqueline, who had overheard, preparing to descend. She turned a scared face on her lover. He caught her
hands and drew her quickly into a dark corner of the landing.

'There is nothing wrong, *mon coeur*,' he said, but despite all

779

his efforts his voice and manner belied his words. 'I am urgently summoned to Glenmoriston on affairs. No,' he sank his voice, 'nothing has been said to your father about us – 'tis not that which causes my departure. I'll be back here, please God, before very long, and we'll get his blessing and fix the marriage day. But if I do not leave at once there may be no home to take you to when that day comes.'

' 'Tis you I want, not the home,' cried Jacqueline rather piti-fully.

In a shadow of a curtain which hung there Hector pressed her to him. 'I hope, my darling – ' he began, then seemed to stop himself from saying more, and, catching his breath, kissed her passionately. Disengaging himself, he rushed into his room at the other end of the passage, and could be heard dragging open drawers, and presumably flinging their contents into his valise.

A quarter of an hour later that object was being strapped behind the saddle of his horse, already at the front door, and Hector, cloaked and booted, holding his hat and cane, was bending over Grizel's hand uttering mingled thanks and apologies.

'Be sure, Mr Grant, to let us know how your business prospers,' said old Invernacree genially, as the young man mounted. 'And if you come south again this way, do not pass this door without knocking upon it. You say that you are to meet Ian upon the road – good!' Standing at Hector's stirrup he touched the long and solid cane of polished wood in the rider's hand. 'Do you usually encourage your horse with so stout a switch, young man?' he asked. 'I wonder he does not throw you.'

' 'Tis not for my horse, sir,' Hector assured him with a rather curious note in his voice. 'I have found it useful ere now against animals more noble ... or less, according as you look at the matter. Again a thousand thanks to you, sir, and to Miss Stewart, for your hospitality; and present my compliments, if you please, to Miss Jacqueline.'

He lifted his hat, bowed from the saddle with a somewhat

foreign grace, touched his horse with the spur and went down the avenue at a trot.

'Well, whatever has gone wrong with that young man's affairs let us hope that he will succeed in putting it right,' observed Invernacree, looking after him. 'A good seat on a horse – but he rides as though he were glad to escape from us!'

'Preserve us! if he has not jumped the gate!' exclaimed Grizel aghast.

'Young fool!' commented her father, turning round again with a frown. Then all at once he looked at his middle-aged daughter, with something a little wistful in his gaze. 'Yet I was young once, Grizel, and did many a thing as mad. But one forgets ... one forgets as the years go by.' And shaking his head with a sigh, he went back to his own room to wait for Ian's return.

Chapter 12

'OUT, SWORD, AND TO A SORE PURPOSE!'

1   *Aug. 19th (continued)*

AFTER his exhibition of horsemanship, of which, directly it was over, he felt somewhat ashamed, Hector Grant rode at a hard, pelting pace for about a mile and a half along the lochside road to the north. Then he pulled up to a slower gait, and went glancing about as though looking for someone or something. The light had waned a little, but for hours now it would not greatly diminish; over the loch on his left hand a clear saffron sky extended behind the peaks of Morven. On his right the road was pressed towards the water by slopes and thickets.

At last he came to a place where the shore widened considerably, because a stream had formed a small delta there. A rough bridge spanned this stream where it crossed the road, and by it a man was standing waiting. Hector pulled up.

'Is this the place?' he asked.

Ian nodded. 'If you will dismount I will lead your horse down to the shore; it will be best not to leave him here.'

Hector swung off, and young Invernacree, taking his horse's bridle, led the animal down a rough path to the shingle below. Here he hitched the reins on to a tree stump projecting from the bank.

'No one passing can easily see him from above, I think. I can find no spot convenient for our business in the wood beyond the road. But the shore is level enough, and will serve.' Ian's voice was perfectly expressionless; he might have been reading out of a rather dull book.

Hector looked round. The worst that could be said of the chosen ground was it was stony. At its mouth the little river was continually rearing up a bank of pebbles, which any especially high tide in Loch Linnhe had continually dispersed over the foreshore.

' 'Twill serve very well, provided we are not interrupted,' he pronounced. 'Here is my sword; you had best handle it a little to become accustomed to it. I have brought the sword-stick of which I spoke for myself.' Laying his sheathed sword on the ground, he took hold with both hands of the stout cane on which Invernacree had commented, touched a spring and drew out a long, sharp steel blade.

'I cannot accept your sword,' said Ian, with at last a sign of life in his dead voice, 'the weapons are not evenly matched. Give me the other.'

For since no resident Highland gentleman might possess any arms, this coming bloodshed had only been rendered possible by the chance of Captain Grant's having brought with him on his travels a swordstick, as well as the more usual weapon at his side. Up under the pine clump, after Ian's accusation had provoked him to the blow which rendered a meeting inevitable (provided neither of the two had tried to strangle the other out of hand, which for a moment or two seemed probable, though actually they did not touch each other again) this expedient had been decided upon, and the pretext for Hector's sudden departure invented also.

But Hector would not subscribe to this theory of inequality.

'No, on the contrary I assure you they are well enough matched,' said he. 'See, the length is the same, or very near.' He unsheathed the sword, and held the blades up together.

'No, no, I will not use your sword,' declared Ian. 'The swordstick has no guard, for one thing; you could not parry with safety to your hand.'

'Then, since you think it inferior, I cannot consent to your using it either,' retorted his opponent. 'In that case, what are we to do?'

His tethered horse – the nobler animal or the less noble – turned its gentle, intelligent head and looked at them with the air of mildly wondering what he had been brought down here for. Then, swishing his tail, he resumed his search for nourishment among the stones. Nearer the loch a pair of oyster-catchers, disturbed in their fishing, were running to and fro like mechanical toys and keeping up their insistent cry. And for a moment, under the influence of this disparity of chances, when either duellist was unwilling to take a supposed advantage for himself, and the whole tension of the situation was lowered by their having to make and discuss their own arrangements – formalists were wise who did not allow parties to a quarrel to speak to each other again after the challenge – even, perhaps, under the influence of the peace and loneliness which brooded over this lake shore, it seemed as if some kind of truce might have been patched up. In fact the hot-tempered Hector actually made a step towards that consummation.

'I suppose,' he said in a voice shackled with embarrassment, looking at the oyster-catchers by the water's edge, 'I suppose, Mr Stewart, that you would not be willing to apologize for what you said to me – which I cannot believe that you really meant?'

'Apologize – after a blow!' exclaimed Ian, flushing up; and in spite of himself his hand went to the little abrasion on his lip which Hector's signet ring had set there. 'No, by Heaven – not even if you apologized for striking me!'

Hector stiffened at once. 'There is no question of that,' he returned coldly. 'Apologize because you insulted me, *parbleu*! – Take my sword, and let us delay no longer!' And laying down the two blades, he tore off his coat and waistcoat.

But Ian had put his hand into a pocket and now held out a coin. 'Let this decide the question of weapons. Otherwise I insist on having the swordstick.'

'Very well,' agreed Hector. 'Do you spin. Head, you take the sword – shield I do.'

Ian threw up the florin so that it fell tinkling upon a flat stone at his side. The young men both bent over it. His Majesty King George II, whose effigy was to decide this matter for subjects who denied his suzerainty, presented to them his unbeautiful profile,

'The sword is yours,' said Hector with relief. 'Now you need hesitate no longer, sir. And don't fancy,' he added, 'that you have the advantage on account of it, for I wager I have had more practice at this game than you.'

He only meant to appease his over-scrupulous adversary, but his words savoured too much of patronage to be palatable to the latter. Ian said nothing openly in reply, but, inwardly cursing the speaker's insolence, he flung off his outer garments until he, like Hector, was in shirt and breeches, caught up the naked sword, tested the poise and made a pass or two with it in the direction of the bank. Then, perceiving that there was more breeze blowing than he had thought, he laid it down again and, removing the ribbon from his queue, tied his hair back more securely, lest a loose wisp might blow suddenly across his eyes.

Captain Grant meanwhile was carefully examining the surface of the ground which they had chosen, picking up or kicking away a loose stone here and there. He had no mind that either of them should slip and bring about a catastrophe, for he intended merely to give his calumniator something to remember him by, no more. To inflict a serious wound upon the brother of his lady-love, however badly that brother had behaved towards him, would scarcely be a passport to the good graces of anyone in the family. Before he had come down from the hillside where they had quarrelled Hector was aware of that awkward fact.

But Ian had no such consideration to restrain him. The recognition of his own culpable folly, which he had had plenty of time to make, did not, for all that, tend to repentance. The child nature which survives in all of us cried in a small, ashamed but angry voice that just because he had been 'naughty' he would go on being 'naughty' still; and all the more so because he was faced with the possibility of a very unpleasant payment for his naughtiness. That he was in the last resort hazarding his life in this course must atone for the wilfulness. Never in all his days had he suffered the indignity of a blow, or imagined one being offered to him; and he shut his eyes to the knowledge that never in all his days had he afforded another man such justification for dealing him one.

Hector, having now ceased his scrutiny of the ground, had picked up the swordstick and was rolling up his right sleeve in a business-like manner. Since he wore a wig he had no need to emulate Ian's precaution; yet even so the sea breeze suddenly lifted the ends of his lace cravat. He untied it, threw it off, and looked at his antagonist.

'Are you ready?' he asked. Ian, without a word, saluted and came on guard; and in the silence the blades clicked together and engaged.

They had not clicked many times before Ian became aware that his adversary's recent boast (as he termed it) was justified. If not a better theoretical swordsman – for young Invernacree had learnt of a good *maître d'armes* – Captain Grant was a much more experienced duellist ... and small wonder. Ian had never fought in earnest before. The knowledge angered him extraordinarily, and even the realization of the peril in which he consequently stood, instead of sobering him, merely infuriated him still further. Yet, lunge or parry as he might, he could not get rid of the menace of that ever-shifting steel at the level of his breast, directed by the same hand which had given him the recent blow across the mouth. He felt, in fancy, the tingle of it still. God! if he could only mark that handsome, intent face opposite as his had been marked! He began to consider by what feint he could best get past Captain Grant's very competent guard to accomplish this amiable design; neglected his own defence for a second – and immediately paid the penalty. Quicker, almost, than the eye could follow, Hector's watchful point had slipped over his blade, and was sliding and tearing its way along his forearm to bury itself above the bent elbow ... It was plucked out again at once, and Hector, springing back, lowered his sword.

'It's nothing!' cried Ian furiously, though the sensation was like redhot wire, and the blood was streaming down his bared arm. Yet he managed to retain hold of his weapon. 'Come on – we have not finished!'

'No, that must be tied up first,' declared his opponent, his point nearly on the stones. 'Have you a handkerchief?'

But something told Ian that if he stopped for bandaging he would never be able to continue. Already it was difficult to grip his sword. All the more, therefore, did he say threateningly, 'On guard again, if you please, Captain Grant! This is not the end!'

But Hector, instead of complying, held up his left hand for silence. *'Chut!'* he said in a quick whisper, 'I heard voices! Someone is coming along the road up there.'

'Damnation!' muttered Ian. But in that at least he and his foe were at one; neither had any wish for witnesses. He too listened, he too heard voices . . . Clutching hold of his right arm – the hilt of the sword was now sticky with blood – he went reluctantly towards the bank, which, when one was close under it, would probably shelter one from view. Then only did he let fall his weapon, and thereafter himself sat down rather suddenly upon a large stone projecting from the bank. The loch had all at once begun to glitter strangely; indeed it seemed to be invading the shore with its brightness. But the voices on the road above, instead of coming nearer, died away altogether. He fumbled vainly with his left hand at his right shirt-sleeve, essaying the impossible task of tearing off a piece of the linen to staunch the blood. Then someone else seemed to be tying up the wound, and, though the process hurt, the fingers were not, he felt, ungentle. Ian leant his head back against the bank and shut his eyes. After a space there was the taste of brandy in his mouth.

'Have they passed?' he heard a voice asking – perhaps his own.

'Some time ago,' was the reply made to him. 'But, Mr Stewart, we cannot continue this affair. It is out of the question.' He knew this voice now for Hector Grant's. It sounded grave, and quite near him. Ian opened his eyes, triumphed over the strange difficulty he found in focusing them, and saw his late opponent kneeling on one knee beside him, with a little flask of eau-de-vie in his hand. He himself was still sitting against the bank. From Captain Grant's face his gaze went to his own right arm, round which were neatly and tightly fastened two pocket-handkerchiefs, both considerably reddened.

787

'Why is it out of the question?' he asked stupidly.

'*Corbleu*, look at your arm!' expostulated Hector. 'You are worse hurt than you know, though I think it is only a flesh wound. Moreover, we *have* fought. For myself I regard my honour satisfied ... and I am willing to express regret for having struck you.'

Ian thought, in what seemed left to him of mind at the moment, 'I suppose he expects me to say that I am sorry I practically charged him with espionage,' but he knew that he was not going to. Out of his pallid lips there came only a muttered, 'If only I had learnt to fence with my left hand too!'

The successful swordsman took no notice of this aspiration. He seemed to regard the business at an end, for he rose to his feet and said, with a certain visible anxiety, 'I do not quite know, Mr Stewart, how you are to get home again.'

'What does that matter?' asked Ian, looking at his bandaged arm, which now seemed to belong to someone else – and yet, every now and then, to be only too unpleasantly his own property. 'Naturally, I shall return as I came.' And he rose to his feet, only a little care being necessary for this proceeding. 'There is your sword,' he said, pointing to it, for it seemed wiser not to attempt to pick it up. 'You were right after all; there was not much advantage in its possession.'

Hector stood in front of him. 'I beg of you,' he said earnestly, 'to accept the loan of my horse as far as your own gate. I will accompany you on foot, and afterwards – '

'Indeed you will not!' said Ian sharply. 'I am perfectly capable of walking back to Invernacree on my own feet.' And, passing Hector, he returned to the spot where he had thrown down his coat and waistcoat, but made no comment when Hector, hastening after him, picked them up and assisted him into them in silence. But when the operation was finished the victor made a last appeal.

'Mr Stewart, I was greatly in your debt once. You helped me to freedom. I beg of you – '

'Debt?' said Ian harshly. 'I think you have remembered that somewhat late. No,' he added, his better self rising for a

788

moment to the surface, 'I will not say that; I brought this on myself. But I ask you to excuse me the further humiliation of returning to my home as the captive of your bow and spear. I wish you good speed on your journey; I'll be about mine.' And, slightly raising his hat with his left hand, he walked with a firm step away from his antagonist across the little strip of shore, and went slowly up the path by which they had descended, Hector making no move to follow him save with his eyes.

But standing there alone in his shirt and breeches, he swore softly to himself in French, adding, '*Eh bien*, if Monsieur Lucifer falls by the wayside, as I think he probably will, *Dieu sait que ce n'est pas ma faute!*'

'It is clear,' he soliloquized, as he untethered his horse a moment or two later, 'that they are right who regard green as an unlucky colour. Though I suppose, *mon ami*, that it is your favourite one!' He wrenched down a handful of grass from the bank, gave it to his steed and then tugged him up to the road above. There was no sign upon it of his wounded antagonist; so Hector flung himself into the saddle, and was off in the other direction on the second of his quests, the settling of his score with Finlay MacPhair of Glenshian. But now it was a double score.

2

Monsieur Lucifer, however, did not fall by the wayside. It was not indeed easy, that mile and a half back to Invernacree, but Ian compassed it somehow, and, about three-quarters of an hour later, stood upon the doorstep of his own home, sick and giddy, full of the miserable knowledge that he had behaved abominably, that he deserved sympathy from none, that his father, when he learnt how he had treated his guest, would feel inclined to disown him, and that Jacqueline, whose life's happiness he had probably jeopardized ... But Jacqueline, at least, he did not intend to encounter.

With a swimming head and patches of mist floating most inconveniently across his vision, he opened the outer door. And there, mist or no mist, there was Jacqueline in the hall, caressing his spaniel. Ian paused irresolute on the threshold; then, leaving the door open, he advanced, fending off the bounding dog with his left hand.

'Ah, there you are, Ian,' said his young sister. She looked as if she had been crying. 'We did not wait supper for you, but – Mercy on us, how pale you are! What has happened?'

'I have met with a slight accident,' said Ian confusedly. 'Nothing to be alarmed about.' Encountering a settle, he sank gratefully upon it, and, as Jacqueline stared at him in dismay (for in truth his appearance was enough to alarm any female, sister or no) Roger, the spaniel, completed his overthrow. For, putting his forepaws on the settle, he poked his nose violently under his master's right elbow in order to draw attention to himself. A cry which he could not wholly suppress broke from Ian; he half rose, fell back again, and then, to Jacqueline's horror, slid completely off the settle and lay in a huddle at her feet. Roger, with tucked-in tail, first fled to a safe distance, then turned and barked long and furiously, on which there came out Invernacree, anxious to know if Ian had returned; and what he saw was the son from whom he had recently parted in anger lying motionless on the floor, with a young girl clasping one of his hands and crying his name distractedly to ears which did not hear.

Chapter 13

CASTLE DANGEROUS

1   *Aug. 21st–27th*

IT was two o'clock of the afternoon when Hector Grant, in the
rain, rode his weary horse up to the doors of the House of
Invershian and, without giving his name, demanded to see the
Chief. On being told that Mac 'ic Fhionnlaigh was out at the
moment he said firmly that he would await his return, and was
shown in to do so.

Finlay MacPhair, for all his importance, possessed no dwelling commensurate with his dignity – but that was not his fault.
The ancestral castle of the MacPhairs had been half destroyed
and gutted before his day; after the Rising still further vengeance had been wreaked upon its ancient stones, and the Chief
of Glenshian consequently lived in a house scarcely to be distinguished from the farm of a well-to-do tacksman. He talked
very largely about rebuilding at least the keep of Castle Shian,
but it was not evident whence the money was to come for this
reconstruction.

The old man who now ushered in Captain Grant dwelt with
apologetic intent upon the transitory nature of the present habitation, but Hector happened to know that the old Chief,
Finlay's father, had also lived in these modest surroundings –
and no shame to him. If the English had rendered the pile
reared by Red Finlay of the Battles a mere resort for owls and
toads, its owner still abode almost within sight of what had been
for centuries the home of his race.

For some time Hector walked restlessly about the room, his
wrongs reviving within him. At last he heard a voice outside the
door saying in Gaelic, 'A gentleman to see me? Aye, I know
who it is; I have been awaiting him. Bring him to me in the
other room, and fetch a stoup of wine also.'

791

Awaiting him, forsooth, and a stoup of wine! Not much of Mr MacPhair's wine was going to pass *his* lips! But Glenshian could not have been expecting him; it was a mistake.

The old servant entered and said that Mac 'ic Fhionnlaigh would receive Mr Maitland.

'But my name's not Maitland!' cried Hector. The old man, however, either heard not or decided to pay no heed, but flung open a door; and as Mr MacPhair would soon discover who this alleged 'Mr Maitland' was, Hector stepped into his presence with a certain pleasurable anticipation.

The room, surprisingly large and long for the size of the house, had a deep hearth at one end on which, in deference to the bad weather, a newly-lighted fire was burning. The Chief had evidently just flung on some fresh fuel, for a blaze shot behind him as, turning round quickly, he came forward a few steps and said, 'I bid you welcome, Mr Mait – ' Then his jaw dropped, his outstretched hand also.

'My name is not Maitland,' said Hector, beginning to enjoy himself. 'You were not expecting me, Mr Finlay MacPhair, were you? We are now going to have the explanation which you have owed me since May, '53, and in addition a fresh one of the slander you put upon me not many weeks since!'

'Explanation!' repeated Glenshian haughtily. He had recovered from his surprise. 'Do you really imagine, Mr Grant, that you can come and demand "explanations" from me in my own house?'

'I do, indeed,' retorted Hector. 'But I can well believe you will find them so difficult to give that this,' he tapped his sword-hilt, 'will prove the only key to the situation.'

'If you are planning another murderous assault upon me,' observed his enemy, 'let me warn you that – beside not being able to run away after it this time – if you so much as touch me – '

'A cock that won't fight, eh?' queried Hector contemptuously, 'Don't be afraid, Mr MacPhair. If you must shelter yourself behind a hedge of gillies, then you are not worth the crossing swords with again. Nevertheless, I intend to have satisfaction, in some form or other, both for your black treachery in London two years ago, and for your libelling me here in the Highlands before Ian Stewart of Invernacree!'

'Will you be so good as to leave this room?' inquired Finlay in a tone of suppressed passion.

'When I have had what I came for, not before!' retorted Hector.

'You may very well get more than you came for!' said his involuntary host threateningly. 'Set down the wine, Roderick,' for the old man had just come in with the stoup, 'and show this gentleman out at once!'

'If I consent to go now,' declared Hector, 'I warn you, I shall remain in the neighbourhood, and tell you before witnesses – not servants – what I think of your conduct!'

But at this the young Chief merely turned his back and went and held out his hands to the fire.

The action infuriated Hector beyond bearing. He strode up to him, swung him round by the shoulder, and said through his teeth, 'I *will* have it out with you, you go-between and traitor!'

The old man near the door uttered a shrill exclamation, flung it open and called out in Gaelic. Almost instantly the sound of running feet could be heard in the passage, though Hector, occupied in glaring into eyes which glared back at him, was scarcely conscious of the sound. But Finlay heard it, and, without removing his wolf's gaze, called out a brief order to those whom the feet were bringing:

'Remove this gentleman to some place where he will not molest me!'

Then did Hector become aware of his danger. Six or seven shaggy and unkempt individuals were precipitating themselves into the room from the door at the farther end. But he had small intention of being 'removed' tamely. Springing back from the Chief's vicinity, he tugged out his sword and faced the gillies, gratified to see that the two foremost, who appeared to have no weapons, showed marked signs of hesitation at the appearance of the naked steel. The next moment a shock ran along his arm and his sword snapped off short near the hilt. Glenshian, half behind him, had snatched up the long, heavy bar used for stirring the peats in the big fire, and brought it down upon his blade. And the famous swordstick was fastened to his saddle outside . . .

Hector flung the useless hilt at Mr MacPhair's face and launched himself unarmed into the thick of the Chief's retainers, in a gallant effort to fight his way through them to the door. He never reached it; at least not of his own volition . . .

Five minutes later the Chief of Glenshian sat down by the hearth in the now empty and quiet room, with the stoup of wine beside him. The hilt of a broken sword still lay on the hearth-stone; he smiled scornfully, and pushed it away with his foot. Then, pouring himself out a glass of wine, he pulled forth and re-read a very dirty and ill-written letter with the Edinburgh post-mark; and afterwards, drumming his fingers impatiently upon the table, sat looking into the fire with a frown.

'He *must* be on his way by this time,' he muttered. 'He dare not neglect to come'; and so sat, the glass of claret untasted at his elbow.

2

Four empty wine-barrels (on one of which stood an unlighted candle) and one empty keg; a pallet with a couple of blankets, a rough ewer and basin and an armchair which, being up-holstered in red leather, was, even if shabby, scarcely of a piece with this retreat – these, its only furniture, the occupant of that retreat was this morning surveying, for perhaps the two hundredth time, with the emotions proper to a captive of singularly unresigned temperament. But he had ceased to relieve that temperament by swearing, for even the resources of three languages had by now proved unequal to so prolonged a strain upon them, since this was the morning of the sixth day which Hector Grant had spent in the Chief of Glenshian's disused wine-cellar. Partly below the level of the ground, it had all the disadvantages pertaining to that situation, save that it was not especially damp;

but it was cold, and filled at the brightest hour in the day with an extremely depressing twilight, and at all hours with a chill draught which filtered into it through a small grating about a couple of feet from the floor.

Hector was leaning, silent, against one of the walls, his hands in his breeches pockets, looking at the wine-casks. He was thinking what delight it would have given him, had they been full, to remove a spigot and let Finlay MacPhair's good wine run about the floor, not to speak of drinking a proportion of it. But alas, neither French wine nor French brandy were his for the broaching; that keg of Nantes had long been dry. Having the first day, however, heard the sound of liquid falling into a vessel, he had stooped and peered through the grating, and had made out, in what seemed to be another cellar, the rotundities of barrels which were not, evidently, empty like these in his prison. And once every day, after that, there had come thither for a supply of wine – as he could see by screwing himself into an uncomfortable position – the old man called Roderick, who had both admitted him to the House of Invershian and summoned the retainers to eject him from the Chief's presence.

If Captain Grant was at all tamed by the experience to which his rough handling by these gentry had been the prelude, no sign of it had been vouchsafed to any eye which so far had rested upon him. Whatever fits of rage, indignation or quasi-despair passed over him in secret lay between him and the regard of heaven; most certainly the mocking gaze which he must shortly encounter would be permitted to discern nothing of these emotions. For about this time Glenshian daily arrived in person to inquire of his contumacious prisoner whether he had yet come to his senses and to a proper recognition of the outrageousness of his behaviour. The moment that he was ready to apologize for this and to withdraw his allegations against the Chief, Hector was given to understand that his stay among the barren wine-casks was over.

If this were the only gate through which he could regain his freedom, Hector saw little prospect of ever beholding the blue sky again, for even had Glenshian's finger been on the trigger of a pistol held against his breast, the young officer would not have consented to apologize nor to withdraw his charges. And since his attempts both at breaking out unaided and at bribery had proved futile, and the chances of rescue (seeing that no one knew for certain where he was) were exceedingly small, the only real hope he cherished was that his obstinacy would in the end wear down Glenshian's patience, and that he would at last set him free of his own motion. But that consummation was unlikely to occur just yet, since this – curse it! – was only the sixth day of captivity.

Think of the devil ... was that Glenshian's step already? Hector started away from the wall, passed a condemnatory hand over his chin – he had no razor – congratulated himself (in the absence of a comb) that he was wearing a wig and not his own hair, pulled down his waistcoat, and, going over to the ancient chair, seated himself therein with an air of being much at his ease and quite content with his surroundings.

The door was unlocked; Somerled, the stalwart, bearded gillie who was in charge of him, entered and stood aside, and when Glenshian had stepped in, closed the door and stood with his back against it. Finlay surveyed his prisoner for a moment under half-lowered lids, his head thrown back – a favourite attitude of his. A faint smile just touched his lips.

'Good day, Mr Grant.'

'Good day, MacPhair,' responded Hector, in the cheery tone which one might use to a superior servant come for orders. He knew quite well that any display of rage was merely gratifying to his captor, and had very soon abandoned even the sulky dignity in which he had at first clothed himself. His present attitude was that his sojourn in this cellar was perfectly indifferent to him; and if this pretence did not lack transparence, it undoubtedly gave his enemy less ground for open triumph.

Very stately and upright, Finlay continued to look at him. He, on his side, was now sustaining the role of the just, patient and not unmerciful judge, who is still amenable to some sign of penitence in the reprobate.

'Well, Mr Grant,' he said at length, 'are you ready to apologize and withdraw?'

'I beg your pardon?' inquired Hector, leaning a little forward, as though he did not quite catch the words. Then, their meaning having apparently penetrated, he smiled indulgently. 'My dear Mr MacPhair, I should really have credited you with more intelligence than to waste your time like this! Surely you have something more profitable to do with it – some other man of your own party whom you could vilify to his associates behind his back! Fix up a notice here in your best handwriting inviting me to do as you say – 'twould be every whit as effective – or send a gillie each morning with the invitation. 'Pon my soul, I am not sure that I should notice the difference!' he concluded drawlingly.

The Chief of Glenshian took no notice of this piece of rudeness. He said, in a manner which combined the most lofty-seeming detachment with a subterranean grimness which was not at all detached: 'You anticipate my intentions in the most remarkable way, Mr Grant. This *is* the last time that I am coming in person to offer you so simple means of regaining your liberty. I have been much too easy with you; had you lived in the time of Red Finlay of the Battles you would certainly not be alive five days after laying hands on the Chief of Clan Mac-Phair – no, not one day! So you are going to learn something of the methods which – if he had spared your life at all – Fionn-lagh Ruadh nan Cath would have employed. After a short experience of them you are likely to desire to exchange them again for mine; but you will then have to send and beg me to receive your apology.'

'Indeed?' said Hector, crossing his legs. 'It still has not dawned upon you that when I am traced here there will be a pretty heavy reckoning to be paid by the present Fionnlagh Ruadh?'

'As I observe no signs of your being traced anywhere,' retorted Glenshian with perfect truth, 'I am not disturbed at the notion. And if they do come, your friends will undoubtedly find that you have already procured your release on the terms which

I have stated. I will, therefore, wish you good day ... until you send for me.'

He was gone, and the captive was left again to the uninspiring society of the wine-casks. The only bright spot in the twenty-four hours was Hector's brief daily passage of arms with his enemy. And now he was apparently to be deprived of that. He was faintly uneasy also; what change for the worse in his circumstances was Glenshian proposing? The times of that early and bloody-minded MacPhair, Red Finlay of the Battles, had not been remarkable for humanity, as Hector well knew, and his descendant now seemed disposed in some way or other to revert to them.

' 'Tis preposterous!' exclaimed the captive, leaping up from his chair. 'Glenshian is downright mad – he ought to be in Bedlam ...'

Perhaps, but he was not in Bedlam; he was at liberty, and a petty king in his own way. Hector, had not as yet suffered any actual bodily ill-treatment, beyond that incurred in the initial struggle with the Chief's gillies; surely it was not possible that Glenshian, in this civilized eighteenth century, was really contemplating a return to the barbarities of the fourteenth!

Yet a distinct chill, creeping over his intrepid spirit, reminded Hector that he could do nothing to prevent such a reversion. For the first time he began seriously to wonder whether it was possible that he should never set eyes on the inheritance which had been left to him – never see again the charming Appin girl whom he designed to bring there as its mistress ...

'Nonsense!' he thought, squaring his shoulders. 'Things which could be done with impunity in Red Finlay's day cannot be done now. For one thing, there is the English garrison at Fort Augustus to reckon with. If only I could communicate with them in some way ...' And then, with genuine dismay, he realized what he was doing – he who had never lost an opportunity of denouncing the presence of the Sassenach invader, with his hated redcoats, in the Highlands ... It was something of a shock, and he sat soberly down in his shabby armchair again. All the same, if Governor Traupaud only knew ...

His rather shamefaced pursuance of this thought was broken into by a clinking sound which came through the grating. That was old Roderick fetching wine – and not drawing it from the cask this time either. There must be bottles of it also in the adjacent cellar; Hector felt he could well have done with one in his. Voices too ... Somerled, his gaoler, had evidently gone in after Roderick – a conjuncture which had never taken place before. Hector had not, therefore, had the opportunity till now of discovering how clearly he could hear what was said in the next cellar, even in Gaelic, a tongue of which he had a good working knowledge, but which, owing to his residence abroad, he rarely had the chance of speaking, and did not indeed follow with quite the same ease as English or French. But he quickly made out that Somerled was giving expression to precisely his own sentiments about the wine.

'Though indeed,' Hector heard him add in his big, gruff voice, 'I have drunk it, and that not longer ago than last June.'

'You surely did not steal a bottle, Somerled!' said the aged retainer in shocked tones.

'Indeed no! But Mac 'ic Fhionnlaigh sent out a bottle from his own table that Seumas and I might drink his health. You cannot have forgotten that, Roderick. 'Twas the night he came back so late from Ardroy with those two missing steers of his.'

The old man gave an exclamation. 'Aye, I remember that now, to be sure. Indeed, I do not know how I came to be forgetting it, for I was asking myself at the time why Mac 'ic Fhionnlaigh should be doing such a thing when there was plenty of usquebaugh to hand.'

Hector, attracted by the mention of the word 'Ardroy', had pricked up his ears. What on earth had Finlay been doing with steers at Ardroy – buying some from Ewen?

'Usquebaugh!' Somerled was saying with a contemptuous laugh. 'That evening's work was worth something better than usquebaugh, and so the Chief thought. By St Bride, you should have seen the laird of Ardroy's face when Seumas showed the brand on the beasts!'

'Aye, I heard of that,' assented Roderick. 'Ardroy's men had stolen the steers – though he swore they had not. No doubt Mac 'ic Fhionnlaigh was glad to be getting them back; I remember his look at supper that night. And yet,' he pursued, with the persistence of an old man, and one who was jealous of his master's best wine, 'yet I do not know why you and your half-brother should have been given a bottle of this claret, which Glenshian brought specially from London with him last year.'

'Do you not, then!' retorted Somerled half-mockingly. 'What if I were to be telling you – ' But here he stopped, and, no doubt pointing to the grating, said, in a lower tone, 'The gentleman within there can hear us, I'm thinking.'

'No matter if he do,' retorted old Roderick. 'He is but a French officer from over the sea, and will not have the Gaelic, though he has the English well enough. There's no word of Erse in his mouth, now, is there?'

'No, that's true.' Evidently reassured, Somerled went on: 'Well, then, we drank the Chief's health that night with a will, for it's he that has the cunning; and we pledged each other too, Seumas and I, for doing his work to his liking.'

'For bringing back the steers, you mean. *Dhé!* that was no great feat.'

'Nay,' said Somerled with a laugh, 'for something better than that. For putting them there for the Chief to find!'

'Putting them there! *putting them there!*' repeated Roderick incredulously.

'Aye, Seumas and I had driven them over two nights before, by Mac 'ic Fhionnlaigh's orders. 'Twas not difficult, for there was a moon. And we left them in the grazing grounds of Ardroy's own cattle – two good steers such as a thief would have chosen. And when Ardroy in his wrath had all his beasts collected together to prove that the Chief's were not among them – ' He broke off, perhaps with a gesture to complete his meaning.

Moving like a shadow, Hector went on to his hands and knees and took a quick glance through the grating. He could see old

Roderick's back, with the end of a bottle showing under either arm. Somerled he could not see.

Roderick was cackling appreciatively. 'I wish I had been there . . . he, he, he! And Ardroy never guessed?'

'How should he? He thought that his men had been helping themselves to Mac 'ic Fhionnlaigh's cattle without his knowledge – which was just what the Chief wished him to think– and he was exceedingly angry and ashamed. It was a good jest.'

'And it was only for a jest that the Chief was after doing it?'

'Why else?'

'Because he is so clever,' quoth Roderick admiringly. 'Cleverer than the old Chief, God rest him. I am wondering, therefore, why he should have taken so much trouble.'

And Hector, listening open-mouthed, was wondering too.

'Was it not worth trouble to humble the Cameron, who had sworn that his men were not cattle-thieves?' inquired Somerled. 'It was a good hour for a MacPhair like myself, that, and to Mac 'ic Fhionnlaigh it was even better, as I could see.'

'Well, I never heard the like,' commented the old man, beginning slowly to move towards the door with his bottles. 'Yes, 'tis no wonder he was pleased, and sent you the wine.'

'Here, don't be leaving your keys, man!' said Somerled, 'otherwise I might be helping myself to another bottle of the Chief's claret; or my fine gentleman in there, if he should take a fancy to try again to break through the grating, would find the door unlocked. Not, indeed, that he will be able much longer to play any such pranks.'

'Why not?' asked the old man, stopping; and it is certain that Hector prepared every nerve of hearing to catch the answer. He also took another comprehensive look through the grating in question; and so, both men now being within his range and vision, he saw with disappointment the hitherto incautious Somerled stoop his bearded lips to old Roderick's ear and whisper something inaudible. The old man gave an exclamation of surprise. Somerled laughed, drew back, and laid a finger on his own lips; upon which Roderick, shaking his head with what appeared to be disapproval, hobbled out without another word, followed by his informant.

On the other side of the grating Hector raised himself slowly from his hands and knees, and sat back frowning. That was an extraordinary affair – that of the steers ... but he wished very much he did not feel that he was soon going to hear of one perhaps even stranger, in which he himself was destined to play the central part.

Chapter 14

'WILL YOU WALK INTO MY PARLOUR?'

1

Aug. 28th

AND meanwhile he *was* on his way, the man whom Finlay
MacPhair had been expecting. He was not even very far off, but
his progress had been delayed by a recurrence of the fever of
which he had spoken so lightly to Olivia Campbell that day at
Kilrain. It was in fact a recurrence so severe that David Maitland had collapsed at the door of a little cottage near Let-
terfinlay, on Loch Lochy, four days before Hector Grant
made his ill-fated attempt to settle his score with the Chief of
Glenshian.

It was to require ten days' stay with the very poor but hos-
pitable couple who lived in that miserable dwelling, and such
rudimentary care as they could give, before Maitland was well
enough to think of resuming his interrupted journey to Invershian. Just a week after Finlay the Red had sat reflecting over
Hendry Shand's epistle announcing that he had seen and contrived to discover the identity of the gentleman who had given
him the fateful letter for the Lord Justice-Clerk, Maitland himself, intending to resume the road next morning, was re-reading
with a sombre and harassed face a missive which he, too, knew
by heart already. It was short and stabbing.

Dear Sir,
Circumstances having put me into posession of yr. Secret,
which I should supose you would pay any price to kepe from
the knowledge of your Frinds and of yr. Enemys also, if you
wish it to remain a secret you will please come to confer with
me at my house of Invershian as soon as you conveniently

803

*may. If you dow this I shall show you a way of disposeing of
it that it shall troble you no longer.*

> *I have the Honour to be, Sir,*
>> *Yr. frind and wellwisher,*
>>> *MacPhair of Glenshian.*

*If you dow not come I shall be forced to other Steps which
will not prove so agreeable to you.*

This letter, whose phraseology seemed engraved upon his
brain, David Maitland put back at last in his breast, his face
gone greyer than before, its delicate and attractive features all
pinched as though by cold. And indeed he was cold, cold to the
marrow of his bones – but not from his late indisposition. 'God
have mercy upon me!' he whispered to himself, and leant back
in his rough chair, his eyes closed, his hands open on the table,
in the attitude of a man beaten, defenceless and despairing.

His surroundings were indeed not out of keeping with despair
– the dark little room, with its floor of trodden earth and its
walls blackened by years of peat smoke, the rickety old table at
which he sat, the few poor necessities for cooking and eating,
all evidence of the most grinding struggle to live. Through the
half open door there streamed in the damp, sweet, soft air, and
the cries of children playing outside, which he was in a mental
region too far away to hear. He was not, therefore, aware of the
sudden hush which had fallen upon these shrill voices, nor of
the sound of wheels upon the rough road below, and started
violently when there came a quick step outside, a peremptory
knock upon the open door, and a voice asking in Gaelic, 'Is
there a sick gentleman staying here?'

Not understanding Gaelic, Maitland could not reply to an unintelligible query; all he could do was to say in English, 'Will you
not come in? The good people of the place are out in the croft.'

'Ah! you are perchance yourself the man I am seeking – Mr
Maitland of Strathmory?' asked the voice at once, and the
speaker stepped in – as well as could be seen against the light, a
tall, red-haired young man carrying himself very upright, and
by his attire a gentleman.

Maitland got up, a hand to the table less because of his weakness than because he was come, he suspected, very near the brink of the precipice.

'You will be perhaps from the Chief of Glenshian, who has heard that I am here, sir?' he inquired. For, owing to a misunderstanding of the scanty English of his hosts, he had received a totally wrong impression of Glenshian's personal appearance, and never divined this fine and well-built young man to be the Chief himself.

The newcomer stared, and after a second gave a brief laugh. 'Yes, I am certainly from the Chief. He desires me to bring you to him, if you are well enough to travel the remainder of the way. I ... he is very sorry to learn of your indisposition.' He came further in, and Maitland saw him better, and liked him less.

'I am at Mr MacPhair's disposal,' he said quietly. 'Indeed, I had fully purposed resuming my journey tomorrow.'

His visitor, who had been studying him very hard with eyes whose like the elder man had never seen before, now transferred his gaze to the convalescent's wretched surroundings. 'You'll not be sorry to be out of this hovel, I should think,' he said contemptuously. 'What a sty! I have no shieling, I think, on my estates as miserable as this!'

'The good man and his wife here, despite their poverty, have done their best for me, and I am very grateful to them,' responded Maitland, resenting the tone, though he knew that the place was a hovel. And then the newcomer's last words came home to him with fresh meaning. 'Are you then perhaps Mr MacPhair of Glenshian himself?' he asked.

'Well, Mr Maitland, since I have no wish to keep the fact from you, I am,' admitted the young man with a careless laugh. 'At your service, and vastly sorry if this long journey, which you have been good enough to take at my suggestion, be the cause of your indisposition. I have only just heard by chance of your presence here, or I should have made shift to remove you ere now to better quarters. I have an equipage waiting now upon the road, so if you will allow me ...?'

He was urbanity itself. Maitland looked at a knot in the table and spoke with difficulty. 'Could we not have our conversation here, Mr MacPhair?'

'And be interrupted by *that* every moment?' queried Glenshian, swinging an arm towards the door, round which a bevy of dirty and awestruck children was collected. He came nearer to Maitland. 'Moreover these walls do not even keep out the wind,' he added meaningly. 'Don't you think that, for your own sake, something more solid is desirable?'

David Maitland bowed his head. 'I will come with you. Let me but get my effects together and find and thank the kind folks who have tended me.'

The young Chief strode instantly to the door, the children scattering wildly at his approach, and called out an order; then, turning, asked, 'Have you a horse, sir? One of my gillies shall ride it – or, if you prefer not to entrust it to a servant, I will do so myself.'

Maitland's pale face flushed. 'I *should* prefer you to ride him, Mr MacPhair, if you would be so good.' For so he would be alone in the chaise, and defer yet a little longer the moment that was coming.

Solitary, as he had designed, in the chaise bumping its way a quarter of an hour later along Lochy side, David Maitland stared in front of him with blind eyes. He could not understand Glenshian's manner to him, for the young Chief had not treated him as an outcast whom no decent Jacobite would admit within his doors – he seemed to be welcoming him with every civility. And yet he knew . . . or said that he did. A wild hope showed its head every now and then above the choking waves of shame and misery, a hope that Glenshian did *not* know that secret which was eating his soul away, and that his letter had referred to something else. But to what else could those guarded phrases have reference, save perhaps . . . Yet that was scarcely possible; for *that* secret was none of his, did not even concern himself directly, and was no burden to his conscience. Indeed, until this moment, the idea had never occurred to him since he had received, at Strathmore, the summons which had brought him here. Well he remembered that sunny day; he had hardly been aware of the sun since . . .

But how the Chief of Glenshian had got upon his track Maitland could not imagine. He had not put any name to his own letter of intelligence on that March day more than two years past, nor had he taken the letter in person to Lord Tinwald's door; and though it was true that he had acquaintances in Edinburgh, whither he was accustomed to go about twice a year, that was no solution of the mystery. He was not there frequently enough for his face to be familiar to the town caddies and chairmen who were reputed to know everyone and everyone's business; he was sure that it was not familiar to the rather dingy messenger to whose charge he had committed the letter. Yet it was undeniable that Finlay MacPhair's summons had reached him a couple of weeks or so after his recent visit to the capital, whither he had gone to consult a physician about his wife's malady. Nevertheless, as the chaise conveyed him on towards whatever it was that Glenshian wanted with him Maitland put that particular question from him. It was more important to be resolved to walk warily, in case there should be a door after all . . . Yes, he must walk warily when he came to grips with this smooth-spoken young man who had written that he would show him a way to dispose of his burden . . . O God, if only he could!

2

There was no sign of coming to grips during the good meal which followed Maitland's arrival at the House of Invershian. Much solicitude did the young Chief show, on the contrary, in pressing meat and drink upon his guest, advising him, now that he was free from fever, to eat in order to strengthen himself, and recommending the claret which, as he said, he had brought from London last year. But at last, when Maitland, who had drunk little enough, and eaten less, would drink no more, Glenshian rose.

'Well, now, sir, if you are not too much fatigued, will you

come to my own room, and we can have our discussion, which I'm in hopes you will find not without profit to yourself!'

He was so damnably pleasant about it! Could it – could it be something else ... not *that*? Yet Maitland passed out of the door which his host held open for him with the feelings of a man going to the gallows, an impulse to get the business over quickly. None the less he knew that he ought to resist that temptation to leap from the cart, as some did, in the hope of breaking their necks at once; for there might be a reprieve. There *was* another secret which he knew ...

In his own room Finlay MacPhair drew a couple of chairs up to the fire which burnt there, arranged tobacco and two long pipes on a small table between them, and then went and locked the door.

'Now we'll not be disturbed,' said he cheerfully. 'Pray sit down, Mr Maitland. Do you use tobacco?'

Maitland, complying, said that he did not.

' 'Tis a solace at times,' observed the Chief, filling one of the pipes. 'When a man has something on his mind, for instance. But perhaps you are not troubled in that way, Mr Maitland?'

'No,' answered Maitland defiantly. 'Not unduly. But you, sir, I observe that *you* use tobacco!'

'To be sure I do, for I *have* something on my mind,' avowed Finlay with frankness. 'Poverty, Mr Maitland, for all that I'm Chief of Glenshian, with lands that run from the Great Glen to the sea. You have but to look at this house to see that I am absurdly poor for my position.'

Taken aback, Maitland murmured he knew not what.

'Aye,' went on his host, 'I'm in the case of a man wanting something he has not. And you' – here he turned full upon his guest those curious light eyes of his, 'you, on the contrary, are in the case of a man who has something he would give a deal to be rid of. Am I not right?'

After all, reflected Maitland bitterly, he must know that I would not have taken this journey at his bidding unless he were right. It was not much use fencing, when it came to it. 'Will you not be more explicit, Mr MacPhair?' he asked, digging his farther hand deep into the pocket of his coat and clenching it there. But he did not look at him.

'Indeed I will, since you thus invite me,' replied the Chief pleasantly. 'Time, they say, is money – though I have not found it so ... Well now,' his voice dropped, but was no less suave, 'well now, would you not gladly be rid of the responsibility for a certain letter which on a night in March of the year before last you caused to be delivered to the Lord Justice-Clerk in Edinburgh, a letter which – '

He paused, for it did not seem necessary to continue. Maitland had pulled out that clenched hand and put it over his eyes; the other he stretched out in a wavering gesture. 'You need not go on.' His voice was quite quiet. Then that hand too joined its fellow, and both covered his face as he bent forward, his elbows on his knees. This *was* the gallows after all.

Finlay MacPhair sat on the other side of the little table, pushing the tobacco down into the bowl of his pipe. At moments his lips were compressed; at moments there was a smile about his mouth, especially when he cast a glance at the bowed figure on the other side of the hearth. Time passed; the fire glowed; Finlay lit his pipe with a pine chip and began to pull at it.

'Come, Mr Maitland,' he said at last, removing it from his mouth, 'I hope you do not think that I have caused you this long journey either to reproach you for the sending of that letter, or to spread the knowledge of it. There's but one man besides myself, I suppose, who knows that you sent it, and he is a nobody who would not be believed.'

The hands fell. 'Then why *did* you cause me this journey?' asked Maitland in the voice of the dead.

'Because,' replied his host equably, taking another pull at his pipe, 'I thought you might be glad to be quit of the memory of that letter – if it irks you.'

Maitland looked at him across the fire. 'Do you by chance fancy yourself to be Almighty God?' he asked bitterly. ' – Yet even God Himself could not compass that!'

'On that I can express no opinion,' replied young Glenshian. 'But I see that you're not quite easy lest it be known that it is you and none other, a declared Jacobite, who have upon your hands the blood of that excellent if misguided man, Doctor Archibald Cameron of Lochiel.'

' "Not quite easy"!' repeated Maitland. 'My God, you have a gift of phrase!'

'I have no wish to exaggerate,' said Finlay modestly. 'Nor to wound your feelings. If I did not put the matter strongly enough, I apologize.'

'You have not put it even correctly,' said the other, with sudden passion. 'Although, when I took the step I did, I never thought – nay, as God is my witness, I never even dreamed – that it would mean the scaffold for Archibald Cameron, yet I have suffered so much these two years that I could scarce suffer more if what I did became public, and if all men, Jacobite or Whig, turned and hounded me out of Scotland! And how you, a Jacobite and a Highlander, who know what I did, can have broken bread with me passes my comprehension!'

For the first time Finlay MacPhair appeared a little perturbed.

He laid down his pipe and leant across the table. 'Mr Maitland, you would do well to compose yourself, and not to give way to such feelings. I have broken bread with you because I desire to help you, not to denounce you. – I trust that you do not contemplate denouncing yourself? That would be madness!'

'I sometimes think it would be the only sanity.'

'*Dhé!* What good could it do to you or anyone else?' expostulated Finlay. 'What's done cannot be undone now. You had your motives, doubtless, for writing that letter; 'tis not for me to inquire what they were. At any rate they were not mercenary ones, for since you never signed your name to it you cannot have expected payment for your information. Or did you put in a claim for reward afterwards?' There was a real anxious inquiry in his eyes, and he leant a little farther over the table.

'A claim for reward!' exclaimed David Maitland, his delicate features contorted with disgust. 'You think I *sold* him!'

Relief, a profound relief, was perceptible on the young Chief's face. 'No, as I say, I am sure you did not. Yet, had you allowed your name to be known, you would not have found the English Government ungrateful. They were desperately anxious to capture Archibald Cameron. But I might have known that you were above taking money for your action ... I suppose you are ... still of that mind?'

Maitland rose suddenly from his chair. 'Mr MacPhair, I don't know what this conversation is aiming at, but you cannot be ignorant that it is exquisitely painful to me, and I should be obliged if you would cut it as short as possible. I am in your power; is it a written confession that you want from me?'

Finlay was up too. 'No, no! Pray sit down again! You quite misapprehend my attitude, sir. I want no vengeance on you; it may be that after all you did not do a bad day's work!'

'*You* can say that!' exclaimed Maitland, almost in horror. '*You* can look at it in that light – the light in which the Devil showed it to me!'

'Oh, I would not be so sure it was the Devil! I am a trifle more behind the scenes than you fancy, Mr Maitland. However, to recur to my purpose. You have read, I suppose, of the scapegoat of the Jews, on which were laid the sins of the people? ... What would you say to my finding you a scapegoat for yours?'

In sheer astonishment Maitland sat down again. 'I don't understand you!'

' 'Tis plain enough. A scapegoat – one who would be ready to shoulder the blame of the deed, if necessary; to swear that it was he who sent that letter to the Lord Justice-Clerk – you of course furnishing him with the requisite details, lest his story should be challenged. Surely that is simple?' His face was eager.

'I'm not a rich man, Mr MacPhair,' replied Maitland drily. 'Nor would such a piece of pretence ease my mind in the least. How could it? Nothing can alter the fact that it was I who wrote that letter.'

'But only I and one other – a nobody – know that!'

'I have said that I almost wish, sometimes, that all the world knew it!'

'That's a mere sick man's fancy,' pronounced Finlay rather scornfully, yet again with visible uneasiness. 'You, a gentleman well thought of, a Jacobite that's been "out" – did you not tell me so? – to brand yourself publicly as an informer without reflecting what it would mean to your family and relatives – for I suppose you're not without kin of some sort – pshaw, my dear sir, you've the fever still in your veins! And all the while you could rid yourself of the burden with such ease, and do a good turn to a poor devil who –'

'*Do a good turn!* Are you crazy, Glenshian?'

' – who wants to earn a little money,' finished the young man quickly.

'I've told you I have none to spare. And, if I had, do you think I would pay a fellow-creature, even the lowest, to take my guilt upon his head?'

' 'Tis not a question of *your* paying him, man!' exclaimed the Chief, sounding rather exasperated.

'Then who *is* going to pay him? You?'

Finlay's eyes began to gleam, and his manner became all at once charged with excitement. 'I? – I, to whom . . . No, by God! The English Government, who contrive to get inestimable services for nothing, who make promise after promise, and because a man cannot prove up to the hilt that he carried out his work to the very end, sit on their money-bags, damn them, and draw up the strings the tighter! 'Tis they that would have to pay!'

'And how, pray,' asked Maitland coldly, 'have you this knowledge of the methods of the English Government with its spies, Mr MacPhair?'

Like a rider who has been giving his horse too much rein, and suddenly perceives it, Finlay MacPhair pulled up. He said somewhat shortly, 'Because this poor wretch of whom I spoke was in their pay – or rather, was not paid.'

And at that there came over Maitland's ravaged face the look of one who begins to guess that he has stumbled upon a nest of something poisonous and unclean. 'In their pay . . . and in your confidence!'

'In my confidence, no. But I cannot avoid knowing his circumstances. He is . . . a kinsman of mine, on the wrong side of the blanket.'

'And you wish to do him what you call a good turn – enable him to claim from the English Government blood-money which he did not earn?'

Glenshian bristled at the tone. 'He all but earned it,' he retorted sulkily. 'All the preliminary work was done by him, and if you had not had the luck to forestall him by being in Glenbuckie at the right moment – '

Maitland sprang up, pushing his chair so violently that it screeched on the uncarpeted floor. 'I cannot go on with this conversation, Glenshian. It brings me near vomiting!'

Finlay jumped up too. 'Sit down again,' he snarled suddenly across the table, 'sit down again and remember what you are yourself! How dare *you* ape virtuous indignation! How dare you, just because you were too timid to claim the money – how dare you come and play the saint over a better man than yourself, who had not your luck!'

David Maitland stood quite still, gripping the back of the chair, his eyes fixed on the figure of the angry young man, who was leaning over the table and emphasizing his points by banging it with his fist, so that he broke the pipe lying there. Horror and incredulity were in the elder man's gaze; then his face stiffened into a mask of despair and self-loathing.

'Is it possible?' he said hoarsely. 'You – *you* want the blood-money yourself – *you* were in the pay of the Government! Now I *know* that I am in hell!' He subsided again into his chair and once more buried his face in his hands.

Finlay MacPhair, with a touch that was not quite steady, took up the two halves of the snapped pipe, threw them into the fire, and flung himself down with outstretched legs and hands deep in his breeches pockets. For some time he studied the flames playing round the tobacco in the bowl; at last he removed his hands, sat up and said briskly:

'Well, now that we know the worst of one another we can get to business, Mr Maitland. Perhaps you are by this time come to a proper appreciation of the service I propose to do you?'

Maitland dropped his shielding hands. 'I believe I do appreciate it at its proper worth,' he said very slowly. 'And I will take my leave of you, Glenshian.' For the third time he stood up, horribly pale, but quite composed.

'Nay, 'tis too early to go to bed,' said his host without moving. 'Moreover, we have not arrived at an understanding.'

'I think we have,' answered Maitland, still more quietly. 'And I was not proposing to go to bed under this roof. I prefer ... anywhere else.'

And at that Finlay rose too, looking dangerous.

'Indeed? If I choose to risk the contamination of my house by harbouring an informer, that is surely my affair, not yours!'

Maitland faced him unflinchingly, though his features were fallen in like a corpse's. 'Your house harbours something worse than an informer, MacPhair. Even I have not sunk to enduring the society of a paid spy who is trying to get the credit of a crime which he never committed – for money!'

'You'll have to endure it,' retorted Finlay coolly. 'The door is locked, Mr Informer, and the key is in my pocket.'

'Yes, I know that. But I am going nevertheless.'

'The last man who offered violence to me,' observed Finlay menacingly, 'is regretting it now. He too thought he would leave at will – and could not.'

'I should not dream of offering you violence,' replied his present visitor. 'I would liefer not touch you. If you are afraid to let me go you must, then, keep me prisoner. But at least I shall not in that case be your guest.'

'Afraid?' Finlay took him up. 'Afraid of what? That you will go and drop hints about the countryside? You can't do that without publishing your own indubitable shame; and nothing that you can say against MacPhair of Glenshian is going to be believed out of *your* mouth! Why, even Ard – even a man with a clean record who has a private grievance against me dare not air it in public. (And, by the way,' he added to himself, 'his record will not be so clean presently.) You are a Lowlander, Mr Maitland,' he finished loftily, 'and must be excused your ignorance of the position of Mac 'ic Fhionnlaigh in the Highlands!'

Maitland said nothing, but stood waiting. Finlay changed his tone a little.

'Mr Maitland, I have been at a good deal of expense and trouble to secure this interview with you. Come, sit down again and reconsider your foolish and hasty decision! You can leave this house, if you wish, to all intents and purposes cleared of your guilt. You have only to – '

'I prefer to leave it with my guilt upon my own head!' broke in Maitland with all the impetuosity of a young man. 'At least it is my own shame. And I will not be implicated in another man's infamy. Informer as I am, *I* never took pay from the English Government.'

'And who's to prove that I did?' retorted Glenshian with an insolent tilt of his head. 'You are a double-dyed fool, Mr Maitland, for I have you in my hand, body and soul. And yet all I desire is to come to an accommodation with you.'

'Either give me the key of this door,' said Maitland sternly, 'or summon your servants and have me made captive, if such is your intention. I will not resist them. But to stay longer in the same room with you is a punishment too great for my sin, and I'll not endure it!'

'And what will you do to prevent it?' inquired the young Chief with a sneering smile. 'If I have a fancy to contemplate Doctor Cameron's murderer for a while longer, you cannot hinder my indulging it. 'Tis a privilege given to few ... Are you not anxious to know how I came upon your track? No? Is there then nothing I can do to pass the time for you? Details of the execution – you have had all those, I expect, being naturally anxious to know how your plan succeeded, but if I can furnish – '

'Will you give me that key?' demanded Maitland. 'If you

keep me here till Judgement Day I shall not consent to what you propose!'

A sudden gust of rage – the rage of the defeated – swept over Finlay MacPhair. He pulled out the key and flung it on the table between them. 'Go, then – and take your shame elsewhere! I am glad to be rid of a fool as well as a scoundrel!' He turned his back; Maitland picked up the key and without a word went straight to the door, opened it, and was gone.

And the man who from the moment of Archibald Cameron's landing in the Highlands had sent the English Government all the information in his power about him, and yet had failed to secure the reward for his apprehension – and had failed again now – began to hammer the remaining pipe which lay upon the table with his clenched fist until it was in a score of pieces; and continued, his face distorted almost to frenzy, to hammer until his hand was grazed and bleeding, and the little table rang and tottered with his blows. The fortunate chance meeting with Hendry Shand in Edinburgh on which he had so congratulated himself had brought him no luck at all – on the contrary; and the thought of those unremunerative guineas was like vitriol on a wound.

Chapter 15

ON THE VERGE

Aug. 28th (*continued*)

RAIN – fine, driving, soaking rain. David Maitland was glad of it; it was clean . . . a kind of lustration.

But no. No rain, no water in the world could wash him clean again – less now than ever, after that hour with Glenshian. For two years there had been blood on his hands, those delicate, scholarly-looking hands which had tied a noose about a man's neck as surely as the English hangman; this fact he had known, had faced, had kept at bay every hour of those two years. The only weapon which he had against it was the knowledge of his complete innocence of such an intention, for he had very truly told Finlay MacPhair that he never dreamed he was sending Archibald Cameron to death. He had thought that in informing the Government of his whereabouts he was merely condemning him to imprisonment, removing thereby the menace of a recurrence of that terrible and useless waste of life of the Forty-five, in which he himself, as a Jacobite, had played his part. Should another such hopeless attempt be made, fostered by the endeavours of Doctor Cameron, he knew that his own young son would be sacrificed in it, and many another like him. But, through a chance meeting on a March day of 1753, an angel had put it in his power to prevent such a calamity by checkmating the conspirator who was working to bring it about. Racked with scruples, yet arguing that he must not let them stand in the way of the good of hundreds of his countrymen, Maitland had posted off to Edinburgh, written a brief, unsigned message to the Lord Justice-Clerk, found a casual messenger to deliver it . . . and had soon learnt that there are two kinds of angel . . .

And now to the blood upon him was added mud. He seemed to have stepped into some festering bog of infamy. He himself

817

had played the informer it was true, yet – ironical though it appeared in view of the consequences to his victim – he had played it with the best intentions. But behind him in the house which he had left was a young Jacobite of high standing, the head of a great Highland clan of like traditions, who had apparently been in the pay of the English Government for God knew how long, who regretted that he could not show to them his fellow-Jacobite's blood upon his hands in order to get paid for the stain, and who, to that end, had planned how best to simulate the appearance of it there! It was so nearly incredible that once or twice, as David Maitland stumbled away in the wet dark from the House of Invershian, he began to wonder whether the whole thing could be a delusion. But there came over him again the shuddering remembrance of the words, the looks, the innuendoes – of the final half-involuntary disclosure and the assumption of a common bond of turpitude. *'Now that we know the worst of one another.'* Yes, that was hell – to be condemned by one's own act to the company of those even more vile than oneself, who had the right to call one comrade.

Maitland had now come, he perceived, to the borders of the loch by which he had driven that afternoon, and heard, though he could not see, the little waves, whipped by the small wind which blew the rain against him, flinging themselves gently along the shore. Water, water on every side; for he heard the voice of a burn also, lamenting in the night. And he came to a stop. Why not the loch? The deed would have some semblance of purification. If his body were found it would only be supposed that he had stumbled in by accident in the darkness. He had but to wade out into that whispering water which he could not see, save as a kind of greyness. Wife, son, friends and kindred – no one need know otherwise. Only the man whom he had just quitted might guess differently.

But merely to walk into the loch would not be sufficient, for he divined it too easy to turn back and to drag himself to land again, though he was not a very good swimmer. He needed a bank from which he could throw himself, not a flat shore like this, and the weight of stones in his pockets in order that this resolution, if it shrank from the cold embrace of the water, should shrink in vain. And he remembered having seen, as he drove along this afternoon, the ruined keep of a castle, standing above the loch on higher ground than this. It could not be very far from here, that loftier shore, and the ruin would supply him with his other requisite.

Maitland walked on again, and pictures went with him through the half-darkness – his ailing wife, his son, so full of promise, whom ... it seemed such bitter irony ... he had named after the Prince, Olivia Campbell, whom he loved as a daughter, the man whom he had betrayed. On the scaffold Archibald Cameron had said (so Maitland had heard) that he forgave any who had helped to bring him there. Perhaps he himself would soon learn if that had been a mere figure of speech.

The world seemed a trifle lighter now, though the rain kept on as steadily as ever. Maitland, a man just recovered from a long bout of fever, was by this time wet nearly to the skin. Well, he would be wetter soon ... He plodded on, and found that his memory had served him correctly. He was going slightly uphill, and before long there loomed upon his left hand the dim shape of some high building, doubtless the tower he had seen that afternoon.

He went up to this and stood there until he could make out a little more of it. Its base seemed to be thickly fringed with nettles and brambles, and was probably rich in fallen stones and fragments of stone. Groping, and getting stung and scratched, and wondering that he should care enough to be faintly annoyed at these small tribulations, his last on earth, Maitland found several bits of masonry of a size to stuff into his pockets. These were half filled when he suddenly gave a violent start and dropped a stone which he had just disembedded from the nettles. Surely that was a cry!

It must have been, for in another moment a voice, a man's voice, a little muffled but not, apparently, very far away, called out:

'Is anyone there? If so, come here to me, for God's sake!'

'Where are you?' asked Maitland after a moment's astonishment. 'What is amiss?'

'I am inside this old tower, on the ground,' replied the voice eagerly. 'The entrance is on the side away from the loch. Come quickly – but do not let anyone see you!'

'There is no one who can,' answered Maitland, looking round as he made this statement, which it was too dark to substantiate or contradict. He began to take the stones out of his pockets, but slowly. Did this mean that he must renounce his purpose – for the time?

'Are you not coming – are you in his pay also?' asked the voice on a note of desperation. 'If you go away and leave me you may have my death at your door!'

'One is enough,' thought Maitland with a grim humour somewhat foreign to him. The stones clattered down from his pockets. 'I am coming to you immediately.'

For all that his progress was largely a matter of groping. It was naturally even darker inside the tower, roofless though it was. A portion of one floor still remained in place about twenty feet up, and this projection was discernible, from below, against the sky.

'Where are you?' asked Maitland, once well inside.

'Here,' replied the voice, which came from his left hand. 'Down by the wall, under the shelter. I can just distinguish your figure. Do not fall over me.'

Maitland at that remembered that he had his tinder box with him, and that it was probably dry, since he usually carried it, when travelling, in a wrapping of shagreen. He got it out, and after some difficulty succeeded in obtaining a momentary illumination. It showed him a sufficiently startling sight – a man whose clothes, though draggled and dirty, were well cut and of good materials, a young man too, despite what looked like a week-old beard, sitting against the naked masonry of the tower among nettles and stones and debris. Then all was dark again.

'What is wrong?' inquired the surprised Maitland. 'Cannot you rise – have you injured yourself?'

In the darkness the young man gave a somewhat unsteady laugh.

'Could you rise if you were chained by your middle to the wall? I can lie down – on these damnably hard stones – and I can kneel (and will kneel to you with pleasure if you'll get me away) but more than that I cannot do.'

'How long have you been here?'

'Two days and a night – no, a night and a half now, I should suppose.'

'Good God! And who – no, I think I can guess that,' said Maitland, for suddenly he remembered a hateful voice saying something about a man who 'found he could not leave at will'. 'But are you not starving?'

'No, only hungry. I have a pitcher within reach, and they bring me bread once a day; but I must fight to keep the rats off it. If you have any humanity in you, sir, waste no time, I implore you, but go to – '

'Wait a moment,' interrupted the older man. 'Now that I am here I can surely do something towards freeing you?'

'Not unless you have the strength of a giant, or suitable implements,' said the prisoner discouragingly. 'I have spent hours in wrenching, and taken most of the skin off my hands.'

'Nevertheless, you must allow me to try,' responded Maitland, and again he procured a spark from his flint and steel. It was not of much use. 'I must feel, then,' he said; and kneeling down in the nettles traced the stout chain which encircled the prisoner's waist, too tightly to be slipped off, to the point, about three feet away, where it was fastened immovably to a staple in the wall.

'Like a monkey, eh?' asked the young man, speaking with a somewhat forced lightness. Maitland took up a stone and hammered, but he could not make the slightest impression on any link; nothing but a file or very powerful pincers could do that. He desisted and got up again.

'But have you not shouted?' he asked, in a sort of disbelief at this extraordinary thing. 'Have you not cried out for help? You are not gagged in any way?'

'I shouted nearly the whole of yesterday, till I was as hoarse as the crows which came and looked at me from the top there. But this tower is believed to be haunted, and not a Gael will come near it – superstitious wretches that we are! – and the less if they hear any cries coming out of it. My only hope has been that a party of soldiers from Fort Augustus might pass within earshot, but they naturally take the other side of the loch where Wade's road goes; and perhaps none have passed, at that ... Whatever good fortune sent you this way, sir, at so late an hour, too?'

To this question David Maitland might have returned a sufficiently startling answer, but in point of fact he made none. In any case he had for the time been shocked almost out of thoughts of his own affairs. He said with determination, 'I must get you released at once. Where is the nearest house or village?'

'You'll get no one to help you here,' opined the voice from the ground. ' 'Tis all Glenshian's territory, where he is absolute king still, although the English have taken away the hereditary jurisdiction of the chiefs. You must go on farther, into Cameron country – best of all, go if it is not asking too much of you, to my brother-in-law Ewen Cameron of Ardroy on Loch na h-Iolaire. The shortest way to get there – '

Cameron, Cameron – the name beat in David Maitland's ears like a gong, and he hardly heard the directions which were emanating from the captive among the nettles.

'But do you think,' he objected, when at last their purport became clear to him, 'that I shall find my way in the dark over this pass you speak of, which is quite unknown to me?'

There was silence for a moment. 'No, that is quite true,' said the captive. ' 'Tis to be feared you might not, and I would not have you endanger yourself for me. Yet the other way to Ardroy is so long – for after this loch comes near seven miles, I should suppose, of Loch Lochy, before you bear away to Loch Arkaig through the Dark Mile. After that – ' He proceeded to give further instructions, and ended: 'At any rate, sir, if you push on until you find yourself in Cameron country on Lochy side, you may come on some dwelling whence you could send on a messenger to Ardroy. I do not myself know the district well enough to indicate any particular house, but I am sure you will find one somewhere along the loch before you come to the Water of Arkaig and the Dark Mile.'

'I scarce like leaving you,' said Maitland, hesitating a moment. 'Are you sure that the man who put you here will not have your throat cut . . . I know something of him.'

'Do you? I am sorry for you! No, he'll not do that, if only for one reason that a man with a slit gullet cannot apologize, which is what he is hoping I will do . . . and which,' added the captive with concentrated fire and fury, 'is what I shall not do even if I have to sit here until I am a skeleton!'

'We'll have you away before that,' Maitland assured him. 'I had best be off, then. You can reach the pitcher and platter? — May I learn your name, by the way?'

'Hector Grant – Captain Hector Grant of the régiment d'Albanie in French service . . . God bless you, God bless you, sir!'

The words rang after David Maitland somewhat hollowly as he felt his way out of the keep and once more set his face south-westwards against the wind and the fine rain. He had already repressed a shiver or two of cold as he stood talking to the unfortunate prisoner. Like a fool (as he said to himself now) he had walked straight out of the House of Invershian without his cloak, which was with his other baggage in his bedchamber there. Well, it did not much matter, provided the exposure and exertion did not bring on a recurrence of ague before he had fetched help to the young man – help from a Cameron source! What would any of these Camerons into whose territory he was going say if they knew his own story? He would be dirked, if there were any dirks left in Lochaber . . . But that, again, would not greatly matter.

Dirks of another sort were beginning to stab through his veins and limbs as he hurried on in the rain. He almost wished that he were going to attempt the shorter way by the pass of which young Grant had spoken, but his legs would certainly not compass an ascent, though they would carry him awhile yet on the level. But would they ever carry him far enough on this much longer route of which he rehearsed the various stages to himself? He had not yet come to the end of the loch which he had thought to make his grave; then there should be a couple of miles without the companionship of water until the length of Loch Lochy began. And, nearly at the end of Loch Lochy, if ever he got so far, he was to turn aside and go through this strangely named Dark Mile. He might be in it now, for all the light he had, mental or physical. Only, at the end of the tunnel in which he felt himself, there did shimmer a light of some kind, though whether it were death or the accomplishment of his present mission he could not tell.

Whatever it was, it had sufficient power still to drag him forward, an hour and a half later, drenched and stumbling, under the flanks of the relentless, stream-scored mountains whose feet were in the grey glimmer of Loch Lochy, mountains over whose base he crawled onwards like a fly. The Dark Mile, the Dark Mile ... It was not one, but many ... and it had been two years long.

Chapter 16

ANOTHER IN THE TOILS

1

Aug. 26th

ROGER, the Invernacree spaniel, had taken very little exercise of late, his master having so inexplicably retired to his bed. Hence, in default of longer rambles, he was glad this morning to accept an invitation to accompany Miss Grizel Stewart down the avenue. It did not seem much of a walk, but she might, for all Roger knew, be meaning to go farther than the gate, for he noted that she had a basket in her hand. Deciding to assume that she was, he inaugurated their departure from the house with the displays usually reserved for greater occasions.

'Foolish dog!' said Miss Stewart indulgently.

Roger moreover went through the pretence of discovering all sorts of novelties in the well-known undergrowth; and at the end of the avenue he did come upon something not of quite daily occurrence – a couple of horsemen advancing up it. As in duty bound, he barked at them.

Grizel, who had been absorbed in thoughts of Roger's master and the events and anxieties of the last week, looked up at the sound. The foremost cavalier was her cousin Ewen Cameron, the second his young piper and right-hand man, Angus Mac-Martin.

'Cousin Ewen!' she exclaimed. 'What a pleasant surprise!'

Her kinsman rode up, uncovered and, stooping from the saddle, gave her a cousinly kiss. 'I was wondering when you were going to become aware of me, my dear Grizel,' he said with a smile. 'You appeared buried in thought.'

'So I was,' admitted Miss Stewart. 'Or perhaps I am growing deaf. I'm not so young as I was, cousin.'

'We none of us are that,' agreed Ewen. But he himself, being ten years her junior, swung lightly out of the saddle with no

825

sign of the encroachment of the age. 'Were you going out?'

' 'Tis of no consequence,' said Grizel (speaking for herself, and not for Roger). 'I'll turn back to the house with you.' And she began to walk beside him and his horse. 'And why have we the pleasure of seeing you today, Ewen?'

'Because I want some advice from Uncle Alexander,' replied her cousin.

'Papa went to Duror this morning; I wonder you did not happen upon him as you rode through. But he may be back at any time.'

'Is Ian in the house, then? If so, I'll have a talk to him first.'

'Ian? . . . You have not heard about him, I suppose?'

'What about him? Do you mean that he is from home also?'

'No – very much at home,' answered Grizel dryly. 'Ian has met with a misfortune . . . a sort of accident.'

'*Dhia gleidh sinn!* I had not heard. A serious one?'

'There was a day,' said Grizel gravely, 'when the surgeon talked of the possibility of his losing his arm – his right arm.'

'Good God!' exclaimed Ardroy, stopping dead. 'What happened to him?'

'Perhaps he would rather tell you himself. Oh, he's much better now, thank God; he left his bed yesterday, and was out of doors a while this morning, but we have been very anxious . . . Well, since Captain Grant is your brother-in-law, which perhaps makes it a little awkward for Ian to approach the matter with you, I will tell you this much: a week ago the two of them had a . . . a disagreement – a quarrel, in fact, and a meeting down by the loch in which Ian was wounded in the arm, rather severely – or so it proved in the end.'

Ewen smote one hand into the other with a vexed exclamation. 'Will nothing cure Hector of being such a firebrand? – And, by the way, I did not know he had been here; I have been wondering where he was. – But to quarrel with Ian! Over what did they disagree?'

'If anybody was a firebrand I am afraid it was Ian,' said Grizel. 'He confesses to having behaved extremely badly. They quarrelled over Jacqueline ... Yes, it appears that Captain Grant is in love with her, and she with him; but since Ian admits that he insulted our guest beyond bearing, one does not know whether, after that, he will ever return to ask for her hand. (I can't think what came to Ian; he must have been fey.) And Jacqueline, poor child, has been terribly distressed over Ian's condition – she's with him now – and my father too, because in some way which I cannot fathom, he seems to think he was partly to blame for the episode. However, it may distract and cheer him to learn that you need his advice, Cousin Ewen.'

Her tall kinsman had listened to this recital with an ever tightening mouth, which at this deduction tightened still more. 'I very much doubt that, Grizel,' he said with a good deal of grimness. 'And I doubt whether Uncle Alexander can really do anything to help me, and whether in a few weeks' time you may not be ashamed to be seen walking with me.'

'I – ashamed to be seen walking with you!' exclaimed Grizel, openmouthed. 'You must be crazy, Ewen! – What have you done?'

'Precisely nothing. But the difficulty is to prove it!'

2

Grizel Stewart had not used the language of exaggeration about her brother's condition. The wound which his folly had gained him, though painful enough, might not have proved dangerous had the weapon which inflicted it been clean. But there must have been rust on the seldom-drawn blade of the swordstick. Ian's arm on the second morning was swollen from wrist to shoulder; by nightfall he was delirious, and the whole household in despair. The surgeon said that nothing but a miracle could save the arm – could indeed save the young man's life if drastic measures were too long delayed. There were periods when the unlucky duellist was able to comprehend what was hanging over him, and declared that he would sooner die than lose his right arm – was even understood to say that he did not much care if he did die ... Yet by the morning the swelling had begun to subside, the patient, if corpselike in appearance, was in his right senses, and the surgeon, who had spent the night at Invernacree (sharpening his knives in readiness, as Ian afterwards surmised) averred that he had had the greatest surprise of his professional experience.

It *was* a miracle; Ian recognized that. He put it all down to Jacqueline's agency – to her prayers, to her tears, to her sweet and entire forgiveness of the wrong he had done her, all of which had enveloped him in so healing an atmosphere that it had seemed to push away from him the heavy clouds of fever, remorse and pain. And he had come out of them once in that long, terrible night, during Jacqueline's watch, to find his young sister's tears upon his face and to hear her saying distractedly, 'Ian, Ian darling, only get better and I'll give him up . . . I'll try never to think of him again!'

Drenched with sweat, Ian had opened his eyes and managed to utter the words, 'I will bring him back for you, Jacqueline . . . Only say you forgive me . . .'

He felt her cool face pressed instantly against his burning cheek. She kissed him with a long, clinging kiss, and gradually he fell asleep, really asleep, with his head on her arm.

After that he became unwilling to let her out of his sight, and so, on this afternoon of Ewen's arrival, though Ian was sitting in a chair in his room, having indeed already walked a little about the garden, Jacqueline had to sit beside him. She had even at his request attempted to shave him, but her nervous handling of the razor had been so unsuccessful and even dangerous, that a gillie had had to be summoned to finish the operation. So now she was mending one of his shirts, and Ian, looking at her bent head, sat thinking of Olivia and Hector, interwoven and flitting thoughts which dazzled in his brain like the patterns in a kaleidoscope.

'Ian, here's a visitor,' announced Grizel, opening the door.

The young man looked round, saw who it was, flushed up with a quick flush of the convalescent, and attempted to rise.

'Don't get up!' said Ewen, and, 'Don't think you have to

explain to Ewen,' said Grizel simultaneously. 'I've told him. Jacqueline, has he had his broth?'

'Yes, and finished every drop. Good day, Cousin Ewen.' Jacqueline tendered her cheek. 'Oh yes, you may talk to him as much as you like. 'Twill do him good; he's had overmuch of women's society of late.' She threw her brother a glance which showed that she neither meant nor believed this, and slipped out of the room. Grizel had already gone.

'My poor Ian!' said Ewen after a moment, looking down at the invalid and his bandaged arm.

'My poor fool, if you like,' responded Ian, but without bitterness. ' 'Tis good to see you; sit down, and rate me as much as you wish. I have been worse than a fool. But I hope to make amends.'

'Did Hector try you past bearing?' asked his cousin. 'I have known him to be pretty irritating.'

Ian leant back in his chair. 'It was not he. It was something which had naught to do with him, and that is why my conduct was so indefensible. Directly I can use my hand I shall write him an apology, or better still, make it in person.'

His penitence was evidently not going to be content with half measures, and, considering that he had had so much the worst of the encounter, Ewen admired the spirit of it.

'I do not suppose that you can do either just yet,' he said. 'Moreover, there's another difficulty. Where *is* Hector?'

'At his new property in Glenmoriston, I imagine.'

'But he's not! The factor sent to me the day before yesterday to ask if I knew when he was coming, as he was aware that he designed to leave France some little while ago. He thought that Hector might have gone to Ardroy to visit us on his way farther north, and Alison and I, indeed, half expected him. I did not know he had been here. What day did he leave?'

'Or, more correctly, what day did I drive him away,' interposed Ian. 'It was last Friday.'

'Nearly a week ago! Then I fear some mishap has befallen him. Do you chance to know whether he meant to visit us at Ardroy, or was he going straight to Glenmoriston?'

Ian drew his brows together in an effort to recall some half forgotten words of that disastrous day. Suddenly the colour flooded over his face. 'Ewen . . . I seem to remember something . . . I don't believe he was going directly either to you or up to Glenmoriston. He . . . yes, I am sure he said something about going to see Finlay MacPhair at Glenshian first.'

An expression of anything but relief dawned on Ardroy's face. 'What a crazy thing to do, alone! Glenshian and he last met at the sword's point, as I told you some weeks ago. I greatly fear some harm has come to him.' He pushed back his chair and began to walk about. 'Why, why was he so mad?'

Ian too got up, and with an increased pallor. 'Ewen,' he said, 'if harm has come to Mr Grant it is my fault. I . . .' he choked over it a trifle, 'I had the meanness – there is no other word for it, I am afraid – to taunt him with that accusation about the stolen letter which Glenshian made in front of me that day at Ardroy, a charge which you told me was baseless . . . and which I nevertheless feigned that I believed. I fear that it is more than possible that Captain Grant has gone to Glenshian to call him to account for that slander.'

His kinsman sat heavily down again. 'Ian . . . what possessed you?'

'I do not know,' replied the young man, standing very still. And then he added, but to himself, and with his head a little turned aside, 'Yes, I do know . . .'

Ewen Cameron had excellent hearing, but the observation was plainly not meant for his ears, and he took no notice of it. 'Sit down again, at any rate, *'ille*,' he said gently. 'Still and on, if you said that to Hector, I don't wonder at anything which followed.'

'No,' said Ian as he subsided into his chair again, 'nor do I. At the time . . . well, all I need tell you is that he struck me in the face for it.' And, sincere as his penitence appeared to be, he still could colour painfully at the remembrance of that blow. 'And I am afraid that he may have gone to Invershian with the idea of doing the same to Finlay MacPhair if he gets the chance. Ewen,

Ewen, if ill has come to him it is my doing ... and there's Jacqueline to think of!'

'No, 'tis not entirely your doing,' replied Ewen consolingly. 'Knowing Hector as I do, I strongly suspect that he may have had it in his mind to pay a visit there in any case. On my soul, there's something of the spider about Fionnlaigh Ruadh, for he has got me into his toils too!'

'You – good God, how?'

Ewen told him, thereby pretty well driving thoughts of Hector and remorse out of his cousin's head for the time. And when Alexander Stewart, returning, came up to his son's rooms he found Ian saying rather excitedly, 'This convinces me that there was, as I have always thought, a great deal more than met the eye in that business of the steers found among yours.'

'What's this?' asked Invernacree, as he shut the door behind him. 'Ewen, my dear boy, I am very glad to see you, though I hear that you are in trouble of some kind. Someone else has been in the same condition,' he added, laying his hand on his son's shoulder in a way which showed Ardroy that in their relations there was not now much amiss. 'However, we'll not go into that. I thank God the consequences were not worse. What is your difficulty, Ewen?'

'This,' said his nephew, the blue of his eyes seeming to deepen, as always when he was moved, 'that Glenshian intends to cite me before the Sheriff Court at Inverness for stealing some seventy or eighty head of his best cattle – unless I pay him their full value before Michaelmas Day.'

'Has Glenshian gone daft?' exclaimed Alexander Stewart. '*You* – steal his cattle! In any case you can easily disprove such a preposterous charge.'

'No, not easily,' replied Ewen grimly. 'Glenshian has seen to that. Two of his beasts were found among mine last June.'

Old Invernacree dropped into a chair and stared without words.

'The question is, how they got there,' put in his son. 'None of Ewen's people will admit to stealing them.'

'Seventy or eighty head!' repeated the old laird, recovering speech. 'And what, pray, are you supposed to have done with so large a number?'

'Hidden some, and sold the most.'

'Glenshian must bring some evidence of the selling.'

'I dare say he can contrive to do that. The buyers will prove to be MacPhairs – ignorant, of course, of where the beasts came from.' Ewen gave a mirthless laugh. 'His word is law round Invershian. But pay him what I never took I will not; though if he fulfils his threat and the case goes against me, I'm a ruined man. Do not imagine, however, Uncle Alexander' – Ardroy drew himself up to his great height – 'that I will accept one Scots penny from you, for I will not. I only wished you to learn of the agreeable situation in which Glenshian has me. I do not know whether you can see a way out, for I cannot.'

Chapter 17

DELIVERANCE

Aug. 28th–29th

Two evenings afterwards the worthy Mrs MacGillonie, the wife of a tacksman on Lochiel's forfeited estate on Lochy side, was congratulating herself on having beneath her roof Cameron of Ardroy, the late Chief's cousin, and the latter's near kinsman, a Stewart of Invernacree, though not a little curious as to the errand which had brought them up this western side of the loch, less frequented by travellers, since there was no good road here, as upon the other. But she was not surprised that they had asked for shelter, seeing that it was growing dusk and was raining, and that the younger gentleman had his arm in a sling and got off his horse as if he were tired. She tried, without effect, to prise some information out of the gillie who had come with them, but found Angus MacMartin, for all his youth, as impenetrable as her own John could be when he wished.

Even had the good woman listened at the door, after removing the meal which she had brought up to the travellers, she would not have heard much to enlighten her. Ewen's chief preoccupation was now to induce his convalescent kinsman to convey himself quickly into the box bed in the wall which was to receive them both; moreover they had already thrashed out the two questions of the moment so thoroughly, both at Invernacree and during their two days' ride, that there was really no more to say.

Alexander Stewart had been unable to help his nephew except by upholding his already formed determination of defying Finlay MacPhair, and refusing to pay a penny of what practically amounted to blackmail. Fury shook the old Highlander at the thought of so impudent a claim; but its impudence did not preclude its being a very serious matter for Ewen. Both

833

of them knew the ease with which Glenshian would be able to get his own dependants to come forward and swear what he wished. Invernacree's indignant sympathy over the wrong threatening Ewen had been the chief reason for his consenting to his son, with a half-healed wound, accompanying him back to Lochaber; for the fact of Ian's presence at the original 'finding' of the steers might be of some value to Ardroy, though it was difficult to see exactly how. But Ian had another project in his own mind – to assist in the search for Hector Grant; and he had in consequence proved so obstinate when, nearing Loch Arkaig on the second afternoon, Ewen had tried to send him off to Ardroy with Angus – and Angus had shown such signs of rebellion at being required to desert his master – that Ewen yielded, stipulating only that they should none of them go much farther that evening, and in fact, claiming John MacGillonie's hospitality in less than an hour after that decision.

Ian was indeed by no means sorry to dismount at the tacksman's door under shadow of the green mountain wall; and after the meal, inserting himself with no great reluctance into the box bed, was asleep in a few minutes. But Ewen remained a while at the window, with an unuttered prayer in his heart that a vision which he saw painted upon the rainy mist outside might not come true, the vision of a man driven to sell the place dearest to him in the world, his home, through the deliberate and heartless fraud of an enemy.

He did not know how long he had lain asleep by his cousin's side when a persistent thudding sound penetrated his slumber. After a moment he realized that someone must be knocking on the farmhouse door, which was immediately below their window – and failing, it seemed, to attract anyone's attention. For a few seconds Ewen lay idly listening to the wayfarer's efforts; then, remembering the rain which was, or had been falling, he got out of bed, opened the window and looked out.

Down below he could make out in the grey light – for it was now after dawn – a man leaning against the door in an exhausted attitude, having momentarily ceased to beat upon it. But when the window above him opened he lifted his head.

'At last!' he said, in a hoarse and scarcely audible voice. 'I can go no farther . . . you must send . . . Cameron of Ardroy . . . at once! And for God's sake . . . open the door.'

'I will come at once,' responded Ewen. He got a light, hurriedly threw on a few clothes, said to Ian, who had awakened, 'There's a man outside asking for me – it might be news of Hector; I'm going to let him in,' and ran down the stairs.

None of the farmhouse people were stirring, so, rushlight in hand, Ardroy unbarred the door. The man outside all but fell against him. Ewen put an arm about him and led him to a settle; then, lighting a couple of rushlights on the table from his own, got a better view of the wet and exhausted stranger lying back there with closed eyes and blue lips.

'Send to Ewen Cameron of Ardroy,' said the newcomer after a moment, and said it like a child repeating a lesson. 'Ewen – Cameron – of – Ardroy.'

'There's no need,' observed Ewen, stooping over him. 'By good fortune I am myself Cameron of Ardroy. What do you want with him?'

David Maitland opened his eyes. 'Tell him . . . in a ruin on the loch there . . . I do not know how far . . . my fever's on me again . . .'

'Yes?' said Ewen, controlling his impatience. 'Castle Shian, I expect. What of it?'

Maitland made a fresh effort. It was equally difficult to summon his words from a confused brain and to give them utterance through chattering teeth.

'There's a young man there . . . his name . . . Grant . . . chained to the wall . . . chained fast . . . two days . . . must get him away . . . I went there to . . . to . . .' He looked up rather wildly into the keen blue eyes. 'But . . . that is . . . of no account . . . He said . . . Ardroy . . . Cameron . . . set him free . . . I tried . . . too fast . . .' A violent shiver went over him and his own eyes closed once more.

Ewen turned his head and became aware of Ian standing behind him. 'Why, 'tis Mr Mait – ' began the latter, but his cousin was already addressing him.

835

'Did you hear, Ian – Castle Shian, that's where Hector is ... chained to the wall, by Heaven! – But first we must get this gentleman to bed; he's ill. I will carry him up to your room. – I think I can do it best alone, if you will hold the door open ...'

He lifted Maitland from the settle like a baby, got him over his shoulder, and went slowly and steadily up the steep and narrow staircase with his burden. Ian followed.

'Castle Shian, you say, and chained to the wall! It's impossible!'

'We'll soon have him away,' said Ardroy. 'But first – see – we must get his messenger's clothes off; he is soaked to the skin. The bed is still warm, and he can have my nightshirt. The woman here must look after him until we return ... unless you will, Ian? It would be better, you know.'

But Ian, helping him to undress the practically unconscious Maitland, shook his head with decision. 'I am coming with you. Do you think Castle Shian is guarded?'

'I don't know – useless to ask *him* now. I will raise some men though, as we go ... If Finlay MacPhair does not pay dearly for this! – Ah, here's Angus. Take your horse, Angus, go and rouse MacKail at the smithy up the loch, and tell him to get together the necessary tools for filing or undoing a chain. I will follow shortly. – What did you say, sir?'

The exhausted man in the bed had muttered something, but all that Ewen could catch was, 'ocean' ... 'blood' and 'hand'.

'Fever,' he commented, shaking his head as he turned away. And then, as the tacksman's wife appeared in the doorway, 'Mrs MacGillonie, pray do your best for this poor gentleman; he has rendered me a great service. Well, Ian, if you insist upon coming with me I suppose you must. Clothe yourself properly, at any rate.' He himself threw on the rest of his attire, ran down the stairs, and could be heard calling for MacGillonie to help him saddle the horses.

Ian went again to the bed in the alcove. Yes, it was undoubtedly Olivia's Mr Maitland: impossible to mistake that delicate, rather worn mask. He guessed him to be drowsy now, rather than unconscious. What could he have been doing here?

Whatever it was, his presence had served Captain Grant well. Chained up in Castle Shian! Finlay MacPhair must really have gone mad!

He observed as much to Ewen as they rode fast along Loch Lochy side in the prevalent damp greyness. Ardroy said so little in reply that Ian hoped Finlay himself would not be encountered on the expedition, for, if he were, violence would probably take place despite all Ewen's vows. Two or three times Ardroy dismounted and went into a cottage, roused the man living there and gave him orders. Here, in Lochiel's country, Lochiel's cousin had no difficulty in getting any clansman to follow him. Last of all they turned up a little gully to a tiny forge, to find Angus and the smith waiting outside.

'Take him up on the crupper behind you,' said Ewen to his attendant. 'There are other men following us on foot, but we will not wait for them. They may not be needed; indeed, I hope not.'

He was clearly alive to the disadvantages of an encounter with the MacPhairs, which would inevitably bring down upon both clans the hand of the English Government, firmly established in its military representatives on either side of them at Fort Augustus and Fort William. Otherwise, as Ian could see, he was spoiling for a fight.

'I must tell you, Ewen,' he remarked suddenly, 'that I have already met the gentleman who so nobly brought us this news. His name is Maitland, and he comes from Strathmory.'

'You have met him already!' exclaimed his cousin, turning in his saddle to look at him. 'Why did you not say so earlier? Where, and when?'

'There was not time to tell you,' said Ian, answering the first query and not the others, which he did not mean to do – at present. 'And I cannot tell you aught about him, save that he is a Jacobite, was "out" in the Forty-five, and is a friend of ... Campbell of Cairns, whose coach, as you have heard, met with an accident near our house.'

'I wonder what he was doing on Glenshian's territory at that time of night, and on foot,' remarked Ardroy, but Ian could not tell him, and he himself was naturally more concerned with Hector's plight than with the man who had revealed it to them, so the subject was not pursued. Indeed the three horses and their four riders came, about half an hour later, in sight of their goal, and must exercise caution in case they were observed. A quarter of a mile or so from the ruined keep they pulled up, on Ewen's command, and dismounted. Angus, to his disgust, was left with the horses and instructed to detain the men, when they came up, unless they were summoned forward to the castle. Meanwhile, Ardroy and Ian, and the indispensable blacksmith, would go forward very quietly, almost in the guise of scouts, for, though there was no evidence of such a thing, the tower might be guarded.

Slowly and quietly they approached the ancient fastness. In the east a faint red line hinted at sunrise. A number of hoodie crows flapped away from the broken battlements, and out of the very entrance, just before they reached it, scurried a rat carrying something white, possibly a bit of bread. But there was no sign of human presence, except what met their eyes when they got inside the ruin – Hector Grant, almost unrecognizable under his young beard, sitting amongst fallen stones and nettles, his back against the damp, bare wall and his head fallen forwards upon his breast in sleep, the most forlorn figure imaginable. A rustling and squeaking, added to a sudden agitation of the jungle round him, hinted at the hasty departure of further animal life.

Under his breath Ewen swore a terrible oath. Next minute he was on one knee by the captive, who had not wakened, or at least had not moved. 'Hector, Hector, we are here! you are saved! Hector, you are not injured, are you?'

And then Hector raised his head and looked at him vaguely. He had now completed a second night in this place, and was in considerably worse trim than when Maitland had come upon him several hours earlier. 'You'll not be able to free me, Ewen,' he said dispiritedly. ' 'Tis only waste of time to try. Someone came and tried ... the damned chains are too strong. But if you could only keep the rats away!'

Ewen put his arm round him. 'A little patience, *'ille*, and you'll be free. I have brought a smith with me. Come along, MacKail.'

'A smith!' exclaimed Hector, a spark of animation coming into his dead voice. 'Oh, Ewen!' For a moment his head went down on Ardroy's shoulder, and when he raised it he drew the back of his hand across his eyes.

Ewen got up and went to Ian, who had remained awkwardly and remorsefully in the entrance, thinking that Captain Grant might not like to feel that his late, if defeated, antagonist was viewing his present ignominious situation. 'Will you stand on guard here with this?' asked Ardroy, producing and holding out a pistol. Seeing his cousin's look of surprise he added, 'Have you forgotten that Lord Stowe procured me a "protection", and that I can carry arms again? But do not use that if you can possibly avoid it. Please God no MacPhair is stirring.'

When he returned to the inner chamber the smith was kneeling in the nettles examining the chain. He looked up.

'If the gentleman will allow, Mac 'ic Ailein,' he said respectfully, 'it will be easier to get this chain apart where it will be going round the gentleman's body.'

'The gentleman will allow anything;' responded Hector with a laugh, 'especially as he has no desire to appear in public trailing a chain about with him. Set to work, blacksmith! You might help me off with my coat, Ewen.'

'How long will you take about it, think you, MacKail?' asked Ewen.

'I'm thinking it might be the matter of half an hour,' replied the smith in an apologetic voice.

'Half an hour! that's no time at all!' observed the captive. 'You'll get well stung by those nettles, I fear, honest man. – Oh, Ewen,' he went on, talking in French, 'I doubt if the angel who released St Peter from his chain was half as welcome as you are!'

And in that tongue, which Ewen also spoke fluently, he gave his cousin a brief account of his adventures while the blacksmith's tools clinked and grated about him. Towards the end

Ewen went again to the entrance, where Ian Stewart stood guard, pistol in hand. But all was quiet, save that a few black-headed gulls were screaming noisily over the loch behind.

'All the better,' commented Ardroy. 'Unless Glenshian should come here in person, in which case we could have the smith chain him up here in Hector's place. By heaven, I wish he would!'

'Whom were you talking to out there?' asked Hector, looking up as Ardroy came back.

'To my cousin Ian.'

'He's here with you – he has recovered, then? – For I suppose you know all about that affair?'

'He has almost entirely recovered, though it seems that he might have lost his arm over it.'

'Lost his arm!' repeated Hector, looking rather shocked. 'I am extremely sorry to hear that. Believe me or no, I tried to do him as little harm as I could.'

'I am not blaming you at all,' Ewen assured him. 'And Ian – but I will leave him to speak for himself, later. Is that really giving, MacKail?'

For answer the chain slid like a heavy snake into the trampled weeds.

'*Ah, mon Dieu!*' exclaimed Hector, with a catch in his breath. He tried to get up, but was so stiff and cramped that Ewen had not only to assist, but partly to support him.

'Come, we'll get away as quickly as possible, and as quietly,' he said, holding the captive up. 'I have some of the clan a little way back, but you will understand, Hector, that though I would willingly throw Glenshian into the loch, I must for others' sake avoid a collision with his people, if possible.' Hector nodded; not even vengeance attracted him at this moment.

At the entrance he came face to face with Ian Stewart. But Ian was holding Ardroy's pistol in his one available hand, and could not therefore extend that hand and take Hector's in silence, as was his impulse, for by the time his cousin had relieved him of the weapon it looked for a moment as though the rescued captive was going to collapse entirely, and the opportunity was gone.

Holding him up between them, the two hurried him away towards the horses, unseen by any MacPhair. Yet neither then nor afterwards was Captain Grant heard to regret the ease and tameness of his eventual removal from Castle Shian and the revived methods of Red Finlay of the Battles.

But when the rescuers, riding slowly, and close on either hand to the rescued (lest, in spite of his disclaimers, he should slip off his horse) reached MacGillonie's farm, and Hector had been set down to a sound meal, his first for a week, Ewen turned his attention to the man to whose good offices the prisoner owed at least a speedier release than he might have had. It appeared that he was now asleep; but Mrs MacGillonie reported that in a sensible interval the gentleman had told her that he had only a day or two left his bed after a week's illness, on hearing which Ewen became very uneasy, and formed a plan which he immediately communicated to Ian.

'I propose,' he said, 'that you and Hector ride on with Angus to Ardroy, while I remain here with Mr Maitland – is not that his name? Mrs MacGillonie, it is clear, has but the slightest knowledge of sick nursing. When you reach Ardroy you shall send hither that old chaise of mine, and I will bring Mr Maitland back with me directly it is possible. He cannot be left here uncared for, perhaps to undergo another illness as the result of what he has done for Hector.'

'No, indeed,' agreed Hector between two mouthfuls. 'I'll never in this world be able to repay him for that. I cannot imagine what he was doing near that pestilential old ruin so late at night, but whatever it was I am thankful for it.'

'Was he actually the only person who had come near you for two days?' asked Ardroy.

'Yes, except the gillie in the morning with food and water – and the rats.' Hector gave a slight involuntary shudder. 'The place has a name for being haunted, I was told.'

'It is the most monstrous, the most intolerable behaviour that ever I heard of!' exclaimed Ewen anew, 'and Glenshian shall be made to pay for it somehow!'

'I hope he will,' agreed Hector. 'I should prefer to make him pay in person, but I do not think, now, that such a course will be easy; he's too surrounded by gillies, to whom his word is law.'

'Yes,' said Ardroy with a gloomy intonation, 'gillies who would swear, no doubt, to anything they were ordered to swear to.' He looked across at Ian. 'Fine talk on my part, is it not, to speak of making Glenshian pay for this outrage, when, before the year is out, it's likely he will have robbed me of every penny I possess, and more.'

'*Au nom de Dieu*, how?' asked Hector with his mouth full.

'By proceeding against me at Inverness for stealing I know not how many head of his cattle. And since you too testify that his gillies – '

But Hector had reached across the table and gripped his brother-in-law's wrist in the clutch of extreme excitement. 'Cattle!' he broke in, gulping a little. 'Cattle! That's the reason, then, I suppose ... cunning devil! ... But were there only *two* steers?'

'What do you mean – what do you know?' asked Ewen staring at him with some of the same excitement. Ian had jumped to his feet.

'I mean this,' said Hector, very fast. 'Two branded steers of Glenshian's were found in your herd some time ago, were they not?'

'Yes, yes. But how in heaven's name did you learn that?'

'By means of my Gaelic and the indiscretion of one Somerled MacPhair, who helped to put them there. Those steers, Ewen, were actually driven over to Ardroy two nights previously by Finlay's orders. Then that redheaded – '

'I was sure of it!' cried Ian exultantly in his turn. 'I was sure there was something of the sort behind that affair! Ewen, you are saved! He cannot, he dare not proceed, now that we know this!'

The colour mounted into Ardroy's face. 'I think I am, perhaps,' he said, looking at the late captive in a rather dazed manner. 'Tell me that again, Hector – tell me every syllable you overheard!'

Chapter 18

IAN DOES SOME HARD THINGS

THE greyness and the damp had lifted, even before the riders entered the gloom of the Dark Mile, and the length of Loch Arkaig, when they came to it, was sparkling in the sun and the breeze. At first the two young men said little to each other, though Hector spoke from time to time in a flippant and rather self-defensive manner about his experiences, much in the same spirit in which he had made Ewen's horse, which he was riding, caracole at starting, with the idea of showing that he was perfectly able to sit it, about which Ewen had expressed himself a little dubious. And indeed those same experiences had left their mark upon Hector, both in pallor and in the loss of his customary military trimness, though he had somehow contrived to get hold of an indifferent razor from John MacGillonie.

Why, Ian Stewart wondered now, was it so difficult to make the apology for his own past conduct on which he had firmly resolved? Perhaps because it would have come more simply in that moment at Castle Shian, which for other reasons was impossible; perhaps on account of his ex-enemy's present attitude. Yet, though beginning was not easy, he was going to make that apology.

'You must guess, I think, Captain Grant,' he said, in the first convenient pause which ensued, 'that I wish to say something to you. I desire to apologize without reserve for what I said that day on the hillside about your lost letter. I never believed it; I was crazy when I spoke.'

'Oh, never trouble about that!' replied Hector easily. 'I thought you were not yourself that day ... As I was saying just now, this man Somerled – '

He was off on his own experiences again, and Ian, who had

843

found his words of regret hard to bring out, harder than he had anticipated, felt distinctly provoked. Surely an apology, made at considerable cost, merited a little more attention than this!

At the next opportunity he resumed doggedly: 'I the more regretted what I said, when I heard that you had disappeared and were probably gone to Glenshian, for I feared that it was my repeating his slander which had sent you there to have it out with him.'

'Then you were distressing yourself unnecessarily,' Hector assured him, 'for I should have gone there in any case. I had an old score to pay off. You are too punctilious. Moreover, we settled our difference by Loch Linnhe side – in a way rather unsatisfactory for you, I fear.' He glanced at his companion's sling. 'I, on my part, am exceedingly sorry to learn that your wound proved so much more serious than I intended – than I knew,' he corrected himself.

Why, again, was it that Hector Grant always seemed to him to say the wrong thing? 'You had, in short, intended to let me off more lightly?' inquired Ian with colour in his face and rather dryly, and, before Hector could reply, added, 'Yes, I had my lesson,' and went on to talk of other subjects. By the time that their way turned northwards from the shore of Loch Arkaig and began to mount, the two had subsided into comparative silence. Yet Ian had meant to let his companion know that it was anxiety on his behalf which had led him to take this journey from Appin, in none too good trim himself; but he was not going to do that now. If Captain Grant had shown the slightest curiosity as to why he was here, his wound still imperfectly healed . . . but no! One must, however, make allowances for the strain of the last week in duress.

Trying to do so, Ian's thoughts flew to Mr Maitland, and thence, naturally enough, to her whose image, for all his efforts, was not long out of them. The bog-myrtle still lay near his heart – brittle now and very fragile. He supposed that the time would come when, if he continued to carry it upon him, there would be nothing left of it but small dry fragments. Better to burn or bury it . . . on the day, perhaps, when he learnt that she was married – if he ever came to hear of that inevitable happening. And by this channel his thoughts returned once more to Maitland. But it was absurd, he told himself, to imagine that there could be any question of *that*; Mr Maitland was too old, and for all Ian knew might be a married man, though somehow he did not think he was.

Suddenly his heart beat faster. When Mr Maitland was brought to the House of Ardroy he would talk to him, if he were well enough, about Olivia, but without revealing his secret. On that he prayed that no obstacle would occur to prevent that gentleman's speedy transference to what Hector Grant, before setting off just now, had not inaptly characterized as a hospital. And soon afterwards they themselves arrived at that destination, to the surprise and joy of Hector's sister, Alison Cameron, the satisfaction of Miss Margaret Cameron, who foresaw work for her skill in the general appearance of the one and the beslinged arm of the other, and the inconvenient curiosity of Donald and little Keith, as to how Cousin Ian's arm came to be in that sling at all.

2

There followed two days of quiet – of quiet and of waiting for the arrival of the master of the house with the third invalid. Hector was a good deal taken up with his sister, and Miss Cameron decreed that Ian (whose long ride had not done his imperfectly-healed wound any good, if it had caused no actual harm) was not to exert himself. Indeed, now that the excitement of Hector's rescue was over Ian had no desire for further forays, and would sit for long periods by Loch na h-Iolaire with a book in his hand which he never read, thinking of his lost love. And also, with an increasing sense of dismay, of Jacqueline's lost lover . . . whom he had driven from her.

For though Hector Grant was perfectly friendly, and though he was here in the flesh within reach of speech, Ian was completely in the dark as to his present matrimonial intentions, which indeed Hector was hardly likely to confide to him again, even if they were unchanged. The position began increasingly to torment the young man; yet how could he, who had told Captain Grant to his face, and with a gross insult, that he should never marry his sister, how could he bring himself to say that he now only hoped that Captain Grant would do so? And yet, unless Hector himself gave some sign, he would have to say that, for Jacqueline's sake.

So Ewen Cameron, coming, the third afternoon, upon his cousin by the loch, sitting propped up against a tree trunk with his eyes closed, stood looking at him rather ruthfully. Hector, whom he had already seen, appeared in his usual health and spirits, the latter heightened, if anything, by the rage which had been simmering in him since his release. But Ian looked so wan; he ought not to have been brought away from Invernacree ... Ardroy came quietly nearer and Ian opened his eyes.

'You!' he said, looking up at Ewen in surprise. 'When did you arrive? Have you brought Mr Maitland with you?'

'Yes. I got here about half an hour ago. I am sorry if I woke you.'

'You did not wake me. I heard a sound, but thought it was Donald. He was about here a little time ago.'

'Was he? Ian, how goes that arm of yours?'

'Excellently, under Miss Cameron's care,' answered his cousin. 'And now I suppose she will have another patient to tend. How does that poor gentleman?'

'He was well enough to be brought here, and that is all one can say. Aunt Margaret now has him in her clutches. I don't think he was sorry to return to bed again, and, I flatter myself, to a more comfortable one than Mrs MacGillonie's. I could not question him when I was with him there; I felt a delicacy about it, and moreover he was too ill. But he told me his name – which you had already done – and from some confused remarks which he let fall when feverish I could not avoid gathering that he had been an invited guest at Invershian, and had left hurriedly on account of some disagreement with that hound Finlay MacPhair. He seemed in considerable distress of mind to boot. You say you have met him before?'

'Yes,' said Ian, arranging his sling with care. 'I met him as I came back from Glasgow not long ago. He was then on his way to these parts.'

'And he is, you told me, a Jacobite and a friend of Campbell of Cairns? That's an odd combination,' observed Ardroy. 'But I suppose it was Cairns himself who gave you that piece of information when he was at Invernacree?'

'No,' admitted Ian rather unwillingly. 'I did not know of this Mr Maitland's existence then. It was Miss Campbell who told me ... afterwards.'

'The lady you pulled out of the coach,' said Ewen, smiling. 'I heard about that from Jacqueline the other day. And that feat, my dear Ian, might have proved the beginning of a very proper romance if the lady had not been of Clan Diarmaid. So it was she who told you this gentleman's history? ... But what exactly do you mean by "afterwards"? After you had met him? Where then *did* you meet him?'

There was no answer for a moment.

'Ewen,' said the young man then, speaking with difficulty, 'did my father say anything to you about ... Miss Campbell?'

'Not a word. What should he tell me of her?' But Ian seemed unable to inform him. Ewen reached across and laid a hand on his wrist. 'Good heavens, Ian ... not that you *did* fall in love with her?'

But his cousin did not meet his gaze. He was looking across the loch. 'That seems like Donald, climbing the *creag ruadh*, yonder,' he observed in a dulled voice. 'I hope he will not slip.' And then, as Ardroy did not even turn his head in the direction of his adventurous offspring, he met his eyes at last, and said, with a little gasp which he could not control, 'Ewen, I wish I were dead!'

Ewen said nothing for a moment, but continued to look at him with those steady deepset eyes of his. After a silence he removed his hand. 'I am glad you told me,' he said gently. 'Forgive me for my thoughtless words.'

The breeze set the birch foliage over them swaying, and a

cone fell with a thud from a neighbouring pine. 'This arm of mine,' went on Ian at last, without much coherence, 'that is the reason ... though Captain Grant does not even know of Miss Campbell's existence – from me at least. It was because I had said farewell to her for ever – that was up at Kilrain in Perthshire – and I was devilridden because my father had been so harsh. (But that matter's all put right now.) Yet, Ewen, I have perhaps wrecked Jacqueline's happiness too, for I have no notion now whether Captain Grant still intends to ask for her hand.'

'Leave Hector to me,' said Ewen with a consoling imperturbability. 'I'll see to the matter; don't torment yourself over that. 'Tis only natural he should not speak to you of it. But, my poor Ian, I am more sorry for you than I can say. For, of course, there's nothing to be done.'

'Nothing,' said Ian, leaning his head back against the tree. He thought for a second of their conversation that June night at Invernacree. 'Nothing. I recognized that at once. I did fight against it ... My father has been kind ... but I'll have to make my suit to Miss Maclean in the end ... Sometimes I feel as if I were dead already, and that all this – even your beautiful loch – is an illusion. The last real water I saw was a burn in a wood at Kilrain.'

His cousin did not try to offer him any consolation, for which Ian was grateful. What would be the use of being told, 'You will forget her in time'? Either he should never do so, which was what he firmly believed, or he would hate to think that his memory of Olivia Campbell could ever be dimmed, were it by the passing of centuries.

'I think I see Hector coming to find me,' said Ardroy, breaking the silence. 'He is eager for a conference as to the next move against Glenshian. Shall we have it here and now?'

Ian nodded and got to his feet. Before Hector came up a mute handclasp – no more – had passed between the cousins over the grave of Ian's stricken romance.

3

But for twenty minutes or so after that the quiet shore of the little Loch of the Eagle rang with the expression of Captain Hector Grant's desire for vengeance, all the more fiery for having been kept some days in leash. And yet it was difficult to see how this desire was to find fulfilment, since Hector would not hear of any civil suit against Glenshian, his pride not enduring the prospect of having to stand up in court and admit that he, a Grant and a soldier, had been chained by the middle to a wall like a bear or a monkey. On the other hand, personal and individual vengeance, as he had just learnt to his cost, was too short in the arm to reach the well-guarded Chief, and a clan foray was impossible in these degenerate days. At last Ian, who was really more concerned with his cousin's case than with Hector's, suggested that the latter might perhaps find his best available satisfaction in checkmating Glenshian's monstrous design of ruining Ardroy – which must lie near the Chief's heart since he had taken so much trouble over the preliminaries. By what Hector had overheard, however, *he* now held the key to that position. And having learnt from his sister and Miss Cameron of the cloud of anxiety under which all at Ardroy had lately been living, Captain Grant agreed to this course, luke-warmly at first, abandoning with reluctance his taste for proceedings more violent and personal; then with a rush of something like remorse for not having sooner regarded the situation from Ewen's point of view.

'Indeed, my dear Ewen,' he said, 'I might have had the good feeling to think of this before, after your coming the way you did, almost single-handed – '

'Don't forget Ian,' put in Ardroy.

'Faith, no, I'm not forgetting him. – We will do that, then, *Eoghain mhóir*, having such an excellent stick to threaten Mac 'ic Fhionnlaigh with. Yet, by the powers, I'm not going to leave him my horse and valise as a gift! You must demand those back, Ewen.'

'I will,' said Ardroy. Like Hector, he would much have preferred a more personal reckoning, but on the other hand he could scarcely yet fathom the depth of the relief which had come to him from the possession of that 'stick' against Glenshian's machinations. Life had taken on a different complexion these last few days. 'I will write a letter to Glenshian without delay, saying that I know he had those steers driven in among my cattle, and for what purpose; and that if he proceeds further against me not only shall I bring forward this damning fact, but Captain Grant will take action against him for assault and unlawful detention. That ought to give him his quietus – even though the part about Hector be only a threat. I will also demand the return of your horse and effects, Hector, by the hand of the gillie who takes the letter to Invershian.'

They were all walking now in the direction of the house, but Ewen being intercepted, when they got round the loch, by one of his tenants who desired to speak to him, the two younger men found themselves alone together for the first time, as it happened, since they had ridden to Ardroy.

They went on in silence for a little while, Hector pulling a grass stalk thoughtfully between his teeth. At last he said, as if to himself, 'Yes, I ought to have seen it in that light before. Poor Ewen, to think of that scoundrel having him on the rack all these weeks! Then you were here, Mr Stewart, when the steers which he had sent on purpose were found – that almost incredible piece of villainy?'

Ian nodded. For the last minute or two his thoughts had left Finlay MacPhair and his victims to think of his own – Jacqueline. Ewen had indeed announced his intention of broaching that topic to Jacqueline's swain in order to save his cousin from drinking the worst of the draught which he saw ahead of him; but was *that* keeping his own promise to his little sister? The prospect was damnably unpleasant, but there was a strain in Ian Stewart which made him contemplate doing the thing for that very reason. He looked round; Ewen had gone off with the tacksman and they were unlikely to be interrupted.

'Captain Grant,' he said, coming to a stop beneath a birch tree, 'I have apologized to you for my . . . indefensible conduct, and you, I think, accepted an apology. But there's something else . . .' Here he stuck.

'Yes?' said Hector, throwing away the grass stalk.

'The . . . the original matter in question – I want to speak of that. My own extreme folly has made that difficult now.'

'You refer to your sister,' said Hector at once. 'My suit to her offended you. I never thought that you in your heart believed the monstrous charge you made against me, and you have acknowledged that you did not. But you must pardon me for thinking that, if you had recourse to such a weapon in order to show your disapproval, you would dislike me as a brother-in-law very much indeed.'

He had in truth put the case in a nutshell. Ian studied the heather at his feet. 'I was crazy that day . . . And now, having paid pretty dearly for that madness, I have to ask you – ' It was almost impossible to bring out the words.

'Whether I mean to pursue my suit,' finished Hector quietly. There was no ungenerous exultation in his manner, but nothing, either, to blink the fact that it was this moment, and not that on Loch Linnhe shore, when he had run his traducer through the arm, which was repaying him for those wild words under the pine-clump. 'But, Mr Stewart, if I am to have your continued enmity on that score to reckon with – '

Ian's face was drained of colour. This was a strain alike on pride and on bodily nerves. 'If that were the case I should not have accompanied Ardroy from Appin with some hope of helping you out of Glenshian's clutches.' It was not agreeable to plead this fact, especially as Captain Grant immediately responded, 'You mean to say that you left home in that condition,' he pointed to the sling, 'on my account?'

'Only partly,' muttered Ian. 'Yet 'twas the least I could do, in the circumstances.' Then he set his lips to the cup. 'Mr Grant, knowing now, as I did not earlier, my sister Jacqueline's sentiments, I can only hope that you – that you will fulfil the intention you announced of approaching my father on the matter.'

The frustrated suitor was staring at him with such a curious expression that Ian felt a terrible sinking at the heart, and thought, 'I have done it – I have ruined Jacqueline's life ... unless she gets over her feeling for him!' and the blood beat so in his brain that he surreptitiously put out his only available hand towards the tree near him in order to steady himself. After a moment he saw, to his surprise, that Hector Grant was holding out one of his.

'Egad, I could not have done that!' he was saying frankly. 'Mr Stewart, I give you best! Let me also have the honour of telling you that I have not wavered an instant from my intention of asking for your sister in marriage.'

Ian removed his left hand from the satin-smooth birch trunk upon which it rested, and it went into both of the late victor's.

Chapter 19

FINLAY'S TOOL...?

NEXT morning Ewen stood by David Maitland's bedside and asked in his deep, gentle voice whether he was well enough to receive Captain Hector Grant, who owed so much to him, and desired to render thanks in person.

To Maitland, lying there clear at last of the circling mists of fever and weakness, his host appeared about eight feet high. A splendid fir-tree of a man – he remembered his carrying him up some stair or other; he remembered too, if dimly, his care of him in the succeeding two days. Now he had even more to thank Ewen Cameron for, and with a less clouded consciousness of it – his recent transportation hither, into the guardianship of this competent elderly lady. Camerons both, it was true; but he *had* done them a service . . .

'I shall be very pleased to see Captain Grant,' he answered now; 'but indeed I have no need of thanks.' What would this handsome auburn-haired giant say if he were to add: ' 'Tis I who ought to thank Captain Grant, for I owe him, in a sense, my life?'

'Well, I'll not let him thank you overlong,' said Ewen, smiling down upon him. Gratitude apart, he found this Mr Maitland, with his refined and scholarly face, an attractive person even in illness, and the fact that he himself had nursed the poor gentleman for two days, without any adequate feminine aid, gave him a kind of proprietary feeling about the invalid.

At the door he turned, remembering something.

'By the way, sir, I am just on the point of sending a messenger to MacPhair of Glenshian demanding the immediate return of Captain Grant's horse and valise. Am I right in supposing that your effects also are at Invershian, because in that case I shall very willingly – '

He stopped, astonished at the hot colour which had flooded over the delicate, bloodless features on the pillow, at the look, as of extreme distaste, which contracted the mouth and brow.

'I . . . I thank you, Mr Cameron. I prefer to hold no communication of any kind with Mr MacPhair . . . I doubt not that later on – ' He broke off, biting his lip.

'Certainly, we will leave the matter exactly as you please,' said Ewen soothingly. 'Communications with Glenshian are no pleasure to me either. – Yes, Hector, you can come in, but you are not to stay for more than ten minutes.'

If the late captive was debarred by this fiat from spending long in the sickroom he made the best use of his time, and there was no doubt of the sincerity of his gratitude. Never, he declared, would he have suggested to Mr Maitland such a journey, upon so wet a night, too, had he known that his benefactor was only recently risen from a sickbed. Maitland felt that this frank young man would probably have welcomed some corresponding frankness on his own part as to what he, fresh from that retreat, had been doing in that lonely spot in such weather and at so late an hour; but he naturally did not enlighten him, even though Mr Grant showed, by what he said, that he supposed the invalid's previous illness to have taken place at Invershian, and though he gave him a summary of Finlay's behaviour to himself, without, however, acquainting his listener with the precise nature of the slander which he had gone to force Finlay to retract.

When he had left him David Maitland lay for a while in a kind of shuddering irritation. Why would everyone speak to him of Finlay MacPhair, that spider from whose web he had just broken free? He desired never to hear his name again. Glenshian might keep his horse and clothes for ever, for all he cared; he had sufficient money with him; he could buy or hire another horse and no doubt borrow a cloak. Yes, he had broken out of Finlay's web; that infamous schemer did not, probably, know where he was now, and he much preferred to feel that it was so. The air seemed easier to breathe.

For all that, Maitland was scolded when Miss Margaret Cameron came in, to find him flushed, and was told that he might have no more visitors till the morrow. And gradually the silence, the peace of the old house and his own weakness all worked to banish those repugnant memories; he ceased to see the sneer and the uncomfortable greenish-yellow eyes looking at him from the foot of the bed, and sank into a beneficent torpor and forgetfulness.

Next day his wardress pronounced herself more satisfied with him, and that no doubt was why, between sleeping and waking, he had a brief glimpse of a lady, still young, with an infant in her arms and a beautiful dark-haired child clinging to her skirts; and for one moment he was dreamily back in Italy years ago as a young man, looking at an altarpiece in a little mountain church and wishing, for all his staunch Presbyterianism, that he could take it home with him. Then he realized that this was no Popish Madonna; it must be Ewen Cameron's wife with her children. The little boy seemed much interested in him, and his mother, smiling, had to whisper to him to come away.

In the afternoon, feeling much more himself again, he was lying listening to the childish tones and laughter which floated in now and then with the sunlight through the open window, when there came a discreet tap at the door, a male voice asked permission to enter, and there walked in, to Maitland's surprise, the young man whom he had last consciously seen with Olivia Campbell upon the hill road at Kilrain. He had his right arm in a sling.

'Mr Stewart – Mr Stewart of Invernacree, is it not?' asked the invalid, slightly raising himself.

'The same, sir. I am glad to hear that you are so much better. I have Miss Cameron's permission to pay you a visit. I hope I have yours also?'

'I am so completely in Miss Cameron's hands,' replied Maitland, smiling, 'that, even if I wished, I could scarcely withhold it

– not that I wish to. Sit down, pray, Mr Stewart. It is a surprise to see you here.'

'I visit here occasionally, for Ardroy is my first cousin,' explained Ian, not enlarging upon the special reasons for his presence this time. But Maitland, now beginning to feel in a dim way that he had caught sight of him that night at MacGillonie's house, asked whether he had not played a part in the rescue of Captain Grant from the ruined castle. Ian replied that he had, though a very minor one; on which Maitland not unnaturally said, 'I suppose you took some injury to your arm in that business? I did not know that there had been any affray over it.'

'Nor was there,' replied Ian, colouring. 'I got this injury otherwise.' He talked on indifferent topics for a while and then asked whether Mr Maitland had lately received any news of Miss Campbell. A few minutes sufficed to make it clear, even to the perceptions of an invalid, that Miss Campbell was the very subject about which he had come to converse. But this did not surprise David Maitland. Had not his 'god-daughter' stayed a week under old Mr Stewart's roof, and had not this young man been given the priceless privilege of rescuing her from a position of danger? If he had lost his heart it was not to be wondered at; what concerned Maitland was the state of Olivia's. What had the two, for instance, been saying to each other up the brae at Kilrain – why, in fact, had Ian Stewart been there at all? Olivia was kindhearted, but she did not suffer suitors overgladly; yet Maitland knew from Mrs MacUre that his present visitor had not only called at the cottage that morning and borne Olivia off for a walk, but had also had an interview with her alone the day before. So, lying there, he paid particular attention to Mr Ian Stewart of Invernacree, and came to the conclusion that he liked what he saw of him, reserved young man as he seemed, but with a smile – probably rare – which quite transfigured his dark, intent face.

And when he had gone David Maitland lay thinking of Olivia, of Olivia whose home he had not visited (as she had pointed out at Kilrain) for more than two years – not since he had had blood upon his soul. But he still breathed the same air as she did. Should he not thank God for having held him back from the sin of suicide? Dulled by illness, his own self-loathing had grown a little less sharp since that night; and he knew that Finlay MacPhair would never betray what he knew of him because it would go counter to that horrible and mercenary hope of his, which, for all that Maitland knew, he might still be cherishing in some modified form. This revived interest in Olivia's future stirred in his heart as the snowdrop's little green spear pushes through the frozen soil. If Olivia were really clinging to this young Stewart, and if he were worthy of her (or approximately so) then he might consider the means of aiding him. There was, it could not be denied, the gulf of clan and political hostility to be bridged, if possible. If only he knew what Olivia herself felt about the matter! Young Invernacree had not confided in him – why should he? – and had given him no inkling of the terms on which Miss Campbell and he had parted. He must learn more of him; in the days which must elapse before he could leave the house of Ardroy he might, perhaps, be able to penetrate his reserve. He wondered if Mr Stewart's cousin, his host, knew anything of this attachment?

Maitland was vaguely thinking of Ewen Cameron, of this home of his, which seemed so pleasant, and the children – he supposed that they were his – whose prattle he had smiled over, when he heard Mr Cameron's very voice, unmistakable in its tones, somewhere close below the window. It sounded hurried.

'Ian, Ian, I want you! Where were you? Listen; the gillie I sent to Invershian with my letter has just returned empty-handed. It appears that MacPhair is away from home – or so he was told by those at the house. Consequently he had to leave my letter until such time as Finlay should return, and to come back without Hector's horse and effects.'

The invalid heard his late visitor give an exclamation of annoyance.

'And Hector must delay his visit to Glenmoriston no longer,' went on Ardroy. 'He is much needed there. I will lend him a horse.'

'Do you think,' asked Ian Stewart's voice, 'that Glenshian is really from home?'

'How can one say? Probably not ... but he finds it more convenient at this juncture to feign absence ... Yet he is no coward, Finlay MacPhair, for all that he betrayed Archie to his death.'

Maitland, rigid, held his breath.

'But, Ewen,' began Ian Stewart in lowered accents, so much lowered that nothing of what he said was audible in the room above save four words at the end. And they were: 'unknown man ... information' and 'Glenbuckie'.

'Yes, I know that,' responded Ardroy's deeper tones. Evidently he had no idea how far they carried. 'But that man was Finlay's tool, probably his paid tool – I am convinced of it. Sometimes I dream that I am meeting him, and – ' He checked himself. 'But enough of that subject. You must help me to persuade Hector to delay no longer, but to set out at once for his inheritance. I had rather, too, he were gone from these parts lest, after all, he and Glenshian – ' The two moved away out of hearing.

Above, in Ardroy's best spare bed, David Maitland lay like an effigy upon a tomb. Even here! ... Yet, of course, here – for in any Cameron house he might expect to hear talk of Doctor Cameron's fate ... But not to find it known that someone had sent intelligence from that obscure glen in Balquhidder. *'Finlay's tool ... his paid tool.'* *'Sometimes I dream that I am meeting him.'* Ewen Cameron had no need any longer to dream that. 'O God!' said the betrayer, and threw his arm across his eyes.

2

A couple of days later, in the early afternoon, Ian and Ardroy came slowly back from Loch na h-Iolaire with their fishing rods, and with five-year-old Keith trotting between them, holding a hand of each, and making them laugh by his development of a theme of his own about caterpillars, in which creatures he was at this epoch deeply interested.

Hector, on the horse the loan of which had been more or less forced upon him, had been successfully persuaded to set off for Glenmoriston. Before he went he had sought out Ian, and had told him that he intended to present himself at Invernacree in about a couple of weeks' time to make a formal demand for the hand of his younger sister, and that he hoped he might rely upon Ian's support in the matter. Ian not only promised this, but offered on his own return to try to prepare the ground a little, on which the grateful suitor brought out a letter addressed to his lady-love. If Mr Stewart would have the goodness to charge himself with that . . .

'But I am not returning home for a while yet,' Ian reminded the writer. 'Perhaps you would rather find a speedier messenger?'

'I doubt if I could,' Hector had replied. 'And I could not find one to whom I would sooner commit my correspondence.'

'You honour me,' replied Ian, not formally, to match the words, but giving his late foe that smile which was, as David Maitland had guessed, so telling if (or perhaps because) it was somewhat infrequent. And he took the letter. 'None the less, if I have the chance, I will, if you permit it, send this on, for I am sure it is eagerly awaited.' And as a matter of fact, he had found and seized such an opportunity soon after Hector's departure.

So he had fulfilled his promise to Jacqueline and laid at last the ghost of that unworthy impulse to deny her the happiness which he might not have himself. He hoped that she *would* be happy with Hector Grant; he had never thought to like him so well as he had the last few days . . .

'Mr Maitland is out of bed today, is he not?' he now asked suddenly. ' – Very well, Keithie, if you think you can jump that little juniper you can but try!'

'Yes,' answered Ardroy. 'But, though I suppose he is better he looks little better to me. He has at times so unhappy an air, as though he had somewhat on his mind. And from various things he let fall during those two days at MacGillonie's, I am sure he has, though I've no notion what it is.'

'Something to do with his sudden departure from Invershian,

perhaps,' suggested Ian. 'Although, to be sure, even before that he looked . . .' He stopped reflectively.

'There is certainly something much amiss in that quarter,' agreed Ewen. 'And it was uncommonly odd of him to refuse the chance which I offered him the other day of recovering his horse from Glenshian. I told you, did I not, how the very idea seemed to horrify him? Yet I suppose – since he did not deny it – that his horse *is* at Invershian, and his clothes? He can hardly have travelled thither completely without effects. Was he mounted when you came upon him on your way back from Glasgow?'

'Yes, and had a valise on his saddle. The horse, of course, may have been hired.'

Ewen shrugged his shoulders. 'Well, 'tis no concern of ours, and I would not for worlds have Mr Maitland think either that I am curious about his private affairs or that, owing him so much on Hector's account, I grudge him a nightshirt and razor, and the loan of a horse when the time comes. If he has quarrelled with Glenshian I but think the better of him for it. – Donald, haven't you yet learnt that it is useless to try and outrace Luath?'

For here his eldest son, who some while ago had vanished ahead, panted up breathless and crimson-cheeked in the wake of the great deerhound with his long easy motion.

'I wasn't racing him,' he gasped, thrusting his hand into his parent's. 'Father, do you know, there are soldiers coming up the avenue!'

Such potent memories of old perils hung round the phrase that Ardroy instinctively stopped, and even changed colour a little.

' – But I think one of them is Captain Paton, and I like him,' finished Donald, regaining more breath. 'There's a lady too, riding with him. Perhaps the other soldier is an orderly, for he is riding some way behind.'

'A lady? Mrs Paton, perhaps. – The child gave me quite a fright,' added Ewen under his breath to his cousin.

'You were not the only one alarmed,' confessed Ian. 'Who is this Captain Paton approved of by Donald?'

'And by me also, for the matter of that. He is an old acquaintance of mine from '46 – a very good fellow. Surely I have told you about him before now? He has been quartered at Fort William for some time, and occasionally rides over to pay us a visit; but he has never brought his wife with him before. She must have come to inquire after Alison – very civil of her.'

By the time, however, that the little party got round the house to the porch only one scarlet-coated figure was to be seen there, just remounting with the reins of the other two horses over his arm. One of them bore a lady's saddle. Seeing Ardroy the soldier saluted.

'I was just about to take these 'orses round to the stable, sir, if convenient?'

'Do so by all means,' said Ewen; and, aside to his cousin, 'Did you ever expect to see me saluted by a *saighdear dearg*? As a matter of fact he *is* Paton's orderly. I expect we shall find Paton and his wife with Alison in the parlour. I should like to make you acquainted with him.'

Outside the parlour door, when the two fishermen had got rid of the traces of their pursuit, they found Donald, a self-posted sentinel, important with information.

'It is Captain Paton, Father – I thought it was! But 'tis not Mrs Paton with him – 'tis a lady come from Fort William to ask news of the sick gentleman upstairs.'

'News of Mr Maitland,' said Ewen, looking down at his heir. 'Well, fortunately we can give the lady a tolerably good account. I wonder who she is – his wife, perhaps ... What, are you not coming in after all, Ian?'

For his kinsman, a moment ago close upon his heels, was now several feet away, looking as if he had received a shock of some kind.

'I ... yes ... it would be strange if ... no, it cannot be!' was his not very coherent reply. Then, making an effort to pull himself together, he said in a more rational tone, 'Yes, I am coming in with you.'

Chapter 20

IN A GREEN RIDING HABIT

IAN STEWART had thus had a moment's warning of whom – incredible though it seemed – he might find in Lady Ardroy's parlour. But the girl in the green riding costume who sat talking to her hostess in the large sunlit room, with the English officer standing beside her chair, had received no warning at all of who was to find her there. And looking up as the door opened, she saw behind the master of the house a figure ... The colour rose in her face with the shock, rose and stayed there, burning ...

'Ewen,' said his wife, 'let me present you to Miss Campbell of Cairns, who has come over under Captain Paton's escort from Fort William to inquire for Mr Maitland, an old family friend.'

'Yes, I told Father outside that was what she had come for,' observed Donald in a satisfied undertone.

Ewen bowed; Olivia curtseyed. Then it was Ian's turn. In a dream he heard some words or other of presentation; he fancied he heard Olivia saying that they had met already – at Invernacree. Her face swam before him under the little three-cornered riding hat which sat so deliciously upon her dark curls. The last time he had seen that face ... Unbelievable, impossible! ... it had been very close to his, upon his breast. Still more incredible – he had kissed it ...

But now she did not meet his eyes – chance or design? She had seated herself again, and was talking with animation to her host and hostess. On one side the long green habit lay in folds upon the floor, and Keithie, approaching, stationed himself upon it and looked at her gravely. Olivia put an arm round him as she talked, and he leant against her – a beautiful, dark-haired child such as one day, perhaps, she would have for her own ...

862

a child such as they two might have had. It hurt so bitterly that Ian could not bear the thought nor the picture which had suggested it, and he quietly removed himself so that he was more or less behind her, and could not see the little boy at all.

All these miles to visit Mr Maitland! And supposing that he himself had been out, hours away on the hills, and had returned to find her come and gone? How much better! ... No: a perfect sea of desolation engulfed him at the mere thought of such a disaster. Better this – though he could scarcely endure it – better at least to be able from where he stood to see the turn of her neck, the little tendril of hair by her ear ... Why had he not kissed that too when he had the chance?

Distinguishable words now broke through the sort of coma which enwrapped him. They were in Alison's voice.

'You would no doubt like to see Mr Maitland himself for a few moments, Miss Campbell? I will go and ask my aunt about it, and prepare him for your visit. – You need not start back for a while yet, I am sure, Captain Paton.'

'We must not delay too long, madam,' said the soldier, as he went and opened the door for her. He had hardly shut it again before Ardroy was bending over the visitor.

'Miss Campbell, I want to ask Captain Paton's advice about a horse of mine. Will you forgive us if we leave you to be entertained by Mr Stewart, since he already has the privilege of your acquaintance? Paton, you will not object, will you? I cannot make out what is wrong with the beast. – Come along with me, boys, to the stables.'

He removed his younger son, who showed signs of reluctance, bodily from his station against Miss Campbell's chair; and in about thirty seconds Ian and Olivia were the only people left in the room.

Ian came forward then; he had to. Olivia also turned her head a little; and then they both said the same thing in voices of varying degrees of embarrassment:

'I had no notion I should find you here ...'

Despite the fact that of the two Miss Campbell was the more seriously handicapped by her memories, she was the first to recover from that embarrassment – or, at least, to affect recovery. She said, changing her position a little, and with some of her natural vivacity, 'You have been told why I am here, Mr Stewart, but I am still in the dark as to why you are!'

'Ardroy is my first cousin,' said Ian briefly, as he had said to Mr Maitland. But in Maitland's presence he had not felt so breathless.

'I did not know that!' remarked Olivia in a tone of surprise.

'But why are you in these parts at all?' asked the young man, words coming more easily now. 'I thought you were returning home from Kilrain.'

'It was my intention. But, before I left, there came a letter from my father enclosing one from my kinswoman Euphemia Campbell, who is married to an officer stationed at Fort William, proposing that I should visit them. My father wished me to go, so I went thither direct from Perthshire. And there, after a day or two, I heard that Mr Maitland was lying ill at a farmhouse on Loch Lochy. My host was good enough to send a messenger to inquire, and the news was brought back that Mr Maitland had been conveyed by Mr Ewen Cameron of Ardroy to his own house. And while I was uneasy, wondering how he did, and how I should obtain further news of him, my kinswoman remembered her husband having mentioned to her that a brother officer, a Captain Paton, was a friend of Mr Cameron's; and so this visit of mine has come about. But I did not guess . . .'

The even fluency of her explanation of her presence failed suddenly, and she sat looking down at her hands in silence. Ian was silent too. The same memory was in the mind of each, the same place before their eyes, the same sound in their ears – the murmur of a tiny burn in a little oak wood. And it was plain what Olivia was thinking of, for a lovely colour began to rise once more and stain her cheek.

Suddenly she lifted her eyes. 'You are an invalid too, I see, Mr Stewart, for you carry your arm in a sling. I hope the injury is not serious?'

'I shall soon discard the scarf,' said he, gazing at her.

'I am glad ... It was good of Mr Cameron to bring Mr Maitland here. I wonder how he came on him.'

'Mr Maitland did a kinsman of his a service – Lady Ardroy's brother, to be exact. My cousin was only too glad to take charge of him.'

'Has he been very ill – Mr Maitland?'

Some perverse impulse tempted Ian to reply, 'Not so ill as I have,' but he conquered it and contented himself with saying, 'He was already better when he was brought here, and does well now; he has left his bed. But you will soon, doubtless, see his state for yourself.'

Olivia was now looking across the room, out of the window. 'This is fine country. I have enjoyed my ride. The sun shone all the way.'

'Even in the Dark Mile?' asked Ian.

'The Dark Mile?' said she, struck by the name. 'What is that?'

'Only a stretch of the road between Loch Lochy and Loch Arkaig which goes by that name – I do not know why, save that, what with trees and high crags, it is gloomy there.'

'I think I remember the place,' said Miss Campbell. She rose and went slowly to the window. Ian stayed where he was. Sitting in a chair in Alison Cameron's parlour, Olivia Campbell was a gentlewoman of birth and breeding come to pay a call; over there, standing by the open window, with the air of the hills blowing in upon her, she might resemble too much the Highland girl whom he had helped over the stepping-stones, and he might a second time ... It was safer not to risk it. Yet he laid hold of the back of a heavy chair as a kind of anchor.

Then the door handle turned and Lady Ardroy came in, to find half the room between the two. But the danger was over, and Ian did not care at that moment what Alison thought of his manners. She went over to the guest.

'I see that you are looking at our prospect, Miss Campbell. It would be a great pleasure to Mr Maitland to see you, and my aunt thinks it would do him good. Will you please to come with me?'

Olivia thanked her. Ian held the door open for the two of them, and Miss Campbell, as she passed him, the folds of her habit on her arm, looked at him with a smile which he could not interpret. He stood there a moment like a dummy, still clasping the doorknob; then he shut the door rather hard. Next he found himself gazing at the chair where she had sat. He touched it; it was still warm, and, as no one could see him, he bent suddenly and kissed one of the arms.

After that he wandered about the room, thinking, Is she seeing him alone, and what is she saying to him? and trying to deduce, from Alison Cameron's continued absence, that she perhaps considered herself necessary as a duenna in the sick man's chamber. Then Ewen and Captain Paton came in again, and Ian made the better acquaintance of the English officer, who was after all a Lowland Scot. He and Ardroy seemed on very good terms, but Ian knew that this was less a testimony to the measure of peace and settlement which was gradually coming to the Highlands, than to their own earlier relations during the Forty-five.

And then both Lady Ardroy and Miss Cameron came in. So Olivia *had* been left alone with Mr Maitland after all! Jealously the young man counted the minutes by the clock – eleven, twelve, thirteen. At the fourteenth the door opened and she entered. Nearly a quarter of an hour!

Refreshments were brought, and there was much talk of the part Mr Maitland had played in Hector's affair, and of Ewen's gratitude on his behalf. Ian stood aside from it. Shortly afterwards, as he had foreseen, Captain Paton said they ought to be starting back, the horses were ordered round, and everybody gathered outside to see the riders off. It was Ewen who had the honour of mounting Miss Campbell, but Ian handed her her riding-switch, and for a moment his fingers touched hers.

'I hope your arm will soon be completely recovered, Mr Stewart,' she said kindly.

'I thank you, Miss Campbell,' he replied with formality, and stood back at once, to circumvent an insensate desire which had rushed upon him to lay hold of her bridle and detain her.

Then she rode away down the avenue, his lost love, the scarlet-coated officer very attentive. Ardroy thrust his arm through Ian's as they returned to the house, but he said nothing; nor did Ian thank him for so considerately and swiftly removing Captain Paton and the children from the room. For one thing, he was by no means sure that he had reason to be grateful.

'So that is the young lady you rescued!' observed Alison. 'She is so charming that I vow I forgot she was a Campbell!'

'And no kinswoman of Mr Maitland's after all, as I hear,' said Miss Cameron. ' 'Tis plain, therefore, that she came all this way in order to see you, her rescuer, Mr Stewart.'

'Since Miss Campbell had not the slightest notion that I was here, madam, that can hardly be,' replied Ian as indifferently as he could.

'As if she would have avowed her knowledge of it!' scoffed Aunt Margaret. ' 'Tis pity, though, she had no chance of a word with you alone. Alison, you should have contrived it!'

'But – ' began Alison – and was silenced by a look from her husband.

'Well, I expect to find the gentleman upstairs, who did see the bonny young lady alone, greatly set up thereby,' announced Aunt Margaret, as she began to mount the stairs again, leaving the young man to whom that privilege had also been vouchsafed, by no means set up by it.

Chapter 21

TORMENT

NOR, really, was it a condition of exhilaration in which Olivia's visit had left Mr Maitland. Keen as his pleasure had been in seeing her again, much as he wanted, for her own sake, to discover her feelings about Ian Stewart, if she had but come two days earlier, before he had overheard that conversation beneath his window, he could have given her what she had always had from him – his whole attention. But almost every moment since that conversation had been for him a long and torturing warfare. There was a moral question to which he could find no certain answer. Was he bound to betray and incriminate himself in order to clear Finlay MacPhair from Ewen Cameron's accusation – Finlay who was only too anxious to claim the guilt of it, Finlay who had behaved so atrociously in that regard? Was *he* to tell Ewen Cameron whom he was harbouring, merely in order to lift the charge of final accomplishment of that bitterly regretted deed from the man who had 'done the preliminary work' for it, and who would have given so much to have had Maitland's 'luck' – the chance of sending that message about Glenbuckie? Must he do this?

It was not fear for his own physical safety which held him back; Maitland was beyond caring for that now. It was the thought of the fearful shock which he should give to all in this house, where he had been made the centre of so much care and gratitude. His soul quailed at the idea, just because he liked them all so much, from his tall host down to his younger son, that little Keithie who had now been permitted to visit him in his room, and had there brought him an offering of a large moth and some exceedingly damp moss in a saucer.

He could face the prospect still less after Olivia's visit. She also would hear of the terrible revelation, through Ian Stewart if from no other source. It was too much to expect of him. In intention Finlay *was* guilty. He himself must get well and leave the neighbourhood as quickly as possible. The sooner therefore that he recovered the full use of his legs the better; and so next afternoon, half against Miss Cameron's wishes, he left his room and came downstairs.

In the big, pleasant parlour he found his hostess with her baby in her arms, the two boys playing in a corner, and Ardroy himself, who seemed just to have come in, for he had a fowling piece in his hand. Young Invernacree was not there. Warmly welcomed, the convalescent was conducted to the most comfortable chair near the hearth; there was question of lighting a fire for him; the children came running and little Keith showed a disposition to climb upon his knee.

And then all at once Maitland's eyes, straying up to the high mantel in front of him, beheld there, hanging under the antlers, a framed engraving which he might not have recognized but for the inscription. But that showed all too clear: 'A True Effigies of Doctor Archibald Cameron, who lately suffered Death at Tyburn for High Treason.'

It was like a blow on the head. The room whirled round him, yet still, by some awful magnetism, the picture held his gaze. He instinctively repulsed little Keith.

'I see that you are looking at the portrait of my unfortunate kinsman, Doctor Cameron,' said Ardroy's voice through the mist. 'I bought it last October in Edinburgh, although it little resembles him. But I had no other likeness.'

Maitland wrenched his eyes away, murmuring some confused words of sympathy. The room had steadied itself, but his mouth was dry. Not that he feared discovery; for discovery – unless he betrayed himself – was practically impossible.

'He – Doctor Cameron – was a kinsman of yours?' he stammered out.

'He was my second cousin. But he was dearer to me than an elder brother would perhaps have been,' answered Ardroy quietly, but with a note in his voice which made Maitland

869

shiver. How could he ever tell him who was sitting there among them all?

It was too horrible. He wished with all his heart that he had remained in his room. He managed to answer the questions addressed to him by Miss Cameron, who fortunately came in at that moment, thereby creating a diversion; then, glancing at the window, he said, trying not to show the sense of suffocation which he felt:

'It seems a fine day; would it be possible for me to take a turn outside?'

'By all means,' responded his host instantly. 'I will come with you; you'll certainly need an arm. Donald, go and fetch Mr Maitland a plaid or a cloak.'

Maitland could not refuse that arm; indeed he was glad of support, for he found himself a good deal weaker than he had anticipated. Well, he had only to keep his head – and hope that there would be no more actual talk of Archibald Cameron.

But unfortunately, Donald, who had come out with them, seemed inclined to pursue the subject, even if his father did not. For as they paced slowly to and fro in the sun in front of the old grey house, Maitland leaning slightly upon Ardroy's arm, the little boy on his other side remarked:

'Doctor Cameron came here once, Mr Maitland, to cure Keithie when he was ill, and after that he was hidden in Angus's cottage up at Sloc nan Eun. – Oh, Father' – he peered round the invalid – 'perhaps that is a secret, and I ought not to have told it?'

'It does not matter now, Donald,' said his father, with so much sadness in his voice that Maitland was like to withdraw his arm. 'Moreover, Mr Maitland is one of us; he's a Jacobite too.'

So Donald resumed: 'And the redcoats took Father to Fort William because Doctor Cameron had been here, and he was there in prison a long time, and Uncle Hector too, and then they – '

'Never mind, Donald,' interrupted Ardroy. 'It will not interest Mr Maitland to hear my adventures. And I think you had better run off now; you are fatiguing him, hanging on like that.'

'Am I, sir?' asked Donald, looking up at the convalescent with his clear child's eyes. 'I am so sorry.' Maitland was not ready with an answer, but he held the boy's hand tighter because in truth he did not wish to find himself alone with Ewen Cameron just then. But Ewen himself said, a little peremptorily, 'Off with you, now!' and Donald, trained like most children in those days to instant obedience, said cheerfully, 'Yes, Father,' and ran back to the house.

'Nevertheless I am glad that my sons are able to remember Archibald Cameron,' observed Ardroy after a moment, 'though they will never know the full extent of the loss which they sustained when he laid down his life. As a Jacobite, Mr Maitland, you must recognize the greatness of the blow to the Cause, but, had you known Archibald Cameron personally, you would deplore much more than that – the death of one of the best and noblest-hearted men whom you could possibly have met. – But I do not know why I am assuming that you were not acquainted with him? You may have met him somewhere, perhaps, during the Rising?'

Maitland had to pause to get his voice. Even then it came with a gasp. 'No . . . never.'

Ewen looked at him in anxiety. 'You are fatigued, sir – this exertion is too much for you. Let me help you to that bench yonder.' His arm under the invalid's, he guided him to it, and Maitland sank down, looking ghastly enough to give colour to Ardroy's deduction.

He *was* near fainting, and yet he was not, for his senses were not numbed; they felt sharper than usual and more swift in operation. At the impact of that direct question his first impulse had been an instantaneous, crazy desire to say, 'Yes, I knew him,' and then to confess everything, whatever might be the consequences to himself. But, almost as swiftly, came the knowledge that that relief was impossible. As he had already felt, and felt now ten times more acutely, to say, 'It was I who betrayed him,' would be like driving a dirk into the breast of the man

871

beside him. It might be a sort of expiation for himself, but it could be nothing but a tragedy for Ewen Cameron. Even if he desired vengeance, as, being a Highlander, he probably did; even though he could now have it in full measure, Maitland knew in his soul that gratified revenge itself would be as nothing, weighed against the shock of the revelation. So there remained only one thing to do: to deny ever having met or seen Archibald Cameron.

'You should not have come out into the air,' said Ewen solicitously, as he bent over him. 'I'll go and fetch you a cordial, and then take you back to the house. Are you comfortable so? I will not be long.'

He hurried off. The warm sun streamed down on to David Maitland, but he felt as cold as the dead. The heather-clad slopes in the distance smiled impassively; his presence was nothing to them. But the great deerhound lying, not far away, in front of the porch, watched him with vigilant, half-suspicious eyes. And the informer looked about him almost in desperation. He must get away at once from this happy household in which he felt like a poisonous snake, whose tongue might wound at any moment and shatter all its peace. But it was obvious that he could not get away yet; he was not strong enough in body for the attempt, and this semi-collapse of his would not make his kind and unsuspecting hosts any the more ready to let him go.

That of course was exactly the case, for in a moment Miss Cameron as well as Ardroy came hurrying out to him, and Maitland soon found himself banished anew to his own room, and scolded for having attempted a feat beyond his strength. Lying back in his chair there he wondered frantically how this was going to end. Once or twice his thoughts dwelt upon the loch which he knew lay behind the house. But, even if he succeeded in reaching it undetected, he could not drown himself in it, he saw now, without cruelly wounding several people – among others his poor wife, to whom he had written again since he came here, and Olivia Campbell – and without involving

Ewen Cameron in who knew what unpleasantness, even suspicion. No, he could not take that way out. There *was* no way
out.

Only yesterday Olivia had said half teasingly to him in this
very room, 'You find yourself, dear Godfather, as I did, in a
perfect nest of Jacobites, but with more justification for your
presence in it than I had at Invernacree.' More justification!
Great God, if she had only known!

He remembered now how he had caught at the name Invernacree and tried to get her to talk of the son of that house, now
present in this. He had met with singularly little success; Olivia
had slid away from the subject, but so naturally that he could
not discover whether it was from real lack of interest in Ian
Stewart – or from too much. Well, Heaven knew that he, David
Maitland, was hardly now in a position to lend a helping hand
to such a match! Yet, partly because her happiness was always
so much at his heart, partly in order to keep at bay for a little
that hungry shadow at his back, he speculated on the problem,
and for the first time it occurred to him to wonder in what light
Ian Stewart regarded his, Maitland's, intimacy with Olivia. It
was true that he might be putting upon it either of two con-
structions, each equally wide of the mark. Those at least he
could correct if he had the chance.

Olivia, sitting there smiling in her green habit, Olivia, come
all this way to see him! And yet she would not confide in him,
not even a little. She had used to, sometimes. It almost seemed
as if she had known what he was now. Impossible! ... And, if
he could ever pray again, that should be his prayer, that she
might never know!

2

At this stage of his reflections Maitland heard a curious soft
undecided knock at the door, and a fumbling at the handle,
followed by the appearance of that engaging little boy,
Ardroy's younger son.

873

'I comed,' he announced, running across the bedroom, 'to bring you something, Mr Maittan'. It's in here.' He held forth a small wooden box.

'Another moth?' asked Maitland, and even out of his despair could not keep a smile from his lips.

'Not a moth. A cattlepillar. You must keep it in this box and not let it get out. But when it is a moth you can let it fly about.'

'I hope – I mean I expect – that I shall be gone before it becomes a moth.'

'Oh,' said the donor, rather dashed. 'I thought it would like to be with the other moth ... Where is the other moth?'

'I think your Aunt Margaret must have taken it away.'

'Naughty Aunt Margaret!' said the entomologist severely; and then, placing the box on Maitland's knee, removed the lid and with his small finger drew his attention to its rearing occupant. Meanwhile, someone pushed open the door which he had left ajar.

'Keithie,' said a man's voice, 'who told you that you might come in here?' It was Ian Stewart who stood in the doorway. 'I apologize for him, sir.'

Keithie turned round with a commiserating air. 'Poor Mr Maittan' had to go back to his room, and I knowed he was all alone, so I brought him my *best* cattlepillar.'

'That was very kind,' said his cousin. 'I am sure Mr Maitland is very much obliged to you. But suppose you leave it with him now and go to Morag, for I hear her calling for you.'

Little Keith shut up the box and thrust it at Maitland, about the middle of his waistcoat. 'Good night,' he said, and held up his flowerlike face, evidently expecting a kiss.

If young Invernacree had not been there in the doorway, Maitland believed that he would have contrived to get out of giving it. As it was he bent and kissed the child of Archibald Cameron's race feeling as if he were indeed the snake of his own tormented fancy. And he envied the young man on the threshold, catching him up in his arms and repeating the salute with unsullied lips.

'There, run along to Morag. I am sorry, sir,' added Ian as the little boy pattered away down the passage. 'It seems very hard to protect you from these children.'

Anything to keep his own thoughts at bay a little. 'Do not go, pray, Mr Stewart,' said Maitland quickly, as the young man was about to close the door. 'Will you not come in and sit down awhile? I am not so really so relapsed as might appear just now. 'Twas only the effect of the fresh air, and the weakness of my legs. Tomorrow I shall do better, I hope; for indeed 'tis full time I returned to my wife and family.'

'Your wife!' exclaimed Ian in a tone of great astonishment.

'Yes. Did you not know that I was married? Why, I have a son not so many years younger than you, I should suppose, Mr Stewart; that is to say, he will soon be of age.'

This unexpected news drew Ian within, shut the door behind him and placed him in a chair almost without his realizing it. 'I ... I thought somehow that you were unmarried, sir,' he said apologetically, 'I do not know why.'

'On the contrary, I am quite an old married man,' replied David Maitland. He reached up as he sat, and, putting the little wooden box upon the mantelshelf, added, 'Does that fact make any difference to you, Mr Stewart?'

He heard the young man draw a sharp breath. 'Any difference? What do you mean, sir?'

Maitland looked at him. 'This, that being, I suppose, nearly twice your age, and married to boot, and an old family friend of ... of a lady whom I think you admire, I wondered if I could prove of any service to you.'

But young Invernacree did not meet his eyes. He was sitting near the door; Maitland near the window, but with his back to it. And almost instantly Ian Stewart left his chair and went and looked out of the window, saying nothing. His face was invisible. Maitland began to be a little sorry that he had obeyed the impulse to say what he had, though he had done it for Olivia's sake. If she ... yet she had given him no clue.

'I am very much obliged to you, sir,' came at last rather stiffly from the window. 'But I fear you can do nothing. I ... I a great deal more than admire Miss Campbell, but circumstances make it impossible for me to ... in short, Miss Campbell is not for me.'

'You mean by that, I suppose,' said Maitland, screwing himself round in his chair to look at the speaker's back, 'the general circumstances of your family's divergent politics, now and in the past?'

Ian turned from the window. 'I mean a great deal more than that, sir. You are a Jacobite and were "out", I believe – as I was, though a mere lad then. You may remember therefore that Campbell of Cairns commanded the Campbell militia at Culloden, and where they were posted. My brother Alan, the heir, fell at Culloden. It is quite inconceivable that I should bring Miss Campbell home as a bride to the house which should have been his.'

He was standing quite rigid, with his hands at his sides, staring straight out of the window again. The attitude, the hard, strained voice told David Maitland a good deal. He got up from his chair and came and laid a hand on the young man's shoulder from behind.

'Mr Stewart – believe me, I have the right to ask, though I am neither her father nor, indeed any relation – does Olivia love you?'

Ian stood unyielding under that hand. 'No,' he answered uncompromising, and went on almost immediately, 'I believed so once. Perhaps for a moment she may have done so. I did think ... But now that I have seen her again I know otherwise. And it is much better so, sir – much better, since I could never marry her, with that between us.'

The elder man sighed and removed the hand. 'I hope you pardon my intrusion into your affairs, Mr Stewart. 'Tis not mere curiosity, I assure you. What you have told me of the unfortunate barrier between you explains much. I think it partly explains why Miss Campbell would not speak of you when I saw her the other day – beyond expressing surprise at finding you here. But I think her silence meant also that you are wrong, and that she does care for you. I may, naturally, be mistaken.

Yet I reflect that there have been times when she has not with-held her confidence from me – when it was of no importance.'

Ian swung round. 'Mr Maitland, don't torture me! Of what use to suggest such a thing! It can make no difference. I have done with her; it ended at Kilrain. She is a Campbell and the daughter of the man who has my brother's blood on his hands. God himself cannot wash that away from them.'

He spoke with anguish and passion in his voice, and he was pale. But David Maitland was paler still. He went back silently to his chair and put a hand over his eyes. Ian once more looked out of the window; then, roused by the silence, glanced round, saw his attitude, hesitated a moment and went over to him.

'Are you indisposed, sir? Shall I summon Miss Cameron?'

The convalescent dropped his hand. In the sudden grey pallor of his face his eyes had a strained, bright look. 'No, no, I am quite well. I was only thinking how true, how terribly true your words are. Blood spilt can never be gathered up again – no, not by God Himself! All that one can hope for, Mr Stewart, is that at the Last Day there may be some crumb of pardon for a man who never meant to spill it, but on whose hands, nevertheless ...' He stopped abruptly. He was looking at his own. Ian thought his manner exceedingly strange, till he remembered that, as a Jacobite, he might have something of the same feeling about Campbell of Cairns, though he was his friend.

'I have my own opinion of the Campbells,' said Ian slowly, 'but I will admit that Campbell of Cairns did not direct his men particularly to kill my brother. Some might uphold that he was only doing what he conceived to be his duty.'

David Maitland, looking at him with those bright, sunken eyes, and with the strangest expression in them, began to laugh. 'His duty! That is the greatest snare of all, Mr Stewart. When the ill angel who masquerades as the good suggests *that* – but I think I am talking nonsense. Forgive me – there's a breath of fever still in my veins. Suppose we turn to pleasanter subjects. You did not see what your little cousin gave me?' And he reached up an unsteady hand for Keithie's gift.

Ian thought the abrupt change of subject odder still, and almost wondered if Mr Maitland's illness – his two successive illnesses – could have affected his mind. At the beginning of this conversation he had seemed so particularly well-balanced. He judged it time, at any rate, to leave him; perhaps to say a word about him to Miss Cameron.

'I thank you very much, sir, for your interest in my ... in me,' he said. 'But that is all a closed book now; and I am afraid that I have tired you. I'll say good night.'

'Good night,' echoed Maitland after a pause. He looked at his visitor again with haunted eyes. 'No book is ever closed ... so long as we remain alive, Mr Stewart. Remember that – to your profit!'

Ian shut the door gently behind him. He seemed to be back on the road to Kilrain, where he had first seen the cousin of that look.

And Maitland remained staring at the little wooden box which he held, the sound of his own words in his ears. No, no book is ever closed till death turns the last page. And is it closed then? ...

A little later there was another knock at the door, and in came Miss Margaret Cameron with a glass upon a tray.

'Now pray, Mr Maitland, do not rise! I have but come to see how you do and to bring you your draught; and also to suggest that after your fatigue of this afternoon you would do well to retire early to bed. I'll have your supper sent up here.'

'I daresay, madam, that it would be well,' acquiesced her patient. 'But indeed you must not think anything of my having shown a slight weakness the first time I took the air.'

Miss Cameron was turning down the bed. ''Tis a pity you ventured into the air at all so soon. I had my doubts about the wisdom of it. And my niece tells me now that you have previously seemed distressed at the sight of the likeness – or rather of the unlikeness, for 'tis a mere libel on his features – of our unfortunate but heroic kinsman, Archibald Cameron. She told me how moved you appeared at it, sir, and it does you honour;

but an invalid should not be called upon to endure sudden shocks.'

'Shocks,' repeated Maitland rather faintly. 'Shocks ... why – yes, yes, it was unexpected, I'll admit. Though of course,' he went on, trying to work off his agitation unperceived through speech, 'such a portrait may very naturally be found in a Cameron household.'

'Aye,' said Miss Margaret, busying herself now with a water jug, 'and may well be found, above all, in this one. Do you know, Mr Maitland, that my nephew Ardroy, who was devoted heart and soul to Archie Cameron, and nearly got himself killed in the effort to save him from capture in Glenbuckie, was actually on the scaffold with him, wearing the dress of the minister who should have attended him thither, and that 'twas he who received the Doctor's last words, and heard him with his own ears pardon his murderers ... Bless us, what's wrong with you?'

She set down the ewer with a thud, and hurried across the room. David Maitland had fainted.

Chapter 22

THE COUNTER THRUST

'NOT the smallest article has been performed of what was expected and at first promised,' declared Finlay MacPhair with emphasis, 'not the smallest article! Not only is the five hundred pounds per annum boggled at – though God knows 'tis a small enough sum to ask, considering my position and influence – but the very journeys I took for the late Mr Pelham are still unpaid. And as for the intelligence which I sent three years ago concerning the coming of Doctor Cameron and my cousin Lochdornie to the Highlands, I might as well have kept it to myself. On my soul, 'tis the most infernal treatment!'

Thus declaiming, the misused Chief tramped up and down the stone floor of his dining-room in deep indignation. The day was drawing to its close; supper was finished, but the recipient of this plaint still sat at the table finishing his wine, a neat, middle-aged gentleman in a particularly close grey wig, a sober blue coat and snuff-coloured breeches. Mr Bruce looked something between a merchant and an attorney, and had small appearance of being what he really was, a 'court trusty', a secret agent deputed by the English Government to keep an occasional eye upon another secret agent. What was odder still, the latter, who had just so passionately bewailed his treatment by that Government, was perfectly aware of the fact, and Mr Bruce knew that he was aware of it. The position was thus robbed of much of its awkwardness.

The guest emptied his glass and wiped his lips carefully with his napkin. 'My dear sir,' he observed in a pleasant voice, 'you know that I desire to serve you in any reasonable manner. It is undeniable that you suffered a great loss in the death of your patron, the minister, last spring, particularly in no longer having

him to urge your merits upon the Government. I am but a poor
substitute for the brother of my Lord Newcastle.'

'Yes,' said Glenshian moodily, 'the cursed erysipelas which
carried off Mr Pelham has much to answer for, in putting a
Highland gentleman to shifts for money, when money is actually owing to him!'

Mr Bruce raised his eyebrows. 'Shifts? You are in difficulties
again?'

'I am never in aught else,' growled his host, 'since the fines on
my estate are not remitted – and that's a scandal almost as bad
as the other! You may remember that about this time last year,
when I succeeded to it, you obliged me with a small loan?'

'Aye, that I remember very well,' assented Mr Bruce with a
little smile. 'Very well, indeed. 'Twas in Edinburgh, about mid-
October, the very day that you told me you had a scheme on
foot ...'

'It came to naught,' said Glenshian with a hasty scowl. 'It
came to naught because in the end I had to do with a fool ... I
had spent money on the business too.'

'I am sorry to hear it,' said his companion, still equably, 'and
I regret, too, that my own circumstances do not permit me to
tear up your note of hand.'

'I should not wish you to do so,' responded the Chief haughtily. 'I prefer to honour my obligations. And I hope soon to do
so, for I have another scheme which, if it succeeds, should bring
me in a comfortable sum and very likely rid this neighbourhood
of a most pestilential enemy of mine, or at least cripple him ...
and disgrace him into the bargain.'

The 'court trusty' shook his head. 'Are you already quarrelling with your neighbours, Glenshian, and you not yet settled
here a twelvemonth?'

'This "neighbour" has been in my path these two years,
before ever I came up here,' answered Finlay with his lip curled
back, kicking as he spoke at a stool, ' – he and his kinsman by
marriage. But I have him at my mercy now. By Michaelmas
Day the laird of Ardroy will not be holding his head so high, I
fancy. That's one of the matters which took me to Inverness, so

that I had not the pleasure of being here to welcome you upon your arrival.' Warmed, apparently, by the thought of his transactions in Inverness, from which he had only returned a couple of hours ago, to find Mr Bruce already arrived to see him, Glenshian sat down once more at the table and refilled his visitor's glass and his own. 'Come, pledge me, good "Twenty-one", as you pledged me last year when you assisted me with the rent-roll after the old man's death.'

The court trusty complied with much amiability. 'To the success of your undertakings, Mr "Pickle"! And, speaking of rents, how do they come in now?'

But at the question Glenshian scowled anew. 'Very ill. Since the troubles, many persons have come on to my land and taken possession of what farms they please; and it is the devil's own work either to uproot them or to get them to pay. I have an unopened letter about one such encroachment in my pocket now.'

'But,' said Bruce with the flicker of a sidelong glance, 'you have come to a very advantageous arrangement with some of your wadsetters, have you not?'

Finlay put down his wine glass. 'What do you know about that, pray?' he asked suspiciously. 'Whom have you been talking to?'

'Nobody in particular,' replied Mr Bruce mildly and mendaciously. 'You forget that the doings of a powerful chief like yourself are public property in the neighbourhood. I understand that you succeeded in persuading some of your wadsetters farther west to give up their mortgages and pay rent, did you not?'

'Aye,' said the young Chief; and he added with a contemptuous smile, 'the fools! To be frank, however,' he went on, 'I failed with my wadsetters in Glenshian itself. I shall be even with them some day yet for that ... Now, look you, Bruce, to come back to this five hundred pounds per annum which, as I was saying, I must absolutely receive from the Government before I undertake to do anything – five hundred pounds paid twice a year without fail. But you can tell my Lord Newcastle that for that sum there is nothing honourable he can think of, but I am able to perform. For instance, I would be willing ... But come, we'll discuss that by the fire, unless you will drink some more claret? No? Find yourself a seat, then, while I take a glance at the letter I spoke of, for it came in my absence.'

Thus invited, Mr Bruce got up and went towards the hearth, followed by his host, who had brought out the letter from his pocket, torn it carelessly open, and was beginning to read it as he advanced. But all at once he ceased advancing ...

At the string of curses in Gaelic and English which some high unfamiliar voice was pouring out behind him, Bruce whipped round to see Glenshian, with a distorted, livid face, holding a paper in his hand as one might hold a wriggling serpent.

'Good God, what's amiss?' he asked in alarm.

'Amiss – amiss!' Looking round blindly as though to find some object on which to vent his wrath, the young man caught hold of the end of the linen table-cloth hanging in a long point over the edge of the supper-table, tugged at it and then flung it violently back, sending plates, wine and glasses into a confused, clattering heap in the middle. '*Amiss!* Everything has gone agley ... ruined ... all my careful plans! May the devil cut the ears off Hector Grant and the tongue out of Seumas's mouth! ... But the latter I'll do myself!' He strode furiously to the bell which stood on the far end of the table and began to ring it like a tocsin.

In the middle of the clangour appeared old Roderick, out of breath.

'Roderick, you old fool, how long ago did this letter come for me?'

The ancient considered. 'I am thinking it would be about two days after you went away.'

'Did you know that it came from the laird of Ardroy?'

'Yes, Mac 'ic Fhionnlaigh. That is to say – '

'Then why the devil did you not say so when you gave it to me? I thought it was only about that Cullachy affair ... And why in the fiend's name did you ever admit that damned spying Captain Grant to this house? You're at the bottom of the business after all, you doited old carline!' And he actually shook his aged retainer till Roderick's few remaining teeth clacked together. ' 'Tis Hector Grant who has wrecked ... no matter what ... and I cannot settle with him! But I'll settle with Seumas that he'll not go chattering again in a hurry! Send him to me in my own room!'

'What has Seumas been doing?' inquired Bruce, as after a horrified glance at the supper-table, the old man shuffled out again.

'Talking!' replied Finlay fiercely, ' – a thing it will be long before he does again!' And without apology he went striding out, pausing only to snatch down a heavy riding whip from the wall.

The guest thus deserted stood a moment rubbing his chin, more than a little uneasy at this tornado of rage and its possible consequences. Yet if the Chief of Glenshian chose to flog one of his gillies for misdemeanour he could hardly interfere. So he finally sat down by the inviting peat fire; yet, looking again over his shoulder at the havoc on the supper-table, observed half aloud, 'I wonder if by chance our "Pickle" is a trifle unsettled in his wits?'

And, not having been idle in the neighbourhood before Glenshian's return, he thought of the stories which Colonel Trapaud of Fort Augustus had related to him over a bowl of punch – stories of the Chief's haughty and overbearing behaviour alike to the English garrison there and to his own tenantry.

'He has refused my officers the right to shoot over his land because, not having taken the oath to the Government, he may not have a fowling-piece himself – as if that were *my* doing!' said the Governor indignantly. 'And he has forbidden his tenants to sell us any peat, which does more harm to those poor devils, whose only chance it is of earning a small pittance, than it does to us, since we are to be supplied with coal next year. I have pointed that out to them and drawn the moral – not in Glenshian's favour, as you may imagine. And then that sharp practice with his small wadsetters, about which I have told you

– that has not made him popular; when he tried the same game nearer home they refused stoutly to give up their rights. Yes, he is alienating all but the most devoted, so that I have hopes his own arrogance will be his undoing.'

The secret agent had listened to the soldier, nodded thoughtfully and said little. He was pleased; and he was not pleased. For if Glenshian's undoubtedly great local influence diminished, so would his potential usefulness to the English Government. This dilemma engaged his reflections now, by Glenshian's fire. Fionnlagh Ruadh's overwhelming sense of his own importance – though he *was* important – joined to the crazily violent temper of which he had just given a specimen, made him a difficult instrument to handle. And yet ... he had his points. A confessed and trusted Jacobite – and in English pay since 1750 – it needed craft, a cool head, and a certain amount of personal courage to combine those positions for five years without arousing the suspicions of a single soul.

Mr Bruce picked up a peat with the tongs, lit his long pipe, stretched out his legs to the blaze, and wondered idly where the flogging or other chastisement was taking place. Perhaps Glenshian's personal retainers liked that sort of thing; perhaps the adage should run, 'A woman, a gillie, and a walnut-tree ...' All the same, *he* would not care to lay a horsewhip about the shoulders of some of the natives here. But then he was not MacPhair of Glenshian ... Five hundred pounds per annum! He wouldn't get it!

Nor, if he really were a trifle unbalanced in his mind, would he be worth it. Mr Bruce slowly brought out a little pocket-book and made in it a short and cryptic memorandum.

2

'Beat me – kill me if you must,' said Seumas, unresisting in his master's grip, 'but as God sees me, I have never breathed a word of that journey to a living man. Then how much less before your enemy?'

Finlay loosed him almost with reluctance. He had not yet

used the whip on him. For, after all, Seumas, abuse him as he might, was of an almost abject fidelity, proved, now, by some years of ill-paid service in France and England.

'Would you swear that on the iron?'

'Aye, and pray to God to send me to a dishonoured grave in a far land if I spoke not the truth!'

'Then who *has* talked? The laird of Ardroy has written me a letter in which he says that Captain Grant – maledictions on him for forcing himself in here and obliging me to keep him prisoner! – overheard the story of the driving of the branded steers, and so, if I proceed with my intention of summoning Ardroy himself before the Sheriff Court – ' Glenshian did not finish, but ground his teeth. 'Someone must have talked before Captain Grant – and he having the Gaelic all the while! Who was it?'

Seumas offered no suggestion.

'Who went with you that night?'

'My half-brother Somerled.'

Finlay gave a sort of snarl of comprehending rage. 'And it was Somerled whom I put in charge of Hector Grant. The dirty traitor! Fetch him here!'

'Mac 'ic Fhionnlaigh ...'

'Fetch him here!'

Seumas went; and in a little returned with that stalwart gillie whose face at one time was only too familiar to Captain Grant. That officer would, however, have been gratified to observe the apprehension upon it now.

Evidently his half-brother had already acquainted him with the reason of his summons, for before Glenshian had time to get out his furious question – if indeed he even meant to ask one at all – the culprit had confessed.

'Aye, I spoke of it, Mac 'ic Fhionnlaigh – I spoke of it one day to Roderick ... because it was so clever a trick to have played upon the Cameron –'

'You spoke of it to Roderick! When – where?'

'It was one day when he came for wine,' faltered Somerled.

'For wine – in the very next cellar to Mr Grant! You fool, you fool, did you not know of that grating!'

'I knew of it. But Roderick was sure that the gentleman had not the Gaelic.'

Glenshian consigned Roderick to a much deeper place than a wine-cellar. 'How dare he make such a statement! But you – ' he had Somerled by the throat now – 'do you know what you have done? Ruined all my schemes, lost me hundreds of pounds, and my revenge on Cameron of Ardroy – my just and well-planned revenge!' He threw the big gillie from him and snatched up the whip.

Somerled made no resistance; he only tried to keep his arms across his face to shield it from the rain of blows. He uttered no plea for mercy nor even a cry of pain; the only sounds were Finlay's own hard breathing and the whistle and thud of the lash. But at the end Somerled was crouching, not much more than semi-conscious, in a corner; and it was at this stage that Seumas, who had stood and gravely watched the execution of justice, ventured to come behind his irate Chief and catch his arm. Finlay turned like a madman and struck him on the mouth. But he had been checked for a second, and in that second the wretched Somerled slid completely to the floor and lay there on his face.

'Mac 'ic Fhionnlaigh, is it not enough?' pleaded Seumas, the blood running down his own chin. 'Of a truth he has deserved it all, and more – but if you kill him, they will perhaps hear of it at Fort Augustus . . .'

'Take him away, then!' said his master, out of breath. He flung the whip on the floor. 'Throw him outside somewhere – then come back to me.'

Seumas, tugging at his dazed kinsman, got him somehow to his feet and helped him from the room. Finlay, as though he had not been within measurable distance of murder, was already absorbed in the re-reading of Ardroy's letter. Then he put it back in his pocket, and stood biting his nails in an even blacker and deeper absorption, and suffering the pangs of an emotion which very seldom troubled him – regret. He was bitterly sorry that he had ever kept Hector Grant a prisoner and so given him an opportunity of overhearing what he had. The mortification of learning, nearly a fortnight ago, that the captive had been rescued with such ease from Castle Shian had been bad enough, yet there had been a certain element of compensation in that cup. The forcible removal of Captain Grant had in fact ended a situation which was becoming awkward for its originator, faced on the one hand with his prisoner's absolute refusal to submit to his terms, and on the other with the impossibility of keeping him indefinitely a captive. Wounding to his pride as was the episode of the rescue, it was not nearly so galling as to be called to book by Governor Trapaud of Fort Augustus and reported to the English Government for his high-handed conduct – a consequence which was well within the bounds of possibility. But now he had not only been deprived of his prisoner but, with the prisoner, of the secret which formed the corner-stone of his nefarious plot against Cameron of Ardroy.

It was only too true; he was checkmated. He dared not move further in the matter. He would have to send to Inverness to stop the pending proceedings. All the time that he had recently been there this accursed letter, lying at Invershian, had been making a fool of him. Once more he took it out and read its short, uncompromising phrases. No, he would get no damages out of Ewen Cameron now, no sweet revenge for that glove flung into the gutter in Edinburgh last autumn, nor for the accusation Ewen had launched at him in June ... in fact, unless he were careful, Ewen Cameron might get damages out of him. 'Assault and unlawful detention'; yes, since the English, damn them, had taken away the old jurisdiction of the chiefs, a jury was very unlikely to pass over his chaining up of a gentleman in a ruined castle on the plea that that gentleman had obtained admission to his house and uttered threats against him ...

Moreover the immediate return of Captain Grant's horse and valise was demanded, and he would have to comply – damn Ardroy and all his kin! Finlay tore the letter to pieces, threw the pieces on the floor and ground them with his foot.

Glancing up he saw that Seumas had returned, and was standing looking at him with gloomy interest.

'For God's sake wipe that blood from off your mouth!' said his master irritably. 'Listen! That horse of Captain Grant's – I suppose it is still here – must go back to him at Ardroy without delay. Do you hear?'

'Yes, I hear,' answered Seumas, who was well inured to this manner of address. 'It shall go. And is the other gentleman's horse to go at the same time?'

'What other gentleman? Do you mean Mr Maitland? But, you fool, he is not at Ardroy – Heaven knows where he is.'

'He *is* at Ardroy, Mac 'ic Fhionnlaigh – that is to say, he was there when the laird's letter was brought.'

'Nonsense!' said Glenshian sharply. 'That's the last place in the world he would have gone to.'

'Nevertheless,' persisted Seumas, 'he is there, ill ... unless the gillie lied.'

His master's face suddenly lit up. *Could* it be true – Maitland fallen into Ewen Cameron's hands? 'My God!' he said under his breath, 'what a jest that would be! How did you come upon this tale, Seumas?'

'I learnt it from the gillie of Ardroy's who brought the letter,' responded Seumas promptly. 'While you were away I had already heard a rumour that the gentleman whom you had fetched here in a chaise was lying ill at some farm on Loch Lochy, where it was said that Ardroy himself was nursing him. I asked the Cameron if this were true, and he answered that not only was it true, but that the laird was just after bringing this Mr Maitland to his house as a guest, and that he was in the best bedchamber and was having every care.'

'The best bedchamber ... every care ... *Maitland!*' The young Chief went off into a wild burst of laughter. But he stopped laughing as abruptly as he had begun, his yellow-green eyes dilated and, as if wishing to hide, even from this *âme damnée* of his, some idea too visible on his face, he swung on his heel and went from him towards the empty hearth.

'Yes,' he said after an instant, in a slow tone of enjoyment, 'in that case, Seumas, I shall certainly send Mr Maitland's horse to Ardroy. (I wonder whether he will ever ride away on it.)' Then

889

he turned and faced the gillie. 'See to it that a trustworthy man sets off with both beasts tomorrow morning, and that he takes the valises of Captain Grant and Mr Maitland as well. – I'll have no one accusing me of larceny,' he added to himself. 'There will also be a letter for Mr Cameron of Ardroy ... yes, there will undoubtedly be a letter.' He smiled, stood a moment in contemplation of some vision of his own, and then roused himself. 'You can go now, Seumas. But be careful that someone goes with the horses who can keep his mouth shut better than that cursed half-brother of yours.'

Seumas, instead of taking his dismissal, came nearer, his thin, swarthy face transformed with eagerness. 'Grant me a favour, Mac 'ic Fhionnlaigh! Let *me* take the horses and your letter!'

'As you please,' answered Finlay carelessly. He had already gone to an escritoire and was unlocking it. 'No, you cannot go; I may be needing you tomorrow.'

'Ah, Mac 'ic Fhionnlaigh, I beseech you to let me go!'

'In the devil's name why, man?'

'Because it might be,' responded Seumas with a dark, inward look, 'that I could wipe out the disgrace which Somerled has put upon us ... and show you that one of my father's sons knows how to be faithful to his Chief, and to his Chief's inmost wish.' The last words were so low as almost to be inaudible.

'I don't doubt that *you* are faithful,' said Finlay carelessly. 'Yes, you shall go then, for you have perhaps the wit to bring me back certain intelligence from Ardroy: how for instance – But I will give you instructions in the morning, and the letter which you must convey, and give into the hands of the laird of Ardroy himself. Come to me betimes tomorrow.'

Seumas was murmuring thanks. He picked up the horse-whip and laid it on a table. 'You were right to use this, Glenshian. And when I return you shall use it on *me* if I have not pleased you.'

But the Highlander's protestations appeared to make little impression on his master; he had already sat down to the escritoire with a pen in his hand. For some seconds after Seumas had gone he sat there nibbling the end with a malicious gleam in his eyes. It was in this very room that that fool of a Maitland had refused to comply with his suggestion. And now, through some chain of events not yet clear, Maitland was an honoured guest at Ardroy, of all places in the world! Ewen Cameron had brought to his own house – had, if report were true, himself tended in sickness – the very man who ... And Ewen had accused *him* of being the cause of his precious kinsman's execution!

Finlay burst, for the second time, into a loud laugh; began to write slowly and carefully; paused, surveyed what he had written, then dashed off a few more words at the end, signed the letter with a flourish, folded it, and sealed it with care and a sort of relishing slowness.

When he went back to the other room Mr Bruce was comfortably smoking by the fire.

'You have been the deuce of a time away,' he observed, but with perfect placidity.

'I ask your pardon for it. I had some business to transact which involved ... the writing of a letter.' He showed the sealed, addressed letter in his hand.

'More business relating to your ... financial schemes?' hazarded Bruce.

'No,' answered his host, looking down at the letter. 'I doubt there's money in this, for I am making restitution.'

'Paying back, in short?' observed Mr Bruce, knocking out his pipe.

'Aye, paying back, as you say – and with interest ... paying two men at the same time!'

'Egad, I'm sure that's very laudable,' replied the court trusty, beginning to refill his pipe. But half-way through he stopped, and fell to studying his companion with some intentness. The young Chief, half sitting on the arm of his chair, was staring down into the peats on the hearth with a secret little smile which even to the rather phlegmatic Bruce – who was, however, no fool – contained something sinister and cruel.

And indeed the red heart of the fire seemed to the gazer to

hold a possibility even more seductive than he had foreseen when he had penned his letter. David Maitland was but a poor scrupulous creature, and, despite the fact that he had crossed him, he did not really care very greatly what happened to him ... though something would undoubtedly happen when this letter reached its destination. But, when one remembered what Doctor Cameron's memory appeared to mean to Ewen Cameron, was it too much to hope that he might in a moment of ungoverned fury, wring Maitland's neck? And then – could the dreamer himself plan a more satisfying revenge than that which the law would take upon his enemy, without his having to lift a finger? He saw in the fire the man who had lectured and insulted *him*, a common criminal flying from the neighbourhood to which he could never dare return – there was no amnesty for murder; he saw him leading a hunted life of shifts and disguises, and then he saw the inevitable end – quite soon, it might be – on the gibbet erected for a crime less easily exonerated by the world than Jacobitism. The Grassmarket at Edinburgh ... a shifting, vociferating crowd, awaiting the hangman and the tall, pinioned murderer ... the seed of that possible consummation slept in the letter which he held, with its big, blood-red seal. The sending of it tomorrow was only the putting of a match to a train already laid by circumstances, it was true, yet, in the knowledge that his hand would apply that match, Finlay MacPhair had an almost delirious sensation of power, as of some Olympian chess player bending over two pawns, one of which, at his bidding, should sweep the other from the board, and then be swept itself ...

He got up, slipped the letter almost caressingly into his pocket, and stretched himself like a large cat. 'Let us go to bed, Bruce. I must be up betimes to see that some orders are duly carried out.'

The court trusty rose. 'You have recovered, I perceive, from your recent disappointment?'

'Entirely,' replied his host. 'Matters are turning out more favourably than I anticipated ... Money is all very well, but there is one thing that is dearer ... to a Highlander.'

'And that is?'

Finlay slapped him affably on the shoulder. 'You have lived too long in England, Bruce, to appreciate what it is. Come to bed!'

Chapter 23

THE STREAM IN SPATE

1   *Sept. 9th*

A LITTLE of the nip of September was in the air, though the sun's heat almost kept it under. The Allt Buidhe at Ardroy, coming down from the mountains, had more than a hint of recent rainfall in the pale amber waters whence it took its name; and indeed it had been raining fairly persistently for two days. But the afternoon was bright, if with a windy and an ephemeral beauty, and the young man slowly crossing the foot-bridge over the racing stream stopped to look at the view.

In old days the footbridge had been unguarded, but Ewen Cameron, after his firstborn, a couple of years ago, had fallen into the burn and nearly been carried away, had caused it to be railed for the better safety of his children; and on one of these rough wooden rails Ian Stewart leant for so long that it was plain he was no longer admiring the scenery but thinking. And his expression would have shown that his thoughts were not merry ones.

At duty's call he had said farewell to Olivia Campbell for ever – so he had believed at the time. He had kissed his love and departed; he had found a token from her in his hand and had ridden away. He had been incredibly strong-minded at very searching cost. And yet, ever since Olivia's most unexpected visit here five days ago, he had been at intervals a prey to a strange and inexcusable mood of imagination, much as after his height of renunciation at Kilrain he had come home and picked a quarrel with Hector Grant. He was increasingly hurt, resentful and bewildered because Olivia had seemed changed to him – so light and cold and civil, so concerned about Mr Maitland (though on that score he might certainly now feel easier, since the good gentleman had turned out to be already married) and

894

on such good terms with that redcoat escort of hers. Days had passed, but he could rehearse every word she had said to him – and all those she might have said; every look of hers – for others. She had never loved him. The scene in the oakwood had been merely a surprise to her, it meant nothing. And that she had not spoken of him to that father confessor of hers, as the latter had avowed, meant clearly that she had nothing to confess. Had he not been right after all in his first impression of her at Invernacree –that she was a finished coquette? And on the little bridge, as if wind and stream had brought them, there came back to him the words of the old spaewife, years ago, who had told him that he would love a woman who was other than she seemed.

Why, since he had most definitely refused to think of marrying her, Ian should consider that Olivia was nevertheless bound to a barren constancy, the jealous and illogical heart of a lover alone could tell.

He was leaving Ardroy for home tomorrow, and had come out here – it was about half a mile from the house – to try to settle the thorny question of his behaviour when he reached Fort William and Maryburgh on his way thither. The best course would be to ride straight through, though in the natural order of events he would have stopped at Maryburgh for an hour or two. But he dreaded the neighbourhood while Olivia was in it; he wished there were some other way of getting down to Appin. Yet he did not know which seemed to him the more unbearable prospect, that of chancing upon her as he passed or of not doing so.

Ian propped his chin on his fists. No, he must have the strength of mind to ride straight through without drawing rein. It was the only safe course. All was over; how often had he not declared it – to her, to his father, to Ewen, to Mr Maitland! Why, then, did he so foolishly preserve those bits of bog-myrtle which she had probably never laid after all in his sleeping hand or, if she had, only as a jest to fool him with? It was odd – when she had been here the other day he had completely forgotten his possession of them. But now he pulled out the stolen letter of hers in which they were folded, slid them out into his palm, and looked menacingly from them to the hurrying burn below his feet.

It was easy, almost too easy. One jerk of the hand, and the brittle fragments had vanished in the racing yellow swirl of the Allt Buidhe. The letter too – Grizel's property though it was – he ought to burn it; but this grave would serve as well as a fiery one. With hands that shook a little he tore across and across Olivia's announcement of her coming visit to Kilrain, and went on tearing until a drift of snowflakes fluttered in the breeze, and then sailed like shaken petals down the stream. Gone – the last trace of her ... Ian bowed his head upon his folded arms on the rail. He had no sling now to hinder such a posture.

And thus, a while later, he was found by Donald, as he came running lightly along the path to the burn.

'Oh, Cousin Ian, what are you doing? Are you looking for trout? Angus says there are none in the Allt Buidhe; and I've never seen one there. Besides, the burn is running very fast this morning.'

Ian had promptly raised his head. 'Very fast,' he agreed.

Donald picked up a stick and threw it in. 'Look where that has gone to already! Throw in another, Cousin Ian, and we will have a race.'

Ian roused himself. 'I have already thrown in my offering, Donald, and it is gone.'

The boy looked at him, a little puzzled at his tone. 'You speak as if you were sorry, cousin.'

'Perhaps I am' said the young man. 'Perhaps I am not ... Well, *laochain*, where are you off to?'

'I was walking with Mr Maitland,' answered the boy. 'But he does not go very fast, and he was only in the garden. So he told me to leave him, and I did. Then I came this way, and saw you on the bridge. If you are walking anywhere may I come with you, as you are going away tomorrow?'

'Certainly,' said Ian, laying his hand on Donald's shoulder. He was a charming and promising boy, this young cousin of his. 'Where would you like to go?'

'Let us start by the *bealach* and go down to the place where you can see Loch Arkaig below.'

So they set off, Donald chattering as they went.

'Mr Maitland is much better, isn't he? He says he will be able to start home in a couple of days now. I think he wants to go very much.'

'Well, naturally,' said his cousin. 'He wishes to get back to his family.'

'Keithie is being a nuisance to him, I expect,' resumed Donald with brotherly frankness, 'for he means to give him his very largest caterpillar to take home with him, the shaggy one. The caterpillar he gave him the other day – the day when Mr Maitland was taken worse – was not truly his best one, though he said it was.'

'Keithie doesn't give me any caterpillars to take home with me,' observed Ian. 'But, on the whole, I am not sorry.'

Donald's remark was on a different topic entirely. 'Cousin Ian, did you ever have to hide in a barn, among the hay – after the battle of Culloden, I mean?'

'No, Donald, I did not have to hide anywhere. But your father did.'

'I know,' said the boy. 'But he was very badly hurt, and he could not enjoy it. And he never hid in a loft or a barn – I asked him. It must be so delightful to sleep the whole night all among hay, with nobody knowing that you are there.'

'I suppose it might,' said his cousin rather absently, without noticing that Donald's youthful countenance was that of one cherishing a bright dream not impossible of realization.

The two crossed the burn and walked on the track which wound through the heather. In ten minutes or so they began to approach the cleft in the hills sometimes locally called a pass, though it could hardly claim that dignity. But it had at least the distinction of being the highest point of the rough road coming up from Loch Arkaig, and also the property of acting as a sounding-board, for before Ian and Donald had turned the corner into it they heard the beat of hoofs, and knew that there were riders there. A moment later, when they came into the little damp, rocky defile, they saw them advancing at an easy trot. And they were a lady in a green habit, with a soldier following behind.

'Oh, Cousin Ian, there's Miss Campbell!' exclaimed Donald, very needlessly indeed.

Ian stopped; his heart also, it seemed to him. He looked at his companion, and made up his mind instantly what to do – if Miss Campbell pulled up, as she probably would.

Olivia perceived him, and the trot dropped to walk. Ian uncovered and went forward, and they met. She pulled up.

'Good morning, Miss Campbell,' said the young man, and before Olivia had time to do more than echo the same greeting he went on: 'Will you allow me to send the orderly on ahead, and Donald with him, and permit me to walk with you the rest of the way? I have something I wish to ask you.'

He did not know it, but his abrupt if humbly phrased request was uttered much more like a command. Olivia looked a little surprised, hesitated for a second, and then said, 'Certainly, if you wish it, Mr Stewart.'

Without further words Ian beckoned to the soldier, who had discreetly halted at a distance. 'Orderly,' he said, as the man came up, 'you will go on ahead to the house, and I will escort Miss Campbell thither. Take this young gentleman with you. Up you get, Donald! Will you have him in front of you or behind?'

'In front, if you please, sir,' replied the redcoat, stooping from the saddle.

Mercifully Donald was aglow with pleasure at this prospect. Had he objected he would have found himself astride the orderly's horse all the same. Ian waved them forward.

'You are in a very autocratic mood this afternoon, Mr Stewart,' observed Olivia laughing, but not quite easily.

'You pardon me, I hope?' asked the autocrat, his hand on her bridle.

'There seems very little choice,' responded she. And as her horse moved forward again, with Ian at its head, she asked,

'How does Mr Maitland today? I could not be easy without news of him once more.'

'Then you will be relieved to hear that he is much better; indeed he is at this moment walking in the garden.'

'Oh, I am glad to hear that!' exclaimed Olivia. 'He must in truth be stronger. – And you, Mr Stewart – I am rejoiced to see that you are able to abandon your sling. But to find you here is a surprise. I thought you gone to Appin by now.'

'I go tomorrow.'

A little silence ensued, during which they came out of the fern-clad walls of the defile into the wider stretch of moor and mountainside. Away amongst its trees sparkled Loch na h-Iolaire, and Olivia's eyes were on it. How he would have loved to show it to her – but he never would . . .

'Had I known that you were leaving tomorrow,' she observed suddenly, 'you might have brought me news of Mr Maitland, since you must pass Fort William.'

'But you are such a notable horsewoman, Miss Campbell, that it would not have been necessary.'

Olivia looked down at the top of his head. He sounded cross; was it possible that he was jealous of her coming all this way a second time to see Mr Maitland? Everything was possible with a man, but how extraordinarily foolish, especially when he himself would have none of her. – Foolish and dear!

'How far are we from the house now?' she asked.

'About three quarters of a mile.'

It occurred to Olivia that if she dismounted it would take longer to cover that distance than at her horse's walk. 'I feel a trifle stiff, so I think I will get out of the saddle and walk a little,' she announced. 'And since you have deprived me of my escort, Mr Stewart, I fear you'll have to lead my horse yourself.'

Ian had not foreseen her dismounting, and that he would consequently have her in his arms for a brief moment. He could, however, pretend to himself that it was Jacqueline whom he was helping off her horse. Fortified by this remarkable and not very successful piece of dissimulation he received her as she

899

sprang from the saddle – a light enough burden – and they set out side by side, the wind bringing to them in little warm puffs, the scent of the heather.

Without saying much they came to the bridge, and to an unexpected difficulty, for Miss Campbell's horse showed an invincible objection to crossing it. Ian tugged and urged him, but he would not set a hoof upon it.

'Surely,' said Olivia, 'he cannot imagine that it is too narrow for him! The horse I was riding the other day did not think twice about going over it.'

'Perhaps he will consent to go through the burn, even though it is somewhat in spate,' suggested Ian. ''Tis not very deep here, and the bottom is good.' He scrambled into the saddle and succeeded in getting the animal through without much trouble. Olivia, on the bridge, stood and watched the performance.

'A thousand thanks, Mr Stewart,' she said, as he gained the bank. 'But what a foolish beast – though this is, indeed, a beautiful burn to go through.' She lingered a moment on the bridge gazing down at the joyous little tide of the Allt Buidhe, while Ian, swinging off her horse, and thinking how much he should dislike a side-saddle, stood on the farther bank waiting for her.

'It looks,' said Olivia suddenly and rather mischievously, leaning on the rail, 'it looks as though someone had been tearing up a letter here.' And she pointed downstream to where three or four small fragments of paper, carried by the wind, showed white among the stems of water weed.

Behind her horse Ian coloured suddenly. The next moment he had knotted the reins to the end of the rail and had stepped on to the bridge himself. 'You are quite right. Someone has been tearing up a letter here. It was I; and the letter was yours. And that brings me to what I want to ask you, Miss Campbell.'

She turned a startled face on him. 'A letter of mine! I have never written you a letter, Mr Stewart!'

'I know that. The letter was to my sister Grizel. But I ... I had it in my possession ... till this afternoon. It was foolish of me. Just before you came I tore it up and threw it into the burn and with it something else from your hand I believe which I had kept till then. Of that – and it is what I desired to ask you – you have, perhaps, some knowledge?'

Her cheek answered that question. It was crimson. She said, 'Oh, Mr Stewart!' in a small voice, and clapped her hands over her face like any schoolgirl.

'You did put the sprig of gall in my hands, then?' he asked rather harshly. 'Why?'

Olivia did not answer, and he could not see her face. But a movement passed across her shoulders, and Ian concluded that she was laughing.

'It was, I admit, an amusing prank,' he continued. 'It must be gratifying, too, to learn that I kept your posy so long. But, you see, I have thrown it away at last – of my own free will!' he concluded defiantly.

A very low voice murmured something which sounded like – but surely could not be – 'I think that you have thrown me away also!' There was a catch of tears, or laughter, in that voice.

Ian dared not come nearer; he was already not far off, since the bridge was very small. Olivia removed one of the hands from her face and began to run it agitatedly along the rail; and Ian saw upon the cheek thus revealed something bright ... She had not been laughing; it was ... the other thing!

At that glittering drop he remained staring incredulously, while the bridge for a second or two might have been a boat upon an unquiet sea. Below his feet the Allt Buidhe sped on, with here and there a leap of foam; the tethered horse champed his bridle impatiently. Very slowly Ian approached, and then abruptly caught the little hand which strayed along the wood, bent his head, and put his lips upon it passionately. Pinned to the rail, it contracted and moved beneath the imprisoning kiss.

'What is the use of that?' asked Olivia's voice above him, with a note in it he had never heard, like a child half angry, half sorrowful. 'I cannot be your wife, so why ...' The hand escaped.

Ian lifted his head and looked full at her. The grey eyes and the dark blue met; and the two upon the bridge were plunged into a stream infinitely stronger and swifter than the Allt Buidhe. All consideration of where he was went from Ian, all his costly scruples and his difficult loyalty. He caught both her hands.

'You do love me, you do love me, Olivia? Heart of my heart, little white love, let me hear you say it ... this once!'

2

'But you must know it,' said Olivia softly, a moment or two later. 'You must know that if it were not so I should never have permitted you to ... to kiss me ... And I should not have made you the gift which you have just thrown away.'

Ian's arms tightened round her. He was holding more than her hand now, and the little three-cornered riding-hat rested against his shoulder. He would have liked to take it off, if she would have permitted it, but did not wish to spare a hand for the purpose.

'You did make that gift then!' How brightly the sun shone! 'By what magic did you come there when I was asleep?'

She glanced up at him. 'Is it chivalrous to demand that of such a poor, foolish besotted girl?' she demanded reproachfully.

'Yet how could you know –'

'I did not know! I thought that, having given Elspeth the slip, I should be alone there. You can hardly guess my feelings when I saw that I was not alone! I really fancied that I was bewitched. And then I so feared that you would wake, and learn my foolishness.'

'*I* could hardly have reproached you with that, *mo chridhe!* And yet I must avow that it was mere chance – at least, I believed it mere chance – which led me to the wood. But when I recognized where I was, and remembered' – Ian drew a long breath – 'then I stayed.'

'And fell asleep! Was that remembering?'

'But I dreamt of you, beautiful spirit of the place!' said he eagerly. 'I dreamt that you were standing there – and that could not have been wholly a dream. I even tried to speak to you!'

'Indeed you did not ... or at least, you had no success. You were as sound asleep, sir, as – '

'As Endymion?' suggested Ian.

'You flatter me,' said Olivia, sparkling.

'And myself too, perhaps. But the bog-myrtle? Why did you – '

'Oh, Diana knows, perhaps,' said she, half laughing. Then her look grew dreamy. 'I saw a patch growing not far away, and since it is the badge of our clan ... and you lay sleeping under an oak, your emblem ... I believe I thought it might prove ... a kind of charm.'

'A charm ... to make me stay longer at Kilrain?'

'That,' said Olivia, laughing outright, 'is a question which the panel does not feel bound to answer. Moreover, who knows what a charm may not accomplish in some other, unintended way? At least I thought 'twould puzzle you! Yet I think it must have worked upon me instead.' She looked at him quite serious, the smile gone, but with a light in the depths of her eyes, clear as sea-water, but not of its colour – grey like the dawn. 'Do you know why I fell in love with you ... Ian?'

He caught his breath at the sound of his name in that voice. It came winging to him like a word from Paradise.

'I could not guess ... Who could divine any possible reason for a thing so wonderful ... so unlikely?'

Olivia held him by the lapels of his coat. There was mischief as well as tenderness in her gaze. 'It was because I could not make you do as I desired!'

But at that avowal, which should have lifted him to the supreme pinnacle of pride, Ian awoke and perceived whither the two of them were fast being swept – towards a shore they could never reach. And the bright world turned dun and cold ... For a moment speech was not possible; but he was able to slacken his hold of her, before he said sadly:

'It is not my will that stands out against you, Olivia. It is Fate.'

Her hands dropped instantly from his coat; he saw the colour leave her lips, her eyes change. 'I thought we had done with Fate! If not, why are we – '

'Because we are bewitched,' broke in Ian desperately. 'Because you are so beautiful and I love you so ... and am so despicably weak.'

Olivia Campbell, very pale, had retreated the little space to the rail of the bridge. 'And so – ' she began, with a flash in her eyes.

'And so little a man of honour – say it if you must, for it is true!' he cried, retreating himself. 'Oh, I should have let you ride on ... I should never have spoken to you again! There's nothing left me now, not even your good regard ... I wish the sword which went into my arm a while ago had gone through my heart instead!'

He said it as if he meant it, and he did mean it. A sword thrust in that region would have spared him this moment.

Olivia suddenly twisted her hands together. 'Oh, my grief!' she said brokenly. 'Was I harsh? ... 'Twas because I was bewildered. Ian, Ian, how can you say such a thing!' And she, who rarely wept, broke into weeping. 'Ian, I cannot let you go, I cannot!' Then she stretched out a pitying hand. 'Was it a sword, then, that wounded you? There's a sword in my heart too. Can't you pull it out? ... You could, you could, but you are so thrawn ... and I love you for it, yet I ...' She became inaudible, partly from tears, partly because she had turned away and buried her face in her hands.

Ian stood with his arms at his sides. His resolution was nearly worn down; he dare not touch her again. Yet he could not, could not leave her sobbing like that! The moment he was a trifle nearer – no distances were other than trifles on that narrow bridge – Olivia, still sobbing, turned and clung to him; and he tried to comfort her, not knowing what words he used, save that they were vain.

So employed, it was no wonder that he was unaware of the slow advent of a man along the path to the bridge. Moreover, the bulk of Olivia's horse, which had moved across the end, somewhat blocked the view, even had he been looking that way; and the beast partly hid the couple on the bridge from the newcomer too. But as the horse moved aside at his approach the latter stepped on to the planks, saw them and stopped dead.

The footsteps on the sounding wood did reach Ian's senses. With Olivia still in his arms he turned his head, and saw David Maitland.

'Olivia,' he whispered, 'Olivia, there is someone here – Mr Maitland.'

Even that name did not rouse her as he thought it would; she went on sobbing quietly. After a long moment Maitland came farther on to the bridge.

'Mr Stewart, I do not wish to intrude, but perhaps I can be of some service to you. I know now . . . what I wanted to know.'

Then Olivia did lift her head, putting her handkerchief to her eyes, and trying to restrain her sobs.

'I did not mean you to . . . see me like this, Godfather . . . I came hither to inquire for you . . . and I was . . . tired with my ride . . . I thought I was . . . going to be h-happy . . . and I find I am not. You cannot move a Stewart, I find; his clan is more to him than – '

'For God's sake do not talk like that!' cried Ian, at the end of his endurance, and careless that Maitland heard him. 'You know that I am yours to the last drop of my blood; but I cannot marry you. I would give the rest of my life,' he added illogically, 'if only I could!'

Maitland came quite close and said in a low voice, 'Will you leave Miss Campbell to me for a few minutes? You will not, I think, regret it.'

At any rate, thought Ian desperately, he could not make the case any worse. It was out of the question for the elder man really to help him, but the scene must be ended somehow; he at least could not bear much more. He answered rather abruptly: 'Yes, I will take Miss Campbell's horse on to the house, and you can follow with her at your leisure.' And seeing that Olivia was now looking at him out of tear-drenched eyes, he explained gently, 'I am going to leave Mr Maitland to bring you to the house,' and taking her hand, kissed it almost without emotion.

But as he unfastened her horse's reins he took a last glance at her. She was looking neither at him nor at Maitland; she had moved to the other side of the bridge as if to let the wind which blew downstream play on her tearstained face. Her back was towards her old friend, who was standing gazing at her very gravely. Then Ian, bridle in hand, turned away from the place where he had learnt beyond doubt that Olivia Campbell loved him, and where he had come through the worst moments of the tormented journey begun in the field of daisies on Eilean Soa, which must stretch away in front of him for the rest of life.

3

'Olivia,' said Maitland at last, gently, 'Olivia, my dear . . .'

'Yes, Godfather?'

He came to the rail beside her. 'My dear child, I wish with all my heart that I could help you! You do truly love that young man?'

'I do truly love that young man,' she repeated, as if it were a confession of faith. Her eyes were fixed upon a distant mountain peak. Then, with an effort at once heroic and pathetic, she added, ' 'Tis unfortunate, is it not, since he refuses to marry me. That is to put it bluntly indeed, yet not too bluntly. He says that there is too much to keep us apart.'

'Yes, I know what it is. He told me.'

'You have talked to him about it?'

'Once. I wished to sound his feelings for you. They are sincere; I have no doubt of that. And now I know yours, Olivia.'

'You could hardly mistake them, coming upon me thus,' avowed Olivia, trying to smile. 'But what is the good of learning all this, dear Godfather; though I know it is your affection for me which makes you desire to go into the matter?'

'No,' answered Maitland, looking at her narrowly, 'it does indeed seem of little use. That barrier . . .'

'It is terrible to be so helpless, to have happiness – for I know

I should be happy with him, and he, I think, with me – to have happiness put almost into one's hand and then snatched away.'

'Perhaps,' said Maitland slowly, 'happiness, like most things that we desire, has to be paid for.'

'Ah me!' said Olivia sighing, 'as if I would not be willing to pay for it!'

'Would you? How much, I wonder?'

'I'd pay – Godfather, why do you look like that? You are not a warlock, are you? How could there be a bargain, with a price? But if there were, I'd pay it, gladly!' The tears came back for a moment into her eyes. 'But there is nothing that I can do. I cannot bring Alan Stewart to life again.'

Maitland sighed. 'No, my dear, you cannot. – Well, let us be going to the house, if you are sufficiently recovered to face the kind people there.'

Olivia turned and put her hand into his arm. 'And tell me how far *you* are recovered? What a thoughtless creature I am, keeping you standing thus while I discourse my own woes!'

Chapter 24

'ASK MR MAITLAND ...'

ONCE before, doubting his own resolution, had Ian conveyed himself bodily from the neighbourhood of Olivia Campbell until such time as he could ride away from it altogether; now he did much the same until she should ride away from his. And so, while Olivia was resting, and being entertained by Alison Cameron and chattered to by the little boys, he, her lover, was lying on his face under the pines at the farther end of Loch na h-Iolaire.

He lay there so long, so motionless, so much like a man slain, that the wild things of the wood began to disregard his presence, and from a bracken frond above his head a spider swung down an experimental gossamer and tethered it to his coat collar.

After a long time he stirred and got to his feet, frightening a young hind which had come down to the loch for a drink. Dazzled by the sunlight, he shaded his eyes a moment, then looked at his watch. Olivia must surely have started back by now. Slowly he went along the smiling loch side, and more slowly still turned off towards the house. If she were not yet gone, but upon the point of departure, he risked meeting her if he went by the front of the house, so he bent his steps towards the stable-yard, thinking that he could there discover whether the horses from Fort William were gone.

They were gone; he had successfully carried out his unheroic plan. But in the yard, in charge of an unknown gillie, were, oddly enough, two other strange horses, one of them a grey which nevertheless seemed somehow familiar. So did the other, when he looked at it again. The swart-faced gillie, too, Ian fancied that he had seen before; but *he* came out of a different department of memory. His own mind, however, was so numbed by that hour of seeming death under the pines that he had not much interest in recapturing a more exact recollection. The only feeling of which he was really conscious was the beginning of a bitter ache which throbbed already like a bruised nerve – an ache of reproach for not having said farewell . . . It was too late now.

In the hall he met Ewen.

'Miss Campbell has gone, I think?' he observed listlessly.

Ewen gave him a look. 'About a quarter of an hour ago.' And in a lower tone he added, 'You had the courage to remain away from the house, of design?'

'Or the cowardice,' answered his cousin. He went towards the stairs, but Ardroy stopped him.

'I wish you would come into my room for a few minutes, Ian. I have just had a letter about which I should like to consult you.'

His tone was peculiar, and looking at him again Ian saw that something was wrong. He wrenched his own mind from following Olivia.

'I will come with pleasure. What is it?'

Ewen waited until he had shut the door of his little sanctum behind him.

'The first point is that Glenshian has suddenly sent back Hector's horse and effects.'

'Ah,' said his cousin, 'I thought I had seen that horse out there before. (I came in by the stable-yard.) And the grey, too – is not that – '

'Yes, it is Mr Maitland's,' replied Ardroy rather dryly. 'From the same quarter.'

'But you knew that he had been at Invershian. And the horse has been sent back very conveniently, for Maitland proposes to leave the day after tomorrow, does he not? What is there amiss in that? The surrender of both horses shows, on the contrary, a desire on the part of Glenshian to mend his ways.'

Ewen had sat down at the writing table and was drumming upon it with the fingers of one hand in a manner unlike him. The other, as Ian now saw, was clenched over something. 'Yes,

909

if he had only sent the horses and baggage. But he has written me a letter also.'

'About those damned cattle of his? But he *dare* not now – '

'There's not a word in it about cattle. I think he has abandoned the idea of citing me for the theft, though he characteristically does not say so. And, as I do not put the least faith in anything which comes from him, I do not believe what he has written here, this ... this horrible allegation. It's a lie – it must be! But all the same I wish to God he had not made it.'

'Do you think, my dear Ewen,' asked his cousin, 'that Glenshian is likely to write you a letter of compliment? But what new charge is he bringing against you now?'

'There's no charge against me,' said Ardroy. 'I almost wish there were, for I could better deal with it. But look at this!' And out of his clenched hand came a missive which he smoothed, and threw across the table very much, had Ian but known it, as he had thrown into the gutter another object which Finlay Mac-Phair had touched.

Ian read:

Mr MacPhair of Glenshian presents his compliments to Mr Cameron of Ardroy and its att pains to send him herewith, in addition to Mr Grant's horse and valise, which he has not the liest desire to retain, those belonging to one Mr David Maitland who left his house in haste about fowerteen days since, and hath not returned nor writt to claim them, for the whiche he doutlesse had his own good resons. But Glenshian has no fancy for being putt to the expence of keping Mr Maitland's beast longer, and deputes the charge of it to Mr Cameron, with whom he understands Mr Maitland has obtained shelter.

Here the lofty and impersonal style of the letter suffered a sudden declension, for underneath was written in what seemed to be the same hand, though the slope of the letters was different:

I vow it neer makes me die with laughing when I reflect on whom you are so carefully tending, as I hear. Ask Mr David Maitland what he was about in Glenbuckie (the word was heavily underlined) in the March of '53, or rather, what he did immediately after. You'll find the truth a matter of great surprise to you, as it was to poor A— C—.

At this epistle Ian sat staring, and could feel himself turning pale.

'My God!' he said after a moment. 'He means – no, he can't mean! – that it was David Maitland who sent that information about Doctor Cameron!'

'Don't say that you believe it!' cried Ardroy sharply.

'Of course I do not – any more than you do. The idea is preposterous. Maitland, *Maitland* Glenshian's tool, whom he is now betraying? No!'

'But what,' asked Ewen uneasily, 'has Glenshian to gain by writing such a monstrous thing to me?'

'He has two aims, I think. First, he wishes to perturb you, in which he has succeeded; secondly, to produce some kind of unpleasantness between you and your guest, with whom he has obviously had some violent disagreement. In both he has been actuated by nothing more than sheer malice. You have checkmated him over the cattle; he is bound to have another blow at you.'

'Yes, I suppose that must be it,' acquiesced Ewen slowly. 'It cannot be anything else – dirty traitor that he is, seeking to fix his own guilt upon an innocent man – a man of Maitland's type, too! He might have selected someone more probable.'

'Why not burn the letter and think no more about it?' suggested his cousin.

'No, I cannot do that. I cannot allow Maitland to go in ignorance of what an enemy is saying of him.'

'No, I suppose not,' agreed Ian rather dubiously. 'And yet that is playing into Glenshian's hands. He is no doubt hoping to create an animosity between you.'

'But why should there be animosity? I can make it quite clear to Maitland that I do not believe a word of what Glenshian hints at, especially since I know how deeply Finlay himself was concerned in that betrayal.'

'Where is Mr Maitland now?' asked Ian.

'He has gone on a horse of mine to set Miss Campbell a little on her way. I shall not say anything about this letter until there is a chance of discussing it with him undisturbed – not, I think, until after supper tonight.'

Ian strayed over to the window. How far had Olivia ridden by now; and what had Maitland said to her by the bridge which *he* 'would not regret'? Regret ... regret ... how could there be anything but regret? He was so sorry that Maitland, who had shown him unexpected sympathy, should have this evening to go through a distasteful scene. Life indeed was clouded just now ...

When he turned again Ewen was still sitting at the table frowning, with his chin propped on his fists. 'I wish nevertheless that I knew what it was which took Maitland to Invershian at all, and what drove him so abruptly away,' he said. 'I'd liefer think there was no connection between a man to whom I have taken a liking and one whom I despise and detest.'

'Well, you'll no doubt get the matter cleared up to your satisfaction this evening,' returned his kinsman.

2

Ian happened to be sitting with a book in the window of the living-room at Ardroy when, about half an hour before supper, the other guest came riding slowly back to the house. Maitland's head was dropped upon his breast, and he appeared buried in thought. In other circumstances Ian would have gone out to meet him, but now he felt a certain constraint, due to his recent conversation with Ewen. Besides, the poor gentleman looked tired. So he let him be.

Had he known, it was of him that Maitland was thinking as he returned, of him and Olivia, and so deeply that his own never-failing source of torment, all the sharper since Miss Cameron's revelation of Ardroy's actual presence at Tyburn with his cousin, had for the time ceased to gnaw him. He went upstairs to his room and, never noticing the presence of his recovered valise in a corner, threw himself on the bed, for the ride had fatigued him, and lay staring at the ceiling. What was the right thing to do? Olivia had said that she would pay any price. Would she pay *that* – willingly?

Downstairs Ian continued to read his book, or tried to do so. He had not seen Ewen since their interview, for Ardroy had subsequently gone out. As the clock neared the hour the family began to assemble for supper, first Miss Cameron, then Ewen, than Maitland himself. The latter came over towards Ian and the window, which was still open. It occurred to the young man, on the approach of the convalescent, to shut it, and he was just on the point of doing so when a small figure made its appearance outside, and Donald, seizing his opportunity, thrust in his head.

'Mr Maitland,' he exclaimed, 'do you know that your horse has come back from Invershian as well as Uncle Hector's? I have been talking to the gillie out there, and –'

'Why are you not in bed?' interrupted his father, coming to the window. 'Do you know what time it is? Be off, you young rascal!'

Donald disappeared with celerity. But the pebble of information which he had flung in, though it was not news to Ian or Ardroy, seemed to have struck David Maitland as though it were a real missile. Ian, who was nearest, observed him draw his breath sharply and put his hand over his mouth with the instinctive gesture of one who desires to suppress an exclamation. And Ian knew that Ardroy's eyes also were fixed on the elder man, and that he had seen his discomposure.

'Mr Maitland's horse sent back?' commented Aunt Margaret. 'I think Master Finlay might have been a thought more prompt about it, with Hector already gone off on that beast of yours, Ewen! Did he not send any letter – and excuse about Hector's?'

'Yes, he sent a letter,' answered Ewen briefly, in a tone which plainly implied that he did not wish to pursue the subject. 'Ah, here's Alison. Alison, my dear, do you know that Donald is still running loose outbye?'

'Morag has just captured him,' answered his wife smiling, and

913

they all took their places at the table, where after he had fulfilled his duties as master of the house Ardroy began to talk firmly about a scheme which he had in view of planting that recently introduced tree, the larch. Ian, and Alison too, obediently followed his lead, but Miss Margaret Cameron, always independent, clearly preferred to continue investigating the matter of the returned horses, which, she averred, was of far more general interest to the present company than non-existent trees.

'I feel a certain concern in that redheaded young gentleman since my encounter with him in this room in June. You are sure 'tis horses he has sent this time, Ewen, not steers?'

'I have not seen them, Aunt Margaret, but I imagine that they know the difference in the stables. – Ian, why has Uncle Alexander never taken to the larch?'

'My father's old-fashioned, as you know,' answered Ian, and pursued the larch a while longer. Maitland took little part in the discussion, and did not appear to be eating much ... but that might be ascribed to recent illness. Ian wished that he could avoid observing him, but, sitting almost opposite, he could not.

'Perhaps, Ewen,' suggested Miss Cameron, with mischief in her eye, 'you would do well to ask Glenshian his opinion of larch-planting. Being young, and new to his estate, and knowing nothing about the subject, he'll be sure to have one.'

But here Lady Ardroy turned Miss Cameron's flank by asking Mr Maitland how he found himself after his ride, a topic which immediately diverted Aunt Margaret's attention, though, leading as it did to questions about Miss Campbell, and at what point her escort had parted from her, it was not altogether the subject which Ian would have chosen.

By now the daylight had somewhat waned, and Angus MacMartin, who was serving, lighted the candles.

'The gillie from Invershian is having some supper, I hope?' asked Ewen in an undertone, and Angus replied that he was. Ian, who guessed rather than heard the question, contrived to keep his eyes from seeking Maitland's face across the table ...

though surely it was rather absurd to be so scrupulous. And yet ...

Ordinarily, since there was no drawing-room at Ardroy, the ladies did not retire farther than to another part of the large parlour. Tonight, however, the Fates appeared to have decided to clear the board at once for Ewen's explanation with his guest, for Alison, when she rose, announced her intention and Aunt Margaret's of spending the evening in the latter's bedroom over some unspecified task which male eyes were apparently not to rest upon.

'Very good,' said her husband; and when, after holding the door open for the two of them, he came back to his place at the head of the table, he dismissed Angus in a manner which told that astute and devoted young man that he was not to enter the room again unless he were summoned. So Ian knew that his kinsman was going to bring forward the matter of Glenshian's letter here, and in front of him. He rather wondered that Ewen had not invited Maitland to his own room, where they could be more certain of privacy, but came to the conclusion that he wished to make the business as informal as possible, lest it might look as if he were bringing an accusation against his guest.

So the three of them sat at the long table finishing their claret. Ian, instinctively desiring to postpone the unpleasant moment which was coming, engaged Maitland, with fair success, in small talk. But, the instant it died down, Ardroy, who had taken no part in it, began with his customary directness:

'Mr Maitland, I have this afternoon received a letter from MacPhair of Glenshian, sent with the horses of whose return you have heard. I think you ought to see it, for in it he makes an allegation against you so monstrous that, were I not convinced of its falsity, I should hesitate to acquaint you with it.'

Maitland leant suddenly back in his chair. By this movement of his the hand which had been on the table near his glass disappeared below it. He sat quite still for a second or two.

'Glenshian and I have quarrelled,' he said at last, in a voice so unlike his usual one that Ian had to look twice to be sure that it was he who spoke.

'I guessed that,' said Ewen gravely. 'And I assure you, sir, from experience of Glenshian, that I do not believe a word he says upon any subject. But it would not be just to you to keep this charge of his from your ears.'

'May I ... know what it is?' asked Maitland, in that voice which gave an impression of creaking as it came forth.

Ewen instantly extracted the crumpled letter from his pocketbook and passed it to him.

Whatever devilry on Glenshian's part Maitland expected after this warning – and he hardly knew what he did expect – it was not that which now stared him in the face. For he did not immediately read the whole letter; the underlined word *Glenbuckie* at the end caught his eye at once, and he knew that he was lost. The one thing which he had thought Finlay MacPhair would never do he had done – for the sake of revenge!

Yet, as a man might clutch at a mere tuft of grass before sliding down a precipice, he gained a moment's respite by slowly reading the letter through. Then he looked up ... and did not need to feign consternation.

'I do not understand ... What is this that Mr MacPhair is hinting at? "Glenbuckie"? That means – '

'It means,' said Ewen with visible reluctance, 'that he is accusing you of acting as his tool in the betrayal to the English Government of my cousin Archibald Cameron. I know that Glenshian had a tool – the man who actually sent the letter which brought my kinsman to the scaffold. He is charging you with being that man.'

There was still, perhaps, foothold as well as handhold. 'I am no tool of Glenshian's,' replied David Maitland with emphasis.

'I never believed it for a moment,' said Ardroy with an air of relief, and Ian too was conscious of the lifting of a heavy weight. 'Why, as you told me the other day, you never even knew Doctor Cameron.'

Maitland shook his head, since there appeared to be a tacit

question in the remark. Speech seemed to have withered on his
lips. He brought up one of the hands which had been clutching
the other under the table, and, trying to keep it steady, drank off
a gulp of wine. He did not know that on the back of that hand,
so deeply imprinted as to be visible by candlelight, were the
nailmarks of the other, and that they lasted while he drank, and
a little after.

But Ian, across the table, saw the marks, and they affected
him very unpleasantly. His sensation of relief deserted him
again. Either there *was* something in this charge of Glenshian's,
or Maitland, since hearing of the letter, had been anticipating
some other accusation. For one thing he had not expressed what
one might have looked for, an indignant, a horrified surprise at
the charge; moreover he was obviously in a state of extreme
tension.

Ardroy seemed to be sharing his cousin's renewed uneasiness.
He reached forward and possessed himself once more of the
creased paper.

'Mr Maitland, what is behind this letter?' he demanded rather
sternly. 'I can see that you know. And, as Archibald Cameron's
kinsman, I have a right to know too. You can speak freely
before Mr Stewart.'

Maitland pushed back his chair and looked over his shoulder
at the uncurtained windows behind him, through which all he
could see now was a dark mass of mountain slope topped by a
lighter mass of sky. The view did not help him. He turned
back to the table again. What should he say, what should he
say?

'I begin to believe,' said Ardroy, fixing on him that very blue,
steady and now somewhat imperious gaze, 'that you know who
the informer was!'

Maitland was silent, half mesmerized by those eyes. They
might be merciless eyes too. An immense fatigue had invaded
his brain.

'Answer me, please,' commanded Ardroy. 'Be easy, I'm
making no shadow of accusation against *you*. But you know
who he was . . . and Glenshian knows that you know!'

He must say something! Truth came easiest. 'I know at least why the . . . the informer did it.'

Ewen jerked forward, his hands gripping the edges of the table. '*Why!*' he exclaimed fiercely. 'Good God, as if there could be any reason but one!'

'It was not the reason that you think,' said Maitland almost inaudibly.

'Whatever it was, since you know it, I demand to hear it! I demand it, Mr Maitland!'

Maitland made a struggle, but his heart was not in it. 'You will not believe it, so what use to tell you, Mr Cameron?'

'I dare be sworn I shall not,' answered Ewen scornfully. 'Nevertheless, you will tell me, if you please!'

'Not here,' retorted Maitland, and he gave the fraction of a glance across at Ian. Olivia's lover was the last person he desired to be present at . . . whatever might be about to happen.

Ewen got instantly to his feet. Heavens, how tall he was, and how the candlelight below him threw up the strong lines of his mouth and chin!

'Come to my own room, then, sir, since you are so particular to shield Glenshian's tool.'

Maitland rose. 'I have said already that the man was no tool of Glenshian's,' he answered in a low voice.

Ian perceived the slip. *That* was not what he had said! His blood checked and ran for an instant very chill. Oh no, no, it could not be! . . . He was reading a wrong implication into the difference between the two phrases Mr Maitland had used. For Ewen, already-on the way to the door, had not so interpreted the last. It was true, perhaps, that he had not heard it . . .

Nor did Maitland seem to be aware of what he had said. His face, as he passed out of Ian's line of vision, had almost the appearance of a sleepwalker's, and like a sleepwalker he went out of the door which Ewen held open for him.

Chapter 25

'HE FORGAVE ...'

'WELL, Mr Maitland?'

Ardroy had turned the key in the lock and stood in the middle of the room. By the hearth, with his hand on the back of an armchair, David Maitland faced him; he had refused a seat. For a second or two he could almost see himself standing there, as one sees an actor on the stage, interested, perhaps moved by the situation, expectant of the words he is about to speak, but aware that the whole business is at bottom nothing but a play.

'The man who did this thing,' he began slowly but quite steadily, his eyes fixed on a little frizzle of horsehair escaping from the worn top of the chair, 'this man was once a convinced Jacobite like yourself, and had given proofs of his conviction. But during those sad years after the failure of the Rising he had come, much against his will, to see how utterly vain were the hopes upon which it had been based, and what a disaster to Scotland, to all whom he loved, would be a repitition of – '

The Highlander with an impatient movement cut him short. 'Suppose that after all we leave that part to the end, and that since you know so much of the traitor's mind, you tell me first how he had the chance of doing what he did – and who he was!'

Maitland dropped his hand from the chair back. 'That last I cannot tell you, Mr Cameron.'

'You mean that you will not?'

'Do you wish me to act the traitor too?'

'He was surely not a friend of yours!' exclaimed Ewen in a tone of repugnance.

'I knew him well . . . once,' answered Maitland very slowly.

'Is he still alive?'

919

Maitland nodded.

'And in enjoyment of a pension from the English Government, no doubt,' commented Ewen in a tone of great bitterness. 'Unless Glenshian, the arch-traitor, contrived to keep all the money for himself.'

A fleeting vision of Glenshian's face the other night, lusting after the visionary blood-money, came and went, and with it the unnatural feeling of being exterior to all this departed also. 'The man I speak of did not betray for money, Mr Cameron. He would sooner have shot himself. Yet he has been paid – my God, he has been paid!' Maitland's voice began to shake a little. 'Two years of the most bitter, the most unceasing remorse, when, if he could only have given his own life instead of the life he so mistakenly sacrificed (thinking merely to deprive a conspirator of the chance of doing further harm) he would have asked no greater boon of Heaven!'

He ceased, staring straight in front of him, and the room was filled with an aching silence. But Ewen, very white, had recoiled a little until he was brought up by the table behind him. No one could easily believe that those heartwrung accents came from the lips of a man who was merely pleading for another, even for a friend whom he had known well ... once. The ghastly suspicion provoked by Glenshian's letter, which Ewen had flung aside, now hissed deafeningly in his ear.

'It is not possible that, after all ... it's not possible!' he whispered, out of lips as dry as Maitland's own.

And then Maitland saw, too late, what he had done. The passion and sincerity of his own remorse had betrayed him. Nor could he fight any longer for foothold; he was worn down by the unceasing torment within, by the pressure of this place with its talk and its memories of the man whom he had sacrificed. It was the end; he only longed to make it complete.

There was a pistol lying on the mantelshelf; he had seen it as he came in. He went and took it by the barrel and held it out. 'I do not know if this is loaded. If it is, use it on me, and I will thank you with my last breath.'

But Ardroy made no motion either to take or to repulse

the weapon; he only stood looking at the man who offered it.

'There must be a mistake. You don't mean what you are saying. It was not *you*!' A lock of tawny hair had fallen disordered over his forehead, and emphasized his paleness and the ice-blue of his eyes, full of the profoundest horror.

'I do mean it,' answered Maitland. 'I am the most unhappy man on earth. You would be doing me a kindness.' He continued to hold out the pistol.

And now Ardroy, his eyes still fixed upon him, took it. Away at Invershian Finlay MacPhair must surely have held his breath.

'I will come with you wherever you wish,' added Maitland unemotionally. 'For you were better not do it in here, where the sound of a shot – '

Ewen Cameron gave the strangest laugh. 'Why should I play executioner? And the thing's not loaded. And I swore at Archie's burying that I would not ... Nevertheless, to make sure – ' The heavy pistol went crashing through the window out into the darkness beyond.

'Now sit down,' said its sender, his voice pulsing with a fury and an agony not less terrible for being held in leash, 'sit down where the man you betrayed once sat, and tell me – ' he drew a long choking breath, 'tell me, not about these noble motives of yours, but how you compassed it!'

Maitland sat down where he was bidden. He was not conscious of fear, only of regret for the pain that he was inflicting. He had told himself so many times recently, when confession had tempted him, that it would be stabbing Ewen Cameron to confess. Now he was doing it. He wondered if Ewen would hear him out; he had never seen a man so pale. The pistol was gone, but the Highlander, he knew, could easily kill him with his bare hands. That did not greatly matter; but he hoped he might be able first to finish all he wanted to say ...

Outside the night pressed against the window, and found an entry too, through the shattered pane. Every now and again the twin candle flames on the table bent and wavered, wavered and straightened themselves again.

'I must tell you,' began Maitland, with his eyes upon those flames, 'that my wife, who is partly Highland, had a little property on Loch Voil which she had for some time wished to dispose of. Early in 1753 Mr Ferguson, a neighbouring laird, made an offer for it, and we decided to sell it. That was what took me to the Braes of Balquhidder in the March of that year. And I must also tell you, Mr Cameron, for it has much bearing upon my ... upon the step I took ... how painful an impression I received from the still partly demolished condition of Balquhidder itself, which, as you perhaps know, had suffered a partial burning at the hands of the Government troops after the Forty-five, and in which there were still many poor houses in ruins.'

He paused a moment. Ardroy's gaze, sombre, freezingly hostile, and full of pain, was fixed upon him, but nothing came from his lips. Maitland went on in the same level tones:

'The sale of the property being almost a foregone conclusion, I had brought with me the necessary documents, drawn up by a lawyer. All that Mr Ferguson and I needed, in the little inn at Balquhidder to which we had adjourned after visiting the property, was a couple of witnesses. We were just about to summon the landlord when two persons passed the window – there was some kind of a local cattle fair going forward – and Mr Ferguson said, "There is Duncan Stewart of Glenbuckie; I will ask him and the gentleman that's with him to serve as witnesses for us." In a moment he came back with the two of them, and on his explaining what he wanted Mr Stewart said that he would willingly append his signature to the deed, but that he feared his friend would be unable to do so, having, he said, hurt his hand. This he said somewhat meaningly, I thought, and the gentleman with him, whose right hand appeared quite uninjured, gave a little smile as though he were amused. Mr Ferguson laughed and said, "You mean, Glenbuckie – we're all friends here – that his name would not have a very good appearance upon any legal document just now." And at that I looked again at Mr Stewart's companion, and recognized him for Doctor Archibald Cameron, whom I had seen more than once during the Rising, though I have never spoken to him.'

A pause. Ewen's lips moved. 'Poor Archie!'

'Doctor Cameron said that he would find a substitute, and going out he returned with a farmer of the neighbourhood, and so the deed was signed. Mr Stewart and the Doctor left almost immediately, but from something which was said in talk it was clear that Doctor Cameron was staying with Mr Stewart at his house. I knew already that he was pretty generally supposed to be in the Highlands working for the Cause, but also that his whereabouts had naturally been kept very secret.

'All the way back to Perth I was turning the situation over and over in my mind, with the ruins of those poor cottages at Balquhidder still before my eyes. Here was a man whom I admired and respected doing his utmost to rekindle the fires which should burn the rest of them. For I was as sure as of anything under Heaven that an attempt which had failed when it had had the Prince in person to lead it could never succeed now, wanting him. And what of the waste of lives – of the lives of young men above all? I fear I thought first of my own son, scarce of age, whom there would be no restraining . . . but not of him only . . . I wished with all my soul that I had tried an appeal to Doctor Cameron. But I knew that it would have been in vain. There was no means of stopping him so long as he was in Scotland and at liberty.

'And as I went, picturing another and a more hopeless civil war sweeping once more over the fair countryside . . . more blood, more fire, more ruin, and all to no purpose . . . I prayed that Archibald Cameron, brave and single-hearted as I knew him to be, might somehow be checked in what he was doing.'

'If you had known,' broke in Ewen, shading his eyes suddenly with his hand, 'how little, God help him, he *was* doing . . .'

'And from that,' went on Maitland after a slight pause, 'it was not a very far cry to speculating on the means which might put a stop to his activities. He might, for instance, be recalled – or he might be captured.'

Ewen went abruptly to the dark, broken window. But the speaker continued steadily.

'He naturally ran the risk of capture and of imprisonment

every hour that he was in Scotland. Yes, Ardroy – ' Maitland got to his feet – 'I swear solemnly by the God above us, the God in Whom I firmly believe, from Whom I hope – even I – for pardon, I swear that no vision of anything worse crossed my thoughts!'

But all that Ewen said, and without turning round, was, 'Go on!'

Standing now, Maitland went on. His voice had dropped.

'You can guess the next step … It was at Perth that it came to me that I had myself the power to stop him … All night long I lay awake wrestling with the thought, and whether I were wrestling with angel or devil I could not tell. The idea of giving up a fellow-Jacobite to a captivity which might last for years was so shudderingly repugnant that at first I could not face it. Yet, on the other hand, there was the heavy thought of all the consequences which I have rehearsed to you – '

This time Ewen swung round from his station. 'Captivity!' he said in a hard voice. 'You knew, you must have known, that Archibald Cameron was attained in '46, and that he had a death sentence hanging over him … and you talk of "captivity"!'

'I knew that he had been attained after the Rising. But how many ever dreamt that that seven-year-old sentence would be put into force? Did you, Mr Cameron?'

'The Government might not have been able to enforce it had they brought him to trial. And brought to trial he would have been, as I believe, but for Finlay MacPhair.'

Maitland looked bewildered. 'Ardroy, I am telling you the truth as at God's judgement bar! Finlay MacPhair, whom I have no cause to love, is for nothing in what I did. I had not then made his acquaintance.'

'That was not what I meant,' said Ewen. 'But you have made it now; you have been with him, you have quarrelled with him, you are – In God's name, David Maitland, what are you to Finlay MacPhair?'

'A bitter disappointment, I am glad to think.' Life and animosity sprang into the dead voice. 'You wish to know why I was recently at his house? It was because, having somehow

ferreted out my identity as the sender of that letter to the Lord
Justice-Clerk, Glenshian caused me to go there so that he could
discover whether I had been paid by the Government for the
act, and if not, whether I could be induced to abandon the
credit of it to him, so that he himself could claim the reward.
He wished to recompense himself for the services he had
already done the Government, for which, so he said, he had not
been adequately paid. That, though you may not credit it, is
what Finlay MacPhair wanted with me at Invershian, and why
I walked that night straight out of his house.'

Ewen had come back to his former place, his face alight with
the fierce eagerness of a hunter who sights a long pursued
quarry.

'He acknowledged to you that he had worked for the
Government in this matter – he acknowledged it? – Pshaw, Mr
Maitland, you need not hesitate to give evidence against the
dirtiest scoundrel who walks this earth, when you could do it
against a man like Archibald Cameron!'

Maitland put his hand for a moment over his eyes. 'You hit
very hard, Mr Cameron!' He removed it and added, somewhat
oddly, 'I think I had rather you did ... Yes, Glenshian acknowledged it. Yet, at the same time, as you see, it was not he
who actually informed. I do not say he does not wish it were.
But the belief which I overheard you discussing with Mr Stewart below my window is not justified. Glenshian neither actually betrayed Doctor Cameron nor did any tool of his betray
him ... And now, since you know the truth about me, you
know it about him also.'

'I have to believe that hound cleared of the ultimate charge,
and you – *you* – guilty!'

'Yes,' answered Maitland, but with difficulty. 'Yes. I am
guilty, and he is innocent. No doubt I should have –'

Ewen made a gesture dismissing Glenshian for the moment.
'Go on, if you please, with what you were saying. You were
doubtless about to tell me that by morning, that time in Perth,
you saw yourself as the saviour of Scotland! I hope the mood
lasted. Perhaps not until the seventh of June and Tyburn ...

Saints in Heaven, to think that scaffold, which I trod with him, was raised by *you*!'

' 'Twas partly for your own sake that I did not want you to know it,' murmured Maitland. The words would hardly come out now; he put a hand to his throat. 'I hoped that I could get away from here without your learning it . . . One day more . . . and I should have succeeded. When I came on Captain Grant that night I was about to drown myself . . . I was filling my pockets with stones to that end. If you could have used that pistol just now . . . only God knows I would not make you a murderer also. But since expiation is denied me I know that I am – ' He staggered suddenly.

'Sit down,' said Ewen, catching him by the arms. He put him back in the chair. 'I will fetch you some water.'

Maitland clutched at him. 'No, no! I need none . . . There's but one thing . . . if you could tell me that you believe me when I say that I only foresaw imprisonment for him . . . I suppose I cannot hope for that . . . I can hope for . . . nothing now.'

He lay back and closed his eyes. Ewen gazed at what this last hour had made of the sensitive and beautifully chiselled face. Weakness there was perhaps, but not a hint of baseness. And yet – he had betrayed a comrade.

Nevertheless, a man with that face might have been so moved by the prospect of calamity falling upon his country as to contemplate such a step and remain the while blind to the doom hanging over his victim . . . Ewen tried to think what Archie himself would do were he now in his place – but he knew. He knew it as if his slain kinsman were in this room, where not three years ago he had sat in the very chair now occupied by his slayer . . . he knew it penetratingly.

He took a step towards Maitland as though to lay a hand upon his shoulder and then drew back. No, he could not touch him in that spirit. But he said standing upright and looking a little as if he himself were facing a firing party:

'Mr Maitland, I cannot say that I entirely believe you. But I think I am near believing you and after a while perhaps . . .'

Maitland opened his eyes. 'And when you do ... will you forgive?'

But Ewen turned away without answering.

'*He* forgave,' said the broken voice. 'And you heard him.'

Chapter 26

A LIFE FOR A LIFE

A SOUND like splintering glass which he had heard in the
living-room, where he still remained had made Ian very
uneasy, and he came out into the hall to listen. But he heard
nothing more and going back he waited, it seemed to him, for
an interminable time. At last he thought that he heard someone
go upstairs; and about three minutes later he himself went to
the door of his cousin's room. There was no sound of voices
within: he tapped, there was no answer, so he entered.

The candlelight glinted on Ewen's auburn hair as he sat in
one of the chairs by the hearth, with his head bowed between
his hands, Maitland was not there. Ian came to a standstill.

'Ewen it's surely not that – that Glenshian was right!'

The head made a movement of assent.

Somehow the length of the interview seemed to have told Ian
that already. And then there was Maitland's own slip. Yet all he
said, after one sick moment, was, 'Where is he?' But he did not
mean Glenshian.

'Gone to his bedchamber, I believe,' answered Ewen almost
indifferently.

'Not gone altogether?'

'No. He wished to leave tonight, but I would not have it.
Nothing – not even *that* – can alter the fact that I brought him
here as my guest . . . and am indebted to him.'

He rose very haggard. 'I am going out. I cannot stay under
the same roof with him . . . though he swears he only took the
step he did to prevent a renewal of bloodshed, thinking it would
merely mean imprisonment for Archie! My God, that a man
could be so deluded. It is enough to send one crazy!'

Ian looked at him dizzily. Maitland – Olivia's Mr Maitland –

928

really had done this terrible thing, from whatever motive. He was but dimly conscious of following his cousin from the room, yet a few minutes later he was walking with him in the half-darkness along the path towards the loch behind the house, having indeed some ado to keep up with him, for Ewen walked as though he were driven by the furies. At the margin of Loch na h-Iolaire he stopped, and there, whilst the scarcely seen water lapped at the shadowy reeds, he told Ian the story.

'Just a chance meeting,' he ended, 'a chance meeting – no more – of a few minutes with a man who, if he is to be believed, wished Archie no harm – was moved, one might even say, by high principles and regard for others – and there's Archie, Archie . . .' He obviously could not finish.

'And Glenshian?'

Ewen recovered himself. 'Glenshian had no hand in it. A better man than he played the villain's part.'

'Are you . . . what are you going to do?'

'Nothing. What can I do? I cannot bring Archie back. Moreover there's my oath.'

Ian looked away to the mountains looming vaguely across the loch. He still only half realized the truth. Ardroy now began to walk on again, beside the loch this time, and they had tramped in complete silence nearly to the end of it, when he suddenly gave a harsh laugh, 'So 'twas not Finlay MacPhair after all who twisted that rope. I have been misjudging him, Heaven help me, though one would have sworn that was impossible! Had I not better apologize?'

His tone was so bitter that Ian glanced at him apprehensively. Deep down beneath Ardroy's calm and self-control there coursed, as his kinsman knew, passions stronger than most men's. 'I would leave Finlay alone were I you.'

'Particularly as his regret is that he cannot claim the guilt,' retorted Ewen. 'Pah! – let us not talk of him! I will tell you what I mean another time. My head is so hot that I can scarce think or speak. I shall stay here awhile.' Kneeling down he dipped his face into the water, then, going back a little distance, sat down against a pine bole.

Ian threw himself on the ground at a yard or two's distance; he too found thought difficult. The man so speculated upon these two years, the execrated unknown informer was ... the gentle, attractive David Maitland – Olivia's 'godfather'! He had confessed; so one *had* to believe it.

Ardroy was silent for so long, his arms folded, his head sunk upon his breast, that at last Ian began to think that he had fallen asleep. It must, surely, be very late; he pulled out his watch but was unable to distinguish the figures. The slight movement roused his cousin, who was evidently not asleep after all, for he raised his head at once.

'You are still there, Ian?'

'Yes. Do you mean to return – ' The end of the sentence was broken into by a shrill noise, an unmistakable whinny, followed almost instantly by a sound as though some large and probably frightened animal were plunging through the undergrowth at no great distance.

'Why, that's a horse!' exclaimed Ewen, jumping up. 'How came it out of the stable – there are none loose!'

He looked suddenly in the direction of the house, now nearly a mile away, to which their backs had all this time been turned as they sat. It was still invisible by reason of the intervening trees, but in the sky above was written an awful answer to his question.

'O God!' he said under his breath, and started without another word to run wildly in that direction, and Ian with him.

2

After Maitland had gone up to his room he sat for an un-counted space of time on the edge of his bed, so battered by the seas of emotion which had broken over him that he had now been swept into some deep impassive place where they surged harmlessly above his head, a drowned man ... or one lost for ever in that Dark Mile which had bulked so largely in his feverish journey of a while ago, although he had never reached the actual place.

... Or had he came through it, since there was now neither hope nor fear left for him? No, nor even expiation, for Ewen Cameron had forsworn revenge; he had told him so.

Without moving from the bed he looked out at the night. Not very dark. Ardroy had said that he would not have him leave as he had left Invershian, for he had eaten his salt. That rendered even an enemy sacred. And indeed, unless he wished to burden Ewen Cameron with the responsibility for his death (having laid far too much upon him already) he could not safely set off at night in this unknown and mountainous country. Nevertheless all his impulses were towards doing so. How could he face Olivia's lover tomorrow?

Moving like an automaton, he got up at last from his bed, left the room and went along the passage to the window there, from which he could see the irregular square of detached buildings behind the house – stables, granary and the like. In one of those was his recovered horse. Probably the door was not locked. And he continued to stare out, already seeing himself in the saddle, miles away ...

Suddenly he came to life, gave an exclamation, and flinging open the window leaned out. Was that *smoke* eddying and curling from the bottom of one of those buildings, that on the left nearest to the house? Maitland leant out farther to make sure, for the light was very deceptive. Yes, it was undoubtedly smoke. As he came to that conclusion he saw, though indistinctly, a human form standing below apparently observing the same phenomenon. Fortunately, then, there was someone astir. He shouted down, 'You there, do you know that that place is on fire?'

And at that the half-seen man turned and bounded out of sight into the darkness. Gone to summon help, no doubt. But it was for him, Maitland, to make known without delay to someone in the house what he had seen. He went back to his room, seized a candle and set out. But he could find neither Ardroy

931

nor his cousin anywhere. Then, since the gentlemen of the house had vanished and he was not acquainted with the servants' quarters, he must rouse the ladies. It was quite possible after all that Ardroy was in his wife's room.

He was not, however, for Lady Ardroy, coming after a moment to the door with a shawl about her, said that she did not know where her husband was. She took the news of the outbreak without undue alarm, and on hearing exactly where it was – in the stables – said that it would not be necessary to rouse the children at all and run the risk of frightening them. The great thing would be to get the horses out at once; no doubt by now helpers had been summoned and were doing this, but in case they had not, if Mr Maitland would go and rouse Angus MacMartin – she indicated his quarters – he and the stable lad could set to work.

But it was Maitland himself and a half-naked Angus who some three minutes later were hastily unbarring the door of the burning building. Not only was there no sign yet of other helpers, but even the stable lad was nowhere to be seen, and there was no time to be wasted in shouting for anyone. Kicking and plunging, the four terrified horses were somehow got out, a difficult and dangerous business too, as was proved at the end when the last animal, which had been particularly unmanageable, reared, lashed out violently and sent Angus to earth with a broken arm. Then it galloped out of the policies after the rest, which there had been no time to tie up.

By now Lady Ardroy and Miss Cameron were out in the yard, and both hurried to poor Angus. Maitland helped him up, half fainting and repeating wildly, 'What can be keeping the men?'

'And where in the name of the Good Being is the laird himself?' exclaimed Miss Cameron.

Alas, Maitland, if he did not know the answer to that question, could well guess what had driven him away. He began to shout his name and Ian Stewart's, for already, from lack of helpers and of water it was too late to save the stables; and other buildings, even the house itself, might be endangered.

All at once Alison Cameron gave a scream so terrible that it cut through his own voice like a knife.

'In the loft there . . . look . . . *O God, it's Donald*!'

She ran forward. High up in the stable, in the end facing the house, was an aperture which at first sight Maitland took to be a window. And his blood seemed turned to ice in his heated body, for at it, half veiled in smoke, had appeared the head and shoulders of a little boy.

'Good God, how did he get there?' he exclaimed, loosing hold of Angus and running too. Alison was crying distractedly up to the child, 'Donald, Donald, jump down to us, darling! We will catch you!'

'But we must have a sheet or a blanket,' interposed Maitland hastily. 'Otherwise – '

But Donald's childish tones came down to them sharpened by terror, 'I . . . I can't. 'Tis too far . . . And I can't climb over this . . .'

And then Maitland saw that the supposed window was really of the nature of an open doorway for the reception of hay or corn into the loft, blocked at present, however, across its lower half, by a deep boarding.

'I'll come up to you, Donald!' he shouted. 'Stay there – keep your head out in the fresh air. – A ladder, quickly!'

The chief danger to the child was, he believed, suffocation from the smoke, for there was as yet no light behind him to suggest the presence of flames. From somewhere Miss Cameron and the crippled Angus were bringing a small ladder. 'But, God be merciful to us, it will be much too short!' cried the distracted young Highlander.

This was obvious. 'Is it the only one you can find. Then we must try raising it upon something – that mounting-block yonder.'

It took the four of them to shift the block, for it was the solid trunk of a tree. Even as they got it into place Alison gave another cry: 'He's gone – he's disappeared!' and looking up Maitland saw that it was only too true. Overcome, no doubt, by the smoke, Donald had slipped down out of sight behind the planking.

The ladder was reared up on the block and steadied, and Maitland ran up. It was of no more use than if it had rested on the ground, for he just failed to reach the sill of the doorway with his fingers. And since the boy was no longer visible, and made no reply when he shouted, he could not encourage him to try to climb over the obstacle and let himself down into his arms on the ladder.

'God in Heaven,' he thought as he slid rather than climbed down the ladder again, 'there's nothing for it but to attempt it from the inside. – Is there not a trap-door up to the loft from the stables?' he asked. 'I thought I saw one.'

'Aye,' said Angus, 'and a ladder up to it, fixed to the wall in-bye.'

They ran to the door of the burning building. A volley of thick, suffocating smoke came out at them, as if in wrath at their temerity.

'Get me a rope, if you can!' commanded Maitland. 'I may have to lower him.' He tore off his cravat, steeped it in a butt of water standing there, and tied it over his mouth and nose. Angus came running with a short piece of rope and several yards of cord. As the rope was plainly inadequate, and Donald could not weigh much, Maitland took the cord and wound it round him, Angus, nearly out of his mind, imploring him the while to let him go up in his place.

'No use, with one arm,' answered the elder man. 'This business needs two. But you can come in with me and show me the ladder – I am not sure of the exact spot. And then go back to the ladies ... *Now!*'

They plunged in. Partly owing, perhaps, to the direction of the wind, the actual fire was still confined to the farther corner, where it had originated. But the mere smoke was more thick and deadly than Maitland could have believed possible. Yet somehow he was clambering up the wooden ladder clamped to the wall, and was fumbling to push open the trap-door above his head. 'I have it – I can do it!' he shouted down through his mufflings, and in spite of them paid with a fit of coughing for having attempted speech. Then, exerting all his lately depleted strength, he pulled himself up and through, and found himself on the floor of the loft.

Up here the heat seemed greater. There was not much of the hay which a romantically-minded little boy was like to lose his life for having slept in; it was mostly piled in one corner, and, miraculously enough, had not yet caught fire. Donald himself, a pathetic little figure, lay face downwards by the boarded aperture. A few strides and the rescuer had him in his arms, was raising him up to the fresh air and tying the cord round his body. It was safer than throwing him down to two women and a one-armed man below, and there was not time to wait for the sheet or blanket which, so far as he knew, had not been brought.

Just as he lifted the inanimate child over the planks two men burst into the yard. Yes, there at last, thank God, was Ewen Cameron, breathless and shouting. In a moment he had thrown aside the useless ladder; and it was into his arms that Maitland lowered Donald through the smoke. The cord was not quite long enough; he had to let him drop the last few feet.

Ewen gave the boy one passionate kiss and passed him immediately to his mother. 'Quick, Maitland!' he shouted up. 'No time to lose – the roof's catching, I think. I'll throw the rope up again – no, this cord would never bear you ... Drop, then – drop!'

But, as Donald had flinched from jumping, so did Maitland from clambering over the planks and dropping. It was too great a distance. Not a young man, and newly convalescent, he was now completely exhausted, shaking from head to foot and almost asphyxiated with the smoke. He could not make a success of the attempt; he knew that. Tearing away the cravat from his mouth he shouted down, 'No ... by the way I came ... trap-door!' and ran back across the floor.

Thick eddies of smoke were now curling up through the open trap-door, and, just before he got to it, a pile of hay heaped against the nearest wall suddenly flared up and fell forward like a fiery cataract. Maitland jumped back just in time, but, though he was not actually touched, the mere heat singed the clothes on his body from neck to ankle, as well as the unprotected hands which he instinctively put up to shield his face and eyes . . . Before he even knew it he was back at the aperture, the only possible way of escape now, and was starting to climb over the boarding to let himself drop . . .

Ardroy and Ian, who, on hearing what he had shouted to them, had run round to the stable door in order to drag him out when he appeared down the ladder, had seen, directly they got there, that no human being could come alive by that route, for through the mouth of the trap-door was hanging a mass of blazing hay. They ran back again, and were just in time to hear a cry, and to see Maitland fall sideways from the aperture, betrayed by the unexpected slipping forward of the boards which blocked its lower half.

He came down right across the mounting-block which had been placed underneath for his attempt to reach Donald by the ladder.

Chapter 27

LIGHT IN THE DARK MILE

1   *Sept. 11th*

IT was the second day after the fire, and the wind was flinging
the rain against the window of Ewen's room with such force
that the panes were little but a burl of sliding water. Through
one, indeed, over which a sheet of paper had been roughly
pasted, it was finding a slow entrance drop by drop, brimming
over the window-sill to form a tiny pool on the floor. Ian
Stewart, standing in front of the window with his hands behind
him, watched the process with half-seeing eyes.

Water enough now, and to spare! If only this drenching rain
had come thirty-six hours earlier, could it have arrested the
tragedy? Or if Donald had never been inspired with that fatal
desire of spending a night in the loft – or had been seen as he
slipped from the house to carry it out: or if Alison Cameron
had not decided (as Ian now knew that she had) against having
the children roused when Maitland had given the alarm, since
otherwise the boy's absence would have been discovered, and in
time, perhaps, to rescue him at less cost. Or if Ewen and he had
not left the house that evening under the stress of emotion and
taken themselves out of earshot. Or, supposing a sharper watch
had been kept on that gillie of Glenshian's who had spent the
first part of the night here, and had then so mysteriously vanished, could the catastrophe have been prevented altogether?

A drop trembled on the edge of the sill, detached itself, and
went to the floor. Of what use were a hundred surmises, when
upstairs a man's life was trickling away like this rain-water
which spilled itself with such silent persistence? And two nights
ago this quiet room had echoed to the clash of agony and
passion; yet nothing of all that remained, save the witness of the
broken window, and a fleck or two of blackened paper on the

937

hearth, where Ewen, early next morning, had burnt Glenshian's letter to ashes. Even Alison must never know what it had contained.

Impelled by a sudden draught, several drops now hurried themselves off the window-sill at once. The door had opened; Ian turned and saw Ardroy shutting it behind him. His face was greyed with vigil and strain.

'How is he?'

Ewen looked at first as if he had not heard the question. Then he answered slowly, 'Awake, and asking for you.'

'For me!' exclaimed Ian. The information seemed to set flowing some spring of hope in him, and he said impetuously, 'Ewen, do you not think that, after all, there is some chance for him? There must be, there must be!'

Ardroy's tired face turned a shade greyer. 'There is not the smallest hope; the surgeon said so. You know that his back is broken, besides the internal injuries. Morrison said that the end would be quite peaceful; that he would suffer less and less. Indeed he is in no pain at all now. We have to face it . . . though I don't know how to do it.'

Ian turned away. 'Does he know?'

'Perfectly well. When I said just now . . . he had asked me point-blank whether I had told you of . . . of his action in regard to Archie . . . when I said in reply that it should always remain a secret between you and me, and that if ever he came here again he would be received as what he was, the man to whom I owe my son's life – God knows why one makes these pretences of a future for the dying, but one does – he answered that I must know well he could never come to this house again, because he should never leave it.' Ewen's voice cracked a little. 'Yes, he knows.'

Ian was quite silent. A gust tore at the window and passed on.

'And now,' went on Ardroy, looking down at the hearth, 'he would like, it seems, to see Miss Campbell, if it be possible. I am therefore going to ride over to Fort William at once, and, if she desires it, bring her back with me.'

The colour mounted to his cousin's face. 'Bring her back? I ... I had best be gone before she comes, then.'

'That's as you wish, of course,' answered Ewen, still staring downwards. 'But go in and see him soon. I think he must have something of importance to say to you.'

2

Upstairs it was just as quiet, save for the rain lashing in the same way against the window. And David Maitland's sense of hearing not being in the least dulled, the sound of that assault was very present to him, as he lay there with his eyes closed. It did not distress him; he almost welcomed it, for he knew that he would never be out in conflicting elements again – in any sense. He had forced the surgeon to tell him the truth, though, since he had no feeling below the waist, it had been easy to guess it, directly he had recovered consciousness. The Dark Mile was over for him, and he had come out, against all hope, into a place where there was a glimmer of sky overhead, even, at moments, sunshine. Never, in that wild rush through the smoke, not even in the moment when he saw that he was trapped, had the shadow of an idea of expiation visited him – he had thought solely of the child's danger. But now, lying here waiting for the end, it was impossible not to know, and with a measureless content, that he had been allowed to make reparation after all. If he had murdered Archibald Cameron he had not only saved Ewen Cameron's heir, he had probably saved Ewen Cameron himself also. Ewen had said that, and much more ...

And here was young Stewart. He must rally all his forces for what he had to do.

'Do you remember a conversation we had in this room, Mr Stewart ... not very long ago?'

Maitland's voice, slow, even, and apparently produced without effort, was a surprise to Ian. But the face on the pillow, when one looked at that ... He averted his eyes from it, and found them fixed on one of the injured man's scorched hands, swathed in bandages, which was lying outside the bedclothes.

'Yes, I remember very well,' he answered with some difficulty.

'You cannot doubt, after what happened at the bridge that afternoon . . . how long ago is that?'

'It was but the day before yesterday,' replied the young man, hardly believing it himself.

'Is that all? . . . As I say, you cannot doubt, after that, that Miss Campbell returns your sentiments . . . Are you still of the same mind that you were then? You said, if I remember rightly, that you would give the rest of your life to be able to marry her.'

'Mr Maitland – '

The bandaged hand half raised itself. 'Believe me, I am not torturing you for pleasure, Mr Stewart.'

'Then . . . yes, I mean that – as much as ever I did, God help me. But I . . . I have turned my face from it,' said Ian unsteadily. 'And it does torture me to speak of it.' Then he was ashamed for having spoken of any pain of his own.

The sunken eyes studied him in silence; and when Maitland spoke again it was very slowly.

'Mr Stewart, I have it in my power to put into your hand a key . . . which would unlock the barrier between you and Miss Campbell.'

Forgetting that he was at the bedside of a badly injured man, Ian abruptly pushed back his chair, and sprang up. 'Sir . . . I don't understand . . . how can you – ' Further words failed him.

'Had I not been dying I should not contemplate doing it – yet,' said Maitland, his brows a little drawn together. 'For it means that I must betray a trust. I dare say,' he went on, with a smile about his bloodless lips which was only just not sardonic, 'that you think that must be a small consideration to me, who have betrayed a man . . . but it is not so.'

Ian made some inarticulate sound. He could not believe that he was hearing aright. Or was Maitland feverish?

'And I hesitate again very much to put this key in your

hands,' went on the quiet voice – no trace of fever there – 'because the price of using it is heavy.'

'As if I would not pay any price!' burst out the young man, the sweat beginning to bead on his forehead. 'Sir, sir, if you have any pity . . .'

'I have,' answered Maitland very gravely, 'and that is why I hesitate. For it's not you who will pay that price, Mr Stewart.'

'You mean that she – that Miss Campbell will?'

And on the pillow David Maitland moved his head a little in assent.

'Then do not – ' began Ian, but could not bring out the words. They were too hard to say. He sat down again and hid his face in his hands.

There was a silence; then a long sigh from the bed. The young man looked up. 'Can I do anything for you, sir?'

'Nothing, thank you. Nothing but swear your most inviolable oath that if I give you the means of marrying Olivia she shall never repent it.'

'But,' said Ian with a beating heart, 'if she has to pay so heavily, how can I tell whether she would not repent it?'

'That is the risk,' said Maitland, half to himself. 'But she said, like you, that she would pay any price . . . any price . . . It is treachery to Cairns. Yet if you love one another . . .'

'At least, sir,' besought Ian in an agony, 'at least give me this key, this secret. I need not use it, but give it to me!'

'You think you would not use it?' The smile came again, faint and not untender. 'You are young, and in love.'

Nevertheless, fixing his eyes on the end of the bed, David Maitland began in a voice which, though firm, sounded as if it came from a great distance. 'Listen then, and may God forgive me if I do wrong . . . Olivia is not Campbell's daughter at all, nor his wife's – nay, nor mine neither, don't go thinking that! She has not a drop of blood of Diarmaid in her veins; but she is involved in no dishonour – she is not illegitimate. She is the daughter,' his voice changed slightly, 'of a very beautiful and gracious lady, own sister to Mrs Campbell, who was a Lindsay, and of Robert Urquhart of Drumgarve, the husband who deserted her and was killed in a duel in France the year afterwards.'

'But why then . . .' stammered Ian, his tongue hardly able to articulate.

'Because Mrs Campbell's own daughter died in infancy, and her grief was so great that her husband almost feared for her reason, so that when, soon afterwards, her sister Mrs Urquhart died, leaving a girl of six months old, already fatherless, they adopted the little Olivia. The boys already born to the Campbells were too young to realize that she was not their own sister, and a few years sufficed to make it all but forgotten among acquaintances and servants; particularly as there was a strong resemblance between Olivia and her supposed mother – not unnatural, with so close a tie of blood. Mrs Campbell died when Olivia was five. I believe that Cairns meant to tell Olivia the truth when she came of age, but he could not face it – she was too dear to him. I doubt if he will ever tell her now, of his own free will. That is why I am breaking the silence of more than twenty years . . . for the sake of Olivia's happiness.'

His voice, which had weakened, died down altogether, and there was absolute silence, for even the rain had stopped.

A long time afterwards, so it seemed to him, Ian had sufficiently recovered to ask in awed accents, 'But you, sir, how do you know this secret?'

Maitland was looking at the foot of the bed as though he saw someone standing there. He said, 'She was more beautiful even than Olivia is. I had known her well; but I never saw her again after her marriage. I helped Cairns over the business of the adoption, and we have been friends ever since. And now I am betraying him . . . for Olivia's sake.'

Ian ran his hands through his hair. 'He . . . he may deny it. What proof is there?'

'Proof enough – locked away in my desk at Strathmory. The key is yonder.'

But Olivia's lover stood up trembling. It was like a cup of water held, just out of reach, before the eyes of one dying of thirst. 'O, Mr Maitland, how can I tell her the truth . . . how can

I cause her such a shock, such grief – even though it sets me free
to marry her? If she loves Mr Campbell as a daughter she may
hate me for it! And once done it cannot be undone.'

'Like most things,' came faintly from the bed. 'Well then, Mr
Stewart, if she arrives in time, I will tell her myself. And if she
loves you as I think she does, she will not reck so much after all
of the cost. She will come through the dark to you ... only a
mile or so of darkness ... I am tired; I think I will sleep now.'

3

Down again to Ewen's room and the pool of raindrops. Ian
hardly knew how he got there. He harboured no thought now of
leaving before Olivia's arrival; he was staring at the clock.
Hours before she could be here. And what if she never came, if
she could not face seeing her 'dear Mr Maitland' *in extremis*?
But she was brave; she would come ... to find her old friend
dying and to learn that she was not what all her life she had
supposed herself to be – a Campbell and her father's daughter.

What then if he spared her that disclosure – what if he asked
the dying man not to tell her about her parentage, and kept his
own lips sealed; never, as he had said, used the key? ... But Ian
was not so deluded as to imagine that he would ever be able to
do that indefinitely.

How quiet it was ... and, after all, the sun was coming out!
Upstairs David Maitland, the informer, who had sent a hero to
death, was himself dying the death of a hero. But he, Ian Stewart, in this overshadowed house, could think consecutively of
one thing only – life with Olivia. He hated himself for doing it,
but he could not tame his thoughts. Nevertheless there still ran
between himself and her a chill enough stream, for all that a
bridge had miraculously been thrown across it. Would she set
foot upon that bridge – come ... what was it Maitland had said
... come through a mile of darkness to him? (Odd; could he
have been referring to the *Mile dorcha*, and if so, how had he
ever heard of it, though it was true that he must have driven

through it when Ewen brought him here? Olivia too – but he remembered then that it was he himself who had told her of the place.)

'My aunt is not at all easy about Mr Maitland's condition,' said Alison to Ian at the midday meal, where they were alone. 'I hope Ewen will soon be back.' Her eyes filled with tears. 'All on Donald's account . . . I can't bear to think of it!'

Ian asked where Donald was, and was told that it was thought wiser to keep him in bed until tomorrow, not because he had suffered any physical hurt, but because, though he seemed quite free from reminiscent fears by day, his sleep was haunted by such alarming dreams. For that reason, and also because the pursuit of his fancy had not contravened any actual command, the boy had not been punished – save that from his point of view confinement to bed was in itself a punishment.

The afternoon was endless – sunny and endless. Towards the close of it Alison took him to the sick-room for a moment or two, and Ian saw indeed a great though indefinable alteration. Maitland seemed to have gone much farther away since the morning. He was very drowsy. Yet, as Ian stood looking at him, he opened his eyes, recognized him, and said, 'Has she come yet? . . . No matter . . . do not be afraid!' and then, with a change of tone, 'Where is the little boy with the caterpillars?'

'Do you wish to see him?' asked Alison, hesitating a trifle. He signified by the least movement of the head that he did, and a few moments later Ian heard through the half-open door Keithie's little pipe commenting on the situation: 'Poor Mr Maittan's ill again!' and he was brought in. He was too small to realize the impending presence of death, and was no more frightened or abashed than a bird hopping about on a tree in yesterday's battlefield, but he was sympathetic. 'Poor Mr Maittan'!' he said, as Alison lifted him up. 'I will truly give you my best cattlepillar when you go away . . . Are you going away soon?'

'Yes . . . very soon,' said Maitland faintly, smiling up at him. 'Will you kiss me, little Keith?'

Keith bent forwards at once from his mother's arms, and

David Maitland received that fresh and dewy salute with a look so full of content that Ian turned away with a constriction in his throat.

Outside the door Alison rather anxiously asked him if he thought that the dying man would ask to see Donald also, because she had not prepared the child for any such summons, and ought now to relieve Aunt Margaret in the sick room. So Ian offered to go up to his small cousin and stay with him awhile, and, if he were sent for, to explain to the best of his ability what it meant. 'Though I doubt,' he added, looking at the closed door, 'whether Mr Maitland will ask for anyone further now.'

Not even for Olivia, he thought, as he went up to Donald, to find the late adventurer tossing restlessly in a jumble of bed-clothes which almost engulfed the book he had been reading. When, he asked eagerly, could he get up; when could he come down and thank kind Mr Maitland for saving him from the fire? Later on, perhaps, Ian told him; adding that Mr Maitland might possibly send for him, in which case he must not make a noise in the room, for he was very ill. Deciding not to add anything further until it was necessary, he then offered to read to the boy, and was willingly handed *Robinson Crusoe*.

Page after page of the immortal castaway's doings did he read aloud without taking in more than a few words here and there. But no summons came, and though he tried to listen, while he read, for any sound of arrival outside the house, he heard none.

It was not until Donald had at last fallen asleep that there was a familiar step in the passage. Ian jumped up. The door opened and Ewen beckoned him forth.

'You must come quickly,' he said. 'There is only just time – he is going fast.'

'Miss Campbell –'

'She is there, with Alison. I did not think it would be so soon. Yet perhaps – '

There was no 'perhaps'. They had to stoop to see if he were still breathing. But years and sorrow had so rolled away from the face on which the two who knew his own bitter secret looked down that it was not possible to feel regret. And after a moment Maitland's eyes opened; they first sought out Olivia, and then looked from her to Ian, and he murmured almost inaudibly, 'There is ... no time now ... for me ... but ... tell her ...'

They were the last words he spoke; yet his last look was for Ewen, kneeling at the bedside; and the last faint movement he essayed was that of his bandaged left hand towards him. Ewen put both of his over it. The smile which came then stayed long afterwards.

Chapter 28

THE KING OF LOCHLANN'S DAUGHTER

1

Sept. 12th

COUCHED in the warm heather about half a mile off, Ian Stewart stared at the old grey house which confronted with close-curtained windows the almost incredible brilliance of the September day. It held death – its silence, its blind air of withdrawal, were tributes to the august visitant; and no more than any of its grown inmates was Ian likely to forget that guest. Yet for him it held love too, a love which might soon be flown unless he put out his hand and caught it. But what if, in the capture, he crushed its wings past reparation?

In the night it had seemed to him that he could never bring himself to tell Olivia the secret of her parentage. But because this was a new day, and one drenched in that unearthly beauty of which September holds the secret, so still that the fall of a leaf was an event, and even the murmur of the distant Allt Buidhe faintly audible – because of all this, and because he was young and desperately in love, Ian lay there and pulled at the heather-stems, and knew that he could not let Olivia go away unenlightened. The life which pulsed so strongly in his veins this morning – only in her could it find its full satisfaction; and with Olivia, as he knew, it was the same. Now at last the barrier was gone, and those two streams could mingle ... And yet he could not but dread the moment of disclosure.

Before he came out here, half an hour ago, Ian had talked with Ardroy in the little room where yesterday the rain had found its slow entrance, and where today the drawn curtains made a curious twilight which the radiance without nevertheless found means to penetrate. Ewen was certain now that the fire had been the work of the gillie from Invershian, and when his cousin had objected that, if the MacPhair's aim had really been

947

to burn Ardroy's property, either by his master's direct orders or on his own initiative, he would scarcely have chosen the stables instead of the house, Ewen had replied very grimly that he had *not* chosen the stables, which was why one knew that the fire had not been caused by accident.

'If you go round to the policies and look carefully,' he explained, 'you will find clear proof that he did try to fire the house itself – from the outside. I only discovered it this morning. But there was nothing sufficiently inflammable; and he either could not get inside or was afraid to risk the attempt. So in the end he took the easier course, and set fire to the stables, hoping perhaps that the flames would spread to the house, though he must have known that the wind was in the other direction. I suppose he thought that the horses would at least be burnt, poor beasts, including those he had brought back – perhaps unwillingly.'

'Or,' had said Ian hesitatingly, 'since there was . . . Donald up the ⌐ asleep in the loft . . . do you think he can possibly have known of his presence? Surely not – it is too horrible a thought!'

In the darkened room the two Highlanders looked at each other almost furtively. Both knew that the annals of their native land had in the past been stained by crimes just as horrible. Then Ewen went and twitched the window curtain over a chink of sunlight. 'I like so little to investigate that possibility,' he said in a low voice, 'that I vow I am glad I have not the means to do it. Donald himself, though he does not seem to know the exact time at which he started to carry out his fatal escapade, is sure that he did not see the strange gillie when he went into the stables and climbed up through the trap-door. Whether the gillie saw him is another matter, and one which we shall never know. I could never bring the crime home to Glenshian, because he could always disclaim responsibility for the gillie's action. And even if he is responsible, he has failed. What has been brought about was probably no part of his intention.'

He was silent a moment, while into Ian's mind there shot the memory of a fierce June sunset, gleaming windows, and a small boy crying out: 'Our house is on fire!'

Ewen lifted his head. 'Have you seen *him* this morning?'

'No,' said his cousin.

They went up together, and in the stillest room of all that still house Ardroy removed the cloth from the quiet face.

'I am glad that Archie forgave him, as he did, without even knowing who he was,' he said. 'I wonder if they have met by now?'

Ewen had a downright belief in the next world and a rather disconcerting habit of speaking of his dead friends – and since the Rising he had lost two by violent deaths – as if they were in an adjoining room. For Ian the dwelling-place of the departed was more remote. He looked down at David Maitland and wondered ...

'God rest him!' said Ewen gently, and replaced the covering.

2

Ian roused himself at last from his communion with the heather, got to his feet, and then stood still. The great vista of mountain and moorland before and around him, always fine, was this morning of an unspeakably intensified beauty, serene yet searching, so that between the silver stems of two birch trees, early yellowing, the deep hyacinth blue of a distant peak smote the senses with a stab like pain. What had death to do with a day of such profound loveliness ... And what had human passions? ... Or was it, on the other hand, the trembling nearness of the fulfilment of his heart's desire which gave the day its transcendental quality? Everything that the young man looked at, even his own hand in the sunlight, seemed of a new and troubling significance, as if he and all that his eyes rested upon this morning existed in some other world.

Wondering a little if he were going fey, he set off towards the house, to see for himself that ugly thing of which Ewen had told him. In the golden radiance the wreckage looked more than ever hideous, even though the rest of the out-buildings had escaped, and the heavy rain had soon put a stop to the sullen after-smouldering of the fire. Round the gutted stables the ground was strewn with charred debris and half-burnt beams; but it was not to look again at those that Ian had come here, and after a little search he found, in a dark angle of the exterior of the old house itself, the proof of what Ewen had told him. And it was a sight more repellent somehow than the wider ruin behind it, though there was so little of it – just a few half-burnt bits of wood piled up in a corner, with a slightly-blackened wall above them. By the extent of the discolouration, more fuel must have been used than appeared now; finding his attempt fruitless, the gillie had perhaps removed the bulk of it to escape detection. But enough remained . . .

Ian stood gazing at this testimony to a malice truly devilish with such revolted attention that he did not hear a door open near him. But, something cold and wet being thrust without warning into his hand, he discovered it to be Luath's nose. And the deerhound was not unaccompanied; a little way off a lady and a small boy were standing looking at the blackened skeleton of the stables – Olivia and Donald.

Ian was aware of a great commotion in his breast. Mechanically he caressed Luath's head, and the great dog responded by rearing himself up and putting his paws on young Invernacree's shoulders – always an embarrassing mark of regard. Its recipient heard Donald's fresh voice, untouched by any emotion other than a somewhat awed excitement.

'That was the stable, Miss Campbell – doesn't it look strange? I will show you where I was – up there; you can still see . . . Oh, there's Cousin Ian!'

Ian threw off Luath and came forward to salute her who was not, and never had been 'Miss Campbell', ashamed all at once that he was aware of so momentous a circumstance while she was still ignorant. That blue cloak with the swansdown cast about her – surely it was the same which she had been wearing when he had lifted her out of the coach and had helped to carry her along Loch Linnhe? Ah, he had thought her lovely then . . .

and ever since; but now that face was more than lovely to him.

Olivia responded very quietly but composedly to his greeting. He saw that she was paler than usual, and had wept; yet it seemed to him that a night of grief had but endowed her with a diviner beauty.

'This is painful for you,' he said in a low voice. 'I hope you did not allow Donald to – '

'No,' said Olivia quickly, 'I was already on my way. I wanted to see the place where – '

'I went up to the loft,' broke in Donald eagerly, 'by the ladder against the wall in the stables; but you see, Miss Campbell, that's all gone now – no, here's a piece – '

But at this point his revelations were cut short by the advent of Morag, his young Highland nurse, who apologetically requested permission to withdraw him, Lady Ardroy having sent her to find him. That the summons was instantly if unwillingly obeyed was no doubt due to the presence of 'Cousin Ian'.

Olivia looked relieved as the boy disappeared into the house. 'I thought that perhaps he ought not to come. But he does not know yet, I think, what his going up that ladder cost ... Will you explain to me just what Mr Maitland did, Mr Stewart?'

That 'Mr Stewart' hurt like a knife; but how else, after the parting on the bridge, could he expect her to address him? And in sight of the smoke-blackened remains Ian went through the story of the rescue. He did not say anything about the origin of the fire, and happily Olivia appeared to have no suspicion of incendiarism, nor to have observed what it was that he had been looking at a few moments previously. It was, however, a little difficult to account satisfactorily for his and Ardroy's absence from the house that evening; he could only say that, having something of importance to discuss, and the night being fine, they had walked up to Loch na h-Iolaire for the purpose.

Olivia heard it all without flinching. 'Yes, I see ... I understand. He first tried to reach Donald from outside, then he went up where the ladder used to be, in there. Then in trying to let himself down from the loft ...' She stood awhile in silence, her face working slightly, but she did not break down. And at last she said, 'Just the death I should always have expected my dear Godfather to die, giving his life for another's ... And now there is but one thing more to ask you – what was it that he said you were to tell me?'

It had come, the longed-for, dreaded moment.

'Let us go from here first,' said Ian, paling. 'It is too difficult and too strange to tell you here ... and needs too much courage.'

'Courage?' echoed Olivia. 'But surely there was no lack of courage here?'

'God knows there was not,' assented he. 'But this needs a different kind.'

'In me?'

Ian bowed his head. 'Yes. And in me too. Courage to hurt you – perhaps terribly.'

'I do not feel as if you could hurt me any more,' said Olivia.

And those words, uttered with an exquisite but unreproachful sadness, ended Ian's attempt at disclosure ere it was begun. The smoke-blackened spot where they stood seemed for a second to be shot with myriad points of light, and then grew blacker than before. He took time to breathe and then said quite quietly:

'I will not tell you then. There is ... no need.' (*No need!* cried his cheated hope to him – *no need!*) 'And in that case I – ' He broke off. Was this, out of so many leave-takings, to be the last, the true farewell?

'But I think there *is* need,' said Olivia, looking at him very gravely. 'I should not have said that about your hurting me; for it has not been your fault ... And you must surely do what Mr Maitland desired you to do. "Tell her!" they were the last words he uttered. I must know what he meant; if it needs courage, I must find it.'

Ian was staring at a half-consumed beam upon the ground. 'It is I who have not the courage,' he said, with something like a groan.

'Is it so terrible? Shall I be so unhappy? My dear Godfather would never have wished you to tell me if that were so.'

'No, that is true,' replied the young man more calmly. He raised his head and looked at her again. 'I will tell you, then, as he urged me to do. If he had had the strength he would have told you himself. Only I must implore you to come elsewhere. We are not even very private here. – You have a cloak, I see?'

'I will come wherever you wish,' said Olivia, gathering it about her.

3

It was natural, being already behind the house, to go towards the loch, even without any fixed intention of reaching it. But five or six minutes walking in silence through the still, sun-flecked wood, and they were there.

Loch na h-Iolaire this morning was no loch, but a mirror. Not only were all the tawny heights on the farther side built downwards in its depths, in a similitude no less bright in colour, and in detail no whit less perfect than the originals, but in that crystalline cup there even moved the little waterfall which tumbled down the lowest slope of Meall Achadh – a tiny white snake alive amid the unstirred heather and motionless birch trees of that reflected world. The feeling of being in some other plane of existence again grew strong upon Ian Stewart; the magic of this golden day was so profound that, even at such a moment of crisis, it could penetrate and bewilder senses like his, deeply troubled with the warfare of the mind – with pain and regret and apprehension and faint hope. Yet ... was hope so faint?

Olivia turned at last from gazing. She was waiting, though she said no word. But now he knew how to begin.

'If you will allow me,' he said, standing at a little distance, 'I will go back to the dream I had of you in the oak wood at Kilrain, because it was – that it, it might be – a kind of presage ... You know the legend of the children of the King of Lochlann or Norway, how they were changed by sorcery into seals?'

'Yes,' said the Highland Olivia, 'I know the legend.'

'When you had been a little time at Invernacree,' continued Ian, 'I thought of you as one of those, because, from the first, I was a man bewitched. And you know, perhaps, that, as the tale goes, a seal-woman wedded to a mortal man can always go back to her native element so long as she retains the skin which covered her as a seal; and that therefore the only way in which a man can be sure of retaining this enchanted bride is to possess himself of the skin. In my dream, where you were the King of Lochlann's daughter of my fancy as well as ... Olivia Campbell, I thought that you came and laid the magic covering beside me, as if you were renouncing your privilege for me. And when I woke, I found in my hand, not indeed the skin of the seal, but ... a sprig of bog-myrtle.' His heart was beating hard, but he managed to keep his voice steady.

'How long ago that seems now!' said Olivia almost to herself, looking again at the imaged water. For a moment she said no more; then, her eyes still on those deep-plunged mountain-sides, she answered the thought behind the allegory of his dream. 'But what the gall stands for I have no power to renounce. How, if I wished, could I make myself of other blood than I am?'

He came a step or two nearer. 'No, no one can do that ... And yet, a spaewife told me years ago that I should love a woman who was not what she seemed.'

Now she was startled; she looked straight at him with that beautiful fearless gaze of hers. 'Not what she seemed! Ian, what are you trying to tell me?'

The young man clenched his hands till the nails ran in. 'Something that, though it will make you sad, could make us happy — make us, if you have the courage and the will ... happy together.'

'*Together!* You mean ...?' The colour rose in Olivia's face like dawn over snow; one of her hands too shut itself quickly. 'You mean that ... somehow ... there *is* a way out for us – a way over the river you spoke of that day at Kilrain? Was that what my dear Godfather meant when he said, the last time I was here, that happiness must be paid for?'

'Yes, that is what I mean – what he too meant, no doubt.

954

There is a way; but it is a dark and difficult way for *you* ...
Only, if you would take it for my sake, my very unworthy sake,
when I have told you ... Olivia, will you – will you?'

One starving look at her, standing there in the windless glory,
and Ian dropped to a knee and pressed the hem of that blue
cloak of hers to his lips. In his heart was a silent prayer for
pardon that he should ask her to suffer on his account, and the
intuitive feeling also that he must give her time ... She was a
woman, and would show some reluctance, were it only to repay
him a little of the humiliation of his own persistent refusal. But
when, getting to his feet again, he saw the look which she was
bending upon him, he could have cried out in mingled exultation and self-abasement.

For as this day was not as other days, so was his love not as
other women. She had a soul as nobly clear as the water by
which she stood, and gallant as any paladin's. She did not even
wait to learn the price required of her.

'I think I would come across yonder loch to you – and that
with no bridge at all! Only tell me the way quickly ... I will be
as brave as I can.'

And with a gesture at once simple and royal Olivia Urquhart
gave him her hand.